# RIFT IN TIME

# RIFT IN TIME

# MICHAEL PHILLIPS

Tyndale House Publishers, Inc.
WHEATON, ILLINOIS

Now the Lord God had planted a garden in the east, in Eden; and there he put the man he had formed. And the Lord God made all kinds of trees grow out of the ground—trees that were pleasing to the eye and good for food. In the middle of the garden were the tree of life and the tree of the knowledge of good and evil.

A river watering the garden flowed from Eden; from there it was separated into four headwaters. The name of the first is the Pishon; it winds through the entire land of Havilah, where there is gold. . . . The name of the second river is the Gihon; it winds through the entire land of Cush. The name of the third river is the Tigris; it runs along the east side of Asshur. And the fourth river is the Euphrates.

—GENESIS 2:8-14

*Dedication*
*To Denver C. Phillips*
*1917–1997*
*A father for the age.*

Visit Tyndale's exciting Web site at www.tyndale.com

Interior maps and illustrations by Joan L. Grytness

Designed by Melinda Schumacher

This novel is a work of fiction. Names, characters, places, and incidents are either the product of the author's imagination or are used fictitiously. Any resemblance to actual events, locales, organizations, or persons, living or dead, is entirely coincidental and beyond the intent of either the author or publisher.

Library of Congress Cataloging-in-Publication Data

Phillips, Michael R., date
  Rift in time : a novel of beginnings—a prelude to the end / by Michael Phillips.
    p.   cm.
  ISBN 0-8423-5525-1 (HC)  ISBN 0-8423-5500-6 (SC)
  1. Title.
PS3566.H492R5 1997
813′54—dc21                                97-24138

Printed in the United States of America

07  06  05  04  03  02  01  00
9   8   7   6   5   4   3   2   1

# contents

## A Personal Word and Brief Tribute from the Author

*Every man, every woman, leaves a legacy of some kind behind when he or she passes from this earthly life. There are many kinds of legacies. Life passes on through one's children, through the works one has done, through the words one has spoken, through the friends one has cultivated, through the lives into which one has built. There are large legacies and small ones. There are public legacies and very private ones. But no man or woman exits this earth without leaving behind footprints, though sometimes it takes the keen eyes of love to detect their lasting imprint.*

*The facts of one's earthly biography aren't the truly significant thing. They are merely the specifics God uses to build character. It's the character that remains, not the data of how one ordered his days.*

*Over the years it was a portrait of character that quietly and subtly impacted me as my own father's son. I watched my dad's use of money. I observed him helping people. I watched both my father and mother constantly building into people's lives. There was a whole mutual outlook on life—a Proverbs life, a life of giving far more than receiving—that I first had to learn to see and then later come to respect and honor in both my parents.*

*They worked hard—worked in business, worked with their hands, worked in church, worked long days—always involved with those around them. And they prospered in the full biblical sense. But they built no empire, because they invested their lives in the people who came their way.*

*My father was not a showy man. The older I grew, the more thankful I became for that fact. He lived the Proverbs, plain and simple. That is a pretty wonderful thing to be able to say about any man. So at the end of his life, my father possessed little the world would count significant. It was his attitude of selflessness, his lack of desire for personal gain, that quality that gave of himself so that other people might be able to fulfill their dreams, which over the years built into me my dad's most lasting legacy. Watching him has* infused within me many of the ingredients that comprise my own idea of what kind of man I want to be.

My father was not outspoken about his beliefs. Yet God has never cared as much for talk about spiritual things as he does for what the Bible calls "a faithful man." It is the man who lives the principles to whom God gives honor.

It is easy for sons and daughters to overlook a parent's role in their development. It is especially easy to miss Proverbs-faithfulness as the significant and scriptural example it truly is. As the eyes of my own manhood were gradually opened, I realized that my father was, simply put, a good and humble man. Not merely a good man, but a good man in the full biblical sense—the sort of man whose life demonstrated the living out of God's principles. He was a man who left footprints of goodness, of selflessness, of humility on the paths of the lives of all who knew him, and who, in his quiet way, helped clarify my picture of God as my Father.

I truly see why the Lord chose the father-son relationship as the type of relationship that exists within the Godhead. For those with eyes to seek truth amidst human weakness and frailty, an earthly father can reveal God's character to his sons and daughters in a way no other human being can ever do.

During the writing of Rift in Time, Denver Phillips passed across that greatest and most mysterious of all rifts in the universe—the rift separating earthly from eternal life. Rift in Time was the last of my books the dear man who was my father was able to proofread (as he did many of my books) and then only about the first third. He faded rather seriously after that and died just six days before the manuscript was completed—the day after Easter. What a triumphant time to die!

During the final four weeks of his life, as more and more he was confined to bed, I visited my father and mother in their apartment for two or three hours a day. By then my dad was unable to speak much, but I could talk to him, bring him sips of water or food, and help my mother with other aspects of care, to allow her time to get out, go shopping, or take care of church business (at eighty-one, she was acting senior warden for her church—the youngest eighty-one I've ever seen!)

During those final special weeks, I sat at my dad's bedside and worked on portions of this manuscript in longhand, close by if he needed me, but mostly just so he could see me, realize I was there, and know I loved him. Rift in Time will therefore always be special to me in a unique and timeless way.

Now he is gone. I am sobered by his passing. My mother and sisters and I will miss him. Our families will miss him. He was our friend.

However, I do not grieve. For this time in my family's life represents a fulfillment of an ongoing cycle in God's kingdom, a cycle in which a man's earthly life ends. It is not the end. Faithfulness lives on, continuing to exercise a permanent, though perhaps unseen, impact for God's kingdom. The invisible footsteps of Denver Phillips are detectable in every book his son has writ-

*ten and in whatever books may be yet to come. Because the footsteps of his character have imprinted themselves within my heart and can never be erased.*

*The Bible extols the legacy of a faithful man. We read in Hebrews 11 of the faithful lives of many of the Bible's heroes. But I am convinced that throughout history it has been the similar faithfulness of untold thousands, millions of God's people you and I never hear of, which has been the strongest element in the ongoing spread of Christianity. Quiet, unseen faithfulness does not merely go to the grave and die. Faithfulness always lives on, whether or not that faithful life is written about in a gallery like Hebrews 11, whether or not there is fame attached to it, whether or not anyone ever hears of it.*

*My father's actual life goes on too. For life is eternal. One part of life may be past—life in the shadowlands, as C. S. Lewis calls it. My dad's real life, the life for which God has all this time been preparing him, has now begun. For already the Father has said to him, "Well done, my faithful son. Come, there's a great deal to be done!"*

*God bless you, earthly father! I loved you. All those who knew you and shared life with you love you still.*

# RIFT IN TIME

◆ ◆ ◆

*In the beginning, first day dawned bright;*

*Creation exploded through infinite sky.*

*Not by chance nor random atom flight,*

*But by the breath of El Shaddai.*

◆ ◆ ◆

# The Wilderness of Arabia, 1898

A searing desert sun bore down upon the lone pilgrim whose quest had brought him to the lower slopes of this rugged mountain. Despite century-old traditions to the contrary, he was certain that this was the place of ancient legend.

He paused, then glanced upward.

The glowing ball of fire sat at an angle in the sky not many degrees above the peak toward which he was bound.

He squinted and brought a hand to his forehead, trying to shield the late-afternoon rays so he might make out the jagged summit. The delay was but momentary. He must make haste. The sun had long since begun its downward curve . . . and he sensed he was not alone.

The faithful camel that had brought him this far would be safe here until his descent. He checked the animal's rope again, then shifted the knapsack on his shoulders. It contained charts, maps, miscellaneous equipment, a well-worn black leather Bible, and a single notebook, almost new, containing only a few pages of entries made over the past few days. He hoped to fill in the final pieces to the lifelong puzzle today.

The pilgrim took a swig of tepid water from his half-empty canteen and drew in a deep breath. He had planned to bring one of his two complete notebooks—a set of thick, worn journals of scientific research and personal observations representing twenty years' work. But a last-minute premonition told him he ought not to have such memoirs on his person. He always completed the data in duplicate. Thus his original journal now sat comfortably on a bookcase in his study at Peterborough. His travel copy he had stashed in the hotel safe in Cairo. He would fill in the final discoveries upon his return.

After another moment or two, he set out on tired but eager feet upward out of the valley onto the slopes of Jebel al Lawz.

Atop this mountain would he prove to the world that the new wave of godless science was groundless. Here at last would the world see and have no alternative but to recognize that the truths of the Old Testament were fact. His discovery would culminate a century of scientific discovery and advance, with a triumphant archaeological counterattack against all that had been done over the last thirty years to undermine the Christian faith.

The assault against Christianity had not begun with the publication of Darwin's The Origin of Species thirty-nine years ago. Seeds of atheism had been growing throughout the nineteenth century. Popularization of evolutionary theory, however, had given huge impetus to the rationalism sweeping the land. From every corner of intellectualism and academia were the lies proclaimed that life had come about by chance, that man had evolved from lower biologic forms, and that the Genesis account of creation was groundless myth.

What he was about to divulge to the world would dispel these falsehoods in one sweeping revelation! He would prove—to skeptics and atheists, philosophers and scientists—that man was no descendent of apes but the offspring and handiwork of God.

Forty minutes later he still trudged upward, as rapidly as aching legs and blistered feet allowed. He followed no trail yet knew his way without hesitation—through low-growing brush, around hot gray boulders, and up steep treacherous inclines of rock—breathing heavily from the exertion, sweat pouring off his face, slipping occasionally but always steadying himself and continuing on. He had mentally scaled the face of this mountain many times in preparation, while poring over dozens of maps, some drawn in his own hand.

He paused again, wincing involuntarily in pain. The heavy pack's thin straps bit into his shoulders. No shrugging or shifting of the load seemed to help.

He slipped behind the shade of a boulder. He removed the pack, propped himself against the stone, and exhaled a long sigh. His stamina was fading under the blazing sun. It had been ten hours since he had broken camp this morning. He could feel strength draining from his body. Again he reached for his canteen, opened it, and took several sips. He allowed a trickle to slide down his whiskered chin and onto the half-buttoned, sweat-sodden khaki shirt. He poured a small amount into his right hand and dashed it into his eyes.

There was no denying the fact that he was exhausted. Not that he was too old for the task. The elements of sun and wind had combined on his face to produce a weathered look ten years in advance of his age. But after a year of ceaseless travel and danger, a two-hundred-mile trek through the desert, and now this scaling of the severe volcanic slopes, both body and mind were nearly spent.

He glanced out of the shadows, this time peering backward down the mountain in the direction from which he had come. He'd known he was being followed. By whom and why he had only recently begun to realize. The sinister web was closing about him. That fact could no longer be denied.

Thought of his pursuers sparked a renewed sense of urgency. A small groan of weariness escaped his parched lips as he wrestled on his pack and set out again.

He had studied every precipice of this mountain for more than a year now. Outwardly his perspiring body rebelled against the unrelenting heat. Inwardly his heart trembled in realization of the significance of the destination toward which his steps led him.

This was no modern-day Moses, no evangelical holy man to whom the Almighty had shown his face. Yet nonetheless, he was convinced that God had revealed to him a truth perhaps equally as great for his generation as that shown to the great patriarch of old.

Was it possible? he thought. Might Moses himself have trod this very way on his historic sojourn upward onto the holy mount where dwelt the presence of Yahweh Elohim . . . God Almighty! Where had he slept those forty nights? Or had he slept at all?

The archaeologist's brain was alive with the ancient story as if he himself were reliving it while he made his way steadily upward.

Again his steps ceased momentarily. His glance raised toward the sky. He spied a lonely wisp of cloud hanging about the peak above him. It reminded him of the voice of God as he had written out the words of his Commandments. Had his servant perhaps dwelt within one of the many caves spotting the mountainside, unable to endure the shekinah glory of Adonai, the Lord?

And millennia earlier, the feet of . . .

No, he could not bring himself to even finish the sentence. The idea was too enormous to utter aloud. Not yet.

For years it had been his dream to shout the revelation to the whole world. At last he was close. If his steps indeed followed his, as he was certain they did, then he would—

An impulse caused him to glance back.

A small cloud of dust rose from the western plain, disturbing the otherwise barren landscape. A shiver of fear surged through his frame. He squinted, even as his hands fumbled for his binoculars. A quick look through the lenses confirmed his premonition.

How could they possibly have followed him here?

He had shaken them off in Cairo. He had been certain of it! And on horseback! No wonder they were moving so fast.

He must not delay!

Still clutching his binoculars in one hand, the archaeologist broke into a labored gait, barely fast enough to be considered a run yet sufficient to carry him across the ground at two or three times his previous pace. He must get higher, then hide wherever he could. The Lord would protect him. If this was holy ground, surely God would not allow evil men to prevent his truth from being known.

The fugitive's legs quickly grew heavy with the uphill effort. Suddenly the tip of his boot caught against something partially submerged in his path. The runner stumbled. His binoculars flew forward. He threw out a hand to break the fall, gashing his palm as it smashed against the sharp edge of a rock. A few small drops of blood flecked his stained khakis.

As he scrambled to his feet, the wet drops from his still-bleeding hand missed his trousers, reddening instead the length of root over which he had fallen. But he never saw it, nor divined its significance.

He recovered his binoculars, one lens now broken, and pressed on.

✦ ✦ ✦

A mile and a half behind him, three horsemen now reached the base of the mount where a lone camel sat chewing its cud lazily in the sun, tied to the trunk of a stout wiry shrub. Nothing grew here for the animal to eat. It was indeed a desolate place. Had anything ever grown here?

The leader reined in. Creaking leather and the impatient stomping of heavily shod feet mingled with the heavy breathing of both man and beast. It had been a hard ride from Al Aqaba. Within thirty seconds the riders located their quarry through high-powered binoculars.

He pointed upward, nodded to his two colleagues, then dug his heels into the sides of his desert steed. Again the three set out in pursuit of the footbound traveller. They would track him as high up the slope on horseback as possible.

Twenty minutes later, they dismounted and proceeded on foot, moving quickly. Their legs were fresh and their shoulders unencumbered by packs of equipment. The horses, where they left them, held what food and supplies might be needed when their business was done and ample water for both men and beasts to survive the return journey to the north Aqaba coast. Each of the stalkers carried nothing save binoculars and an Enfield rifle. One purpose had brought them here, and it did not involve discoveries of antiquity.

Above them, much closer than he had been a short while earlier, the breathing of the one they pursued grew labored. Collapse seemed imminent. Glancing back repeatedly now, he was well apprised of his trouble. How they had picked up his trail mattered nothing now, only finding somewhere to hide, if not himself, at least his notes of the last few days. If it was not destined for him to make the proclamation public, the Lord would bring another. He must find a place—

The sharp report of a rifle sounded behind him. The same instant a piece of rock shattered some four feet to his right. Fragments of granite spewed in all directions.

Reflexively he fell to his face. Another shot might follow. He listened. The echo died away. The onetime volcano grew silent.

He crept to his knees, then carefully to his feet, hurrying on, energized by the gunfire to a renewed attempt at speed. They were gaining on him faster than he imagined possible. He was in grave danger and knew it. Nor did he have means to protect himself. Of the diverse tools of his trade he had packed, no gun was included.

Ahead of him the thin path curved. He sprinted ahead.

Another shot exploded. A slug smashed into the side of the cliff just as he turned. A hundred yards behind, a great curse sounded as his pursuer lowered his rifle and resumed the chase.

The small black mouth of a cave, partially obscured by a jutting slab of stone, appeared to his left. He darted toward it, then inside.

Feeling frantically about in the darkness, the archaeologist knew instantly this was no suitable refuge. The cave had no depth, and they would find him easily.

He grabbed at the shoulder straps and yanked the knapsack from his back. At least here his secrets would be safe. He stooped low to stuff the precious canvas bag far back into a corner of blackness. He murmured a brief prayer, then turned, still crouching, and hastened away.

Three strides again brought him erect in the sunlight. He squinted briefly, then dashed once more in the direction he had been bound, the lightening of his burden putting new air under his feet.

But it was no use. The three erstwhile horsemen closed in.

He covered but forty or fifty yards when another echo of gunfire roared in the air, this time accompanied by a cry of pain. The archaeologist crashed to the ground, the calf of his right leg spurting blood.

He struggled to his feet and tried to run, limping dreadfully now. He knew his life was done. If this had once been the mount of the Creator's presence, it could be no less now. He would die happily in this sacred place. He had given his life to the quest for truth and had no regrets. If now was not the appointed time for revelation, that time would yet come.

But he must struggle to get as far from the cave as he could, so they would not—

Another deafening explosion sounded. The blood this time gushed from his back. He fell prostrate on his face in the rocky dirt.

But a few seconds of consciousness remained.

"Lord . . . Lord God," he whispered faintly, "protect . . . secret of this place . . . in your time . . . oh . . . oh, my Lord . . ."

Scarcely twenty seconds later heavy strides ran up, then stopped. A boot kicked at the form lying below him, turning it over onto its back. Already blood was soaking into what thin layer of dry soil existed on this mount of granite.

Two more booted feet approached the evil scene.

"He's dead," said the first.

"What shall we do with the body?" asked one of the others.

"It can stay here to rot for all I care. He's been silenced, that's all we had to make sure of." Even as he spoke, the man kicked the body to the side of the narrow pathway, where it rolled tumbling over the side.

"There's no one in this God-forsaken place except the vultures."

"They're welcome to him now."

The murderer and his two accomplices turned and began retracing their steps down the mountain. Fifteen minutes later they passed over the exposed red-stained tip of a giant buried root, the blood upon it dried now, little knowing that they were walking over the very proof their victim had sought.

But nothing is hid that shall not be revealed. And in the time appointed by him who once spoke from this mount would the revelation be revealed.

# PART ONE

# ARARAT

✦ ✦ ✦

*Sin hid Paradise from God's highest creation;*

*A long season of separation began.*

*Though none knows the day or duration,*

*There will flower sign of his return to man.*

✦ ✦ ✦

_____

# one

# Discovery of the Century

Two legs dangled precariously over a jagged precipice of ice.

A yanking of thin lines stretching above followed in final test of readiness. The ropes appeared too thin for the task. In truth they were strong enough to hold a mammoth.

Then came the command: "Lower away!"

Slowly the figure in the orange down jumpsuit descended from the icy ledge into the no-man's-land of space. Five hundred feet of nothingness spread under the crane arm holding him. Beneath that, mountain peaks and glacial ice extended in all directions.

Far below the daring mountaineer a black mouth in the glacier overlooking Ahora Gorge on the north slope of the mountain—appearing tiny, but wide enough to receive him—possessed a secret about to be exposed to a waiting world.

The target hole, toward which he was being lowered through space, stretched across a mere six feet in diameter. It had been melted through the ice with state-of-the-art torches lowered by the same crane on the ends of two large cables. A third simultaneously sent oxygen into the recess to keep the flame alive, even as the melted water thus produced was suctioned out with a gigantic dentistry tube attached to a fourth. One of the lines also held a remote television camera to guide the efforts of the team perched safely in the encampment above. Coordinated by a sophisticated computer program designed specifically to Livingstone's specifications, the operation combined large-scale NASA engineering with intricate medical ingenuity to perform a space-age archaeological arthroscopy on one of the most remote glacial packs on the globe.

The only potential glitch that neither men nor computers could control was the winds. Always unpredictable at 16,000 feet, they were especially treacherous here in the eastern Turkish highlands. If they whipped up, neither astronaut nor heart surgeon, with any number of computers at their command, would be able to prevent the cables from flailing about wildly.

The winds, however, had behaved according to the optimistic forecasts of the team's resident meteorologist.

The burning was carried out in the early morning hours on two successive days of calm. They then prayed that no unforeseen storm moved in suddenly to dump snow into the void thus created and that the weather would hold for yet a third day.

That would make it possible for a *man* to be lowered in place of torches. He would witness the discovery up close with his own eyes and feel with his own fingers what everyone on the mountain hoped the spectrographic images from the previous spring had indeed discovered, and the subsurface interface radar from two weeks ago confirmed and pinpointed more precisely. He would conduct what tests were possible at the base of the six-foot-wide well, remove a few samples, and then recommend to the overseeing committee how to proceed.

No storm had come. The winds remained at bay. And now, at a little after seven o'clock on the morning of the third bright day in a row, the much anticipated moment had at last arrived.

From the cliff's edge precisely above the target hole, the orange figure slowly descended. No less than fifty video and television cameras recorded the moment from various vantage points of safety about the mountain above.

Archaeologists, historians, and preachers had dreamed of this moment for centuries. Now the potential discovery offered an exquisitely fitting climax to a millennium of technological advance, briefly diverting man's focus from what he might *become* to where he had come *from*. For if the predictions were indeed correct, the seed of all humankind on the globe may have originated right here.

Whether anyone would be the first in the modern era to actually set foot in that ancient place—a site of legend and myth to some, of fact and divine intercedence in man's affairs according to others—probably few of those dreamers in their heart of hearts realistically imagined possible.

Yet modern man's resourcefulness had a way of making impossibilities happen. The foot of a human being had indeed ventured out of a spaceship called *Eagle* to plant itself onto the surface of the moon. In that instant had impossibility become history.

Now had a similar moment of destiny arrived. To archaeologists this day was surely no less significant than in July 1969. Whether the name Adam

Livingstone would be known to posterity with the same prominence as Neil Armstrong only the future could determine.

On this morning, decades after the American spaceman, an adventurous Englishman, archaeologist, explorer, and daredevil dangled in midair at the end of the tether controlling his life. Certainly he occupied center stage of the world's collective attention no less than had Armstrong during his rendezvous with history.

Adam Livingstone's thoughts, however, were preoccupied with the task at hand. Closer and closer, he now approached what signified a major fulfillment of the objective he had set for himself ten years earlier. That was to see, to discover, to set foot inside places unknown to any mortal before him. His dream was to represent to the field of archaeology what Alexander did to conquest, what Columbus did to sailing, what Edison did to technology, what Einstein did to nuclear physics.

At thirty-four he was already well on the way toward achieving that goal. If yesterday's dig—more accurately "melt"—and today's exploration of the shaft were successful, the resultant fame would surely catapult his growing reputation into yet more lofty realms of worldwide renown.

Livingstone glanced below him. The essence of his chosen field of endeavor was digging holes into the past, yet now he was about to enter the most remarkable such *tell* imaginable. It was one he hoped would take him back to the earliest of all beginning points known to man . . . to the sixth chapter of the book of Genesis itself!

He was two-thirds of the way down now . . . another two hundred feet to go. As he gazed below him, all was white, save his two dangling orange legs. Above, the sky shone pale blue in the dazzling autumn morning's sun, only just creeping above the peaks at his back.

The air was breathless. The whole world was quiet. Except for the slight pressure and an occasional tug upon his shoulder straps, he felt nothing. Only a slight sensation of updraft against his cheeks betrayed his downward movement.

Slowly he turned his head around toward the mountains of ice and snow.

This was spectacularly peaceful, he thought. He felt as if he were floating weightless in the air. It was cold. Probably he should be wearing his goggles. But nothing was going to keep him from witnessing every second of this momentous day with eyes wide open.

He had been waiting a long time for this moment.

(2)

The daring archaeologist was not given to premonitions or angst. They were a liability in his line of work.

But as he glanced down into the void below him, the thought flitted through Livingstone's brain—*What if something goes wrong?*

5

What if he tempted fate once too often? Was he ready to face death? Was he prepared, as they said, to meet his Maker?

He laughed the idea off.

This was too beautiful and triumphant a moment to spoil. He didn't believe in immortality anyway, so what difference did it make? Life was life. This was it. Live it to the full. When you died you died. That was it. No need to worry about it ahead of time. As to meeting his Maker, Adam Livingstone was too thoroughly a modern to give the idea a second thought. Once his time came, he didn't plan on meeting anybody. He would get his living done on *this* side of death and waste no time thinking about the other.

Besides, Livingstone thought, he had himself designed this whole apparatus holding him. He had supreme faith in the equipment, in his team, and in himself.

His thoughts turned momentarily to Candace.

Did the living he intended to do include marriage and a family? he found himself wondering. What did he want for himself, for his future—however long or short that future happened to be?

They had lunched together at Harrods two weeks ago, where Livingstone had appeared to dedicate an archaeology display in commemoration of his upcoming Turkish adventure.

"You're quite the talk of London, Adam," she said across the most secluded table they could manage to find once the festivities were concluded. "How lucky of me to have you all to myself."

"You could have any man in England, Candace," Livingstone said with lighthearted laughter.

"Maybe I don't want just *any* man," she rejoined, glancing into his eyes with a teasing smile. "You simply must come round to Swanspond soon," she added. "Daddy is dying to see you again."

Livingstone laughed once more. "I shall try the instant I am back from Turkey."

"Daddy will be disappointed not to see you before your trip."

"Your father is too important a man to expend his energy waiting to see me," he replied. "Are you sure you are not using him to gain your own ends, Candace, my dear?"

"And so what if I am?" she replied, allowing her lower lip to protrude slightly. "Is that so unreasonable of me? A woman can wait only so long, you know, Adam."

He really ought to marry her, Livingstone thought. But did he want to bring a wife into the midst of such a consuming career? Was he ready for marriage? Did he even have time to fall in love?

All these thoughts flitted through his brain in the merest second or two.

A brief flash of light shone below and far to his left, waking the descending archaeologist from his momentary reverie. No doubt a reflection of the morning sun off an ice crystal.

*What am I doing!* he said to himself. This was not a convenient time to consider such questions as marriage and death!

It was time to get on with the business at hand.

(3)

Again Livingstone looked down. Only fifty feet more. The excavated flue of blackness was directly below him and steadily enlarging. From a mere dot as he began, it now showed itself as a duct into the heart of the otherwise unreachable glacier. Everything was going exactly according to plan.

"Easy now . . . I'm nearly there," he said, speaking into the tiny microphone embedded in the suit under his chin.

Immediately a slight tug came upon his shoulders signalling a slowing of descent. Then a stop.

"Are you over it?" came a voice through a miniature speaker attached to the headgear near his right ear.

"Slightly off . . . only two or three feet."

"Which direction?"

"Draw in the crane—can you see me clearly—backward and to my right?"

"Yep, good—making the adjustment . . . *v-e-r-y* slowly."

Livingstone felt himself swing slightly from the pull at the top of his tether .

"Good, that's it," he said. "I'm over it—wait a minute till I'm steady again. . . ."

A brief silence.

". . . start easing me down gradually."

The downward motion resumed.

"All right . . . about twenty-five feet . . . twenty . . . now fifteen . . ."

Again he slowed.

"Ten feet . . . eight . . . six . . . four, three, two, one—stop."

The downward motion ceased.

"Where are you?" came the voice at his ear.

"I thought you were watching me from up there!" said Livingstone. "What do you mean, where am I!"

"We can see you fine," replied Scott Jordan, Livingstone's closest friend, an American who had served as his lifeline and confidant on more adventures and projects than either could count. "We want to know how it looks on *your* end."

"I'm exactly at the top of the shaft. My boots can touch the ice around the edge."

"See anything inside?"

"Just blackness. Wait a minute—I'm going to turn on my spotlight."

Livingstone reached for the halogen lantern strapped to his side, flipped it on, and sent the high-powered beam straight down below him.

"Nothing," he said. "It's deep," he added with a laugh.

"You getting cold feet, Adam!"

"Did I say that! Come on, Scott—*Eagle Two* to Mission Control . . . let's get this show on the road. Start me moving again. I want to see what's down there."

"All right, you're the boss—here we go."

(4)

As the archaeologist resumed his descent, Jordan's private satellite line rang in the tent high above. "Get that, will you, Jen?" he said, keeping his eyes on the monitor in front of him.

"It's Washington, Scott," said Livingstone's other trusted assistant in her musical Scandinavian accent.

"Stuart?"

"Right. What shall I tell him? Surely, you don't want—"

"You bet I want to talk to him," interrupted the handsome black man with a flashing smile of perfectly set teeth. "That man's going to be president someday. I want him on our side when it comes to research appropriations. I told him to call. Put the phone to my ear—I can't take my hands off the controls."

Jen did so.

"Marcos—you there?" said Jordan, still eying the monitor carefully.

There was a brief pause as he listened.

"Yeah, well you almost missed it, old buddy. Look, I can't talk. I'm sort of in the middle of the greatest discovery of all time. I'll have Jen hook you into the line. You won't be able to say anything, but at least you can hear Adam and me live . . . right, good . . . okay, talk to you soon."

Jordan nodded. Jen removed the phone from his ear and did as he had indicated, while Scott returned his full attention to the task at hand.

Meanwhile Livingstone's feet slowly entered the cylindrical well of ice. Now knees . . . shoulders . . . finally his entire body descended below the surface and out of sight from above.

"You're gone from view *now*," came Jordan's voice in his ear.

"I'm still here," returned Adam.

"Got room to maneuver?"

"Think so."

"How deep is it?"

"Can't tell . . . still no sign of the bottom. The lantern's picking up only frozen wall. Looks like I'm inside a vertical pipe of ice—a slight bluish tinge around the edges wherever the light hits."

"I'll turn on the helm-cam."

It fell silent for a few moments. Livingstone continued lowering into the

8

chilly blackness. It was eerily quiet. If anything went wrong now, he was a dead man. But nothing *would* go wrong. This was the moment, the triumph.

He arched his neck to see above him where the six-foot-round circle of faint blue light grew smaller and smaller.

He turned off the lantern briefly. Blackness engulfed him. The quiet inside the ice shaft was entirely different than that of open space. The air was dead, cold, empty. How old were these frozen walls, he wondered.

He had been in dozens of cramped, unusual, and dangerous places in his life. He had studied scores of ice-core rods drilled into glaciers. Now he was *inside* a hollow ice core. This was a sensation entirely new . . . uncanny, full of mystery.

"Hey, what's going on down there? The lights went out!"

"Don't worry, Scott. I wanted to see how dark it was."

Livingstone flipped the lantern back on, then reached up to adjust his helmet lamp. He squinted straight down, following the beam of light. The bottom was somewhere below him. He'd seen it on the monitor yesterday. Yet he could not escape the thrill of adventure, knowing his eyes would be the first to actually *see* it.

Still the lingering question remained: Might what they observed when they'd cut off the torches and siphoned out all the water from the bottom of the well . . . might it be only a horizontal slab of rock? Or perhaps a chunk of prehistoric tree? Only personal inspection could answer those questions.

"Wait . . . I think I see something!" Livingstone cried, surprised at the dull echo of his voice from inside the thin black cavity. He was probably two hundred feet below the opening now. Below him . . . yes, he could make out an end to the round cavity through which he had come!

"It's the bottom . . . . another seventy-five feet."

"We'll slow you up," said Jordan.

"Not yet—get me down there!"

"Give us a countdown then. I don't want to send you crashing onto it."

"Ten-four, Mission Control," said Livingstone excitedly, trying to imitate a NASA accent, "—about fifty feet now."

Silence.

"Thirty . . ."

His descent eased. Was this how Armstrong felt creeping down *Eagle*'s ladder onto the moon, wondering if the moondust would support him? What would *his* feet find when they touched down on the surface below?

"Twenty feet . . . fifteen . . . ten . . ."

Heart pounding with anticipation, Adam Livingstone awaited the final moment.

His searchlight now clearly revealed to his eyes the ancient timbers upon which his feet were about to strike. Was he about to become the first human being to stand upon those miraculously preserved planks, or so he hoped . . . since Noah himself!

"Hold it just a second, Scott—I need to tighten one of these straps."

(5)

Eight hours to the west, it yet remained night.

The sun sparkling off the glacial pack into which Adam Livingstone was at this moment boring like a human ice mole had set only a few hours before. U.S. Senator Marcos Stuart sat in his Washington office riveted in front of a television screen. The speakerphone on the desk beside him, turned to full volume, relayed the historic and dramatic conversation between his friend and the archaeologist.

A knock sounded on the outer door.

"Come in!" he called without turning his head.

The door behind him opened. Stuart heard footsteps cross his secretary's office and walk through the open door into his own. He knew well enough who it was. He would rather enjoy what was left of this evening alone. But his visitor was more responsible for securing him his present position than anyone, and he could not refuse him . . . at any hour.

"Working late, Senator?" said the new arrival.

"Just keeping tabs on events in Turkey."

"Military crisis?"

"Hardly," laughed Stuart. "Archaeology."

"Ah, yes—I'd forgotten your predilection for the sciences. What's going on?" asked Stuart's importune guest. He squinted at the monitor but was unable to make heads or tails of the images being relayed into space and back to earth.

"Adam Livingstone is about to prove that Noah's flood may be more than a fairy tale," quipped the Senator.

The other man did not reply. Stuart did not observe the creasing of his visitor's eyebrows at the words.

"What's your interest?"

"This man Jordan—who's at the controls—he and I go way back."

"What's the connection?"

"We majored in geology together at Colorado. I wouldn't miss this for the world."

"What about Livingstone?"

"What about him?"

"You know him well too?"

"Well enough, I suppose. Look at this—it's amazing!"

"How'd you meet?"

"When Jordan and I went to Cambridge to study for a year."

"Same field?"

The senator shook his head. "Livingstone was working on his master's in archaeology. He wrote a paper Scott showed me once. Other than that I was busy with my own studies."

"And now?"

"We keep loose tabs on one another through Scott."

"Close?"

"Not especially. Scott's a good mutual friend, that's all."

The other took in the information thoughtfully. "Well, no matter—all that's in the past, Marcos," he said. "You're an important man now. Your star is only beginning to rise. You can take my word for that. And some of my people are at last ready to meet you."

"Can't you call my secretary tomorrow and arrange something?" rejoined Senator Stuart. Frustration was evident in his tone as he tried to keep his attention on the set in front of him. The man's timing could not be worse.

"I don't think I need remind you, Marcos, that we do not go through *public* channels."

Stuart nodded and muttered a few words. Just then the voice of his long-distance friend sounded on the table.

"Can't this wait?" Stuart said impatiently, nodding at the screen. "Look, he's moving again."

His visitor did not reply immediately. He listened for a moment, intrigued with the telephone exchange crackling through the night.

"... *okay ten feet ... five ... three feet ...*"

The office fell silent. The only sound was the static over the telephone line.

"I'll be in touch," said the man after a moment. He turned quickly and moved toward the door.

"And, Senator," he added, pausing briefly and glancing back with narrowed eyes, "when my people are ready, I suggest you give *them* your full attention."

Stuart muttered something in reply. But already his visitor was gone.

(6)

The remote place at the immediate focus of the world's attention sat squarely in the center of a nose-shaped bulge in east-central Turkey, twenty miles from the Armenian border, fourteen miles northwest of Iran. The mount of activity lay also within just a few miles of Gruziya and Azerbaydzhan—known to westerners as Georgia and Azerbaijan—and Iraq. It would have been difficult to find a place on the globe more central to forces of change and ancient conflict, sitting at the very hub between Europe, Asia, and the Middle East.

Though sought after through the years by thousands of would-be fame-seekers and Bible-provers, in recent decades the region had remained largely off-limits to adventurers and archaeologists.

There had been, of course, rumors and legends of numerous sightings through the years.

A shepherd lad named Jacob was said to have stumbled upon the ark in 1905 while searching for his lost goats. He drew a picture of a boxlike boat sticking out of the ice near the edge of a steep drop-off. Another young Turkish shepherd named Georgie was reported to have climbed the mountain twice a few years later and actually climbed up onto the structure and peered into its windows.

In 1916 and 1917, Russian soldiers and scientists made one of the first documented expeditions specifically to find the ark. They were said to have walked inside the enormous mythical ship, seen the animal stalls, taken photographs of their discovery, and mapped the area in great detail. Upon returning home, however, they found themselves engulfed by the Russian Revolution. All photographs were lost.

Through the years such stories proliferated, added to by pictures taken from a U.S. Navy plane and many other so-called eyewitness accounts. The navy pictures too, like those of the Russians decades earlier, were never made public.

Somehow photographs *always* turned up missing, adding a certain dubious quality to their authenticity. Thus the exact spot upon the mountain where sightings were said to have occurred could never be pinpointed with accuracy.

At last that uncertainty seemed about to be put to rest. Methods of infrared and multispectral photography had been greatly improved through the years, recently revealing tantalizing clues that could not be ignored. Now the Turkish government, under initial prodding from well-connected political friends and, ultimately, in a deal brokered by Livingstone himself, had two years ago granted its approval to the project now reaching culmination. It was far more extensive than anything yet attempted—a quid pro quo arrangement between several Western governments, three unnamed American firms, a French professional consortium, and four British cabinet ministers, likewise unnamed.

No financial specifics had been disclosed. But Turkish officials expected the windfall to accomplish for their sagging economy—beleaguered by factional strife, weakened by the Kurdish refugee problem, and having a difficult time finding a national compass in the post-Soviet new-world order—no less than what the Marshall Plan had for postwar Germany. If allowing international explorers to poke around in the ice could substantially fatten their nation's treasury and line the pockets of a few of those same officials in the meantime, what could it hurt?

Nor did the Livingstone Cartel, as it was unofficially styled, peer too closely into whatever graft might be involved in the arrangement. Too many questions in this part of the world had never been a wise practice. As long as they were allowed access to the mountain, they considered their investment secure. They would not quibble over details or whatever local politics resulted from it.

They had been granted five years to conduct their research. After that time all would be renegotiated. It was what amounted to a five-year "lease" of sorts on the 16,946-foot mountain known to Turks as Bü Agri Dagi.

Livingstone, it was reported, had been involved in a daring rescue of several high-placed Turkish officials who had fallen into misfortune in Baghdad a couple years earlier. Details of the incident were confidential and sketchy, though there was a clear linkage between it and the sudden relaxation of policy regarding Ararat exploration. If said officials owed Livingstone their lives, after this he would consider himself repaid many times over for his bravado.

A governing committee of seven had been appointed to oversee the interests of the cartel. But Livingstone, ostensibly a nonvoting eighth member, was recognized as calling the shots.

It was his brainchild. Without his prestige, knowledge, experience, and reputation, the expedition would have little chance of success. Livingstone's presence and charisma provided the central ingredient making a lucrative outcome possible.

For anything to capture the public fancy, a personal element was required. The comptrollers for this profit-sharing cartel recognized that Livingstone himself was it—handsome, famous, rich, one of England's more eligible bachelors, and by any standards a brilliant man with visionary objectives. He had received more press recently than the royal family.

To garner American support and enthusiasm, a shrewd media blitz on U.S. television had elevated the status of Livingstone's right-hand man to a near equal level of importance. Most U.S. citizens were unaware that the project was international in scope. Thinking it entirely an American affair, they followed it as eagerly as they had the moon landing. In the States Scott Jordan would no doubt wind up being the more famous of the two men.

Jordan's ethnic background drew high interest from the African-American community, offering beneficial PR antidote to recently growing polarization between whites and blacks, accomplishing for archaeology what Tiger Woods had for golf. And with blond, blue-eyed diminutive Swede Jennifer Swaner—about whom lingered a faint air of the counterculture from her years of schooling in northern California—completing the Livingstone trio, the entire project could not have been more perfectly cast by a Hollywood master script-writer.

If Livingstone returned to England with what his backers hoped were pieces of antiquity itself in his hand, his fame would eclipse that of his Scottish namesake for his African exploration a century before. Moreover, the treasures of unearthed (or "un-iced") wood would be as valuable to science as the moon rocks. According to the few metaphysicists among them, that wood could become even more significant in divulging the meaning of that science.

The only interests conspicuously unrepresented in the project were Jews and evangelical Christians, both of whom it seemed would possess a great stake in the potential discovery. Any number of evangelicals had clamored to get in once news of the project broke on CNN. But several of the principle financial players were outspokenly opposed. They would open no door that allowed religion a role in the expedition. Especially, they said, Christian fundamentalists whose agenda could hardly be considered scientific in nature. Whether Jewish and Israeli interests had been considered or rejected for similar or other reasons was not known.

Motives on the part of all but Livingstone himself were purely financial. Since the fall of the Soviet Union, all the adventure seemed gone out of the world. There hadn't been a good crisis you could sink your teeth into for years. Space stations weren't all that interesting to most people. Mars remained a remote possibility at best.

But Noah's ark!

This was something to capture the attention of the world. And hopefully pay rich dividends later for those who knew how to exploit the business aspects of archaeology. It was personal, televisible, and tailor-made for this era of heightened spiritual interest. Columbus had brought gold into the coffers of Spain and Portugal. Why might not the discovery of the century likewise yield handsome rewards?

As a historic find, this would surpass King Tut's tomb. It would be greater than the ark of the covenant or the chalice of the Last Supper, if either of them were ever unearthed.

There would be books, photographs, television specials, movies, lecture tours, and who could tell how many hundreds of ancillary products created for sale.

And the cartel owned rights to it all.

As long as the discovery was genuine and worldwide interest proved what they were counting on, the investment—which some sources estimated at a billion dollars for the mountain "lease" alone, not to mention funding for the high-tech expedition—would repay itself many times over.

All this, Livingstone's reputation, and several personal and corporate fortunes, hung on the line with the 225-pound weight of explorer and equipment, as all seven committee members and a dozen or more of the cartel's investors stared breathlessly at several television monitors under the expansive tent of expedition headquarters above. Several had been flown in earlier by huge military helicopters from Dogubayazit as soon as morning's light permitted. On the screens before them passed the slowly moving nondescript surface of ice wall as seen by the miniaturized camera attached to Livingston's helmet light.

Within moments they would observe that which they hoped would make them rich men and perhaps etch their names in history as a footnote underneath Livingstone's, or else it would send one or two of them to the bankruptcy courts of their respective countries before month's end.

(7)

A distant mountain climber lowered the telescope from his eye and hastened on. The sun shone in his face. It was reflecting off the lens too much from here to see accurately.

He had to be closer. And get the sun behind him. He needed to see exactly what was going on. He must take a precise fix of the coordinates.

With speed remarkable for his bulk and breathing heavily from the exertion, cold, and altitude, the climber hurried up the steep rocky trail ahead of him, over the stones and around the ice floes of his own personal Mount Maleficent. He, too, had been excluded from an event, which by all rights should have included him. Like Maleficent, he would find a way to make them pay for that oversight.

Over his characteristic khaki garb, he had dressed from head to foot in white climbing pants and parka so his movements would be unseen against the snowy background. His breath, visible in the chill morning air, came in frosty bursts. One of his gloved hands carried an ice ax, the other the telescope. Around his waist clanged an assortment of ice screws, chocks, pitons, carabiners, harnesses, a hammer ax, and other assorted impedimenta of the mountaineer's craft.

He would probably need none of it. His objective on this day was not to scale icy peaks but to gain a vantage point from which he could clearly observe the goings-on across the way.

His smoldering resentment kept his blood warm against the elements. Did they think they could cast him aside so easily?

He would show that he still had a few discoveries left for the world too! He had been here before, once in the 1960s on the Lord Bode expedition and again on several of the more recent Morris ventures into Davis Canyon. He knew Ararat better than any of them. Once he had their location pinpointed exactly, he would return again.

He would not so easily be overshadowed by this young upstart!

Thirty or so minutes later, upon the ledge of an exposed projection of an adjacent ridge of Ararat's treacherous slopes, the hefty lone figure positioned himself on the edge of a narrow precipice. He was separated from the spectacle being played out before the world by a distance of approximately a mile as well as by a deep glacial vault that none but an eagle would be capable of traversing. Standing a thousand feet lower in elevation than his renowned counterpart, he stared into the eyepiece of his high-powered telescope, which now sat on a tripod where he had positioned it on the ledge. He was grateful that the usual cap of clouds was gone today, and visibility was perfectly clear.

The setting was exactly as many of the sketches represented it—a glacially encrusted overhang sitting beneath a sheer cliff of rock overlooked from above by the summit and extending straight down from the site a thousand or more feet.

He could see nothing of the structure from where he stood. But if it was there, Livingstone was approaching it just about the only way possible. Sightings reported a year ago after two years of warmth and glacial meltback had no doubt exposed the protruding end of the vessel, though it had been covered over again by last winter's heavy snows. He was loath to admit it, but he had little doubt that Livingstone was on to the find of all time. The thought filled him with silent rage.

He continued to breathe heavily. The watcher was, in truth, in better shape for this sort of escapade than his size would indicate. Until just a short while ago he had himself been considered the foremost archaeologist in the world. The fact that such a perception was now eroding, notwithstanding his discovery in the Rift Valley, was a bitter one for an ego nearly as large as his frame. It made him more determined than ever to reverse the trend.

For just such an opportunity had he hounded the Livingstone expedition since the moment he learned of its objective.

Nor was he the only one stalking Livingstone's moves. Forces in higher realms had been invisibly tracking the Englishman for years. The Dimension had underestimated the danger of this present expedition, however. But it was about to wake. When they did, powers of both light and darkness would be sent into the battle that would soon be at hand.

(8)

"Ten feet . . . ," came Livingstone's voice over the speaker in the headquarters tent.

Regulating the controls of the intricate system of wheels and ropes, cable and cranes and pulleys, to which a thousand feet of cord was attached, Scott Jordan slowed the rate of descent to a crawl. From here on, he would take it inch by inch.

Not a head moved from the screens. Scarcely a sound could be heard, save a few mumbled comments.

"Look down at your feet, Adam—let us see too!" came a whisper.

Almost as if he had heard the words, though the chief project engineer had spoken nothing into his microphone, Livingstone's helmet camera swung down, revealing the floor of the ice chamber.

A few gasps sounded, followed by exclamations of astonishment.

"Okay, nine feet . . . five . . . three feet . . . two . . . ," came Adam's voice again.

Silence immediately returned. Not an eye moved from the monitors.

"One . . . gently . . . that's it—hold it there."

"What is it, Adam?" asked Jordan.

"I'm down, Scott—I'm touching. I want to test it to make sure it's solid and will support . . . seems fine . . . frozen solid—let out a little more line . . . fine . . . all right, good—I'm standing firmly on the bottom."

At last a cheer went up inside the tent.

"I heard that!" laughed Livingstone.

"Everyone up here is proud of your accomplishment, Adam. So is the watching world. But you must know the question on everyone's mind—"

"What historic words I am going to utter for posterity—let me see, that's one small step for an archaeologist—"

"Never mind that!" interrupted Jordan with a laugh. "What is it you're standing on!"

"That's what I came down here to find out," replied Livingstone. "All right, I suppose we'd better get on with it. Let out a little more line so I can move about freely."

On the monitors, observers and investors now saw Adam kneel down.

"The surface is a brownish gray," he said. "I'm sure you can see too that it doesn't appear at first glance to be any kind of granite, at least nothing I'm familiar with. It's uneven, though not pitted like stone. There seem elongated depressions, a graininess such as you would expect from wood. It obviously appears to be wood—solid, frozen . . . and I would have to say it does not look like a mere tree. It's flat, as would be a cut timber of some kind."

They could see Adam scanning the interior of his tiny cave of exploration.

"I'm taking off one of my gloves. . . ."

All waited in silent expectation. They saw a hand rub back and forth across the floor.

"Hard to tell . . . , " came the voice from below after a moment. "It feels no

17

different than ice. It's covered with a thin layer of the refrozen meltwater from yesterday. The surface isn't exactly level. Up at one end it's pretty clean, and the ice is thicker down at the other end where the residue from the burn drained down."

He paused a moment.

"What's peculiar, though," he added, "—look here, do you see that . . ."

His finger pointed for the camera.

". . . a few spots of blackening. It's almost—but that could hardly be . . . I was about to say that it's almost as if the torches had actually burned the wood in spots."

"Try your hand-burner."

"Right."

Livingstone stood again, unfastened the small propane torch from his waist, ignited it, and knelt again. Carefully he fanned the flame across a small section of surface. He paused to feel it, then burned at the ice again. After two minutes he turned off the burner and set it aside. He removed a small hammer and pick from the equipment strapped to his side and began chipping at the section of floor his flame had probed. The observers saw him reach down and grasp something between his gloved fingers and examine it carefully. He turned it over two or three times.

"Scott, you're not going to believe this!" he exclaimed. At last his voice displayed genuine excitement. "The petrification is not complete! This is wood all right—real, genuine wood . . . the black spots are burn marks—our torches actually burned the surface of this wood!"

Astonished exclamations nearly raised the canvas roof of the headquarters tent.

"Adam . . . Adam, can you hear me above this hubbub here? Everyone is shouting only one question—is it the ark?"

The tent grew silent again.

On the screens Adam knelt again and appeared examining the floor very carefully.

"We'll have to do more tests," came his voice at length. "But it is wood, of that there can be no doubt. That leaves but two possibilities—that somehow an immense tree utterly nonindigenous to this region wound up here. The fact that we are four to six thousand feet above Ararat's tree line would make such an occurrence impossible under any other conditions than a cataclysmic flood of unbelievable proportions. Even if this is a mere tree, its presence here would appear to confirm the flood theory. But the second possibility seems far more likely."

"What possibility!" came the eager voice from above.

"I am standing on a flat, not a round, surface. It can't be a tree. Unless I miss my guess, there are detectable markings different from the grain itself—which to me indicate that I am not the first man to touch this wood."

"What kind of markings?"

Adam bent close to the floor and again pointed below him.

"Such as would come from a crude cutting instrument of some kind—I'm not sure if it was a saw or ax," he replied. "I don't know if you can see what I'm pointing to here, but to my eyes I think it is clear that something or someone actually cut this wood into the flat boards upon which I am standing. And the irregularity of the grain in places gives the appearance of lamination. In other words, it's not just one large plank. Whether it is the ark, I cannot yet say . . . but I would stake my reputation on the conviction that these are certainly boards hewn by man."

The cheering that went around the tent of headquarters now did not stop for three or more minutes.

Immediately half those in the tent scrambled for their satellite-linked cellular phones, for which provision had been made. In less than an hour, four-inch headlines had been set at the offices of no less than five hundred daily newspapers around the world—from Tokyo to Moscow to London to New York—proclaiming NOAH'S ARK DISCOVERED!

(9)

Meanwhile Adam Livingstone busily engaged himself in what further exploration and experimentation were possible in his cramped six-foot circular laboratory.

"Is there any way you can send one of those large burners and the suction cable down?" he said to his chief engineer. "How's the wind up there?"

"Still holding calm," replied Jordan. "What do you have in mind?"

"If I could open up this cavity . . . burn away more of the ice. Any extra foot I can get to might provide the evidence we're after."

"I'll consult with the others. In the meantime, take what samples you can."

Half an hour later, torch, oxygen, and suction cable were on their way down over the ridge, attached to the guideline that had taken the glacial astronaut on his historic descent an hour before.

"Watch yourself, Adam," Jordan cautioned. "That's a powerful torch. You don't want to create too large a cave for fear of collapse."

"This ice is several hundred feet or more thick in every direction. It's not going anywhere."

"There could be cracks."

"I'll be careful, Scott. But this is the chance of a lifetime. I've got to expose as much of this surface as I can."

"If the winds kick up, we'll have to pull you out."

"Relax," laughed Livingstone, "no winds are going to bother me down here."

"If it starts blowing a gale—"

"I'm not leaving here until I'm good and ready," interrupted Livingstone. "Try to yank me out before then, and I'll unhook the rope!"

"Your committee might have something to say about that," laughed his friend. Despite his cautions, Jordan would have trusted Livingstone's judgment with his own life. He had in fact done exactly that numerous times.

"You tell my committee I'm thinking of spending a day or two down here."

"What!"

"It's actually rather cozy. You just send me down food and water."

"You'll need more than that."

"Like what?"

"Air, for one thing . . . and warmth."

"Didn't you say the oxygen line is on the way down? If I get cold you can send me down another parka."

"Some might argue you've lost your mind!" laughed Jordan.

"Don't worry. If the weather becomes a problem, I'm on my way up. But it's taken who knows how many millennia for someone to find this place . . . we have to know. The more I de-ice of this thing, the better chance we'll have."

Jordan did not argue the point further. Everyone wanted the same thing—to learn as much as they could in what time they had available. If conditions deteriorated, they would reassess.

"Matter of fact, why don't you join me, Scott?" added Livingstone. "The hard part's done. Now that we have a secure line from the crane into the shaft, we can move people and equipment up and down with relative ease."

"I wouldn't trust anyone else at the controls."

"How about Figg? Why don't you start getting him suited up? And Jen would like nothing more than to be the first woman since Noah's wife to set foot down here. What do you say, Jen . . . if you're up there listening?"

"I'm on my way!" shouted the young lady, trying to grab the microphone excitedly out of Jordan's hands.

"But don't bring your Birkenstocks!" laughed Livingstone. "It's cold down here."

"Let's see how the initial work with the torch goes first," replied Jordan, reassuming control of the mike. "If you clear out enough room for two or three people to maneuver," he went on, "and if the weather cooperates, we'll see. Figg is already getting his parka on."

In thirty minutes two cables stretched down the shaft to Livingstone, and the suction pump was operating. Adam fired up the torch at minimum burn and set about to enlarge his igloolike cavity. It took several accidental extinguishings and considerable tinkering with the external oxygen flow between Adam below and Jordan at the controls before he managed to get much ice melted. Once the levels of flame, oxygen, and suction were regulated to satisfaction, however, Livingstone began to make rapid progress.

The splashing about of melting ice made it messy work. Within two hours, however, the archaeologist had tripled the area of exposed wood—at one narrow point extending to some fifteen feet against the grain. The flat expanse was clearly wider than the girth of any possible behemoth of prehistoric tree, establishing the surface conclusively as man-made and no mere natural occurrence of a growing thing.

By noon he had exposed enough to establish some order to the planking structure, digging out samples between them of a crystalline resinlike substance of amber color. Though his on-site television 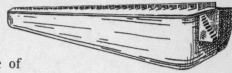 camera captured his every move and recorded every motion of progress, he also shot still photographs of every inch. Color enlargements would be capable of far more detail than mere video.

But it was the discovery made by Adam Livingstone about two o'clock that afternoon as he continued to lengthen the crawl tunnel he had begun excavating from the original six-foot opening, which finally ensured his place in history. Anxious editors circling the globe at last possessed verification that they were indeed on solid ground to run the headlines their papers had set that morning.

# Global Intrigue

(1)

Around the globe, Adam Livingstone's Ararat discovery met with strong and diverse reactions.

Overseas to the west, a newspaper whacked against the front door of a two-story home of classic New England design. Inside, its thud reverberated off the walls of a starkly furnished living room and echoed through an open bedroom door. The abrupt noise roused the slumbering occupant into wakefulness.

Bedsprings groaned. A large-framed man rolled over a time or two and glanced sleepily toward the clock on his nightstand. Seven-twenty.

Now the scents of fresh Yukon Blend brewing in his automatic Braun in the kitchen slowly reached his nostrils. The aroma enlivened the senses inside his head far more than light through windows or paper landing on the porch were capable of.

He drew in a deep breath and exhaled slowly, as if the effort would enable his body to vanquish the grogginess still clinging to every muscle. Its effect, however, was minimal.

He lay several minutes more, gradually coming to himself. Finally he draped his legs over the edge of the bed and dragged himself to a sitting position.

Slowly he rose to his feet, wandered into the bathroom, eyes still mostly closed. With more reflex than decision, he spun the cold-water valve to full velocity. The next moment he climbed into the shower. As an act of supreme, though still sleepy, will, he planted himself directly under the head. There he stood under the icy flow, gasping for air in what could be described as nothing short of self-imposed torture. It was a ritual in which he engaged every morning. Whether he could be said to *enjoy* it was doubtful. But it woke him faster than Starbucks and was always worth the momentary agony thirty seconds later when he stepped onto the bath mat, shivering, invigorated, and ready for the day.

He shaved hurriedly, not because he was in any particular hurry, but because the process bored him. He had no one to whom he needed to look presentable. Neither did he bother combing his rumpled graying hair. He walked back to his bedroom to dress.

His eyes fell on the book about the end times his pastor had lent him, still sitting on his nightstand. He'd only gotten through a chapter and a half before sleep overtook him. Fascinating stuff, he had to admit. He and Pastor Mark had been discussing such things during their previous three Bible studies together. His outlook on many things was changing rapidly following his conversation and prayer time with Mark and his wife, Laurene.

Ten minutes later he eased himself into his favorite overstuffed chair. His fingers stretched around a large mug of strong black Yukon as he opened the morning's edition of the *Boston Globe,* whose arrival had begun his day fifteen minutes earlier.

Rocky McCondy, widower, father of none, friend of few, and acquaintance of many, lived by no routine other than that prescribed by these few morning pleasures. Once two stout mugs of coffee had been downed, the rest of the pot thermosed for the day, and the *Globe* read, he would consult the papers and files on his desk for twenty or thirty minutes. He would then gather what notes, reminders, updates, and files he might need and be off for the day.

Breakfast followed at any of a dozen small cafes between here and Nashua, Manchester, or Concord, in whichever direction his business that day would take him. By nine or ten he would be on the streets doing what he did best—finding out things people wanted to know.

There had been years he'd punched a time clock. But after the death of his wife, he had needed a change. Through the encouragement of a friend on the Boston force, he'd wound up in this most unusual of professions. It was a lonely life at times, though he met interesting people. But despite numerous offers, he'd never been tempted to return to what some would consider a more normal existence.

Today's peaceful morning was suddenly interrupted, however, as McCondy read the astonishing front-page account of the historic discovery that had taken place in Turkey as he'd slept.

He had scarcely known of the expedition. He'd only run across the name Adam Livingstone in passing. But a familiar phrase in the article now slammed into his brain like a freight train out of the distant past.

He set down his mug, threw the paper aside, and leapt to his feet. He lumbered toward the stairs, which creaked as he made his way up to the second floor of the 120-year-old, wood-frame house.

Five minutes later he was rummaging around in the dim light of his attic. A lone twenty-five-watt bulb overhead provided but little help as he sifted through the contents of a long-forgotten chest of heirlooms.

He returned downstairs to his chair sometime later, clutching several sheaves of paper, an old browning photograph, several newspaper clippings, a book with a decaying leather cover, and a few other valuables. He picked up his mug again and began sipping at its remains, his brow creased deep in thought.

The sensation that had come over him was the most peculiar thing he'd ever experienced. The man was a perfect stranger—and a famous one at that. He would *never* get through!

But . . . he had to try.

He'd learned to trust his hunches over the years. True, some of them led to dead ends. But this was no time to take a chance. Hunch or not . . . possible dead end or not . . . a man's life could be at stake.

He could not risk keeping silent.

(2)

Senator Marcos Stuart, feeling vaguely ill at ease, strode up the Capitol steps several hours later the same morning following the Ararat discovery.

Headlines and broadcast specials blared the news everywhere. He had been cornered twice already since leaving home by eager reporters anxious for a quote from the friend of Livingstone's partner. He should be elated. This was Scott's moment of triumph. Jordan had celebrated with him last November following his own landslide victory.

But something had gnawed at Stuart ever since last night in his office. He'd detected a different timbre in Mitch Cutter's voice . . . and wasn't sure he liked it.

He had hardly noticed it at the time, for he had been distracted by the broadcast from Ararat. But as the brief interview played itself over in his mind, Stuart realized there had been a veiled tone of threat around the edge of the conversation. Nor did the inquisitive bevy of questions settle well within him. He had revealed nothing that wasn't public record. Yet something about the exchange didn't feel right. Why was Cutter so interested in Livingstone when he'd hardly seemed to know what was going on?

Two words repeated themselves over and over in Stuart's brain—*my people . . . my people . . . my people.*

For the first time, he felt himself more than a little nervous. Who were these "people" anyway?

He had known, of course, that a day of reckoning would come. When those whom Cutter represented threw their invisible weight behind a candidate of Stuart's stature and national potential, expectations accompanied the package. He'd been around the political game long enough to know how things worked. He'd tried to convince himself there wasn't much difference between this and any powerful political action committee. Down inside, however—and maybe last night's tone finally made him realize it—Stuart knew Cutter represented no mere PAC . . . but the power that controlled *all* the PACs.

Being beholden to *them* meant that no tiniest slice of your life was yours again. You were owned. It seemed an easy price to pay back then—with no hint of repayment.

Now Marcos Stuart wondered.

As the senator tried to extricate such worries from his mind, already the man who was at the center of them was seated in the first-class cabin of a plane bound nonstop from Dulles to Zurich.

(3)

Meanwhile, far away—almost due east of the discovery site itself by some three hundred miles—a man of distinctive appearance, striking features, and confident gait, entered and strode across the lobby of an ultra-modern, glass-and-steel highrise office complex.

It had been a busy morning and afternoon. Most in these new government offices were gone for the day. But not the man recognized as one of the most powerful individuals in the new republic, second in influence only to the president himself.

There was a great deal to be done. He had kept his smoldering wrath in check all day, but the effort was becoming more and more difficult by the minute. Today's events proved even worse than he had imagined they might be. The exploration so close to his homeland was bad enough. But he had not dreamed they would actually find anything. The discovery was sure to cause him trouble, exactly as he had feared. Though he might still be able to deflect most of the potential damage.

The elevator took him rapidly to the seventh floor, where he walked briskly down a deserted corridor and into his expansive office. In New York, London, or Rome this would hardly be considered a skyscraper. Yet a building of such height was unusual in this region of the world. For now it was the tallest building in Baku, capital of the new sovereign nation of Azerbaydzhan.

It was a city few in the world had even heard of. But it would not long remain in the background on the world's stage. The time approached when the skyline here would rival New York's—if not in scope, certainly in grandeur.

The title indicated on the door he had just entered did not sound particularly significant—Interior Minister of Works. Yet the decisions made in this room had more daily effect on life in the small country—created earlier this decade by the breakup of the former Soviet Union—than anyone's, including President Voroshilov's.

And his present role was merely a stepping-stone. Such would not be his position much longer. Momentous times loomed ahead. He occupied this role for the present only as a means toward an end.

Early this morning he had watched the televised account of the Ararat climax from his villa south of the city overlooking the bay. He had kept tabs on it as his schedule overseeing several construction projects allowed. By day's end embers of anger had grown hot within him.

He had known for a year or more that any significant discovery on Ararat would threaten to expose his own activities prematurely to the attention of the world. He had thus kept close watch on the English archaeologist for some time, doing his best to prevent the Ararat exploration from materializing at all. But to no avail. The man had the favor of the world and more lives than a cat.

Once the gaze of cameras and lights and throngs and newspeople was brought down upon them, there would be questions—questions it would not be good for the world to ask. The international press was a more inquisitive lot than the people of Azerbaydzhan.

The world *would* take note of this critical global juncture. The moment for that unveiling approached rapidly, and with it, his own personal destiny.

But that time was not yet. Livingstone must be stopped before he ruined everything!

He crossed the room briskly to the bar, poured himself a drink, then strode, deep in thought, toward the large picture window. He stood overlooking the city and harbor where much of his modernization work was focused. He took several deep breaths, trying to calm himself.

Livingstone was too close. Across the Muganskaya Steppe, over the Zangeszurskiy Khr at the Armenian border . . . hardly more than a stone's throw.

The Englishman's high-profile proximity was inescapable. Already news teams were booking rooms in Yerevan and Kirovabad in anticipation of expanded efforts on the Turkish mountain. If things continued, it was only a matter of time before they also descended into Baku.

He could *not* afford the prying eyes of the world's press. The publicity certain to be focused upon this region of the globe would prove disastrous. Theirs were schemes that depended on stealth. Light was doom to their design.

He'd seen danger two years ago. He had put someone on Livingstone then and had attempted by various subtle means to ruin his cartel, as he had successfully done many times before with other expeditions. He'd even tried to get his old friend Saddam to pressure—or threaten—the Turkish government. But the Englishman's plans progressed in spite of his efforts. Livingstone was proving a capable and potent adversary.

He would try another tack. He had to put a stop to all this. He must strike before this thing got out of hand. From here on he would handle it personally.

His two colleagues in Holland and Switzerland would no doubt disapprove. But they did not have so much to lose as he. The eye was one of their symbols.

They watched everyone of significance on the world stage. Henceforth he would concentrate *his* eye on Livingstone.

He stood gazing out the great window a moment longer, then spun around and reached for the phone.

Two brief calls sufficed for his purposes. A third call was to the airport, where his private jet stood by twenty-four hours a day. He would fly to Baghdad tonight and on to London in the morning.

(4)

On the continent of Europe, other eyes also watched.

They were the eyes of the two foremost members of the highly secretive Council of Twelve, to whom had been entrusted the indoctrination of mankind in preparation for a new-world order. These two were not merely powerful in this invisible realm, they were also among the world's most influential financial and media giants, able with the stroke of a pen to effect the global economy and communications networks.

They had been watching for years . . . their predecessors for centuries.

Those of their Order were not anxious over momentary rises and falls in their Master's vast scheme. Unlike their ambitious colleague, they were not concerned on this day over the attention the incident drew from the world. The masses were fickle and small-minded, easily manipulated in any direction that became necessary. The enemy might appear in a thousand simultaneous visions around the world, and it would not increase belief in him nor endanger their cause to any significant degree.

There were deeper matters involved, of more far-reaching import. They were part of a timeless design. The passage of years mattered little to the ultimate success of The Plan. Yet a climax approached for which long preparations had been made. The era of their Millennium was at hand, and nothing must threaten the promise of its dawn.

"I have felt strange rumblings in the Dimension," said a tall, stately woman whose eyes were alight with vision beyond the ordinary. She appeared middle-aged. To have called her attractive would not have been untrue, though her countenance and demeanor exuded quiet potency and unassailability far more than beauty. She was one capable of transfixing the mind, not the eye.

"I was awakened in the darkness," rejoined her counterpart, a greying man of dignified bearing. He was sixty-two and well fit, and his face bore a like expression of command. "My Wise One was calling me," he added.

"My Spirit Guide likewise spoke in the early hours" said the woman. "The message was a single word—*beware . . . beware!*"

"My Wise One cautioned—*the door must not be opened!* His face wore a grave expression. A vision came to me the likes of which I had not before seen."

The woman nodded. Her Guide had come to her with similar countenance.

As of one mind, the two turned toward one another where they sat, extended their hands until their fingers barely touched, then closed their eyes. They must seek further illumination from those who had gone before and who now apprehended deeper levels of the Dimension than could their earthbound eyes.

The woman began to softly hum a strange otherworldly melody. The man's lips moved in silent repetitive cadence to open the channel to his Wise One.

The next sounds several minutes later came from voices eerily unlike the two out of whose mouths they came.

"*A door tightly shut for eons,*" said a strange voice through the woman's lips, "*. . . must not allow the origin of the breach to be found . . . threatens to awaken mysteries of power kept secret since the dawn of time. Keep the door of that truth sealed. Find it . . . discover the source and destroy it.*"

The idea of such a secret coming to light had indeed caused Lucifer's legions to rise and take note. Nor were these the only two being summoned. That secret represented the *true* light—the light of Truth, where good and evil were born—not the darkness that such as these *called* "light." Such were no mere matters of transitory whim on the part of the enemy's people, but they touched the very foundation of their existence.

The eyes of mankind must *not* discover the portal to that truth!

Over the potential emergence of this truth the Dark Dimension was not merely uneasy—the Livingstone discovery had set the spirit realm atremble!

His discovery on Ararat could unravel a century of careful work discrediting the enemy's primacy over life itself. The evolution of man into a higher consciousness of godlikeness lay at the very root of their scheme. They could *not* allow such an important cornerstone in their framework for world control to be weakened in the public mind.

Yet what Livingstone might *next* unearth represented the ultimate peril, extending back not just a century . . . but to the beginning of their Master's season of domination.

"*Few things imperil our ultimate success.*" It was a man's voice speaking now, softly, as from a great distance. "*That to which his eyes will soon turn represents the most dangerous. Long has the Master feared it.*"

For a long while it was silent. Those from the other world slowly retreated. The messages for this day were complete. The two withdrew their hands, sat back, and opened their eyes.

"Is it the ark itself . . . is that the danger?" said the woman in her own voice now, reflecting as if to herself. "We knew this might come. I find these warnings unexpected. We were apprised of Livingstone's plans. One of our people is in his cartel."

"Perhaps we misjudged the spiritual import," rejoined the man, also reflectively. Both found themselves strangely at a loss to understand these tremors. "The finding of the ark does prove the enemy's Book true."

"That fact is of limited danger. The Book has been proven true many times."

"But what might Livingstone do with that knowledge? Had one of the evangelicals made the discovery, we would have little cause for worry. In Livingstone's hands, however, it could prove a dangerous revelation."

"That may be the message of our Guides, that it will point him toward the door that must not be opened."

"I thought Livingstone safely ours."

"My Wise One says his allegiance is in jeopardy, that the enemy is at work, that others are now involved."

"Perhaps we have taken Livingstone's affection for granted. We must alert the baron."

"I remain confident the girl can turn him."

"Hopefully it will not come to that. All she need do is keep him from being turned toward the enemy and gradually bring him into our orbit."

"The marriage will make him one of us. I have no fear of his ultimate loyalty."

"The Scottish order will be the best route of initiation, a logical next step in his career progression."

"It may be time to call the Twelve," said the woman. "I sense stirrings also within the Council."

"My Wise One says one of our number may be straying from The Plan."

"Was identification given?" asked the woman.

"Only to the extent of warning us to look to our own. He said none must be allowed to betray the Master's cause."

"Betrayal always comes from those closest at hand."

"We must be watchful."

More silence followed. At length the two rose and left the windowless room separately.

From this day they would heed developments with heightened diligence. And they would bring all the mysteries of ancient Babylon to bear that *they* might first discover the place where their power could be undone . . . so as to destroy it.

The enemy's people occasionally ventured too close. A formidable menace had come a century earlier. They had eradicated the threat. But they had not been able to discover the man's secret. He had gone mad with desert wanderings and had led them nowhere. Now they must not allow further exploration toward what had almost disastrously been revealed back then.

They had waited for centuries for their strategy to unfold. Time now advanced inexorably toward the revelation of the Master's anointed one. They could allow a threat to his invincibility no slightest foothold.

Wherever the place of their vulnerability was, Adam Livingstone must not set foot there.

_____

# three

# No Fairy Tale

(1)

The morning dawned bright and warm.

It was a perfect day to be up in the city. The Royal Tournament at Earl's Court Centre would highlight the family holiday.

The moment the horsemen had completed their military spectacle, mother and father, daughter and son eagerly sprinted to their waiting borrowed car. Laughing, they scampered in. The boisterous father turned on the engine and sped toward Green Park. They hoped to arrive in advance of the horsemen, who would complete their day's event with a special ceremonial salute to the queen and the honored quests invited to that afternoon's garden party in the private and secluded gardens of Buckingham Palace.

Perhaps they would catch a glimpse of the queen herself!

All about were bright images of happiness, laughter, smiling faces. It seemed long ago. Like a story from a distant fairyland.

London indeed was so colorful, radiant, warm, and exciting that day.

They parked as near the palace as possible. They ran toward the crowd, squeezing through, inching close to the great front gate. Father led the way, behaving like a playful child. The four peered about, hoping for a sign of activity behind the ornate gold-and-black bars.

Behind them, the rousing music of a marching band grew louder. The straight lines of horsemen now approached, entering the Mall from along Constitution Hill.

"When will the queen come, Papa?"

"I don't know, Son. Keep your eye on the front of the palace."

In the dreamy images of the daughter's mind—she was twenty-three now but young at heart—the day was like a fairy tale. Such spirited music. Such a festive atmosphere. Papa was so fun! Mama said she had never seen him so gay as on this special outing.

"Come . . . come with me," he said, working his way to the front of the throng. "Let's dash across the street where—"

Dissonant sounds suddenly interrupted approaching trumpets, trombones, and drums.

Shouts . . . now the high-pitched revving of a car speeding toward them . . . a few screams . . .

The crowd scurried. The car sped forward.

Whistles sounded and mingled with several policemen's yells. More yelling . . . more shouts.

The music stopped . . . rearing and whinnying horses . . . gunfire . . . terrified screams.

"Death to the monarchs and tyrants!" came a cry from the speeding black car. A hooded man leaned out with something in his hand.

"Run, children!" cried the father, "back to the car!"

Screaming and pandemonium . . . everyone running . . . people falling . . . police whistles shrieking . . . sirens blaring . . .

All four were running now . . . running away. But the commotion followed. There was Auntie's car . . . they would be safe—

Images of panic and confusion . . . evil sounds . . .

Suddenly a deafening explosion erupted followed by terrified cries . . . then another . . . something fell in front at her feet . . . she stumbled.

All blurred with confusion. Reality faded into vague hazy movement. Sounds grew distant.

She glanced down. Blood dripped from her hands! Horrid red everywhere . . . but she felt no pain . . . only numbness.

Now it was *her* voice above the others . . . screaming, screaming.

Police ran and chased, leaping over bodies strewn on the pavement, but their boots made no sound. Grotesque faces filled her brain, but all now became silent.

She opened her mouth wide to scream . . . great tears streaming down her face.

"Papa . . . Papa!" she tried to cry, but her voice had grown mute. No sound would come.

Why would he not open his eyes! What were these bloodstains covering everything about her?

At last her voice returned. "Papa, Papa, *please* wake up!" she wailed aloud . . . the sound of her forlorn shriek echoing into silence.

✦ ✦ ✦

"Juliet . . . Juliet, dear," came an urgent but soothing voice.

Hands gently roused her.

"Juliet . . . my dear, wake up . . . you've had a nightmare—"

Her eyes opened. The thin light of a lamp revealed a bedroom momentarily unfamiliar. Slowly the reality of the dream's events surged back upon returning consciousness. The young woman, an adult but feeling very alone and childlike, broke out in great sobs of anguish.

The tender woman at her bedside reached down. She took the girl in her arms, gently stroked her hair, and allowed her to weep.

Five minutes passed.

"I'm sorry, Auntie," said the young woman at length. Still crying softly, wakefulness now became complete. "I'm sorry for disturbing your sleep."

"Don't even say it, my dear."

"I feel like such a little girl again."

"At times like this, it's perfectly right to let yourself be young. No one ever leaves childhood entirely behind. The most hurtful moments remind us that we are all children. You've lived through a horrid experience. It will take time."

"Will I ever stop dreaming about it?"

"Even after more than fifty years, I still remember the terror of the bombs during the war. But my nightmares eventually stopped. You will never forget—but yes, eventually the nightmares will go away."

"Oh, Auntie, but what am I going to do!" moaned the poor girl.

"You will stay with me for now, Juliet, dear."

"I don't want to be in the way."

"You must put the future out of your mind. It will take care of itself. Until then, you are welcome with me. Now, would you like some tea?"

Juliet sniffed, took a tissue from the table next to her bed, and blew her nose. "Yes, yes, I think I would." She nodded. "I am so cold. I've been cold since that day. Tea sounds good. I don't want to go back to sleep right yet, even if it is the middle of the night."

"I will go down to the kitchen and put on a pot for us."

"You don't have to stay up with me, Auntie. I will keep the lights on awhile."

"I want to, dear. We shall both take naps tomorrow."

The faint sound of a telephone ringing somewhere else in the house interrupted them.

"Whoever in the world can that be at this hour," remarked Juliet's aunt.

The older lady rose and hurried from the room, leaving her niece sitting upright in bed, drawing several deep breaths to further calm herself. Downstairs, though she did not get to the phone until the tenth or twelfth ring, Mrs. Graves found the persistent caller still on the line.

"I'm sorry, he is not here," she replied to the inquiry, "—but how did you get this private number?"

An answer followed that hardly satisfied her.

"I really have no idea," she said after another moment. "Please, you will have to call through normal channels. Good night."

She set down the receiver with an inward *humph* at the fellow's manner, though his accent more than half explained it, and set about with the tea.

33

(2)

The triumph of the Livingstone expedition to Ararat, as the media were calling it, kept London electrified for a week and a half. The U.S. networks had round-the-clock news teams assigned to the story as well, running nightly television updates. Still the archaeologist-adventurer had made no appearance in his homeland or anywhere else.

There were those who called the week of near-windless sunshine a divine miracle on a par with that performed by the Almighty in the tenth chapter of Joshua when he stopped the sun in its course. Or rather, had the ancients understood the physics of the heavens more accurately, when he stopped the earth in *its* course.

Most of those on the mountain simply called it good fortune. In either case, the calm allowed Adam Livingstone, eventually followed by two assistants, to remain in the ice cave almost three days and two nights, excavating sights never before seen by modern man.

With the location pinpointed and the lay of the huge icebound structure becoming known, nothing would keep Livingstone's team from returning to complete the task so well begun. That it was a massive and ancient sailing vessel astonishingly to the specifications of the biblical craft there was no longer doubt. Already talk was under way of controlled explosive charges being set at strategic points on the glacier to chip at the gigantic ice pack and thus render the structure more accessible. Talk also circulated of establishing a closer base camp, perhaps on the ark glacier itself. There it would be easier to coordinate further exploration. Both these sensitive and risky maneuvers remained in the planning stages and would have to wait until the following year, when the winter storms and winds abated.

One thing was sure—this was archaeology of the highest order, and it had captured the imagination of the entire world.

The weather eventually turned as expected. The exploration team had been evacuated. The makeshift camp had been broken up. All personnel and equipment were returned by helicopter to the more permanent headquarters for the mission established at Dogubayazit. High winds and a dense cloud cover now engulfed Ararat.

Planning for phase two of the incredible adventure, which could take years, now began in earnest—the ambitious attempt to excavate the ark from the ice without damaging the partially petrified yet exceedingly fragile structure. The mere groundwork for this stage would consume the months between now and the following summer. Meanwhile, Livingstone was already looking ahead to several winter digs in Africa—long planned—that would take up much of the intervening calendar.

Anxious to meet with his whole team as well as the cartel's managing committee, Livingstone was realist enough to recognize that inevitable public attention would dog his heels. He took it mostly in stride. His already distinguished career had accustomed him to occupying the limelight.

Realizing that news teams were about to descend upon the small Turkish city in droves, after two days Livingstone and Jordan made a night getaway from Dogubayazit to Ankara. From the Turkish capital they reportedly flew to Rome for a hastily called meeting of the cartel's principals. Before the press could locate him there, again the archaeologist disappeared.

Rumor had it that he and Jordan had successfully flown incognito into Prestwick, then driven down the M6 and the M40 into the city, and were actually in London at this very moment. From the day after his touchdown at the base of the historic ice shaft, the roads surrounding Livingstone's home had been snarled with newspersons camped out, awaiting his eventual arrival.

After ten days, however, still there was no sign of him. If he was in London, he had managed to stay hidden. Whenever and wherever he finally emerged into public view, his was surely the most anticipated arrival of an Englishman anywhere since the four mop-topped young Liverpudlians took New York by storm in 1964.

(3)

Mitch Cutter's trip to Zurich lasted less than twenty-four hours.

He always met the Swiss executive at a different place of her designation. When he called the private number, only a tone met his ear. His numeric code followed, punched in by telephone keypad. That was all.

He received his instructions on an Internet site within two hours. To the eyes of the uninitiated, the words would have appeared nothing more than junk cybermail. From them, however, he discerned date, time, and cross streets for the rendezvous. Always in the Swiss metropolis. If he deemed the matter urgent, an extra two numbers after his phone code designated the tryst for the following afternoon.

Even the simplest of matters were handled face-to-face. Telephone and computer transmissions were too easily intercepted. Cost of travel was negligible. Money mattered nothing. Secrecy was the foundation of everything.

Cutter could be summoned to Europe via the Internet as well. He checked the coded site every morning immediately upon rising.

She was his contact. They all had contacts. He didn't know how high she was in the clandestine Society, though he had his suspicions, or even how high *he* was. He realized that he was far lower on the heirarchy than she.

On this particular occasion, at the appointed time and place, Cutter recounted his recent discussion with the senator.

"You were right to contact me," said the lady, whose aura emanated command. "We have been watching developments carefully."

"Are you concerned—what he said about the flood?"

35

"Such matters are of concern but contain only minor significance."

"Minor?"

"It is not of high importance."

"What is?"

"That is not for you to know. But you have done well—this may be an angle for infiltration we can use to our advantage."

"What shall I do?"

"I have someone in mind whose wiles may be useful to us. I will have her here to meet you tomorrow morning. We will explain to her then what we have in mind for our friend in Washington. I think perhaps it is time I also meet your friend."

(4)

Mrs. Andrea Graves and her niece Juliet Halsay sat at the breakfast table of the estate where Mrs. Graves was employed as live-in housekeeper. The younger woman had been with her now almost a week.

"Oh, Auntie, what am I going to do with myself?" sighed Juliet. "I can't just sit in my room and take walks in the garden forever."

"You need rest now more than anything, dear," replied her aunt.

"Maybe I should get a job."

"There's no hurry for all that."

"But I have no money," the girl added. She shivered and pulled her cardigan more tightly around her.

"I thought all that was settled. You are with me now, dear. You mustn't be anxious about money."

"I have to make a change sometime, even if it's only standing behind the counter at a fish-and-chips stand."

"You didn't take those college courses so you could sell fish-and-chips."

"I'd do *anything* to keep from thinking . . . remembering," moaned the girl.

"Give yourself time to heal."

"That's what the counselor says. But time only gives me more thoughts . . . more nightmares. I wonder if being busy and working might be a better way to heal than going to counseling and support groups."

Mrs. Graves noticed her niece scraping at her hands again. The movement came upon her sporadically since the accident, was usually accompanied by a terrified look in the eyes, and was always followed several hours later by a severe headache.

"On the other hand," sighed Juliet, "everything seems so uninteresting now. Maybe all I'm good for *is* a fish-and-chips stand. What did college really prepare me for other than looking at maps and rock collecting?"

"At one time you were interested in earthquakes," said her aunt, trying to find some subject that might pique her interest.

"I suppose I was," consented Juliet lethargically.

"And I thought you were looking into technical writing as a way to pursue your interests, even if it wasn't actual research?"

"I considered it. But getting established seemed so hopeless."

"What does your counselor say?"

"That I shouldn't worry about the future, that the government has programs to help victims of tragedies."

"The English take care of their people, no doubt about that."

"She said I need to give myself permission to grieve, whatever that means."

"Perhaps she is right, dear."

Juliet looked away and sighed. "Daddy didn't approve of taking handouts unless there was absolutely no other choice," she went on after a moment. "He said it dried up the human spirit. But the counselor keeps telling me that victims need to learn that their lives may never be normal again."

Again her hands began to rub unconsciously at themselves.

"Why don't you talk to the career-guidance and placement people at the college and see what they can do for you?"

"I did last year, several times."

"And?"

"The interesting jobs go to university graduates. People like me clean test tubes, not conduct research, and file reports rather than write them. I could never hope to get into the field and really *do* anything. And no one would hire *me* to write a report about anything that mattered."

"That was last year. Try again."

Juliet nodded without enthusiasm, then rose and left the kitchen.

Thirty minutes later she walked out the back door of the house and wandered aimlessly toward the garden, still chilled though the sun was rising high. But she did not look up and neither beheld the blue nor felt the warmth surrounding her.

Maybe the counselor was right, and she was a victim of a terrible injustice. Perhaps she should content herself in that fact and forget trying to get a job.

(5)

Adam Livingstone's housekeeper was busy herself in the kitchen of Sevenoaks when a young lady in her early twenties—stocky but with a pretty face and curly black hair—bounded up from the basement below.

"I'm expecting a visitor, Mrs. Graves," she said. "Will you please ring when he arrives."

"Your electronics friend?"

"Yes." The young lady smiled. "He's working as a computer technician not far from here. He's coming over for lunch."

"Where will you be, Miss Wagner?"

"I'll be working downstairs."

A look of momentary concern passed over the housekeeper's face.

"But don't worry," the girl went on, a little too breezily to alleviate Mrs. Graves' anxiety, "I know the laboratory is off-limits to everyone. I wouldn't *dare* take him there. We'll eat upstairs in the office or maybe outside."

Mrs. Graves nodded. Adam's assistant returned to her duties.

The visitor of whom she had spoken arrived an hour later. The girl hurried upstairs the instant the housekeeper notified her. She found him waiting silently in the entryway with a watchful Mrs. Graves.

"Hi, Dexter—did you bring your lunch?" she said.

"Got it right here," replied the young man.

"Let's go upstairs to the office. We'll be able to talk."

She led the way toward the stairs. The newcomer made little attempt to keep from being heard as he commented on his reception at the door.

"That lady watches this place like a hawk."

"Shhh, Dexter . . . keep your voice down. She's just doing her job."

Their voices faded as they reached the landing and disappeared. Mrs. Graves watched them go, then shook her head imperceptibly and returned to the parlor. She liked her employer's assistant, but the girl was too preoccupied with men for her own good and not a very good judge of character besides. She didn't like the looks of the fellow. Mrs. Graves knew well enough that the girl's mother did not approve of him. But the girl bristled whenever anyone mentioned her mother. Parental approval was the last thing on her mind when it came to choosing her friendships.

If the housekeeper had been asked, Erin's involvement with that young man couldn't help but spell trouble. The girl had been here less than a year, and Mrs. Graves seriously doubted she'd last much longer. She could not help feeling responsible, since it was she herself who had recommended her.

The telephone rang as she reentered the parlor. She recognized the voice immediately. It was the third time the man had called.

"I will tell you again, as I've told you before, sir," said Mrs. Graves, doing her best to keep a courteous tongue, "I do not know when he will be back. And, yes, I still have your telephone number from the last time. But I cannot assure you that—"

She listened as the caller again stressed the importance of his message.

"It may be urgent to you," she said in a slight huff. "He is a busy man. All I can say is that he will get the message. Good day."

"Some people cannot take no for an answer," she mumbled as she walked away. She had not taken more than three or four steps when the telephone sounded again.

*Will that man never cease!*

She was relieved to see the light flickering from the business line, indicating it had been answered upstairs.

Thirty seconds later the lab assistant walked into the room from upstairs. Mrs. Graves glanced up.

"Someone's on the line saying you granted an interview this afternoon," she said. "He wanted me to confirm the time with you."

Mrs. Graves stared blankly. "Me?"

"He said he had spoken to you earlier. He asked me to find out if three o'clock was still agreeable."

"I spoke to no one about an interview," said Mrs. Graves, rising with a concerned expression and walking toward the phone. She lifted the receiver and pushed the button for the office line.

"Hello, sir . . . this is Mrs. Graves—"

She stopped.

"That's odd," she added, slowly hanging up the phone. "The line's gone dead, Miss Wagner."

A puzzled expression came over the young woman's face. "I'll check the phone upstairs," she said, turning to go.

The housekeeper glanced down at the parlor phone. None of the lines were lit.

Forty minutes later she heard the two young people descending the stairs. Miss Wagner let her guest out. A moment later she poked her head into the parlor to inform the housekeeper that there'd been no one on the phone. Whoever it was hadn't called back.

# four

# Triumphant Return

(1)

Contrary to rumor, Adam Livingstone had not yet arrived in London at all.

Everything about the reports that had surfaced was true, except that he and Jordan had stopped for the night in High Wycombe. Once they were situated and had enjoyed a cup of tea, his friend slipped out to pick up a take-out order of fish-and-chips and visit a newsstand. The two then spent what they knew might well be Livingstone's last undisturbed evening for some time in the peace and solitude of one of the cartel member's homes.

They had been alerted to the fact that *Time* magazine planned to devote an unprecedented twenty pages of its regular weekly issue to the find. Today was the scheduled day of release.

Jordan could not keep from grinning as he paid the cashier for the copy in his hand. The cover featured a close-up of Adam Livingstone superimposed upon a sweeping panoramic view of Ararat. A close-up side box contained one of the photos taken inside the exploration chamber.

"There you are, for all the world to see!" he said, tossing the magazine into Livingstone's lap as he walked back into the house.

Adam glanced down briefly and chuckled. "Never mind that," he said. "What I really want is in that bag you're holding—I'm starved. I can smell those chips from here!"

"Then dig in—you want to look at the article?"

"You read it first. You can warn me about any nasty bits I ought to skip."

"*Criticism!* Of Adam Livingstone?" exclaimed Jordan. "Don't you know, you're a national hero, man?"

"Nevertheless," Livingstone laughed, "you read it first."

Jordan unwrapped his large slab of cod as he flipped through the magazine. Breaking off a large, satisfying bite, he began reading the account in which he was one of the principle actors in the historic drama.

"Science and religion have engaged in a stormy relationship over the past hundred and fifty years. The feud for supremacy has been a bitter one. Late in the nineteenth century, on the heels of rapid advances in every field from astronomy to zoology, rationalists made the bold assertion, 'Science disproves the Bible.'

"Except for a minority view of Christian fundamentalists, it would seem to have backed up that proclamation in the decades since. During the past three generations science has, indeed, successfully persuaded most modern thinkers of the truth of its claim of supremacy over the ancient religious Book. Nearly one hundred forty years after the publication of Darwin's *The Origin of Species* in 1859, evolution is considered *fact,* while creation is taught in the textbooks of the world as *myth*.

"Not so fast, say those who teach that a supernatural Presence, not random chance, created the universe. Such creationist spokespersons maintain that the Christian God is a presence, in fact, *so* personal that he spoke to the ancients he fashioned from the dust and even intruded himself into their affairs.

"The verdict is not yet in, they say. The Bible may have light to shed on our beginnings after all.

"Has religion suddenly turned the tables on this long erosion of its credibility? Has there been a divine shake-up of modernism's hold on truth? Has science been suddenly thrown to the mat, finding its shoulders pinned by the unexpectedly vigorous power of its newly muscular religious adversary?

"So it would seem.

"Suddenly *science itself* has come to the rescue of religion's shaky reputation! Across the globe headlines everywhere are being rewritten to read, 'Science *proves* the Bible!'

"Alternative conclusions are difficult to postulate in light of the unparalleled find made a little more than a week ago some fifteen hundred feet below the summit of Turkey's Mount Ararat. There, renowned British archaeologist Adam Livingstone (cover photo) led a team representing the most advanced expedition in history to the discovery of what appears nothing less than the massive ark described in the sixth and seventh chapters of the book of Genesis.

"Descending by rope from a crane located at the expedition camp perched high above and aided by favorable weather, Livingstone, a veteran of hundreds of archaeological digs over the past decade since his graduation from Cambridge, was lowered into a six-foot-wide shaft burned through the glacier (see article on p. 47, 'High-Tech Exploration: Archaeology Enters the Computer Age') by what amounted to a much theorized but heretofore never attempted system of sophisticated blowtorches.

"'We planned and schemed and did our best to cover all the variables,' Richard Dewhurst, chairman of the Livingstone Cartel, which funded and organized the expedition, said at expedition headquarters in Dogubayazit, fifteen miles southwest of the summit beneath the shadow of Ararat. 'Yet I don't think any of us quite realized how successful the outcome would be. Suffice it to say that we are very, very pleased.'"

"You've got to read this," laughed Jordan. "They're quoting Dewhurst. They make it sound like he single-handedly planned the whole operation!"

"What—do you mean he didn't?" replied his friend with an amused smile.

"You know as well as I do that the totality of what our friend Richard Dewhurst knows about archaeology would fit on the head of a pin!"

"There's no denying he's good with the press," replied Livingstone wryly.

Jordan continued reading: "Setting the stage for last week's unprecedented attempt was a series of photographic sorties flown the previous spring. From those flyovers, advanced X-ray technology located, trapped far beneath impenetrable layers of ice and apparently wedged in a crook between two adjacent depressions of base granite long since covered by snow and ice, what the cartel dared hope was a form vaguely suggestive of a bargelike shape (see photo, next page).

"Before last week's incredible series of events, what exact material comprised the mystery shape could only be conjectured . . . *until* the foot of Livingstone reached the bottom of the melted cylinder. Could he have set himself down upon the oldest verifiable link with the Hebrew and Christian Scriptures ever discovered? (See related story, 'Egypt, Babylon, and the Ark: Verifying the Bible by Archaeology.')

"Tiny fragments from the structure were flown immediately to independent laboratories in six different nations. These laboratories have all universally acclaimed the age, both of petrified and nonpetrified samples, by carbon-14 dating methods to be between 6,200 and 8,100 years old. This is not considered prehistoric by archaeological standards, for tools and pottery have been discovered twice that old. Yet broken shards of a water vessel hardly compare with a ship one and a half football fields in length, which sets this remarkable find in an archaeological class all its own.

"According to the account in Genesis 6, God commanded the man Noah, well past the midpoint of his life somewhere between his five and six hundredth year, to construct *'an ark of gopher wood.'* The Almighty, it is said, went on to instruct: *'And this is the fashion which thou shalt make it of: The length of the ark shall be three hundred cubits, the breadth of it fifty cubits, and the height of it thirty cubits. A window shalt thou make to the ark, and in a cubit shalt thou finish it above; and the door of the ark shalt thou set in the side thereof; with lower, second, and third stories shalt thou make it'* (KJV).

"The New International Version of the Bible interprets the size of the ark in dimensions more readily understandable: *'Make yourself an ark of cypress wood; make rooms in it and coat it with pitch inside and out. This is how you are to build it: The ark is to be 450 feet long, 75 feet wide and 45 feet high. Make a roof for it and finish the ark to within 18 inches of the top. Put a door in the side of the ark and make lower, middle and upper decks.'*

"The ships with which Columbus first sailed the Atlantic were less than a third the length thus described.

"The exact meaning of the word translated 'gopher' or 'cypress' wood is uncertain in the Hebrew. Each of the six laboratories has established that the samples from Ararat cannot be linked conclusively with any known contemporary species of tree in the Middle East, though DNA tests reveal similarities with an ancient variety of *Pinaceae sempervirens,* sometimes known as *Cupressus sempervirens,* or Mediterranean cypress, found in two chief forms in the Middle East. Centuries later, Alexander the Great constructed his ships from this fragrant wood, and it has traditionally been used for sailing vessels. Likewise, tests performed on the resinlike substance Livingstone dug from between the planks found it to be bitumen or pitch, in correspondence with the Genesis account, probably from a more resinous coniferous tree, perhaps some local species of pine."

Jordan glanced up from the magazine.

"Had you heard anything conclusive on the wood analysis?" he asked. "I didn't know the results were in."

"They're not. Only a preliminary report from the lab when we were in Rome," replied Livingstone.

"This article gives the impression that the identification is complete."

"What do they say—Mediterranean cypress?"

Jordan nodded.

"I'm sure that's accurate. Maybe they got to one of the labs. I'll reserve judgment until we have a chance to conduct tests at home. I'm anxious to get Erin on it."

"She's expecting us?"

"I called her from Prestwick. She can't wait to get her hands on our suitcase of samples."

"She'll have the time of her life! What a dream for an archaeological chemist—ice and rock and wood from the grave of Noah's ark! Do you think Erin's up to the task?"

"She's young and a little distracted at times by the trouble with her mother. But I've got a fond spot for her. And I think she knows her stuff. No better way to learn than with a find like this."

Again Jordan returned to the article.

"Despite the preponderance of apparent evidence, however, yet one additional clue remained hidden behind a wall of ice as Adam Livingstone first knelt upon what were laminated boards, presumably hewn by Noah and his three sons. Several hours later, enlarging his cavity of exploration by means of a great burner lowered from the encampment above, Livingstone melted out a crawl space extending across the width of ancient planks to ascertain that he had indeed discovered more than a gigantic cross-section of log.

"By late morning he came to an opening through the wood planking—whether man-made or from decay it was impossible to tell—into a lower level of the structure. By now having summoned two of his colleagues to join him in the expanding ice cave, Livingstone set about to explore downward into this intriguing new hole.

"Melting the ice by fire and removing the resultant water by suction tube without damaging the structure proved no hasty or easy task. By day's end, however, Livingstone had enlarged sufficient space within this lower room of the vessel to discover a series of vertical wooden bars, perhaps tree branches, set between the planking above and a second level of planking he eventually reached below him. (See cutaway drawing of excavated area.)

"Confident the weather would allow it, Livingstone and two companions remained within the heart of the glacier, working through the night and all the following day taking minimal breaks for sleep as needed. Eventually they satisfied themselves that they had discovered nothing more nor less than a network of animal cages. A few samples of a substance conjectured as fossilized animal dung are also being analyzed. The results of these tests were not known at the time of this printing.

"'Here at last,' declared Livingstone, 'is a confirming link to the ark of Noah!' Did you declare, 'Here at last is the confirming link to the ark of Noah!'?"

"I don't remember saying that," replied Livingstone.

"I didn't recall hearing it, either."

"Livingstone and his colleagues remained in the heart of their historic 'dig' for three days and two nights, managing to de-ice and photograph what Livingstone believes are substantial portions of the upper and middle decks of the structure. Further expeditions are planned, although weather at the top of the troublesome mountain will remain the most critical factor in scheduling them. All that can be ascertained at this point is that the Livingstone team plans a return next summer. Further exploration this year appears doubtful.

"See related stories: 'Unlocking Ararat from Turkish Bureaucracy: Speculation about Financial Aspects of Livingstone Expedition' and 'Evangelical Reaction to Ark Find. *The Bible Vindicated!* Cry American Fundamentalist Leaders.'

"Beleaguered by years of adversity and declining prestige and still reeling from last month's mysterious bombing outside Buckingham Palace in which seven people were killed, an exuberant British crown seized upon the discovery as an opportunity to bolster national pride. Hoping, no doubt, to also boost the image of the royal family, the queen hailed Livingstone as a national hero. A spokesman for Her Majesty has indicated that an audience between the queen and the archaeologist is being planned.

"Speculation has it that . . ."

Tiring of the account, Jordan skipped ahead to the last paragraph.

"A biographical outline of Adam Livingstone's life, as well as the highlights of his career, follows in the story, 'The Man Who May Make Archaeology a Household Word,' p. 53."

Jordan set the magazine aside with a chuckle. "If there is one thing I don't need to read," he said to Adam across the room, "it's a biographical sketch of your life. I've lived half of it with you!"

"Here, let me see that," rejoined Adam. "You've finally got my curiosity up—I want to see what's being said about me. I suppose I'd better be up on my own stats. Although I'll wager the U.S. edition has a sidebar about *you*, not me!"

(2)

The following morning Adam Livingstone and Scott Jordan embarked on the final leg of their homeward journey. It was less than a two-hour drive.

As Jordon drove up the narrow lane leading to the Livingstone estate outside the town of Sevenoaks, he found the way nearly impassable. Cars jammed the way, parked on both sides of the road, in fields and alongside fences, wherever they could squeeze in, sometimes in the middle of the road itself.

Inching his way through automobiles and people milling about, he turned into the private drive and approached the high-fenced estate. One of the BBC television reporters finally recognized him.

"It's Scott Jordan!" he cried.

Immediately cameras rolled. Within seconds the car was swarmed by newsmen and newswomen, halting Jordan's progress altogether.

"Come on, Glendenning," Jordan said through the partially open window as the journalist did his best to shove a microphone toward him, followed on his heels by a BBC cameraman. "No interviews. Just let me through."

"Is Mr. Livingstone with you?"

"Obviously not," replied Jordan. "You can see as well as anyone that no one else is in the car."

"He could be in the boot."

Jordan laughed. "Adam will get a kick out of your suggestion. Believe me, he's not in the trunk of my car."

"When will we see him?"

"Very soon, Alex—believe me, *very* soon. Help clear these people out of my way and just *maybe* I'll put in a good word for you with Adam."

The reporter backed away from the car, making a halfhearted effort to disperse his colleagues.

"And spread the word, Glendenning," Jordan called out of his window, "that anyone who tries to enter the grounds when I open the gate will be barred from this morning's news conference."

"*News conference*—why, yes . . . yes, sir—I'll see to it, Mr. Jordan!" replied Glendenning, suddenly alert to the prospect of what his cooperation might gain him. He was immediately willing to do anything to raise himself in Jordan's estimation. "You heard Mr. Jordan," he called out. "Stand aside everyone . . . stand back . . . let him pass—and keep out of the estate!"

Meanwhile, Jordan took opportunity of the momentary diversion to punch the secretly numbered code into the digital gate mechanism in the box sitting at car-window height beside the drive. Slowly the heavy, black-iron gate rolled back. Carefully he drove through, amazed that no one *did* attempt to sneak in alongside his car. Once clear, he stopped the engine and got out while the gate automatically closed.

Slowly he walked back toward it. Two or three dozen reporters clustered toward him on the other side of the bars.

"Yes," he said pensively, as if continuing the previous conversation, "I think if you keep your eyes open, you might see Adam Livingstone just about any minute now."

"Look!" cried a voice at the back of the crowd. "Look . . . up there!" he repeated, pointing into the air. "Look . . . it's him!"

All eyes now glanced toward the sky. There they saw the leading edge of a brightly colored paraglider canopy swooping down in a wide arc above them. The faint sound of an airplane engine retreated in the distance.

Two or three upward and downward bends and wide graceful swoops followed, and in less than twenty seconds the much sought form of Adam Livingstone lit smoothly on the grassy expanse of lawn in front of his own house, in full display of two dozen television cameras that were running live feeds of the spectacular arrival.

(3)

Adam cleared himself of the canopy and ran forward to join his friend.

"Well done, Adam!" laughed Jordan. "Perfect timing—a very nice touch."

"Why, thank you, my good man," replied Livingstone. "I say, who are all these people? Do we have guests?"

No longer was the coterie of journalists content to remain silent. Suddenly errupted a volley of fifty voices at once. Nearly as many microphones, held by eager hands, came toward them through the iron bars.

"You owe Glendenning one," said Jordan. "He helped me get inside unscathed."

"All right, Alex," said Adam, walking forward toward the crowd, "what's on your mind?"

"What is on everyone's mind, Mr. Livingstone," replied Glendenning. "What was it like?"

"I'm not a religious man," replied Adam, "but I have to say there was an unbelievable sensation down there."

"How do you mean?"

"A profound sense of awe is the only way I can describe it."

"Is it the ark?"

"Surely you don't expect a scientist to rush to a conclusion on so momentous a matter." Livingstone smiled.

"Either it is, or it isn't."

"Things in our world are rarely quite *that* simple, Mr. Glendenning."

"What do you *think,* then?"

"I reserve judgment."

"What other credible theory can explain your find than the ark of Noah?" asked another voice, whose decidedly Christian views were known among the entire London press corps.

"I pose no other theory, Mr. Halliday," replied Adam. "I say only that as a scientist I must await further evidence."

"What additional evidence do you need? You set foot inside the thing. You saw its dimensions. You saw the animal pens. The implications are not only obvious, they are staggering."

"What implications, Mr. Halliday?"

"Just this, Mr. Livingstone," the journalist answered, then paused. "May I ask you another question first?"

"Of course."

"How big is the vessel you found? Describe it to us."

"The thing is huge," replied Adam. "Enormous beyond anything shipbuilders have constructed throughout man's history until well into this very century. It positively dwarfs anything manufactured by the Spanish or Dutch or Portuguese in the sixteenth and seventeenth centuries."

"And those nations were skilled shipbuilders, would you not agree?"

"Certainly."

"Exactly my point—the implications I referred to," rejoined the journalist. "How did a man, a mortal, come to build such a craft all those years ago? Do you see what I mean? How did one man, without modern tools, prior to any sophisticated metalworking we are aware of, without technology, and perhaps with only three sons to help him—how did they possibly build such a thing?"

There was a brief moment of silence. Neither the archaeologist nor Halliday's fellow journalists had a ready answer to his query.

"Who's to say only four men built it?" asked Adam after a moment. "Even if you accept the Noah account, why couldn't he have hired others to help? Who's to say an entire community didn't participate?"

"I don't think the biblical account supports such a view," rejoined Halliday. "But I concede the point. It hardly matters. For that's not the most staggering of the implications of this discovery."

"What is, if I may ask?"

"It's the *why,*" replied Halliday. His voice quieted as he spoke. Those listening sensed an indescribable awe inherent in the word. A hush descended over the gathering. As it did, most of those present turned to the man standing in front of them for some response. But Adam Livingstone possessed no answer to the probing question.

"Why do you think that question is the most significant implication of what we found on Ararat?" he asked after a moment.

"Why did they build it?" repeated Halliday rhetorically, only too happy to continue in the spotlight. "How could they possibly have fathomed the engineering required to construct a seaworthy vessel of such magnitude . . . and why? How did they know rains of such tremendous power and duration were going to come, such as would lift their ship to the top of a sixteen-thousand-foot mountain? Do you see what I'm getting at, Mr. Livingstone? The questions and implications involved in your discovery are enormous."

"It would seem that we've created more conundrums than we've answered!" laughed Adam.

"What is the single question that is foremost in your own mind, Mr. Livingstone?" asked another of the reporters present.

Adam smiled, again with a pensive expression.

"You've hit it squarely on the head, Mr. Stokes," he replied. "I don't even know if I know myself. I haven't allowed myself to stop and consider that one. I suppose I'll have to sooner or later, though, won't I?" he added with a chuckle.

Adam thought for a moment. "Archaeology is about more than mere discovery," he went on at length. "If that were all there was to it, I suppose we could make robots capable of handling shovels."

A ripple of laughter went through the crowd.

"But it's not only about digging holes in the earth—or in the ice—to see what we can find. Once we find things from the past, then, as Mr. Halliday so aptly pointed out, we begin asking what they mean.

"Who were the people that had to do with these things we find, and why did they behave as they did? We're right back to Mr. Halliday's question. When it comes to the matter of the ark, I suppose there is a host of unanswered questions. At this point, I can't tell you what it all means. But I'm not sure a spiritual connection is imperative, as I think Mr. Halliday would suggest. The Egyptian pyramids are certainly magnificent, yet no one suggests that God and the pharaohs had dealings together."

"The situations are entirely different," said Halliday, now speaking up again.

"How so?" asked Livingstone.

"The builder of the ark had to have had help of some kind that cannot be accounted for by any human means."

"Upon what do you base that conclusion? I still see little difference between the ark and the Pyramids. The pharaohs had help too. It was called slave labor."

"I'm talking about help outside human knowledge—supernatural help, if you will."

"Why is that necessary?"

"Because there had to be a reason he built it. How did he know the rain was coming and that he must construct this ship?" replied Halliday. "There aren't very many ways to answer that question. Then how could he have built it? How could he possibly have known the dimensions and symmetry with which to build a three-story-tall, seaworthy craft the size of a small football stadium, when all around him the only boats he was familiar with were probably little more than hollowed-out logs? The engineering of the thing staggers the imagination beyond comprehension. This boat had to be seaworthy for a year. The technology would seem to be far beyond that of the Pyramids. How could he have done it . . . again, without help? And again, how did he know the rains were coming? It's an enormous mystery if you only look at it from the human point of view. These questions have no simple answers that mere rationalism can spin out."

Halliday paused, then added, "There is only one possible way to answer these questions, and it is the very antithesis of a so-called rational response."

"Do you mean, God speaking to him—is that what you're suggesting?" asked Livingstone.

"I leave the conclusion to you," rejoined Halliday. "How would you reply if I asked you such a question?"

"I would certainly not say that God spoke to him," countered Livingstone, quickly and with a slight edge to his tone. This press conference had gone in a direction he wasn't altogether comfortable with. Suddenly he was anxious to have it done with. "To say that not only presupposes belief in a Supreme Being . . . but also one who talks to men. That's quite a leap. In no way am I prepared to endorse that interpretation of my discovery. I think that will be all for right now, ladies and gentlemen. You will be hearing more from me soon."

Livingstone turned, and he and Scott Jordan walked away from the gate, unloaded a few things from the trunk of the car, and now made their way toward the massive stone house in front of them.

(4)

"I'll take this case of samples down to Erin," said Adam as they entered, still agitated from the unexpected turn the encounter with the press had taken. "I'm sure Crystal has been watching all this at the window. I'll be up in a minute."

Jordan nodded, and the two men parted. Adam turned to his left into a wide corridor, then after only ten or fifteen feet quickly turned again to his right, descending a broad flight of stairs to the basement where his private laboratory was located, presided over by his staff technician Erin Wagner.

Entering the basement corridor with briefcase in hand, he took several large strides along it when suddenly the door of the lab opened ten feet in front of him. A girl he had never seen before in his life walked into the hallway. She was of athletic build, with light brown, slightly wavy hair, and stood probably five feet seven inches or so, with well-proportioned and attractive features.

He stopped and froze in astonishment, as did she. For the briefest of seconds the two stood staring at one another.

The young woman's face reddened, and her green eyes widened. She knew who he was—she had seen the *Time* magazine too. He, however, hadn't a clue as to the identity of this intruder into his private and state-of-the-art domain. Livingstone was the first to find his voice.

"What were you doing in there?" he demanded, now walking slowly toward her. The authority in his voice was unmistakable. It sounded anything but friendly.

Knowing she had been caught where she didn't belong and terrified by the unexpected and imposing presence of the great man, she struggled in vain to find her tongue.

"Who are you?" he said. "I want to know what you are doing here."

"I . . . I . . ." but no more would come.

Reaching the door and still eying her skeptically, he half opened it, then peered inside as if his lab assistant might be able to shed some light on the mystery of the mute girl's presence. The next instant Livingstone turned back once more to the stranger.

"Where's Erin?" he said.

She shook her head. She had come downstairs with a message for the technician, found the place deserted, and had been unable to keep herself from a quick look about.

"Well, I don't know who you are or what you're about, but I have to get these things inside. Go back to wherever you came from—I presume you have some reason for being here. In the future, stay away from this laboratory. Do you understand?"

A timid half-nod was all she could muster in response.

Livingstone walked inside. He closed the door behind him, leaving the frightened girl's eyes wide and threatening tears.

Ten minutes later Adam emerged, locking the door behind him. Quickly he strode back to the ground floor, continuing up the stairs to the first floor of the same wing of the building where his offices were located. He found Jordan, Wagner, and his secretary, Crystal Johnson, laughing together over one of Scott's tales from the recent expedition.

"The conquerer returns—welcome home, Adam!" said Crystal warmly.

"You have samples for me?" cried Erin.

"That I do," replied Adam. "I've already been downstairs with them. By the way, who's the girl I found just now snooping about the lab? I certainly hope she's got some connection with you and isn't one of Sir Gilbert's spies."

Crystal and Erin both glanced at one another with puzzled expressions.

"On the solid side, brownish hair, above-average height, glasses, eighteen or nineteen, I would say," added Livingstone. "And so timid I couldn't get a word out of her."

At last Erin's face displayed recognition.

"It's my fault, Adam—I'm sorry. I came up here a few minutes before Scott walked in. I wasn't thinking and left the door unlocked."

"Who's the girl?"

"She's harmless enough," Crystal added. "But Mrs. Graves should fill you in."

Still puzzled, Adam nodded hesitantly but did not press it. "The first of the samples are in a case on the counter to the left of the freezer," he said. "Scott and I will go over them with you—" he paused to glance at his watch—"in about an hour. How's that for you, Scott?"

"Sure."

"All right, then. That should give time for Crystal to fill us in on everything here in the office. Jen checked in yet?"

"She called a couple days ago," replied Crystal, "but isn't back in the city yet."

"Mind if I look over what you brought me?" asked Erin.

"Not at all," replied Livingstone. "We'll be down in a while."

Wagner left the room.

"So, Crystal—what do we have? Messages, letters, faxes—anything urgent?"

"The urgent ones number maybe fifty or a hundred . . . those that can wait a day or two, probably a thousand!"

Livingstone laughed. "All right," he said, "we'll get going with the most urgent of the urgent right away."

"There are more invitations and requests for interviews than we've had in the last five years. There is one, however, I've kept at the top of the stack."

"Why's that?"

"It bears the royal seal. It was delivered by personal messenger from the palace."

"Ah . . . that does sound intriguing! Let's open it and see what the queen has to say. Then we'll work our way through the rest of the fifty."

Livingstone paused briefly. "Come to think of it," he said, "perhaps I'd first better go have that talk with Mrs. Graves. She should know to expect me for dinner. Dust off that pile of messages and start some tea brewing. I'll be back in a few minutes."

(5)

Adam Livingstone found his housekeeper in her apartment on the first floor of the south wing.

"Good day to you, Mr. Livingstone," she said. "Welcome back to Sevenoaks."

"Thank you, Mrs. Graves. All is in order I trust?"

The housekeeper nodded.

"I ran across a girl downstairs. Crystal said I should seek an explanation from you. She was snooping about the lab."

Mrs. Graves's face filled with anxiety.

"Oh, I am sorry, Mr. Livingstone," she said earnestly. "I am certain she meant no harm. I sent her downstairs with a message for Miss Wagner. I did not know there had been a problem."

"Who is she? What on earth is she doing here?"

"She is my niece, Mr. Livingstone, the daughter of my sister . . . from Brighton."

"Oh . . . oh, I see," replied her employer, his annoyance moderating. "She is here . . . for a brief visit?"

"Yes." Mrs. Graves nodded. "Well, actually," she went on, "perhaps a little more than that, if you have no objection. I am afraid I took the liberty while you were gone, sir, of inviting her to stay with me for a time. She is rather destitute at the moment, you see, sir."

"She hardly looks a pauper, Mrs. Graves."

"That is just what she is, Mr. Livingstone—or close to it. Certainly in her heart she is as poor as is possible for a body to be, sir. When someone's heart is broken, there's not much good a fat bank account will do them, now will it, sir? And my poor Juliet's a pauper in both places—heart and bank. That is why I brought her here to stay with me."

"I'm sure I am very sorry for whatever trouble she has, Mrs. Graves. But I still must confess you haven't done a great deal to enlighten me nor to answer my original question. That's her name, is it, Juliet?"

"Yes, sir—Juliet Halsay."

"And she is, what . . . about eighteen?"

"Twenty-three, sir. You knew of the bombing at the palace, Mr. Livingstone?"

"In July—yes, certainly."

The case remained unsolved, and no terrorist organization had claimed credit.

"They were there on that day, sir—Juliet and her family. On holiday, they were . . ."

Mrs. Graves' voice began to quiver. At last Adam Livingstone began to suspect the truth.

"They were in the middle of the crowd, sir," she went on, eyes filling with tears. "Juliet's father and younger brother were in front of the others. They were all running, trying to get away . . . when the blast went off. . . ."

She glanced away, unable to continue, reaching for her handkerchief.

"They were both—"

The woman nodded.

"—killed?" said Adam at last.

The housekeeper continued to nod, weeping softly.

"And her mother?"

"My sister and Juliet were unharmed," answered Mrs. Graves through sniffles, after two or three attempts to regain her composure. "But there were debts they knew nothing of and no insurance. The house was sold off. They were left penniless. Juliet's mother went to my other sister in Bedford. She has but a small flat and space for only one. We're a working family, Mr. Livingstone, as you know, without means. After their affairs were all settled, I invited Juliet here to be with me—I thought it would be all right . . . for a short while. She's so . . . she's feeling so insecure and unsure of herself."

"You did exactly the right thing, Mrs. Graves," said Adam sincerely. "I am very glad you felt the freedom to do so. Where might I find the girl?"

"I don't know, Mr. Livingstone. I put her in the guest room down the hall there from my little parlor, until I could speak with you, sir."

"That will be fine, Mrs. Graves. Thank you for clarifying the situation for me. I'm sorry I was brusque to begin with."

He turned to go.

"Before you leave, sir," Mrs. Graves answered, "I should tell you that there has been a man calling for you—on the private line, sir, and most persistent. I have done my best to dissuade him, but he will no doubt call again."

"What's it about, Mrs. Graves? A reporter, I presume?"

"I don't know, sir. He refuses to say. He used the private number, Mr. Livingstone."

"How could he have gotten hold of it, I wonder."

"I think he's an American," Mrs. Graves added, emphasizing the word as if that fact were sufficient to explain everything.

"Well, if he calls again, we shall find out soon enough."

(6)

Adam Livingstone strode down the corridor of the staff wing of his home in a considerably subdued mood. He had been on top of the world for the past two weeks, rarely pausing to think about those who had perhaps recently lost their whole worlds.

With gentle step he approached the guest room Mrs. Graves had indicated. Softly he knocked on the door. There was no answer.

He glanced about. The parlor door next to it was ajar. He went to it, touched the door lightly, and pushed it slowly open. Inside he saw the form of a young woman huddled on one of the two couches, face turned away, apparently weeping.

He stood a moment at the door, then spoke softly.

"Miss Halsay?" he said.

The form on the couch started. She had not heard the door swing open or the soft footsteps enter. She glanced up and spun around, eyes bloodshot, face red, fumbling to put her glasses back on. Seeing who had interrupted her, her eyes filled with fright. He saw the expression and was stung.

"Please," he said quickly, "don't be anxious. I'm not here to scold you again. I've had a talk with Mrs. Graves. She has explained everything to me. I want to say that I am sorry for speaking discourteously to you downstairs. I suppose I was a little out of sorts after an interview outside with the press. Please accept my apology. I am very sorry, as well, to hear about your father and brother. I want you to know that you are welcome here at Sevenoaks for as long as any of us can be of help to you."

Realizing she would probably still not find her voice for yet a while longer, Adam punctuated his statement with a smile and a nod.

He turned to leave the room. A scarcely audible "Thank you" sounded from the couch behind him.

(7)

It did not take long for Mrs. Graves' prognostication to come true.

Later that same evening the phone rang again. She knew the voice at once. The man gave her no chance to cut him off.

"I know Livingstone's home, lady," he said quickly. "I've got someone watching for me. It's all over the tube about his arrival. So don't tell me he's not available. I know he's there, and I want you to put him on the phone."

Huffing, Mrs. Graves complied, not without considerable annoyance at the man's importune manner. But what else could be expected? At least it would be good to be rid of him.

She found her employer in his private lounge where he was perusing several recent magazine articles about the expedition.

"The man I told you about is on the phone again, sir," she said when he answered her knock on the door.

"Thank you, Mrs. Graves. At last we shall see what this is all about."

He walked across the floor and picked up the receiver.

"This is Adam Livingstone," he said.

"Mr. Livingstone," said a voice at the other end of the line, "you don't know me. I'm calling from the United States. Please give the lady who answered my apologies. I'm afraid I've been rather insistent with her this past week, calling at all hours. But it was urgent I speak with you personally."

"Well, now you have me. What's this about, Mr. . . . . er—"

"I'd rather not give my name just now," replied the caller. "I can't give you any details, either, about what I'm about to tell you. If I'm right, it wouldn't surprise me if your phone's already bugged, so I'll keep it as short as I can. It's this, Livingstone—I've recently stumbled across information, again, I can't tell you what exactly because of who might be listening—"

"No one's listening, I can assure you," interrupted Adam. "This is a secure and private line." Adam paused a moment, then added in a puzzled tone, "But then . . . how *did* you get this number?"

"That's not important," replied the American. "I have my ways. What is important is that your life may be in danger."

"Oh, is that all," laughed Adam. "My life is always in danger!"

"I'm serious, Livingstone."

"I do dangerous things for a living."

"I'm not talking about falling into the hole of a dig somewhere or slipping off a glacier on Ararat."

"What are you talking about then?"

"There are powerful people who may want you dead, especially now."

"Now . . . why now?"

"Your discovery changes everything. I can't say more without putting both of us at even greater risk. You're going to have to trust that I'm no kook. This is on the level."

"If you'll forgive me, it sounds pretty bizarre. Someone in my position is always being threatened."

"This is different, Livingstone—believe me. They may try to kill you."

"I'll take my chances. I'll be prudent. But without more information to go on, there's not much I can do."

"I honestly don't have more than what I've told you. I wish I did. Just be very careful, Livingstone, be very, very careful."

The caller hung up, and Adam was left to ponder the cryptic message as he returned to the stack of magazines beside his chair.

(8)

Three evenings later Adam Livingstone sat in his lounge reading through the flood accounts in several books he had picked up from the library—reflecting Christian, Jewish, and secular theories. He had studied the flood before. Now suddenly the desire to understand it more fully had become very personal.

Since the telephone call from the United States, he had not been able to get out of his mind the mysterious fellow's statement: "Your discovery changes everything."

How true those words were proving to be. But he had not anticipated that the greatest change would come within himself. The American's words, along with Halliday's persistent *why*, were making him squirm.

The exchange with the journalists outside his home had provoked a whole new line of inquiry he had not anticipated when planning the expedition to Ararat.

What did the ark mean?

Thus far to Adam Livingstone, the question was unanswerable. Nothing in his philosophical framework was capable of shedding light on an answer.

But the huge fact of the thing stared him in the face. He had found something that could not be ignored. If Halliday was right with all his talk of implications, then perhaps Adam Livingstone's philosophical framework would have to be overhauled.

Why had he gone in search of the ark in the first place?

Sure, it had always intrigued him. But now that he stopped to consider the matter in retrospect, hadn't he been like many others who, if pressed, would have admitted to considering it a pretty far-fetched quest? He had seen people chuckle at his mention of a literal ark you could touch and feel. What made him think he had a chance to really find it?

He had delivered the counterargument to such naysayers persuasively. "Look," he had said, "we have found all manner of fossils and bones and tools and artifacts from far earlier in earth's history than Noah's time. Geology confirms evidence of a massive flood, perhaps global in extent, sometime during the last ten thousand years. Legends about the world tell of eight survivors. Therefore, what is so remarkable, if these other artifacts have been preserved, that the ark of myth and legend might also be preserved—especially if encased within a glacial ice pack?"

It all sounded plausible enough. But he had staked out his ambiguous philosophical position, as it were, in the vacuum of conjecture. Suddenly there were actual *facts* to deal with. What was he going to do with them?

Now the question loomed so much larger. For at root one's response depended on what level of faith he or she placed in the biblical account. The exchange with Halliday made him realize that he hadn't ever placed much faith in it. Had he been a scientist going in search of a legend? What kind of "science" was that?

Now suddenly a whole new range of issues presented themselves. Did one believe that Noah's ark existed in the first place? That was the question. If it existed, then of course it might someday be found. But what if it had never existed at all? What if the tale was nothing but a myth?

Adam now had to admit to the possibility that he might never have actually believed it. He had gone in search of the ark . . . yet was nearly as astonished by what he had discovered in the ice as the rest of the world. He had been a skeptic and hadn't even known it! Yet did not his response now—an unwilling denial after it was too late to be skeptical—reveal that he had never really believed it in the first place?

What did the ark mean?

There he was, back where he had started. The discovery had implications, as Halliday had said.

The questions forcing themselves upward into his brain made Adam Livingstone uncomfortable. But he knew that he could not rest until he resolved them satisfactorily, if not to the world, at least to himself.

# PART TWO

# LONDON

✦ ✦ ✦

*That in a new age men truth would require,*

*From sin through flood were delivered the obedient.*

*On holy ground I AM appeared in smoke and fire,*

*Their seed expects pending parousial event.*

✦ ✦ ✦

# five

# Toast of London

(1)

Andrea Graves sipped quietly at a warm cup of tea. She gazed out the window of her private first-floor lounge onto the grounds of the Livingstone estate stretching behind the house. This was the time of day she enjoyed most—after breakfast when all the kitchen things were done. She always came upstairs for an hour to be alone with a fresh pot of tea and the newspaper.

Painful things occupied her mind on this day, however, and the daily news held no interest.

Accidents happened. She knew that. No amount of faith could remove calamity and uncertainty from the world. But when trials came close, it provided small consolation that heartache pressed daily upon the hearts of millions of others.

On this morning, Mrs. Graves felt her niece's loss more keenly than usual.

She, too, knew the grief. She had lost a brother-in-law and a nephew. And she was well acquainted with the loss her sister was experiencing. She had lost her own husband ten years earlier. Nor could she help blaming herself for Juliet's momentary row yesterday with her employer.

Not one of these factors, however, was sufficient in itself to explain her feelings as the housekeeper gazed out upon the trim hedges and stone pathways and bordered flower gardens. What weighed on her mind most heavily was the simple question, Why couldn't it have been *her* instead?

She was widowed and had no children. She may not yet be what people considered *old*. Yet most of her

life was behind her. Why was she not taken? After a few tears, she would not have been missed by more than a few. Mr. Livingstone would be able to find a suitable replacement.

Why had half her sister's happy young family been so suddenly and cruelly snatched from the earth?

It was no mere question of fate. It *should* have been her!

They had all planned to go to Earl's Court and Green Park together. Her sister's family had driven from Brighton up to Sevenoaks. Then she had come down with a dreadful cold that morning, and the family had gone ahead into the city without her. They had driven *her* car, which had been destroyed in the bombing. Scotland Yard was still holding it, for ongoing tests, they said.

Slowly Mrs. Graves' eyes filled with tears.

It was so sad for poor Juliet. She had witnessed the explosion and been thrown to the ground by it. What she went through! The police could be so insensitive with all their interrogations and questions.

She had come in for quite a lot of their questions as well. The police hinted—though such a thing could hardly be—that her car had actually been a target.

Almost immediately the social workers descended upon Juliet and her mother. When it was learned that Juliet's father was the sole provider and that their small house was rented, the various agencies lost no time in coming to their aid until they were settled. Now Juliet attended two support groups, was taking medication for depression, besides seeing a grief counselor once a week.

Soft footsteps sounded behind her. Mrs. Graves turned to see Juliet standing in the open door, cardigan over a pullover. It was a warm day, but she could not get rid of her chill.

"Hello, dear."

"I didn't want to be alone, Auntie," replied Juliet. "I hope you don't mind."

Mrs. Graves' eyes went immediately to the girl's moving hands.

"Of course not," she replied with a smile. "Would you like some tea?"

"I suppose," sighed her niece, sinking into the nearest chair, "although *nothing* sounds very interesting."

The housekeeper walked across the room and poured a cup from the pot she had just brewed.

"Are you all right, Juliet, dear?"

"I don't know. I wonder if it will ever go away."

"You are still anxious about the incident with Mr. Livingstone yesterday?"

"Oh, he was nice about it. He seems a very understanding man. But . . . nothing I do takes away the terror of that day. If I'm not thinking about it when I'm awake, I'm dreaming about it when I sleep. And I can't help feeling like I oughtn't to be here, that I'm going to be in the way and that people won't like me."

"Please, dear—you mustn't talk so. Does the counseling help?"

"I don't know, Auntie. She tells me it is healthy to let my feelings, even my anger, vent themselves. But hour after hour I sit staring out my window, or trying to read but unable to concentrate. Sometimes I just wish I could shrivel up and die."

"Do you share your feelings with the people in that group?"

"Oh, yes," she sighed. "We're all supposed to talk. But it won't bring Daddy and Joseph back for me to be miserable and to keep talking about my misery. Yet every time I go to the group, I'm afraid *not* to be miserable. That's what everyone expects. Sometimes when I do forget for just a few seconds, a ray of light peeks through. I think I might start warming up inside. Then I remember again, and the iciness comes straight back into my bones."

"Time will change all that."

"Will I ever stop being cold?"

"Yes, dear, I'm certain of it."

(2)

No loftier dream existed in any loyal British subject than one day to be invited to a garden party attended by the queen.

Merely receiving an invitation to such an event, in the private gardens of Buckingham Palace, was more than many politicians and aristocrats dared to hope for. But to be the singularly honored invitee at a gathering *hosted* by the queen—no higher pinnacle of renown existed in all the realm.

The center of attention and guest of honor at the gala reception on this warm September afternoon gave every appearance of being nothing less than royalty himself, yet was not. Surrounded as he was by a questioning and admiring throng circulating through the gardens and had marriage been on his mind, dashing archaeologist Adam Livingstone could have had any nobleman's daughter in Britain. Personable, witty, and intelligent, he could likewise have easily won a seat in the House of Commons from any constituency in the land.

Neither wife nor political clout, however, ranked at the top of Livingstone's present list of ambitions.

The modern-day explorer had dressed for the occasion in white tails and grey top hat, with a red rose pinned to his lapel. Full, sandy blond hair to the length of his ears protruded from beneath the brim, catching and glimmering occasionally in a ray of sunlight.

At six feet two and a hundred and eighty-five pounds, Adam's physique was well proportioned and powerful and could not but stand out in any crowd of his peers. The features of his face were unremarkable, though not from mediocrity but rather from their approach to perfection. Eyes of deep blue and a well-proportioned nose set off clean-shaven and angular cheeks, tan by acquaintance with the elements. A well-established jaw and high cheekbones indicated decisiveness. The even mouth of straight horizontal lines was equally comfortable at rest or in speech. It enclosed wide teeth and his smile contained the merest unintended hint of subtle mystery and was enough to melt a woman's heart.

At first glance a stranger would have taken him for a film star, not a scientist, though his rising fame had already begun to blur that distinction in the public consciousness.

It would have been unwise, however, to draw the conclusion from such a princely carriage, that Adam Livingstone's heart beat with any less vigor for his work. His passion was antiquity, not fame. At the same time, he was a pragmatist and recognized the occasional, and even necessary, linkage between the two. Confident and comfortable beside kings and presidents, prime ministers and financiers, he was a man supremely at ease with himself. Given his choice, however, he would sooner be out in the field in the middle of a jungle or a desert, Jen and Scott and Figg beside him, a shovel in one hand and a brush in the other, engaged in the work to which he had devoted his life—digging backward in time . . . in quest of the past.

Today was Livingstone's first public appearance since the return from Ararat. Everyone who was anyone in London was in attendance, and even a few who weren't—lords and ladies, members of Parliament, bankers and barons, earls and dukes, dames and duchesses and their husbands and wives, a few famous sportsmen, many of London's business elite, an international clique of journalists, small in number though influential, and every additional segment of British society. Owing to the scientific nature of the celebration, the gathering also included heavy representation from Oxford and Cambridge.

Nor did the invitation list ignore the international cooperation that had been required in the Livingstone project. Americans, Russians, French, Italians—were all present in good number, along with several high-placed Turkish diplomats and officials. Livingstone's entire field team and research staff had, of course, been included, as well as all members of the funding cartel except a few who desired to remain anonymous and stayed away.

To one side of the garden an eight-piece ensemble was engaged in a spirited rendition of Handel's *Water Music,* reported to be one of Livingstone's favorites. Capturing the nuances of the composition's subtleties was an ambitious undertaking for so small an orchestra, yet this day had been set aside to celebrate the triumph of ambitious ventures, and thus far, the musicians seemed to be carrying it off with the vigorous confidence demanded by the inherent complexities of the piece.

The highlight of the day would be the queen's receiving Livingstone for a private audience, after which both would address the gathering.

No one had yet seen Her Majesty. The entertainment thus far, such as it was, consisted of that tedious occupation called "milling around." On a day such as this, however, at the very center of the empire, surrounded by the elite of the elite, none of those in attendance found it other than stimulating. At least such an impression they tried to convey. For those uninterested in the scientific or spiritual dimensions of the subject du jour, there was always plenty of society gossip to catch up on.

"Hello, Adam," came a smooth and beguiling voice. An intent to captivate could not have been more unmistakable, though a mere two words had escaped the bright red lips.

The guest of honor turned as a tall, thin, gorgeous woman of approximately twenty-seven approached, flashing a radiant smile as bewitching as her tone. She was accustomed to occupying the center of attention and did not hesitate as she moved straight toward him. The small gathering around the archaeologist naturally opened itself to allow her entrance as she glided forward. That she required no invitation was more than obvious by the familiarity of her address.

"Ah, Candace!" exclaimed Livingstone. "It is wonderful to see you—and how lovely you look!"

He took the hand she offered, then bowed imperceptibly as he lightly kissed the back of it.

"I was hoping you would have called before now," said the newcomer. She withdrew her hand daintily from his grasp, feigning the sort of pouty expression with which a flirtatious woman is well experienced.

"Planned to, my dear," replied Livingstone with casual aplomb. "Unfortunately the press of my schedule has been unending since my return to the city."

"And quite a return it was! I saw the replay on the telly," she said, moving now to Adam's side with an intimacy that seemed altogether natural.

Lady Candace Montreux, daughter of Lord Harriman Montreux, member of the House of Lords and wealthy financier of a very old English family of Norman roots, was known to most of those in attendance. Lord Montreux's daughter, one of London society's most dazzling single women, had been presented with more proposals of marriage than were good for any woman. But she had eyes only for Adam Livingstone, with whom she had enjoyed a friendly relationship—though not so close as she would have liked—for the past four years. Her father had at first opposed the notion of a match between them. He insisted that no less than a viscount could possibly be suitable for his daughter, preferably an earl or a marquis. Of late, however, he had begun to look upon the archaeologist with more favor, no doubt enhanced by the latter's expanding reputation.

"But tell me, Adam," she went on, "when *are* you going to call at Swanspond? Father said just the other day that he hadn't seen you in ages."

"He is here today, is he not?" said Adam, glancing about.

"Oh, yes—he's off talking with someone."

"Then I shall see him later."

"But you still must call, Adam. Daddy's feelings are almost as hurt as mine," she added with a coy glance upward into his face.

"I doubt very much if *your* feelings are capable of being all that hurt quite so easily, Candace," Livingstone replied with a smile containing power equal to her own expression. "The way I hear it, you have a steady stream of admirers who keep you well entertained."

"Oh, Adam, you are so amusing!" she laughed, inching now closer to his side and slipping her hand through his arm. "Unfortunately, none of them is as charming as you, nor does Daddy approve of any like he does you."

"Your father honors me with his esteem," rejoined Adam, taking the pause that followed to turn toward another of those nearby with a remark.

(3)

On a shadowy dusty street in Baghdad, a furtive figure entered a nondescript earth-colored building, quickly descending two flights of stairs to a basement deep under the bowels of the city. Opening a thick steel door, he walked into a small but obviously high tech room. Computers, printers, telephones, and fax machines sat on several desks.

A young bearded man of undeterminable age glanced up.

"Did you get it?" he asked.

The messenger walked forward, reached inside his coat, took out a small sheaf of papers that had been folded several times, and handed it to his questioner. The seated man opened them hastily and perused the contents.

Both men wore beards and head coverings. Their eyes burned with the fire of Muslim fundamentalism. Their present jihad, however, was no holy war aimed at the destruction of the great Satan America, but was rather against the desecration of what had suddenly become a holy mount in their eyes. That Ararat had never mattered to the terrorist organization Il-Khadim before was an inconsistency neither paused to consider. In fact, the Turkish mountain was historically no more holy to them than the computers they used, though they hated the society that had spawned the technology to create them. Consistency was no necessary element in the creed of their radicalism.

Suddenly here was something the public cared about, an object of worldwide esteem and renown. If it could be sabotaged and destroyed, it would suit their purposes and give them a twisted, evil satisfaction. Destruction, not meaning, drove them. The fact that this great object was treasured by Christians and Jews, whom they hated above all others, made it all the more appealing a target.

They had been offered a huge sum from their neighbor to the north to carry out the treachery, a fact that certainly heightened their devotion. They could buy guns, bombs, much ammunition, and possibly secure the freedom of several of their number held in various European and Israeli prisons. If they were idealistic when it came to giving their lives, they were pragmatic in the way of finances. And the powerful one promised to pay them well. It was not their first dealing with him. They knew he would deliver as agreed.

"This is all?" the man asked bluntly. "It is not much of a map for our purposes."

"They assure me we can get to it. The locals who took the big man up the mountain, there where it shows—" he pointed to the drawing on one of the papers—"they will take us there again for the right price."

"We do not need to scale this mountain, but the one opposite."

"They assure me that with the right guides there is nowhere upon Ararat we cannot reach."

"*With* our supplies?"

The other nodded.

"And be able to get out before we are buried?"

Another nod.

"Good . . . make the arrangements."

(4)

Most of the milling going on in the Buckingham gardens subtly directed itself toward the constantly fluctuating circle swarming about Adam Livingstone and his associates, with the dazzling Lady Montreux now having made herself one of the select coterie.

There was one among the guests who watched Livingstone from a distance, making no attempt toward personal approach. He stood mostly to one side of the gathering, chatting superficially with an occasional diplomat with whom his position in one of the new republics of the former USSR made him acquainted. All the while he kept one eye shrewdly following Livingstone's movements. He had not come here to curry the man's favor. Something of far different intent lay on his mind.

Among the rest, however, even those who knew nothing about archaeology and cared even less hoped to be able to say that they had spoken personally with the discoverer of the ark. Such little fragments of conversation were the trophies to be gathered in such a setting, though one mustn't appear too eager.

"I say, Livingstone," remarked the duke of Arundel, who, though he had made most of the arrangements on behalf of the queen, had only just been successful in penetrating the inner circle of discussion surrounding the honoree. "I read the other day where you said that God told Noah how to build the ark. I didn't know you were one of *them.*"

"One of whom, Duke?" asked Adam.

"One of those fanatics who sees God behind every prehistoric rock."

"I am not sure I am. Just where did you read the quote in question?"

"I don't remember exactly, possibly the *Mirror.*"

"That explains it," laughed Adam.

"Were you misquoted?"

"I never made the statement at all."

"Where did they get it?"

"An energetic discussion of the ark's spiritual dimensions took place outside my home the day I arrived back in London. I did remark, I believe, something to the effect that the discovery of the ark opened up more questions than it answered."

"Come now, Livingstone—what can spirituality have to do with it?"

"Considering that it may be the ark of Noah, I would say perhaps a good deal."

"What more did you have to say?"

"I was not the one raising most of the questions that day. Kelley Halliday posed the query of how the man Noah *knew* to construct a ship and how he was *able* to build it. I have to admit that these questions suddenly loom large, it seems to me, in the way of the implications of the find."

"Oh, well . . . *Halliday.* That accounts for it! He does look for God under every rock."

"At first I found myself a little annoyed as well," said Adam. "But as I have reflected upon it, I would have to say that I think Mr. Halliday's questions valid and important ones for consideration."

"And do you answer them by saying that *God* is the reason he knew these things?" asked Fred Marks, a producer of BBC documentaries, to whom the reporter Glendenning had recounted every word of the gateside exchange with Livingstone.

"I reserve judgment," replied Livingstone evasively, echoing his earlier answer to Halliday.

"A shrewd reply," commented Stanbridge Dunbar, aristocratic publisher of an avant-garde scientific journal who had come hoping to secure a future interview with the archaeologist.

"Honestly, Baron," said Adam, "I don't know. Halliday *is* right in that the ark has implications. Believe me, I have been asking myself many things I had not considered before."

"And what conclusions have you reached?"

"None as yet. But might this not be a question science has to reconsider? I simply throw out the question as a research query."

"*Science* consider what is primarily an issue of *faith?*"

"Isn't *everything* a matter of faith in the end?" rejoined Adam. "You have put your finger on what seems to me one of the greatly misunderstood points in the debate between science and faith, to use your terms. What about the faith we scientists put in our own science? Science takes just as many leaps across the void of unprovability as do Christians. And besides, Darwin hardly explained everything, did he? His book may, it seems, have been singularly ill titled, for true origins is one thing he did not address—where did we come from . . . originally?"

"What has that to do with the ark?"

"Everything! Where did everything come from—the ark and all the rest? Can we afford to limit the scope of our quest, now that we have found the ark, and not try to learn why it is there? I think not."

"By the way, Livingstone," added Marks, hoping for a little hard news as long as he had the man's momentary attention, "what's next on the agenda?"

"My team's been planning a little junket to Africa while waiting for next year's warm spell in Turkey."

"In search of what?"

"Ah, Mr. Marks." Adam smiled. "An archaeologist never knows the answer to that question until he has found it!"

"You must have some idea."

"Let's just say there are certain hypotheses I have been speculating upon for several years that I am eager to put to the test of on-site research."

"I understand there is an invitation pending from the White House," said Marks.

"Scott Jordan is involved in some arrangements in that regard, along with the scientists there who were involved in the project with us. It truly was a group effort, not only between America and Britain, but many other countries as well. I just happened to be the one coordinating it."

"So you are convinced the structure on Ararat is indeed the ark of Noah?" asked a woman who did not seem eager to let the conversation stray from what the occasion had been called to celebrate. Adam did not recognize her, but she had shown a keen interest in the discussion.

"Yes, I think I am," he replied.

"Your use of the word *think* is not very convincing," she added with a smile.

Adam nodded. "Like many rationalists in the world," he said, "I am finding that the implications of the find take time to get used to. I am convinced it is the ark described in the Hebrew Scriptures. Yet without fully knowing what the presence of Noah's ark really means, without a more thorough understanding of the whys involved, and what role a Supreme Being of some kind may have played in preflood events—you must understand, these unresolved questions force a certain ambivalence into my response. I don't know if that makes sense. I am afraid it is the best I can do at the moment. I am still wrestling it through myself."

"Surely you had considered these issues before? Why would you have gone in search for Noah's ark if you had never stopped to consider the Genesis account?" The questioner was one Rev. Felix Holderness, high-ranking bishop in the Church of England and one of the queen's personal spiritual advisors.

"A very probing question, Bishop," answered Adam, whose tone now became very thoughtful. "I suppose Noah's ark has always represented something like the holy grail of archaeology," he went on. "It is so extraordinarily unique and unmistakable. Of course, there are many discoveries that are potentially huge. Johanson's discovery of the bones called Lucy in '74 was groundbreaking—yet the whole find consisted of only a few bones."

"Not so small. The site yielded more than two hundred fossil specimens, if I'm not mistaken."

"You are up on your archaeology!" laughed Livingstone. "But as to the point I was making—let us take your own field, Bishop. If we found some stone tablets that were purported to be written on by the finger of God, or if someone claimed to have discovered the real Holy Grail, these are items about which there really could be no conclusive proof able to convince everyone in the world that the objects were genuine. In such matters there are always doubters. Even Lucy has her skeptics."

"And if the discovery did have to do with a so-called religious artifact such as the tablets of Moses," interjected the bishop, "science would dismiss it with a wave of the hand. Scientists tend to reach massive conclusions based sometimes on very scant evidence. But when a man of faith comes up with evidence that might be even more persuasive, they tend to disregard it."

"Are you saying the scientific community is not objective?" asked Dunbar.

"I think science tends to blind itself to the potential veracity of anything that comes out of the religious arena," Rev. Holderness replied. "In so doing, science abandons its objectivity. Yet when scientists are looking at something that they want to see or really want to find, they find a way to prove it with very little evidence indeed. Lucy is a case in point."

Livingstone's face brightened as he glanced around the group listening in rapt attention.

"This is exactly what makes this find truly unique," said Adam, now resuming the dialogue. "It links science and faith in a way nothing else could. Imagine—a boat four hundred and fifty feet long with animal cages and dated between seven and fifteen thousand years old," he went on, eyes alive and voice animated. "That is pretty difficult to fake. I was there. I saw it. I felt it. Nothing so old and so huge has ever been found. And found so high up an inaccessible mountain with no possible logical explanation of how it could get there except a cataclysmic event such as a massive flood. It's staggering. The evidence is so strong as to be almost indisputable. It is in a class all its own. It is absolutely singular and unequaled in all archaeology. There has never been a discovery to compare with it."

Again he paused and drew in a breath, his countenance calming and growing pensive again.

"All these factors contribute to the magnitude of this particular quest," he continued. "The ark has always been a natural focus of interest for everyone who studies archaeology. Yet as I say, I had not stopped to consider the spiritual dimensions beforehand. I don't know why I hadn't. You are right, Bishop—not to have done so before now seems ludicrous. They suddenly seem so obvious. But my energy prior to this time was directed simply on the hunt, the journey, the research, the science itself. Now I find myself wondering, as Halliday articulated, why is it there . . . what does it mean?"

"You obviously place great stock in your find," remarked Dunbar. "Perhaps the ark will become your Lucy, placing all your other finds into perspective."

The archaeologist did not have the chance to comment immediately.

"Come, come, Livingstone," said a crusty voice now entering the conversational cadre, "if you continue with this sort of philosophical drivel, you shall give our profession a bad name. We can't have them think we're all a batch of canting spiritualists."

All eyes turned to see a hulking man bearing down upon them. With trademark gray panama hat tied up on one side, khaki shirt and trousers, and well-worn boots, he wielded a drink in one hand and looked as if he had stepped out of an African safari rather than into the midst of a Buckingham garden party. Long, gray, sandy hair pulled back into a small ponytail completed the offbeat image, topped to perfection by a single earring of a serpent dangling from the left ear.

The circle opened again, though not this time in awe of Lady Montreux's elegance, but rather in unconscious self-defense. If those present did not make room, the fellow could mow them down like a charging rhino, of which his ponderous and ungainly approach could not help but remind them.

"They certainly shan't say that about you, Sir Gilbert!" laughed Adam, turning toward him.

As Sir Gilbert walked into the group, Candace Montreax took the opportunity to glide away unnoticed. The observant foreign guest had caught her eye, and she now moved casually in his direction. She could tell he had been watching her and was intrigued, though thought it best to initiate no contact. She would get close enough to hear his voice and see if she might learn something. His English was perfect, she could tell that instantly, though it contained the merest trace of his Irano-Armenian roots. What was the man's connection to the Ararat expedition? she wondered.

Meanwhile, Adam welcomed the bulky man who had just approached his circle of conversation. "How nice to see you again, Sir Gilbert," he said, shaking hands with the newcomer. "It's been a couple of years."

The khaki-clad colleague did not reply directly, shaking Adam's hand with what looked like more enthusiasm than he actually felt. A probing search of his keenly expressive black eyes would have revealed less camaraderie than the impression he sought to convey to those observing the significant exchange between rival associates.

"Still giving the Christians what for, Bowles?" asked Dunbar.

"Only when they deserve it."

"Which, according to you, is all the time, am I right?" put in Bishop Holderness good-naturedly.

"Not so far off the mark," laughed Bowles. "I am always willing to make an exception in the case of open-minded priests—especially when they are good sports like you, Bishop. But I am a scientist first. I am guided only by verifiable facts. When fundamentalist religious types persist in ignoring them and devising ridiculous theories in defiance of the evidence, then I feel it my duty to take them to task for it."

"So what do you think of the fact of Noah's ark?" asked the BBC's Marks. "We were just discussing the implications of the find before you stepped in. Your colleague Mr. Livingstone said he did not know quite what to make of it. Where do you stand?"

Bowles did not reply immediately. He was still irritated at losing the limelight so soon after his own discovery. He must guard his words. But he had found out what he needed to on his own private little excursion. And he would find out more.

"I suppose that is a question that will take a good while for us all to answer," he replied at length.

The response satisfied no one. But the man's tone made it clear enough that he would offer no more detailed opinion in that direction.

# Breach of Security

(1)

Sir Gilbert Bowles turned the ancient human skull in his hands, almost as if staring into the two eerily empty eye cavities for some transcendental communication from a long-dead ancestor.

What did his find mean now? he wondered.

Was the significance of this object he personally had dug out of the earth and now cradled in his palm, this object upon which his recent fame had been built . . . was it all now to evaporate? Was he to be reduced to second fiddle in the world of human historical exploration?

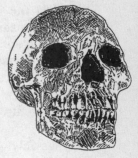

The past month had been particularly unnerving for the forty-eight-year-old paleoanthropologist. It was not merely the question Marks had asked him at the queen's reception. It was the whole convulsion that suddenly turned his world topsy-turvy.

Just when his own reputation as England's most noted authority on human antiquities seemed secure—had not the queen herself knighted *him* three years ago for his groundbreaking work?—this young Cambridge upstart Livingstone had scooped both him and his theories all at once. Notwithstanding that he had received an invitation to last month's festivities at the palace, it was clear no one wanted to talk to *him*. Even the queen had positively snubbed him. Such a short time ago she had called him the pride of the British Empire. No matter how high he rose professionally, in his own mind he never quite forgot his common roots. He always suspected that people looked at him differently as a result, and the gathering at the palace seemed to confirm it.

*Livingstone, Livingstone, Livingstone!*

He was sick of the name. It was on everyone's lips—that's all they were talking about. Livingstone and the ark.

Ark his foot!

73

The whole thing smacked of flummery! He would like to get *his* hands on some of those so-called ark samples. He would prove the whole thing a hoax in a minute!

He would get his hands on them, too, now that he knew where the ark was. He may have been bested momentarily. But he would not let Livingstone get away with such a thing again. He would watch his adversary's moves more carefully from now on.

In the midst of his smoldering ire, the man's gaze wandered across the room where sat a stack of his best-selling book, *Homopithecus: The Link Is Found*. Perhaps the most influential treatise on evolution published since Darwin's *Origins*, the book was no stuffy archaeological diary. Rather, the scientist had managed to pen a readable and entertaining account of his seemingly indisputable disproof of the existence of a Supreme Being, wrapped in a thin cloak of scientific validation based upon his African expeditions.

The success of the book startled the entire publishing world. It sold 2 million copies in cloth and another 8 million in paper. That success led to one Hollywood movie, three BBC specials, and two PBS documentaries. As a result, Bowles had become almost overnight one of England's wealthiest men and the world's most vocal spokesman against religion on behalf of evolution and natural selection.

In his own right, Bowles was a first-rate archaeologist and had been in on a number of important finds through the years. But when his research team unearthed the immense graveyard on the savannah of the Ngorongoro Crater in Tanzania, discovering several intact *Homo* skeletons—neither exactly *Homo* nor *Australopithecines* but combining many of the features of *A. boisei, H. habilis,* and *H. ergaster*—as well as hundreds of miscellaneous bones and no less than twenty skulls representing all ages—the stage was set for a major new step forward in human evolutionary research and migratory postulation. It was the greatest find since Lucy, and Bowles was hailed as a genius.

In digs only one year later, Bowles made another discovery in the African Rift Valley north of Lake Rukwa, not so large, though significant enough, and again postulated a new subspecies of *Homo,* which he styled *erectus sapiens*. Dating the new remains almost entirely between 195,000 and 215,000 years, Bowles astonished the scientific community by refuting both commonly held theories regarding early *Homo sapiens*—the view that all modern peoples descended regionally from *Homo erectus,* evolving distinctly in different parts of the world, and the view that the species called *Homo sapiens* entirely replaced *Homo erectus* in Africa between 100,000 and 200,000 years ago, which then spread out eventually to populate the entire globe. These were known as the *multiregional* and the *out-of-Africa* views. There had been speculation either of an in-between but yet unknown species between the two. Others held to the likelihood of a different species altogether, which led from *erectus* to *sapiens*—sometimes called early *Homo sapiens*. But until Bowles' startling discovery, nothing to validate this view had been found.

In actuality, neither of Bowles' finds and subsequent theories was quite so revolutionary as he allowed the public to believe. Neither *Homopithecus* ("man ape") nor *erectus sapiens* had been altogether accepted into the scientific vocabulary as yet. No one was suggesting outright fraud on the level of the Piltdown man of 1911, and there were many who believed his migrations theory was precisely on target. But many said all he had found were additional samples of *H. sapiens* archaic. And Bowles' use of the word *link* in the title of his book conveyed more, as was his intent, than the facts of the case supported. The so-called missing link between hominoids, or apes, and hominids, commonly known as ape-men—of which *Australopihecus afarensis* Lucy was the most famous, though no longer the oldest known example—yet remained undiscovered.

It was not, therefore, the science of the finds or of his book that had made of Bowles a celebrity and his book a best-seller. It was instead the apparent authority with which he spoke out his crusty and humorous atheism, given credence by his knowledgeable scientific references and data.

Bowles was a Will Rogers–like Carl Sagan, making the science of evolution fun and understandable. He placed fundamentalist Christians as the butt of his every reference to small-minded and backward thinking. Scientists took much of what he said with a humorous wink, though his finds were genuine enough. And it could not be denied that fund-raising had grown easier as a result of Bowles' having put archaeology on the front page.

He was revered by humanists and liberals and genuinely hated—to whatever degree their adaptive bending of the gospel would allow it—by most conservative Christians.

Bowles' personal carriage contributed all the more to his colorful reputation. He always looked the same, whether his shirt was stained with perspiration from a day under the hot African sun, or whether he had put on a clean one to deliver a lecture at Oxford. If such a thing existed, Sir Gilbert Bowles represented the world's stereotypical image of an archaeologist. The only thing gradually changing about his appearance was that his six-foot-four-inch frame and hefty build were being added to with yet more girth during the recent years of banquet speeches that had resulted from his fame.

Bowles took a slow puff from the fat cigar in his mouth, then blew the smoke at the fossilized skull, watching it drift around and through the orifices where eyes and a nose once existed.

This Livingstone find could undermine everything he had worked all his life to prove—namely, that no God existed in the universe, only atoms that behaved according to rational science.

He was not about to let that happen.

(2)

Adam Livingstone sat back in his chair in his office, sipping a hot cup of tea and glancing at the morning edition of the *Times*.

He had barely gotten himself comfortable when he flew up and back to his feet.

"What!" he exclaimed. This couldn't be!

He shot out the door, ran down the hall and into the offices of his team.

"Scott—have you seen this piece on page 2 of the *Times*?"

He thrust the paper toward him without awaiting an answer, jabbing the page with his finger. "Explosion, Avalanche Rock Ararat," Scott read.

"Do you know anything?"

Scott's bewildered expression of concern was all the answer he needed.

"Crystal," said Adam, spinning around toward his secretary, "get me Kate Cody in the foreign secretary's office on the phone."

Adam paced about the floor nervously as she made the call. "Our people in Dogubayazit should have called us with this immediately. I don't like to run across something like this in the newspaper. And why didn't the *Times* call about this?"

"Oh, no!" exclaimed Adam's secretary. "They did . . . but I thought it was just another interview request. I forgot to tell you. Adam, I'm sorry."

"Well, it's done now—get me Cody anyway."

In thirty seconds Crystal handed him the phone.

"Kate . . . Adam Livingstone," he said. "There's a piece in this morning's *Times*—an explosion on Ararat. You know anything?"

He listened intently.

"Uh, huh . . . okay . . . yes, right—I see . . . yes, I was extremely concerned. You'll update me? Right . . . good. Thanks, Kate."

He handed the phone back to Crystal, exhaling in evident relief.

"False alarm," he said. "Well, not exactly a false alarm—something happened, but no damage was done. The incident came lower down the mountain and on a different slope."

"What set it off?" asked Scott.

"No one knows. Bit of a mystery at this point. Shepherds reported hearing a loud sound like an explosion. Whatever it was set off a localized avalanche. There was quite a buildup of soft powder from last week's snowfall. That's it. No bodies, no explanation."

Scott took in the information with interest.

"See if you can get through to Dogubayazit, Crystal. Talk to Figg. See what he has to say."

Already Crystal had the phone in her hand again.

"Well," said Adam, "I was just about to have a cup of tea and engage in some gray-cell work. I'll have to see if I can get the mood back after that little panic."

(3)

Adam sat down in his office again. The cup of tea beside his chair was no longer steaming but was still drinkable. He took a swallow and let his thoughts wander.

It had been six weeks since the Ararat expedition. The birches lining the driveway of the Livingstone estate had exploded with gold, and occasionally leaves floated gracefully to the ground. The evenings held a hint of chilling frost. The air smelled different. Even the songs of the birds seemed preparing for the change that was at hand.

Winter was on its way to London and would soon descend upon the entire Northern Hemisphere, including Turkey. Any thought of further exploration was out of the question for three-quarters of a year or more. Hopefully there would be no more freak avalanches in that time. Livingstone's thoughts, as they always did after a triumph, had lately found themselves gazing toward the arena of the new challenge he had set for himself.

He glanced up at the huge relief map of the world that occupied one entire wall of his expansive study. There was the place of his work—it was called the planet Earth.

With the African trip approaching, his brain was now free to conjecture more expansively concerning his rift theory. The enthusiasm was mounting at last to pursue it aggressively.

There was a complication, however, to another expedition of such magnitude at this time. And it was not scientific in nature.

He smiled as the face of that complication arose before him.

He turned from the map and glanced toward her photograph on his desk. He needed to figure out where Candace fit into the matrix of his future. He needed to figure out where the rift region in Africa fit into his future as well. He had seen Lord Montreux's daughter several times since the Buckingham reception. There was no doubt of her intentions.

Again came the question that had occurred to him on the way into the glacier—was he ready to share his work with a wife?

He knew that Candace was counting on a formal proposal soon, no later than sometime in the spring if they were to be married next autumn. He had better be sure of himself.

He sat back, took another sip of tea, and fell into a reminiscent mood. He was indeed a fortunate man. He was thankful for his life and the opportunities that had come his way. He had seen much of the globe. If only he could probe beneath its surface into the past as clearly as he could visualize the landforms on the wall.

Adam Livingstone's passion was antiquity. He loved all things old. Specializing in both history and archaeology at Cambridge, during the course of his studies he had delved deeply into every branch of humanity's story, from ancient Egypt and Judaism, to Greece, China, the American Indian tribes, and the Roman Empire. He eventually acquired multiple master's degrees and was at work on his doctoral thesis when boredom with the academic life finally overtook him.

He left Cambridge for the field and never looked back. Nor did he regret his decision. On the wall behind him opposite the map hung several honorary doctorates that had been awarded him since. In the ten years after leaving the university, he had traversed the world many times over, driven by an ever more ambitious desire to understand man's beginnings.

A dozen theories swirled in his brain about migrations, languages, human evolution, and the mixes of peoples and races on the earth.

The library on the third floor of the Livingstone home contained, besides an enormous array of books, a vast accumulation of notebooks and manuscripts and research diaries. Eventually he planned to write books himself. But as yet his hypotheses remained in the research stage. His life was too full to sit down and write. He would synthesize his findings on paper someday. For now the hunt itself possessed him.

Adam lectured from time to time at various British and American universities but regularly had to turn down scores more invitations than it was possible to accept. Along with his charismatic aristocratic image, he was a fascinating speaker and was recognized as a compelling authority on a dozen subjects. A student of anthropology and paleontology, Adam had studied biology and the details of evolutionary theory. He had kept track of Sir Gilbert Bowles' movements with keen interest. He had studied physics, astronomy, and meteorology sufficiently to lecture convincingly on the big bang and related theories of cosmic origins. With the help of Scott, who had majored in geology at the University of Colorado, he had become well versed in the earth's formations that had occurred since earliest ages.

Both the prestige of his reputation and the wide range of his expertise ensured that Adam Livingstone could have been offered a permanent professorial chair at any university in the world. Had such been his ambition, any of a dozen think tanks, research groups, or European governments would have paid him a multiple six-figure salary in pounds sterling to call him their staff consultant.

On a case-by-case basis, he did consulting work for such organizations and was handsomely paid. Such remuneration, however, proved nowhere near sufficient to offset the costs of his own expeditions and research adventures. Except for Ararat, his trips were mostly funded from his personal donations. The freedom to be on his own remained a more appealing and practical motive than any offer of a fortune. It would feel like the ring of someone else's control through his nose. If someday he failed to raise funding for a project his heart yearned to follow, he would ponder other financial options. He hoped it would never come to that. For the present he was a man happy and content with the lot, station, and career that life had presented him.

Furthermore, Lord Montreux was said to be one of the richest men in England, and Candace was his only child. Adam was too much a gentleman of principle to marry for money. Yet the fact could hardly be overlooked that as Lord Montreux's son-in-law whatever expeditions he chose to undertake in the future would hardly want for capital.

Adam's many insatiable interests had gradually fused into a hunger to get to the bottom of history's earliest moments—synthesizing existing knowledge into a unified theory of beginnings. He hoped to bring the fields of history, archaeology, geology, anthropology, and paleontology together as Einstein's relativity had harmonized light, mass, and energy.

His dream was to discover truths of man's existence that had elluded all who preceded him, to find and understand and bring to light truths never before known. And perhaps, with a lifetime of such discoveries behind him, someday in the future he would write a magnificent chronicle of beginnings on earth such as none other had ever conceived, a unified history of humankind, which posterity would place on a level with Einstein's unified theory of the universe.

Adam saw ancient history as comprised of a scant one percent solid information, with 99 percent of the space devoted to gaps in the record. It was his dream to gather the data necessary to rectify that imbalance and write an encompassing theory that placed his findings into an overarching historical perspective.

As yet, however, Adam Livingstone's paleoanthropological $E = mc^2$ had eluded him.

There were those who called him a modern-day Renaissance man, like Leonardo or Einstein, always with some new theory or idea to try out on whomever would listen.

Adam only laughed when such comparisons reached his ears.

(4)

An hour or two later, Adam was returning from a pensive walk in the garden behind the house when Crystal called down to him from the office balcony.

"Adam," she said, "your mother's on the phone."

Adam waved up to her with a smile, breaking into a light jog across the lawn and toward the back door. He took the call in the breakfast room off the kitchen.

"Mum," he said, "I didn't know you were back in the country!"

"I only flew in two days ago," replied his mother on the other end of the line.

"Where are you—are you in London?"

"I'm calling from Lady Percival's in Birmingham. She and I just arrived back from Alaska. She asked me to stay on a few days."

"When will you be back home—I'll drive up and bring you down."

"You'll do nothing of the kind, Adam. I'll ring you when I'm settled."

"Why don't you come stay at the estate for a while? Mrs. Graves would love to see you—so would we all."

"My flat in the city will suit me fine. Why, Adam, you've turned Sevenoaks into a three-ring circus. I wouldn't know what to do with myself."

"What are you talking about?" laughed Adam.

"All your theatrics—that's what I mean. Goodness, flying in like a bird! We were in Vancouver when you returned from your expedition. It was all over the telly. Wherever I went, the moment people heard my name they asked if I knew you. I'm his mother, I said, though I was embarrassed to admit it. And then did they make a fuss! From the looks of it, Adam, I would think you were some American film stuntman!"

Adam laughed with delight. "Is it really so embarrassing to be my mother?" he chuckled.

"I've learned to live with it. But what would your father have said? He was always so distinguished."

"I should hardly think you would complain. Where do you think I got my adventuresome spirit? You're more a world gadabout than I am. Why, Mum, it wouldn't surprise me to hear that you'd taken up parachuting or skydiving. I've never climbed the Matterhorn."

"Mrs. Ludgate and I have been talking about trying a bungee drop."

"There—you see! My mother, Frances Livingstone, the daredevil." Adam laughed again. "But, Mum," he went on more seriously, "tell me—how are you? And how was Alaska?"

"Gorgeous . . . unbelievable."

"I want to hear all about it. Why don't you come over for dinner when you are back in the city?"

"I'll be much too busy, Adam."

"Breakfast then?"

"I'm chairman of a clothing drive and will be working night and day. I'm certain I told you about it."

"I haven't seen you in months, Mum."

"We're taking a boatload of clothes and supplies to India in three weeks. As soon as I'm over this jet lag, I'll have to devote every minute to it."

"The price of being a philanthropist!"

"But sometimes society people can be so exasperating. Do you know that silly Lady Batham actually gave us a sequined stole—for orphans in Calcutta!"

Adam could not help laughing again, though his mother obviously did not find it humorous.

"How long will you be there?" he asked.

"I don't know—a week, perhaps two."

"Then you will be home for Christmas?"

"I've made arrangements for a little tour into the northern mountains," his mother went on, "with a stop to visit some very interesting monks high up on the border between Nepal and Tibet."

"Mum, I didn't know you cared about religious things."

"I don't. I haven't stepped inside a church since your father's funeral eighteen years ago. But these monks have great influence. I hope they can be helpful in our work with the orphanages throughout India."

"Well, if anyone can enlist their cooperation, it's you, Mum!" said Adam.

"Have you seen Claresta?" his mother asked.

"No—not a word. Is she still in Germany?"

"I haven't heard from your sister in three years, Adam," replied Mrs. Livingstone, a hint of pain coming through in her voice. "I was hoping she might have contacted you."

"I'm sorry, Mum. I don't know any more than you do. You know I would do anything . . . if I could."

"I know that, Adam."

A brief silence followed.

"But what's this I hear on the news about your going to Africa?" asked Adam's mother, resuming her carefree tone.

"I want to check out certain hypotheses I've been speculating on."

"Come now, Adam—don't give me the same line you gave the press!"

Adam grinned. "You should be a journalist, Mum."

"We don't report the news—we make it. Isn't that what your father used to say?"

"Something like that."

"So what's it all about?"

"I've told you about my theory," replied Adam. "It's finally time to investigate it in more detail."

"It sounds boring to me. You really should direct your energies to something that will benefit mankind. All this digging around does nobody any good."

"What about the benefit to scientific knowledge?"

"There are hungry mouths to feed, Adam. Knowledge won't feed them."

"Knowledge helps produce food, Mum."

"I doubt archaeological knowledge does. But I won't criticize your profession, Adam, even though I consider it a waste of time. But I must run. Lady Percival is calling for tea."

"Give her my regards. What about breakfast or at least tea in the city?"

"I'll ring you when I'm back in the city. We shall get together before I leave for India, I promise. Take care, Adam."

"You too, Mum."

Adam put the phone down with a smile, then exhaled a long sigh.

His mother was certainly a whirlwind. She had scarcely stopped since his father's death. She often said that she was in the third stage of her life. The first had been living for herself. The second had been doing everything for her family. The third was doing what she could for the world. Adam wondered if there would be a fourth.

Reflecting on the conversation, he returned upstairs to his office.

(5)

Juliet Halsay walked down the corridor in the Livingstone home and knocked on the door of the housekeeping workroom.

"You wanted me, Auntie?" she said as she entered.

"Oh yes, Juliet dear," replied Mrs. Graves, glancing up. "Would you please take these ironed linens to the second floor for me?"

"The linen cupboards in the big storage room?"

Mrs. Graves nodded. She loaded Juliet's outstretched arms with what could be comfortably carried. Then Juliet turned to go.

Mrs. Graves watched her leave. Her niece was doing better, she thought to herself. She was doing her best to keep her busy. Still the girl constantly wore both pullover and cardigan, even on the warmest of days, and continued to rub at her hands. Mrs. Graves doubted the counseling was doing much good.

As she entered the west wing on her way to the stairway, Juliet passed the administrative and secretarial offices, where Adam and his small full-time staff had informally gathered and were now engaged in enthusiastic conversation about the work recently completed and what lay ahead.

The door stood partially opened. With arms full as she walked past, Juliet heard voices from inside. She continued on and turned up the stairway to the second floor, where she deposited her cargo.

Descending the stairs two or three minutes later, the voices from the office below had grown louder. Juliet was able to make out various threads of the conversation.

". . . can't do anything more until next summer . . . Ararat will be under a half mile of snow . . . , " said Scott Jordan's voice.

". . . need to bring that adventure to closure for the present."

". . . only until the summer thaw?"

". . . nothing will keep me off that mountain when the time comes!"

One of the women spoke next, but Juliet could make nothing of what was said. Then Adam's voice resonated into the corridor.

". . . got to make sure the planning for next year continues while we're in Africa."

"Figg and the cartel people will stay on top of it."

Juliet slowed. Fascinated by what she heard, her steps unconsciously came to a stop, and she sat down on one of the stairs.

". . . want to find out once and for all if my rift theory holds water."

"When do we leave?" asked Jen excitedly.

"Within the month?"

"Do you really think it's there?" said Crystal.

"I don't know." Adam laughed. "Tantalizing to think about . . . flora of antiquity too, not just fauna . . . first relics of humanity . . . need to complete the picture . . ."

"Why not bring in Bowles to join us?"

". . . all we'd need!"

Laughter circulated through the room.

"His interest in Genesis would only be to debunk and discredit me as a lunatic."

". . . knows the Ngorogoro Crater and Olduvai Gorge better than anyone . . ."

"You're right, Crystal . . . helpful to tap his expertise."

". . . can't trust him," came the voice of his assistant.

"I agree with Jen," added Jordan.

"He is responsible for a great deal of the progress since Lucy." It was Livingstone speaking again. ". . . but Eden—he would laugh at the very notion."

"He's not the only one," laughed his secretary, ". . . set the whole scientific community on its ear when they learn what we are going to Africa to look for."

". . . say what they will. Besides, Scott, no one is going to find out until we have hard evidence . . . don't want to hear the word *Eden* spoken outside this room . . . all understand?"

Another brief silence followed.

". . . not a word of any of this to anyone. The purpose of our junket has to remain secret . . . do you hear me, Erin?" Livingstone added, "That boyfriend of yours is too curious for his own good. Every time I see him he pesters me with questions . . . didn't know better I'd think he was a reporter."

Juliet could hear Erin laugh in the background and say something in reply.

". . . just knows computers inside out . . ."

This was intriguing. Juliet wanted to go stand right beside the door and listen to every word!

From her studies she was familiar with the rift region of Africa. To actually go there! That was just what Mr. Livingstone and the others were talking about!

More conversation followed, which she could not hear. Then came Livingstone's voice again.

"... the computer model ..."

"... not perfected yet," replied Crystal. "... think I'm getting close to what you asked for."

"Keep at it ... foundational to the whole theory ... weather patterns ... dramatically changed through centuries—you know, the Sahara syndrome ... never pinpoint precise location, yet still would be incredible to demonstrate a connection."

"Crystal ... finalize plans with our people in Africa—and we've got to get hold of Dr. Cissna ... with Scott on contacts at Olduvai."

All at once Juliet heard chairs shuffling as if people were standing. Suddenly she came to herself. She jumped to her feet and hastened the rest of the way down the stairs as noiselessly as possible, heart pounding, and back to her aunt's quarters in the east wing for another load of linen.

(6)

Adam Livingstone had not seen Lord Harriman Montreux for six months, except for a handshake and a few brief words at Buckingham.

As he now drove his dark green Mercedes convertible the final two hundred yards up the winding, tree-lined drive to the Montreux estate of Swanspond, he recalled his previous visit. A formal dinner had been followed by a private interview between the two men over Napoleon cognac.

Adam came away from the evening knowing that Candace's father had been looking him over more seriously than ever before as a potential son-in-law.

The memory amused him. Adam smiled as he recalled the questions Lord Montreux had put to him, almost as if from a list of qualifications for a job at

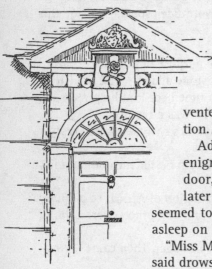

his firm. He wondered if today's luncheon would prove a continuation of the same. The subject of marriage came up in discussions with Candace, of course, for she was a forward young lady who knew what she wanted and was not afraid to take the steps required to achieve it. Thus far Adam's work had prevented serious consideration of a move in that direction. But he could not forestall a decision indefinitely.

Adam walked toward the house, glancing at the enigmatic design engraved on the stone above the door, and rang the bell. He was met a few moments later by the butler, a slender graying man who seemed to require constant effort to keep from falling asleep on his feet.

"Miss Montreux is in the garden, Mr. Livingstone," he said drowsily. "She asked that I direct you there."

"Very good, Phelps. I shall find my own way."

Noticeably relieved to be spared the long trek to the rear entrance, Phelps retreated in the direction of his quarters. Smiling to himself, Adam walked briskly along the wide corridor through the middle of the huge house.

He came at length to two double doors opening out onto a well-manicured lawn, giving way on one side to a high-hedged formal garden of flowers and low-growing shrubs. Lord Montreux's daughter stood in the middle of the grass awaiting him. A silky, purplish, floral dress hung closely, as she intended, to every curve of her body. She held a large yellow sun hat between her hands.

She heard the door open behind her, turned, and approached him wearing one of her hypnotic smiles. She walked straight toward him and snaked her arms around him. Adam slowly returned the embrace. They stood for a few moments in silence, then separated. She placed her arm in his and slowly led him in the direction of the garden.

"I am so glad you could come," she purred.

"Have I ever turned down an invitation to lunch?"

"What concerns me is what you might have done was lunch not included in the invitation."

Livingstone laughed at the insinuation.

"I hardly ever see you anymore, Adam."

"It's this ark business," he said with affected annoyance. "It's suddenly taken up my whole life. Why, do you know, Candace—I've endured ten interviews in the last two weeks alone. It's positively debilitating. There has been little time for lab work or to sit down and elaborate on my notes."

"Still, one would think you could find some time for poor little me."

"I shall, my dear, I promise. The schedule is already beginning to let up."

"And then you shall be off to who knows where again! I read in the news that you are to fly to Africa soon."

"Unfortunately that is the life of an archaeologist."

"Really, Adam—that I should see it in the paper, and you not even tell me you are leaving again."

"The work doesn't come to you—you have to go find it."

"I don't know if I could ever be the wife of a scientist," said Candace with pretended innocence.

"I was not aware you were considering such a future."

"Oh, Adam, don't toy with me!" she said. She pulled away and gave his shoulder a playful slap with her palm.

"Toy with you, Candace? I would never dream of such a dangerous thing. You are not a woman I would dare make an enemy of."

She gazed at him full in the eye, then slowly lifted one eyebrow and smiled wickedly. The expression confirmed his every word, and both knew it. She was not only a beautiful woman, she was a determined one as well, one in whom Adam Livingstone had met his equal, if not his superior, in the charisma of personal power.

They continued to walk a few more minutes, chatting comfortably about nothing in particular, while Candace did her best to respin the web of her charm about Adam, the prey she had feared losing.

(7)

The bell sounded from the house behind them, announcing that luncheon was served.

They turned and made their way inside. Lord and Lady Montreux awaited them in the glass-enclosed terrace to the south of the house.

"Adam, how good to see you again!" said Lady Montreux, a tall woman of handsome and dignified bearing, whose graying hair gave her a look of royalty rather than age.

Adam embraced her lightly. He then shook hands with Candace's father, three or four inches shorter than his wife. His midsection had grown in proportion with his financial success. The crown of his head had lost its once-thick crop at about the same rate as his girth had added its late accumulation of poundage.

"Lord Montreux, you are looking well, as usual," said Adam.

"And you are a terrible liar, young Livingstone," he rejoined. "I'm feeling devilishly out of sorts today."

"I am very sorry to hear of it," said Adam. Each of the four took a seat.

The maid placed plates in front of them. They began delicately partaking of the light cold fish filets and greens, served with a slightly chilled Chardonnay from the Mosel Valley.

"You are quite a famous man since we last saw you, Adam," said Lady Montreux.

"I will take your word for it, Lady Montreux," laughed Adam. "I feel no different, though I must admit it grows increasingly difficult to escape the press."

"What are your plans now, Livingstone?" asked Lord Montreux. The question contained several levels of intended meaning. Candace again lifted an eyebrow and glanced toward their guest with an unmistakable expression.

"To tell you the truth, Lord Montreux," replied Adam, "when I came here today I thought the visit might perhaps offer suitable opportunity to discuss my future with you. However," he added with a pause, "only a few moments ago Candace told me she doubted she could ever be the wife of a scientist, so I suppose there's really no point."

"Oh, Adam!" cried Candace playfully. "I said no such thing!"

"You said those exact words," rejoined Adam. He turned toward her in apparent surprise.

"But I didn't mean them!"

"Ah . . . ," he replied. He drew out the expression and nodded his head as if at last grasping the significance of their earlier dialogue for the first time. "Well," he added, turning again toward Lord Montreux, "you can see my perplexity, sir. When I consider the matter of my future, and the beautiful face of your daughter enters the picture, only confusion results."

"Adam, you are impossible!" exclaimed Candace.

He glanced across the table toward her. At last he allowed his own magnetic smile to play around the edges of his lips.

"Seriously, Lord Montreux," said Adam, turning to Candace's father, "as you know, my work is very demanding and takes me all over the world. Next summer there will, of course, be extensive work on Ararat as we attempt to clear away as much of the glacier as is safely possible. Between now and then we will be designing and fabricating equipment for the job. We hope that the ark might be excavated in full. One or two additional projects besides will keep me away from London a good part of the next twelve months, notably in Africa. In fact, I will be flying out in two weeks. I feel, therefore, that it would be premature and unfair of me to involve myself more deeply relationally at this time."

Lord Montreux's eyebrows raised imperceptibly as he gazed across the table.

"Having said that, however," Adam went on, "I would hope when the pace of my current research tapers off, probably sometime late in the fall of next year, that you might consider allowing me to call more seriously upon your daughter."

Candace smiled to herself. It was all she wanted to hear. At last it appeared that she had been successful and that her patience would be rewarded.

Somewhere behind them in the house they heard the faint sound of a telephone ringing. A minute later Phelps appeared, carrying a cordless phone.

"Excuse me, Lord Montreux, it is Eric Frome calling."

"Frome! He's the last man I want to talk to. Tell him I'm busy, Phelps."

"Forgive me, sir," replied the butler. "But under the circumstances, I thought you might want to take it."

"Confound it—what the devil circumstances are you talking about?"

"I think you should hear it from him, sir."

With exasperation, Lord Montreux took the phone.

"What's this all about, Frome? I'm in the middle of—"

He stopped. Within seconds he was listening intently, his sour mood instantly moderated. The others fell silent. As he took in the information, slowly his black eyebrows lifted toward their guest.

"No, uh . . . I've seen nothing of him."

A brief silence.

"No—I have no comment to offer."

He clicked off the phone and set it on the table. The others waited while Lord Montreux took a slow and deliberate sip of the dry Chardonnay.

"I just lied for you, Livingstone," he said, setting down his glass. "Otherwise they'd be upon you before you could make your escape."

"Lied . . . why?" asked Adam.

"What's it about, Father?" said Candace.

"It seems the good Mr. Livingstone is again in the news."

Adam continued to gaze bewilderedly at Candace's father.

"That was Frome, of the *Daily Mail.*"

"A real newshound," remarked Adam somewhat cynically. "I've had more than one run-in with the fellow."

"Adam is their headline story for this afternoon's edition," continued Candace's father. "They've got wind of what you'll be looking for in Africa." Lord Montreux eyed Adam intently as he spoke. Candace's father had more reasons than he divulged for being concerned with this latest development. "He said that he was aware you were having lunch with me and called to see if I had any comment. You heard what I told him, that I had nothing to say."

Already Adam was halfway to his feet, even as he spoke. "You will excuse me?" he said, glancing at Lady Montreux.

"Of course, Adam, but—"

"Thank you very much for the invitation," he added, hastening toward the door. "The fish was delicious. But I've got to see if I can stop this! I'll ring you, Candace."

He disappeared around the side of the house, breaking into a run.

A minute later his Mercedes spun about on the gravel entryway. Its tires squealed down the paved drive to the main road, where Adam turned the wheel almost without slowing, then revved the engine to full throttle in the direction of London.

(8)

Frome's story ran as planned.

By the time Adam reached the offices of the *Daily Mail,* the papers had already hit the newsstands, vendors all over the city shouting his name to sell their wares.

Cringing as he did so, he bought a copy, hoping he would not be recognized from the six-inch picture of his face on the front page. The headline alone was enough to make him sick. All hope for the confidentiality of their trip was lost.

Gilbert Bowles would love this. From the Ararat triumph, now the name Adam Livingstone would be a laughingstock. Bowles would make sure of it. Now he would be considered a religious nut intent on proving the Bible.

He read nothing of the article but sped out of the city and back to Sevenoaks. He hoped he would beat the rest of London's press corps to his home.

He was not so fortunate.

The front of the estate swarmed with cars, vans, television crews, and more than a hundred newspeople. This time he had no airplane and parachute standing by.

Honking as he went, Adam pressed his way through the throng toward the front gate, which had only seconds before closed behind Erin Wagner's car.

"Let me through . . . please . . . stand away!"

"Mr. Livingstone . . . Mr. Livingstone!"

"I have no comments—please . . . stand aside."

"Just a few questions!"

"No interview."

Voices shouted from all directions.

"Is it true you have located the Garden of Eden?"

"What!" Adam turned to the questioner. "Where did you get that?"

"The *Daily Mail* quotes you."

"They didn't quote me! I never said such a thing."

"Do you deny such is the purpose of your upcoming trip to Africa?"

"I deny nothing. I confirm nothing."

"Just tell us whether you do have evidence about the location of the Garden."

"I have nothing further to say!"

Somehow Adam managed to open the gate. He inched his way inside. The moment the gate closed behind him, a volly of shouts erupted behind him. He sped to the house, jumped out of the car, and ran inside with newspaper in hand.

He flew up the stairs two at a time, reaching the main office just on Erin's heels. A quick glance around the room at the faces of his other three staff members gathered awaiting his arrival told him they knew of the story.

He threw the paper down on one of the desktops, where three-inch headlines blared for all the world to see: LIVINGSTONE DISCOVERS GARDEN OF EDEN! That Adam was angry there could be little doubt.

"Believe me, Adam," said Scott, "we are as upset as you. We've been wrestling this thing around among ourselves for the last hour trying to figure out where the leak could have come from. None of us have said a word to anyone."

"Then how did Frome get this stuff!"

Adam sank into a chair, reluctantly picking up the paper and scanning the details of the article.

"Look at this—have you read it!" he exclaimed in disbelief. "There are direct quotes from every one of us. Even me—and I know I didn't talk to anyone!" He glanced toward his lab assistant, still standing and hastily reading the article. "Erin, are you absolutely sure you didn't—"

"I haven't seen Dexter in a week," she replied quickly. "I promise, I never talk about my work with him."

"Does he ask?"

"Not much, really. He's mostly always been interested in what computer programs you use, that's all. He really loves computers, but I don't think he's all that into archaeology."

"Need to complete the picture of the first relics of humanity . . . ," he read aloud, "set the scientific community on its ear when they find out we have the hard evidence that will pinpoint the location of the Garden of Eden—how did they get this? Those are quotes!"

"But they're not accurate!" said Jen. Even the lilt of her accent could not hide her ire.

"When did that ever stop the press?" said Scott. "I think they're worse here than in the States—and that's saying something!"

"What worries me is that they're close," said Adam. "We were talking along those very lines, although Frome's twisted them about. And look—they even know where we'll be setting up base camp. That's just great! They'll be there like bloodhounds before we even arrive!"

"It's as if somebody was listening when we were making our plans," said Crystal.

Adam set down the paper with a dejected sigh. He didn't want to read more. The damage was done.

"What are we going to do?" asked Scott at length.

"I don't see anything else we can do except go ahead, ride out the storm, and hope the press doesn't interfere with our work."

"We could postpone."

"We've been planning this too long. Everything is in motion. Besides, I will not let inaccurate or ill-timed news stories dictate what we do or do not do. No—we move ahead as planned."

# seven

# New Vision

(1)

The months since Ararat had been thoughtful, even difficult, ones for Adam Livingstone. He was not unaccustomed to wrestling through weighty conundrums. His brain took on intellectual complexities with relish—the more impossible a solution, the better.

But this was different. All at once he *himself* occupied the center of the mental and emotional vortex. The man named *Adam Livingstone* lay beneath the microscope of his probing eye, not some abstract theory.

The American caller, the one who had warned of danger, had certainly spoken prophetically about the Ararat discovery changing everything. Kelley Halliday's query about implications had finally become inescapable.

What did the ark *mean* . . . had *God* spoken to Noah?

Those questions lay at the root of all the others. Close behind them was the very personal query: If he himself *didn't* believe, why was he trying to find Noah's ark and the Garden of Eden? His own motivations had become suddenly vague and uncertain.

On the other hand, if he *did* believe, then—

Then . . . *what?*

He didn't even know how to finish the question. What *was* on the other side of the belief-unbelief fence?

Everything had been fine until setting foot in the ark. Why had that suddenly so complicated his life? Again came the question—what business did he have looking for something he didn't know if he believed in? What had so drawn him to look for fact beneath myth?

Why not just put it to rest? Forget the Garden of Eden. Ninety-five people out of a hundred would scoff at the notion of Eden's existence anyway. Absent personal belief, what compelling and legitimate reason did he have for thinking such a place had ever existed? He might as well tell people he was going on an archaeological expedition to Kansas to look for the Land of Oz! The very idea of Eden was altogether too incredible to *really* believe in.

Or was it?

If there was nothing to it, why had the subject always fascinated him—and not as a myth—but fascinated him with the potential reality of the account? It was not something he could escape.

Could he then say he *believed* in Eden?

No, he could not go so far quite yet. Suddenly he didn't know. *Belief* . . . *faith* . . . he had never given such things much thought. Now they seemed to matter a great deal.

Many in his profession took the Gilbert Bowles approach, pitting science *against* faith, and therefore adopting a generally antagonistic outlook toward the supernatural. Atheism, or at best agnosticism, was the personal creed of choice among most of his colleagues.

But he found nothing so rationally absurd about *faith*. If the Bible turned out to be true, it would be ridiculous to rant and rail against it. Truth was what mattered. One couldn't pre-form conclusions and then call what followed a serious search for truth.

A week ago, he had been ready to cancel the African trip altogether. It would be intellectually dishonest, he said to himself, to search for something he could not say he believed in.

During the past week, however, Adam had gradually moderated his outlook. What if the search itself would illuminate more fully where truth existed? Would that not validate the quest?

All right, he said to himself, so he *didn't* understand everything . . . so he *couldn't* answer every question that popped up out of the unknown or that popped unexpectedly out of some journalist's mouth. He could still go forward.

He *would* go forward—with both *scientific* and *spiritual* integrity. If he was honest with himself, he must explore every possibility. He would look for insight and truth in *both* areas at once and see what came of it.

He was not afraid to admit there were things he didn't know. He would keep asking questions . . . and keep looking for answers.

Then this journey would be fun. He would relish this dual quest. Why should a spiritual search be less challenging and exciting than a scientific one?

He would delight in what lay ahead, as much as he had in other, more purely scientific, endeavors.

(2)

The English archaeologist who was its subject was not the only one angered by Frome's story in the *Daily Mail*. There were others with just as much to lose by what it revealed . . . perhaps more.

Many relationships existed within the Council of Twelve. Necessity and circumstance joined now two, now three, now four of its number to refine this or that element of their global strategy, each of whom would return to his or her sphere of influence to carry out the Universal Will as it was communicated to them.

The two men of ancient familial bond whom developments had brought together had known one another for years. That which was on their minds had been planned for nearly a decade. But now arose suddenly a new sense of urgency and imperative concerning its implementation.

One of the two had descended from the Mayer line that had brought the ancient order of the Rose and the Cross to England late in the eighteenth century from the continent. The offshoot of the line that had come to him through his grandmother no longer bore the name, a fact that allowed him an anonymity useful to their designs. But the blood of Rothschild flowed in his veins as surely as any in the progeny of the Red Shield and assured the centuries-long loyalty to the oath of secrecy that bound those of the Society together. He continued to be styled *baron,* in honor of his Austrian ancestor, when those high in the Order held council together.

Their highest creed was secrecy. The Order infiltrated nations and cultures and societies with its occultish mysticism through the many branches of Rosicrucianism, alchemy, Freemasony, Perfektibilisten, and the Scottish knighthood. The powerful invisible network was held together by a shadowy mysticism in which it cloaked its pretended wisdom. Thus had all its tentacles become of particular use in more recent times to the carrying out of the Will of the Dark Dimension, whose clairvoyants in these latter days came masquerading as Prophets of Light, heralding the dawn of a new age of peace.

But though these new age oracles were soothing and beguiling, darkness and secrecy ruled all they did. Their message of deception came from the pit of blackness, where dwelt the Great Lie of the universe who had stolen the Life of mankind at the foot of the Garden's tree.

The English lord's counterpart, the Germanic spelling of whose name still bore reminders of the continental branch of the intricate familial web, had flown over from Amsterdam and arrived an hour before.

The two men had been sitting facing one another for some time in a small, dim room, eyes closed, outstretched fingers touching lightly. Their lips had moved and sensations had been felt, but no audible guidance from the Dimension had come to either. At length they sat back.

"Have more developments surfaced since the article?" asked the Dutchman.

"None. He did speak to me more directly about the marriage."

"That is good news. It must take place without delay."

"I fear it will be at least another year."

"That is a long time, Baron. Forces are attempting to lure him away from us."

"I have felt that of which you speak."

"We have monitored his research for some time, watching for troublesome indications. We have planned this alliance too long to let him slip away. What about your daughter?"

"She grows impatient as well."

"Then she must use her allure on him, and you your persuasiveness."

"I shall see to it."

"He is an influential man. In the enemy's hands, he could work great ill."

"He shall not fall. He shall be brought into our circle."

"Time grows short. Much culminates with the approach of the Dawn. We must not allow the enemy to have such a man whose voice carries so far."

"He will be ours."

"He *must* be ours . . . or no one's."

(3)

Adam had awakened early, as was his custom. It was a crisp morning in early November. Leaves were falling in earnest now, and cold was in the air.

He sat down in his office to finalize the written prospectus for the African expedition. It was time to put the hubbub over the newspaper article behind them and put his personal quandaries on hold pending further revelation. He wanted to get down to mapping out a detailed strategy for the winter.

He and his trusted field team of Scott Jordan and Jen Swaner always worked from a written outline of objectives and specific schedule to keep them focused on goals, as well as to guide their assistants and hired labor. In their business, they hoped to unearth the unexpected. They therefore learned to expect it. But without a well-organized road map, the work too easily diverted into random and tangential directions. Later in the morning he would bring in his two assistants. They would go over their final notes together and formalize plans for the next three months. He would then give it to Crystal to key in. He also needed to set Erin's agenda for lab work downstairs with the various wood, rock, and ice samples from Ararat during the time they would be away. He needed the results of some of those tests to fill in a few missing equations in his Eden theory.

Beside him sat a thick notebook, compiled over many years, whose cover merely read *Large-Oval Eden Theory*. Some of the information contained in it had been entered into his computer files. But much in the notebook predated his own use of a computer. Thus most of it existed only here, among his private handwritten papers. There were dozens of hand-drawn maps, some mere hasty sketches of unidentified portions of the globe; hundreds of queries to himself; a few formal articles he had written; extensive historical and bibliographical references; and a summary of the key archaeological findings in the region through the years extending all the way from the Taung child to what Sir Gilbert Bowles had recently unearthed. A map of the entire rift system placed every known archaeological dig in the region over a seventy-year span.

For years Adam Livingstone had been fascinated with the biblical account in early Genesis. He had not paused to ask himself where the interest had come from. He had received no religious training as a child. Yet as one fascinated with beginnings, the Creation story had always been there, if only as a mythical counterpoise to Darwinism and one additional aspect of the literature to consider.

It hadn't seemed to matter before now whether he believed it or not. It was history he was after, not theology. There was sufficient evidence to suggest that the biblical record contained bits and pieces pointing in a generally accurate direction. To his mind, no honest scientist could afford to ignore it.

Most of the pure "religious" sections he had considered to be mere legendary remnants from a superstitious nomadic people who chanced to preserve their history for later generations. But did that mean he could neglect what aspects of the account could be useful?

Many within the scientific community did exactly that—ignoring the entirety of the Bible just because it was the Bible. Such had always seemed to him a flimsy rationale for discarding such an ancient and massive body of work. Adam Livingstone could not do so. It was a historical document. Any thinking and rational individual had to account for both its existence and its content.

But now since Ararat, new thoughts were assaulting his brain with increasing force. The question concerned where those origins came from. The uncertainties that had arisen among the waiting press the day he arrived home and later during discussion in the Buckingham gardens, now loomed very large as he considered his future as a scientist and archaeologist.

Who began life's origins? How did beginnings begin? Where did origins originate?

The big bang explained nothing concerning those questions. The view held by the most passionate of evolutionists was that what were called "conditions" existed on earth capable of spawning life from nonlife. Those conditions, they maintained, caused inanimate matter to coagulate together over billions of years and one day somehow miraculously (though they would never use that word!) to begin to breathe.

But such was a scientifically absurd notion. It violated the most basic principle inherent in the second law of thermodynamics. How his thinking colleagues in the scientific community could accept such nonsense was beyond him.

Besides, where did the inanimate matter come from? The original *where* remained unaddressed.

Yet though he pondered such inconsistencies, still the implications of the questions "who? where? how?" struck no deep root within his soul. For the moment they remained abstract queries. He realized the folly of a purely inanimate origin to life. Yet he had not considered in depth what must be the only other possibility—an animate explanation.

He was thinking in new directions—that could not be denied. He had not yet considered where that subconscious self-interrogation might be leading.

(4)

Everything was looking new and different for Adam Livingstone.

The query of a Being at the root of all science, all history, all beginnings—an actual living Creator—was no query that could forever remain impersonal. Even Adam himself could not foretell just how much his life was indeed destined to change in the months to come.

The mere fact that the Jewish chronicle purported to start at what it called "the beginning," with the creation of the world, made it of enormous interest to an archaeologist. The first chapter of Genesis with its supposed six-day creation Adam had always taken for myth. So must be the dust-and-rib creation of man and woman, the conversations between God and Adam and Eve, as well as the serpent and temptation portions of the third chapter.

Even his own sharing of name with the first biblical man had not caused Adam Livingstone to actually believe that such an individual really existed. He had always assumed the Adam of Genesis 2 probably to be only a symbolic representation of man, as the origins of the name suggested.

Nonetheless, he had always been intrigued by verses 8 through 14 of the second chapter of the Bible's first book. Here was one of those passages that intimated something other than myth. Adam considered it to represent one of those slices within the biblical account around which clung the faint whiff of truth.

For years the possibility had haunted him: Could the amazing account have a factual basis?

Adam was well familiar with the words.

They were found on the first page of his notebook, written in his own hand, and his own rendition of translation, while a graduate student at Cambridge. Whether or not he believed in a literal "Adam" made from the dust of the ground—these were words to tantalize the brain and stir the blood of any self-respecting historian and archaeologist!

> *Now the Lord God had planted a garden in the east, in Eden; and there he put the man he had formed. And the Lord God made all kinds of trees grow out of the ground—trees that were pleasing to the eye and good for food. In the middle of the garden were the tree of life and the tree of the knowledge of good and evil.*
>
> *A river watering the garden flowed from Eden; from there it was separated into four headwaters. The name of the first is the Pishon; it winds through the entire land of Havilah, where there is gold. . . .*

*The name of the second river is the Gihon; it winds through the entire land of Cush. The name of the third river is the Tigris; it runs along the east side of Asshur. And the fourth river is the Euphrates.*

With a trip to the region at last now imminent, Adam's heart began to beat with excitement for what possibilities might exist for actually finding some portion of the place spoken of in the ancient account.

(5)

Meanwhile, in her own room, Juliet Halsay had also woken early.

She now lay almost as wide-eyed as Adam, though contemplating a very different series of developments—concerning, not the history of the world like Adam, but the history of her own being, her own soul . . . and her own future.

It had been almost four months since the accident. Her father and brother were dead. Nothing could change that. She and her mother had been forced to separate temporarily. Nothing could change that. Life would never be, could never again be, the same. Yet she had begun to feel ready to move forward again. She had gradually come off the medications and was helping her aunt with more and more of the housekeeping chores.

She had seen many schoolmates blame their parents, their circumstances, the system, or just what they called "rotten luck" for their lot in life, whatever it was, and thus for their own failure and lack of vision. If anyone had the right to succumb to defeated thought patterns, surely she did. No one would blame her. She was entitled. Circumstances had indeed dealt her a severe blow.

But on this particular morning, as wakefulness returned and a stray ray of sunlight silently shot through her window from the sun creeping above the horizon, it wasn't anger or depression or defeat that quietly welled up inside Juliet's heart. Rather it was an unexpected, momentary burst of joy.

With it came the question—how long did she want to be a victim of the tragedy? Might there not be good things in life that were still worth celebrating?

Juliet glanced out the window. The morning was bright and cheery. What did that ray of sunlight mean if it was not that the sun still shone . . . just like before?

Her circumstances had changed, but the world had not. The sun still rose, day after day. Its light still warmed the earth. Its rays still gave light. The flowers still bloomed. Even though winter and cold were coming, the birds still sang. She could hear them outside about their morning business.

Despite what she had been through, might life not once again become a good and precious thing?

Gradually a sense of quiet peace began to steal upon her, like an invisible inner blanket of calm spreading over her soul to cover the turmoil and upheaval of her recent emotional state. She breathed in two or three times deeply, still staring at the beam of light. Slowly she allowed a smile to come to her lips.

Juliet Halsay had not thought about God in what could be called a personal way before this moment. Her family, like her aunt, were faithful to services every Sunday morning. She believed in the Church of England and the Christian doctrines to which it was dedicated. She had memorized the creeds and had always done her best to live by them. But rarely had that vague sense of belief penetrated beyond the level of intellectual assent, church tradition, family custom, and what she knew to be the difference between right and wrong.

But suddenly on this day she felt something . . . and instinctively sensed that it was God's peace come to comfort her and raise her out of her season of grief.

As she lay on her bed, the peace and contentment deepened. Gradually the realization came into her heart that God's peace had not just settled vaguely upon the house on this particular morning, but that it had come . . . to her. It had been sent to comfort her. God cared about Juliet Halsay as if she were the only person alive. He loved her personally.

She continued to lay there, allowing that peace to spread through every corner of her consciousness, making no attempt to understand or rationalize it. For the moment she was content to drink it in. She could not have explained what she felt, nor did she care to. It was enough that a blanket of peace had covered her heart.

At last she found herself whispering, though the words seemed to come from some deep reservoir within her that she hardly knew existed, "Thank you."

It was the first time she had spoken to God as if only she and he existed in all the universe. She knew beyond any doubt that he was listening.

(6)

For several long minutes Juliet stared at the beam of sunlight, watching as it was joined by another, then another. Quietly the multiplying rays spoke into her heart about new opportunities that would come to replace the hurts of the past—opportunities that would come, if only she would rise to meet them.

She could keep looking backward and miss them. Or she could look to the continually rising sun of the future, open her eyes to the wonders it presented, and make something of her life.

Yes, she would do that. It was a new day. If God cared enough to invade her with this new sense of peace, then she could do her part and rise to face this new season of her life with optimism.

Juliet climbed out of bed, wrapped her robe around her, then put on her glasses and sat down at the small dressing table. She gave a long serious inspection of herself in the mirror, then spoke to her reflection in a voice of decision and renewed confidence.

"Juliet Halsay, it is time to take stock of yourself," she said, sitting straight and looking objectively at the young lady before her. "You've given yourself some time and space. You've felt your sorrow. You've wept your tears. You still miss Papa and Joseph."

She stared straight into her own eyes.

"But look at you," she continued. "Everything's not black and dismal. The sun is shining outside, and on this day you feel the joy of the living inside. You're a healthy young lady. You're reasonably intelligent. You've had some good training. You can take care of yourself—even if it does mean working at a fish-and-chips stand. But who knows what new opportunities might come along?"

She scrutinized the face a bit more carefully, lifting a hand to move a few stray strands of dark brown hair. The attempt ended in a smile.

"And despite how your hair looks at this minute," she said, "you're actually not too bad looking. All right, from now on, you will remind yourself of the happy times. You will remember Papa's smile and laughter. Yes, it's been a rotten few months. But you've landed on your feet here with Auntie Andrea. Look where you are—on an English estate with one of the most important men in the empire for a landlord."

Her commanding demeanor gave way to a girlish smile.

"And a very handsome one at that!"

She picked up the hairbrush sitting on the table and began tugging at her shoulder-length dark hair.

"Today I will see about getting on with my life," she said, speaking now to herself rather than to the alter ego of her reflection. "I will begin looking for a job in earnest. When I can, I'll get my own flat. Eventually I'll bring Mum to live with me. And I will remember that God cares about me."

She rose and walked to the oak wardrobe that stood on the adjacent wall, opened its two doors, and surveyed the contents. She chose a green corduroy skirt and white blouse. She grabbed a red pullover sweater to put on later. She would take a quick walk about the garden in the bright dawn. The sunlight had called her into a higher form of wakefulness than merely from the night's slumber. She had felt a new peace, a new closeness to God. She would go out and enjoy the morning.

She turned to leave the room, then glanced once more at her reflection.

She pulled herself up straight and tall, thrust her shoulders back, smiled determinedly, and gave the girl in the mirror a quick salute of firmness and resolution. Then she left the room and walked down the stairs and out the back door.

The peace of God that had come upon her now joined with the vigorous exercise of Juliet's will to prompt one of the most energetic and miraculous acts that distinguishes the human animal from all others—the decision to grow and become.

That exchange between the human and the divine within the depths of her being would prove a turning point in her existence. From this day forward, all would indeed be new.

Juliet Halsay had decided to live.

(7)

Half an hour later Juliet had completed her morning stroll and wandered contentedly back inside and toward the kitchen, where she knew she would find her aunt.

As she walked through the door, she heard the voices of Adam Livingstone and Scott Jordan in the midst of lively conversation concerning their upcoming trip. She stopped when she saw them and began to make a retreat. But they glanced up and noticed her.

"Good morning! You look bright and cheerful today, Miss Halsay," said Adam ebuliently, his spirits reflecting the rejuvenation of his mood now that serious planning was under way.

"Yes—actually I am feeling very well," Juliet replied.

"Please, come in and join us."

"Thank you, Mr. Livingstone." Hesitantly, but returning his smile, Juliet walked forward.

"We won't be much longer," said Adam. "Scott and I got to talking and never took our things into the breakfast room."

"Tea, Juliet?" asked her aunt, approaching from the stove.

"Yes, thank you, Auntie. And do you have anything to go with it? To tell you the truth, I am famished."

Suddenly her face lit. "Auntie," she exclaimed, "I just realized—my appetite's back . . . and I'm not wearing my pullover!"

"I noticed it in your hand the moment you came in," Mrs. Graves replied.

Already Scott and Adam were engrossed once more in conversation. Juliet sat down quietly at the other end of the table and was soon listening intently.

"The traditional view among biblical historians," Scott was saying, "is that the first men originated in the area of the Fertile Crescent. Going public with your theory will have evangelicals down your throat."

Adam laughed.

"I'm serious," Scott went on. "They'll brand you an evolutionist if you give such primary credence to the African fossil record."

"Nothing new about that. Besides, most modern students of human origins consider the Mesopotamian view simplistic," replied Adam. "Sir Gilbert would deny it vehemently!"

"He would deny anything with biblical connection vehemently!"

"In this case, I think he is right—though only partially. The Fertile Crescent is only one part of the story. The most plentiful fossilized remains of pre-

*Homo sapiens* occur in eastern Africa, not up in the Middle East. The evidences of human antiquities must be more than coincidental."

"Supported by the climate along the equator."

"Exactly—it's the climate that offers one of the keys to the whole thing."

"Do you mind if I ask a question, Mr. Livingstone?" said Juliet, who had just taken a sip from the cup her aunt had given her. Both men, along with Mrs. Graves, glanced over in surprise that she had spoken.

"Of course not," he replied. "Go right ahead."

"What does the climate have to do with the fossils?"

"Everything," answered Adam. "The equator is approximately the same temperature year-round. It's the perfect locale to have supported the earliest forms of such a fragile species as humans and prehumans—naked and without thick natural coats like most of the animal kingdom. If there was such a place as Eden, it had to be near the equator."

"If there was such a place," she repeated. "You doubt there was?"

"I don't doubt it," rejoined Adam. "I don't necessarily believe it. I am simply intrigued. That is why I hope to discover evidence to make a further and more definitive determination."

"But Auntie showed me the article," said Juliet. "I thought perhaps—"

"That we had discovered the Garden of Eden?" said Adam laughing. "I'm afraid not."

"But you are going to search for it?"

"We are going to see what we might see. I will say that much."

"If you don't believe it is there, why would you go search for it?"

"I have always been curious about Eden."

"Why?"

"It's simply intriguing. The equatorial belt offers the perfect place to sustain human life, not only from a climatic standpoint, but from an agricultural one as well. On the equator vegetation thrived as nowhere else on the globe. There is debate about when rain first came to the earth, but whether it rained upon Eden or not, there were surely abundant moisture and sunshine. We still see remnants of that truth in the jungles and tropical rain forests that cluster about the equator, though much has obviously changed since earliest times. So if the Genesis Garden story holds truth, or even if it were a myth carried down the human ancestral line, where else but an equatorial and tropical location could the account possibly describe?"

"I . . . guess I see your point."

"Let me just say I have a strong suspicion that something very well might exist in support of the Genesis account. I have to see if I can find it."

"Surely you don't intend to search the entire equator! Isn't that . . . more than twenty-five thousand miles!"

Adam laughed again. "Hopefully our efforts won't prove to be utterly a stab in the dark!"

"Tell her about the rivers," said Scott.

"Right—it's the rivers that make this particular place on the globe intriguing, not to mention that such an abundance of fossil remains exist there," said Adam.

"Which rivers?"

"The four rivers in Genesis. They have always puzzled biblical researchers," said Adam, "for only the Tigris and Euphrates have remained known down through history. The other two are enigmas. But I have studied and researched that whole region and have devised a theory based on changing weather patterns and geologic structure."

"What kind of theory?"

"Of a huge oval-shaped Eden, not merely a Mesopotamian garden, but one combined with an equatorial Eden."

"I want to hear it," said Juliet eagerly, inching forward in her chair. Mrs. Graves noticed the change in her niece. How long had it been since she was so interested in something?

"What if the original Garden were more enormous than anyone has dreamed?" said Adam, his eyes widening to recount his theory to one who had never heard it before. "What if in the beginning it extended from the region of the Tigris and Euphrates all the way down to the equator?"

"It would be huge, just like you said."

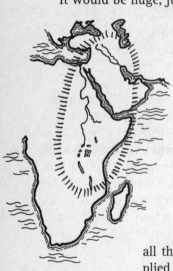

"And why not? If the Creator, as the story has it, put not only man in it, but also all the animals? It would have had to be enormous, merely from the standpoint of feeding and grazing requirements."

"But—"

"I know what you're thinking—the deserts, right?" Juliet nodded.

"What if this entire Garden stretched three or four thousand miles in length by two or three thousand miles in width? What if the entirety was lush and filled with life, like our current tropical rain forests? What if it possessed an abundance of freshwater lakes and animal and plant life? What if, in short, it possessed everything necessary to sustain the life of all the thousands and thousands, eventually as they multiplied even millions, of creatures living in it?"

"I never thought of that."

"Then, what if the desertification brought about by changing weather patterns, what I call the Sahara syndrome, gradually turned much of the expanse of that original Garden, including the whole of the Arabian Peninsula, into a virtual wasteland over the centuries? So obviously, if such were the case, it would be unrecognizable today?"

"But you were talking about the rivers."

"Ah yes—the rivers. It is the rivers that hold the key. Where are the two missing rivers?"

"I have a feeling you think you know," laughed Juliet.

"I just might," rejoined Adam. "If my theory is credible, the original Garden occupied portions of two continents. It might have been as big as 2 or 3 million square miles—approximately the size of Greenland or even almost as big as Australia. If that were so, the search for the rivers must obviously be widened. In other words, those who search for the missing rivers in the immediate vicinity of the Tigris and Euphrates will never find them. They aren't there. The Garden was much bigger."

"Where are they then?"

"One of them I believe to be the Nile. It flows from the Kenyan highlands and Lake Victoria northward to the Mediterranean and presents an obvious link to the Genesis account. Genesis 2:13 says that the river Gihon wound through the entire land of Cush, or Ethiopia. To my ear that's a reference to the northeast quadrant of the African continent, now comprised of Kenya, Ethiopia, Sudan, and Egypt—exactly where the Nile flows."

"Do you see what perfect sense it makes!" said Scott enthusiastically to Juliet.

"The river Pishon of verse 11 presents more of a problem," Adam went on. "Yet there are clues to its location as well."

"Clues?"

"A study of ancient gold deposits reveals that one of the largest ancient regions where gold was found lay in the Precambrian Aqaba Granite Complex that occurred on the shores on either side of the Red Sea."

"That's right!" exclaimed Juliet. "And the sedimentary rock of Egypt derives from it. Of course—that's where the pharaohs would have got their gold."

Suddenly she paused, realizing what she'd said. Her face reddened.

Scott glanced at Adam with a puzzled expression. Both broke out in amused smiles.

"That had to be more than just a lucky guess!" laughed Adam. "What do you know about the Aqaba Granite Complex?"

"Juliet studied geography and geology at college," said Mrs. Graves.

"No kidding!" said Scott. "Geology's my field!"

"Well, you're exactly right about the sedimentary formations in Egypt. And the same kind of rock is found farther to the north, up into Palestine. But the gold connection with the Eden account gets even better!" said Adam. "Do you know where I think the Havilah of Genesis 2 is?"

Juliet shook her head.

"The mysterious land called 'Havilah' shows ancient links with the western portions of Arabia northwest of Yemen."

"Along the Red Sea!" exclaimed Juliet.

"Exactly!" exclaimed Scott. "I could hardly believe it when Adam told me."

"So the first Edenic river mentioned in the account," said Adam, "the Pishon, could in fact have been the largest of the four and might originally have flowed in the channel now represented by the Red Sea. There's been gold found recently in the Atlantis II Deep in the middle of the Red Sea. There is still gold there!"

"Wow—they didn't teach us that in my geography classes!"

"The origins of both words *Pishon* and *Havilah* suggest exactly such a connection, especially in that millions of years ago, the Red Sea wasn't a 'sea' at all."

"What then?"

"The Arabian Peninsula was initially connected to the African continent. Originally the Red Sea was a river, which through time widened, eventually splitting Africa from Arabia except for the tiny remaining link at Suez. So there you have the final Genesis river, flowing through a land where there was, and still is, gold."

(8)

A thoughtful silence of a few seconds followed.

"You said you had devised a theory of a large Eden," said Juliet after a moment. "I understand what you say about the equator and the four rivers. So how do the ancient civilizations found in the Fertile Crescent fit into it? Two of the rivers are up there."

"That area represents the second half of my theory," replied Livingstone, "which is why I call it a large-oval theory. Egypt and the Mesopotamian crescent hold keen interest as well as the region nearer the equator. You're exactly right—the most advanced of known early civilizations rose and fell in those areas. Babylon, near modern Baghdad, and both the Tigris and Euphrates were all identified very early in the Genesis account. The Ur of Abraham was in modern Iraq. And of course the ark of Noah, we now know, came to rest on Mount Ararat in present-day Turkey."

"So how do you correlate the two regions? They're so far apart."

"That's why I theorize the original Garden to be huge. I think man's beginnings originated in both places, between Lake Victoria in eastern Africa and the Tigris/Euphrates valley of northern Arabia, stretching, as I said, over two or three thousand miles—in all of it! Not both as in two separate places, but both as in the one gigantic whole. Obviously the Garden had a center where perhaps life began. But from that center, I believe it spread out and gradually encompassed a garden much larger and much different than a garden plot behind the house."

"Is that your theory?"

"In a nutshell, I suppose. I believe that if such a garden as Eden existed, it occupied a huge oval extending from the Fertile Crescent in the north (the region of the Tigris and Euphrates), southwest across the Arabian Peninsula into the land of Havilah and the river Pishon (Arabia and the present Red Sea), and finally southward into the fertile equatorial region of the Nile (the Gihon of Genesis), the present lush equatorial belt of central Africa. A gigantic flourishing greenhouse of origins for every species of creature to establish itself, and then roam and spread out, eventually to cover the entire earth."

"And you think the evidence supports it?"

"It supports it exactly!"

Adam leapt up. "Wait here," he said and ran from the room. A minute or two later he returned carrying a globe stand, which he set down beside the table.

"Look," he said excitedly, standing beside it, "according to the archaeological record, earliest man was intriguingly clustered along a line roughly approximating the rift region of eastern Africa, extending gradually northward. Look—right here . . . from the Lake Victoria region of Tanzania—well, actually from all the way down into South Africa, too—then northward through Kenya and Ethiopia on up all the way to the Strait of Bab el Mandeb."

His animated fingers pointed across the African landmass as he spoke.

"There are the finds from Taung up to Olduvai Gorge in Tanzania, Lukenya Hill, Rusinga Island, Samburu Hills in the Kenyan badlands where Miocene strata are exposed . . . Baringo/Chesowanja, Laetoli, Lothagam, Omo . . . all the way up to Maka and Belohdelie in the Middle Awash Valley in Ethiopia near Hadar where Lucy was found. Discoveries have been made all over the region! The most ancient and clustered hominid and *Homo sapiens* bones and relics have all surfaced in the region of rift rupture of the earth's crust. I am convinced there is truth enough in Genesis 2:10 to explain why the earliest bones of *Australopithecus afarensis* as well as later *Homo habilis* and *Homo erectus* and Bowles' *Homopithecus* and *erectus sapiens* all come from this very region. Man's origins clearly originate in an equatorial rift of eastern Africa."

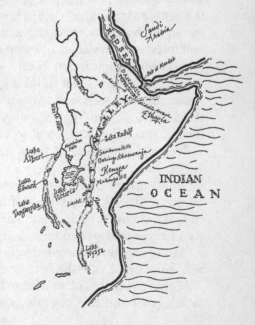

"I thought there were fossil relics everywhere on the earth."

"There are. Of course, eventually man spread everywhere as did all the rest of the creatures—both Genesis and the fossil record tell the same story. But the most ancient evidence of biped hominid species all comes from Africa, mostly from the rift region of Tanzania, Kenya, and Ethiopia—right here!" Adam's finger ran excitedly up and down the thirty-fifth longitude between Tanzania and Ethiopia.

"And look at this," he went on, pointing in a circle. "Lakes remain throughout the rift uplift, reminders of that prehistoric time. And even the simple fact that zero degree latitude runs directly through the vast Lake Victoria," he added, running his finger horizontally along the equator as he spoke, "is indication that this was one of the few continental locations temperate enough to have supported earliest life."

"The presence of so many animal species in Africa also speaks of origins," added Scott. "Central Africa is the world's most ancient zoo. It's like a window back into the past, all the way back to the beginning. Somehow the species have survived there like nowhere else."

"Exactly!" added Adam. "I am convinced the southernmost extremity of the Garden is there."

"I still don't understand how that accounts for the Tigris-Euphrates region."

"My huge Eden oval encompasses both. We have a southern portion—" he drew a circle with his finger around the African rift system—"and a northern portion." He now did the same around the Fertile Crescent of Mesopotamia.

"The world's most ancient civilizations were all found in the northern extremeties of my oval, in early Mesopotamia—the Sumarian civilization, then Egypt, Canaan, Nineveh, Akkad, then the great Babylonian Empire, Phoenicia, and Persia. Eden, therefore, stretched throughout the entire oval."

"But the whole middle portion is desert."

"Right, because the climate changed. As time went on, man gradually spread from this enormous Eden of origins throughout the globe. As he did, the earth was changing. Oceans cooled, continents gradually shifted, many of the warm, wet forested regions shrank. Climates became more seasonal. Tree and forest cover lessened. Open savannah and woodland replaced much of the high-canopy tropical rain forest.

"All these factors and shifting global weather patterns gradually brought desert conditions to much of the north African continent, eventually creating the Sahara, Libyan, Nubian, and Arabian deserts. Some think it began when the Panama Isthmus rose and separated the Atlantic and Pacific."

"You mean because of the different salinity levels of the oceans?" said Juliet.

"Right again!" Adam glanced toward Juliet with something like amused admiration. "The sinking of the North Atlantic current froze the Arctic cap and caused a cooling and drying in Africa. You do know your stuff, Miss Halsay. And I know that was no lucky guess!"

"I took a couple of meteorology courses too," laughed Juliet, surprising herself with how at ease she felt. "But go on with your theory."

"These changes," Adam resumed, "effectively erased any sign of the vegetation and hospitable conditions throughout the central half of the former

Eden that had existed. That is precisely the reason we do not find the fossil relics there as we do in Africa. Desert sands and dirt and scrub and rock covered them over. I am sure there are plentiful bones of early man in these arid regions too. In the Faiyum Depression of Egypt's Sahara, enough sand has been stripped away that an *Aegyptopithecus* was unearthed. But this is the exception. In Arabia and Mesopotamia they're mostly buried too deep to be located.

"Eden was, in a sense, cut in half by this vast desert and by the widening of the river Pishon to become the Red Sea. All that was left to trace man's beginnings were the fertile regions of the Tigris and Euphrates valley—in the north, where civilizations flourished—and the rift region of Africa—in the south, where hints of the lush conditions and diverse animal life of bygone days managed to prevail.

"There in Africa, the uplift of the rift system and the two halves of the African landmass slowly thrust up the earth's surface to reveal the secrets of man's ancient beginnings. So that is where the most ancient evidence of man's presence has been archaeologically excavated. It isn't that man's origins are limited to the rift region of Africa. That's just where we're lucky enough to be able to uncover the most evidence. If we knew where to look, we would discover equally exciting and ancient finds all the way from Lake Victoria to Ararat.

"In other words, we have been left with the northern and southern remnants of the original Eden, both yielding distinctive clues and links to man's earliest days upon the earth, but with most of that northern area, as well as all the middle portion, turned into a desert. In a way, perhaps that single fact is the most intriguing of all."

"What fact?"

"That it is the heart and center of the Garden that is most hidden from our view. The southern rift portions seem to reveal their secrets, while the center portions hide theirs. It's puzzling, now that I think about it."

"But why did man migrate to the northernmost regions of your oval to build towns and cities and civilizations?" asked Juliet. "Why didn't similar civilizations spring up in the southern African portion?"

"I'm afraid that remains a mystery to me," replied Adam. "I honestly have no theory on it. As you say, the earliest civilization was limited to the line between Egypt and Babylon. I am nonetheless convinced that the original

Garden of Eden encompassed the whole. Whether man was divinely placed there, or how he came to be there if such is not the case—that is something upon which I cannot conjecture. In any event, this region is where man's existence on the earth began, accounting for both the civilizations of antiquity in the north and the fossil record of man's beginnings in the south."

The kitchen fell silent. Even Mrs. Graves was fascinated with what she heard, to the extent she could makes heads or tails of it.

"What is it you hope to accomplish with your expedition?" asked Juliet at length.

"In anticipation of further study we shall focus our attention to the south, near the equator. That is where the most ancient relics are located. It seems a more fruitful field of inquiry than Mesopotamia, which like the Sahara, has became desert. I doubt much will ever be found in Iran or Iraq. But in the rift uplift and Kenyan highlands and in Tanzania and all around Lake Victoria, because of the gradual expansion of the earth's crust that gives the region its name, evidence remains to be discovered. And more is being thrust up continually. I am convinced great finds are yet to be made there."

"I see."

"This area may represent only a very small portion of the original Eden, but it is a portion where I think links to Genesis can yet be found."

"How do you expect to find them?"

"Ever heard of the bristlecone pines?" asked Scott.

"I've heard of them—the oldest known plant."

"It is positively fascinating," said Adam. "Here are species of flora almost five thousand years old! Can you imagine how old that is? Scientists have taken core samples and literally counted the rings. And they're still living! The very thought is staggering. I travelled to California to observe these oldest of all living things a few years back. They call the spot where the greatest concentration of them is located the Methuselah Walk."

"Are bristlecones growing in the rift too?"

"Not bristlecones themselves. Perhaps something even better!"

"What?"

"I don't know yet. But why might there not also be such species of living things also extant in the rift? If we can find ancient flora—as old, perhaps older, than the bristlecones—to accompany the ancient human relics already discovered, that would be powerful evidence that perhaps the region was indeed part of an ancient garden made up largely of forest. Is such not implied in the Genesis account: 'every kind of tree that is pleasant to the sight, and good for food'? It's all about trees! If we're going by the evidence presented to us in Genesis, then perhaps it is trees we should be looking for rather than bones. It might be more accurate to call it the Forest of Eden."

"I never noticed that before," said Juliet. "The Garden of Eden does sound very much like a forest."

"Precisely—an equatorial, tropical rain forest."

Adam gave the globe a spin, then returned and sat down again at the table.

"Well, there you have it, Miss Halsay," he said. "That's our objective, to find the African equivalent of the bristlecone pine, perhaps a species even older, that we hope will provide a link to those very worlds, or even some species that was actually part of the original Eden—a missing link of flora, as anthropologists have sought the so-called missing link in the evolution of the world's fauna."

"So you're going to Africa not to look for bones or fossils but for plants?"

"Exactly. Which is why on this trip we're hoping to become botanists rather than paleoanthropologists, right, Scott? It should keep Sir Gilbert out of our hair," Adam added with a smile toward his friend.

"He'll get wind of it and think you've turned into a nature lover," said Scott.

"Have you written about any of this?" asked Juliet.

"Not for the world to see," replied Adam. "I've got extensive notes, of course. When I find some verifiable link to antiquity—but not before—I will then go public with my large-oval, split-Eden theory."

"But not through the *Daily Mail!*" said Scott.

"Positively not."

"If Eden was originally as big as I believe is the case," Adam went on, "no man will ever locate some exact place to say, 'This is the Garden of Eden.' That is not even the goal."

"Just think," said Juliet, "if someone could set foot in what was the center of it!"

The room grew eerily quiet for a moment.

"That would be an archaeological triumph equal to, if not even greater than, the finding of Noah's ark," Adam said pensively.

He paused and smiled. "In any event," he added, "the Garden, if not its precise center, is now my quest."

"Thank you for telling me about it," said Juliet.

Adam suddenly realized that he had prattled on for an hour, describing their very sensitive plans and theories.

"Not a word of this to a soul, Miss Halsay," said Adam. "You do understand that requirement now that you are here with your aunt?"

"Yes—yes, of course," she said.

Scott rose. "I should be getting upstairs," he said.

"I'll be along in a minute or two," said Adam. "I think I'll just have another cup of tea. Mrs. Graves, please boil a fresh pot of water."

(9)

Scott left the room.

It was silent a moment as Mrs. Graves brewed a fresh pot of tea. Adam glanced toward Juliet.

"Your interest in the work surprises me," he said at length. "Although I am delighted. You seem to know a good deal about it."

"I suppose I am feeling more interested in everything than I have been in a good long while. And I feel good not to be wearing my pullover," she added.

"To what do you attribute this heightened sense of enthusiasm," asked Adam with a laugh, "other than it is too warm a morning for a sweater?"

He looked at their houseguest with an expectant expression.

"Do you really want to know?" asked Juliet.

"Of course. I'm constantly in search of new depths of meaning, whether it lies beneath the earth's crust or hidden within the heart of man or woman. Please, tell me . . . yes, I am interested."

Juliet thought for a moment. "I don't suppose it is much more complicated," she said at length, "than that I decided it was time for me to move forward."

"A worthy resolve," remarked Adam. "What brought on such a decision?"

"A ray of sunlight through my window."

"A ray of sunlight?"

"Just an hour ago," laughed Juliet.

"What did that have to do with it?"

"It wasn't really the sunlight itself. It was the peace it brought into my heart. I felt God's presence with me, and a quiet peace filled me."

"Ah . . . I see." It wasn't exactly the answer Adam had been expecting.

"More than that," Juliet continued, "I felt he had sent his peace to me for just that reason, to get me on my feet again. I realized that God was good. I realized that he cared for me and that life could still be a good thing. Maybe even a happy thing again."

Adam mused over her words. She made it sound altogether too simple. His housekeeper poured him a cup of tea and set it in front of him. She was glad to see her niece so improved. Yet she was concerned about the propriety of Juliet's sitting at the table chatting so freely with the master.

"You say God cares . . . for you? You make God sound very personal," Adam reflected.

"I'd never thought much about it before this morning," replied Juliet. "But you're right. It was a very personal kind of peace I felt. And now that I do think about it, if God wasn't personal, how could he be God at all?"

"I'm not sure I follow you."

"How could he be God if he didn't take an active interest in our lives?"

He nodded slowly, puzzling over her words.

"I have to admit, it's all new to me, Mr. Livingstone," Juliet went on. "But I know God cares about me. Even when bad things happen. Once I realized that, I began to see that life could be good and that it was time for me to be glad for that. I'm sure I will be sad again whenever I remember that my father and brother are dead. You don't get over things like that overnight. But I'm going to do my best to remember that God is good, even when I am sad, and no matter what happens."

"It's a remarkable story, Miss Halsay. Although I confess, I still don't altogether understand it. I don't think I've ever heard anyone say what you just did—that God must be personal or he can't exist at all."

"It's obvious, isn't it, Mr. Livingstone? Your own discovery proves it."

"My discovery—how so?"

"God told Noah that he was going to flood the earth and then told him what to do in order to preserve the creation. How can it be more personal than that? God and man talking together about how to build a boat. Why, Mr. Livingstone, you've proved that God is personal yourself. And if you find the Garden of Eden, even a tiny little part of it like you said, just imagine how personal that would be. For Genesis says that God walked and talked with Adam in that very Garden. Imagine, Mr. Livingstone, God himself walked and talked in the Garden of Eden with a man who had the same name as you. And now you are going in search of that very place!"

It fell silent for a few moments. Then Adam heard the front door open.

"Oh, there's Jen!" he said, relieved to be spared further comment about his having proved something about God's existence. He didn't even know if he believed in God at all. Now here was Mrs. Graves' niece saying he had proved him! He would have to think about that later.

He gulped down the last half cup of tea, then jumped from his chair and ran toward the door.

"Thank you for the breakfast, Mrs. Graves. Jen . . . Jen, I'm in here."

He hurried out of the room. "I'll walk up with you. Scott and you and I need to go over our final plans. I've been working on them this morning."

The two voices retreated out of hearing. Juliet was left listening, part of her longing to follow. She would love to hear more about the research they were going to do in Africa.

She rose and walked slowly to the globe sitting where Adam had left it. For several minutes she stood pondering with wonder the region of the large oval Adam had drawn with his finger.

What secrets might the region hold? she wondered. What secrets might it be about to divulge to Adam Livingstone?

# eight

# Missing Link

(1)

Takeoff for Nairobi was scheduled in two weeks.

Adam eased into bed and propped a few pillows behind his back. He wasn't sleepy enough yet to call it a day. He opened the issue of *National Geographic* that had come that morning.

As he began perusing the magazine, Adam was instantly struck by a short piece detailing a strange botanical phenomenon in the desert at the far westernmost tip of Saudi Arabia. Without water of any kind, an unknown plant had sprouted unnoticed out of the desert floor at the base of a long-dead volcano. When first noted sometime later, it had already grown into a stout seedling, thriving as if nurtured in a greenhouse.

That had been three years ago. In the time since, the original plant developed rapidly and soon sent out branches and leaves. Green year-round, it had now become a tree eight feet in height, with a trunk unusually massive for so small and fast-growing a plant. The most astonishing fact about the case was that the tree seemed to possess sylvan powers beyond itself. For all about it, to a distance now extending several hundred yards in every direction, the desert itself blossomed with greenery, grasses, shrubs, and a host of other unusual flora.

Strange sensations crept over him. Something was here that defied reason. Even as he read the unbelievable account, an inner voice whispered to Adam Livingstone that one day he would have to investigate.

Still no streams brought water to the place. No underground spring or well was known. Nor had a drop of rain fallen in two years. Neither had the tree spawning the strange germination out of rock and sand been identified as any known species. Several botanical experts and horticultural historians were called in from universities in Cairo, Amman, and Riyadh, but they were without success in making a characteristic designation. All proposed theories fell short in explaining the sudden flourishing oasis in the middle of such a wilderness wasteland. No analysis produced a clue. It remained a mystery how the sandy, rocky soil could produce such verdant life.

Every day, the article claimed, new sprouts, seedlings, and shrubs came to life. The extent of the oasis widened. More trees took root, of many distinct types, though none like the original. Within a few years, said the author, if the present trend continued, the place would become a forest.

A full-page picture of what was dubbed "ancient Arabia's mystery tree" was shown. It was unlike anything Adam had ever seen.

The sight sent an inexplicable shudder through his frame. He stared at the photograph for two long minutes.

At length Adam smiled.

*It's too bad old Harry Mac couldn't live to see this!* he thought to himself. He hadn't thought of the fellow in years, not since his university days when he had worked on the paper about the old archaeologist. But this article triggered his memory.

Perhaps it was the location. Or was it the supernatural talk surrounding the occurrence? According to the article, the nomadic inhabitants of the desert were proclaiming the oasis a holy place, investing the tree with divine powers. It had reportedly already been responsible for several healings and two visions.

The region of growth had sprouted, as if by incredible accident, behind a chain fence surrounding a supposed archaeological area. It had thus far contained the oasis and kept the tree at its center from pilgrims, tourists, or mischief-makers. No enclosure, however, could forever contain the steadily expanding pattern of greenery that gave no sign of slowing its progress.

Adam set down the article, eerily fascinated, and turned out the light on his bedstand.

(2)

Adam awoke suddenly. His clock showed 3:36 A.M.

He knew immediately that sleep was out of the question. Within seconds he was on his feet. He dressed in haste, then made for the staff office.

Two hours later he still sat in front of the computer screen.

Light now shone through the window from outside, though the rest of his house and the entire town still slept. But Adam Livingstone had been awakened with a jolt through his brain of seismic historic and archaeological proportions. The electric current from it still ran through his veins as if supercharging his limbs, his blood hot with aroused insight and vision.

Three phrases rang through his head.

At half past three in the morning all had surfaced out of the depths of sleep, bringing with them new and staggering implications of the Ararat find.

The comment he had heard in the queen's garden sometime earlier had lodged deep in his subconscious. It had chosen this night to emerge. *Perhaps the ark will become your Lucy.*

Added to it was what the Halsay girl said. Imagine *his* proving that God was personal. It was a seriously unnerving notion! Her words came back with force upon all his spiritual preconceptions. *If you find the Garden of Eden . . . just imagine how personal that would be!*

Mostly, however, it was the proclamation about Arabia's mystery tree he had read before falling asleep that coursed through him from an energy source he could not explain. *"It's a miracle!" proclaim desert natives.*

*Miracle . . . miracle . . .*

The words repeated themselves over and over in his brain!

*Miracle*—what did the word imply?

Was Eden a *miracle?*

Was the ark a *miracle?*

Was life itself a *miracle?*

Suddenly *everything* seemed infused with higher meaning that no rationality or logic could explain.

Adam sat at the computer station in the expansive workroom where Scott, Crystal, and Jen all had their desks. He had scarcely moved for the past two hours.

His fingers clicked across the keyboard of the Power Mac 9800 as if with a vengeance.

Folders and notebooks sat beside him, notably his Eden file. In the hours he had been awake, he had entered much from his years of accumulated notes, entering every scrap of data from the Ararat discovery, rechecking much of his research during the year leading up to the expedition.

His eyes glowed with the passionate fires of new discovery. He could not get the picture of that tree from his mind!

The thoughts now speeding through his brain at warp speed were staggering, unbelievable. He was in the midst of realizing that more threads to his theory existed than he had imagined. He had not beheld the larger picture . . . until now.

This morning's new glimpses opened as windows into another dimension of awareness. He could barely maintain his focus sufficiently to type words and numbers and coordinates into the program. Before he could even begin thinking of conclusions or of running simulations, he had to get all the data into place. From there he would formulate new models and hypotheses.

He had been playing with his large-oval, four-river Eden theory for years. But all this time he had seen but the tip of Eden's iceberg. The scope of the quest and its implications and eternal import, were much larger than he had imagined.

What if, in fact, the entire future of the human race rested upon the *meaning* of Eden . . . and what would be the result if it ever were found?

First one, now another, seemingly unrelated piece interwove through his brain into a gradually cohesive and credible, though astonishing web. It was an awe-producing paradigm with a personal and purposeful element at its core.

*Personal and purposeful.* He had spoken to Juliet about weather shifts and random changes in the earth as if they were accidents of nature. But what if there were more causitive foundations behind the covering of Eden's mysteries? What if some deeper intent was at work? Something—or *Someone*—perhaps very personal indeed?

The thing was too fantastic to contemplate. Even the ark paled in comparison.

Yet it was the ark that made this revelation possible, for its discovery opened his eyes to the *spiritual* component in the Eden equation.

Adam had never considered such an integration before. Yet it was only in the spiritual dimension that either Eden or the ark could be understood.

The first Adam and Noah had to be intrinsically linked. Eden and the ark could not fit into a historically valid pattern without one another. He had all along approached them as isolated events. But the linkage was unmistakable. A linkage on more levels than mere science could ever apprehend.

It was a *spiritual* key that unlocked the mystery, not a scientific one. That spiritual component changed everything.

Had a *personal* God instructed a man to build a gigantic boat and then left it on top of a mountain after the receding of the flood he had caused?

And was it now perhaps God himself who was causing this new desert phenomenon—to all appearances "natural," yet deeply mysterious—possibly with supernatural origins?

Perhaps *purpose* ruled the universe after all. Where would *that* put the evolutionists, with their dance of amazing chances and random flow of atoms?

In what astonishing new directions were these new thoughts suddenly pointing him?

Adam's fingers paused. He leaned back momentarily in his chair and exhaled deeply. He thought for a moment, then grabbed the Bible from the shelf above him.

It opened of itself to the opening chapters of Genesis. This was the only part of the so-called sacred book that had interested him and, then, only as a historically useful text to shed light on his work. Now he found himself digesting the words with newly hungry purpose.

*Here,* at last he realized, not in the dirt or ice or sand or granite of the earth, would he discover the unified theory of beginnings, which had always been his dream . . . in this book!

*And the Lord God made all kinds of trees grow out of the ground. . . .* he read.

Then once more the words he had gone over and over and over a dozen times during the past two hours: *In the middle of the garden were the tree of life and the tree of the knowledge of good and evil.*

Two trees . . . in the middle of the garden.

Would the end of the age be signalled when all would have to choose between the two?

What brought such a thought into his brain? The end of the age—he had only heard the phrase in connection with religious fanatics. Could something of such historic magnitude be approaching? It could hardly be doubted that people the world over were looking to the coming of the new millennium with enormous significance. Might this be it? If so, he was looking in the wrong place for light on the end of the age. Genesis was the book of beginnings, not endings!

How did all the pieces fit together?

*A river watering the garden flowed from Eden, and there it divided into four headwaters.*

Explosions were going off in Adam Livingstone's brain. Still he apprehended but vague glimpses, as his mind spun out more questions than it had answers.

(3)

Over and over Adam pored through the words, turning back and forth through the first eleven chapters of the book, between the accounts of Adam and Noah, searching the text like a starving man for morsels of nourishment. He sought insight from the record as if he had stumbled across a long-lost written account of those very antiquities to which he had devoted his life. His archaeologist's brain examined every word as if uncovering verbal stones in a dig—squinting, sifting, scooping, brushing—hoping under each to behold some previously undetected grain of truth.

*The Lord God had not sent rain on the earth.*

Here was evidence for the preflood canopy theory.

Then came the remarkable words he had never stopped to examine with clarity before.

*So the Lord God banished him from the Garden of Eden. . . . After he drove the man out, he placed at the east side of the Garden of Eden cherubim and a flaming sword flashing back and forth to guard the way to the tree of life.*

Eden's center had been covered over on purpose. The hiding of the Garden . . . the flood—these were no geological or meteorological accidents.

The Almighty had caused the Garden to be sealed, to be split—caused it for reasons known only to him. As the Garden had been given, it had been taken away. It had remained hidden all these years, its entrance barred by angels.

But hadn't he heard a verse sometime . . . yes, something about hidden things!

Frantically Adam turned to the back of his Bible. Though it had not been greatly used, he knew what a concordance was and quickly located it. A few seconds later he was flipping through the pages, trying to find the book of Mark . . . there it was! Chapter 4, verse 22.

Yes, that was it: *Whatever is hidden is meant to be disclosed, and whatever is concealed is meant to be brought out into the open.*

Meant to be disclosed!

Was it possible that someday . . . the actual Garden might be found . . . was it meant to be found?

Could he dare dream of such a possibility?

(4)

Shortly after awakening, Adam had opened several new files in his computer. Immediately he began entering the morning's new rush of ideas along with what actual data he possessed, collating and combining it with yesterday's work.

Sometime about five years ago Adam had first begun reading a little of the creationist literature. He had never put much stock in what he considered the pseudoscience of the biased effort. As an archaeologist of antiquities, however, he was drawn to any and all sources that might shed light on the ancient literature.

Suddenly the hypothesis that a biblical worldwide flood caused the raising of the mountain ranges and the deepening of the ocean floors and the laying down of sedimentary rock formations worldwide and some actual continental drift along with it held a wholly new fascination. The scientific side of his brain had never been able to admit to the possibilities these authors proposed. Now he was newly intrigued. For he now recognized the global flood to be more than mere legend.

His creationist reading had led to research into the whole subject of dating antiquities and dating methods. He was well familiar with carbon 14 and the radiometric potassium-argon methods. More recently he had begun postulating some new ideas of his own. The scientific community's theories and the literal creationists' theories could not be further apart. Scientists said it took 17 billion years. Creationists claimed it was six thousand. He had always subscribed to the former as one of the cornerstones of evolutionary theory.

Could either extreme be validated more accurately through dating evidence? If the flood possessed the cataclysmic geologic impact that now seemed likely, substrata could have been overturned and recombined and made to appear much older to traditional geology than it actually was. Likewise, the flood could certainly have changed and reversed rivers or obliterated them.

And caused a rift in Eden by turning the river Pishon into the Red Sea.

It was the discovery of the ark that synthesized these various opinions into a credible thesis that both evolutionists and biblical literalists could not dispute.

The ark seemed to prove that the book of Genesis was fact, not myth. Once that foundational certainty was established, the way was opened to backtrack from the factuality of the sixth chapter to the factuality of the second chapter. Could Adam selectively keep certain segments and omit others? What gave him the right to wield such a truth scalpel? Did not the discovery of the ark compel acceptance of the entire Genesis account? If part of Genesis was true, why should not all of it be true?

It was a quantum jump. That question involved a majestic leap backward from a known and verifiable historical event to the point of beginnings itself!

In the Eden account, Adam had landed just a few verses from the origin of everything.

He had dedicated his life to beginnings. Now here he was staring the first great Beginning in the face.

This could establish all known science on a completely new foundation—a literal, factual book of Genesis . . . all the way back to Genesis 1:1. What breathtaking words for an archaeologist to read, when he read them as fact: *In the beginning, God created the heavens and the earth.*

(5)

There had been many significant finds in Adam Livingstone's field of endeavor. His Ararat adventure had to rank as one of the greatest. But it was not the first to be so hailed.

Many had already been the claims to the title *Missing Link* before now. Both the 1924 Taung child and Lucy in 1973 had briefly been given the title. Then came Sir Gilbert's discovery of the *Homopithecus* graveyard, which he wishfully touted as the true "missing link" between the *Australopithecus* and *Homo* species. But none of the three was close to providing a verifiable connection between the ancestral line of pongid and hominidae during the Miocene epoch.

The ark was the true missing link. The link between men and history and events and archaeological findings, and—dare he even think it!—man's first encounter with God himself.

Ararat had provided the most significant archaeological find to date. Unlike the many fossil discoveries whose significance required enormous, and sometimes flimsy, conjecture, the ark proved itself. It simply was. And Eden would be an even greater find.

Thought of his colleague brought a smile to Adam's face. Significant as was Sir Gilbert's find, it didn't come within a mile of connecting hominids with apes. But Bowles was happy to let the public think his discovery of more import than it was.

Adam glanced over to his own autographed copy of *The Link Is Found*. Bowles was so evangelical in his atheism. Wouldn't he love to get hold of what Adam was thinking now!

The reflection brought a certain realism to his thinking. What if he did succeed in finding some portion of Eden to his own satisfaction? Without proof, all sides would dispute any new theory on the basis of their preconceived conclusions. There would be many who would expend great energy to suppress or discredit any public proclamation.

Well, thought Adam, he would just have to give them proof they couldn't dispute.

The dimensions of this thing were so vast it would change the way people thought. It could eclipse Darwin in importance. It could establish the foundation of a whole new scientific argument for divine creation. And it seemed— though Adam would have to think this through in more detail—that it would scientifically prove once and for all that evolution of humans from other species could not possibly be true.

Again he paused to consider the implications.

If he were right, there were people who would not want to see this evidence made public. It was a sobering realization. The forces supporting man as an evolved creature had made powerful inroads into every corner of society. Evolution and natural selection were two of the foundation stones upon which modernism and humanism had been built. There could be very real dangers involved.

He couldn't worry about any of that now. He had to figure out what it all meant. Anyway, he had no intention of allowing any of this to leak to the media.

He returned his attention to the computer screen and set his fingers again to readiness on the keyboard.

How could he run a computer simulation of postdiluvial drift, factoring in weather changes . . . and according to what time scale? More sophisticated programs would be needed than what he presently possessed, but he could get a good start.

For another two hours Adam sat, fingers flying, brain on fire, adrenaline pumping into his brain, collating information onto his hard drive from dozens of files and from a lifetime of reading, work, and research.

Eventually most of the data was in place.

At length Adam stood and stretched, then exhaled a long breath of air. Mental fatigue had set in. He needed a break.

He glanced toward the clock. Seven-twenty. Mrs. Graves should be up and about by now. He'd go have tea and some breakfast.

"Well, my friend," he said quietly, gently placing a hand on top of his monitor, "you're going to tell me your secrets before this day is out. It may be that you and I have more shocking possibilities to tell the world even than Noah's ark!"

Scott walked into the house forty minutes later. Adam heard him from the kitchen and hurried out to join him.

"Good morning. I'll go upstairs with you," Adam said. "Just wait till you see what I've got hatching on the computer."

"What is it?" asked Scott.

"I'm rethinking my whole Eden theory—literally from top to bottom," he added with a laugh.

"What—just since yesterday!"

"There's a whole world to it we've never seen before . . . never even looked for before because we had no idea it existed. Come on, I'll show you."

They took the stairs two at a time.

"Are Erin and Jen here yet? I want them to see this too."

# nine

# Terror Too Close

(1)

Adam and Scott walked into the office. Crystal already sat at her desk. Erin and Jen arrived for the day two or three minutes later.

"Have I got exciting news!" said Adam.

"Our African visas came through?" asked Jen.

"No," laughed Adam. "Crystal is working on that. By the way," he added, turning to his secretary, "where *do* we stand in that regard?"

"A week . . . ten days at the most," replied Crystal.

"That's cutting it close. Jen and Scott and I are scheduled to leave in two weeks."

"They'll be ready."

"Passports up to date—," he added, glancing toward his two assistants. "Both of you got your shots?"

"After Turkey, we can go anywhere in the world," laughed Scott.

"Good, Scott, you're working on the shipment of the equipment?"

"Yep. We're mostly set. There are a few people I have to see once we set up camp in Tanzania."

"Jen, you're working on the daily work schedule and mapping details?"

His assistant nodded.

"And you're in contact with our botanist in Cairo?"

"I'll be talking to him tomorrow. His office said he was free these dates and would love a chance to work with us."

"So, what's the delay?"

"Dr. Cissna's out in the jungle with some peace corps team from the States. I haven't been able to reach him yet."

"Leave it to the Americans!"

"Careful!" laughed Scott.

"I'm sure he meant present company excluded," said Crystal.

"Right," rejoined Adam. "But we really need an African botanical expert," he added. "He's supposed to be the best. Keep trying, Jen."

"I will. But what's the exciting news?"

"A series of connections between the ark discovery and the Eden theory," replied Adam. "I've been up since three-thirty plugging in data. I need more of the drift information. Come over here. I'll show you all what I've been playing with so far. Look at this proposed map of my large-oval Eden area."

Excitedly Adam strode across the room and sat down at the computer where he had already put in several hours. Scott, Jen, Erin, and Crystal gathered in a semicircle behind him.

Adam brought the desktop back into view on the screen, then double-clicked on the new folder he had recently created called "Expanded Eden." The icons of several documents came into view as the contents of the folder appeared.

Moving the mouse rapidly, he double-clicked to open all three.

Suddenly a message appeared: The system has unexpectedly quit because a type 1 error has occurred.

Groans filled the room. "Oh no!" cried Adam.

"I hate when that happens!" exclaimed Scott.

Adam sank back in his chair as if suddenly deflated of power to support his body. He stared at the screen in disbelief.

"You didn't overload your RAM?" asked Crystal.

"This 9800 has more RAM than we would use by triple if we put every file from every computer in the house on it," replied Adam.

He continued to eye the dead screen. He had a bad feeling about this. Slowly he summoned the energy to sit forward. Again he took hold of the mouse and began moving and clicking it.

Nothing.

"I was afraid of that," Adam sighed.

"Restart," suggested Jen.

"I doubt it will do it. I'm afraid the system's dead. Crystal, what's the restart command?"

"Control, command, power."

Adam pressed the three keys. The screen went black, followed by the on-tone. A moment later a sad-faced Mac icon appeared.

More groans sounded. They all knew that icon meant the worst.

"Looks like a full-scale crash," said Adam.

He leaned back in his chair again, hands clasped behind his head and exhaled in frustration. "I don't even want to think what I might have lost!"

"Don't worry. We'll get to the bottom of it," said Crystal. Already she was gently easing Adam out of the chair and taking his place in front of the computer.

Like a balloon deflated of its air, Adam slowly rose with the weight of the world on his shoulders and relinquished the chair. The elation with which he had bounded up the stairs moments before was gone. A lump of rock sat in his stomach. He was going to be sick.

As much as computers could do, this was one part of it he could never get used to. There was no feeling quite so horrible in the world as the helplessness following a major crash. Especially in that it always seemed to follow a burst of creative energy. His panic-stricken chest told him the early morning's exciting work was gone . . . or that he was having a heart attack!

Scott was already on the floor under the desk checking connections. Crystal's fingers experimented with the keyboard and mouse, attempting to restart the machine using any of a half-dozen tricks of the trade. Nothing succeeded except in again bringing up the sad-faced Mac icon.

"You saved your work?" said Crystal over her shoulder.

"Of course," replied Adam. "Before I quit for breakfast. But saved won't matter if the hard drive is damaged."

"We're not going to lose anything," called out Scott from under the desk. "We'll get to the bottom of this."

"You guys do what you can," said Adam dejectedly. "I'm going for a walk."

He turned and left the room, descended the main stairway, and was soon strolling aimlessly about his garden.

(2)

"We've *got* to get to the bottom of it," said Jen as soon as Adam was out of the room. "I've never seen him like this."

"He hates computers," said Scott. "He loves what they do. Actually, he's pretty good with them. But he can't stand being at their mercy."

Adam returned upstairs an hour later.

He knew immediately from the subdued atmosphere in the office that his team had made no progress. Only Scott's legs were visible. Wire and cables lay strung about the floor, while he tested various other pieces of equipment. Crystal still sat at the keyboard. Jen's head was buried inside a technical manual. Erin was on the phone.

Adam looked in her direction.

"She's talking to her boyfriend at Computers, Ltd.," said Jen, glancing up.

"I'm afraid it's time to get a technician out," sighed Adam.

"That's what Erin's calling about," said Jen.

Erin looked up from the phone. "Dexter says they can't get anyone out until tomorrow."

Adam walked across the floor and took the phone.

"Dexter," he said, "let me talk to the manager."

He waited. A moment later another voice came onto the line. "Right, Adam Livingstone here," he said. "We've got a rather serious problem, and I'm afraid it can't wait. We've got a service contract. . . ."

"We're jammed up busy as can be all day, Mr. Livingstone," said the man. "What model is it?"

"The modular 9800."

"Why don't you bring in the hard drive?"

"You have someone who can look at it?" asked Adam.

"Right—just no one I can send out."

"I'll have it sent right in."

"Be best to bring it yourself, Mr. Livingstone. You can walk the technician step-by-step through what happened."

"Well . . . if that's the best way to get it repaired."

"Bring your backup files too. What external drive are you using?"

"A Quantum 4280."

"Unplug it and bring it along."

"What do you need it for?"

"We'll have to check the information when we retrieve the hard drive of your 9800. Make sure the files correlate. We want to make sure the retrieval is complete. By the way, did you run Norton?"

"Just a minute. He wants to know if we've run Norton," Adam said to Crystal.

"Every way I could think to," replied Crystal.

"Yes," said Adam into the phone. "It wouldn't boot with the Norton disk either."

"Bring everything in then."

"I'll be there in less than an hour."

Adam hung up the phone.

"Start disconnecting the hard-drive laptop module and the 4280," he said. "Looks like I won't be able to show you my exciting new discoveries right now after all."

(3)

Thirty minutes later Adam set the external drive into the large metal briefcase laid open on the top of the desk beside the troublesome computer. Scott handed him the hard-drive module. He closed the lid with a sigh.

"Guess that's what they'll need," he said. "I hope they can restore it."

"It doesn't matter how bad the crash, if your hard drive's intact, usually the information can be retrieved, unless you've been hit with a lethal virus."

"I'll be back as soon as I can." He glanced around at his forlorn staff, then headed for the door.

Suddenly Erin's face lit.

"Would you like *me* to take in the equipment, Adam?" she asked.

"They told me to bring it in personally."

"I was right here. I saw everything. I can tell them what happened."

"Anything for an excuse to see Dexter!" laughed Crystal.

"Oh, I *see!*" said Adam, drawing out the word as at last he made the connection. "Hmm, well . . . I don't see anything wrong with that. I wasn't relishing a drive into town. Sure, you take it, and if there are questions, have them call me."

Erin skipped merrily toward him to relieve him of the case.

"I'll walk you down," said Adam. The two left the office and headed for the stairs.

"They should have our service contract on file," he said as they walked. "You saw exactly what happened—the computer was on, I tried to open a couple of documents and got the system-unexpectedly-quit-type-1-error bomb. Remember that—it was a type-1 error. The screen froze. We tried to restart. Then the sad-faced Mac."

"Got it," said Erin.

They reached the front door and emerged outside. Adam stopped, then handed her the briefcase. Erin walked across the cobblestones in front of the house toward the car. Adam glanced up and saw Juliet coming from the garden behind the house, returning from her morning's walk. He gave a brief wave, then turned again in Erin's direction.

"You stick to business!" called out Adam after his lab technician. "You and Dexter are getting paid to fix my computer, not make eyes—"

The final words never left his lips.

As Erin turned to flash a smile from his good-natured tease, the unthinkable shattered Adam Livingstone's well-ordered world.

His own metal briefcase suddenly exploded with a deafening roar.

The girl's bright smile froze Adam's consciousness for a hundredth of a second, then disappeared forever in a blinding burst of red orange flame and gray black smoke. She did not even scream.

The violence of the blast threw Adam onto his back. He would later be thankful for that fact. It prevented him from witnessing the horrible seconds that followed.

Raining down from above, even as the echo reverberated in his ears, tinkled a hundred tiny pieces of what was left of his briefcase and computer.

Adam tried to pick himself off the stones. He crawled to his knees, then groped to his feet. Haze clouded the scene.

"Erin . . . Erin!" he yelled, half dazed, then staggered forward.

*Erin!*

Already he knew she was dead.

"Erin . . . ," he cried. He tried to run.

Blood was splattered everywhere, all about the ground and on fragments of clothing and metal. And there were worse sights still.

Queasy, gagging, and knees buckling, Adam instinctively removed his shirt to cover what he could of Erin's body.

Screams of horror echoed, and running feet came hurrying frantically downstairs.

Adam straightened to his feet. He staggered around, bare-chested, tears streaming down his cheeks.

"Get back!" he yelled. Limping forward, eyes cloudy and blinking back hot tears, he held up his hands to barricade approach.

"Don't—"

He gagged again. Struggling, he forced out the words. "Don't come closer!"

His hands fell. He bent at the waist, clutching his knees for support as he vomited on the pavement. Scott ran toward him.

Crystal and Jen ran from the front door, and Mrs. Graves from a side entrance. All stopped halfway out from the house, weeping . . . moaning, hands clasped to their mouths . . . crying in disbelief and horrified shock. Now the butler came sprinting clumsily from around a side of the building.

Fighting the urge to break down himself and just managing to keep his stomach in control, Scott placed a steadying hand on Adam's shoulder and tried to lead him away.

He glanced up. "Beeves, call the police," he said. "Mrs. Graves, bring us some blankets. . . . You girls, get back inside."

As the dust cleared, on the opposite side of the explosion stood Juliet on the edge of the lawn, still as one of the stone statues behind her, in complete shock from what her eyes had witnessed.

As he regained his feet and began limping toward the house, an impulse caused Adam to glance around. He saw her paralyzed there, unable to move.

He paused, motioned to Scott, then turned and slowly made his way, limping badly now, across the battle-scarred entryway to his home. As he approached, she looked into his face with huge green eyes of helpless disbelief and anguish.

Heedless of his own condition, instinctively Adam wrapped his arms slowly about her. Juliet melted into his protective embrace. It took but a moment. Her body trembled slightly. Then she burst into a catharsis of sobs.

Adam led Juliet to her aunt. Juliet was put to bed, and there she remained for two days.

# Surprising Acquaintance

(1)

The deserted London street under the shadow of the Chelsea Bridge was not a friendly place. The slow-moving Thames, dreary and somber even in bright sunlight, grew black and forboding as dusk descended upon the city.

A young man stood waiting, his back to the river, nursing a cigarette. He looked up and down the street nervously, then glanced down at his watch.

A thin fog began to creep shoreward along the water's surface. It would be a cold night.

Ten minutes more he stood. He lit another cigarette and took several long puffs.

An imported Mercedes, black as the ancient river, came slowly along Grosvenor Road. The young man looked toward it. The headlights played eerily in the gathering mist. They appeared as two sinister eyes probing the twilight . . . searching for him.

Involuntarily he shivered, then stepped back a foot or two from the curbside.

The auto approached, slowed, then stopped. Slowly the back door opened.

*"Get in,"* intoned a baritone voice. To describe the sound would be to probe the ageless mystery of earthly power. Deep and resonant, the ominous order was scarcely audible above the idling engine. It was not a voice one thought to disobey.

A momentary hesitation followed. Then the young man threw down the butt of his cigarette and complied. The driver pulled away from the curb. The car resumed its way along the Thames.

For several seconds it remained silent.

The Voice spoke first.

"You thought you could go into business for yourself," it said in measured and dispassionate cadence. The menace of the tone was unmistakable.

Unconsciously the young man shifted in the seat. He dared not glance beside him. He had met the speaker only once before, at night. He had no clear idea what the man looked like, though his voice betrayed the hint of Russian background or perhaps some Slavic country.

"What do you mean? I did exactly as you said." The lad's rapid speech gave away his anxiety. "Didn't you see it in the papers?"

"Of course I saw the papers. But Livingstone *himself* was the target, not merely his data," rasped the Voice in disgust and derision. "You failed completely."

The young man's heart stung him at the reminder. Sure, he had done it for the money. But he had let himself begin to think too much of Erin. He had hardly been able to live with himself since.

"How was I to know—"

"You are a fool!" interrupted the Voice, aroused finally to anger and thus increased volume. "You should have foreseen every possibility! But," the man went on, his voice lowering again, "I saw *both* newspaper accounts. It is that of a week *before* the accident to which I referred."

"What . . . I don't—"

"Shut up! Do you think me a fool? I have eyes and ears everywhere. Do you imagine I am unaware where the story came from."

"I don't know what you're talking about."

Suddenly he felt the hand of his recent employer grab his forearm from beside him. The fingers squeezed his flesh in a vise grip of unbelievable strength.

"Don't lie to me," the Voice growled. "I know well enough where the *Mail* got its undisclosed lead. When you virused the hard drive, you also planted a listening device. I authorized the former, not the latter. You hacks think no one is wise to your little schemes. I presume you thought you could make a little on the side?"

"Let go—you're hurting my arm," the young man said, almost whimpering.

"It was not my intent to have such things spoken of in the light of day."

"What was the harm?"

"Now the whole world knows what it was our desire to keep secret." rasped the man beside him, tightening his grip still more. "All because your foolish little brain could not be satisfied with what I offered. Well, my greedy friend, you shall pay for the trouble you have caused."

(2)

Erin's funeral, four days after the incident, in Hillingdon, was mostly a family affair, though the entire Livingstone staff was in attendance. Only Juliet remained at the house.

The six drove out together, Beeves at the wheel, Adam in considerable discomfort in the rear seat. Both left leg and right bicep had been struck by flying bits of metal, which had been removed that same afternoon at the hospital.

The shrapnel had sliced deep into muscle and would cause him pain for a while.

No one knew how to contact Dexter except through Computers, Ltd. Crystal conveyed news of the funeral to the establishment. No one there had seen him, nor did he appear at Hillingdon. Owing to the peculiarities of the case, Scotland Yard was engaged in a thorough investigation of the shop, its staff, and its ownership. Nothing had yet come to light.

Erin's hiring had originated through Mrs. Graves' acquaintance with Erin's mother, and Adam's housekeeper visited with Mrs. Wagner at some length following the service.

Most of the return drive to Sevenoaks along the M25 was silent. Mrs. Graves and the two girls wept off and on. Beeves, Scott, and Adam remained content with their reflections. None except Mrs. Graves had known Erin that long. But when death intruded so close and with such sudden cruelty, its finality and mystery left an indelible mark on the soul, which each had to deal with in his or her own way.

Adam was especially somber. It was obvious the bomb was meant for him. He was alive and Erin now was resting in the ground where they recently left her, because of a quirky last-minute change of plans. He wasn't quite sure where to place all that in his consciousness.

He had hardly thought about God since the morning of the bombing. All the revelations he thought he'd been having seemed remote and dreamlike. Maybe he hadn't woken up at all. Maybe he *had* dreamed the whole thing.

None of it seemed to matter now. Both computer and backup drive were destroyed. He'd forgotten everything anyway.

If God was out there at all, surely he controlled *death,* thought Adam, more even than arks or gardens. Then came the ageless human cry, that inevitable unanswerable that intruded into the midst of heartache. . . . *Why?*

Adam possessed no answer. Who did?

Where would Miss Halsay's optimistic picture of God fit into something like this? If he cared about her, as she said, why not for Erin?

Where were Erin's rays of sunlight?

Practical man that he was, Adam did his best to force his thoughts toward areas where there were things to be *done.* Gradually his reflections returned to the work. He had already settled on what to do, but he had not yet told the others.

"I've decided to postpone the trip," he said at length.

Jen and Scott nodded. They had expected it.

"We'll make a final decision in a few days—maybe reschedule in another three or four weeks."

It would be best. They would not be able to concentrate on the thousand details of a research expedition until they had time to get over Erin's death.

They reached the estate. A few reporters clustered about, but they stood back quietly as the gate swung opened and allowed entrance without incident.

(3)

When Candace Montreux called an hour later, she was let in the front door by the housekeeper. She stood waiting in the entryway while Mrs. Graves went in search of her employer.

The older woman had but set foot on the first stair when a moment later Adam appeared at the top of the landing. Descending slowly at his side— rather *close* at his side it appeared to his waiting guest—was a girl Candace had never seen before.

The thing was hardly more than a child and obviously a commoner. Yet the sight of the two of them together involuntarily raised the hair slightly on the back of Candace's neck. The fact that Adam did not immediately apprehend her presence and seemed altogether engrossed in conversation with the girl certainly did nothing to alleviate her quiet displeasure at the scene.

Adam and Juliet had but started down the stairs when Adam glanced up and saw Candace below.

"Excuse me, Miss Halsay," he said, "we'll talk again later."

He left her and quickly strode the rest of the way down to the ground floor. As he came, Candace kept her gaze focused on the girl. As Juliet followed Adam's movement, her eyes were caught momentarily by Candace's penetrating stare.

Only for an instant did the two sets of eyes meet. Juliet looked quickly away, turned, and hurried back up the stairs the way she had come. In certain matters the aristocrisy and the working class spoke a common language. And there could be no mistaking the message Juliet had just received from Candace Montreux.

"Miss Montreux to see you, Mr. Livingstone," said the housekeeper as he passed.

"Yes, I can see that—thank you, Mrs. Graves."

"Oh, Adam, I am so sorry about what happened. But who . . . ?" Mrs. Graves heard Lady Montreux say before she and Adam disappeared outside on their way to the garden.

Two Scotland Yard inspectors were about the grounds most of the afternoon. They had more questions about Computers, Ltd. and conducted a few chemical tests out on the stones at the site of the blast.

(4)

Mrs. Graves and Juliet climbed the stairs together after breakfast. It had been a week and a half since the explosion.

The incident had rocked everyone at the Livingstone estate. But Mrs. Graves' niece was now back on her feet and actually returning to herself more quickly than Crystal or Jen or her aunt.

Juliet was *not* going to allow this new terror to cause her to sink back into the hole out of which she had recently climbed. It was terrible, but after two days in bed, she was reminded of God's peace and remembered once again her determination to see life as a good thing in the midst of heartache.

"I think I will take a drive today, Aunt Andrea," said Juliet. "Perhaps down to Brighton to see a friend or two, then to Folkestone. I know the police are still about and everyone is nervous. But I need to get out. Get some fresh air, feel the wind on my face."

"That will be nice, dear," said Mrs. Graves. "It's a lovely day."

"I think I may drive into the city as well, to see about any job openings."

"You will be back for tea?"

"I'll try, Auntie. I need to look ahead, now more than ever. I need to keep reminding myself that God is good."

"I understand, dear. . . ."

The woman hesitated. An odd expression passed across her face. Juliet knew her aunt wanted to say something more. She assumed it had to do with Erin's death, for the housekeeper had been visibly shaken.

Juliet waited.

"Do you mind if I ask you a question," said Mrs. Graves as they entered her parlor together, "—a personal question?"

"No—no, of course not, Aunt Andrea."

"I've . . . I've never heard you talk about God like you did the other day to Mr. Livingstone. I—that is, I could not help being somewhat taken aback."

"I suppose it *was* rather bold of me."

"It was wonderful how you could express yourself so openly. But I was surprised."

"Why . . . surprised?"

"Someone like *me* could never speak with such familiarity to one so far above me."

"Above you? You mean because he's a gentleman and you are from the working class?"

"Of course. But I know you young people today don't think the same way my generation does."

"Nobody cares about station these days, Auntie. People are people. Everyone's equal."

"You cannot deny that men such as Mr. Livingstone on the one hand, and you and I on the other, Juliet, dear, are very, very different. We must remember our place."

"I didn't think about any of that when I was talking with him. He seems like a natural enough man. He doesn't put on any airs."

"Indeed, he is a very good man. But nothing can change the fact that we come from completely different backgrounds. Equal in God's sight, perhaps, but not in the eyes of society. Nor, I dare say, in the eyes of Mr. Livingstone himself, however natural he seems. We work *for* him. We can never be altogether on the same level as he."

"I know, Aunt Andrea, but people don't think so much about those sorts of things now. These are new times."

"That was not the only reason I was surprised," Mrs. Graves went on.

"What else then?"

"Neither did I know you felt that strongly. Your mother and father were never so vocal about—you know—about things of faith."

"I suppose you're right," said Juliet thoughtfully.

"How long have you felt like that—as you were explaining?"

"It just came out as Mr. Livingstone began asking me questions. When I woke up and saw that beam of light, somehow I realized like never before that God really *was* good. I felt such a peace inside. And that one little fact suddenly made such a difference."

"Not such a *little* fact—if we could believe it was always true," sighed her aunt, speaking out of her own doubts during the past week.

"I hadn't been thinking that much about God before," said Juliet. "I just started talking about him. I felt like I was waking up. Seeing God in a new way was part of it—knowing that he cared personally for me."

"Well, dear, as I said, Mr. Livingstone is an important man. I sometimes don't know quite what to make of the boldness of youth. But one thing is certain—not everyone would have the courage to speak with such confidence. Thank you for letting me ask, dear. Now you go on and enjoy that drive of yours. And I'll do my best to remember that God is good too. It *is* difficult just now."

"I know, Auntie—but he is . . . I am sure of it," she added brightly, "even though at times like this the clouds block the rays of sunlight for a while."

Mrs. Graves nodded and did her best to return Juliet's optimistic smile.

Thirty minutes later—with Beeves' help getting through the gate that had again been engulfed with a crowd of reporters—Juliet was on her way south toward the channel coast in her aunt's car.

(5)

Candace Montreux and her father were cut from the same cloth. Both were thoroughly adept at the art of getting what they wanted. The daughter's method was more straightforward, the father's more subtle. In the end, the results achieved by each were not so very different.

Candace was well enough aware that she was the centerpiece of a scheme to ensure Adam Livingstone's ultimate loyalty to her father's clandestine cause. She scarcely knew what that cause was, though in time she would be drawn more deeply into its web.

Had she been told all, little would have changed in her outlook. She had wanted Adam Livingstone herself nearly as long as her father and his people had been observing him. What difference would there be if her own designs fit in with her father's? Little did she realize, however, the extent to which her father was willing, and intending, to use her.

The odds were now shifting against both father and daughter in the Livingstone stakes. For too long they had employed the subtle approach. Adam had proved independent and more than a little obstinate. Confident that the hook was well set, it was time to reel in the catch.

Lord Montreux wondered, as did certain other members of the Council of Twelve, as to who might have so clumsily tried to dispatch Adam Livingstone. Eliminating the man was not part of the plan—but using him for their own goals was.

"Ah, Candace, my dear," said Lord Montreux as she entered the sitting room, "I have been giving serious thought to our friend Adam Livingstone. Tell me—are you in earnest about marrying him?"

"I thought that was the idea, Father."

"Of course, but now he seems ready to move in that direction."

"Yes, and it is about time."

"Do you love him?"

"Of course, I love him."

"Are you content to wait until next year before he commits himself definitely, as he indicated the other day? You are not getting any younger, you know."

Candace bristled at the remark.

"No, I am *not* content to keep waiting," she rejoined testily, doing her best to stay calm. Her father's insinuation and tone irritated her nearly as much as Adam's ambivalence.

"Then perhaps we should see if we cannot persuade our young friend to accelerate his plans."

She hardly needed her father to tell her how to win a man's heart, Candace thought to herself. She could spin Adam's head any moment it suited her. She had merely been playing it coy so as not to frighten him off.

"What does the date of a wedding matter to you?" she asked. "You have never shown any urgency before now."

"I have my reasons for wanting Livingstone to join our family, shall we say, at the earliest opportunity, as I am sure you do."

Candace did not reply. Her father was right. She was more than a little annoyed that Adam's affections seemed so dispassionate.

"I want you to see what you can do," her father went on, "to get his mind off all this biblical research. It's not healthy to become so preoccupied with myths and old wives' tales. People will call him a lunatic if he continues with all this Eden nonsense."

About that her father would get no argument. She couldn't agree with him more!

"What does he find so fascinating about religious tales?" he added.

"I don't know, Father. It's a side of Adam I've never understood."

"We can't have you the wife of a priest, for heaven's sake!"

"Don't even say such a thing!" Candace shuddered.

"Are people close to him poisoning him with these absurdities?"

"I don't know."

"Find out. And put a stop to it. Get his mind off this daft poppycock. Garden of Eden be dashed! Surely your feminine charms are capable of dangling some apple in front of him he cannot resist."

"I will do what I can."

"He needs to settle down to the life of an English gentleman. The sooner he realizes that, the better off we'll all be."

"And a wealthy one, too, isn't that right, Papa?" said Candace with a sly smile.

"True—but I hope not to resort to outright bribery . . . that is, unless there is no other alternative."

The two understood one another well enough.

(6)

Marcos Stuart had had misgivings about this social gathering from the moment he received Mitch Cutter's invitation. Instructions would be more accurate. It just didn't feel good. But in the end he had known he had no choice but to attend.

So here he was. The setting was a country estate in Maryland's hills about forty minutes from D.C. He did not recognize anyone present. The place reeked with wealth—expansive pool and lawns and gardens, chandeliers in every room—the whole place was easily worth a million five. This was no poor politician's house, that was for sure.

Drinks were flowing freely by the time he and Cutter arrived.

"So, at last we get to meet our senator," said one Lars Witjansund, as Mitch introduced the two. The word *our* rang oddly in Stuart's ear in light of the man's rhythmic, musical Scandinavian accent. Marcos doubted that the stranger was from his home state of Pennsylvania. The stranger could be an American, perhaps from Minnesota or Wisconsin. But it was unlikely.

A few trivialities followed. Cutter turned away momentarily, then reappeared. He thrust a glass in Stuart's hand. "Scotch and water, Senator?"

"That will be fine." Marcos nodded.

"Come with me. I want you to meet some of the others. Marcos . . . Sophia Lennox, and here is Lawrence Mobuto . . . ah, Ciano, my dear!" Cutter exclaimed, turning to face an attractive woman, perhaps an Italian, who now walked toward them.

Her black eyes sparkled as Cutter introduced them. More introductions around the room followed, as gradually the two newcomers worked their way outside onto the huge brick-and-tile patio.

The foreign flavor of the gathering was unmistakable. Everyone was comfortable and at ease in mannerism and surroundings. Whenever Marcos inquired, all seemed willing for him to think them Americans and adroitly deflected his questions concerning background. Yet they made no attempt to hide their global interests and affiliations or the diversity of accents they brought to the English tongue.

"Tell me, Senator," said a dark-skinned man whose name had been given as Lebrun Inonu, "I understand you are close to the Livingstone Cartel."

"Not really," replied Marcos. "Actually I know nothing whatever about the cartel."

"Mitch has said you know Adam Livingstone personally." Now the speaker was Ciano Bonar, who had followed them outside.

"That is true, Miss Bonar. I know nothing of the business aspects of his expeditions, though Livingstone himself is an acquaintance."

"That is fascinating," she replied. "You must tell me about him."

"More than a mere acquaintance, isn't that right, Marcos?" Cutter smiled. "You can tell them—we are among friends here. You and he were old school pals, were you not?"

"We knew one another. Mostly we had a mutual friend."

"Ah yes—of course."

"That would be Livingstone's assistant Scott Jordan?"

Stuart turned as a tallish stately lady whom he had not met approached.

"Yes, that is correct, uh—," replied Marcos.

"Anni D'Abernon," she said, shaking his hand. "I am most pleased to meet you, Senator Stuart."

"You know Scott?" he asked.

"I am afraid I have not had that pleasure," the lady replied. "Perhaps one day you might introduce me to him."

"You are interested in archaeology, I take it?"

"Upon occasion."

It was an odd reply, thought Marcos to himself, as was the woman's expression. But as the conversation moved into other channels, he thought no more of it.

"My, but everyone seems extraordinarily interested and well-acquainted with Adam Livingstone's exploits!" laughed Stuart.

"We are interested in many things," rejoined D'Abernon. "Anything of international import holds interest to our . . . to such as we."

"But we are most interested in you, Senator Stuart," said Miss Bonar.

"That is why these friends have come, Marcos," added Cutter breezily. "They were all influential in your campaign in one way or another. They have wanted to meet you. They believe you are a man of destiny, a man of the future. They are anxious to help you lead our country forward into the new century and the new age."

"Here, here!" chimed in Lennox and Witjansund, raising their glasses.

"To the future of Senator Marcos Stuart!" added Mobuto.

"To Marcos Stuart!" repeated the others. "The only one of the gathering who did not participate in the toast was the enigmatic D'Abernon, who continued to observe, as from a distance, as if not so anxious as the others to commit herself.

Gradually Marcos warmed to the occasion. How could he not, with such gushing approbation lavished upon him?

An hour later, Mitch Cutter observed the senator moving across the lawn on the far side of the pool, the lithe and entrancing Ciano Bonar on his arm, the two laughing and conversing freely.

Cutter smiled.

His eyes caught D'Abernon's across the way. She too had observed the scene. The most imperceptible nod of his head in her direction, which she returned with a slight raising of one eyebrow, gave indication that the two were pleased to see Miss Bonar's charms achieving their ends.

Both recognized that one of their objectives for the afternoon had been gained.

(7)

An hour after Juliet's departure for the coast, the bell on the front door of the Livingstone house rang. Beeves was not in the immediate vicinity, so Mrs. Graves opened it.

Before her stood a large, somewhat disheveled man she did not recognize. How he managed to get through security at the front gate she couldn't guess. Perhaps Beeves knew something.

"I'm here to see Mr. Livingstone," the man said.

She recognized the grating American tongue immediately. The faintest thinning of her lips was the only hint of recognition she let slip. He was enough a student of human nature, however, to realize she was the woman he had spoken with on the phone.

She turned without a word, leaving the caller in the entryway, and went in search of her employer. Mr. Livingstone had conveyed the man's apology after the prior phone call. It had been only slightly capable of moderating her annoyance at his brusque manner.

Adam descended the main stairway three minutes later. The visitor still stood inside the door. Adam approached with hand outstretched, though also with a look of question on his face.

"I am Adam Livingstone," he said.

The two men shook hands, silently appraising one another.

"The lady probably told you who I am," said the newcomer.

"She said the American who called before had shown up at my doorstep," replied Adam. His lips curved upward in amusement at the reminder of Mrs. Graves' expression while she conveyed the fact. "But I had understood you to say you were calling from the States. I didn't know you were in—"

"I was calling from the States, Mr. Livingstone."

"But then . . ."

"Then what am I doing in London?"

"Precisely."

"I read about the attempt on your life. I booked the first flight I could get."

"I see," said Adam. "I take it, then, you think the incident related to the, uh—the subject of your phone call?"

"Isn't it obvious? They tried to kill you. They'll try again. That's why I came."

A look of concern wrinkled Adam's forehead. He hadn't wanted to accept the reality of it quite so starkly.

"Look, Livingstone," said the American abruptly, yet with sincerity in his voice, "I know the lady who answers your phones and let me in just now doesn't much like me. For all I know, you may be suspicious too—you said before, my warnings sounded pretty cockeyed. But I didn't come all this way at my own expense because I'm some kind of nut. I came to help you, Livingstone—that is, if you want my help. Now I'd suggest you and I sit down and have a talk."

He gazed directly into Adam's face with keen eyes that looked wide awake and without hint of motive beyond exactly what he said. The straightforward honesty of his demeanor told Adam, whether you liked him or not, that this was a man to be trusted. And it could hardly be denied that Erin's murder changed everything. The fellow could well be right.

"Yes . . . yes, of course," Adam said after a moment. "I appreciate your coming and what you've done—what do you Yanks call it?—to try to save my skin?"

"That's what we call it," rejoined his visitor with a smile.

"Certainly—yes, I want to hear what you have to say. Come upstairs to my study. Would you like some tea?" said Adam, turning back toward the stairs and beckoning with outstretched arm.

"I'd prefer coffee if you've got it."

"I'll have Mrs. Graves bring up something," said Adam. He turned and led his guest up the stairs. "I'm sure she can find some instant around here someplace."

The American shuddered inwardly at the thought. But caffeine to combat the jet lag was what he needed more than anything right now. He wasn't particular how he got it. Even tea might help, though he hoped the housekeeper would be able to find something stronger.

"By the way," added Adam as they ascended to the first floor, "if we're going to be friends, don't you think it's time I knew your name?"

"I suppose you're right," said the American. "It's McCondy . . . Rocky McCondy."

# eleven

# Clues from the McCondy File

(1)

Adam Livingstone and Rocky McCondy, as unlikely an alliance as had ever come together in this house, stood together in the archaeologist's private study.

The two chatted informally for a few minutes. Adam offered the perfunctory inquiries about his trip. His guest gazed about the room—full of books, maps, artifacts, and other reminders of the archaeologist's trade—with more interest and apparent understanding than his appearance and manner would readily account for. His questions and comments revealed a shrewd grasp of the more sophisticated elements of the discipline not widely appreciated by the public at large.

At length Mrs. Graves appeared with a pot of hot water, tea makings for Adam, and a jar of stale instant coffee.

"The two of you have spoken on the telephone, I believe," said Adam, introducing them. "Mrs. Graves, meet Mr. McCondy. Mr. McCondy, my housekeeper, Andrea Graves."

"Sorry to have given you so much trouble before, Mrs. Graves," said McCondy, offering his hand, "—you know, when I called. I was mighty worried about Mr. Livingstone."

"No trouble . . . uh, no trouble at all, Mr. McCondy," said the housekeeper, at last allowing the hint of a smile to part her lips. The fellow really wasn't so bad in person. He looked a little gruff. But now that she heard his voice and saw him smile, she supposed he *might* have a pleasant manner about him.

"Thank you for the tea and coffee, Mrs. Graves," said Adam.

The two men proceeded to fix their respective brews, then sat down in two adjacent stuffed chairs.

"I suppose we've beat around the bush long enough, Livingstone," said McCondy as he continued to stir the two spoonfuls of outdated coffee he had put in his cup, trying to get them to dissolve. "I'm a detective by trade," he went on. "Retired mostly, though I'm only forty-eight. I take an odd case now and then, but only when it interests me."

"I've never known a detective—is it like the films portray it?"

"Not really—pretty boring stuff. I used to be a cop, but I got tired of it. I needed a change after my wife died."

"I'm sorry."

"Thanks. Anyway, ex-cops have one of two ways to go if they want to keep their hands in the game, one on each side of the law. They either join the bad guys, or they become private eyes. I did the second. Of course, they can become consultants or security guards," he added, "but then I don't consider that staying in the game."

Adam gazed down into his cup as he listened.

"All that doesn't exactly tell you why I'm here," McCondy went on, "but it might get us going in that direction. Sometimes I've got a nose for trouble. And when I saw you in the news, I knew trouble was brewing. That's when I called."

"You'll have to excuse me if I seem distracted," said Adam after a slight pause, glancing up and taking a sip of his tea. "But the moment you said the name *McCondy,* I recognized it. At least I thought I did—though I haven't been able to place where I've heard it before."

"It's an unusual name—you say you know it?"

"It's something very recent, but out of my past too. I'm sure I have stumbled over it just in the last week or two."

"I can't answer for that. But I *can* tell you well enough why you might have run across the name sometime back—that is, if you studied your archaeology like I don't doubt you did."

"I'm listening."

"My great-grandfather was an archaeologist too, so I know a little about the field."

"I could tell by the way you looked around, by the remarks you made."

"His specialty was biblical research, spent time in the Middle East—"

"Of course—old Harry McCondy!" exclaimed Adam, nearly rising out of his seat. "I *knew* I knew the name!"

"That's him, Grandpa Harry, as he was to my dad."

"And he *did* cross my mind just recently. Have you seen this month's *National Geographic?*"

"Can't say I have."

"Harry Mac—that's what I used to call him to myself—he'd have been interested in something going on in Saudi Arabia."

McCondy nodded. If it had to do with the Middle East or North Africa, his great-grandfather would have been more than interested. He'd have been in the middle of it! That much about Grandpa Harry he knew beyond doubt.

"I had a feeling you'd know him," McCondy said. "He was quite the man in his time."

"Indeed he was."

"His obsession was Mount Sinai, did you know that?"

"Vaguely. Your great-grandfather, Mr. McCondy—you're not going to believe this! I once wrote a paper on your great-grandfather's research during my graduate work at Cambridge."

"No fooling!"

"In fact . . ."

Already Adam was out of his chair. He strode quickly across the room and pulled out a drawer from an oak file cabinet.

"—you might like to see it," he said.

"Very much."

Adam flipped hastily through the files representing his early work. "I haven't thought of it in years," he added, laughing. "I might enjoy rereading the thing myself! Ah, here it is."

He drew out a folder labeled *McCondy File* and opened it.

"That's peculiar . . ."

"What is it?"

"My paper's gone."

Adam went through the drawer again, this time more thoroughly, still without success. At length he closed it and slowly returned to his chair.

(2)

The two men each drank from their cups, but without much apparent interest.

"I can't imagine . . . ," mumbled Adam, still bewildered by the empty file.

"It might not be as peculiar as you think, Livingstone," said the detective. "It might be that paper that's at least partially responsible for putting your life in danger."

"What . . . how could that be?" asked the archaeologist.

"I'm not just some out-of-work gumshoe who got curious when I read about your discovery of the ark," Adam's visitor went on. "I didn't just have some far-fetched *hunch* something was about to happen to you. If that'd been it, I could have sold it to the *National Enquirer*. They pay good money for crackpot notions about celebrities. My being Harry McCondy's great-grandson is no coincidence either. I'm here for a *reason*, Livingstone."

"I'm more than just a little curious."

"Your research. The ark, especially. When you set foot inside that boat, you set a time bomb ticking. I came to try to help you diffuse it."

"If you're talking about the bomb that blew up my laboratory technician, it would seem you're too late."

"That's not the bomb I mean. It's far bigger than that."

"I don't have a notion what you're talking about, Mr. McCondy."

"The long and the short of it is this—I realized I was probably the only man on this earth who knew enough of the pieces and how they fit together to be able to disarm that time bomb. I didn't get here soon enough to keep your lab girl from getting killed. I feel bad about that. I really do. I probably should have come immediately instead of just calling. But even I didn't realize how fast they'd work."

Adam stared, dumbfounded, listening to the cryptic words.

"But I never so much as met your great-grandfather," he said. "I just followed a little of his work, found myself fascinated, and wrote a paper. It probably wasn't even that good. No revelations, no scoops, no discoveries—just your basic term-paper kind of thing. I'd completely forgotten about it until just today."

"It was enough of a connection to put them onto you. But probably it has more to do with your current work. What do you have on tap next?"

"We're planning a trip to Africa."

"For what?"

"I have a notion about the Garden of Eden that I want to explore in more depth."

"The Garden of Eden!"

"You sound astonished. I *am* an archaeologist."

"This could be the key we're looking for! It could be what lit the fuse. The ark . . . Eden—there's a definite connection." McCondy grew quiet again. His brow wrinkled in thought. "Are your plans public?" he asked.

"They are now," replied Adam sardonically.

McCondy eyed him with question.

"One of our scandal sheets—like your *Enquirer*—ran a story a couple weeks ago. I was infuriated."

The detective took in the information with interest. "Before I say more," he went on after a moment, "tell me this—do you trust everyone in this house?"

"What do you mean—of course."

"Staff, servants . . . is there anyone possibly not all the way behind you?"

"Are you suggesting I might have a spy in my home?"

"I'm in the spy business, Livingstone."

"But that's—"

"Look, I think like an investigator. I'm *always* looking for the bad apple in a barrel. Being suspicious keeps me alive."

"Mrs. Graves, my housekeeper, and my butler Beeves—they've both been with me for years."

"You've got research people. I looked into a few of them, like the fellow Jordan—"

"Scott! He and I go back to the university."

"Time doesn't make a lot of difference in the strategems we're talking about. You know what a mole is—I mean a human mole?"

"I've heard the term. You can't possibly think such a thing about Scott!"

"What about the others?"

"I've got two girls—Crystal and Jen. They've been on staff four or five years. Jen I hired after her graduation from Sonoma State University in California. Crystal's husband I've known for years, and he works for the government in the city. She's been with me most of my professional career."

"I'll run checks."

"I don't really see—"

"You want someone else to get killed?"

"Of course not."

"Then let me do this my way. Any newcomers?"

"I suppose there is Mrs. Graves' niece, but—"

"Who is she?"

Adam explained how the girl came to be in his home. McCondy listened with interest.

"She bears watching. I'll check her out."

"Now wait a minute, Mr. McCondy. You can't start investigating everyone just because—"

"Look, Livingstone, I came over here to help you. If you don't want my help, just say the word. If you do, then let me do my job. I won't tell you where to look for the Garden of Eden. You don't tell me how to find the bad guys."

"All right, you win. This spy business will take a little getting used to."

"No problem. Just trust me, Livingstone—I know what I'm doing. Now, I'll run some background profiles. I'm sure your people are clean, but I've got to know."

"How will you do all this investigating?"

"I have connections at Interpol. And I've got a friend in Boston who's tight with some guy at Scotland Yard. I'll get what I need. All right, I want to know a little more about that Eden article."

"It came as a complete and total surprise," said Adam. "I'm still entirely mystified by it."

"How so?"

"It was like someone had been listening while my staff and I planned our trip. It was uncanny. There were near-exact quotes."

"And right afterward somebody obviously got to your computer, both to foul up your hard drive and set some kind of explosive. Although it might have been broken into earlier too, there's no way we can know yet. May have hacked in through the Internet or some other back door. Hmm . . . then they'd have had to steal or somehow access the password. I'll check all that out too. By the way, where were you when you and your staff were having this Eden discussion?"

"In there, next door, in the main suite of offices."

"What am I thinking!" exclaimed the detective. "I *am* an idiot to let us keep talking like this!" He stopped abruptly.

Adam started to speak, but the detective's finger came quickly to his lips. His eyebrows creased in warning.

"Come to think of it," McCondy went on, "I'm tired of sitting. Let's go outside—better yet, why don't you show me some of London? We'll talk as we go."

He rose. "I've got a rental car outside," he said. "I'll drive."

As the room grew silent, the man listening in on the conversation cursed.

He'd decided to make use of the bug in Livingstone's office even though he hadn't originally ordered it. A quick ransacking of his erstwhile young accomplice's flat had turned up the receiving end of the powerful transmitter, which was now in his possession. As yet it had provided him with nothing much of use . . . until now.

This McCondy fellow could be trouble. It appeared that the stranger was now deeply involved somehow.

It was clear there would be no more listening today. But he had access to Interpol, too, and Scotland Yard and Boston and anywhere in the world for that matter. His organization had people everywhere.

(3)

As the two new acquaintances drove slowly along, Adam could not avoid a certain anxiety over sitting in the passenger seat with a sleepy American behind the wheel.

But the detective had insisted they take his hired car. If the house was bugged, he said, so might be any of his automobiles. This was the only way they could converse freely.

"I still cannot see what my research," Adam was saying, "or my paper on your great-grandfather—or Noah's ark or the Garden of Eden, for that matter—why *any* of this would precipitate such danger as this so-called time bomb you're talking about. I take it you don't mean another *real* bomb?"

"No—a spiritual time bomb. Though the danger's real enough, that much is clear. One person's already dead—" he paused—"hmm . . . and maybe more, come to think of it."

"What do you mean?" said Adam.

"Didn't you tell me the housekeeper's niece had been involved in something similar?"

"Yes—her father and brother were killed recently. But that was a terrorist incident. It's completely unrelated."

"Don't be too sure," mused the American.

"Mr. McCondy, really—what connection could possibly exist—"

"Threads exist everywhere."

"I simply do not see what *any* of this has to do with my work."

"I don't know either," replied the detective. "I'm just asking questions, trying to piece together a few threads. After that, we'll follow them and see where they lead. That's how the detective game is played. Find a thread—follow it. We'll get to the bottom of this eventually. Hey, it's really not so different from your line of work."

"And my paper—what connection could *it* possibly have?"

"Again, I don't know. I sure would like to get a look at that thing. Tell me about it."

"I hardly remember the details. I was interested in Harry McCondy's work."

Adam went on to tell what scattered portions he could recall.

"Harry Mac's approach was unorthodox," concluded Adam after a few minutes. "That appealed to me. I think the biblical and religious connections of what he wrote fascinated me as well."

"Why?"

"I don't know. The ancient Hebrew texts struck a chord of intrigue in my brain. I suppose I always wondered if they might hold unknown keys to the past that science would unlock one day."

Adam paused with an ironic smile.

"Though the funny thing is," he added slowly, "until very recently I never stopped to ask myself to what extent I believed them. It was just a detached scientific inquiry . . . though I must say it's becoming more than that now."

"You may have hit the nail on the head, Livingstone," he said.

"What did I say?"

"The key, as you call it, may be that connection between science and the biblical texts. My great-grandfather was a very devout man. His mission was to *prove* the Bible through archaeology and to disprove evolution in the process. He hated evolution with a passion."

"An interesting raison d'être for a scientist," remarked Adam, "—though I suppose much of science back in those days was based on starting with the conclusion one wanted to prove and working backward from it."

The detective's concentration was diverted for several moments by a troublesome intersection involving two congested roundabouts.

"You handled that very well," said Adam when they were clear.

"I'd prefer traffic lights!" rejoined McCondy. "Tell me, Livingstone, where do you stand on matters of faith?"

"I've never considered myself a religious man, if that is what you mean. To be frank," he added, "I would say I am an evolutionist—at least so I always considered myself till now."

"I'm not afraid to break bread with an evolutionist." The detective smiled. "Let my great-grandfather roll about in his grave if he likes."

Adam laughed. The man had a sense of humor too.

(4)

They drove on for several minutes in silence. Adam found himself pondering again his revelations on the morning of Erin's death.

"What about you, Mr. McCondy?" he said at length. "Are *you* a religious man? Is that why you take such a keen interest in your great-grandfather's work?"

"I am a Christian, if that's what you mean."

"I suppose that is what I meant. Aren't they the same?"

"Religion and Christianity? Not at all."

"How so?"

"Let me answer by asking you another question," replied McCondy. "Do I *look* like a religious man?"

Adam glanced over at him, scrutinized his appearance briefly, then chuckled lightly.

"No . . . no, I would have to say you do not, Mr. McCondy."

"If you'd given me any other answer, I'd know you to be a liar!" McCondy laughed. *"Of course* I don't look religious! Could you imagine me dressed up in a clerical collar, singing in a church choir, or even wearing a suit. I'm a private detective. I used to be a cop. I've shot a few people in my time. My profession usually involves crime in some way. It's not a very 'religious' thing I do. But I *am* a believer in Jesus Christ. I do my best to do what he says. That makes me a *Christian."*

"That's interesting," replied Adam. "I never thought of them as different."

"There are all kinds of religions. There are all kinds of religious people walking around who don't give Jesus Christ the time of day in terms of how they live. No, Livingstone, being a Christian is a whole different thing."

"Do you mind if I ask you a very personal question, Mr. McCondy?"

"Heck no. Fire away."

"Do you pray?"

"Yep."

"Every day?"

"Try to. Sometimes I forget. Can't help it. But when I think of it—yeah, I talk to God."

"What about?"

"I don't know—everything. What I ought to do, maybe ask for his help on a case I'm working on, pray for him to help me with something I'm struggling over in my life, ask him to show me things, give me insights . . . anything that comes to mind."

"Are you an active churchman, Mr. McCondy?"

"Active as my work allows me to be. But my being a Christian isn't about going to church any more than it is about being a religious person. It's being a follower of Jesus that makes me a Christian, not being a good churchman."

The silence that fell this time was lengthy. Suddenly his new acquaintance was providing Adam Livingstone a host of new things to think about.

"By the by, Mr. McCondy," said Adam at length, "where are you staying?"

"Some flea trap by the airport."

"You can't stay way out there."

"I was beat when I landed. All I could think of was finding a bed to plop into."

"That's clear on the other side of the city."

"Then tell me someplace closer where I can get a room. I'm not particular."

"Mr. McCondy, for the rest of your time in England you're staying at my house. We'll drive out and collect your things right now, if that's agreeable with you."

"Why . . . sure, Livingstone, thanks—that's downright hospitable of you."

"Go around this roundabout here . . . good. Veer left and take the second road out of it. That should get us heading toward Heathrow."

(5)

Eventually they resumed talking about the reason for McCondy's visit.

"You seem to think there's a link between my paper on your great-grandfather," said Adam, "and my present predicament. But I cannot see anything about it that poses a threat to anyone. The idea is almost ridiculous. Who could possibly care about my work that long ago?"

Unconsciously McCondy rubbed his chin as he thought the matter over.

"They might have thought you knew more than you did," he said half to himself. "Or maybe they just didn't want to take any chances."

"They, they—you keep talking about they and them. But you never say who they are. Who are you talking about, anyway?"

McCondy did not answer for a long several minutes, remaining deep in thought. When at last he spoke again, his voice took on a new and mysterious quality.

"Look, Livingstone," he said, "you and I don't know each other very well yet. I took a risk in coming here. You took a risk in listening to me. I'm going to take an even bigger risk now telling you what I'm about to. My great-grandfather confided in a partner of his named Dubois, only to learn that the man was in league with some very powerful people. That was the leak that put them onto the danger Grandpa Harry represented."

"For heaven's sake, Mr. McCondy—what on earth are you talking about?"

"With these people, you never know," McCondy went on, ignoring the question. "That's why I'm cautious. They've got ears everywhere. They infiltrate where you least expect it. They're in every government, every multinational corporation. They control the banks. I tell you, Livingstone, they're everywhere. I'm going to tell you, because my nose says I can trust you. But wouldn't surprise me if you've had a plant or two in your own home. There might even be one there right now. If not, they've got the computer network of the world in the palm of their hands."

"Who, for heaven's sake, Mr. McCondy? You make it sound like a conspiracy involving the whole world!"

"You've hit the target dead center, Livingstone."

"A worldwide conspiracy! Mr. McCondy—really."

Again the detective was silent. At last he drew in a deep breath, then spoke again. "You ever heard of the Illuminati, Livingstone?"

Adam shook his head. "Is that the international conspiracy you're talking about?"

"Part of it." Rocky nodded. "Though it involves numerous such secret and occult societies."

"A conspiracy toward what end?"

"Control."

"Of what?"

"The whole world—mainly how people think. By controlling how people think, they control society's values and attitudes. That keeps them in power."

"I don't say I believe this, Mr. McCondy. And I can't imagine what any of it's got to do with me. But I'm listening."

"All right, then—hang on, Livingstone, it's going to be a ride unlike any you've ever had. You may have a hard time believing what you're about to hear."

Adam nodded. McCondy began, and Adam listened keenly.

For the next forty minutes the American laid out the most unbelievable story the English archaeologist had ever heard.

"It's an incredible story—positively incredible," said Adam, shaking his head in disbelieving wonder when the detective finally stopped. "It sounds like you stepped out of a John LeCarre story into the middle of my life! A worldwide conspiracy . . . with me suddenly in the middle of it! It's . . . it's just too—turn there, Mr. McCondy," said Adam, "—that's the road."

"Hey, good directions—there's the hotel. I'd have never found it on my own. You must be a native!"

They pulled up and went inside to get the detective's things and check him out.

(6)

"It's all very intriguing, Mr. McCondy," said Adam as they resumed their drive back in the direction of Sevenoaks. "You make a convincing case. But you must admit it sounds just a bit ridiculous. I'm just a scientist, an archaeologist. I don't see how my work threatens anyone. Your story sounds more far-fetched than looking for the Garden of Eden, and a lot of people think I'm off my nut for even thinking such a place ever existed at all! You can hardly blame me if I'm skeptical. I'll research it."

"Livingstone—haven't you been paying attention! You can research this thing till doomsday and you won't find much of anything. It's a conspiracy. Conspiracies are secret. This is the most secret one in the world. You won't find them by uncovering rocks. They're going to be harder to unearth than old *Austrolo*—whatever-it-is kind of old human skull."

*"Austrolopithecus."*

"You bet—harder to find than that! Time's going to come, Livingstone, when you're going to have to trust me—and I figure that time's about here."

The words sobered Adam all over again.

"How long have you been following your great-grandfather's work?" he asked at length.

"I knew nothing about it all the time I was growing up," the detective replied. "But when I read about your Ararat expedition in the paper, suddenly I found myself wondering about Grandpa Harry and what had got him killed. I knew I had some of his old papers up in my attic—"

"You have Harry McCondy's papers!"

"It's the family house. He used to live there, and his effects passed down ever since. Now they're mine. So I went up to the attic, and I found an old journal—"

"A journal!" exclaimed Adam.

"Everything written in his own hand."

"I can't believe it. What a treasure!"

"More a treasure than you think. I spent three days poring over that thing. That's when I knew you and he were on the same track, though you never knew it and though you were following different paths to get there."

"May I see it?"

"Are you kidding! I wasn't about to bring it along. I stashed it in a safety deposit box in Boston. Believe me, once they find out about me, especially what I know, the crosshairs will be lined up between my eyes too."

# twelve

# Another Houseguest at Sevenoaks

(1)

The interior minister of Azerbaydzhan flew back from London in white, silent fury.

Both his attempts to squash Livingstone had failed. Everywhere they were incompetent fools. It served the imbeciles in Baghdad right to be buried under fifty feet of white!

He hated to leave business unfinished in London. But he could not afford to be gone longer. Much needed his attention at home. He would have to bring in more dependable people to deal with Livingstone. *One* skilled operative or, he thought further, someone really on the inside would serve him better than twenty idiots.

Events on his western border were marching toward a climax as well. Perhaps the army's tactical force could arrange an errant missile in the direction of Ararat. He would discuss the matter with General Pervukhin.

He could ill afford more foul-ups. From now on he would use his own people and handle things *his* way.

By the time his jet touched down in Baku, his wrath had moderated. Already he was busy formulating the next phase of his multipronged strategy for takeover and ascendency. He glanced at his watch as he emerged from the plane onto the tarmac. A quick salute followed to the few officials and reporters gathered to greet him. It was past five. He walked briskly to the waiting limousine, then ordered his driver to take him straight to his villa.

A feeling of pride swelled within him as the sleek black automobile threaded its way through the city. Early in the next century, executives, financiers, and politicians would come here for their directives. From Baku they would be sent throughout the world to effect the mandate of the new order.

Empires rose, empires fell. On the horizon of history where the sun of the future was about to rise on a new era, the rays of its destiny would point straight here—strategically selected years, perhaps decades, before as the ideal global locus from which power would extend outward in every direction—northward to

Russia, eastward to that great mass of human potential in Asia, southward to the Middle East and Africa, westward to Europe and the Americas.

*Here* would originate communications, commerce, finance, and decision. Here between the Caucasus and Zagros Mountains at the mouth of the Kura, between the Black and Caspian Seas—isolated but central—a Switzerland of the new age with global reach would be created.

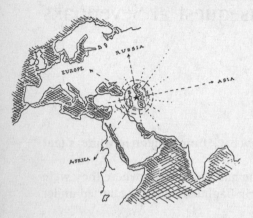

He was already creating it!

Baku would act as the hub, the critical midpoint, not merely of Europe, nor of some post-Soviet confederation of former Warsaw Pact allies, but of an entire new earthly order.

Such had been decreed by those who had placed him here. They were secretly bound together in allegiance to a Power of whom the world scarcely recognized the existence, though the billions of its inhabitants did his bidding every moment of their lives.

And he, Halder Zorin, would occupy center stage in that new-world matrix of rule.

He picked up the telephone.

"General," he said after a moment, "Zorin . . . yes, I have returned. It is imperative that you and I meet. We must consult on some matters of importance."

A brief pause followed.

"Maneuvers—I see . . . yes, it may take some time. Block out an entire morning. Three days from now. That should give you time to gather a complete report on our plans. We will meet at my villa. There we shall be undisturbed."

He set down the private line and again glanced out the window.

A radical new global culture had been ordained. The unifying religion of the new age would draw all nations, all peoples, all cultures, all political institutions together. For such a purpose had his rise to prominence been orchestrated—to prepare the way, to make the paths straight for the One who would lead the united world government—the great teacher, communicator, political leader, and statesman of vision and destiny . . . the Master's appointed oracle.

The conviction had lately been growing upon him that perhaps *he* would be that one. All prophets had to develop their greatness. Why might not *he* grow into that hallowed role? Perhaps *he* was Lord Maitreya, and was even now being prepared for his eventual reign.

He would prove himself worthy! He would carry out his every charge to perfection. Then *he* would become the Man of Peace, avatar, spokesman for unity to whom the world would gaze with acclaim and adoration and to whom it would look as its new millennial global leader.

Who could tell, perhaps the Council of Twelve would soon be informed of his prophetic destiny.

Why else would his colleagues have imbued him with such authority, given him unlimited financial resources? What else could mean their assurances that when the time came he would be given *complete* preeminence over this one nation, which would rise in prominence as nucleus of all the world's nations.

(2)

Zorin's assignment on behalf of the Council had been simple: Consolidate power in Azerbaydzhan.

This he had already well accomplished on a diversity of levels. He had coordinated building programs to establish the necessary infrastructure from which to govern a global confederation. He had quietly imported the technology for a communications network extending worldwide. He had gathered about him a loyal network of subordinates, experts in every field imaginable, capable of instantaneous and unquestioned obedience.

Now he only need wait for the right moment to seize command. Control, when the time came, must be complete.

President Voroshilov, a mere temporary figurehead, would step down. Elections would be held. Zorin's victory would be assured. No hint of autocracy would mar his reputation. When the time came for the world to see him and know him, the very name *Zorin* would ring in the ears of one and all as the epitome of new-world leadership.

He was working on a book—he had not yet divulged this fact to the Council—that would outline his proposals for the new order: *Peace in the New Age: A Humanist Global Manifesto for Unity.*

Prepared simultaneously in fifty languages, he would see that it was ready to flood world markets at precisely the moment of his election, shining the spotlight of international prominence upon him.

He would rise overnight to eclipse the president of the United States, the U.N. secretary-general, even the pope, in prestige, popularity, and influence. The mantel of cosmic messiah would gradually come to rest upon him.

Baku would likewise eclipse Zurich, London, and Amsterdam as banking centers. At the appointed time, all the world's major financial institutions, which their own people controlled, would transfer headquarters and communications systems here. Other businesses would follow. Soon all major stock-market activity would also originate in Baku. New York, Rio, London, Rome, Moscow, Hong Kong, Tokyo would all revolve around this global center.

Toward all these ends, he was quietly seeing to construction of an airport more vast and modern than Denver's and a high-tech subway system connecting the heart of the city with the outlying districts being developed into housing and office complexes. A completely revamped system of roads and highways was under way, with an upgrading of the harbor. Dozens of modern superstructures capable of housing embassies, banks, brokerage firms, communications organizations, and multinational corporate headquarters of every conceivable type and size were being planned. Many were already under construction, extending out from the heart of the city as far as ten miles.

He was, in short, preparing Baku to become a city capable of supporting 2 million inhabitants by the end of the first decade of the new age.

He was also quietly consolidating military force to ensure that Gruziya's coastline gave Azerbaydzhan naval and shipping prowess equal to its preeminent role in the new-age order. Already he was designing highways and high-speed rail systems that would link the two coasts straight through Tbilisi. It was true that Georgia had no large natural harbor on the Black Sea. But he would create one after union between the two republics was assured.

To the scrutinizing eye, an observer might well have wondered why such vast development was taking place in Baku, of all places. Which was precisely why he wanted no outside scrutinizing eyes peering about.

The men and women of Azerbaydzhan asked no questions. Long under the thumb of Moscow, they were generally a backward, obedient people. They were satisfied to be told that such things were an inherent component of freedom. Capitalism meant growth. No one here wanted for anything, in stark contrast to many of the former Soviet republics. Work was plentiful, wages were high. *Why* it was all happening, they neither knew nor cared. Communism had left one enduring legacy—most of its former citizens did not possess a highly developed sense of curiosity. Little did they dream that their tiny nation would rendezvous with the new age to come.

As he reflected on the future and his determinative role in it, Zorin's face bore the countenance of power and command. For such had he been selected by those who determined such things, and the choice had not been without merit. The psychic light from Zorin's countenance was surely a sign confirming his lofty role in the order to come.

Eyes of deep gray, almost black, shone out of a face rough-hewn but handsome, its features strong, its skin only slightly darkened in indication of Middle Eastern blood somewhere in the lineage, though in most respects the image was consistent with his Azerbaijani and Slavic roots. Thick lips, a wide mouth, well-set visible teeth, and high cheekbones all combined to enhance the image of force, vitality, and supremacy. He had indeed been well chosen, for he was a man of imposing stature and carriage who would command attention wherever he went. Thick hair of pure black came down slightly over a modest forehead. It was a face full of expression. The eyebrows, likewise thick and black, accentuated the eyes to yet greater dramatic effect.

More often these days, however, the forehead and heavy brows creased in mounting impatience over the Council's reluctance to impose the new order with greater dispatch. The new millennium was nearly here. It was time!

They said they must await orders. Wisdom from the Secret Dimension must speak. They must allow The Plan steadily, slowly, silently to unfold. Infiltration must progress by degrees. The transfer of the seat of authority to Baku was but one aspect in a vastly more far-reaching strategy of world control.

Zorin had heard it all. Yet ambition had risen up within him. In this he was not unlike another disciple of long ago, whose role was likewise pivotal in bringing a new age to the world in a way he had never anticipated.

Zorin was devoted to the ancient Wisdom of the Babylonian Dimension. But in his view, circumstances could not be more fortuitous. Signs of the holy number were all about. The light of the Millennial Dawn already brightened the cosmic horizon.

The new age was nearly come! Why did the Council continue to drag its feet?

He wanted to move. All was in place. They could be ready within a year, two at the most. If he nudged things along, the other eleven were certain to follow.

(3)

When Adam's new houseguest had been at Sevenoaks several days, he requested a meeting with the Livingstone research team.

Though the pall from Erin's death gradually lifted, each recognized that life at the estate would never be the same. The tears had mostly dried. It was time to move forward. McCondy, however, inisisted that no one remain oblivious to potential dangers that may lurk ahead.

"How much Mr. Livingstone wants to tell you is up to him," the American began. "All I want you to know is that the bomb that killed your friend *missed* its mark. So there may be more incidents. No way to know what kind. You all check out clean, so I got no problems with any of you staying on—for now."

"What do you mean—check out clean?" asked Scott.

"I've been compiling files on everyone in the house—"

"You've been investigating us?" said Livingstone's assistant with incredulity.

"I suppose that's about the size of it."

A few glances and shifting eyebrows went about the room.

"It can't be helped, Mr. Jordan," the detective added. "If I'm going to get to the bottom of this, I've got to know everything I can about everyone. But none of you need to worry—like I say, you all check out clean."

"You did say *for now*. What exactly do you mean by *that*, Mr. McCondy?" asked Adam.

"I always keep sniffing around."

"Would you care to explain," said Jen, more than a little annoyed. "Are you going to be looking over our shoulders every time we do something?"

"Let's just say sometimes people have connections even they don't know they have. Mr. Livingstone had one with me he knew nothing about. That's what I mean. I won't be looking over your shoulders exactly. But I'll keep trying to spot those connections. I'll keep looking for threads dangling around— loose ends, we call them. I've got my eyes peeled for links going anywhere. Who's to say some loose end might not involve one of you down the road."

"I don't like the sound of it," said Jen.

"That's why I'm telling you all this straight," the detective went on. "If you're afraid, I'd suggest you talk to your boss. It could get worse before it gets better. That's all I got to say. Any questions?"

He glanced around the room, then rose to leave.

"Thank you, Mr. McCondy," said Adam. "We're all very appreciative of what you're doing."

(4)

"Whew!" sighed Crystal when the door closed behind the American. "I'm not so sure I like him."

"Me either," agreed Jen. "He gives me the spooks."

"Don't worry. I did call my old friend at Scotland Yard. McCondy's a real pro," Adam said. "And he's only trying to be thorough. He's doing what he can to help us return to a normal routine as safely as possible. And that reminds me . . . I hired a new laboratory technician yesterday. Her name is Emily Stevens. She even passes detective McCondy's approval."

"Three cheers for that," laughed Scott. "I've never been grilled with so many questions in my life!"

"Isn't that the truth," added Crystal.

"He's only trying to protect us," said Adam. "I trust him. The more he can learn to trust us, the better off we'll be. Please be patient with him—and cooperative. Don't forget, Erin is dead. If he's right and we haven't seen the last of the trouble, his thoroughness just may save one of our lives."

"When will we meet this Emily?" asked Jen.

"She'll be here tomorrow."

"Who is she?"

"A graduate student at Kings in London. I conducted some interviews there this week and received recommendations from a couple professors. She is supposed to know her stuff."

"You want me to get the paperwork started?" asked Crystal, opening the employment file. "Full time . . . or what?"

"Four hours a day to start. When she comes, you and Jen show her around, acquaint her with the work up here. Then I'll take her downstairs and have her run a few tests and familiarize herself with the laboratory and our procedures. Scott, you're still looking into the replacements to our computer system?"

"Right—I'm heading into the city today."

"Good, we need to get our files transferred, re-create what we've lost, and establish new backups. Talk to Mr. McCondy. I want him comfortable with any moves of that nature we make."

Scott nodded.

"There is much to do before we can take off for Africa," Adam sighed.

The intercom sounded. It was Beeves.

"Inspector Saul at the door for you, sir," said the butler.

"Tell him I'll be right down."

Adam left the office and walked quickly downstairs.

"Good morning, Max," he said to his longtime acquaintance.

"Sorry to bother you, Mr. Livingstone," said the inspector, "but I thought you ought to know. That blighter that knew your young lady—"

"Right . . . Dexter."

"Turns out his name was Dexter Caine, sir. The chaps at the shop where he worked identified him—though I don't believe you know this yet either, Mr. Livingstone. Seems the manager of the shop's flown the coop now too."

"What about young Caine, Max?"

"Body found this morning, sir—floating in the Thames, washed up under the pilings at Canary Wharf on the Isle of Dogs. It was . . . a broken neck."

"Argh, this is a grisly affair, Max. Any leads?"

"None, sir."

"Well, thanks for the news. Keep me posted. By the by, how's my American friend hitting it off with the brass down at the Yard?"

Inspector Saul smiled. "No one's too keen on privates, sir—least of all Yanks. Word is Captain Thurlow owes someone in Boston—past favors, you know how it is, sir—so we've all been ordered to give your man McCondy anything he asks for."

Adam laughed. "He does seem to have a way of getting what he wants!"

"Ain't such a bad bloke, once you get used to him, though, is he, Mr. Livingstone?"

"No, Max—not such a bad bloke at all."

✦ ✦ ✦

Meanwhile down in the kitchen, before his planned excursion to Scotland Yard, the subject of everyone's discussion was rummaging about when the housekeeper walked in.

"Where's that jar of coffee, Mrs. Graves?" McCondy asked. "I can't find it anyplace."

She opened a cupboard and handed it to him.

He took it with a grimace. "Don't you have a Starbucks anywhere in England?" he said in jest.

"Star what, Mr. McCondy?"

"Never mind, Mrs. Graves—just a brief hallucination. Right now I'd settle for Folgers!"

(5)

Midway through the morning, Adam encountered Mrs. Graves and Juliet on their way across the back lawn to the garage.

"Where are the two of you off to?" he asked.

"I'm taking Juliet to the station," replied the housekeeper.

"Off on a holiday?" said Adam, turning to Juliet.

"No, just into the city for the day."

"Shopping?"

"My mum called last evening. I have to sign some papers at the solicitor's—something about the house."

"It's too bad you couldn't go in with Mr. McCondy—he left a couple hours ago."

"I don't mind taking the train. Besides I'm meeting a college friend for tea."

"When will you be returning?"

"I don't know—later this afternoon," replied Juliet.

"Pick a time and tell me where you'll be—I'll bring you back. I've got to return some things to the British Museum."

"Oh, I couldn't ask you to do that, Mr. Livingstone." Juliet began to show her embarrassment, as much from her aunt's presence as Adam's offer.

"You didn't ask, Miss Halsay. It was my suggestion. I've been needing to get to that errand anyway. I insist. When will you be through with your business?"

"I suppose three or four," answered Juliet.

"I'll be at the Westminster Abbey Bookstore at 3:45," said Adam. "I'll wait for you there."

Sensing quiet disapproval, Juliet glanced toward her aunt with a shrug and sheepish smile as Adam walked off toward the house, as if to say, "What else could I do, Auntie? He insisted."

At 3:40 that afternoon, Adam parked on Great College Street just off Abingdon. He walked toward the great abbey, glancing up at the houses of Parliament on his right. Juliet and another young woman were just emerging from the bookstore as he approached along the walk. Juliet looked taller than usual because her friend was especially short.

Adam paused his step, observing his housekeeper's niece with interest. Juliet was laughing gaily, then handed her friend something. Her demeanor struck

Adam as curious. She somehow appeared as a different person outside the confines of his estate. Here she was in the middle of the loud and busy city, at ease and happy, not subdued and tentative as she always seemed before. He continued on, and a moment later Juliet saw him walking toward them.

She waved.

"Perfect timing, I would say," remarked Adam with a smile. "I hope you haven't had to wait long."

"We've only been here a moment," replied Juliet. "I wanted to give my friend a book. I'd told her about it last year. Jane, meet Mr. Livingstone. Mr. Livingstone . . . Jane Simmons."

They shook hands, the girl obviously embarrassed. Juliet and Jane said good-bye as they parted.

"What book, if I may ask, Miss Halsay?" asked Adam as they turned and began walking back toward Adam's car.

"A fairy tale about a lion and a witch."

"A children's book?"

"A fairy tale, Mr. Livingstone—by C. S. Lewis."

"I've heard of him, but never actually read anything by him."

"I first read it when I was a girl. But I've recently been reading it again. Now I suspect it may actually be more for grown-ups."

"Sounds fascinating," rejoined Adam. They reached the car and got in.

The conversation flowed freely as they made their way through congested afternoon traffic out of the city toward the southeast.

"Did you get your business all settled?" asked Adam.

Juliet nodded. "It was only a few papers to sign that were neglected before."

"How is your mother doing—she's in Bedford?"

"Yes, with my other aunt. She's doing fine, though I think recovering is more difficult for her."

"Do you and she have plans to live together again?"

"When we can—when I get a job," replied Juliet. "My mum's never worked."

"Neither has mine!" laughed Adam. "But that doesn't stop her from being busier than any ten people."

"What do you mean?" asked Juliet.

"My mother, bless her soul, is what might be called a benefactress if we were of the aristocrisy. But since we're not, she is simply a humanitarian who travels throughout the world trying to do good. Sometimes I wonder if her ceaseless activity is more for other people or for herself. All I can do is smile at her adventures. She mixes a playful spirit with her compassion."

"I thought you *were* a titled family, Mr. Livingstone."

"Oh, no. My father was a businessman, not an aristocrat."

"In what kind of business?"

"Imports. He travelled all over the world purchasing interesting things from exotic places to supply London's specialty import shops. He made a great deal of money quite rapidly. He was actually quite a wealthy man by the time he was thirty. Then he died suddenly in India—I was sixteen at the time—and my dear mum has spent the last eighteen years doing her best to give away her husband's fortune."

Adam could not help laughing at his own characterization of his mother.

"Is the estate a family property?" Juliet asked.

"No to that question too. We'd actually only moved out to Sevenoaks from north of London three years before my father died. That may explain why my mother was never very attached to the place. As soon as my father was gone, so was she—off gallivanting about the world in the peace corps, on cruises, climbing mountains, on jungle safaris, helping to build orphanages, involved with disaster relief. My sister had left even before that, so I was basically left with the house and estate myself."

"I didn't know you had a sister—older or younger?"

"Two years older. I'm the baby!" laughed Adam.

"You were alone at the house at sixteen?"

"I was just starting at Cambridge. For the next several years Mrs. Graves and Beeves, with help from the family solicitor, kept the house going. After I was through with my schooling I was old enough to begin assuming more responsibility for it. By then I realized how much I really loved it at Sevenoaks."

"But you travel a good deal, don't you?"

"I do. But having a place to call home is what makes travelling tolerable. And of course I've got to have a place for my offices and research."

"What does your sister do?" asked Juliet.

Adam sighed. "I don't know," he answered slowly. "She's not really in touch with us. She didn't even come back for Dad's funeral. She's in her own world—I don't even know what she's doing now. I've seen her only two or three times briefly in all those years. We're not a very homogeneous family, are we?"

"After what I've been through recently," said Juliet, "I'm beginning to wonder if any family is."

"Good point. Everyone loves my mother, and I've stopped trying to figure her out. I do sometimes wish," he added with a laugh, "that she would leave a little of Dad's money for me. It complicates my work to always have to think about fund-raising, though I'm not complaining. I've been most fortunate. But Mum seems determined to give away every farthing before she dies."

"What about your sister?"

"She wants nothing from either of us. She's happy with her bohemian lifestyle and wouldn't touch a penny of Mum's money if it fell into her lap."

"So the estate is yours?"

"Technically, all three of our names are on it—mine, Mum's, and Claresta's. But both the others seem content for me to treat it as my own, though I'd certainly welcome them anytime. Dad left a small trust to help maintain it. But I'm generally dependent on outside sources for my income."

They continued to talk easily with one another. The hour's drive seemed but a few minutes, and suddenly they found themselves approaching the gate to the estate.

(6)

Lord Montreux was the last person Adam expected to hear when he picked up the telephone shortly after his return to Sevenoaks.

"Livingstone, my boy," said Candace's father, "I wanted personally to extend my condolences on the affair concerning your laboratory girl."

"Thank you, Lord Montreux. That is very kind of you."

"Are you and your people recovering?"

"We are managing to get back to normal, though something like that is always difficult to put behind you."

"I understand. If there is anything I can do, you must call."

"Thank you, sir."

"Candace is very concerned. She fears you may be working too hard."

Adam laughed lightly. "No fear of that. My work invigorates me."

"Perhaps it is time you give thought to widening your horizons."

"I'm not sure I follow you, sir."

"I would like you to attend a dinner with me in the city next week. If you and I are going to spend the rest of our lives as father and son, then it seems time I brought you a little more into my world. I think it might open your eyes to a great many things."

"What sort of dinner?" asked Adam, reflecting that Candace's father had apparently based a great deal on his own statement during their luncheon together.

"Let me just say that many highly influential people will be in attendance who have a great interest in you. You are a respected man. They want to meet you."

"People—what people?"

"Members of an order to which I belong."

"I doubt that I—"

"I know you would find it most intriguing and no doubt beneficial to your research. Your name has come before us, and many of the normal premembership requirements have already been waived. You have been approved. It is a great honor, I assure you."

"I have no doubt. But it seems doubtful I would fit in."

"Some of the most well-known names in England will be in attendance."

"I appreciate your kindness, Lord Montreux, but truthfully, I have no interest in joining a secret order."

"This is hardly just *any* order, Livingstone."

"Nevertheless, I am afraid I must respectfully decline. I am far too busy to take on such an additional commitment."

"Would you attend the dinner with me, then—simply as my guest? It would mean a great deal to me . . . and to Candace."

"I'm sorry, Lord Montreux—I really must say no."

Lord Montreux could find no suitable reply without revealing his annoyance. Instead he handed the phone to Candace, who was standing by waiting for her opportunity.

"Hello, Adam," she said in a silky tone.

"Candace, how are you?" said Adam, doing his best to sound upbeat.

"I don't know. Perhaps you should tell me. Daddy doesn't look pleased. What did you say to him, Adam?"

"I'm sorry, Candace. He invited me to a dinner that I simply have no interest in attending. Please convey to him that it is certainly nothing personal."

"Why don't you want to go, Adam?"

"It's just not the kind of thing I'm interested in."

"What are you interested in?"

"What kind of question is that?" laughed Adam. "You should know well enough. I'm interested in my work."

"Arks and mythical gardens! It's all so stuffy. People are going to talk if you're not careful. You can't get *too* interested in all that religious tomfoolery."

"What if there's more truth to it than we realize?"

"It's all nonsense."

"I'm not so sure."

"Oh, Adam, don't *say* such things. You're going to ruin everything!"

"What are you talking about—ruin what?"

"Oh . . . never mind. I just wish you'd stay away from it, that's all. It's dangerous. People don't like it. I want to be the wife of a respected man, not—" she hesitated, realizing she was about to say more than she intended—"oh, just never mind."

"A truth seeker?"

"That isn't what I was going to say."

"I *want* to be a truth seeker, Candace."

The phone was silent a moment.

"I'm sorry to have upset you, Candace," said Adam at length. "It seems I have offended two Montreux with one telephone call. Would you give me the chance to make it up to you over lunch tomorrow?"

A long pause followed, after which Candace sullenly consented.

(7)

Lord Montreux sat across the room puffing violently on a cigar as he waited for Candace to conclude the call. He was still inwardly fuming. He was not accustomed to being refused. The man was proving more difficult than he had anticipated.

Candace set down the receiver and briefly recounted what Adam had said.

"We *must have him,*" mumbled her father. "The situation grows perilous."

Candace was in no mood to talk. She left the room.

A minute more Lord Montreux sat thinking, then rose and went upstairs to his study. He picked up his private phone. The number he punched in was for the continent and highly confidential. Only eleven others in the world had access to it.

He left a brief message, then waited.

Five minutes later, the phone rang.

"Yes . . . that is correct," he said after a brief exchange of greetings.

"Does a chance remain of changing his mind?" asked the other.

"His reply to my offer was emphatic."

"Might he suspect?"

"I sense no indication. He is an independent thinker, that is all."

"That trait begins to pose a greater danger than we may have realized. And your daughter?"

"She is making no more inroads than I. The alliance that seemed assured but a short time ago now grows tenuous. He now openly comments on the religious notions that seem beginning to preoccupy him."

"We may have delayed too long. It appears the time for stronger measures has come. It becomes imperative that he be turned."

"What can account for the change?"

"He is being lured away. The Dimension is alive with disturbances."

"Yes, and Livingstone appears at the center of them. I remain hopeful his affection for the girl will win out over this nonsense. I will continue to do what I can."

"We will meet with the Council soon."

(8)

Mrs. Graves walked into the kitchen, which she was accustomed to considering her private domain, several mornings later a little after six-thirty. For several moments she could not fathom what it was she was witnessing.

The large form of their houseguest hunched over the counter near the sink. Only his back was visible. He held something in his right hand, though she could not make out what. He was stooped over as if ill.

"Mr. McCondy," she said hesitantly, "is everything all right?"

"Never better!" replied the detective, straightening himself and turning to face her. "Come, come, Mrs. Graves," he said enthusiastically, motioning her closer. "Give your nose the feast of a lifetime!"

Cautiously she approached.

Meanwhile, he continued the delicate operation, which consisted in gently pouring boiling water from a small saucepan over a makeshift filter comprised of two paper towels, in the center of which swam grounds of a Colombian French Roast he had purchased at the market in the town. Underneath, the anticipated brew dripped slowly into the most appropriate container he had been able to find for the procedure, a stray glass beaker from the lab downstairs.

"For a man to be away from his coffeemaker is a sorry state of affairs, Mrs. Graves," he said. "But there are always ways to improvise. I've had to concoct some ingenious methods in my time. But if it works, what matter how you got there—right! Bring your nostrils over that and tell me it isn't the aroma of heaven!"

Mrs. Graves approached as close as she dared, took two or three tentative whiffs, gave a look of disinterest that also conveyed that she was more than a little concerned for the man's sanity, then backed away.

"I'm sorry, Mr. McCondy—it is not to my liking. I'm a tea drinker and an Englishwoman through and through."

"I'll forgive you on both counts, Mrs. Graves!" he laughed. "All a matter of individual preference, I suppose."

Not altogether appreciating his attempted humor, she continued to observe the strange goings-on, while putting on the pot for her own morning beverage.

At length the beaker was nearly full. The detective allowed the last of the water to drip through, then set the towels and grounds on the counter. As if gazing upon aqua vitae itself, he grasped the container and held it up to the window.

"Ah, the hue of steaming coffee is a thing of beauty, is it not!" he exclaimed with wondrous pride in the liquid he had created. Again he drew it to his nostrils and breathed in deeply. He located a cup and now poured himself a full measure of the dark pungent brew from the beaker. He now raised the cup to the window, as if toasting the powers of the sun itself to create such a marvel.

"I never thought I would say it," he said, "but Juan Valdez, I salute you!"

He lifted the cup to his lips, probed at the edge briefly, then took a lusty swallow, closing his eyes with unabashed pleasure.

"Starbucks you ain't, Juan, my friend!" he said, "but in a pinch—oh yeah! That's good!"

Two more swallows emptied the cup, and he poured himself another.

"Well, Mrs. Graves," he said with a smile, "it may turn out that England is not such a cultural wasteland after all!"

She found these words no more humorous than she had his former comment.

That same moment Adam walked in.

"It smells wonderful in here!" he exclaimed.

"Just what I was telling Mrs. Graves," replied the American. "Doesn't your man Jordan drink coffee?"

"He's usually got a Coke in his hand, and occasionally he'll join me for tea.

But no, I don't think he's particularly fond of coffee. What will you be about today, Mr. McCondy?"

"Enough of the mister stuff. You Brits are too formal for a Yankee like me. You've got to call me Rocky from now on, or I will go crazy."

Adam laughed. "All right, Rocky, what do you have planned for today?"

"I'll going into the Yard again—see if I can borrow some equipment."

"I have friends there if you need any more strings pulled. Although I understand they're rolling out the red carpet for you."

"Not exactly," rejoined the detective. "There are still odd looks and glances and an occasional reminder of good old English standoffishness. No cop anywhere is overly fond of private eyes. But they're cooperating, that's what matters. And one or two of them are downright agreeable gents."

"Be sure to give whatever you discover to Inspector Saul. He's been in charge of the case here. I've no doubt he'll reciprocate."

(9)

"General Pervukhin!" said a voice of command. "Is your schedule still free as per our previous discussion?"

"At your convenience, Mr. Zorin."

"Thank you, General," replied the interior minister. "My limousine will be in the parking garage under your building in twenty minutes. I shall await you there. We will drive to my villa together."

Zorin hung up the phone, poured himself half an inch of scotch, downed it in one gulp, walked to his desk where he picked up several files, then strolled to the window, perusing the top one casually.

He already had high-ranking contacts in Georgia representing industry, finance, transportation, communications, the media, and, of course, the military. By the time he made his move, he would have the entire population in the neighboring republic begging for unification with Azerbaydzhan.

Even at this moment subtle reports flowed steadily into Georgia about the land of wealth and opportunity its eastern neighbor had become. His key individuals kept such news constantly lubricating the dissatisfaction, which would provide him his ultimate success.

There would be no takeover, only a peaceful unification process, at the request of the Georgian republic. It would go off without a hitch, accelerating all the more Azerbaydzhan's rise to ascendancy when the new order came.

Five minutes later Zorin was on his way down the elevator.

He sat behind the one-way glass in his limousine, interior light on, reviewing the two files in more detail when General Pervukhin approached, carrying a thin briefcase. Zorin pushed a button. The rear door opposite him opened. He said nothing. The general climbed in and closed the door. Immediately the limo began to move.

"I was just going over the files for our proposed maneuvers to the north-west, should they become necessary." He handed the files to the general, who looked them over. As long as they had known one another, General Pervukhin cringed inwardly at the sound of Zorin's voice. Its portentous sound grew more commanding with each passing year.

"Do you think it will become necessary, Mr. Zorin?" he asked at length.

"We must be prepared for all contingencies," said the Voice. "Give me a status report on your end, General."

The general did so in brief. Nothing much had changed since their previous meeting.

"I have everything in my files—would you like to see them?" he asked.

"There will be time for that later. All the people you would need are in place?"

The general nodded.

"Good," replied Zorin. "We will go over certain details at the villa. In the meantime, I need someone reliable upon whom I may depend at any time for any duty I may require."

"I am, of course, at your complete service—"

"I do not mean you, General. I need an unknown face, able to move throughout the entire world."

"What kind of person?"

"An individual, shall we say, with a wide range of additional skills."

"Special requirements?" asked the general.

"He or she must speak fluent English. I would prefer an Englishman. However, I must not be visible in the affair."

"I understand, Mr. Zorin. I shall be discreet. He will be responsible to . . ."

"He or she will be answerable directly, and only, to me," replied Zorin with unmistakable meaning. "Cost is no object. I want the best."

"Shall I make the arrangements?"

"When I have a name, I shall handle it personally. I will return to England soon. The initial assignment for which I have need is rather urgent."

(10)

Zorin stood at his large window watching his own limousine wind its way from his villa down the hill toward the bay, carrying General Pervukhin back toward the city.

His request of the general turned his mind toward his thought of a few days earlier to secure someone on the inside, close to Livingstone. He turned, strode to his office, and turned on his computer. A moment later he brought up his files on the archaeologist.

He also possessed complete dossiers on every member of the Council of Twelve. He doubted his colleagues would approve. But he was in a position where knowledge was power. He had no intention of missing anything that might be useful for him to know. A few quick clicks of the keyboard brought the names to the screen.

He stared at it momentarily, then initiated a cross-check with the Livingstone data.

Of course—Baron Rothschild, or Lord Montreux as he was commonly known. There had been talk for some time of involving his daughter in a permanent liason with Livingstone. He had not kept close track of developments on that score. Nor had he met the girl. She must be twenty-three or twenty-four by now.

Quickly he entered the name. A few moments later the monitor filled with a color scan of Candace Montreux.

Zorin stared at it a moment, his lips gradually widening in the hint of a grin. More like twenty-seven or twenty-eight . . . a full grown and very desirable woman—the same woman he had noticed at Buckingham.

So this was the Council's strategy for winning Livingstone over!

It was ingenious. She was dazzling. The computer didn't come close to doing her justice. Why hadn't he paid more attention to this connection before? How long had she been working to infiltrate Livingstone's work? Zorin wondered. Or was she an unknowing accomplice to the Council's scheme?

He stared at the unmoving face a long while, still smiling with cunning.

His eyes probed the screen as if he could divine by telepathy what the young lady might be thinking. He detected in her eyes that which drew him. An inner psychic sense told him that he and she might be useful to one another . . . perhaps even more than merely useful.

So this young lady wanted Livingstone.

So did he. Though in a different way.

It was time he met the good Lord Montreaux's daughter . . . discreetly, of course, and see what they might be able to do for one another.

# thirteen

# Threads of a Dark Conspiracy

(1)

As Adam walked down the corridor about seven-thirty one morning, he heard sounds from inside his staff offices. It was early. None of his team had yet arrived. He opened the door and walked in. There sat Rocky McCondy at the computer desk where he had himself spent many hours. Several contraptions and wires were spread about. The lid of the computer was off, and the detective was probing around inside.

"Hey—morning, Livingstone!" he called out over his shoulder.

"Still suffering from that jet lag, I take it," said Adam.

"It's getting better. I also wanted to get in here before your people arrived. But come here—look what I found."

Adam approached. McCondy held a miniaturized instrument resembling a microphone. Its wire was attached to a small sensing device, whose needle bounced up and down as he moved the probe about inside the computer.

"What in the world—"

"What you're seeing, Livingstone, are trace evidences of explosive. Nothing to worry about. Not enough to detonate, just the faintest residue of the bomb that was placed here."

"Do you know where it was?"

"I figure in your detachable hard drive."

"So the bomb was inside the module unit."

"Yep. This handy little gadget I got from Thurlow is a Geiger counter and dope-sniffing dog rolled into one. It's amazing what technology can do these days. I'll run the unit back into the city this afternoon and have its memory analyzed, just to make sure it's the same explosive the forensics boys found outside."

"Now I'm doubly glad we decided to replace this whole system. When you're finished, we'll dump the entire thing on the scrap heap. I told Scott to talk to you before deciding anything definite on a replacement. What do you think happened?"

"You didn't have it out—in the shop . . . anything like that recently?"

Adam shook his head.

"They must have got to your computer—right here . . . don't ask me how," McCondy went on. "But if a guy knew what he was doing, he could have gotten into your module in thirty seconds, then planted a thin strip of highly specialized plastic explosive connected to a tiny battery to receive an electronic signal. The explosive itself is similar to what they use in letter bombs. Doesn't take much. It's lethal stuff."

"Why didn't it blow up inside?"

"It could have been detonated anytime later."

"You mean . . ."

"Sure, from as far away as a mile or two."

"Who would have set it off? How would they have known *when?*"

"My guess is they probably instigated the crash of your computer and were in cahoots with the shop. They'd have known exactly when you were bringing it in. I don't know—it's guesswork right now. Oh, yeah . . . and look what else I found!"

The detective spun around in his chair and reached across the desk. He handed a circular, flat device approximately half an inch in diameter to Adam.

"There's the bug. It was under the desk here. A scanner I borrowed with this other stuff sniffed it right out. *Someone* has been listening in on every word that's been said in this office."

Adam slumped into a chair.

"It makes you feel . . . violated, somehow," he sighed. "The thought that someone we don't even know is . . . right here with us. But what about—," he added suddenly.

"Not to worry. I disarmed it. I'll take it to the Yard to be analyzed too. Pretty high-tech, that much I know. Never seen one like it. This little baby might have been able to pick up conversations even through walls, for all I know—even in your study."

Adam shuddered at the thought.

"One thing for sure," McCondy added, "money's behind this, which confirms my earlier suspicions. You can bet they haven't stopped. With your permission, I'd like to search the rest of the house."

"Yes . . . yes, of course."

"Another interesting thing—your Inspector Saul told me the residue they found from their analysis is from an explosive that was never used in England before last summer."

"That explains why they've been conducting so many tests on the stones outside," said Adam.

"It's sophisticated stuff, like what some of those groups use on the continent. But the IRA's never used it. That's one of the things that has them baffled. Well,

I got as much as I need. I'm going to wrap it up here and get this stuff back to the Yard.

That same afternoon, Rocky sat in Captain Thurlow's office with an open file folder in his lap, looking over the records from last summer's bombing in front of Buckingham.

"It's got us all a bit puzzled, and that's a fact," Thurlow was saying. "You can see the evidence right there—though it makes no sense I can think of."

Rocky stood and handed him the file.

"Thanks, Captain," he said. "Livingstone will have a hard time swallowing this!"

(2)

When Rocky returned to Sevenoaks, he immediately sought Adam to tell him what he had learned. He found him outside near the garage at the back of the house, talking with Beeves. Adam saw Rocky's approach and excused himself.

"You know that explosion in the city a few months back," said Rocky as they walked off together, "the one you told me killed the father and brother of your housekeeper's niece?"

Adam nodded.

"Traces of the *same* explosive from that bombing were found in your computer and outside in front of your house. When it showed up again here, the Yard didn't know what to make of it."

"What could possibly be the connection?"

"No one at the Yard can make anything of it either. No one knows how they tie together. I suppose this explosive is the new favorite for terrorists."

It fell silent as Adam puzzled over the detective's words.

"Would you come upstairs to my study?" Adam said after a moment. "I want to ask a few more questions about this whole thing."

They comfortably seated themselves a few minutes later. Adam spoke first.

"I am still baffled," he began, "about this conspiracy you speak of. You say they have a religious orientation—I should say *anti*religious. For the life of me, I cannot see what interest these people you're talking about or any of them has to do with *me*. I've never made any bones about being a religious sort of man. I've never engaged in anything to sway public opinion, to make people believe one thing or another."

"It's your *work*."

"Archaeology?"

"More than that. Your *recent* work. My guess is that your discovery of the ark triggered something—something deep and far-reaching that threatened their world."

"People have been looking for the ark for years. Why me . . . why now?"

173

"Because you found it. And because Eden is next on your agenda. The two are connected."

Adam recalled his own revelations of early that fateful morning, the information he'd lost and since mentally discarded. He'd been thinking that the ark possessed the key on that day too—though a different key than Rocky was talking about.

"There's no doubt about one thing," McCondy added, "my great-grandfather's research got him killed. The same people are out to stop you."

"How was he killed?"

"Don't know," McCondy replied, shaking his head. "Actually, all that's known for sure is that he disappeared. But I *know* he was murdered."

"That was a hundred years ago."

"The faces change. The motives don't. Believe me, Livingstone, these forces in the world will stop at nothing to prevent certain truths from getting out—truths my great-grandfather was close to finding. They may fear you are about to finish what he began."

"It still all seems . . . unbelievable."

"Once you understand what's going on, it won't seem so incredible. My great-grandfather *knew* things, important things. You never realized the ramifications of his work. You never knew what you'd stumbled into. You ever figure out what was in that paper?"

"I've been racking my brain trying to remember. Your talk of your Grandpa Harry and Sinai has triggered something in my subconscious about it. As I recall, he had a theory of some kind . . . something about an alternate site for the Red Sea crossing and for the location of Mount Sinai . . . never verified and laughed down by most Old Testament scholars. I remember no details. But I may have mentioned it in my paper."

McCondy nodded with deep interest. "That raises some interesting possibilities." He thought for a moment. "You want to hear my theory?" he asked.

"Of course."

"It's just an attempt to piece it together at this point. But we've got to start someplace. All right—the way I've got it figured is something like this," McCondy began. "Grandpa Harry discovered something, or was about to discover something that would have struck a serious blow to their cause. Maybe it had to do with that Sinai thing."

"What *cause?*"

"Evolution, humanism, their new-age world plan. Though the words may have been different back then. So they got rid of him. But they kept a close watch to make sure no one else picked up where he left off. Let's say, just for the sake of argument that they've been keeping an eye out for a resurfacing of his theories all these years—this whole century. Then all of a sudden you come along and write a paper on Harry McCondy. That probably got their attention. It might not have been anything in your paper itself, but just your interest in him. Maybe you *did* inadvertantly put your finger on something—we don't know. We'd have to see the paper to know that. It's my guess they've got it now—and we may never find out when or how they pilfered it from your file. Somebody who's connected to them has been in your house, that's for sure. So we may never get the chance to read it. In any case, that probably got you into their system, back when you were in school."

"You honestly think they've been . . . *watching* me all this time?"

"You bet I do. One of their symbols is the all-seeing eye—they use all sorts of secret symbolism. But the eye is most significant of all. They *watch* everyone."

McCondy paused and pulled out his wallet. He opened it and took out a bill and handed it to Adam.

"Look—right there on the U.S. dollar bill. Do you see the eye above the pyramid?"

"Yes—it's right there in plain view."

"Two symbols of the new age. They were active and in control as far back as the founding of our country, though it wasn't called *New Age* back then. Different terms have been applied to it through the years, but it's all part of the same plan. Wouldn't surprise me if some of their symbols are on your British money too, though I've never thought to look. Look under the pyramid—see that banner?"

Adam nodded.

"Can you read the words?"

*"Novus Ordo Seclorum,"* Adam read aloud.

"How well do you know your Latin?"

"Well enough," replied Adam, "new secular order."

"Their plan is as ancient as the Pyramids and the founding of my country. Those symbols have been on U.S. money since 1782!"

"Does everyone know?"

"Very few have a clue," laughed Rocky. "Take a guess, Livingstone, who designed our money?"

"I have no idea."

"Charles Thompson, a Mason, one of the most secret of all the societies. It's all connected, I tell you. So to answer your question—yes, I think they've been watching you. *Everyone's* in their system—but your interest in my greatgrandfather probably high-profiled you all the more. And then your own research later began moving in similar directions as those that had made them so paranoid back in the 1890s. *You* didn't know that. But maybe they *thought* you did. Then you went and got famous—then they were *really* watching you. Somehow they got hold of your paper out of your files, and that solidified the link with Grandpa Harry.

"But it keeps getting worse—because then you actually found Noah's ark! Then you started talking about the Garden of Eden and stirring up the hornet's nest of their world all the more—that's when they decided to get deadly serious about you, like they did Grandpa Harry. That's when you set, as I called it, the invisible time bomb ticking away. It was only a matter of time before they would try to stop you."

(3)

Mark Stafford had been feeling uncomfortable all day. It had been difficult to keep his mind on his work. The uneasiness grew throughout the evening, though without revealing its cause. He tried to read a few psalms before retiring, but his brain was distracted.

Between three and four in the morning he suddenly woke from a sound sleep.

The face of Rocky McCondy filled his mind. He knew immediately why he had been awakened. His friend needed prayer.

He wasted no time in rising. He put on his robe and slippers and walked into the living room so as not to disturb his wife. He turned on no lamp. Such was not the kind of light required for the business now at hand.

Stafford slipped to his knees beside the couch.

"Father," he prayed in a scarcely audible voice, "I lift up Rocky McCondy into the protection of your presence."

They were the only words necessary for the moment. He had obeyed the summons. Now the Spirit would pray through him when the time came.

Mark Stafford could not know the extent of the battle he had just joined. He was well acquainted with its gravity through countless frontline skirmishes. He was sufficiently aware of the times to realize that all God's praying men and women in these crucial times were no mere believers . . . but warriors. He had taken up the armor years before with seriousness and devotion.

He was one of the few, in the words of his Master, who had watched and had learned the lesson of the fig tree, and who thus apprehended the signs of the age. He realized that the years were rapidly gathering themselves to a culmination. He knew that the great rift in history, the scar across the human soul between good and evil, was about to widen, in preparation for the coming of him who alone was capable of healing it.

"The time of your coming approaches, Lord," he began again after some moments, whispering, though none other could have heard the words. "Time is short. The curtain draws down upon the present age. The enemy is at work, even as you are at work. Eternity hangs in the balance within the heart of every man and every woman.

"Rocky has now entered that battle, heavenly Father. The dear man is hardly more than a babe, yet so precious in your sight. Keep him in your care, Lord, as well as the man he went to see. Protect them both, Lord. Surround them with your love. Hedge them about with angels to guard their steps and *their thoughts. Guide them into your wisdom, as they seek you in the work for which you have chosen them.*

*"In whatever paths you have for them to walk, go before them. Make the way straight. Speak your will, your wisdom, your guidance into their hearts and minds. For whatever purpose you have appointed them during these days of high and eternal import, keep the enemy from thwarting your plan.*

*"Accomplish your perfect purpose through them both, Lord God. Be Father to them. Cause them to look up and apprehend your face, to seek the Father-hood of your ever-present love deep within their beings. Let them know what it means to walk with you in the cool of the day. Walk beside them, Lord Jesus. Let them feel the strength of your abiding Spirit dwelling within their hearts."*

The prayers drifted into silent expressions of praise.

A few moments later shuffling footsteps sounded behind him.

He glanced up. It was his wife, Laurene, approaching from the bedroom. She knelt down beside him on the floor.

"I hope I didn't disturb you," said Mark. "I tried not to wake you."

"You didn't," she said. "I heard nothing when you got up. The Lord woke me a minute ago with the strongest sense that I was to pray. Then I saw that you were gone."

"I've been here praying for Rocky."

"Something's going on, isn't it—something in the heavenlies. I can feel the battle strongly in my spirit."

"I think the time we have long anticipated may be rapidly approaching." Mark nodded. "I have a sense that the Lord is raising up his praying saints the world over to wage war against the enemy."

"Why Rocky? . . . Why tonight?"

"I don't know. I woke up with the strong sensation that I was to pray for him. Somehow I have the feeling that he is squarely in the midst of the battle."

"He is so new at all this, at walking as a man of God."

"Perhaps, but he is utterly obedient. Nothing matters so much in the kingdom as that. Besides, God's choice of vessels is for reasons beyond the ken of man's eyes. And I think Rocky may now be on the front lines."

(4)

As that prayer concluded, a thousand miles away Adam Livingstone sat shaking his head in disbelief as he listened to his new American friend.

"I tell you, there are no secrets from these people," Rocky was saying. "With the Internet and all the other global means of access and communications, they can get into anyone's computer files. Every house with a telephone and modem has an open access line straight into their information vault. No one is safe from their eyes. It's not merely collecting information, it's influence. That's why traditionally it's been financial and media people who've occupied the highest levels. That enables them to control whole economies. They there-fore sway governments and thus dictate how people think. Why do you think the West has become a post-Christian, amoral, atheistic civilization?"

"You're saying they've caused it?"

"They control the flow of information that influences people."

"How?"

"The levels of secrecy surrounding their motives and movements are all but impenetrable. But we see the results all around us—from credit cards to the way banking is done, to the humanist slant given to education, to the inter-pretation of scientific advances—they've got their hands in it all. There's noth-ing in modern society they aren't involved in."

"You make it sound rather frightening."

"It is frightening, Livingstone. But we've got to figure out your connection. And the point is, anything you've been doing, researching, even thinking about on your computer, they probably know all about it."

He paused momentarily.

"That reminds me of something I've been wanting to ask," he said. "Any new data about either the ark or your Eden theories that you entered into your computer recently?"

"Yes, quite a bit, actually," replied Adam. "The morning of the bomb, in fact."

"What was the gist of it?"

"What the Ararat find triggered in my brain—how Eden and the ark might tie together."

"Whew!" exclaimed Rocky, shaking his head. "These people move fast! The morning of the incident?"

Adam nodded.

"That could have been what lit the fuse. If they were monitoring your input, it must have been some dangerous theory you were onto—dangerous for them, I mean. Doggone, I wish we had your paper! You must be intersecting paths with Grandpa Harry's research!"

"I just can't imagine how that could be," said Adam. "I was just a kid when I was researching your great-grandfather."

"Something's ignited a firestorm," rejoined Rocky. "Because after all these years have gone by, all of a sudden—boom!—the proverbial fan. You stuck your foot in it. You got snooping around too close. They couldn't let it go any further. That's when things started to happen. I'm just brainstorming off the top of my head. But that's how I work. I've got to talk through the loose threads until I start to see where the connections are."

McCondy sighed.

"My great-grandfather's work made them very, very nervous." he said. Once again he found himself repeating the facts, as if hearing the words might trigger some new tidbit of information. "So they were watching him and eventually killed him. And now, for better or worse, that same legacy has passed to you. Whatever he was onto, they don't want it revealed. We still don't know the connection between your work and his. But it's there—depend on it. We'll find it eventually."

Again the detective stopped, deep in thought.

"Why have they never come after me all this time?" Rocky mused to himself. "If they were watching you, why weren't they watching me? They had to know I had a record of his work, though come to think of it, even I didn't know, so maybe . . . I don't get it. Why would they steal your paper and not come after what I had?"

Again his voice trailed away, and a thoughtful silence followed.

(5)

"Maybe talking it through like this is helping you piece together the threads," laughed Adam at length. "But you're only confusing me all the more. What was I getting too close to?"

"Genesis, Livingstone—you started snooping around in Genesis! Then all of a sudden a few months ago you set foot right inside the sixth chapter! That's too close for comfort, don't you see?"

"Too close to what?"

"To the beginning. You're getting too close to the beginning of everything!"

"You mean. . . ?"

"I mean the very beginning. Genesis was my great-grandfather's lifework—proving Genesis true. He lived in the era when evolution was hotly debated. He devoted what there was of his life to disproving it. He and Dubois used to be partners, you know."

"I'm well acquainted with the Dutchman's work. Dubois went to the Dutch East Indies in search of the missing link and eventually found the Java man."

"*Homo erectus*—yep, 1891." The detective nodded. "Made him a famous man."

"He and Grandpa Harry split over the evolution controversy. Dubois betrayed him, and the split got Grandpa Harry killed. Precisely how the pieces fit I'm still not sure of. But there's no doubt about the magnitude of the strategy. It's big, Livingstone."

"But we're just two ordinary men sitting here, and you're making it sound like the fate of the world hangs in the balance."

"Sometimes ordinary men and women get caught up in events and causes that do change the course of history. Our being what you call ordinary does not mean there might not be high significance involved. If your research validated evolution," Rocky went on, "you'd have no worries. But your work undermines the humanistic system. That system has grown this century out of an evolutionary foundation and all the subtle implications of godlessness it leads to. Your discoveries threaten to change the way people view the world. The discoveries threaten that evolutionary, humanistic system. And that has immense worldwide significance."

"It's just too incredible to contemplate."

"Livingstone, if you start causing the world to believe in God instead of evolution, you immediately become the number one threat to their whole silent, invisible empire. Proving Genesis true would change the cultural perspective of history more than Darwin's book did. I tell you, you're right between the crosshairs!"

Adam exhaled and shook his head.

"If you make people think about divine origins, your work will undo everything the enemy has worked for centuries to invisibly put into place. Religion as such doesn't threaten them. But applied Christianity does, like I was explaining the difference earlier. If your expedition to Africa is a tenth the success your Ararat discovery was—man, you may be on the verge of proving that the God of the Bible exists and that the earliest portions of Genesis are scientifically and verifiably true. You may not consider yourself a Christian or even a religious man. But whether you like it or not, that is the direction your work is leading."

"But I don't have anything even resembling evidence for a complete theory. I'm merely guessing, hoping—"

"What about the new data you were telling me about? It just may be that you were getting closer than you realize."

"I saved some of it . . . in bits and pieces. I was sloppy and foolishly saved the final work to the hard drive—the one that blew up."

"Can't you re-create it?"

"To tell you the truth, Rocky, I don't remember much of it. My brain was sizzling with new and fantastic ideas. But then Erin's getting killed . . . it was as if along with Erin's life, at the same moment the bomb blew away my new revelations. They didn't seem so important anymore."

"If God was revealing them to you, when he's ready to tell you about it again, it'll come back at just the right time."

"You think your great-grandfather was about to make such a revelation?" asked Adam.

"I don't know exactly what he was onto—he never went to Ararat or got farther into Africa than Egypt as far as I know, so it's not the same work as yours. But there's some connection. Whatever it is, it's a huge one."

(6)

When Candace Montreux stooped down and stepped into the open back door of the limousine that had pulled up beside her, she hardly expected to find herself sliding in beside a man quite so capable of taking her breath away.

The message had been cryptic, though left her little avenue of refusal. Not that she wanted one. Anything to assist in the matter of Adam Livingstone she was eager to explore. For the first instant or two as the limousine slowly pulled away, however, she found her thoughts nowhere near the man she hoped would soon be her fiancé.

She had expected something of a purely business nature. Thus she was altogether unprepared for the suddenly quickening of her pulse and the rush of heat to her head. Candace Montreux was not the sort of woman whose pulse rose for any man, including Adam Livingstone. She was in the habit of turning heads herself, not having hers spun. What love she may have felt for Adam, or thought she felt, lay in another dimension within her being than where originated the fluttering heart of common womankind.

That Candace could probably love there was no doubt. Whether she had actually loved would be another question.

The desire she felt toward Adam was not so much romantic ardor as what might more accurately be called the passion to possess. She would happily turn on the charms of her kind to arouse his passion and would enjoy the ensuing result of his affections. But such feelings were not primarily what drove her. Adam represented not so much man as quarry.

In the merest second or two, all the latent femininity of her nature rushed in upon her. These were feelings she hardly recognized.

Suddenly she felt vulnerable in the presence of a power altogether greater than herself. It was at once delicious and frightening. She both quailed from it and felt herself yielding to it. Adam had never made her feel like this!

It was not love she was experiencing but the force and irresistible lure of raw power. She recognized it as from the same source as her father's. But this was a man so temptingly nearer her own age—in his midforties, she could hardly tell in the subdued light—as to render comparison with her father absurd. It was not mere strength that radiated from his presence but power in the undefinable realm of the occult and mystical. An almost terrifying exhilaration made her tremble, even as she struggled to find breath to respond to his first words.

"Miss Montreux," said the Voice, "how good of you to come." The baritone timbre sent chills down her spine. "I have wanted to meet you personally for some time. I am Halder Zorin."

Rapidly gathering back her wits and hiding the rush of emotions, Candace replied in measured tones. "I am pleased to meet you." She extended her hand in the manner of women who walk in a man's world. But he turned it, and as his eye held hers, lightly kissed it. If she was cowed in Zorin's presence, she was nearly his equal in self-command. She would allow nothing to show. The momentary disadvantage, from which she was quickly recovering, would not be beneficial to reveal.

"What would you say to a drive up the Thames into the country? It would not do for us to be seen together."

Candace gave hint of a bewitching smile and nodded her approval. Already she was regaining her self-command.

"Who might see us?" she asked.

"Your father or one of his people."

"You know my father?"

"I do."

"But you do not want him to know we are together?"

"That is correct."

"What, then, is your interest in me?"

"I should think that would be obvious, Miss Montreux," replied Zorin, now smiling himself with clear intent to beguile. "I noticed you from a distance at the palace garden party and have wanted to speak with you ever since."

She nodded, choosing not to divulge her interest in him that same day.

"But besides yourself," he went on, "I am also interested in Adam Livingstone. I understand you and he are close . . . very close, in fact. Soon to be engaged, are you not?"

"Perhaps," answered Candace noncommittally.

"If such is your wish, perhaps I may also be of some help to you."

"I assume some quid pro quo would be involved."

Again Zorin smiled. This was a shrewd lady. He had not underestimated her. They were of similar mind.

"As I say, I too am interested in Adam Livingstone," he said. "His research intrigues me. I am thinking perhaps you will be able to shed light upon it that I would be unable to learn on my own."

As the car drove on from the confidential rendezvous toward the country, the two found more in common to discuss than merely Adam Livingstone. In fact, the archaeologist did not enter the conversation again for some time.

When Candace stepped out of the limousine several hours later, her world, which had begun to grow stagnant, had suddenly taken on intriguing and exciting new levels of interest.

(7)

In stately, privileged British homes of bygone eras, most servants took their meals in the servants' quarters, often in a separate wing of the house, while the kitchen staff served family members in the formal dining room.

In this new era of equality, however, like many of his generation, Adam Livingstone stood on no ceremony. The last thing of interest to him would have been to dress up every evening to sit through a formal dinner, especially alone. As a single man, like Bronte's Rochester, he had therefore long taken both light evening tea, if he had dined earlier in the day, or a thorough dinner if he had not, with his housekeeper. As Beeves and his wife lived in a detached and remodeled footman's cottage off the garage, this arrangement was obviously a practical matter, for there was no one else but Mrs. Graves with whom Adam shared the huge house. After the death of Adam's father and the beginning of his mother's ensuing world travels, at Adam's request Mrs. Graves took several rooms upstairs for her own. She had since that time gradually assumed a role not unlike that of Adam's aunt.

No amount of generosity on his part toward her, however, would cause the good woman to forget the vast difference in their backgrounds and respective stations. As Rocky learned in the matter of her morning drink and as her niece had discovered in the matter of familiarity, Andrea Graves was a traditionalist.

Occasionally one or more of the research staff remained for tea. But most had families, and all had lives of their own beyond the work. Both the master of the house and his housekeeper, therefore, enjoyed sharing their meals with Mrs. Graves' niece. And now the visitor from America made it a foursome.

Adam and the two live-in guests took their chairs for dinner one Saturday afternoon as Mrs. Graves set the last platter on the table and took a seat next to Juliet.

"It looks delicious as always, Mrs. Graves!" said Adam.

The housekeeper gave a smile and nod of appreciation as she handed the first dish to Rocky.

"What do we have here?" he exclaimed. "It looks interesting."

"Surely you've heard of Yorkshire pudding?" said Adam.

"I thought that was some kind of dessert!"

Adam laughed. "The popover alongside the meat—that's it."

"Then I am sure it will be a treat—thank you, Mrs. Graves." Rocky took a slab of beef, then carefully lifted the airy pastry mound of so-called pudding and set it onto his plate.

Mrs. Graves handed him a bowl of boiled potatoes.

Rocky helped himself to several. He now stabbed a chunk of meat with his fork and opened his mouth wide to receive it. "Great roast, Mrs. Graves! This lady is some fantastic cook, Livingstone," he added, turning again toward his host.

Gradually light conversation followed, mostly between the two men about recent events and the latter's investigation. Juliet listened with interest, but offered little in the way of comment.

(8)

Candace Montreux drove quickly along the A20 toward central London.

She had been thinking a good deal of Halder Zorin since their afternoon together. She had also been thinking about Adam. She had tried to call him twice, missed him, left messages, but neither of her calls had been returned.

The mere fact of Zorin's presence in her life heightened her annoyance with

Adam's nonchalance. Their strained luncheon together last week hadn't resolved a thing. Did he think he could toy with her affections? There were other
men in the world.

Even as she said the words to herself, however, it only made her want Adam
all the more. Her desire to have him grew more desperate in the gnawing suspicion that she was losing control over him. She had flattered herself that he
would do almost anything to please her. The realization that such was no longer the case, if it ever had been, was a bitter one to swallow. At the moment
her father's interest in her future and in Adam's loyalties could not have been
further from her mind.

She flipped on the radio. Candace recognized the melody quickly enough.
Nonsensical though the words may have been, they had become part of
English culture in less than a generation.

> . . . the girl with kaleidoscope eyes . . .
> Lucy in the sky with diamonds,
> Lucy in the sky with diamonds,
> Lucy in the sky with diamonds . . .

The fanciful harmonies of the McCartney/Lennnon tune triggered something in her brain. Who did Adam think he was anyway, the most important
man in the world? Didn't he know that he could lose her if he wasn't careful!

She was well enough acquainted with the famous story about the Beatles'
song blaring out over the Ethiopian desert when the 3-million-year-old bones
were unearthed, which as a result were given the name Lucy, changing the
study of anthropology forever. That tale had become legend in Adam's field,
as had the song in pop culture. But right now the words reminded her that she
was sick of bones and archaeology and history and research altogether!

She remembered something Zorin had said. This isn't only a man's world
anymore. It is a vigorous and appealing woman who knows what she wants
and isn't afraid to go out and get it.

Without pausing to consider the implications, Candace turned off the radio
and the next moment spun her car about and sped back in the opposite direction.

It was time to have this decided once and for all.

Forty-five minutes later she arrived at the entry to Adam's estate in
Sevenoaks, announced herself, and waited for the gate to swing open. She
zoomed in toward the house, her mood, if anything, hotter than it had been a
short while earlier.

"Ah, Candace, my dear," said Adam, a winning smile spreading across his
face as he strode down the stairs toward the door. "What a pleasant surprise."
If he detected the storm brewing on her face, which was not hard to see, he
gave no indication of it.

"I want to talk to you, Adam," said Candace.

"Certainly. Let's walk outside."

The moment the door closed behind them, Candace spoke. Her tone left less doubt about her mood than the thundercloud gathering across her brow.

"Adam," she said, "I've reached a decision. I don't want to wait until next year. It's time for you to decide . . . decide about me."

"You mean, you want me to talk to your father sooner than—"

"I don't care what you do about my father," she interrupted, eyes flashing. "You have to decide whether you want me or not. It has to be me or your work."

It was silent a moment as they walked slowly around the house toward the garden. Adam tried to absorb the ultimatum calmly.

"I . . . I didn't realize the two were at odds in your mind," he said after a moment.

"Perhaps you should have," she replied testily.

"This is a sudden change."

"Not so sudden, Adam. If your eyes could see what is right in front of you, it wouldn't have come to this."

"I don't know what to say."

"It's simple enough. I want us married before your trip."

"Candace, I haven't even spoken with your father definitely. Nor have I even proposed to you."

"My father is wholeheartedly behind the match. I have spoken to him."

"It would seem that is my responsibility."

"Yes, and I've waited long enough for you to carry it out."

"I can't just . . . get married so suddenly."

"Why not? People do it all the time."

"We're in the middle of preparations for Africa—this would disrupt everything."

"Maybe it should. I'm tired of taking a backseat, Adam. I want to know whether you're going to be married to me or to your career. I won't share you forever."

Adam was silent. They continued to walk slowly along side by side, but it felt as if a mile separated them.

For years Adam Livingstone and Candace Montreux had moved superficially in similar enough directions not to realize what distinctive motivations and goals really drove them. Neither stress nor major decision had come to test the character each was in the process of forming. To both it appeared the other had suddenly begun to drift away. In reality, however, they had never been bound toward the same ends in life but had only found themselves walking paths that happened, almost by accident, to intersect for a season.

Now at last had those two very different life-roads begun to diverge.

Candace glanced over into Adam's face. She detected a foreign influence, something from an altogether different world than that of Halder Zorin. All at once Adam was remote and far from her. A gulf had come between them, an invisible rift between two human spirits whose choices had long set them moving toward opposite destinations of character and personhood.

"I . . . I don't think I can make that choice, Candace," said Adam at length. "If and when I marry, it will be because a wife shares my work, not competes with it. I don't think this is a reasonable request for you to put to me."

"A woman has the right to a man's sole affections!" rejoined Candace angrily.

"But, Candace, don't you see—I have no choice but to go forward with my plans." Adam's voice was sad. "I can't imagine what has got into you. This attitude doesn't become you."

"How dare you preach to me!"

"I did not mean to preach, Candace," replied Adam quietly.

"What has changed you, Adam!" It was no question but a demanding and angry exclamation. As she spoke, Candace rose to the full height of her carriage, as if assuming a lofty level of dignity over this man she had once looked up to but who now appeared small in her eyes. "The next thing I know, you will be quoting Bible verses at me!"

Adam did not reply to her words. He could hardly fathom what had come over her. "I sincerely hope you will change your mind," was all he could utter.

Candace spun around and walked to her car. In the distance, across the garden, she caught a glimpse of the same girl she had seen two weeks earlier on the stairway.

If that little minx was at the bottom of that look in Adam's eye, she thought, whoever she was . . . she would make her regret it!

(9)

Adam woke early. A week had passed.

He found himself pondering more quietly his new friend Rocky McCondy and what the American had said about his religious views. Adam's own reflections about God of two weeks earlier also began to return with renewed clarity.

The revelations that morning—at least so he had considered them then—seemed perfectly sensible. Then had come the explosion. In its aftermath the windows into that other world had misted over for a time.

Now here came Rocky saying things like "when God is ready to tell you about it again, he will." What an outrageous thing to say.

God tell him! God say something . . . to Adam Livingstone!

The American's very presence stirred Adam's brain in such unfamiliar directions, along some of the same pathways he'd found himself exploring the morning of the explosion.

He now lay ruminating over the conversations the two men had had together in the past few days. Slowly light penetrated the windows as he lay in bed. Morning stole over the countryside. Gradually Adam became aware of a peculiar smell wafting faintly into his room. It did not take long to recognize it and realize the origin. It was coffee. It came from downstairs.

He rose, dressed quickly, and descended to the ground floor.

Adam walked into the kitchen. There stood McCondy over his morning brew. He turned at the sound of his host's footsteps.

"Hey . . . morning, Livingstone—how's it going?"

"Good morning, Rocky. Your coffee's aroma permeates the whole house."

"Best smell on earth!"

"You're up early."

"My body's suddenly reverted back to Boston time."

"I thought you were over that."

"So did I. Then at four o'clock, all of a sudden my eyes shot open, and I was wide awake."

Adam smiled. "Got extra water?" he asked.

"Fresh boiled, there on the stove."

"Mind if I ask you a question, Rocky?" asked Adam as he threw two tea bags into a stainless pot.

"Heck no. I've asked you about three hundred since I got here. I figure you're entitled to one or two."

Adam poured what remained from Rocky's steaming kettle over the tea bags. "I was lying awake earlier too," he said. "I found myself wondering something."

"Fire away."

"All right, then, it's this—do you believe God speaks to people? I mean . . . today."

"I do," replied Rocky, at last satisfied with the color of his Colombian mixture. He poured himself a cup.

"How does he do it—how does he speak to people?" asked Adam.

"Lots of ways," replied the American, sitting down at the table and sipping at his cup. "Through circumstances, from thoughts, by impressing you with something you feel you ought to do, through other people—he can speak all kinds of ways."

"Only to believers—to, uh . . . Christians."

"Not necessarily."

"Take a man like me, for instance," asked Adam, "might God speak to me?"

"Sure."

"Why would he?"

"I couldn't say. He might have lots of reasons."

"Such as?"

"He might want to use you in some way," replied Rocky.

"Use me?"

"That's how God gets his truth out—through people . . . sometimes the most unlikely, even unsuspecting, of people. Why—has God been speaking to you?"

"Oh, no," said Adam. "Just that morning I was telling you about, before the explosion. My brain was going in a lot of new directions, that's all."

"Don't sell God short, Livingstone," said Rocky. "He may have been trying to speak to you. He just might have something he wants you to do. That's not such a far-fetched idea."

"But why?"

"You're a man of influence. That doesn't make you any better than anyone else. But sometimes God lays his hand on a man or a woman in a special way because of how widely their voice can carry for good and truth. Wouldn't surprise me at all if that's the case."

"Even though I'm not a Christian?"

"Give God time, Adam." Rocky smiled.

"What do you mean?"

"You'll know when the time comes."

It fell silent. Both men sipped at their cups.

"You ought to talk to Juliet Halsay," commented Adam after a few moments. "You and she would have much in common. Mind if I ask you another question?" said Adam.

"Go ahead?"

"How long have you been, you know . . . a Christian?"

"Long enough, though only three or four years what I'd call an active and growing one. Why do you ask?"

"Thoughts of death sometimes make a person think more about God, life after death, and what it all means."

Rocky nodded.

"Watching someone die is a sobering experience," Adam added.

"You been thinking a lot about God recently?" asked Rocky.

"I don't know if I'd call it a lot. But more than ever before."

"A time comes to all people when they find themselves wanting to know about things they've never thought about, things they've neglected till then."

"Do you have people you talk to about God?"

"My pastor."

"It's hard to talk about such things to other men. It would be difficult to talk to Scott like this. Your pastor, is he a friend?"

"Yeah, both he and his wife."

"What's his name?"

"Mark Stafford. A good man."

"Older than you?"

"Younger, actually. He and Laurene helped me a lot after my wife died. That's when I really gave myself to the Lord all the way."

"I'm afraid I don't understand you," said Adam.

"Before then it was just church."

"Just church. What do you mean by that?"

"I mean I was a faithful churchgoer, but God hadn't yet managed to really get hold of me down where I lived. I'm sure he had tried, but probably I wasn't listening like I should have been. But after losing her, and like you say coming close to death, Mark helped me into a personal relationship with Jesus that had been missing before."

*Personal,* thought Adam. There was that word again!

"Now Pastor Mark and I get together every month," Rocky went on. "I still don't know much about doctrinal things. But he is explaining more and more of the Bible to me and how God works. I've been going to church for years, but at last I am starting to see more what it all means."

The two continued to talk for nearly an hour, by which time the conversation had returned to the subject of the postponed research trip.

"What do you suggest I do, Rocky?" said Adam. "I can't just stop my life. I've got to go on doing what I do."

"Who's stopping you?"

"I thought you said I was in constant danger?"

"I did."

"So . . . what about the trip to Africa?"

"The best thing to do might be for you and your people to get away from here. You may be safer there than at home. Besides, maybe that's where you'll uncover the key to this whole thing."

"What about you?"

"I've about wrapped up all I can do here in London anyway."

"I am still dying to get a look at your great-grandfather's journal!"

"Please," laughed the detective, "use some other metaphor than *dying* to convey your enthusiasm!"

"I am eager to see it, then!"

"That's better," said Rocky. "I have the feeling it's in that journal where we have to concentrate our next efforts. I went through it, but so much was a mystery to me."

"Why don't we read old Harry Mac's notes together? With two sets of eyes we could uncover what put him in danger. And I could see if there are, as you call them, intersections with my own work."

"That just might be the best way to get a handle on exactly why these people are after you."

"I've got it!" exclaimed Adam. "I'll fly back to the States with you!"

McCondy thought for a moment or two.

"I'm not sure that's a good idea," he said slowly. "I don't know why, but I've got a feeling it'd be best for you to go on with your plans. I'm sure you're still being watched. I may still be in the clear . . . temporarily. The longer we keep it that way, the better for all of us."

"I certainly don't want to bring danger on you."

"If you and I suddenly flew off to America together, we would really call attention to ourselves. We'd probably have newspeople trying to track us down and watching our every move. The bad guys would wonder what we were up to. There wouldn't be much good I could do you if I became as high profile as you."

"I see what you mean."

McCondy thought again, rubbing his hand back and forth across his chin.

"Tell you what," he said after a pause. "I'll fly home. I'll make a complete copy of the journal. I'll close up my house and see to a few things. In the meantime, you go on with your work as planned."

He drained off the last of the coffee in his cup.

"Then I'll meet you in Africa . . . with the journal," he added. "We'll pursue the investigation from there!"

# PART THREE

# AFRICA

◆ ◆ ◆

*Not harbingers nor signs as seers give pronouncement,*

*But by a wonder long concealed,*

*Of covenant deep buried will be made the announcement.*

*At its discovery, antiquity shall be revealed.*

◆ ◆ ◆

# Mysteries in High Places

(1)

A dozen executives sat around a thick oval conference table, speaking in serious and confidential tones.

Had there been windows, those present would have commanded a breathtaking view of the Netherlands metropolis spread out beneath them. But this top floor of the highrise was windowless by design. Leather and dark mahogany furnishings were dwarfed by the import of the personalities themselves who occupied them. One could sense the collective power emanating from this high perch at the heart of European life.

Though dressed in ten-thousand-dollar suits and looking like investors and bankers, as most were, their minds had joined in concentration rather upon recent events in the field of biblical archaeology that had suddenly so captivated the global public mood. The expedition of Gilbert Bowles' they had financed several years earlier had validated human evolution more conclusively than ever. Their concern now, however, revolved around the recent discovery that had prompted the meeting and seemed on the surface, perhaps, to *disprove* Darwin's hypothesis.

Such a shift in the public outlook they could not tolerate.

Whether the Turkish discovery actually disproved it mattered nothing to this most exclusive and clandestine fraternity in the world, only that such could become the perception of the masses.

But something even more dangerous was in the air. They sensed unsettling forces at work.

Since the discovery itself, events seemed moving toward a renewal of a threat their forebears thought they had dealt with a hundred years earlier. Disturbances in their hidden world were being felt in many realms. The Power of the Air had been stung with sinister reminders of a time long, long ago. Hints of the warming scents of a coming spring had been detected upon the earth. Its stench was foul and made him tremble. The curse of the great rift, the separation of the banishment, and the resultant blight of man's long winter, gave him his power and allowed him his reign. The door to the spring that would signal its end must be found and locked forever. It's warmth would destroy all!

Upon the twelve appointed members of the Council did it fall to eradicate the threat. The Plan must not be thwarted nor delayed.

The twelve representatives of the surreptitious societies affiliated around the globe were bound together in a bond of mystery more ancient even than the rights of progenitry that gave them access to one another. They normally came together in such a manner only once every three years. But with only fourteen months left before the millennial transition, a crisis had come in the Dimension.

Representing twelve nationalities and their respective nations—Japan, Great Britain, Iran, Germany, Switzerland, the United States, Holland, Azerbaydzhan, Brazil, Russia, Egypt, and Iraq—their hold on global finances, communications, transportation, industry, computer technology, and vast other institutions was the world's best-kept secret. In reality it had been well known in certain small elite circles since the fifteenth century, though its roots were far older than that. Even the governments and stock markets who did their bidding, however, knew little of the existence of this formidable syndicate. Shadowy rumors continually circulated, but without injury to their designs.

At a nod from any of the Twelve, the stock market in his or her corner of the globe would instantly tumble by 5 or 10 percent. Any three, had it been their intent, could precipitate an international financial crisis. Such was not normally their objective, though their fathers and grandfathers before them had done so upon occasion, as it suited their purposes.

More than regulating the world's financial institutions, monetary flow, and market trends, their deeper aim—for these most preeminent individuals in the world were players in a far higher conflict of which even they perceived but glimpses—was to control how the people of the world *thought*.

The predecessors of the Twelve had concerned themselves since antiquity chiefly with matters economic and political. They had controlled nations, alliances, empires. They had been responsible for wars, treaties, scientific and geographic discoveries, marriages, alliances, births, deaths. In these latter days, however, the mantel that had fallen to these particular twelve was to usher in the new age of the Third Millennium and prepare the way for him who would rise to lead them . . . and the world.

Their assignment: To ensure that humanism and its multifold ramifications upon culture continued to expand its vise grip on the liberal new mentality of the masses. Upon such ancient occult alchemy was the mystical Order and its worldwide invincibility based. Now had at last arrived the moment for their destiny to be fulfilled. Yet even though their triumph was at hand, undermining influences were rumbling the dark foundations of their origins.

The members of the Council had gathered for this special tryst at the summons of their Dutch leader. Each had arrived in Amsterdam separately and incognito, as they always did. They gained entrance to the private twelfth-floor suite of the building's owner, Holland's minister of finance and owner of Europe's two largest investment conglomerates, Rupert Vaughan-Maier, by his private elevator. Its door opened only upon recognition of the signal from a computer chip unlike any other in existence. Each of the Twelve had implanted such a chip under the skin of the right palm. A similar code of personal identification they were already working to install in the world's populace at large, in readiness for that approaching apex of the new order when he whom they called Master would place his personal mantel upon the Chosen One to reign upon the earth.

Had outside eyes been allowed access, the covert conclave might have appeared to be a séance at first glance, with a single candle burning in the dimly lit room on the table, along with assorted crystals, in the center of the circle in which they sat—an observation that would have been precisely accurate. The table was covered with a cloth of exceedingly ancient date, embroidered at each corner and across the middle in perpendicular directions with symbols familiar to the world but whose occult meaning was known to but a few. They had recently concluded initial incantations, and the invoking of the power of the One Master of the Earth. Now they were discussing the practicalities of the matter at hand.

(2)

"It would seem," the white-haired Dutch financier was saying in English, "that we may have been overlooking the need for vigilance on the scientific front. But first an overview."

He turned around and pressed a single button on the remote control in his hand. The room went black, though the next instant one entire wall of the office burst into computer-generated illumination, displaying a detailed map of the world. Whenever they met, this was the sphere of their strategies and objectives.

"In political power," he said, "our cause has never looked stronger."

He pressed again, and a series of changes swept across the globe, indicating the current state of political ideologies that held sway in the capitals of the world.

"In both democracies and totalitarian states," he went on, "there seem no hot spots of grave concern. The United States has calmed after the '94 scare, thanks in large measure to our colleague Mr. Abrams. The right-wing religious element was quickly discredited in the political arena, and there seems no threat to a continuation of our agenda. At present we are grooming a rising U.S. senator to take over when the Clinton-Gore era has run its course.

A target date has not yet been decided on. Steps, as I understand it, are in progress even now to ensure his yet deeper loyalty to our cause.

"Moving on to world economics and finances—" again the map changed, now to reveal the state of the world's financial markets—"our hold is solid in these areas, as it has been for three hundred years. Even religion—" a new map now brightened the wall—"has never been less troublesome. Our inroads into Christian evangelicalism are slow, but designedly so, as not to be detected. I feel most pleased with our progress. Our ally, the good Mr. Hann, is enjoying his momentary spotlight. He will shortly tumble and bring many of the disillusioned into our camp, though they will not recognize it as such."

He paused.

"In the arts and sciences, however," he went on, "we have been made aware of a recent development, which should not have, but which I am afraid has, caught us off guard. I refer, of course, to the so-called ark discovery in Turkey. We planned to have linkages well established between the various disciplines, so that scientific advances in genetic and molecular research exercised a silent impact on religion and politics. However, we were not prepared for an archaeological discovery that has the potential to alter the religious landscape so massively."

"I doubt it has such potential," commented the Russian member.

"That is because you are not aware of the background of the case," rejoined the stately Swiss woman to his right, Anni D'Abernon, the only woman of the coterie, of an ancient and wealthy Zurich family and now CEO of the manufacturing conglomerate bearing the same name and of immense influence in world financial circles. "The danger is very real and is extreme."

"Perhaps you would fill our members in on the background you speak of," said Vaughan-Maier.

D'Abernon was a tall and physically imposing woman, a modern corporate throwback to that ancient race of Amazons, easily six feet, whose personal involvement in the world of sport had at one time been competitive weight lifting. Her greatest strength, however, lay in the command of her powerful presence. She nodded in acknowledgment of the man's request, then began.

"We have had Adam Livingstone under close watch for years," she said. "We are present in his managing cartel and knew his every move well in advance. The whole affair was an economic one, driven by money, greed, politics, ambition, and jealousy—all which ensured insulation from the enemy's purposes. An unfortunate and unauthorized, high-profile event near the discovery site—"

As she spoke she allowed her eyes to drift imperceptibly toward her colleague from Baku. There was no *proof* he was involved, of course, but she wanted him aware of her suspicions. He coolly returned her gaze without the slightest ruffle.

"—added considerably more visibility than we might have wished. I do not think I must remind you that our design is stealth, coercion, infiltration, and secrecy, not open displays of force. The attempt was unsuccessful, however, and thus attracted little international exposure."

D'Abernon paused briefly again, glancing knowingly toward Vaughan-Maier, then continuing.

"More recently, however," she went on, "it has become apparent that Livingstone's research may be leading in more damaging directions than we foresaw. We did not anticipate the event actually changing the archaeologist himself. Things now appear moving in a direction that lies outside our primary control. Foreign influences are invading. Our power over the man is weakening.

She went on to tell of the archaeologist's research and to further explain its implications to their cause. Her counterparts listened attentively, gradually recognizing those elements that indeed represented a threat to The Plan.

"As I indicated, Livingstone has, for a variety of reasons, been under the scrutiny of the Dimensional Eye for years. He was alerted to us by a variety of Guides and Wise Ones as one with great potential for one side or the other. So we have watched, carefully awaiting opportunity to neutralize him, allowing him certain discoveries, knowing that his educational background would ensure the secularization of his findings. His fascination with biblical research, in fact, represents a great asset for us. For one so influential to attribute to seemingly spiritual things a humanist basis contributes enormously to the world outlook we must maintain. He is a plum for our cause, who would be able to further the Darwinian tradition with great impact.

"But unexpectedly, as I indicated, foreign influence is at work. He has made more than one troubling comment. It now becomes more imperative than ever that he be turned and brought in once and for all."

"What are we doing in that regard?" asked the Russian member.

"A plan has long been in place to neutralize Livingstone through marriage," D'Abernon replied, "and thus not merely to silence him but to bring him all the way into our inner coterie. As one of us, he could become a singular spokesman for the New Millennial Age."

"Are you speaking of full Council membership?" asked another.

"Those high matters are not for us to decide. But there *are* those of us here by virtue of marriage into the ancient familial lines. His future would remain to be determined. I meant that he must be brought into the cause and made one with The Plan, with his own Wise One to guide him."

"I see."

"However," she added, "the intended avenue for securing that level of loyalty has also grown troublesome."

She looked across the table.

"Perhaps Baron Rothschild would care to illuminate the Council further," she added, a hint of annoyance in her tone.

Lord Montreux coughed uneasily, then spoke.

"All is far from lost, I assure you," he said. "The man has spoken to me recently about marriage. I am certain the present breach between Livingstone and my daughter will be short-lived and that plans will procede as we have intended. The affair of the bombing at his home has no doubt upset him temporarily. I assure you, there is nothing to worry about. Livingstone will be ours."

"We all hope you are correct in your assessment, Baron," said Vaughan-Maier, his voice heavy with insinuation. "Your comments remind me of the unfortunate incident you mention. Does any of the Council know more concerning the origins of the event about which we should be enlightened? We have been monitoring Livingstone carefully and closely. We have detected elements in his research and data that are of grave concern. But I remind you that he will be of more use to the Master as one of us, not made a martyr for another cause."

The commanding Dutchman gazed slowly around at his colleagues with a penetrating stare. His eyes hesitated but half a second on Zorin, who returned the gaze without flinching. Vaughan-Maier again beckoned to his colleage to continue.

"Additionally," D'Abernon went on, "another individual has entered the picture besides Livingstone whom we must watch with equal diligence. How he slipped by us all these years I cannot imagine. I have already put my liason and some of his operatives on it. It is possible he may hold a key to much of the uncertainty that has suddenly arisen in the Dimension. He too must be stopped from making a public revelation."

(3)

Rocky McCondy was not the sort of man who got the shivers.

Not only was he big enough and generally tough enough to take care of himself in a scrape, he was not by nature the kind of man given to fear. He had always been too practical to be afraid.

But that fellow on the plane spooked him—the thin cheeks, pale olive beret, effeminate walk, and gray goatee—it was a countenance you couldn't help notice. Every time he'd gotten up to squeeze into the toilet room, he could not escape the inexplicable feeling that he was being watched. By the time his plane touched down at Logan, the sense of apprehension had grown steadily. Rocky couldn't wait to get out of there.

He didn't like it. He preferred to face his fears and the bad guys that went with them—whether criminals waving guns or his own personal demons—straight on, face-to-face, eyeball-to-eyeball, may the best man win.

But this was different. It was a sense of some invisible power. A dozen times on the flight home he'd tried to tell himself he was imagining the whole thing. But nothing could take away the feeling of dread . . . that bad things were about to happen, and that the moment he'd dialed Adam Livingstone's telephone number a few weeks earlier, he'd landed smack into something too big to control.

He retrieved his car and hurried out of the airport. He was dead with sleeplessness but determined to get home before yielding to it. What a relief to get back on the right-hand side of the road! And to drive on highways with lanes wider than eight feet. But the two-hour drive from Boston to Peterborough was as grueling as ever.

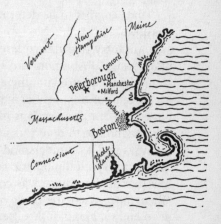

He finally pulled into his driveway, eyes red from constant rubbing. With effort, Rocky staggered toward the door. He would get his suitcase later. He wanted to flop on the bed and get two or three hours' sleep before he did anything. He unlocked the front door and walked in.

All thought of sleep suddenly vanished.

Rocky gazed about at overturned chairs and broken lamps and miscellaneous articles strewn about. His living room had been turned inside out! He wandered toward his bedroom in astonishment. The scene was worse. He turned to the kitchen. Pans, glasses, cups, and plates were broken across the floor. Every inch of the house had been ransacked. Every drawer, every cupboard emptied.

Suddenly he remember the chest in the attic.

Rocky turned and flew upstairs, hardly pausing to denote the condition of the rooms on the second floor, then up the narrow attic stairs.

The attic had not been spared. They had found the chest! Its lid lay back.

Rocky looked inside. The box was empty.

The sight confirmed his worst suspicions—this was the work of whoever was after Livingstone all right or their hired thugs. They had known exactly what they were after.

Luckily he'd removed the most valuable of the contents—his great-grandfather's journal. The next instant he was flying down the stairs again two at a time. He couldn't take the time for sleep yet. He had to find out if they'd gotten their hands on that too.

He'd make a strong pot of Starbucks, straighten a few things around, and walk over to town.

(4)

"We have to move with extreme caution," the founder of a giant Japanese electronics conglomerate, Hito Kawasaki, was saying to the Council of Twelve. "We mustn't forget that it has taken decades, even centuries, to achieve the power we hold. Even Darwin's hypothesis, crucial as it now is to the overall foundation of our organization, took almost a hundred years to infiltrate every corner of worldwide culture and knowledge. Changes of such magnitude develop slowly, silently, invisibly, as gradually the public mind is persuaded without realizing it. We must not be hasty in our response."

"Are you saying Livingstone is not the threat he seems?" asked an Iranian sheik.

"That remains to be determined," replied Kawasaki. "I would think such is possible."

"I am sorry to differ with my colleague," spoke up the white-haired Dutchman. "Miss D'Abernon and I have been following the situation closely for some time. I assure you, there is *much* to concern us. And time, though it has long been our ally, is now a major factor. I need hardly remind you how long have been our preparations for the year 2000. We must not allow anything of this magnitude to divert us at this eleventh hour."

"He is not, as I understand it, a Christian man," put in a high-ranking Iranian banker and diplomatic advisor, whose involvement in this organization, like that of the others, was completely unknown to his colleagues in Tehran. "Remember what the enemy once said, that even someone rising from the dead and speaking of the afterlife before a skeptic's very eyes would persuade men of nothing."

"We needn't worry about the ark, if that is the basis for the concern," added Hector de la Cruz, who had flown in from Rio that morning. "It will all be explained away in time. Livingstone himself may do that work for us. He will gradually rationalize the discovery. His whole background and training will force him to an intellectual response. Eventually he will write about the *science* of it. In time it will fade in the public consciousness as a thing of *spiritual* import. In the end, our purposes will have been *advanced,* not hindered, by the ark's discovery. Spiritual things work *for* us when they are robbed of their power. Disbelief in the face of overwhelming evidence is the most powerful and unassailable form of disbelief of all."

"There are reports, however, that Livingstone is more than hinting at spiritual implications?" commented Wilson Abrams of the United States.

"Exactly as I noted," rejoined Vaughan-Maier. "Indeed they are more than mere hints. What Hector says of the ark is correct, in and of itself. It is the change the discovery is working *in Livingstone himself* that concerns us. And toward what it might lead him."

"Most men such as he involved in high things of national import slip occasionally into metaphysical cogitations," remarked Kawasaki. "But again I emphasize my conviction that the reality of the rational world always seeps back to douse their embers."

D'Abernon now spoke again. Her voice was soft but full of power. That she had quickly come to be recognized as second only to Vaughan-Maier in command was a fact silently resented by some of her colleagues, though none dared speak of it openly.

"It is not the ark or its specific spiritual implications that pose the *greatest* threat to our Plan," she said. "It is precisely as Rupert has indicated—where Livingstone may be led as a result."

"Meaning what?" asked the Voice from Azerbaydzhan.

"Meaning, Mr. Zorin, that he may be on the verge of unlocking secrets that must *not* be made known. There are signs of the age that advance our cause and signs that may signal its demise."

Again the eyes of the two rivals on the Council met and held one another momentarily. But now was no time for open dispute. D'Abernon would deal with Zorin later.

"We managed to infiltrate his system," she went on. "We have sketchy knowledge indicating the direction of his research. The danger is extreme. It has implications far beyond the mere disproof of the humanist view of evolution. Unfortunately we do not know specifics."

The very tone of her voice hinted at deep realms in the Dimension.

"It is as I explained," she went on. "He may have in his hands the power to undermine our influence."

"He will soon be on his way to Africa," commented Lord Montreux.

"For what purpose?" asked Egypt's Saad Gamelli.

"There has been talk . . . of Eden," answered Vaughan-Maier.

It was silent a moment. The very word momentarily jarred the occult bond of their association.

"That fact pinpoints our concern," added the Dutchman after a few seconds. His voice contained a hint of uneasiness.

"The place is a myth," laughed de la Cruz, though his tone contained no humor. "What harm can possibly arise out of such a quixotic crusade? The world will only laugh."

"You should know far better than your superstitious countrymen, Hector, that the place is assuredly no myth but contains a power of which we much be constantly vigilant."

"What is about the Garden that has you so alarmed?" now asked Iran's Razmar Mossadeq. "I have never seen the Council like this. No man will ever find a remnant of that place."

"Do not be so sure, my friend. The enemy may yet again try to bring its location to light," replied Vaughan-Maier. "At the Garden our Master won the victory that gave him preeminence over man and his world. We are not told all concerning such deep things. But I sense through my Guide that its discovery may signify the lifting of a veil, the end of the curse. Such could begin a great loss of power. It may signal the enemy's coming."

"But surely—"

"There will be a victory. The Third Millennium will yet be ours. But the gravity of the times must not be ignored." The speaker was again the woman from Zurich. "Livingstone's research must *not* continue toward its end. The door to *that* place must not be opened. We have long postponed the coming of the enemy. We will continue to delay it as long as we are successful in obscuring the vision of his people with trivialities and doctrines. But this is a foreshadowing of great stirring in the heavens. The enemy is at work. We must redouble our efforts. We must not allow the deeper magic to reappear upon the earth. For when it does, *he* will come. When he does, then it will be *his* Millennium, and our work on earth will be curtailed. Livingstone may, without knowing it, hold the key to the door where that magic has been hidden these many millennia. The magic of the Garden must be kept buried. Its power must not be loosed."

The woman's cryptic words cast a spell over the Council. Even Zorin found himself preternaturally chilled.

They were silent some time, then, as one accord, began chanting quiet incantations and invitations to their Guides from the Dimension.

(5)

Thirty minutes later the discussion again resumed.

"Can Livingstone be turned," asked the Egyptian, turning to their leader, "before his research proceeds too far?"

"Everything possible is being looked into," replied Vaughan-Maier. "The alliance with the baron's daughter is our chief tactical line of offense. And other means, money and prestige, for example, do not seem particularly powerful inducements in his case. Such efforts are hampered by the troubling signs that he is bending his ear toward the enemy."

"With regard to Miss D'Abernon's earlier suggestion of bringing him in," said Germany's Georg Mühsam, "—I must say, with all due respect, that I consider it far too risky. Even as the baron's son-in-law. He is a thinker and a scientist—too independent. The enemy seems far too active around him, with people close by and gaining his affections."

"What are we doing with regard to such individuals?" asked the Iraqi oil magnate.

"All are being watched," replied Vaughan-Maier. "We continue the attempt to implant one of our people inside."

"I agree with Mühsam. The inclusion of such a man would be against everything upon which our secrecy is based," said Abrams. "I support the marriage. But more is out of the question."

"The risk of exposure would be serious. We must not have him mount a crusade. No, he must know nothing of our existence."

"Surely he has heard of us."

"Most have heard rumors. Few *believe* what they have heard."

"Why do we not simply get rid of him?" asked Zorin. His tone made of it an innocent question, but more was on his mind. D'Abernon glanced quickly toward him with a flash of her eyes. Fortunately the Brazilian answered before she found a reply necessary.

"He may still be useful for our ends," said de la Cruz.

"Not if he is dangerous, if we have no power to control him."

"Elimination would be an easy matter, I grant you, but it is out of the question," said Lord Montreux. "Again, we must innoculate and anesthetize, not create martyrs."

"Frankly, I do not see the danger of these spiritual leanings you are all speaking of," commented the American Abrams. "My country is history's most classic case study, unless Mühsam's prewar Germany might also be considered. Spiritual belief, if properly intellectualized and emotionalized, has never posed a threat to our designs, only a nagging annoyance. Unbelieving Christians are our strongest allies. We must do nothing to upset the comfort zones with which their orthodox belief systems surround them. We must not rally them nor anger them nor incite their passions. Martyrs only wake them up. We must keep them asleep."

"Well stated," added Viktor Gomulka, the Russian member of the Council. "The same principle is true of this man Livingstone, whether he considers himself a Christian at present or not."

"Once the raw science of the ark discovery takes over," said de la Cruz, amplifying on his earlier point, "with books and magazines and television specials explaining it from a humanistic perspective—which we will make certain *is* the point of view—our cause will be in an even stronger position."

"As long as more serious discoveries do not follow," added D'Abernon.

"What discoveries?"

"We have already spoken of that place," she replied.

"Let him even discover the Garden," said de la Cruz, ignoring her reticence, "or *think* he has. Nothing will come of it. Whatever implications the thing has against the evolutionary framework will be dissipated easily enough."

"It seems, then," suggested the Egyptian, "that our chief objective must be to discredit Livingstone." He glanced toward Lord Montreux, then toward D'Abernon and Vaughan-Maier.

"For what purpose?" rejoined his counterpart from Great Britain. "The ark has been found."

"The ark has been found before," rejoined the Iraqi. "The Turks have a tourist center already built beside one such discovery at the foot of the mountain."

"Indeed, and its finding will only stir up evangelicals to fight among themselves and argue about which is the *real* ark and soon dissipate any potential spiritual impact. I tell you, Livingstone's discovery will help us in the long run."

"Discrediting him remains an intriguing strategy."

"I ask again, for what purpose?"

"To reveal that he was in it for the money, for the glory," replied the American, picking up on Gamelli's theme, "—perhaps a rumor that evidence was falsified, or even that the whole thing was an elaborately staged hoax. Even if what Señor de la Cruz says about its blowing over and working to our advantage in the end is true, discrediting Livingstone and his find will only benefit those objectives."

"It would likewise serve to lessen the impact of future discoveries," added Gamelli, "as Miss D'Abernon suggests ought to be at the forefront of our concern. It seems a reputational undermining of Livingstone would achieve many of our ends."

A few heads nodded around the table, intrigued.

"Only *if* the marriage to my daughter fails," said Lord Montreux. "By destroying Livingstone, we also destroy his capacity to advance our cause."

"Granted," rejoined Gamelli.

"Suggestions?" said Vaughan-Maier at length, glancing around the table.

"Rumors . . . innuendos."

"Affairs are always useful."

"Nothing new there . . . everyone in British society plays around," said Lord Montreux.

"It remains a powerful means of censure for Christians."

"Not like it used to be—" the American smiled—"at least not in my country."

"True—" The Russian nodded—"which is indication of how successful have been our infiltration efforts."

"Financial scandal?" suggested D'Abernon.

"What we have to do is discredit him as a man . . . discredit his motives, his believability."

"Turning one of his staunchest supporters against him—nothing is so useful for destroying a man as that. It is how we destroy many reputations. Truth matters nothing, only that the charges come from someone very close. A family member is best of all."

"I know just the man to help us," said the Englishman. "And he can be bought. He is not family, but one of my own countrymen—Sir Gilbert Bowles."

"A fellow archaeologist?"

"I tell you," insisted Montreux, "Bowles is our man. If we want to discredit Livingstone, not a better man can be found for the assignment. He knows his science. And he hates Livingstone."

Silence and more nods followed, indicating a general consensus.

Zorin listened to the discussion with interest. He was way ahead of them. He had already used Bowles in the matter of the Ararat affair to locate the exact coordinates of the ark. He knew Bowles' soft spot. The big man's use by the Council could prove useful to him.

"You can arrange it?" Vaughan-Maier said to the Englishman, glancing also at D'Abernon.

"I can."

"As always, make sure the arrangements are untraceable."

"Consider it done."

The conversation continued. There were other matters to discuss.

The woman from Zurich remained mostly quiet through the remainder of the meeting. She was far from convinced the measures they had talked about would accomplish what needed to be done. If Zorin was taking matters into his own hands as she suspected, the measures she was already considering would leave no such fingerprints.

She would meet privately with the two others who formed the triangle of greatest power among the Twelve.

(6)

Rocky McCondy walked into First Fidelity National Bank.

He glanced about nervously. He still had a bad feeling. But at least he wasn't quite so sleepy. He'd catch up on his sleep tonight. First there were things he needed to do.

He walked downstairs and straight to the deposit-box room.

"I'd like to get into my safety deposit box," he said.

"Name?"

"Robert McCondy."

"Back again so soon, Mr. McCondy?" said the receptionist, removing the signature card from her file.

"What do you mean, so soon?"

"You were just . . . oh, no—I see from the record that it was your attorney."

"What are you talking about?" asked Rocky. "I've been out of the country until about three hours ago. I don't even have an attorney."

"Hmm . . . that is odd," replied the lady. "Now that I look at the file, I recall the situation—there was a power of attorney signed by you . . . and he had the key to your box."

"That's impossible—I've got the key right here." Rocky dug into his pocket and produced the key. "I don't suppose it matters now—just let me sign. I'll go check the box."

Two minutes later both keys were inserted into their respective locks and the lady left Rocky alone. He turned the key and pulled out the drawer.

Whoever it had been wasn't concerned about money and was certainly no common thief. His modest stash of Krugerrands was undisturbed, as was his complete set of U.S. silver dollars, save the 1804.

His great-grandfather's journal, however, was nowhere to be seen.

# fifteen

# Dark Schemes

(1)

Juliet Halsay answered the telephone, wondering who could possibly be calling her.

"Juliet . . . Hi—it's Margaret."

"Margaret!" exclaimed Juliet. "It's good to hear from you!"

"I found myself thinking about you the other day and decided I'd try to get hold of you. How are you?"

"Actually, I'm doing pretty well," answered Juliet. "How did you get this number?"

"From one of the social-welfare people you were seeing. She asked about you."

"There was a rough patch there for a while. I'm coming out of it now. I went by your house when I was in Brighton a couple weeks ago but must have missed you."

"Would you like to get together?"

"Oh, I would, Margaret!"

"You know what I've been in the mood for—Arundel."

"I can't think of anything better! We'll have a cream tea in that restaurant up the hill."

"And the antique shops!"

"I hardly have a penny to my name."

"We'll window-shop. That'll be just as much fun. When can you get away?"

"Anytime. I'm not working. Auntie Andrea is good about letting me use her car."

"Day after tomorrow?"

"Shall we meet there—at the restaurant . . . eleven o'clock?"

"Right, good. See you then."

Two days later the friends walked along Tarrant Street in the quaint old English village of Arundel, poking in and out of various shops as they went, chatting gaily.

"There's the walking-stick shop!"

"Oh, I don't know if I can bear it again—remember last time we were here? We couldn't get away from the man for an hour!"

"His whole life is those walking sticks!" giggled Margaret. "I would positively die of boredom if I had nothing more to keep me company than antique canes and sticks and umbrellas!"

"Let's go into the antique bazaar at the church!" rejoined Juliet, leading the way farther down the street. "There's always something interesting there. I might even find some little trinket *I* could afford."

They approached the large stone building, the Congregational Church of the village in Victorian times, now turned into a score of booths for dealers in secondhand goods. Some of the merchants touted their wares as antiques. Others were not quite so bold in their claims.

As they entered, Juliet paused and glanced about. A strange feeling of quiet reverence stole over her in the midst of the commotion and voices buying and selling. How incongruous, she thought—stained-glass windows and a stately old church . . . filled with discarded junk and treasures of a thousand people's lives. Somehow the two images did not fit.

*What might this church once have been?* Juliet thought to herself. *What might have been the messages preached from that platform up front where once there had been a pulpit? Who had stood there? What had he said?* Then came the question, *How could such a once-grand church sink to this?*

She had no time to ponder further. Already Margaret was dragging her toward one of the booths.

Two hours later Juliet and Margaret sat spreading thick clotted Devonshire cream over two golden scones. They had just returned to their table from the ladies' room as their order arrived.

"I am so glad you called me," Juliet was saying. "I haven't had so much fun in ages. I needed to get away and do something different."

"Isn't it terribly exciting being where you are though—Adam Livingstone . . . wow!"

Juliet laughed. "I don't really have anything to do with *him,*" she said.

"But you're still so lucky. I mean, you're there, aren't you?"

"I suppose. But I don't know how lucky that makes me. You heard about the girl who was killed?"

"That was horrible, wasn't it? Nothing like that could happen to you."

"What do you mean? It did happen to me in London, or *almost* did."

"I'm sorry. That wasn't what I meant . . . you know."

"It's okay."

A brief pause followed.

"But you *know* him!" said Margaret. "I can still hardly get over it."

"Who?"

"Adam Livingstone, silly," said Margaret. "He's *so* handsome!"

"He would *never* notice someone like me."

"I don't know whether to believe you or not," laughed Margaret. "I bet he *has* noticed!"

"He has not—I promise."

"Do you ever talk to him?"

"We've talked—yes. Though I've made a ninny of myself a time or two."

"I don't believe it!"

"I have!" insisted Juliet, giggling. "And I made him angry once too."

"What—how?"

"I was in his lab when I wasn't supposed to be."

"Did you get in trouble?"

"Just briefly. Then he felt sorry for me. My aunt told him about the explosion."

"What are you going to do, Juliet?" asked her friend after a pause.

"I'm looking for a job. I can't stay there forever. Mr. Livingstone's leaving for Africa tomorrow. There's an old folks' home in the village that might have an opening for a caregiver next month."

"Not very appealing work."

"I'd rather be helping old people than selling fish-and-chips. In any case, I'm going to do my best to be working and have my own flat before Mr. Livingstone gets back from his trip."

"Why?"

"I don't want him to get mad at me again!"

"I bet he's thinking about you more than you let on."

"Betsy! Don't say such things."

"It's true. I know he is!"

"Stop," laughed Juliet. "He is not!"

"There's something about you that everyone likes. Don't sell yourself short."

(2)

A single day had passed since the meeting of the Council of Twelve.

Rupert Vaughan-Maier, Anni D'Abernon, and Lord Harriman Montreux had, by common consent, agreed that more confidential discussions were urgently needed between the unofficial leadership triumvirate of the Council of Twelve. The latter two had therefore remained over for the night in Amsterdam.

"Others of the Council are slow to apprehend the danger," Vaughan-Maier was saying. "I am perplexed that they were so unmoved by our warnings. I fear some untoward influence is at work."

"You do not mean . . . work of the enemy?" asked the scion of the Rothschild line.

"Nothing of that nature. I mean a division among our own."

"From what cause?"

"What else but pride and the lust for power."

"That is precisely the cause. One of the Twelve has grown to think too highly of himself," said the Swiss woman. "I felt it the moment he entered the room yesterday. It kept the others from heeding the gravity of the situation. It obscured the Dimension."

"I had the distinct impression he knew more about the two incidents than he let on," remarked Lord Montreux.

"Indeed, Baron," rejoined Vaughan-Maier. "I fear our friend Mr. Zorin may have motives of his own."

"The reason for it continues to baffle me. Zorin has been an ally in the cause longer than several of the others."

"Not to mention the fact that it was to him we entrusted the greatest responsibility in preparation for the new order."

"Some thought he would rise in the power of the Dimension to eclipse us all."

"It is those upon whom the light shines most brightly that pride and ambition cause to fall to the lowest depths."

"Our friend Zorin may be taking matters into his own hands," said D'Abernon. "His gambit at present is mere destruction. He threatens to expose us with his juvenile tactics. Our purposes are brought about invisibly, not with bombs."

"I fear the man is obsessed with power," rejoined Vaughan-Maier.

"He has lost sight of the larger purpose of The Plan. He must be reined in. Invisibility *must* be retained."

As one accord they extended their hands, lightly joining fingers.

After a few moments an otherworldly crooning came out of one of the mouths. The sound resembled praying, yet it was a universe distant from prayer to the true God. Gently one of the three rocked back and forth. Eyes were closed, faces blank. Humanity drifted into the background. Others from distant realms in the Dimension now came forward to speak through them. A single candle flickered in the room, sending sparkles about from the crystal beside it. There was no other light. The world of darkness intoned its Will in wraithlike tones.

*Danger approaches . . . that place must not be found.*

Inaudible murmurings, then silence.

*The rift must be preserved, its source hidden . . . life left buried.*

The three voices mingled as their oracles seemed hasty to convey urgent messages of warning.

*Find and destroy it . . . do not let him discover source . . . great danger.*

*The Dawn of the Dimension dims.*

*Must not find door . . . keep it sealed . . . closed for all time.*

Gradually the medium voices trailed away. Humanity returned. Eyes opened.

A lengthy silence ensued in which each of the three tried to absorb what they had heard.

"Could the man really be seeking the Garden?" said D'Abernon after several minutes. In her depths, even as she gave expression of incredulity, she knew it was true. "The thing seems impossible."

"You know it is so," replied Vaughan-Maier. "You yourself alerted me to stirrings and warnings from your Guide before I felt them myself."

She nodded gravely. "Have we information where he is bound in Africa?" she said.

"My daughter is in touch with him," said Montreux.

"This may be an opportunity for her to redeem herself, Baron. Absense is said to make the heart grow fonder. We shall hope it will work in Livingstone's case."

"Our sources have traced a reservation to a hotel in Arusha in Tanzania. In appears his base camp will be in the Olduvai Gorge."

"That tells us nothing. Half the evolutionary archaeologists in the world are digging there. What is he looking for—fossil remains? What will *that* tell him about the Garden?"

"We will maintain surveillance through Bowles."

"Make sure he finds the camp and reports back Livingstone's every move."

"Have *we* any idea where the source of the rift is located?"

"If we knew that we could destroy it before Livingstone gets there. But the old record indicates nothing. The fool was wandering in the desert when our people killed him. There were no entries detailing his destination—only the word *Sinai.*"

"The mountain or the region?"

"There is no peak by that name, only a legendary location in the southern desert of the Sinai Peninsula, with a run-down monastery at its base. We have watched it for a hundred years. Nothing is there, if it is the fabled mount at all. Nor has Adam Livingstone shown the slightest interest in the place. We must be vigilant."

"And Zorin?"

"He, too, like Livingstone, we must watch. It may be that he will eventually have to be removed from the Council."

(3)

The moment Lord Montreux returned to London, he sought his daughter.

"Have you and Adam patched it up?" he asked.

"Oh, Adam—I'm sick of him, Father."

"What do you mean by that?"

"I've decided not to marry him."

"What? Why have you said nothing to me?"

"I am telling you now."

"I cannot allow such a thing."

"I have made up my mind, Father."

"You *must* marry him. I thought that was clear."

"I no longer love him."

"Love has little to do with it. You won't make a better match."

"Why do *you* care so much all of a sudden? What does it matter to you, Father?"

"It has always mattered to me. I have my reasons."

"He's changing, Father. He's getting religious. I don't know if I can stand him any longer."

Lord Montreux took in the information with serious expression.

"All the more reason, Candace," he replied at length. "You must get his mind away from all that. Charm him. Use that smile of yours. You have always been successful before."

"I don't know if I have any charm left for him."

"He is still a handsome catch, Candace. You can't be serious about not loving him. Love doesn't disappear so quickly."

"He no longer attracts me."

"I tell you I want it patched up between you two before he leaves for Africa."

"If I don't?"

"Candace, don't anger me. I don't want to have to force this upon you. It would be better if you would simply see things my way."

"I never agreed to become a preacher's wife."

"I tell you, it is imperative—"

"Whose life is it, Father," Candace interrupted angrily, "yours or mine?"

"Don't be impertinent! We have long had an understanding about Adam Livingstone. If you want to see a penny of my estate, young lady, you will do as I say."

Candace did not reply. To say she was pouting would hardly give accurate indication to the expression on her red face. Unfortunately, her father held the tools to coerce her to his will.

"Do you hear me, Candace?" he said. "I am giving you no choice. We need Adam Livingstone now more than ever."

"I won't do your bidding any longer!" Candace shouted.

"You will do exactly what I tell you," rejoined her father icily, "or I promise you and whomever you do marry will live as paupers. We've *got* to find out what Livingstone is up to."

A long silence followed. Lord Montreux stood still and imposing, waiting for his daughter to come to herself. Candace's anger gradually moderated. Her father was right—she had no choice. She hated to be at the mercy of anyone, especially a man. Unfortunately, she had grown up with this particular man and knew how powerful he was. He did not make empty threats. If he said she would never see another penny of his fortune, she knew well enough that she could find herself cut off entirely by the following morning. Her pride did not extend quite so far as to be willing to see *that* happen. She had grown accustomed to living well and had no intention of altering her lifestyle.

"What do you want me to do?" she said in a soft voice of resignation after several minutes.

"Nothing but what you do best, Candace, my dear," replied Lord Montreux in a tone of renewed fatherly tenderness. "Win over the man's heart, steal his affections . . . and find out where he is going and exactly what he hopes to do in Africa."

"If he will not tell me?"

"He will, my dear. He loves you."

"He is often secretive about his work."

"Do your best. I am sure he will tell you if you feign interest. We will find out what his game is, one way or another."

Candace left the room. Her father thought for a moment. It was obvious they could not depend only on Candace for the information they required. He went upstairs to his study, picked up the phone, and made a quick call. They must use every means possible to obtain the information.

(4)

A strange feeling had been growing upon Andrea Graves for a day or two. Ever since she and Mrs. Beeves had gone out to the butcher's and returned home, she'd been unable to keep from glancing over her shoulder. Maybe it was just because the house was so quiet with everyone so suddenly gone.

Juliet's return late in the afternoon made her breathe a sigh of relief.

"Did you have a good time, dear?" she asked.

"Oh, yes, Auntie," Juliet replied. "It was so nice to just do something fun. Margaret and I laughed and giggled like we haven't since we were schoolgirls."

"I confess it was too quiet around here for me," said her aunt.

"*Too* quiet—what do you mean?"

"Surely you've noticed how different it's been since everyone left."

"Yes, it's not so lively, is it? It's like the spirit is gone. But I thought you would like having the house to yourself again—and being rid of Mr. McCondy and his coffee."

Mrs. Graves did not reply.

Juliet's eyes squinted slightly with the hint of a twinkle, as if she were attempting to gaze beneath the surface of her aunt's visage.

"You miss him, don't you, Auntie?" she said at length.

"Miss . . . miss who, for heaven's sake—the American fellow? Don't be ridiculous!"

"You *do!*" repeated Juliet with a playful smile. "I wouldn't have believed it."

"Juliet, don't you say such a thing," insisted her aunt, turning to leave the room.

Juliet let her go, then skipped up the stairs to her room, still in a gay and happy mood.

A moment later the telephone rang. Mrs. Graves picked it up.

"Hello, Mrs. Graves," said the caller, "this is Candace Montreux."

The housekeeper said nothing. She had never liked the Montreux girl. With Adam gone she needed to maintain no appearances of friendliness.

"May I please speak with Adam?" said Candace.

"I'm sorry, Miss Montreux, he is gone," replied Mrs. Graves guardedly.

"Gone . . . gone where?"

"Left on his research trip."

"He's left already—for Africa?"

"He flew out yesterday."

Candace could hardly maintain her composure. Adam had left the country without settling things between them, without even saying good-bye.

"Did . . . is there a telephone number where I could call him?"

"No, I'm sorry."

"But what—what work will he be conducting?"

"I really cannot say."

"Is there any way I can reach him, Mrs. Graves?"

"Really, Miss Montreux, he is in the middle of Africa somewhere. I don't even know myself where he is going."

Candace put down the phone in a white fury. The meddling old woman! If she didn't know where Adam was, you could bet someone in that house did. She would find out! It wasn't merely her father's desire to know any longer. Candace's pride now rose up in the face of the housekeeper's obtrusiveness.

She determined to learn what they were trying to keep from her.

And Adam . . . how dare he leave without a word!

Meanwhile Mrs. Graves entered the kitchen, the phone call already fading from her mind. Prompted by the exchange with Juliet, things other than Candace Montreux occupied her thoughts. By force of habit she put on a pot of water. She began rummaging around the cupboards for something to go with tea, although, in truth, she wasn't very hungry.

There, stashed in a corner, was Mr. McCondy's half-empty canister of coffee. She eyed it for a moment, then reached in and drew it out. Unprying the plastic edge, she lifted off the lid and brought the open can toward her face. She bent her nose toward it, then slowly inhaled the pleasurable aroma.

The nostalgic moment was over as quickly as it had begun. The next instant the canister was back in its corner, and the housekeeper was busy again with her tea. Nor did she pause to reflect further on what the brief incident might signify.

Outside the estate, from a vantage point down the street in a van with tinted glass, a watcher lowered the binoculars with which he had been observing the house. He had kept track of the girl's movements all day and had managed to get hold of her purse at the restaurant just long enough to obtain what he needed. There didn't appear much more he could do now.

He'd keep watch . . . and await his opportunity.

(5)

A mist had begun to descend an hour earlier.

Now the silently thickening fog made its way off the water into the city, muffling sounds and blurring whatever shapes loomed in the distance. Now and then a foghorn sounded, accented by the shrill cry of an unseen gull somewhere. Tiny waves slapped faintly against the hulls of the few large ships and the many smaller fishing boats moored nearby.

A curious looking man, by the appearance of his soiled trousers and grimy hands a hardworking Irishman yet whose subtle visage betrayed hints of a look altogether foreign to this dock region of Belfast, walked casually along the narrow street through the darkening mist, cap pulled low over his forehead, then strode aimlessly into the Lucky Doubloon.

Any pub or street corner in Belfast would have served the purpose equally well. But prying eyes were everywhere, and the man he was supposed to meet was not exactly the sort who blended unnoticed into the scenery. Nor did the fellow's renown help. In London he would probably be stopped for an interview or an autograph. On the Belfast docks, however, few would know him, and those who did would care even less.

Setting up the meet here was also bound to add a certain level of intrigue and potential danger in the other man's mind. It would utterly throw him off any track if he tried to discover the identity of those who had contacted him. So much the better if he thought there were Irish connections. It would prevent him from asking too many questions. That was the one thing above all his employers desired to avoid. They were not of the sort who sought the spotlight. Their power had been perpetuated through time by anonymity.

The supposed Irishman glanced around.

There was no mistaking the huge man. He sat in a darkened corner hunched over a tall mug of thick dark Guinness stout.

Hesitating but a moment to accustom himself to the dim light, the newcomer walked first to the bar, picked up an empty mug, then strode forward and sat down in the rickety wooden chair opposite the man. Without a word he poured his mug half full from the remains in the pitcher that stood in the center of the table, then drained it down his throat in a single swallow.

Setting down the glass, he glanced up and stared straight into the other man's eyes with an expression intended to intimidate.

"Mr. Bowles," he said in his best Irish accent, "the people I represent have asked me to make you a proposition."

"What kind of proposition?" the archaeologist gruffly returned, annoyed at the half an hour he had been waiting and feeling out of sorts from the gloominess of this place. He had endured poisonous spiders and snakes by the hundreds, faced a charging lion once, rhinos twice, and had had malaria three times, and taken it all without much fuss. But this was different. He didn't trust the IRA and relished being here less by the minute. The fact that this fellow looked like he would kill him for the rest of the beer on the table didn't help steady his nerves.

"One that should be to your liking," the man replied. "One that will make you a rich man."

"I am already a rich man," rejoined Bowles. "I have no need of money."

"Tax-free money?"

"No money is tax free."

"The cash in my pocket will be tax free, if you choose to take it."

Bowles' thick eyebrows lowered slightly as he eyed the man with skepticism. He then nodded cautiously, bidding him continue.

"There will be other incentives," the man said.

"Such as?"

"Restoration of your reputation as Britain's leading archaeologist."

"My reputation needs no help," rejoined Bowles more calmly than he felt.

"That is not how I hear it."

Again Bowles was silent, doing his best to swallow his irritation.

"Get on with it," he said at length. "What is your proposition?"

"The assignment, in its simplest form, is to discredit your colleague Adam Livingstone."

Bowles took in the information with keener interest than he allowed his face to show, though his eyes flashed at the words.

"Discredit?" he repeated.

"However you like. The means, the specific ends are up to you. My employers want his name and image damaged beyond repair. They are not scrupulous about the particulars."

"Why me?"

"It is thought, knowing the field as you do, and bringing to your aid, shall we say, your own personal motivations insofar as Livingstone is concerned, that you would be the most suitable man for the job. It is also thought that you might be capable of bringing a level of ingenuity to the case. What is required is no mere rumor of sexual impropriety or news leaked that he cheats on his taxes, but something so damning as to destroy the credibility of his ark research."

The eyes of the large archaeologist now shone with an unmistakable light.

"I have suspected that very thing," he replied. "It may all be a hoax."

"We wondered if such might be your view. My people are convinced that you, and you alone, possess the credentials to bring such news believably to public light. We also want this new expedition of his undermined."

"The Garden!" said Bowles, shaking his head with a grunt. "It needs no discrediting. It's the most absurd idea I've ever heard."

"My people are not altogether convinced. Before the damage is done, therefore, they want you to learn all you can of this present quest."

"I tell you, there is nothing behind it."

"Nevertheless, such is their wish. We must know where he goes and what he is looking for—specifically. My people must know exactly where Livingstone's research leads him. If he finds anything at all—anything!—we must know it the moment he does. You will report your findings to me."

"Bah! He will find nothing."

"As you know, the reality is not as important as the perception. We even want to know what he thinks he might be finding. Even this may be useful to us, if it can add to the public perception that he is a religious fool."

"That should not be difficult," huffed Bowles.

"It is his influence we want damaged, whatever he does or does not find."

"Do you have a plan?"

"Follow him to Africa and find out what he is up to."

"And then?"

"We will know how best to make use of the information."

"Who would I be working for?" asked Bowles.

"Tut, tut, Mr. Bowles, look around you." The man smiled. "Do you think I would have arranged to meet you here if my principals wanted full disclosure of their identity? You will be contacted."

Bowles nodded. "If I am successful?" he asked.

"You may name your price."

"Do your employers own a bank?" smiled Bowles wryly.

"My employers own all the banks, Mr. Bowles," replied the man significantly, holding Bowles' eyes.

Bowles dropped his look to the table and laughed lightly, not knowing whether to believe the man or not. Involuntarily he shuddered. "As I said," he replied after a moment, still chuckling nervously, "money is not my chief interest at present. I will consider your offer. But don't think I can be bought. I'm no patsy."

"You will be rewarded in many ways, Mr. Bowles. You may even find yourself in Parliament one day."

"I take it they own governments as well as banks," said Bowles with attempted humor.

The man did not laugh.

"Let me just say," he replied, "that whatever they wish to accomplish can be arranged."

# sixteen

# Into the Rift

(1)

Adam Livingstone ducked under the flap of his tent, wiping the sweat off his brow with one hand and beating back the insects with the other, then exhaled.

His shirt was drenched. He could never remember feeling so lethargic. *How could it be so hot here in the middle of the winter!*

Surely he would acclimatize to the change in humidity and heat any day. He'd been exhausted, whether from the temperature or the flight, since their arrival. Now that the camp was set up and they were ready to get to work, hopefully he'd soon be back to himself.

He sagged into the rickety chair at the equally rickety table, a map of eastern Africa spread out before him, and let his eyes roam over it.

The very sight brought a brief surge of energy, if not to his limbs, at least to his brain.

Here it was, he thought—not just a map of the rift region of Africa but perhaps a chronicle of man's beginnings. The thirty-mile-long gash in the Serengeti Plain of Tanzania one hundred miles east of Lake Victoria known as Olduvai Gorge had long given archaeologists prospecting for hominid fossils their richest finds.

He and his colleagues were looking for something different. They would not seek it at Olduvai. Yet the place provided an ideal central location from which to base their research and throw those inquisitive about his purpose off track. They had flown into Nairobi four days ago and rented both vehicles they would need and certain other equipment. They arrived here and set up base camp the day before yesterday. Computers and what equipment had been shipped would arrive in another two or three days at the hotel in Arusha, some seventy miles east. They would maintain a room there as a secondary base of operations.

The sound of a jeep approached. Adam stood, turned, lifted the flap, and glanced out into the afternoon heat. It was Scott.

"You had a message at the hotel to call McCondy," said his friend as he jumped out and approached.

"Urgent?"

"Didn't say."

"I'll get to a phone tomorrow. I'm still trying to firm up plans with Dr. Cissna in Cairo. I'll call Rocky at the same time."

Thought of the American brought a smile to Adam's face. Already he missed his new friend.

"You get the books?" he asked

"Yep—in the jeep. Where's Jen?"

"In her tent—taking a nap. This heat's knocked her out too."

"What's with you two?" laughed Scott.

"I wish I knew."

"You might have picked up a bug."

"It's just the heat," said Adam. "Let me give you a hand with that stuff," he added as Scott began unloading the supplies. As they worked, an odd expression came over Scott's face.

"What is it?" asked Adam.

"Oh . . . just being in Africa, I suppose. Roots and all that, you know. It 0-always catches me off guard how different it feels here."

"How so?"

"In the States and in England," replied Scott, "our working together—my being black, your being white—doesn't matter to most people. Or maybe people's reactions come in ways you expect because you've spent your whole life getting used to it. I guess subtleties of racism exist everywhere, for more reasons than just skin color."

"Of course," said Adam. "In England I'm not so sure our class structure isn't more prejudicial in its own way than your white-black problem. But we disguise it with the British highbrow manner and a gloss of culture and refinement, so no one notices. We're so disgustingly polite."

Scott laughed. "I never thought I'd hear a Brit admit such a thing! Are *you* prejudiced, Adam?" he asked jokingly.

"Against blacks or my inferiors?" said Adam.

"Ah, so you admit there *are* those who are your inferiors!"

"I admit to no such thing!" He grinned. "Not that I admit to any superiors either," he added with a wink.

Both men laughed.

"But seriously," Adam continued, "I don't suppose any of us is completely free of prejudice. But I do hope I've managed to move beyond most of mine. But go on with what you were saying a moment ago."

"Well . . . here, it's like I'm looked at differently."

"In what way?"

"I don't know, almost as a traitor because I work *for* you."

"You really feel that?" asked Adam.

"It's subtle. I don't suppose anyone but an American black could pick up on it. I don't know, maybe I do imagine it. Yet you can't help but pick up the occasional odd glance, the stare full of question."

"You're reading too much into it."

"Maybe you're right. But it's funny—with all the emphasis lately on being African-American and roots and everything, I feel far more *American* than I do African. I'm out of my element here. For all I know, African blacks feel similar odd sensations when they come to the States. Just having black skin and having the same ancestors two, three, four hundred years ago, doesn't make all blacks the same any more than white skin does a German and an Englishman."

"No, I don't suppose it does."

"There's variation in the skin color of blacks just like whites. And historically it's been a source of division among us. Prejudice exists *within* races just as surely as *between* races."

"What about our common ancestry in Noah? That really takes it back a few generations!"

The two friends laughed at the thought.

"You walked the gorge yet?" asked Scott.

"A little. I'm going out again later."

That evening, as twilight gradually spread over the Serengeti, Adam Livingstone walked alone, contemplating the remarkable finds made here. Along the gorge at Olduvai over one hundred separate tool or fossil sites were located. The separate discoveries here numbered in the thousands. It was a unique break in the earth's crust, unmatched anywhere for exposing glimpses into the past between one and two million years ago. Woodland and savanna had once spread over the region. But it was the history of the water that Adam found most intriguing. Evidence suggested that a great salt lake once covered the area but had later given way to an intricate system of freshwater streams and ponds.

*What if the geologic signs hadn't been caused by a salt* lake *at all,* thought Adam, *but from a massive global flood?*

These and many such questions flitted through his mind as he walked. Casually he flipped at the pebbles beneath his feet with his walking stick.

A smile crept over Adam's lips.

What if suddenly his stick overturned something that would prove to be the next Lucy? He'd better keep his eyes open!

What would he name *his* great find—Candace . . . Jennifer . . . Juliet?

Candace would probably *not* be flattered to have a pile of old bones named after her, Adam thought with a smile.

It wasn't the bones of another Lucy he was after, though.

What he'd really like to uncover was some fragment of *wood* that revealed an equally incredible story. *That* would truly pioneer new ground. *Everyone* came here looking for hominid fossils. At this very moment there were probably more than a dozen separate archaeological digs in progress along the main and side gorges of Olduvai, not to mention elsewhere in the African rift.

But no one, to his knowledge, was seeking the other half—the botanical side—of the ancient equation of life. He wondered if anyone else had even paused to consider its significance.

It wasn't that Adam seriously thought he would find anything here at Olduvai. During the last five hundred thousand years, according to accepted dating, there had been a gradual shift to a more arid climate throughout Africa, which had turned much of it into a virtual desert. He called it the Sahara syndrome. This dry, rocky ground over which he walked was evidence of the change. It had been good for preserving fossils but not for growing vegetation.

He would find nothing *here*.

But after setting up camp at Olduvai, he would gradually carry his investigation farther afield, westward toward Lake Victoria, perhaps onto the slopes of the great African mountains, then toward the rain forests westward into Zaire. With Dr. Cissna's help he would see where the research led.

By the time Adam wandered back to camp, a full moon had risen over the dark blue horizon, appearing bigger and brighter here than anyplace on earth. The African plain was really a unique place—so huge, so quiet yet with the distant noises of animals coming from every direction, so empty of human habitation, so full of everything else . . . and with such a sense everywhere of antiquity and mystery . . . so wild. All these qualities were most evident at night, when the sounds of the nocturnal kingdom came to life.

Scott and Jen sat outside the tent under the light of a lantern. Jen held a book in her hand.

"What are you reading?" asked Adam.

"One of the psalms," replied Jen. "Psalm 8, actually."

"Why a psalm? I didn't know you were a student of the Bible."

"I suppose because of this."

She handed Adam a small card. "Erin's mother knew of our plans. She sent it to me before we left," she said.

On it Adam read the words *Have a great trip—God bless you!* On the opposite side, beneath the scene of a magnificent mountain lake with the solitary figure of a man walking beside it, was the Scripture verse *What is man that you are mindful of him . . . ? O Lord, our Lord, how majestic is your name in all the earth!* (Psalm 8:4, 9).

"I thought I would like to know what the whole psalm was like," said Jen.

"Read it to us," said Adam, unfolding a third chair and sitting down beside her.

Jen did so. When she finished, no one spoke. It remained silent among them. Each beheld the landscape, glowing now under the light of the huge rising silver moon, and drank in the peaceful wildness of the African plain, contemplating the significance of the Hebrew poem they had just heard.

No words seemed appropriate, and no more were uttered. An hour passed. Finally Jen, followed by Scott, and then finally Adam rose, and each walked slowly to his or her tent for the night.

(2)

Adam woke early. In the distance he could hear an occasional cry of hyena or roar of bull elephant. Farther away he heard the shrieking of monkeys.

What had awakened him, however, were the last words he had heard the night before. He had slept soundly all night, and his fatigue was gone. He rose, dressed, and went out into the morning.

Across the plain, in the mist of the faint predawn light, a herd of giraffes moved as if in slow motion. Elephants and zebra were also visible. There was no place on earth like this, thought Adam. He had come here in search of beginnings. How could anyone argue that the abundance of animal life, surrounded by evidence in whatever direction one turned of man's antiquity, reminded one of creation itself.

Adam walked slowly away from his tent into the still misty air. *How had it all come about?* he wondered. *Where had it come from? How had it begun?*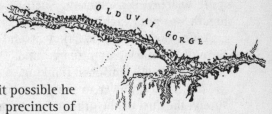

Incredible as was the thought, was it possible he could perhaps be standing within the precincts of the original Eden, changed and made unrecogniz-able by eons of climatic shifts? He could articulate his theory convincingly. Yet when it came to walking along the ground and actually saying "Eden was here," he wasn't quite so confident. Who could possibly make such a bold claim?

If only he could lay his hands on some tangible proof.

*Creation.*

Adam paused, knelt down, and scooped up a small handful of the rocky, dusty soil beneath his feet. He gazed at the inanimate matter—a handful of mere dust.

Many of his colleagues here at Olduvai and in other such locations had knelt down as he had just done. Instead of rock, they had reached to the ground and laid hold of some bone or bit of skull that had once been part of the skeleton of prehistoric man.

Adam continued to gaze pensively at the dirt in his hand.

What was the difference between the rock around him everywhere, this dirt in his palm, and the fossilized bones that were so plentifully scattered about the region? The bones and fossils they found were no more alive now than rock.

What was the difference? Could rock from the earth ever become human bone? What distinguished the two? Not mere chemical composition.

The difference, of course, was . . . life.

Somehow, at some distant time, the fossils and skeletons of men and women had been alive. Rocks could never live . . . but the creatures who had walked this region long ago had been alive.

How had bones been given life? What caused a living, breathing, loving, reproducing, thinking, deciding man or woman to come into existence from all this nonalive matter they called dust?

Surely that life had come by no mere accident and chance. The thing could not be possible.

Adam smiled, reminded of the words. *The Lord God formed the man from the dust of the ground and breathed into his nostrils the breath of life, and the man became a living being.*

A moment more Adam beheld the handful of dirt he had picked up. He brought his hand toward him and blew lightly upon it, sending up a small cloud of dust.

He watched it a moment. Such a simple act, yet so full of mystery. His breath was not capable of giving life.

Adam now spread his fingers and allowed the remaining dirt to flow through them back onto the ground.

He stood and continued thinking.

Man had no power to create life out of the dust of the ground. Just as surely, the dust of the ground had no power to generate life of itself.

But life existed. It had come from somewhere. How could it have originated if not from a Creator's hand?

And man was the greatest living creature of all—a being who could think and yearn and love and decide and, to a limited degree, even create. What magnificent power had been placed within the human species, far beyond that in the giraffe and elephant.

Something had to account for that uniqueness. Evolution could not explain it. All the finds in the Olduvai Gorge for another thousand years would never explain it. Man was more magnificent . . . man had to be more magnificent than all the rest of creation.

The explanation could be no other than Eden . . . and that puff of creative breath out of the mouth of the Almighty into the man he had made—and the command to live.

Adam's quest was not merely for the place of man's beginnings, but for the Source of those beginnings . . . the divine *why* of those beginnings.

As if answering the questions he did not even know how to ask, Adam Livingstone found himself repeating the words of the psalm Jen had read the previous night. The words came as from some inner well within his own soul.

*What is man that you are mindful of him . . . ? You made him a little lower than the heavenly beings and crowned him with glory and honor. You made him ruler over the works of your hands; you put everything under his feet: all flocks and herds, and the beasts of the field, the birds of the air, and the fish of the sea. . . . O Lord, our Lord, how majestic is your name in all the earth!*

It was all so visible . . . right here! Was that because . . . it had begun here? What was man . . . ?

The words of the Scripture reminded him of the meaning of his own name— Adam . . . man.

Unconsciously the passage repeated itself in his brain—What is Adam . . . ? Then came the whole sentence—What is Adam . . . that you are mindful of him?

*God,* he thought—addressing the words more to himself than to another— *are you truly mindful . . . of me . . . are you mindful of Adam Livingstone?*

He recalled Juliet Halsay's comment, which struck him as unusual at the time, about God's caring about her. Here were words saying that very thing about all mankind . . . and—if he put stock in it—of him personally.

Suddenly the question burst forth, and this time he could not deny that it was a prayer, *"Oh, Lord, where was it you did these things? Where did you make man ruler over the animal kingdom? Where was the Garden where you walked with Adam?"*

He hardly realized what he'd done. Adam had never prayed aloud in his life. Suddenly the words had come forth from some deep reservoir inside him. This was no mere scientific exploration. Adam Livingstone had embarked upon a journey from which there was no return. His life seemed to have brought him to a giant flowing river. He now felt he was standing on the bank gazing into its moving waters. An unseen impulse told him to jump into the center of its tide and trust where it would take him, though he could see nothing of where it led.

Perhaps Eden was no place man was meant to find on the earth. Perhaps it had disappeared so that the descendents of the first Adam would discover Eden elsewhere . . . within their own hearts.

*Well,* thought Adam, shaking off the mystic thoughts, *perhaps if for no other reason than by virtue of my name, I am going to try to find both places— the earth garden and the heart garden.*

*Though,* he added to himself with a smile, *at this moment I don't know where either is located!*

He had walked a good distance. The horizon was brightening. The sun would soon explode over its eastern edge, and the heat of the day would return.

It was time to get back.

(3)

"Good . . . right—you have the core-boring equipment, Dr. Cissna?"

"I'll bring everything we will need, Mr. Livingstone," replied the botanist. "We'll have a variety of increment borers and extractors. I've got a special Swedish borer over forty inches long. I've contacted some specialists about your request for plastic tubing for preserving the samples rather than the standard metal ones. It is a little unusual. Most ring counting is done on site because the cores are so fragile. But I think we shall be able to manage it. You'll see to the permits?"

"I've cleared our research with authorities in Kenya and Tanzania already. I'll get on the phone immediately to the Congo."

"And Uganda? We need to go to Murchison Falls Park."

"I have good relationships with everyone. Though unrest and refugees and fighting might pose a problem in some of these countries. But I hope we will be able to avoid it as much as possible."

"I am looking forward to the diversion," replied the professor.

"You should just be apprised of the uncertainties involved."

"I understand. It will be a pleasant change from my normal routine and a new challenge. I am eager to know more about your work."

"How long will it take us?"

"I shall be able to show you most of what you're looking for within a week. That's all the time I have to spare. After that you will be well capable of carrying the research forward on your own."

"I will look forward to seeing you in a couple of days then, Dr. Cissna. We will meet at the hotel in Arusha. Thank you."

Adam glanced at his watch. He wanted to make one more call. He hoped it wasn't too early. He informed the hotel operator of his request, then sat down as the call went through.

"Rocky . . . it's Adam."

"Hey, Livingstone, good to hear from you!"

"Likewise—hope I'm not calling too early."

"I needed to be out of bed, anyway. You all set up over there—I gather you're calling from Africa?"

"That's right. We're making progress, still getting used to it. What are your plans?"

"Not quite sure. Had a surprise waiting for me when I got home."

"What kind of surprise?"

"My place had been trashed."

"Oh, no! Serious?"

"Yeah, and they got Grandpa Harry's journal."

"I thought you said it was—"

"Yeah, in a bank box. They got to that too. Used a forged power of attorney document."

"What do we do now?" exclaimed Adam.

"I don't know, but this thing's starting to snowball. I don't like it."

"Nor do I. Not to minimize the damage to your house or the danger you must be in," said Adam, "but I really had my heart set on seeing that journal."

"You're not the only one."

"What are your plans now? With the journal missing, that changes everything. Are you still coming here?"

"The whole purpose was for us to go over the journal. I doubt I'll do you much good tramping around in the forests—that is, unless whoever's behind this has followed you there."

"I've seen no sign of danger," laughed Adam.

"There's not much use in my coming without the journal. I'll lay low for a day or two, try to get a handle on this thing, and put my house back in order. I'm going to see if I can get a lead on who broke into my place. If the trail's not too cold, hopefully I'll be able to pick it back up."

"I've got a favor to ask. If you do come, which I hope you still will, would you stop by my estate for a few days, just to make sure everything's all right there?"

"What's up?"

"I don't know. If they are following you now, too, it's obvious that whatever this is about isn't going away. Let's just say I'm concerned."

"Fair enough. I'll nose around here first. My priority at the moment is to see if I can find out who stole the journal. But I'll make tentative plans to come. When I do, I'll lay over a few days in London."

"Call and leave me a message again here at the hotel."

"I'll be in touch."

# seventeen

# Strangers in Peterborough

(1)

Rocky was sure it was the same guy from the airplane.

From this distance he couldn't be absolutely sure. But he could hardly mistake the same thin carriage and peculiar walk, and he thought he recognized the odd-looking cap.

He lowered his binoculars a moment and thought.

What were the odds that a European—of course, he didn't know that for a fact, he hadn't heard the man's voice, but he *looked* foreign—on his flight back from England, would wind up in Peterborough? And then hang around, apparently watching his house, just like he had watched him on the airplane.

*Zero in one hundred,* said Rocky to himself.

The fellow was following him, all right!

He'd just have to turn the tables. Besides, it was the only lead he had.

Rocky considered his options another moment or two, then jumped up and left the house. He didn't exactly have a plan, but he'd had experience watching people out of the back of his head. It wouldn't take long to tell what the guy was up to.

He crossed the street and headed toward the cafe. Peterborough was a quiet little New Hampshire town of less than three thousand inhabitants. He could practically see the whole town from his front porch—with its white houses and white picket fences and white snow on the ground—though a certain inevitable sprawl of buildings lengthened beyond his visibility along the two highways that crossed in the center of town.

He entered the cafe, glancing casually over his shoulder as the door closed behind him. Back across the street, the man's gaze had definitely followed him to the cafe. The mysterious stranger now turned and walked to the telephone booth between the gas station and grocery store.

"Hey, Darci," said Rocky toward the perfumed and pleasingly plump red-head at the counter, then sat down at a window booth and lifted a menu to his

229

face. Rocky continued to observe the man's movements. A minute later he came out of the phone booth, cast a quick glace in Rocky's direction as if to make sure he was going to be occupied for a while. The stranger then turned and walked in the opposite direction toward the town's single hotel.

Rocky gave the fellow a chance to get inside, then rose.

"Scramble me up some eggs, will you, Darci?" he said to the waitress. "And a couple English muffins. Give me about fifteen minutes."

"Sure thing, Rocky," she replied with a smile to her favorite customer. "Nice to have you back, by the way." She unconsciously tossed a couple of red curls back in place above her ear.

Rocky returned her smile as he walked toward the back of the room, past the rest rooms, and through the back door. Once outside, he crept carefully around the building. A moment he hesitated, then lumbered across an open lot into an alley extending parallel along the backyards of several houses fronting the main street. He passed two of them, then let himself into the yard of the third by means of an unlocked latch on a low wooden gate. Immediately the high-pitched bark of a terrier sounded frantically. The sound's owner came scurrying toward him.

"Shut up, Bugsy—you want the whole town to know I'm here! Good morning, Mrs. Hanks," he added with a smile, nodding to the woman whose inquisitive gaze now filled the frame of the back door she had just opened. "I hope you don't mind my using your yard."

"Not at all, Mr. McCondy. I didn't know you'd returned. But whatever are you doing?"

"Just trying to get to the hotel without being seen, Mrs. Hanks. Keep Bugsy off my ankle, will you?"

"Bugsy . . . Bugsy—come here!" she cried. "I declare, Mr. McCondy," she went on, speaking to Rocky again, "I don't know what to make of you and all your pranks. It's a mercy I mind my own business."

Rocky laughed at the remark. "It is indeed, Mrs. Hanks. You are better off not knowing."

"You hardly set my mind at ease, Mr. McCondy."

"The Lord gives some men strange things to do to put potatoes on their table, you know. I'll be over to mow your lawn for you at the first sign of spring."

Rocky continued on into the lady's front yard, then paused.

From here only the nondescript wall of the hotel was visible. Nor did any of the second- and third-story windows face this direction. He hurried across the street, approached the wall of the building. He now crept forward carefully, pausing as he drew gradually alongside the edge of the front veranda.

Still contemplating his options, Rocky heard the hotel's front door open. Footsteps crossed the wooden planking. He stepped back and ducked low out of sight.

". . . he'll be there awhile. Let's go up the road and get something to eat . . . going stir-crazy in this dump of a place." A muffled reply came in a foreign-sounding voice. It almost sounded like a woman.

Two figures now descended the steps and walked away from him toward the hotel's small parking lot. Rocky inched his way upward and peeped up over the railing of the veranda. The green beret was walking toward a car with someone he didn't recognize. He couldn't tell whose voice had been whose.

He ducked down again and waited.

(2)

A minute later the car drove away. Rocky stood, walked around to the front, then up the steps and into the hotel.

"Morning, Weiderman," he called out to the clerk at the desk. "How's the tourist business?"

"Not like September, Rock, that's for sure. Not much to see around here in the wintertime—unless you're partial to snow. Nobody wants to climb Monadnock in this weather."

"Those two who just left," said Rocky, nodding toward the door. "What rooms are they in?"

"Come on, Rock, you know I can't—"

"After all the business I bring you."

"Yeah, I know. . . ."

"And saving your hide in that scam by the guy who was going to pay you a million dollars for this place but who was just stringing you along for a sucker. You owe me big time, Weed."

"I know, I know, but—"

"Just a couple room numbers. Nobody'll know—especially those two. They're up to no good, Weed. All I'm trying to do is put a stop to a crime before it happens."

"What kind of crime?"

"Could be murder."

"Murder!"

"Yeah—and it might be *mine* if I don't find out what they're up to!"

"All right, you win," said the man with resignation. "Rooms 23 and 24."

"Thanks, Weed!"

Rocky turned to go.

"Hey, Rock . . . you want the keys?"

"Don't think I'll need them. Besides," he added with a wink, "I don't want you to get in trouble."

"With whom?"

"The boss."

*"I'm* the boss!"

"Oh, yeah . . . right!" said Rocky with a wink.

"Thanks for nothing, Rock."

(3)

Rocky glanced up and down the hall, more from habit than nervousness, then inserted a small hooked lever, one of the tools of his profession, into the lock of room 23.

This was one part of his work he was having more and more trouble reconciling with being a Christian. He'd probably have to give the business up one day because of it. It had never bothered him when he was a cop. But things were different now. It got harder every time he broke in somewhere he wasn't supposed to be, even when lives were in danger. He always had a litany of arguments to parade out at such times about doing good and saving lives and foiling the bad guys. However, they were accomplishing less and less to soothe his conscience.

But things were heating up. He wasn't about to resolve the ends-and-means debate and which justified what right now. He wasn't even going to try. At this point the ethical debate would have to wait.

The hotel door swung open. Rocky let himself inside. An eerie sensation swept through him.

He couldn't put it into words. He knew at once that something was going on here on a different level than he'd ever encountered before. It was no feeling his brain could rationalize. It was something he *felt* . . . and it made the hair on his arms stand on end.

He walked toward the bureau. He pulled out a drawer or two. Nothing.

He glanced around. A suitcase stood in the closet, closed and upright. He pulled it out, set it flat on the floor, and opened it.

Bingo! Identification papers, from the looks of it . . . and more besides.

Hurriedly he glanced through the papers, the leather passport satchel, the photographs and maps, and the envelope of odds and ends. He was tempted to take everything but thought better of it. There were only two things here he *had* to have . . . and those he had a *right* to have. They'd been stolen from his own attic.

This was more urgent than he'd realized. And exactly as big as he'd told Adam.

Rocky jumped up and continued a hasty look around. In another minute or two he was searching the room next door. It proved nearly as significant a trove.

Five minutes was all it took. But when he was done Rocky was perspiring freely, notwithstanding the cold outside. He hadn't felt fear very many times in his life, but he recognized this as unlike anything he had ever been up against.

Rocky ran from the room, barely remembering to lock the door. As it turned out, he hadn't exactly told the hotel owner the truth. They *would* know he'd been there.

He couldn't help it. He wasn't about to add that unintentional fib to his conscience's problems now.

He took the stairs two at a time and bounded across the lobby for the front door.

"Thanks, Weed!" he called out as he passed the desk. "Debt paid in full. Now I owe *you* one!"

(4)

A minute later Rocky ran into the cafe.

Sorry, Darci," he said, "those eggs are gonna have to wait!"

"But Rocky, they're—"

"On second thought, my dear . . . take them over to Weiderman at the hotel. Matter of fact, put on a big juicy T-bone to go with them!"

"You serious?"

"He just may have saved my life. You fix him the biggest breakfast you know how to make. Give yourself a twenty dollar tip . . . and put the whole thing on my tab."

"Thanks, Rocky!"

Already the detective was back out the door.

"But, Rocky," the waitress called after him, "when will I see you—"

"Don't know, Darci. I'll be in touch. And if any strangers ask about me, you never saw me this morning!"

She watched him go. Then a faint, lonely smile crossed her lips, as a finger twirled at the unruly red strand that had fallen again.

Even while he managed the closest thing to a sprint he was capable of across the street back to his house, Rocky realized he had thirty or forty minutes at most. After that, he couldn't tell what they might do. Obviously the second person was the one who had trashed his house. After what had happened in England to Livingstone's lab girl, it was clear there weren't too many limits to these people's scruples.

He ran inside and straight to the attic. Five minutes later he was hauling the great trunk down the stairs and toward the back door. He put into it what few things he possessed of value, as many of his records and files as he could, and a few personal belongings he especially wanted kept safe. He had to find someplace they'd never think of to stash it.

Twenty-eight minutes later, Rocky locked up the last of the doors tight. The trunk was in the car.

As he'd packed it he'd decided on his next step. He'd go see Pastor Mark. He was in over his head. He needed some spiritual advice before he made another move. The more help he could get in figuring out what God wanted him to do, the better.

He missed his wife, though he was glad she wasn't facing this danger with him. She had always had a sixth sense about spiritual matters. But the Lord had given him Mark and Laurene in her place. At times like this he was especially thankful for them.

# eighteen

# Origins and Eras

(1)

Adam Livingstone and the man he hoped would widen his knowledge of African flora took off in a small chartered plane from the airfield in Arusha. A versatile and experienced pilot, Adam himself sat at the controls.

Today would be an opportunity for the two men to establish their bearings and get an overview of the region, before circling back and touching down in two or three hours at the dirt airstrip near Olduvai. Adam had rented the plane for a week.

"I appreciate your making room for me in your schedule, Dr. Cissna," Adam said as they rose steeply.

"What little you've told me over the phone is so intriguing," rejoined the botanist enthusiastically, "that I could not possibly pass up such an opportunity. What exactly is it you hope to find?"

"In a word, Dr. Cissna—old living organisms. *Very* old. And not fossils—current specimens."

"I sensed a certain reluctance to divulge details of your research when we spoke before."

"I am sorry about that," said Adam. "I have learned to be guarded. Lately we have had some serious security problems. I scarcely trust telephones now! I thought it best that a detailed explanation wait."

"We could hardly be more alone now, Mr. Livingstone," laughed the professor, gesturing out the window of the Cessna 150. "I am eager for whatever you feel at liberty to tell me. What is the purpose of your expedition? It hardly seems the normal quest of an archaeologist . . . looking for *living* things."

"My quest, as you call it, has one objective, Dr. Cissna," said Adam. "Eden."

The botanist's head turned toward Adam with an expression of incredulity. He studied Adam's face a moment, as if searching for some indication that the man was pulling his leg. All he could find returning his look of inquiry were eyes of utmost sincerity.

"The biblical Garden?" he repeated in disbelief. *"The Garden of Eden?"*
Adam nodded.

"I want to find the oldest species of plant life on the globe," continued Adam. "If my theory is correct, it will exist somewhere here in the rift region, possibly extending northeastward up toward the Red Sea."

"You say your *theory*. What exactly *is* your theory?"

"I call it the large-oval Eden theory," replied Adam. He went on to explain the basic premise.

The botanist listened as one caught up in a sudden new world of unbelievable possibility and adventure, hardly able to contain his enthusiasm over the simplicity and logic of Adam's deductions.

"You truly may be onto something, Mr. Livingstone," he said excitedly. "You are absolutely correct when you say that huge worlds of potential lay hidden in vast jungles and rain forests, undiscovered plant forms, extensive root systems, vines and fungi capable of growing downward and outward literally for miles and miles. The possibilities are boundless. We know so little about this earth of ours, in spite of all our study and research. Indeed— why might not evidence of Eden still exist . . . if we could just locate it? In fact—"

He turned toward Adam.

"What do you have in mind for us today?"

"Nothing specific. Just get an overview of the region and discuss the work."

"Then turn south," said Dr. Cissna, pointing his hand off to the left.

Adam obeyed instantly and banked the small plane steeply to the south.

"We'll start at Lake Manyara just a short distance from where we are now. We'll drive over there tomorrow. It should come into our view within ten minutes. There are more elephants there than trees. We'll see the herds easily from up here."

"There is vegetation as well?"

"Mostly what grows nearby is acacia. But still, the west shore near the volcanic rock of the Crater Highlands supports some very interesting high-groundwater forest vegetation with some instances of *Adansonia digitata*, which will be a primary quarry. I want you to fly over it and get an overview. Manyara will be an excellent place to begin. Then we can fly up to Mount Kenya too. There we will find many more varieties."

"I can tell you are enthusiastic about your work, Doctor."

"And yours. I am very intrigued by your theory. But how versatile is this plane—will we be able to get in and out wherever we need to? I expected that you would have a Piper."

"I thought this would be more comfortable at first. But if we have difficulty, I'll find a Supercub to rent. It's the best of the tail-draggers for our kind of work. They can land anywhere."

"In any event, there is truly no better place to conduct your inquiry. The flora of eastern Africa is truly fascinating."

"So you are optimistic?" asked Adam as they flew.

"It just may be the tree known as the baobab that holds the key to what you are looking for," the botanist replied. "They have only been found up to twenty-five hundred years old, but with luck we may do better. Some say they are the oldest living things. It is diffi-cult to get accurate readings, however, because the wood is often spongy."

"Why is that?"

"They tend to hollow out inside, accu-mulating large reservoirs of water. Ele-phants will attack and destroy old trees to get at it."

"I see how that could make our job diffi-cult."

"But they *are* huge and old. Their hol-lowed-out trunks have even been used as houses. There is a famous story of one baobab used as a bus stop. Thirty people could cram inside its trunk!"

"Remarkable," laughed Adam. "How do they compare in age with the bristlecone pines?"

"It is a heated debate. Counting rings is not so exact a science as one might think. One section of a tree will die while another goes on living. One side will be struck by lightning or hit with some blight, which will affect the ring count. Oftentimes you have to take cores at different angles and try to match rings in different samples that overlap one another. And as I'm sure you know, we have other methods we have for determining age."

"It's a complicated science."

"Indeed it is. I also want you to see thorn trees and the giant euphorbia in Queen Elizabeth Park. It is actually a form of cactus but may be ancient be-yond our capacity to determine age, so I am sure it will intrigue you. Africa, Mr. Livingstone, is mysterious and ancient wherever you look. Its antiquity does not merely point in the direction of human fossils, but includes flora and fauna and geology and nearly all the diciplines. And I do not speak merely be-cause I am a native Egyptian and prejudiced in favor of my home continent. It truly is, in my opinion, the continent of beginnings."

"The more research I do, Doctor, the more inclined I am to agree."

"Of course you also must see the giant heather trees of Mount Kenya and the giant groundsel. Do you know the groundsel?"

"I've heard of it."

"Most unique bark structure. Neither it nor the heather is as old as the bao-bab. But they should interest you as well. *Everything* in Africa is interesting, and most, if you know how to trace origins, is quite old as well."

By the time they reached the gorge itself, both men were engaged in vigorous discussion about their plans for the following week.

✦ ✦ ✦

In her sandals and khaki shorts, Jen came running out of her tent, blond braids bouncing, as Adam and Dr. Cissna drove up in the jeep. Adam knew by the expression on her face that she had news, although he couldn't tell whether to anticipate good or bad.

"Let's have it," he said. "I can tell you're bursting with something."

"You'll never guess who just set up shop less than a mile away," she said.

"You're right," laughed Adam. "I won't."

"Gilbert Bowles."

"Sir Gilbert!" Adam exclaimed. "What on earth is *he* doing here—and practically right beside us!"

"Your guess is as good as mine. We heard about it from one of the other camps. Scott's walking over now to see if he can find out anything—you know—the casual friendly approach."

"Bowles won't buy it for a second. He'll be more suspicious of Scott than we are of him. But, Jen, meet Dr. Petiri Cissna from the University of Cairo. He's going to lead us to the oldest living things on the face of the earth."

The vibrant young Swede shook hands with the gregarious professor, who was no more than an inch taller than she. Having a dark complexion and a thin black moustache, his wiry frame seemed to possess an energetic enthusiasm that could not be contained. His English was nearly perfect, though it contained a distinct Mediterranean accent, enhanced by the mischievous smile constantly playing about his lips and the sparkle that came from his active eyes.

"I made no such promises, Mr. Livingstone," laughed the Egyptian.

"I have faith in you, Dr. Cissna!" rejoined Adam. "I did a thorough background check before contacting you. I know both your reputation and your talents."

(2)

The following morning, their leisurely camp breakfast was interrupted by the sounds of several jeeps and Land Rovers rumbling toward an adjacent campsite.

"What's all the commotion?" asked Scott, standing and peering toward the noise.

"That's the direction of Bowles' camp," said Jen.

"What is our esteemed colleague up to now?" laughed Adam, rising also and following the others' gazes. Already Scott had grabbed his binoculars and walked some distance to a rise in the ground that gave him better visibility.

"I can't make out a thing," he said, returning in a minute.

"A friend of yours?" asked Dr. Cissna.

"He may be a friend of Adam's, but not mine," rejoined Jen.

"Sir Gilbert's harmless enough," said Adam.

"I've never met the man. This should be an experience," exclaimed Dr. Cissna.

"You're not going to meet him now either. Come, Dr. Cissna—let's have a closer look. I'll explain as we go."

They set off across the gorge toward the Bowles' camp, which lay only some thousand yards away across rocky terrain of scraggly wild shrubs and scattered small trees. As they drew within a hundred or so yards, Adam paused, shielded by a moderately sized cropping of rocks and growth, to see what was going on.

"Hand me those binoculars, will you, Scott?"

Scott did so. Adam peered through them, then gradually began to chuckle.

"You're not going to believe this," he said. "It looks like the press has followed him here . . . or else Sir Gilbert has called a press conference. Three carloads of reporters just pulled up, and they're all piling out."

"What a publicity hound!" groaned Jen.

"Give him the benefit of the doubt," laughed Adam. "He may have had nothing to do with it. They may have followed him."

"I bet he set the whole thing up."

"Let's stay out of sight. The press hasn't followed us here, which is fine with me. Gilbert Bowles is a respected archaeologist in his own right. There's no reason why the press wouldn't be all over him if he's about to embark on a new dig."

"Which he has no intention of doing," rejoined Jen. "I don't trust him. I tell you, Adam, he's here to spy on you."

Adam laughed again.

"I don't know about the rest of you, but I'm going up for a closer look," said Scott. "With my complexion, I'll blend right in with all the local reporters."

"Are you crazy?" said Adam. "I can't let you—"

"I'll be careful. I want to know what Bowles is up to. I'm not so sure Jen is wrong in her assessment."

"They'll recognize you."

"Nah," rejoined Scott, already walking off.

"Dr. Cissna and I will head back to camp," said Adam with a reluctant smile. "I can't afford to be seen. I certainly do *not* want anyone asking questions about Dr. Cissna's presence. We can't have inquisitive reporters putting two and two together. Come, Doctor, let's you and I get back."

"Jen, you coming with me?" asked Scott, as Adam and their guest headed back the way they had come.

"Sure."

The two emerged from their hiding place and traipsed across the uneven ground with expressions of a schoolboy and schoolgirl up to some mischief.

A few minutes later, having worked their way unseen around behind the group of journalists clustered about Sir Gilbert Bowles, Jen and Scott casually approached the clearing where the archaeologist had set up his camp. Still unseen, they sauntered to the back of the entourage. The hulking figure of Sir Gilbert stood thirty or forty feet away—his trademark hat, khaki garb, ponytail, and dangling serpent earring setting him apart wherever he happened to be. He was obviously enjoying himself and had already begun fielding questions from the group.

". . . and as you know, the remains I found in this valley a few years ago prove beyond question that man as we know him today evolved over millions of years."

"That's old news," called out Kaci Lyle, science editor for *World* magazine. "You called this press conference and dragged us out into the middle of nowhere. Give us something new."

A number of voices raised in agreement. It had indeed been a long trip, and many would encounter disgruntled editors upon their return if this junket did not reap worthwhile news.

"Just wanting to lay a little groundwork," assured Bowles. "All right, how is this for hard news? I am here to prove that there has been a continuous, uninterrupted settlement of hominid and later *Homo* species in this valley and its environs much longer than the 1.2 to 1.9 million years previously thought."

"How much longer?" asked someone.

"Perhaps up to 5 or 6 million years," answered Bowles, "predating the period during which a salt lake covered much of this region."

"How will you prove your hypothesis?" asked the *World* editor.

"My team of experts is on its way, Miss Lyle. What we are doing—and already this work is in progress by computer in London—is documenting and cataloguing and dating all bits of fossil evidence that have been found at Olduvai over the last forty years—since the Leakeys' time. Their discovery here at Olduvai in 1959, as you recall, was dated at 1.8 million years. My results will reveal a clear picture of an unbroken history of man and conclusively demonstrate evolution's incontrovertibility. My hope, in addition to the benefit of such anthropological sequencing data, is to dispel the Creation myth once and for all."

"Come on," called out a reporter, "you're going to *prove* evolution? Even Darwin would laugh at that."

"You Americans," retorted Bowles, "are long on intuition and short on facts. I doubt anything can be proven to you. But the rest of the world will take note."

Laughter spread through the group. Bowles was known, and generally liked, for his sharp, though sometimes biting, wit.

"What about the recent finding of your colleague Adam Livingstone?" asked the tall American.

"What about it, Adrian?"

"His discovery of an actual ark supports the biblical version of a worldwide flood. How does that correlate with your theory that early biblical history is nothing but moonshine?"

Sir Gilbert smiled. He had been waiting for the press to go in this direction.

"My dear Mr. DeWald," he said, radiating a countenance of patronizing pity. "Finding *one* structure on *one* mountain hardly leads to the conclusion of a worldwide flood."

He paused and smiled again.

"Let's see," he said. "How may I put this delicately? Instead of letting facts verify or disprove his hypothesis and lead to rational conclusions, I am afraid our good friend Adam Livingstone has allowed mythology—and I use even *that* word generously—to contaminate his theories. Then he looks for support of his fantasy-laden constructs in fields and under glaciers, or under his bed, for all I can tell. But boogeymen and fairy tales have no place in science. And besides, the point is—if there *was* a flood, it was obviously localized. But I do not even accept that explanation."

"You're telling us, you don't buy the ark business?"

"I don't know if I would put it that way, Charane," replied Bowles with a playfully devious smile. "Can't you tell, I am doing my best to be gracious toward my colleague? But you are at least correct in your conclusion. Really, my good people, surely you can see as well as I can that our dear Mr. Livingstone, for whatever reason, has come down with a terminal case of religion?"

"Do you deny the finding of Noah's ark?"

"Excuse me—*Noah's ark?*" rejoined Bowles. "I do not deny that he found something. And yes, it appears to be a large, boat-shaped object. But who says it is Noah's ark? There have been so-called boat-shaped objects found on and in the neighborhood of Ararat before. Obviously, early civilization in that region possessed skilled boatbuilders."

"It must mean something."

"Oh, to be sure, Miss Douglas. Everything means something. But the devil, as they say, is in the details. Or, in our line of work, the devil is in the interpretation."

"And you say Livingstone's interpretation of what he has found is wrong?" asked the noted Johannesburg journalist Eliza Douglas.

"Consider the evidence logically, Eliza. For myself, as I have travelled around this globe, I have never ceased to be amazed at the accomplishments of our forefathers," said Bowles, now assuming a dignified, professorial tone. "If the Egyptians can build a pyramid in the desert, and if the Incas can establish an advanced civilization so far from other human habitation high up in the Andes, what is to prevent the ancients of Turkey from building a boat?"

"What about Adam Livingstone's search for the Garden of Eden?"

Again Bowles smiled, then gradually began to laugh. After a few seconds his huge frame was fairly shaking up and down with unsuppressed jocularity. His delight with the very question proved contagious. Soon all but the two standing unnoticed at the back of the group had joined in.

"I can't stand that man!" fumed Jen between gritted teeth.

"Just keep smiling," whispered Scott. "Adam's reputation doesn't need any help from him."

"We're going to be calling him Rev. Livingstone before long!" Bowles finally said through his laughter.

"Do you think there's anything to it?" asked the young woman he had called Charane.

"Of course not. The Bible's a fairy tale. I won't even dignify it by calling it a myth. It's pure fancy. My own work and that of ten thousand scientists for the last hundred and fifty years categorically proves it."

"Livingstone might disagree with you."

"Yes, and the way he's going, I expect him to tell me to repent of my sins or I'll be on my way to hell anytime now!" chortled Bowles. "I can't imagine what's got into the man. He used to be a decently straight-up fellow. Maybe he snuck off to a revival service somewhere!"

In the shuffling that accompanied the laughter and joking banter at Bowles' ribbing of his colleague, the *World* editor chanced to glance behind her. A momentary expression of confusion crossed over her face, followed by gradual recognition.

She turned and began walking slowly toward Jen and Scott, still apparently debating with herself if she was actually looking at whom she thought she saw. Realizing they'd been spotted, the two now began nonchalantly backing away to beat a hasty retreat.

"Wait a minute!" called Lyle, increasing her step. "Hey, it's Scott Jordan! What's up here? Jordan, wait . . . I want to ask you some questions! Have you defected to Bowles' team of experts?"

By now she was hurrying forward. It was obviously too late to get away. At her shouts, the entire entourage had turned and now followed her.

Behind them, a disgruntled Bowles—not laughing now—watched them go. Suddenly he felt very much alone. He did nothing to display his annoyance, however. He would get the last laugh yet.

"Oh, boy, there goes our cloak of secrecy," whispered Jen, as they backed away. "Adam's going to kill us!"

"Don't worry," said Scott, "we still have a few tricks up our sleeve. We've just got to make sure they don't learn about Dr. Cissna. That would kibosh everything."

"If we can convince them we're here for some good reason."

"They'll never suspect what Adam's really up to."

"Hey, you two," said Lyle, as she approached, "care to share with the rest of us what you're talking about between yourselves? What are you doing here, anyway?"

"You're on, Scott!" said Jen.

(3)

When Mark Stafford opened the door of his house and saw his friend standing on the porch, his face went momentarily pale. He stared at his visitor for a second with blank expression.

"What in the world?" exclaimed Rocky, not knowing whether to be serious or laugh. "You look like you've seen a ghost!"

"I . . . I'm sorry, Rocky," said Stafford, recovering himself. "It's just that— this may sound bizarre, but to tell you the truth, Laurene and I wondered if we'd ever see you again."

Now it was Rocky's face that filled with a bewildered stare.

"Come in . . . come in, Rocky," said the pastor warmly. "I can't tell you how great it is to see you! Honey!" he called back inside as he led Rocky into the living room, "you'll never guess who's here!"

"Rocky!" exclaimed Mrs. Stafford, entering a moment later from the kitchen with a dish towel in her hand. She went straight to him and embraced the private investigator. When she stepped back, Rocky saw that tears filled her eyes. "We've been praying for you," she said softly, though it was with obvious difficulty that she struggled to get the words out.

"What is this?" said Rocky with almost a nervous laugh. "If I didn't know better, I'd think I had just returned from the grave."

"I'll make coffee," said Laurene, turning back toward the kitchen.

"And I'll explain," added her husband. "Have a seat, Rocky."

"I don't know which I want most—the coffee or the explanation."

The two men sat down. "We thought you were in danger," said Stafford.

"I was . . . I suppose I still am."

"From the business with the British archaeologist?"

Rocky nodded.

"I'm sure that's why the Lord put it so urgently on our hearts to pray for you. We sensed that you were in the middle of something big. We've been lifting you up in what I can only call strenuous prayer every day."

"I appreciate that."

Gradually Rocky's story came out as the two men continued to talk. The pastor's wife listened from the kitchen, and a few minutes later reentered the living room with a tray of mugs and a carafe of fresh coffee.

(4)

A minute or two of informal chatting followed as they each poured cups of coffee and stirred in their preferences of enhancements.

"I have a favor to ask," said Rocky.

"I had the feeling, if and when we did see you again, that it would be more than a mere social call," rejoined the pastor.

"I'm afraid it is serious," said Rocky. "I'm sure I'm still in danger, like I said. Other people are in danger too. I'm going to have to leave town for a while."

"London again?"

"Initially. To be truthful, I'm not sure where it will lead. I may be heading for Africa after that."

"Our friend, the world traveller."

If you don't mind, I'd like to give you the key to my house and ask you to keep an eye on it while I'm gone."

"Not at all," replied the pastor.

"There could be some risk. It was broken into a few days ago."

The pastor and his wife glanced at one another, concerned.

"We'll be careful," said Stafford.

"And I need to store a trunk of valuables and files."

"You can leave it here."

"No. Too dangerous. What would you think of the basement of the church?"

"Good idea. There's nothing much of value down there anyway. It would be easy to hide with all the old chairs and boxes and clutter. But who are these people?"

"I don't know specifically. That's one of the things I'm trying to figure out. But they're dangerous. I'm sure they're connected with the end-times things you've been telling me about recently."

The pastor and his wife exchanged meaningful glances.

"Could we take the trunk over now?" added Rocky.

"You *are* in a hurry."

"I'm leaving town this afternoon," said Rocky.

"Then we'll take it right over," replied Stafford.

"First, I'd like to ask you about these," said Rocky. He pulled some papers out of his pocket and set them on the coffee table in front of them.

The pastor and his wife leaned forward. Each picked up two or three of the papers at a time, studied what they saw for a moment, then handed them each to the other. Both grew pensive.

"What is it?" said Rocky. "Your serious expressions have me worried."

"I think you ought to be worried . . . well, worried or excited perhaps," replied the pastor.

"Those two things hardly seem to go together."

"It depends on how you interpret events."

"How do you mean?"

"From what you've shown me, along with what we were talking about prior to your previous trip—I would say these indicate that something momentous, something truly significant, in the spiritual realm may be at hand. And you, my friend, would appear to be right in the middle of it. Do you sense the same thing, Laurene?" he added, turning to his wife.

"Absolutely," she replied. "I am feeling very strange right now. We are not alone. I know the Holy Spirit is here with us. But there are other forces present too. A real battle is under way."

"What are you talking about?" said Rocky. "You're giving me the shivers."

"It's no cause for fear, Rocky," said Mark. "But it is cause for vigilance. Laurene is right—we're in the midst of a battle. The Lord will go before us—the Lord is going before us even now. But we must have our weapons ready as well."

"I still hardly know what you're implying."

"I think we need to have a talk—a long talk—now, before you leave. But not here, if, as you say, you may be being watched."

"Before we do anything," said Laurene, "we must pray."

Immediately she closed her eyes and began to speak. *"Holy Spirit,"* she said softly, though in her voice was also the tone of confidence and command, *"we thank you for your presence here among us. We join our hearts in the name of the Lord Jesus Christ to bind the power of the enemy. May the blood of Jesus cover our every thought and prayer and the steps we take together. Protect us, Lord God. Fill us anew with your power to confront the wiles of the enemy and his legions. For we know that you have already won the victory. Give us courage to stand tall as we wield the weapons of warfare you have given us. Let us not quail in the face of fear but humbly walk in the might of your ultimate triumph. You have promised that the devil will flee when we resist him. In the name of Jesus and in the power of his shed blood, we do resist the devil and command him to be gone from among us. And now, Holy Spirit, show us your truth. Guide us into all truth. Anoint Mark with wisdom as he shares with Rocky about this time of battle that is upon us."*

A hush fell over the gathering as Laurene's tongue fell silent. Each sensed that the Lord was about to speak important truth to them in answer to her prayer.

"About that talk," said Mark at length, "what about if we meet at the church in twenty minutes."

He looked toward his wife with questioning glance, to see if her spirit bore witness to the suggestion. She nodded briefly.

"We'll leave here separately," the pastor went on. "Laurene and I will drive around a bit, perhaps stop in for a few minutes on Mrs. Woodcock. That should give you time to get there and unload your trunk. Back up to the fellowship hall, under the overhang. I don't think you'll be seen there. Then we'll stash your trunk and meet in my office."

"But—what's going on?" asked Rocky.

"You're about to come face-to-face with what may be the most astonishing story you've ever heard," replied Mark.

(5)

Face red with suppressed anger, Gilbert Bowles remained stock still, watching the entourage disappear out of his camp in pursuit of more lucrative journalistic quarry.

After answering a few questions, Scott and Jen realized they were digging themselves into deeper holes of double-talk than they were comfortable with. They glanced at one another, nodded, then turned suddenly and lit out running across the rugged terrain. The newshounds piled into their vehicles and tore off after them, doing their best to keep the two Livingstone assistants in their sight.

A minute or two later the dust clouds settled back to the ground, and the sounds of engines and shouts died away. Slowly Bowles walked toward his tent and threw back the flap.

"Relax," said a deep voice from inside.

"What do you mean, relax!" Bowles spat back. "Did you hear what happened?"

"I heard every word. We will use it to our advantage."

"What advantage! I've got to find out what he is up to. I'm supposed to call Cutter tonight and let him know what I've learned."

"Cutter . . . Mitch Cutter?"

"He didn't tell me his first name. He just gave me a number and told me to ask for Cutter."

The other man smiled. So, he thought to himself, Anni D'Abernon had associated herself more closely in the details of this little plot than he had realized. If her private lackey was involved, the Swiss woman wasn't far behind. She and Vaughan-Maier must be even more concerned about Livingstone than they'd let on. That would make matters interesting.

"Forget Cutter. I'll handle him."

"You know Cutter?" said Bowles, lifting an eyebrow.

"Of course."

The archaeologist's eyebrow remained cocked. This was one man he'd begun to regret getting mixed up with.

"But he musn't know I'm here, Bowles. Do you understand?"

"I know, I know—everything's always a big secret with you, Zorin."

"You make sure it stays that way."

The Voice made no attempt to mask its tone of menace. Bowles understood the man's meaning clearly enough.

(6)

Thirty minutes had passed.

Rocky's trunk of possessions was safely stashed in the basement of Peterborough Community Fellowship. He and Mark and Laurene Stafford had gathered in Pastor Mark's office.

"We were talking before about the conspiracy against God and his purposes and plan," Stafford began. "What I told you several weeks ago, before you left for England, was only the tip of the iceberg. I assumed we would continue to get together periodically. I planned for us to talk about what I believe this conspiracy is leading to. It would seem that the moment has arrived more quickly than I anticipated. In any event, these are things I believe you must hear . . . and now. This is no mere theological discussion. Your life may depend on your understanding of these things."

His wife nodded. "Truth in such matters is given to the saints so that we may combat the enemy effectively," she said. "It is far from just an intellectual exercise."

"What it's leading to?" repeated Rocky. "Are you talking about the end of the world or something?"

"You may not be far wrong, Rocky," replied Mark.

"Really?"

"Don't be alarmed. Not the end of the world, really. But certainly the coming of a new time, a new era."

"You're not doing much to reassure me."

"I'm sorry, my friend. It's something we have to face. I am not trying to reassure you—but warn you. The simple truth of the matter is this: I would stake my life on the fact that we are rapidly approaching the close of our present era on the earth—and soon."

"What happens then?" asked Rocky.

"A new era will begin."

"It's no secret that times are changing," commented Rocky, almost as if the vague rejoinder would make the pastor's unsettling revelations easier to swallow.

"Mark doesn't mean something like the Industrial Revolution or what people call the computer age," now put in the pastor's wife. "He's referring to something hugely more significant—on an eternal scale."

"Exactly," rejoined Mark. "I'm talking about eternal eras of God's vast plan."

"You're saying that one of those eras is about to end?"

"That is just what I am saying, Rocky. I think those papers you found confirm it. I think you may have stumbled across a trip-lever that may trigger events of worldwide significance, leading to . . . well, the end of the present age."

Rocky leaned back in his chair and exhaled a long sigh.

"That is," the pastor added seriously, "if they don't kill you first."

Rocky continued to shake his head back and forth slowly. He wished Livingstone could hear this firsthand. Unfortunately the man was thousands of miles away.

"All right, Mark . . . Laurene," he said, glancing toward his friends. Rocky's voice was soft and equally serious. "I'm listening."

"Everything has to do with time," the pastor began. "Time is the great definer of eras. All biblical truths function within a framework of time. What kind of statement described the creation, Rocky?"

"Uh, something about time?"

"Presicely. The first era—the era of creation—began with a statement of time, 'In the beginning . . . ' Do you see what I mean?"

Rocky nodded. "The beginning . . . of time?" he said.

"Right. And then what followed was broken up how?"

"By days?"

"Exactly. Creation was described in units of time—whatever duration those days may have had . . . however long that age of creation lasted. It's all about time. Do you see what I mean, Rocky?"

"More or less. You're saying that time is at the root of how God works."

"I couldn't have said it better. Now, back to the eras I mentioned. These eras I speak of are defined by the slow passage of time. But when a certain epoch reaches a conclusion, that point of finality comes all at once."

"In other words, they progress slowly, but conclude suddenly?"

"Right. Then a new long, slow stage begins. And there's one very telling factor that always accompanies these rapid moments of change out of one season and into the next."

"Which is?"

"The new epoch is always completely unlike what has come before. We're not just talking about the gradual, developmental maturing of the earth and its inhabitants. There are those who interpret history in that way. But it's inaccurate. History involves periodic jumps, quantum changes that thrust man forward from era to era. The changes don't just sort of happen. They don't gradually flow from one to the next—the changes come by means of specific breaks. This is another reason why evolution cannot be true—it violates the intrinsic method by which God works."

"No side roads, Mark," said Laurene with a light laugh in the midst of the serious mood. "You don't want to confuse Rocky with one of your tangents."

"Correction noted and received," said Mark with a smile, glancing toward her. "All right—the point I was making is that we're talking about fundamental changes that take place from one division of eternal history to the next, moments of transition that literally change everything about how man functions."

"I'm afraid you're losing me. Can you give me a specific example?"

"May I answer his question with an example from a woman's experience?" said Laurene.

Both men nodded for her to continue.

"Take a baby in a woman's womb," she began. "It lives there for nine months, cozy, warm, insulated. It's a world it is used to. During this nine months, in a sense, like Mark says, it is a season in that baby's life that progresses slowly."

She paused briefly.

"Then all of a sudden the change comes. The moment of birth is quick, cataclysmic, painful, and completely disrupts that former world, which is instantly gone. A new stage in the cycle of life has come."

"That's a great analogy," said her husband. "And death would complete the picture of another such moment of change."

"I see what you're getting at," said Rocky.

"History progresses like that," Mark went on, "although the changes are on a spiritual plane and thus not as easily seen. Let me give you the examples from Scripture. The first age was the era of creation. Whether you believe it lasted 17 billion years or six twenty-four-hour days you can decide for yourself. The point is, this was a span of time during which God fashioned the universe. In this stage, he inhabited the earth with vegetation and animals.

But then after creation was complete, it was time for a change. So then came a new interval of God's work—the age of early man. It was not a gradual change, but a quantum change. Evolutionists will argue with me, but I contend that in a moment of time, God made man and gave him what we call a soul. This was the first epochal shift. History now embarked upon a second era."

"The progression from out of the womb into the sunlight of the world!" added Laurene.

"Suddenly the old was gone," her husband went on. "Everything was new—just as it is for a newborn child. There was a new creature to whom the whole earth was given as dominion—a creature who could think and act and reason and decide and love and choose and grow and learn and speak . . . because he had been created in the image of the Creator himself. Everything changed as a result. The second era was completely unlike the first. Now that man was present, it was an entirely new world from what creation had been *without* man.

"This new epoch progressed. Many generations went by. Time again went by slowly. Many thousands of years passed. Then the flood came. A cataclysm in time. In an instant, except for eight faithful individuals, early man was wiped out. Again, everything changed. A new era came upon the earth—one in which God spoke and revealed himself to man and instructed him in worship and in life. In this third era following Noah, both civilization and the Jewish faith were born.

"But you see, it's not completely parallel with human life in having just two times of change—birth and death. The history of God's creation has gone through a number of stages, with still more ahead.

"After the flood, again time passed slowly until the moment came for the *next* and third eternal cycle—the era of the covenant. God called a man named Abraham apart and established a whole new basis of relationship between God and man. The covenant was given in a moment, as God spoke to Abraham. It did not just slowly evolve into Abraham's consciousness.

"Again time passed. Again another moment eventually arrived for a transition into the age of salvation. God sent his Son to the earth. And again, everything changed. The entire basis for life changed. Faith replaced works. The blood of Christ replaced the blood of lambs and goats and bulls. It is this era in which we still live. Just as the era of the covenant lasted something very close to exactly two thousand years, it has now been two thousand years since the life of Jesus. The previous two eternal eras have each been two millennia in duration."

"Are you leading up to telling me that the slow progression of history is about to be interrupted again?" said Rocky. "Is one epoch coming to an end, and another about to begin?"

"I believe such is exactly the case."

"Will it be a catastrophic ending, like the flood?"

"That is, as they say—" Mark smiled—"the sixty-four-thousand-dollar question, Rocky. Bible scholars have been debating that one for centuries."

"What is your opinion?"

"Catastrophic in the sense of occurring quickly—yes. But visible and recognizable like the flood—no, I don't think so."

"A complicated answer," commented Rocky.

"To explain in more detail will take a little longer than the time for what I have just said about the various eras in time."

"I can take the time if you can. If my life hangs in the balance, I want to know all I can."

Pastor Mark thought a moment.

"Hmm . . . now that I think about it, if these people in town you've told us about are watching you, they might spot your car. Where are you headed to-night?"

"I thought I'd get lost in Boston."

"Let's go for a drive, then. We'll continue our talk as we go."

Rocky rose from his chair.

"Why don't you head on out of town. Laurene and I will follow after a while. We'll meet at the church in Wilton and take a drive in our car from there."

Rocky headed toward the door.

"You be careful, Rocky. We've grown attached to you, you know."

"I'll watch myself. The two of you just keep praying for me."

"Always," said husband and wife in unison.

(7)

Adam heard frantic shouts before he was aware that a bevy of reporters was about to descend upon him. He half suspected that no good would come from what they had observed at the Bowles' camp—just not so soon.

He glanced about. There came Jen and Scott running across the ground to-ward him from the direction of the gorge.

"They recognized us . . . the jig is up!" cried Scott, as they ran into camp.

"Sorry, Adam," said Jen breathlessly. "We tried to throw them off by run-ning in the wrong direction at first. But I'm afraid it's only a matter of time."

Two or three minutes later, the sounds of engines approached. Two Land Rovers and three jeeps soon appeared and rumbled toward them, followed by a cloud of trailing dust.

"Here they come!" groaned Scott.

"Dr. Cissna," said Adam, turning to their guest, "would you mind staying in the tent and out of sight? If they see a renowned botanist here among the world's most famous fossil graveyard, there will be altogether too many un-comfortable questions."

"Not at all. Reporters give trouble in my line as well." He turned, disap-peared into the tent, and let down the side flaps.

Adam strode toward the oncoming vehicles to keep his camp from being overrun with dust.

"Hello . . . hello—you're all a long way from home!" he greeted them cheer-fully, recognizing several, as people began tumbling and piling out and hur-rying toward him.

Several voices were shouting at once.

"It's Livingstone!"

"So, you are here, Mr. Livingstone."

"Where else would I be but out in the field? This is what I do, you know."

"Mr. Livingstone, I presume," said one, running forward now ahead of the others.

Adam laughed. "Very good, Sorenson! The perfect greeting here in the heart of Africa."

"What are you doing here?"

"Oh, you know, the usual—bones and fossils. But actually, Shawn, I ought to ask what you are doing so far out in the field with your long-endurance colleagues!"

Some of the others laughed.

"Even one in my end of the business has to get out and sweat once in a while," replied Sorenson good-naturedly. "But does your research here have anything to do with the ark?"

"All history ties together," replied Adam. "But we do not plan to resume our ark research until next summer."

"What about your Eden theory? Is that why you're here?" now asked Kaci Lyle.

"You don't actually believe what's in the tabloids, do you, Miss Lyle? By the way, how's that brother of yours doing—still running everyone ragged?"

Lyle laughed and nodded.

"Do you actually think Eden's here in Olduvai?" asked DeWald.

"You never know." Adam smiled.

"Look at it. Everything's dry and barren. There's no Eden here."

"When archaeologists search for something," replied Adam, "we don't always find it where we expect. So you have to learn to look in the unexpected places. But I do place great importance on the animal life here in East Africa."

"Did you come here so soon after the bombing at your estate to get away from the danger?" asked Eliza Douglas.

"This trip has been planned for more than a year. But I would like to express my condolences once again to the family of Erin Wagner."

"Do you think you may be in danger here?"

"Just the usual . . . you know, lions and tigers and snakes, oh my!" he singsonged in reply.

The interview continued for some time, but Adam Livingstone managed to skirt around anything of substance. In the end, most of those present felt that between the two archaeologists, they had made the trip for nothing.

(8)

A few hours after their first discussion, pastor, pastor's wife, and private eye drove leisurely along a deserted country road in southern New Hampshire. They were engaged in a vigorous resumption of their previous conversation.

"I'm not necessarily a proponent of what are called the dispensations," Mark was saying, "although I don't suppose it's so very different than the eras or epochs I was telling you about. To me, the history of time organizes itself by common sense. If you look at the highpoints of change in Scripture, it's a very logical progression. It's kind of like taking a bird's-eye view of the history of the world from God's perspective."

"Tell me the different divisions of history simply. Just list them for me so I can keep them straight in my mind," said Rocky.

"All right. First, you've got the era of creation. Second, the era of early man. Third, the era of primitive civilization and religion. Fourth, the era of the personal covenant. And finally, the era of salvation. I see these five eras about which the Bible speaks—the latter two, as I said, were each of two-thousand-year duration."

"And they each have an abrupt, sudden end point, like you were saying?" asked Rocky.

Mark nodded. "Early man's season began the moment God breathed life into Adam's nostrils," he replied. "The flood, too, was a sudden event. Well, it lasted a year, but in terms of history that is sudden. So also was the covenant with Abraham. It was an event that occurred on a specific day in history. And these events were all followed by the birth of Jesus. All moments in time, out of which eternal change took place."

"And you think we are on the brink of another such moment?"

"A moment of eternal destiny—yes, I do."

The car was silent a moment as each of the three considered the implications.

"How privileged we are!" said Laurene softly at length. "Thank you, Lord!"

"Amen," added her husband. "If we truly are living at one of those critical junctures in the eternal plan," he went on, "we ought to try to understand what it is like at those moments when time splits history apart, and a new era begins."

"I have the feeling—" Rocky smiled, glancing over from the passenger side of the car—"that you have thought about this enough to understand it, as you say, to your satisfaction."

"Do you want to hear what I've concluded?"

"You bet."

"The first fact we observe is that some people do indeed live on through the change. Some lives span the two eras. Granted, only eight people survived the flood. But most of the world lived through the birth and death of Jesus.

"This leads to the second fact we observe, which I find incredibly intriguing. It is this: Most of those who do live through it—and, of course, the flood is exceptional in this regard too—do not recognize the magnitude of the change that is occurring, even though they are right in the middle of it. An entirely new age of eternal history has suddenly come to the universe . . . and most never see it. The people of Jesus' day hadn't a clue that the era of salvation had come, that the entire basis for life on the earth had changed as of the moment of the Crucifixion. Are you following me, Rocky?"

"Pretty much."

"I'm explaining this in such detail because I think it will give you a clearer understanding of your present situation."

"I think I'm with you so far," replied Rocky.

"Good . . . okay. Then, additionally, these changes we're talking about are not what anyone could have anticipated. Only those few individuals whose spiritual focus and obedience leading up to the change are in tune with God's ways will truly understand what is happening. The men of preflood times could not have envisioned the change that was coming, and they scoffed at it when they were told. They were not one with God. Therefore, they were left behind when the change came."

"But like you said, they didn't live through it."

"You're right. The flood gave a visual image to the principle that the change is cataclysmic and that only a few individuals of faith are destined to be taken through and raised up into the new era of relationship with God that follows. But that was only the case with the flood. Thereafter the imagery has changed to a spiritual level, not an actual literal level."

"Huh?"

"When Jesus came, for instance, the rest of the world continued on about their business as if nothing had happened. You'll recall that even the disciples didn't understand at first either. The era of salvation was so different from anything they could envision. Because the change occurred on a spiritual plane, not a physical one like the flood, people didn't see it.

"The people of Old Testament times, even the devoutly religious Jews of Jesus' time, could never have anticipated a salvation based on the shed blood of God himself. It was too astounding a thing—how could they anticipate it? God provided *himself* as the sacrifice! To the eyes of man, a peasant Nazarene simply died a gruesome criminal's death. But the entire universe was turned upside down in the unseen realm of the Spirit. Satan was defeated. The heavens rocked with the change—salvation had come to the universe! The Creator, God himself, shed his own blood to bring that salvation!

"Yet the very men and women who witnessed those events never knew their meaning. Only a few of those living during the first century were taken up and over that chasm from one era into the next. The others, you could say, were left behind in the previous epoch, even though their physical lives continued on. They could have seen. All men and women have that opportunity. God doesn't arbitrarily select some and reject others. Being what is called "chosen" by God is a choice that man makes. But only a few in every era do choose to open their spiritual eyes.

"In Jesus' day, a new season of spiritual awareness had come. Most were not destined to be part of it. Eventually they died, still apprehending only the old . . . and the new continued on without them."

(9)

The drive into the countryside west of London felt different to Juliet today than upon other recent excursions.

This errand was different. This was something she had been wanting to do, and today was finally the day. If the loss of Papa and Joseph was going to have any meaning in her life, she felt she ought to use the experience, whenever the opportunity arose, to comfort others when similar griefs came to them.

She found the house with a minimum of difficulty.

"Yes," said the woman at the door with a pleasant but questioning look, in answer to Juliet's knock.

"I, uh . . . hello," she said. "My name is Juliet Halsay. I have been staying temporarily at the Livingstone estate in Sevenoaks. I . . . knew Erin, and I thought . . ."

The lady immediately sensed that the girl had come to offer sympathy. She smiled and reached forward to motion her inside.

"Come in, Miss Halsay," she said. "I am happy to meet you. I am Katie Wagner. Please, would you join me for tea?"

"Thank you, Mrs. Wagner. That would be nice."

Erin's mother led her through a dark corridor to the kitchen. Two complete walls of it were comprised mostly of windows, and the morning sun streamed cheerfully into the room. There was a small alcove with built-in seats and a table nestled in one corner. Mrs. Wagner motioned to it. Juliet sat down while her hostess put the kettle on the stove to boil. She then joined Juliet at the table.

"It was lovely of you to come, dear," she said. "You must know Crystal and Jen and dear Mrs. Graves—how are they?"

"Oh, fine. I didn't know you were acquainted with the household."

"Yes—I've known Andrea Graves for years. That's how Erin began working for Mr. Livingstone."

"Mrs. Graves is my aunt."

"I see. I knew she had sisters but knew nothing more of the family."

"I wanted to say how sorry I was about Erin," said Juliet. "You see, I know something of what it is like. I lost my father and brother in a bombing in London a few months ago. It has been a struggle for me since."

"Oh, I am so sorry," replied Mrs. Wagner tenderly, placing a motherly hand on Juliet's arm.

The water kettle began to whistle after a moment. Mrs. Wagner rose and poured the boiling water into the waiting teapot. She added another cup to the

255

tea tray, then brought it over and set it on the table. Juliet quietly watched Erin's mother busy herself with the milk.

"Sugar?"

"Yes . . . please," replied Juliet.

She was a lovely lady, Juliet thought to herself. She possessed a beautiful smile and a smooth and elegant manner of moving about, though in appearance her features were plain enough. An indescribable quality of grace hung about her, though Juliet couldn't quite put her finger on its cause.

"It would seem we have a great deal in common," said Mrs. Wagner as she poured the steaming tea into two cups. "I suppose it would be more pleasant if we both had red hair or enjoyed a similar hobby or some such thing. It's not a very happy thing we have in common, is it?"

Juliet glanced down and shook her head.

"It has been hard for you, hasn't it, dear?" said Mrs. Wagner.

"It's been so difficult," replied Juliet. "Not only were my father and brother killed, I didn't know my mother was alive until the next day. The police had so many questions, and we found that my father had debts. So we lost the house and had to separate. Just when I was getting back on my feet, there was that terrible day when Erin . . ."

Juliet's voice quivered involuntarily. She glanced up at Mrs. Wagner with huge watery eyes.

The next instant, Erin's mother rose from her chair and sat down on the bench seat beside Juliet. She wrapped her arms around her. Juliet could not help herself and now wept freely. After two or three minutes, she gradually pulled away, dabbing at her eyes with her tea napkin. Mrs. Wagner eased away and returned to her chair.

"I came here thinking I might be able to offer some comfort to you," said Juliet, embarrassed, trying to laugh through red eyes and wet cheeks. "Here I am crying my eyes out."

"You've brought me more comfort than you know, dear."

"How can that be? All we've talked about is my grief."

"Oh, but my mother's arms have ached to hold Erin again, to hold her close to me, to protect her."

"I am sorry."

"It's not only Erin's death that has prevented me from holding her. She pulled away from me about a year ago. Though she lived here with the rest of the family, she really wanted nothing more to do with us. You can't imagine how it broke my heart to see her change so. I don't know if you will understand, Juliet, dear, but I think the pain of her change in heart was almost worse than her death. The loss of a loved one is always difficult. But when hearts are one, there is a certain comfort one is able to take, even in death. But the grief that comes from strained hearts has no consolation."

"Why did she pull away, Mrs. Wagner?" asked Juliet.

"The usual reasons, I suppose," sighed Erin's mother. "Growing up, independence, changing loyalties and associations. She made new friends that turned the direction of her affections away from her upbringing."

She sighed, and in her eyes was a look of melancholy sadness. "I warned her about that young man she was seeing. But Erin didn't want to hear it. Her judgment was clear and focused, and mine was selfish and critical—in her eyes it seemed so."

"Dexter Caine?"

Mrs. Wagner nodded. "He seemed nice enough on the outside. Erin was completely taken with him. But there was something about the spirit of him that I recognized. He was an unhealthy influence for Erin, but she never saw it. By then she had stopped trusting my insight. She resented my saying anything and became blind to very real dangers."

"The spirit of him?"

"Yes." Mrs. Wagner smiled. "I often sense a person's spirit. Oh, I don't mean a hocus-pocus kind of thing. But I pray for the people I know. I pray for everyone I meet, and the Lord often gives me insights."

Mrs. Wagner saw from Juliet's expression that the statement bewildered her.

"I'm sorry, dear. You probably think me a strange one. I am a Christian, and I love the Lord Jesus very much. My faith has helped me through many rough patches in life. Are you a believer, dear?"

"I do believe in God, if that's what you mean, and lately I have had a sense of his peace about me, reminding me that he is good and that he cares about me."

"That is wonderful."

"I have the feeling, however, you meant more than just that," added Juliet.

"You're right, Juliet, dear. What I actually meant was whether you had invited the Lord into your heart—in a personal way. You see, that peace you felt was God's voice, what is called the Holy Spirit, speaking to you something beyond mere peace."

"What was he saying?" asked Juliet.

"Just what you said, dear," answered Mrs. Wagner, "that he is a good and loving Father and that he cares about you. But even more than that, I believe he was saying that he wants to live more intimately with you now than before."

"More intimately . . . how?"

"He wants to be your very own Father in a more personal way. It's what Jesus came to tell us about—that our Father in heaven wants to love us. He speaks that message to everyone at some time in their lives, in some unique way. For you it came through a sense of peace. It comes at different times and in different ways. It can come at fifteen or fifty, through happiness or grief. But when that moment comes and through whatever circumstances it comes, then has the most important moment of decision of life arrived."

"You think that time has come to me?"

"It may be, dear. It's often a time of sadness or tragedy or change or personal crisis, such as you have faced, that brings it about. When such a moment comes, it is then that we must decide what kind of man or woman we want to be."

An expression of question on Juliet's face was her only reply.

"Do we want to live for God or for ourselves?" added Mrs. Wagner. "That is the decision before us."

"And if we decide we want to be God's man or woman?"

"If we let him, God's Spirit will live in our hearts always. That's the message Jesus brought to us—that God is our Abba . . . our very own personal Daddy."

"I've never though of God quite like that. To me he always seemed more like a grand old man."

"As heartbreaking as it is to lose a loved one, especially a father, it may be that God wants to use this time in your life to become even more a Father to you than your earthly father was. That is the difference between childhood and adulthood, Juliet, dear—recognizing who your true Father is and becoming his child. Most men and women spend their whole lives striving for independence. They never grow up, never become spiritual adults, because they never recognize what comprises true manhood and womanhood."

"What is it supposed to be like?"

"True maturity only comes when we relinquish the desire for independence, the obsession to rule our own lives, and become the sons and daughters we were created to be—who choose to make themselves dependent upon someone else to rule their affairs . . . their heavenly Father."

"That seems backward from what everyone thinks."

"It is exactly backward. Everything in the spiritual life is backward from the world's viewpoint. The last shall be first and the first last, and all that. Everyone knows the verse by heart, but not very many do anything practical about it. That is why so few people perceive the deepest spiritual truths."

"What is the deepest truth?"

"Life lived with God—lived every breath with God."

"How does one do that?"

"The highest life to which the human species may attain is the life of relinquishment. The life the Creator intended for his creatures, right from the first moment when he placed them in the Garden, was a relationship of divinely blissful childship with God."

"Childship?" repeated Juliet.

"It was the life of a trusting son that Jesus lived, to demonstrate that Garden relationship. He said, 'I do nothing but what my Father tells me. I do nothing but his will.' Only by becoming children of the Father again can we step into mature adulthood. We were created to become dependent, trusting children. We were given free autonomous will for just that purpose, that we might lay down that will into the higher and more perfect will of another. To become a man, a man must become a son. To become a woman, a woman must become a daughter."

The kitchen fell silent a moment. Juliet was doing her best to absorb the full yet puzzling words of Erin's mother.

"I think I understand what you are saying," she said at length, "though it is bewildering. I've never heard that before—that to become a man or woman, we must become a trusting child."

"It's just what Jesus said, isn't it? You've heard the words *'Anyone who will not receive the kingdom of God like a little child will never enter it.'"*

"Yes . . . yes, I suppose I have." Juliet smiled.

"If you want to understand, ask God to help you," Mrs. Wagner went on. "There is no prayer he desires to answer as much as the honest cry for deeper insight into his character and his ways."

"It is hard to imagine that my father's death might actually help me in some way."

"You will always miss him. There will be pain at the memory. Yet when God dwells in our hearts, he turns all things for good if we let him. He wants to be your Father even more now. He wants to wrap the arms of his love even more tightly around you and draw you into a higher life than you knew before. You are his daughter now, God's daughter, and only his daughter. I believe, Juliet, that the day will come when you will thank God, not for your father's death exactly, but you will thank him for what he has been able to do in your life as a result."

Juliet remained the whole morning in Mrs. Wagner's kitchen, asking many more questions about what she had heard. When she left after a light lunch several hours later, she felt as if a whole new life had just begun—as indeed it had.

(10)

"I think I see what you're saying, Mark," said Rocky after a pause in their conversation. "But what does all this have to do with me right now?"

"Everything!" replied the pastor. "If we are indeed living at such a time, it will be no different than it was in the first century—some will be aware that a cataclysmic shift has come to the spiritual realm. Most will not. Some will be taken into the new era, so to speak. Others will continue living as if nothing has happened. They will never realize that the whole universe has been altered. They will not recognize the eternal rearrangement that has taken place."

"Why?"

"Because the change is not one that can be anticipated," said Laurene, "nor seen with merely the eyes. It can only be apprehended in the spirit."

"But Christians are constantly talking about the end times and studying the Rapture and the Tribulation and looking for the Antichrist, and all that."

"I know" Mark smiled. "Our church is full of such individuals. They have everything outlined in detail."

"That's my point exactly," said Rocky. "It seems they are completely aware of what's coming."

"If it all comes about according to their preset notions," rejoined Mark. "But I have my doubts."

"You think the prophecies wrong?"

"Not wrong, just that the interpretation misses the bull's-eye. That's why I've studied these eras and have prayed long and hard about the transitions between them. I am convinced that they're not so easily predictable, even by those poring over the Scriptures. History tells us that most of those who study the future are invariably in error, religious soothsayers along with all the rest. Of course, I have no choice but to put myself in that category too, because I'm telling you what I see in the future. I suppose we will all miss the bull's-eye. But some will be closer than others."

"So what do you think is going to happen?"

"The very foundations of the universe will tremble because a major rift in time will have come. But many of the prophecies with which we are familiar may, in fact, not be predictions intended to be taken verbatim."

"Do you mean they might not happen?"

"Oh, no—every word of Scripture will happen. But much will come to pass differently than many expect—on levels of spiritual, not word-for-word, fulfillment. Those who interpret every prophecy with a letter-of-the-law rigidity are akin to the religious prognosticators and prophets of the first century who proclaimed that the Messiah would trample Rome's power and reestablish the glory of Israel throughout the world. In their spiritual pride, these people wanted Israel to replace Rome so they might rule the world instead. They sought no Calvary road where the cross must be borne, but rather a road of earthly conquest paved with stones of seemingly pious principles. But such is not God's way. All *his* victories go through Calvary.

"Because of their failure to see the deeper truths contained in the prophetic utterances, Israel was destroyed altogether—earthly, worldly Israel—in order that a new and spiritual Israel could be born. But those unable to discern the deeper meanings of God watched the Savior of men pour out his life for the sin of mankind . . . yet never had an inkling who he was. The rift had come, but most of the Jews knew it not. It is entirely possible that this new era about to come will be accompanied by just such blindness in the eyes of the ecclesia, today's church and those who watch for superficial signs."

The pastor paused, then exhaled a long sigh. It was clear what he was about to say gave him pain, not pleasure.

"It is more than just possible," he added. "I would say it is probable, when the next cataclysmic shift comes, that it may well be Christians who will not recognize it. As it was in Palestine long ago, once again God's people will be straining their eyes in the wrong direction. They will not see the Calvary road that God has given his people to walk through the change. They will not see the face of their coming Messiah."

"Surely God has given his own people eyes to discern these things?"

"He gave prophetic words also to his people, the Jews, so they would be able to discern the times. But they did not know the truth when he came. They had turned a blind eye to the deeper meaning of God's ways and thus misread both the prophecies and the times. Thus, when the end of their era came and a new dawned, they were not among those taken up into it."

(11)

On her way back to Sevenoaks, Juliet smiled to think that she had gone on her morning's outing to offer Mrs. Wagner comfort, little realizing what she herself would be given in return.

The return drive of a little more than an hour and a half was a pensive one. Without consciously pausing to frame the conclusion, Juliet Halsay sensed that a corner in her life had been turned, that a great change had come—or more accurately—was about to come.

Her spirit was calm.

The sunshiny peace she had felt several weeks earlier had returned. But now the feeling was even more personal than she had expressed that morning to Adam Livingstone. She realized it was more than mere "peace"—it was the loving arms of God the Father wrapping themselves tightly about her. She was ready to invite the Son to live within her as Erin's mother had explained. She was ready to give her life completely to him.

Many of Mrs. Wagner's words repeated themselves over and over in her brain. She still did not understand all she had heard. But she understood enough to know that God's voice was speaking quietly to her.

"Do you acknowledge God intellectually, or have you made him Lord of your life?" she could still hear Erin's mother saying. Juliet smiled as she remembered the woman's next words, "With all due respect to Shakespeare, that is the question."

"What does it mean to make him Lord?" she had herself asked.

"That's the relinquishment," Mrs. Wagner had answered. "To make another Lord means giving up your right to sit on the throne, to make the decisions, to set your priorities, to determine your future. Who is in charge? Who makes the decisions? Who is master? There can only be *one* Lord in any human heart. If you are your own master, there's no place on that throne for the Savior of men. It's the decision who will be the permanent occupant of it that eventually comes to all. And upon that decision all the rest of life hinges."

Gradually tears began to fill Juliet's eyes as she recalled the recent conversation. They were not tears of sadness but of comfort and peace and a deep, quiet joy. With them came the conviction that the moment of decision Mrs. Wagner had spoken of had arrived in her life, a realization that it was no longer enough to passively bask in God's peace but that the time had come for her to respond personally to it . . . to him . . . to her Father.

She took the next exit off the M25. She was somewhere around Leatherhead, though she had been paying little attention to the road signs, as she sought the first available road south into the countryside. At the first opportunity, she pulled off onto the side of the narrow road and stopped the engine.

Juliet leaned back in the car seat, closed her eyes, and breathed in deeply. She was weeping freely now but felt as if the tears were washing and cleansing from her soul the grief, that she might move onward and forward into new dimensions of her dawning womanhood.

For several long minutes she remained in contented silence, heedless of the cars whizzing by, heedless of all but that she knew she had a Father again.

She drew in a long breath, exhaled slowly, then began to pray.

"God," she said, "thank you for opening my eyes to see that I am not without a father as I have been thinking, but that you are there, as my Father . . . even more a father to me than Papa was. I loved Papa and love him still. I miss him. But it is time for me to be yours now. And I want to be, dear God. At last I know how much I want to be your daughter and your woman. No longer do I want merely to believe things about you. I want your Spirit to live with me now . . . and always. I do not want to merely acknowledge you intellectually. I want you to be wholly and completely my Lord."

Juliet paused, gazing out the window momentarily. It was a chilly day. The hills beyond the Dorking Valley were of an intense blue and the sky was pale. In the distance she heard a train's whistle as the train came into Leatherhead station. The sound was sweet and nostalgic in her ear and somehow struck the chord in Juliet's consciousness that she was at that moment being carried across a frontier into a new country.

Again she prayed.

"So I give my heart to you now, Lord," she whispered. "Thank you for the peace you have given me. Fill me with more of you, so that I can know you even better, know you closely, not just as a grand old man in heaven. Be my Abba, my heavenly Papa. Make me a grown-up and mature daughter of yours. Whatever is to become of me, whatever my future holds, I leave it in your hands. You know what is best for me. You know what you want for me, for you are my Father. If I feel your arms about me now, surely I can trust you for my future. Do whatever you want in my life . . . for I am yours and no longer my own."

Again quiet tears of joy welled up inside Juliet's eyes. She felt a new sense of maturity growing within her, the feeling that comes of desiring only to be God's and of relinquishing all to him.

(12)

Dusk fell over Sevenoaks.

Darkness came even earlier on this particular evening because of the thick storm that had been raining down over southern England all afternoon.

About four o'clock a lone automobile had parked a quarter mile down the road from the entryway to the Livingstone estate.

There it had remained. No one had come or gone from it. Nor had there been sign of life connected with it. It had not even been seen. With Adam Livingstone out of the country, the news teams had packed up and gone, a number of the journalists already in Africa. Nor had Beeves or anyone else ventured out in the downpour.

All evening the car sat motionless. About ten o'clock one of the doors opened.

A black-clad figure emerged, dressed for the rain in a wide-brimmed hat, raincoat, and boots. He made his way toward the iron entry gate, surveying the large house as it gradually came into view. Most of the lights were off. The place gave every appearance of being asleep for the night. His information had it that only two women were present in the main house.

He paused, pulled from an inside pocket a small piece of paper, and shone a penlight briefly onto the numbers scrawled upon it. He entered the numbers onto the keypad, following them with the alarm deactivation code.

The gate rolled back. He walked inside. Thirty seconds later the gate closed behind him. The night and the rain continued to hide his movements from human eye.

The figure turned and now made his way toward the house.

Reaching the front door, he paused under the overhang to remove hat, coat, and boots. Every item underneath was likewise black from head to foot. Gloved hands now removed a key, the impression for which had been made from the key taken, along with the access code, from the handbag of one of the two inhabitants of the place during her recent excursion to Arundel.

A moment later he was inside. He glanced about quickly to get his bearings. The ground floor would be unoccupied. The two women should be in their private quarters on the east wing of the first floor.

Noiselessly he moved toward the main stairway on soft-cushioned feet, making not the whisper of a sound.

(13)

Mrs. Graves and her niece had enjoyed a pleasant evening together in the housekeeper's parlor, casually watching a two-hour Hercule Poirot special on the BBC, while trying to keep up a game of backgammon.

The mystery finally ended. Neither of the two, however, felt very much more enlightened by the detailed summation given to the principle players in the drama by the diminutive balding Belgian detective.

"Mr. McCondy would no doubt have followed every clue," laughed Mrs. Graves. "But I was befuddled from the very beginning."

"Me, too," replied Juliet. "I thought the writer fellow did it. I never trusted him. I don't think he ever really wrote those books he said were his."

"I was sure it was that sinister professor who kept hanging around asking questions."

"It couldn't have been him, Auntie," said Juliet. "Don't you remember, he was in Cambridge the night of the murder."

"He said he was in Cambridge. But there was that anthropology student, who was accidentally in the library when the librarian found the book missing, because her class had been cancelled."

"That's right! I'd forgotten."

"No one actually saw him at Cambridge, on that day or the next?"

"Well, I never would have guessed it to be the librarian herself," said Juliet. "She hardly had anything to do with the dead man."

"That's always the way with these detective programs."

"The clues are so ambiguous. It's always someone removed from the center."

"But then she was in love with the professor, after all," concluded Mrs. Graves, "which, I suppose, does explain it halfway satisfactorily. I would hope that Mr. McCondy would solve his cases more straightforwardly."

"I wonder if he's ever investigated a murder," said Juliet.

Almost the instant the word *murder* left her lips, a tremendous crash of thunder rocked the house. Both women started.

Suddenly Juliet felt very chilled and realized what a spooky night it had become.

She pulled her pullover about her shoulders, rose, and walked toward the window. She shivered as she looked out.

"I didn't know it was so wild and stormy," she said.

A few more minutes of conversation followed. It was thus moving well on toward eleven when the two women began making moves toward retiring, later than was their custom. Neither seemed anxious to leave the comfort of each other's company. The prince of the power of the darkness outside had managed to slip inside and bring the mood of the storm with him.

They sat several minutes in silence. A few more peals of thunder crashed overhead. At length Juliet determined to summon her courage. She would not let a little wind and rain get the better of her.

"I think I'll just go down and get a small glass of milk before bed, Auntie," she said. "May I get you anything?"

"No, thank you. I am so drowsy. All I want to do is get under my blankets. Good night, dear."

"Good night, Auntie."

Juliet left the sitting room. Instead of turning left to her bedroom, she turned right along the corridor and walked in the darkness toward the main staircase.

She would not let this storm make her feel afraid. After her prayer yesterday afternoon, a new confidence, a heightened sense of inner strength, had risen within her. She wouldn't let a little storm make her forget that God was her Father. He was Lord over storms as well as over women. Besides, she could see well enough to find her way down the hall. She would flip on the stairway light when she reached the landing.

A flash of lightning momentarily filled the window to her left, followed two seconds later by a great crash. Juliet nearly leapt out of her skin. The wind moaned and whined around the corners and chimneys outside. Again she reminded herself there was nothing to be afraid of.

Passing by Mr. Livingstone's office, a sound that was not from the storm caught her ear.

She paused, heart beating now with a pulse echoing in her ears almost like the thunder echoing through the corridors. She glanced to her right. Light came from under the door!

Who could possibly . . ?

Trembling, she stepped toward it. She reached out her hand to test the latch, then gently pushed the door open a crack.

Across the room a strange man, dressed in black, knelt with flashlight in hand poring through the bottom drawer of a file cabinet! It was obvious from an instant's glance about the office that he had been busy. The place was a mess.

"What are you . . . who are you?" Juliet stammered weakly.

The intruder had sensed the door open. He turned to face her and now rose quickly to his feet. In his eyes was a look of menace and evil intent.

Juliet backed through the doorway.

"Come back here, you little—"

Juliet turned and fled down the hall.

"Hey—wait, you!" he cried.

Behind her Juliet heard him crash through the door. Heavy footsteps now followed along the corridor. A scream broke from her lips, even as another crash of thunder exploded outside.

"Auntie—Auntie Andrea!"

The next instant a great hand clasped itself over her mouth from behind.

"Shut up, you little wench!" rasped an evil voice in Jamaican accent. Juliet found herself squeezed tightly to the intruder's body. Something sharp suddenly poked her ribs. "You keep quiet or I'll put a slug inside you—you got that!"

Juliet tried to nod. She was shaking too badly to control the direction of her head's movements.

The storm—following on the heels of a spooky movie—had gotten under Mrs. Graves' skin, despite her last words to her niece. Thought of sleep instantly vanished the moment she heard the scream from Juliet's mouth.

The sound of more footsteps than could be accounted for sent the clear-witted housekeeper immediately to the phone. Already she had punched in the emergency police number and was waiting frantically for an answer.

"Hurry, it's the Livingstone estate . . . we've had a break—"

"Put the phone down, lady!" said a commanding voice from the door.

The housekeeper glanced up, face white as a sheet. There stood a stranger of Caribbean complexion dragging her niece into the parlor. He held her tight with his left hand, while with his right he held a pistol pointed straight toward Juliet.

Trembling, Mrs. Graves dropped the receiver to the floor, then sank heavily back onto the couch, her kind, round face drawn into a pale mask of astonished and terrified shock.

# nineteen

# Hostages at Sevenoaks

(1)

As Rocky McCondy drove up the familiar road, the first thought that came into his sleepy brain was that Adam must have returned unexpectedly, drawing a crowd of reporters.

As he approached closer to the Livingstone estate, however, he knew something was wrong. There were television crews all right. But the BBC didn't carry guns.

It looked like a SWAT training film. But he could tell in an instant, even through the rain, this was no exercise.

He parked some distance back of the hubbub. He bundled up, climbed from his rented car, and walked toward the front gate under a large black umbrella. There, under a similar covering, stood Max Saul.

"Hey, Inspector, what's going on?"

"Oh, it's you, McCondy—thought you'd gone back to the States."

"I'm back. Just flew in. Looks like you got some kind of trouble."

"You're right there—hostage situation."

"Hostages—who!" exclaimed Rocky.

"Housekeeper and her niece, and—"

"The Halsay kid! What in the heck happened?"

"Had a break-in last night—right in the middle of the storm. They heard the bloke and managed to get on the emergency line before he stopped them."

"Anyone hurt?"

"Don't think so. Local boys got over here before the blighter could get out. They called us right in. We got the place surrounded. Meanwhile, he's in there with the two women."

"Any progress?"

"Not much. He's a cool one, he is."

"Livingstone been notified?"

"He's out in the field. Haven't been able to reach him. Left a message at some hotel. Won't be anything he can do."

Rocky thought for a minute, then glanced around, taking a hasty survey of the place. All hint of jet lag was gone. He walked toward the gate.

"Hey, where you going, McCondy?" said Saul behind him.

"Inside."

"You can't."

"Somebody's got to."

"Captain Thurlow won't let you anywhere near that house."

"Let him try to stop me."

"He will if he catches you."

"Look, Inspector, I've had a little experience with this kind of thing."

"It just may surprise you to know that so have we," said a voice walking up behind him. Rocky turned to see the captain approaching.

"Hey, Thurlow, how's it going!" said Rocky.

"Not so good at the moment, McCondy. Not only do I have two hostages, it seems I also have an interferring American cowboy who's just arrived on the scene."

" I can get them out."

"So can we. Our methods just may be a little calmer, that's all. And a little less prone to risk."

"Look, Thurlow. I'm more familiar with the inside of the house than any of your men. I know the back corridors and stairways. If you can keep him busy in a front room, I can get to him."

"*If* he doesn't see you go in."

"Like I said, you'll have to keep him busy."

"If you fail?"

"Then you can do it your way."

"If somebody gets killed in the meantime?"

"Come on, Thurlow—nobody's going to get killed. I know what I'm doing."

"What's your plan?"

"Work my way around back while he's occupied trying to keep track of you in front."

"How will you get in?"

"Just open the gate while some of your men walk toward the house. That should get his attention. You head toward the door. While you're talking to him, I'll slip through the shrubbery along the fence toward the back until I'm out of sight. By the way, where's Beeves—in his place?"

"Only the missus. The guy's got the butler, too. We've had a man in the Beeves' place watching the back since we got here."

"What room are they all in?"

"Don't know about the hostages. The fellow's been yelling down to us from a first-floor window above and just east of the main door."

"I know the place." Rocky nodded.

Captain Thurlow thought a moment, then motioned to Saul and three or four others to follow. The iron gate rolled slowly open. The captain and his men began walking slowly toward the front of the house.

(2)

Rocky crept from behind several large shrubs next to the gate, then walked briskly across the lawn toward the back of Adam Livingstone's house.

His flight was arrested halfway by movement to his right. There stood the butler's wife at the foot of the stairs leading to their flat above the garage. Her face was pale and her eyes red.

Rocky paused, then jogged heavily toward her.

"Don't you worry, Mrs. Beeves," he said, placing a reassuring hand on the poor woman's shoulder, "we're going to get them out of there safely."

She nodded, lips trying to speak but without success. Again her eyes filled with tears. She handed him a key and pointed toward the main house.

"Ah—good for you, Mrs. Beeves. That will save me some time. Now you just stay here and pray that I am able to keep my wits about me."

Again she nodded vigorously.

Two minutes later Rocky was inside the breakfast room and closing the door carefully behind him.

He let out a breath of air and glanced hurriedly around. This wasn't exactly how he'd envisioned returning to the estate. All right, time to get down to business.

He listened intently but heard nothing. Carefully he removed his shoes. Most of the corridors in this place weren't carpeted. He didn't want to take any chances.

He crept to the door, listened again, then eased his way into the kitchen. He wasn't far from the front staircase, but he couldn't risk using it. If the guy heard him and got a drop on him halfway up, he'd be dead meat.

He heard a voice faintly coming from upstairs. Thurlow must still have the guy talking.

That was good.

*Let's see—what would be the best way . . . probably that narrow stairway down at the end of the west wing.* To get there he'd have to go out into the main corridor off the entryway.

Rocky shuffled his way slowly out of the kitchen. Throughout the ground floor the corridors were oak. He should be fine, if he didn't fall on his face walking in his socks—a not altogether unlikely possibility. Mrs. Graves kept the wood so highly polished it was sometimes slippery.

". . . that helicopter out there within thirty minutes . . . ," a voice echoed down from somewhere above him.

Rocky's hand crept inside his jacket toward his gun. He kept a wary eye peeled toward the staircase while hurrying along the ground-floor hallway into the west wing. He heard Captain Thurlow calling something up to the man from outside but could not make out the words.

In another minute he was again out of range of both voices.

Now he could relax briefly. He revolved in his mind how best to disarm the intruder. He'd have to hope the man didn't have any of the three prisoners actually in his grasp. That would make his job almost impossible. If the man stood and the door to the room was open, as Rocky suspected from the sound of the voice he'd heard, then he should be able to get the drop on him.

He reached the stairwell at the end of the hall, climbed the stairs one at a time, then paused at the top to catch his breath. His mind was wide awake, but the slight exertion reminded him that his body was tired.

*It will be over soon,* he thought. Then he would lie down and sleep the rest of the day.

He began walking again toward the center of the house. If the guy now suddenly decided to leave the room where he was talking to Thurlow, he'd be in big trouble. Sauntering down the corridor like this he was a sitting duck.

Rocky removed his pistol from the shoulder holster inside his jacket and continued foward cautiously, his hand poised in readiness.

Gradually the voice came into his hearing again. It seemed to be coming from the first room to the front of the house off the east-wing corridor. From the sound, he thought the door was open, but he could see nothing from here.

Inching his way along now with his back against the wall, Rocky stopped where the two wings joined at the landing of the main central staircase. He exhaled a silent breath, then leaned his head out around the corner.

". . . tired of this stall!" he heard in an accented voice. "Don't forget, I got three people in here. If you don't bring me that chopper and get me out of here, I may just start throwing them out the window!"

There stood the open door, thirty or forty feet away.

Rocky crept from his hiding place. Inching forward, his fingers now unconsciously fidgeted in the neighborhood of his gun's trigger.

*Keep the lowlife talking, Thurlow!*

Almost as if in response, he now heard the captain's voice from outside.

"Twenty minutes—I just got the confirmation. It left Scotland Yard downtown about thirty seconds ago."

Rocky eased to the open door, hugging the wall, then slowly snuck around it.

"Twenty minutes!" barked the man.

There stood the man looking out the window. His back was turned toward Rocky. He was alone!

Behind him in three chairs, the two women and Beeves sat tied up with some kind of light rope.

"It's eighteen miles," replied Thurlow. "Relax—it'll be here."

(3)

Carefully and silently Rocky eased his frame through the door, crouching down to one knee. Steadily he raised his pistol in both his hands and drew a careful bead on the intruder.

Out of the corner of her eye, Mrs. Graves detected the movement. She turned her head. Her eyes suddenly opened wide as saucers.

There was the American detective, gun in hand, coming to their rescue!

Rocky let loose the barrel of his gun with his left hand just long enough to bring a finger quickly to his lips. He shook his head slowly back and forth. The housekeeper understood well enough, though no injunctions to silence could reduce the size of her eyes.

"You just make sure it gets—"

"Drop it!" said a calm voice of command behind him.

The intruder froze. The hand holding his own gun rested on the wide sill of the window through which he had been talking. The nerves in his arm immediately tensed, though its muscles betrayed not the slightest movement.

"Drop the gun!" Rocky repeated.

Juliet and Beeves now also turned their fearful expressions toward their former houseguest and now their knight in shining armor. Their relief was almost matched by continued terror over what might yet be the result.

"And if I don't, Yank?" snarled the man, slowly turning his head to face his foe. His hand remained poised where it was.

"Then it will go worse for you," growled Rocky.

"You don't look like you got the guts for it. I can see it in your eyes. You won't shoot."

"Don't make me prove it."

"Ha—I can always tell the shooters from the cowards."

Rocky said nothing.

"I may take one of these with me before you take me down," rasped the intruder with a wicked grin.

"You're not taking anybody anywhere. Now drop the gun before—"

The man turned suddenly from the window. In the same motion he drew back his hand and spun to fire.

But Rocky's pistol was no bluff.

Even as screams of terror sounded from the two women, a single deafening shot echoed through the room.

Shattering glass and a cry of pain accompanied the splash of blood on the windowsill and carpet. Rocky jumped up and scrambled forward. He had the man's remaining good arm tightly in an iron grip even as his gun clattered onto the stones below.

"Got him, Captain," Rocky called out the window. "You'd better send up a doctor. He's bleeding pretty bad. And I think his arm's broken."

"Oh, Mr. McCondy, Mr. McCondy," Mrs. Graves was already babbling in relief and terror all at once, "where did you come from . . . how did you—but what on earth . . . oh, I don't even know what I'm saying!"

"Take it easy, Mrs. Graves," said Rocky.

He tugged his prisoner across the room, then released his arm while keeping him carefully covered with his pistol. Rocky backed up a few steps, and with his left hand now fished into his pocket for his knife, which, with some difficulty, he managed to open. Carefully he slit a few of the cords holding Juliet to her chair until she was able to wriggle free.

"How are you, Miss Halsay?" Rocky asked calmly, as if nothing whatever was out of the ordinary.

"Whew . . . very well—now!" Juliet laughed uneasily and breathed in a deep sigh, though the sight of blood was doing funny things to her stomach. "We are all very happy to see you. There—I think I can manage now."

"Untie the others, will you? Here, toss me that little tablecloth there. Stop bleeding, you!" he barked at the man, walking back to take hold of him again and now giving him his full attention.

Within a moment, Juliet's aunt was free. Juliet moved toward the butler. Mrs. Graves jumped up and threw her arms around Rocky and clung to him as if she were still in danger, tears streaming out of her eyes and babbling incoherently.

"I was so afraid, Mr. McCondy! Then when I saw you there . . . and I saw your gun . . . and I saw him jump like that . . . I was so . . . oh, I'm so glad you're safe. Thank you, Mr. McCondy! I don't know how I'll ever be able to repay you . . . oh, thank you. . . ."

Rocky chuckled, attempting to free himself from her embrace so as not to lose the man who was swearing fiercely.

"All in a day's work, Mrs. Graves. Shut up, you!" he spat at the man. "You watch your tongue—there are ladies present. Don't make me stuff something down your throat!"

At last managing to free himself from the housekeeper's arms, Rocky moved toward the door.

"I'll take him downstairs. Hey, Beeves," he added, giving the butler a nod, "how's it going?"

(4)

Rocky reentered the room several minutes later. He was attacked with hugs and handshakes, exclamations and questions, from Juliet, Beeves, and Mrs. Graves.

When the butler's wife appeared a moment later, she and the housekeeper temporarily took complete leave of English propriety and decorum, Juliet coming in also for her share, with renewed chattering and joyful, tearful expressions of relief and gratitude.

By now it was midmorning. Everyone had had a relatively sleepless night—Rocky in the plane, Mrs. Beeves in her flat, and the three captives in this same room. The three hostages had had nothing to eat in more than twelve hours. All five were exhausted and famished.

Gradually coming to herself, Mrs. Graves began to think of practicalities.

"We must have breakfast. Mr. McCondy, you must be starving after your trip," she said. Though still agitated and breathing deeply, she did her best to bring her wits back into control. "Come, Mrs. Beeves—you and I shall cook up a proper English breakfast."

The two women left, as Captain Thurlow entered the room.

"The bloke's in the ambulance and on his way to hospital," he said. "What do any of you know about that character?" he added, glancing around the room.

"I just stepped off a plane and walked into the middle of this," laughed Rocky. "I was in Boston yesterday."

"Me, I just came over to the house a little after eleven last night," said Beeves. "Me and the missus had just gone to bed. I heard voices and shouts over here. Then sirens in the distance. So I got up and came over. What with Mr. Livingstone gone, sir, and me being the only man about the place, I was worried about Mrs. Graves and Miss Juliet. I let myself in. But I couldn't find Mrs. Graves in the kitchen. That's when I heard voices up here. I crept up the stairway, but I don't guess I was as crafty as I might have been, sir, because the man heard me, and next thing you know he pointed his gun at me, and I was sitting there tied up and helpless with the others."

"You did just fine, Mr. Beeves," said Juliet. "You were very brave."

"Just seems I ought to have done something."

"Wasn't anything you could do," said Captain Thurlow. "In these situations, the best thing you can do is remain calm and do what you're told. What about you?" he said, turning to Juliet.

She explained the sequence of events leading up to Beeves' half of the story.

"And you've never seen the man before . . . know nothing about him?"

Beeves and Juliet shook their heads.

"Well," he sighed. "Show me where he was prowling around. We'll check it out and see if we can find what he was looking for, though we'll probably have to wait until Mr. Livingstone returns to get very far on that. Meanwhile, we'll find out who the fellow is."

They turned toward the door as two detectives entered. Thurlow pointed them toward the window, then left the room with the others.

"I'm not going to ask you about your firearm, McCondy," the captain said. "I don't know how you got it past our people at Heathrow. But I'd put it away if I were you."

"I told you out at the gate that I'd get him. How did you think I was going to do it?"

"I didn't know you had a gun!"

"Now you do."

"I don't want to have to run you in and lock you in the same cell with that fellow you shot. So just don't let anyone see it again."

"Sure thing, Captain," replied Rocky with a grin. "Anything you say."

Thirty minutes later, Beeves, Juliet, and Rocky entered the kitchen.

"Ah, Mrs. Graves, what have you created? It smells wonderful in here!" exclaimed Rocky.

"Nothing but a proper English breakfast for our guest," replied the housekeeper.

"More than a guest, Auntie," added Juliet. "Mr. McCondy saved our lives!"

"Weren't you afraid, Mr. McCondy?" asked Beeves' wife. "Mrs. Graves has told me all about it, that you actually had to shoot the man. I would have been frightened out of my wits!"

"We were!" said Juliet.

Rocky laughed. "Sure, you get afraid," he replied. "But when you're in a fix like that, you don't stop to think about it. It just comes, and you do what you have to do. Before you have a chance to stop and realize you're afraid . . . it's over."

"Well, you just sit down there—at the head of the table," said Mrs. Graves. "As today's guest of honor. We have eggs, scrambled just the way you like them—"

"How do you know how I like my eggs, Mrs. Graves?" laughed Rocky.

"I watched and listened to you last time you were here, Mr. McCondy."

"These are perfect!" exclaimed Rocky as she set a plate down in front of him. "You were paying closer attention than I realized."

"—and toast, bacon, broiled tomatoes, tea for all the rest of us," she went on, not acknowledging his comment. "Sit down, Juliet, Mr. Beeves—sit down, all of you. Everything's ready. All but one thing, I should say," the housekeeper added. "But I did not want to attempt *that* without the help of an expert."

She turned away momentarily, then returned with the canister from the cupboard.

"If you will just show me the proper measurements, Mr. McCondy, I believe I will be able to manage the rest."

"Coffee! Mrs. Graves, you are a woman after my heart! Surely you do not intend to use my old beaker-and-paper-towel method."

"I purchased a coffeemaker since you were here, Mr. McCondy," she replied. "I thought you would probably visit us again. But I have not used it yet."

"Then let me show you how it is done!" said Rocky, rising from his chair enthusiastically. "On one condition, that is, Mrs. Graves," he added.

"After what you have done this morning, how could I refuse?"

"That you will allow yourself just one small sip with me."

Juliet watched the exchange with quiet amusement. Her aunt's face now reddened slightly. She nodded an agreement less reluctant than she tried to pretend, as an embarrassed smile escaped her lips. Then the two set out to prepare the American brew, Rocky explaining every detail as if his new protégé in the matter were a child.

A minute later the two resumed their seats. Bubbling and gurgling gradually began to sound on the counter behind them.

"Ah . . . the aroma," said Rocky, "don't you love it? I can smell it already."

"Yes, Mr. McCondy—" Mrs. Graves nodded—"I believe it *is* beginning to grow on me."

"I realize it has not been the custom here, at least from my brief time with you," said Rocky, "to pray at mealtime. But if you don't mind, I would like to thank the Lord this morning for his care for us through what has happened *and* for the delightful breakfast these two lovely women have prepared."

He bowed his head and closed his eyes. The others followed his lead, and Rocky began to pray.

*"Lord, we thank you for watching over us all and getting us through this little scare unharmed. I thank you for these good people here, my friends. Thank you for your love for us. We ask that you'll continued to protect us, and watch over Adam wherever he is too. And thank you for this wonderful provision you've given us to enjoy. Amen."*

As Mrs. Graves opened her eyes and glanced up, it was with a new feeling of respect, even awe, that she looked upon their American houseguest. She hardly even noticed the tear that had fallen from Juliet's eyes during his simple prayer.

Gradually they began to talk. Rocky dug enthusiastically into the contents of his plate. By the time breakfast was over, all were chatting and laughing freely. Little doubt remained that this boisterous American had indeed brought renewed vigor and vitality, as well as safety, back to the Livingstone household. Thought of sleep could not have been further from anyone's mind.

(5)

Rocky remained in the Livingstone home two days.

Gradually the mood lightened, though Rocky continued inwardly concerned. Obviously the intruder hadn't found what he was looking for. Whoever was behind this had successfully penetrated the Livingstone security twice now and was likely to try again. Despite round-the-clock protection by Scotland Yard, Rocky knew he could not again leave the women, Beeves, and Adam's research staff alone.

Late one night as he lay in his bed reflecting on what he ought to do, Rocky's mind returned to his discussion with Mark and Laurene Stafford before leaving New England. Now that the jet lag was subsiding, his mind was working again. He knew there must be a connection between everything they had said and these events sweeping him up in their train. He'd told Livingstone as much himself on their long drive out to the airport. Yet he had been slow to realize just how widespread the connections were.

Mark and Laurene were right. The danger was real. Rocky was now convinced that these occurrences were part of a larger scheme . . . much larger.

He needed to talk to them again. He needed to know more.

At noon the next day, after his first sound night's sleep again on English soil, Rocky telephoned New Hampshire from a pay phone near the estate. He knew Mark and Laurene would be at breakfast together after their prayer time.

"Mark, it's Rocky," he said when the pastor answered.

"Hey, Rocky—good to hear your voice!"

"I need to talk to you and Laurene again. Do you have time?"

"Now . . . on the phone?"

"It can't wait. There's been another incident. Things are heating up."

"Yes . . . certainly I have time," said Pastor Mark, his voice concerned. "We just finished breakfast. What happened?"

"Another break-in at the house."

"Was anyone hurt?" he asked seriously.

"No. It's all under control now."

"How can I help?"

"I've got to ask you some more questions. I need to know more."

"Just a minute," said the pastor. "I'll put Laurene on the other phone."

"Hello, Rocky," said Mrs. Stafford after ten or fifteen seconds.

"Hi, Laurene—sorry to interrupt your morning."

"Don't even think it, Rocky. This is what we're here for."

"Go ahead, Rocky," said Mark, "what's on your mind?"

(6)

Rocky collected his thoughts and refocused them on the subject of their earlier discussion.

"You were telling me about the ages, or epochs, that have come and gone in the world's history," he began.

"Right."

"Okay," Rocky went on, "if we are approaching another of the change points you spoke of, or even if the year 2000 signifies it, I want to know what to expect. What is the new era that is coming next?"

"Many will disagree with me," replied Mark. "Most believers are expecting something altogether different. But I expect it to be an era of deception."

Rocky took in his pastor's words thoughtfully. "What about God's reign?" he said after a moment. "I thought the Tribulation was going to usher in the Lord's victory on the earth."

"These aspects of the eternal timetable will come," replied Mark. "There *will* be an era of God's rest."

"But not yet?"

"In my view, that is correct—that era yet lies in the future."

"But I've heard people talk about the six thousand years now drawing to a close. The coming Millennium I thought was going to be God's thousand-year reign."

"All that will happen, as I said," replied Mark. "But those who think we are approaching the season of God's rest misread the signs. It is the *fifth* era that is now drawing to a close, not the sixth. The *sixth* epoch is about to dawn, not the seventh. And you know what the number 6 symbolizes?"

"What?" said Rocky.

"Imperfection, division, opposition to God . . . deception."

"Hmm . . ."

"We are about to embark upon the sixth era or day in history—an era of deception, not the millennial reign of Jesus, at least in my opinion. Then later in the future, *after* Satan is exposed and the deception is undone . . . *then* will the seventh era dawn."

"That makes sense."

"Then will the number 6 yield to the number 7. Then will come the Millennium of rest."

"So that's still thousands of years away?"

"I don't say the era of deception will last a thousand or two thousand years. It may. It may only last a hundred. Actual duration means very little. It is the *eras* in God's timetable that are significant."

"How long *do* you think it will last?" asked Rocky.

"Only as long as God's people remain deceived. Hopefully that will *not* be a long time. When they rise up against the deception, then will the enemy no longer have power over them."

"*God's people?*" repeated Rocky. "I think I'm confused."

"It is those expecting to be wondrously transported out of this time and into the period of God's rest who are likely to be those most susceptible to the deception of all. Because they do not see it coming, they are the least protected against it."

"Are you saying it's not the world that will be the deceived during the sixth era?"

"The world is *already* deceived," replied Laurene. "Of course the world is included in the deception, but the world has *never* recognized truth. There's nothing new about that."

"The greatest deception, and what will distinguish this era, will be that which falls upon those who consider themselves God's people," added Mark.

"All Christians?" asked Rocky, still trying to get a grip on this new twist to his perception of the end times.

"No. A remnant will discern the times and will rightly read the prophecies so as to know what is happening. But only a small number. Most misread the prophecies altogether. Those few, like Noah and his family, will be those who will enter the ark of God's protection and, if I may continue the metephor, sail across the waters into the future, bridging the rift from the one era to the next."

Mark paused and reached for his Bible.

"There is a passage in 2 Timothy 3," he said as he flipped through the pages, "in which I believe Paul is speaking exactly about this sixth era that will lead to the end times. Listen to his words: *'There will be terrible times in the last days. People will be lovers of themselves, lovers of money, boastful, proud, abusive, disobedient to their parents, ungrateful, unholy, without love, unforgiving, slanderous . . . having a form of godliness but denying its power.'* Do you see, Rocky? He is talking about Christians, not the world. He went on: *'They are the kind who worm their way into homes . . . who are loaded down with sins and are swayed by all kinds of evil desires, always learning but never able to acknowledge the truth.'*"

"I've never thought about those kinds of warnings as applying within the church."

"I believe," Mark replied, "that many Christians will become so deceived about truth and falsehood that they will actually take on a cultlike behavior, even in the midst of a very righteous-sounding pietism. But it is just such individuals Paul is warning about. He says the attack will come specifically on families. And the most venomous and slanderous attacks will come against the families of those who most vigorously stand for the principles of God's Word and seek to obey them."

"And right after that passage, Paul tells Timothy what are the characteristics of the godliness that will combat the deception. A remnant of obedient men and women God will entrust with his truths," added Laurene. "They will proclaim, not raptures nor tribulations, but obedience and sacrifice and Christlikeness."

"Thus will these of the remnant, by their lives and their obedience, expose the lie of the deception, though not until those of the deception have done all they can to destroy them and their families. This obedient remnant will reveal the number 6 for what it is, not mistake it for 7. These will be those who shall pave the way for the coming of Christ in power," Mark said.

"This remnant you speak of—who are they?" asked Rocky.

"They will come from all segments of Christ's body—evangelicals, charismatics, Catholics, Baptists, Episcopalians, Seventh-Day Adventists, Presbyterians, liberals, fundamentalists."

"And the deceived?" asked Rocky.

"They will likewise be well represented from all these same segments, and, sadly, in far greater numbers. More will remain oblivious to the change that has come than those taken forward into the new era."

"But some will be taken forward into it?"

"Every rift needs its families of Noahs to bring truth into the new era. Especially will it be true in this case, to shine the light of truth into the darkness of the deception so that eventually the church can rediscover its true Head."

"What does all this have to do with the papers I showed you back at your house?" asked Rocky.

"The allies of the demonic conspiracy are the chief earthly perpetrators of the deception. Those who ally themselves with this cause have been given great power in the world, even great spiritual power to deceive. We're all well familiar by now with the term *new age*. That's exactly what is coming—a new era, the 'new age'—which is actually not new at all!—which will be sold to the world—which the church will also embrace—as an era of peace and enlightenment. But it is a bill of false goods."

"What could I possibly have to do with it?"

"I think it is possible you have stumbled into the middle of this hornet's nest at the very highest levels of the conspiratorial and satanic heirarchy," replied Mark.

"As Mark said, many Christians will be swallowed up in the deception as well," added Laurene. "They have no idea. That is what *makes* it a deception. Even now they don't see what is happening. This has exactly been the plan of the enemy's forces for centuries."

"For millennia," added Mark. "It began in Babylon."

"Yes," Laurene went on, "to lull the world to sleep, even as the enemy gains control, to subtly dictate how people think, how they perceive truth."

A lengthy silence followed.

(7)

"That's why evolution is such a foundation stone for the deception strategy," resumed Mark, after a pause. "Under the guise of science and truth, God is carefully squeezed out of the matrix of the world's considerations."

"Why, then, am I in danger?" asked Rocky. "Why is Adam Livingstone in danger?"

"I suspect because you threaten to expose the deception. Lights are being shined in places where the Great Lie of humanism gains its strength. Your friend Livingstone is stirring up waters the conspiracy wants left murky."

"I don't see how—he's just another archaeologist."

"The central role of evolution in the enemy's ploy explains why your great-grandfather was drawn so specifically into it. And now Adam Livingstone, and you along with him. Their research and now the ark's discovery threaten to bring down that humanistic world around their ears."

"So evolution is at the foundation of the battle?"

"No—*truth* is. Evolution is merely one of the key tools the enemy has chosen to use to undermine truth. Very few realize how greatly their entire perspective is colored by the evolutionary theory and by the humanism that lies at the root of it."

"Evolution, in a sense," said the pastor's wife, "gave the world permission to disbelieve."

"I'm not sure I see what you mean," said Rocky.

"It took God out of the creative equation," answered Mark. "As soon as that happened, people no longer felt an obligation to be accountable to a higher power in the universe, and a slide of disbelief resulted. Truth then became fuzzy in *other* aspects of life. Evolution has been used by the enemy, not as a thing of extreme importance in and of itself, but as a tool to rob truth of its power. Evolution triggered an ethical domino effect against faith. And on the other side of it, as soon as an individual acknowledges that God is real, he or she becomes accountable to the Ten Commandments and to the words of Jesus. Suddenly ethics and morality matter again."

Rocky quietly took in Pastor Mark's words.

"The loss of absolutes, the loss of the relevance and significance of personal decisions and accountability—these are results that affect Christians along with the rest of the world. Gradually, without our even seeing the shift, lies and falsehoods come to be called truth. Even Christians who don't believe in evolution per se have allowed the nonabsolutist mind-set to engulf them."

"Christians don't see the approaching rift of deception," added Laurene, "because it creeps upon them so subtly. They do not see the accomodation and compromise gradually engulfing our world, and their own values and standards and attitudes along with—"

She stopped abruptly. "Mark," she now said in an urgent voice, "I have the strong feeling that we need to pray."

"Then let's pray."

The three joined their hearts over the miles in a threefold cord of prayer.

*"In your name, Lord,"* prayed Mark, *"we bind the power of the enemy over your servant Rocky McCondy and over all those with whom he is associated right now, especially Adam Livingstone. Go before them both and guide their every step. Protect them, Lord, and accomplish your purposes through them."*

The pastor's wife now prayed.

*"Dear Lord, we know that your preparation of seeing a remnant people will not be in the visible ways those who would profit from your Word proclaim. Such explanations will not seek your heart, but they seek only sensational signs and wonders. They are the dill, mint, and cumin of prophetic utterance, the mere outsides of pots and cups and vases. They represent the words the Lord has given his prophets to say, not what those sacred words mean. Lord, we ask that those who interpret events by shallow lights of interpretation will discern the deep import of what you, Lord, would say to your church.*

*"Otherwise, they will miss the rift in time because they know not its true meaning. Lord, give signs to those who see with discerning hearts. Help us to*

*be vigilant, to be wary, to be watchful. Help us heed the times, for many of the Lord's people will be deceived. We know that your Word says that lies will be called truth, sons will be stolen from fathers, daughters will be stolen from mothers, and authority will be despised. We know that your Word says that the hearts of the saints will break on the altars of those days that are coming. Thieves of the truth will be those who call themselves the Lord's people but who do not know the Lord's heart. They have not made the Lord's ways their ways. Dear Lord, allow a season to come for the healing of rifts. If it be your will, Lord, allow the day of your return to draw near. We feel this in our hearts, O Lord. To those who know your ways, Lord, give us a wonder. Allow unseen growth to sprout from long-hidden roots . . . verily, from the root of life."*

As she spoke, tingles went up Rocky's spine.

*"Lord, I do not think the sign will be as many of us might imagine,"* she went on. *"I fear that few will recognize it. But, dear Lord, accomplish what is your purpose. Let it be like a sign as a baby born in a manger. The Pharisees gazed about for a sword-wielding warrior-king. They did not recognize the birth of their divine Babe. We know that your salvation came quietly, and we will quietly look for the sign of your coming again."*

The room fell silent. There was nothing more for any of the three to say except, "Be it unto me, Lord, according to your will."

# twenty

# The Quest Begins

(1)

Captain Thurlow of Scotland Yard was not able to reach Adam Livingstone personally until twenty-four hours after the incident, and then only by contacting the small nearby airstrip.

Adam nearly threw down the telephone on which he had returned Thurlow's urgent message and ran in search of the rented two-seater plane being fueled at that moment to take him and Dr. Cissna to Nairobi.

"Take it easy," assured Thurlow. "The man is in custody. There is nothing you can do."

"I ought to be there," insisted Adam.

"I know it's difficult, Mr. Livingstone," said Thurlow, "but stay about your work. Your American friend is keeping an eye on things. We've posted a twenty-four-hour guard around the estate. Nobody comes or goes without our knowing it. We'll keep you informed. For now, everyone's safe, and no harm's been done."

Shaken but realizing the sense of Thurlow's words, Adam returned to camp and told the others what had happened. Half an hour of somber discussion followed.

"I'll be happy to fly back to England, if you want, Adam," said Scott.

"I don't know," sighed Adam. "I hate being out of touch like this. But Thurlow's probably right—we'd just be sitting around there too, not really doing anything to help. But I feel much better knowing Rocky is there."

"Whatever you want me to do," said Jen. "Like Scott said—I'll fly back too if you think I could be of any use there."

"Let's give it some time and see what develops. Meanwhile, we've got both the plane and Dr. Cissna. I suppose we ought to make the best use of them we can—right, Doctor?" he added, glancing toward the Egyptian.

Dr. Cissna nodded.

"Then let's you and I be about the quest for beginnings!" said Adam, rising and trying to put the telephone call out of his mind. "We had planned to tromp through the forests of Mount Kenya today. Shall we be off?"

"I am at your service, Mr. Livingstone."

"I think I will drive over and make contact with Sir Gilbert before we leave," said Adam. "I ought to speak to him face-to-face. Do you think I'll encounter any curious reporters?" he said.

"I haven't seen anyone for a day or two," replied Scott.

"Do we dare hope they've packed up and gone?"

"Not a chance," rejoined Scott. "They'll be back, I'm sure."

"I think I'm going to risk it. I'll be back in less than an hour," said Adam. He rose and a minute later drove off toward the Bowles camp.

❖ ❖ ❖

"So, Sir Gilbert, we meet again in the African rift that made you famous," said Adam as he jumped out of his Land Rover and walked toward his prodigious colleague who was standing in front of his tent, cup of tea in hand.

"Not so famous as you, Adam," rejoined Bowles, doing his best not to allow his annoyance from the other day to show. He had at that very moment been thinking of Livingstone, wondering just how he was going to learn what he was up to. So this could not have been a more fortuitous visit. He knew Cutter would be growing impatient, although Zorin had disappeared yesterday and hadn't been back. Bowles was glad for that, at least.

"A mere fleeting burst of interest in the fickle public's mind," said Adam. "I'm sure that's all the ark will be."

"Tut, tut, Livingstone." Bowles smiled. "You make a very bad liar."

"I understand you are here to establish a more detailed chronology of man's evolution in the region?"

"That is correct."

"How is the work proceeding?"

"Very . . . uh, well. My, er—my associates will be arriving shortly."

"Evolution is on shaky ground, Sir Gilbert." Adam smiled. "Surely you have read Dalton's book on the debunking of Darwin's hypothesis."

"Nothing but hogwash."

"You really owe it to yourself to get more in step with the times, Sir Gilbert. It seems the Bible may be true after all, and we scientists of the twentieth century have missed the mark."

"Spoken like a scientist taking leave of his senses. It is you, Adam, who should get in step with the times. Progress marches forward, not back. So . . . now that we have discussed my project, what is it *you* are working on?"

"Ah, Sir Gilbert," said Adam, "colleagues though we are, archaeologists must remain secretive about our hunches, you know!"

Bowles winced imperceptibly. He had been too obvious.

"But come—you can play it straight with me," Adam went on. "There's more to your being here than merely cataloguing Olduvai. Surely you are here upon some other errand than that?"

"Now I must throw your own words back on you, Adam. You do not expect me to divulge *my* next great find to one with an ambition to match my own?"

"Touché!" laughed Adam good-humoredly. "I see we understand one another, Sir Gilbert. We really ought to collaborate on a project one day."

Bowles made no immediate reply. He really could think of nothing that would interest him less. In his mind no one had the right to be as good-looking and highly regarded as Adam Livingstone.

"I understand you brought in someone from Cairo to assist you," he said, sipping at his tea. He lifted one eyebrow in Adam's direction.

"You are well informed, Sir Gilbert," replied Adam, now having to keep his own reaction in check. How could the man have discovered that?

"Olduvai has a life of its own—people talk, you know. Everyone up and down the gorge is curious what you are up to."

Adam smiled. Sir Gilbert was curious, that much was obvious. He rather doubted anyone else cared. But if Dr. Cissna's identity was learned, all hope for confidentiality would be lost.

"What's the man's field?" Bowles added. "At least you can tell me that much."

"You're a shrewd one, Sir Gilbert. Let me just say that we're off on the quest this morning, and you're welcome to follow . . . if you can keep up. But I do have to go now. Happy hunting, Sir Gilbert!"

Bowles watched him go, swore under his breath, tossed out what remained of his tea, and lit a fat cigar.

He glanced about, wondering if and when he'd see Zorin again. He knew about Adam's airplane. As soon as he was gone, he'd drive over to the airstrip and see if he could bribe anyone for information.

(2)

"Keep an eye on Bowles," Adam said to Scott and Jen, as he and Dr. Cissna got out of the Land Rover at the small airstrip. "I don't want him to know what we're looking for."

"Will do, chief!" laughed Jen, sounding as American as Scott in her usage, though with a melodic lilt in her tone.

"Then drive over to Manyara and try to take some core samples," he added to Scott.

"How high up should we drill?"

"DBH," replied Dr. Cissna.

"What's that?" asked Jen.

"Diameter at breast height—four and a half feet. It's standard."

"That will be a good starting point," replied Adam. "I would like to get some at ground level for comparison as well—as deep into the root system as you can go—from the baobab there. We'll do the same on Mount Kenya, as well as from other species. We should be back tomorrow or the next day."

They boarded the plane as Jen and Scott took the Land Rover back to camp.

"If you don't mind," said the botanist as they situated themselves and accenting his statement with a yawn, "I was awake a good deal during the night. I think I shall take the opportunity to get another hour's sleep."

"Just adjust your seat and put on this eye mask. The drone of the engine will lull you off in no time."

As their plane took off ten minutes later, Sir Gilbert Bowles followed its ascent with his gaze. They were heading north, but that fact told him little. The rift valley stretched three thousand miles northward from here. They could be going anyplace.

They rose into the sky and Dr. Cissna dozed off. The mountains and volcanic craters and valleys and lakes and plains of northern Tanzania gradually spread out below them. Adam's excitement grew as he looked down upon this unique four-thousand-mile north-south scar on the earth's crust. It had revealed so much about the past already, yet it no doubt contained many untold mysteries that might never be revealed.

From Mozambique in the south to Lebanon in the north, the rift was the product of subterranean forces that had slowly torn apart the earth's crust,

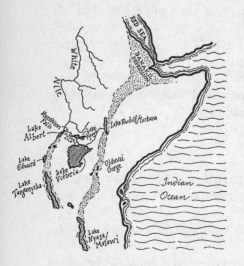

cutting apart wide valleys that sank between parallel cliff-edged fault lines. At the same time volcanic eruptions forced up liquid rock from deep below.

The stretching and tearing was still in progress. Adam could see evidence of this fact as they now flew northward. Steam and smoke rose here and there about them from semiactive volcanoes, steam vents gushed, and sodium carbonate springs boiled throughout the region. Occasionally could be seen the white glare from soda flats and the reflection of the sun off bitter salt-and-soda lakes.

At this point in its history, the enormous fissure stretched approximately thirty miles in width, though in central Ethiopia it widened to some three hundred miles in the Danakil Depression south of the Red Sea.

Adam had himself stood on the cliff edge of this portion of the rift valley many times and at different places. He had gazed down two thousand feet over the flat rift plain. On most days he had been able to see at the opposite side another almost vertical wall like that on which he stood. The great trench was so colossal as to invoke awe into the heart of all who gazed upon it.

Nor was Africa the only continent affected. The northern extremity of the rift was Israel's Jordan River valley, from whence it ran southward through the Red Sea trench into the Ethiopian highlands, continuing south through most of eastern Africa. There it branched off into a lesser western rift containing Lakes Albert and Tanganyika. Majestic Lake Victoria sat almost exactly between the two rift scars.

No more diversely active geologic location existed on the face of the globe. It was hardly any wonder, thought Adam as they rose into the sky, that such a high percentage of archaeological discoveries concerning man's past had been made here.

Staring down over that great scar, Adam found himself reflecting once more on the theory that had brought him here—that the location of the original Eden was connected with this part of the world. Was the rift part of it? If, for reasons of his own, the Almighty had chosen to divide, split, or hide his original Garden, what more natural way to accomplish it than to cause the earth itself to carry out the task?

As he flew, in his mind Adam could envision the earth changing over the centuries, the continent gradually widening as a result of the rift and continental drift . . . Africa separating from the Middle East, rivers becoming seas . . . the earth still splitting and tearing. And now in his mind's eye the image became superimposed with another rift . . . separating humans from the Garden, separating the two trees of the Garden . . . a rift separating men and women from their Creator.

According to the Bible that lay back in his tent, the Creator had driven the man and the woman from the Garden and hidden its location ever since.

Likewise, the earth below him had changed and shifted and hidden the secrets of its past, revealing its hints only in tantalizing pieces.

Could the two hidings be one and the same?

Was now the time for such a revelation?

Adam drew in a deep breath, humbled at the thought that he might have something to do with such a momentous possibility. Yet it seemed within reach, almost as though he had been chosen for the task. The ark. The ice cores he had taken. And now, perhaps, the samples he and his botanist colleague would collect. They would all help tie his theory together.

He looked down on Ngorongoro Crater and the three other volcanic craters just to its north. On the other side of the range sat Lake Manyara. Even now he thought he could see a herd of elephants near the lake, the region of the highest elephant concentration in all the world. Far beyond that, eastward over the expanse known as the great caldron, rose the forbidding 19,000-foot summit of Kilimanjaro.

He turned his attention back forward and to the controls of the plane and glanced over at his sleeping passenger. It was a clear and windless sky through which they flew. Steadily they climbed, rising above Mount Lengai, which had erupted in 1966. The wide Serengeti Plain spread out to their left. Beyond in a westward direction just beyond their vision lay fabled Lake Victoria.

Everywhere here in eastern Africa was such contrast. Lush jungles and rain forest. Rocky, desert areas. Cauldrons of hellish hot springs. Vegetation so thick, how could it be other than Edenic in origin. Now they were flying over Lake Natron, its northern end defined by the Kenyan/Tanzanian border. Soon they passed over the Nguruman Escarpment and began a gradual northeasterly bearing that would take them past Nairobi, over the Aberdare Mountains, and down into Nanyuki. From there they would drive up onto Mount Kenya.

As they flew, Adam recalled his conversation with Scott only the day before.

"I tell you again, Adam," Scott had said, "I've never known quite what to make of your interest in biblical archaeology, all the way back to that fellow you were so interested in at the university."

"You can't deny that the rift valley contains all kinds of biblical geological connections."

"I don't deny it. I just don't know why your interest is so keen on them."

"Don't you find it fascinating that if the earth truly is splitting apart, the Old Testament might confirm it more than any other document or evidence we possess?"

"I suppose. What else but a sudden subsistence could have engulfed the Egyptians in the Red Sea when they were chasing Moses and the Israelites," consented Scott. "Though you have to *believe* the story first, which most scientists don't."

"There is another explanation for that one."

"What's that?"

"A divine miracle, perhaps," suggested Adam. "Isn't that the gist of the biblical story?"

"But I'm talking as a geologist," rejoined Scott, "explaining *how* the Almighty might have caused some of these things to happen—caused them, I mean, through the processes of nature. There's no denying that the Red Sea is sitting smack in the middle of the rift. So rift action could be the unseen factor *behind* the miracle of the Red Sea crossing. And there's Sodom and Gomorrah just south of the Dead Sea, also right in the middle of the rift. That story sure sounds to me like a volcanic eruption of sulpher."

"Lake Natron, too, can't help but remind you of fire and brimstone. Who knows but what Sodom and Gomorrah weren't the only places rained down upon."

"And why not a rift volcano to explain the biblical account?"

"Can't you imagine a gigantic fumarole like Mount Dallol spewing out fire and salt and sulfer over a city? Not to mention Karum salt lake and Lot's wife. When I hear stories like that, I think less of myth than I do of eyewitness accounts of great cataclysms coming on the earth."

"You're right. I'm convinced," laughed Scott. "All it takes is a little time in the rift valley to make you realize how violent and sudden some of the stretching and shaking must have been."

Dr. Cissna came awake as the sound of the engine slowed, and Adam's thoughts returned to the present.

"You had a good sleep," said Adam. "We're on our final descent."

(3)

By midafternoon the botanist and the archaeologist were tramping through dense undergrowth on the lower slopes of Mount Kenya, some two hundred and thirty miles north of Olduvai.

"There are so many ancient species here, I'll never be able to show you them all," Dr. Cissna was saying. "It's so dense and thick. Actually we don't even know half the species between here and what's left of the rain forest over in Zaire, what used to be the Belgian Congo."

"It's the Congo again—or haven't you heard?"

"Of course," laughed the professor. "Just when I get used to one political name change, up pops another."

"Anything as old as the bristlecone pines and the baobab?"

"Those are the two leading candidates for the oldest living thing title. Nothing's really been conjectured specifically to the contrary. There is at present a living specimen of bristlecone dated at 4900 years."

"Remarkable. That would place it before the time of the Hebrew patriarchs."

"More remarkable even than that," rejoined the botanist. "Dendrochronologists have compared samples from living and dead bristlecones and have managed to build up a continuous series of growth rings dating back beyond 6000 B.C., over *eight* thousand years ago. According to the old Ussher chronology, both these dates would precede the Genesis flood itself."

"You don't hold to that dating scheme?"

"No, but it's intriguing nonetheless. I have my own theories."

"Care to share them, Dr. Cissna?" said Adam striding up alongside him as they came to a relative clear stretch.

The botanist smiled. He seemed to consider his next words carefully, though when they came, they were hardly ambiguous.

"I think flora will one day be found here twice as old as the bristlecones."

"That is some theory!" laughed Adam. "I can see I have consulted the right man. You are speaking my language, Doctor."

"Most people have no idea how lush this whole area is," Dr. Cissna said. "Yet still how virgin and unexplored. Two hundred miles around Lake Victoria has received a lot of attention since Grant and Stanley's explorations, as well as the Scots geologist John Walter Gregory. He explored farther east in the rift. As lush as it is, there is research to suggest that it was far *more* so millennia ago. I can only conjecture what it must have been like then. It makes me tingle with—"

He paused. "Well, let me just say that I become excited to consider the possibilities."

"I am tingling to listen!" rejoined Adam.

"It is such a vast continent," Dr. Cissna went on, "and still largely unknown. Whenever I am working down here, I envision that some special creative energy was placed into the earth here, which is still here . . . and continues to burgeon forth with life and vitality."

(4)

Before Adam had opportunity to respond to Dr. Cissna's curious comment, they crested a small hill. Suddenly the energetic botanist broke into a run. Adam hurried after him.

"This is exactly what I was hoping for!" he exclaimed, approaching a tree of astonishing girth. "Just look at this baobab! And it looks healthy. Hopefully it won't be too hollowed out."

Adam had seen plenty of baobab in his life, but never one so positively huge. "It is such an odd looking tree," he remarked, "with the massive straight, thick trunk, which suddenly branches out in a hundred directions."

"Odd, perhaps—yet can you not feel its antiquity?" rejoined Cissna. "Especially this hoary old fellow. The notion that such trees may have been . . . well, the mere thought sends shivers down my spine."

"May have been what, Doctor?"

"Never mind. You would only laugh."

"May have been among the trees that grew in Eden?" suggested Adam.

The botanist shot him a strange glance.

"What makes you ask such an improbable question?"

"Archaeologists are an imaginative lot, you know," Adam replied with a smile.

"So I have heard. And yourself preeminent among them."

"You mentioned a creative energy a moment ago, Doctor? Do you mean God?"

"I'm a botanist, not a metaphysicist, Mr. Livingstone."

"Your words might be taken to indicate a reference to a lost, prehistoric garden," suggested Adam, glancing toward the doctor.

"That much would be to severely stretch my words," laughed Cissna.

"All right. I admit to stretching your words. Would I still be privileged to receive a response?"

"You win," said Dr. Cissna cheerfully. "Yes, I admit to believing that all this life is not accidental."

"Care to elaborate?"

"I believe God placed it here—on the earth, I mean," he added.

"So do you believe such a place as Eden once existed?"

"Let me answer by saying that it is impossible to travel throughout the interior of Africa and not have one's mind continually drawn to the ancient account. However, I will not be lured into a debate on the *location* of the Eden of Genesis."

Adam laughed. "Does it seem I am attempting such a thing?"

"Aren't you?" Dr. Cissna's eyes twinkled with fun. The two men were already finding a deep level of camaraderie with one another. "I do marvel at what I am priviledged to see, Mr. Livingstone," Cissna went on. "I consider myself an extremely fortunate man."

Adam knelt at the huge, gnarled, multitrunked base of the tree and inspected it carefully for several minutes.

"Shall we drill a core sample, Doctor?" he said.

Both men removed their packs and began setting out the increment borer, cutting bits, handles, tubing, and extractors for the operation.

"All this reminds me of the most unusual article I read in the *Geographic* recently," said Adam as they began. "Have you been following that strange growth phenomenon up in Saudi Arabia?"

"Following it! I've been out there five times. That was my photograph in the article."

"You took that! Tell me about it."

"Nothing to tell. Strangest thing I ever saw—a complete mystery."

"Have you taken core samples?"

"The Saudis won't let us."

"Can't they be persuaded, in the interest of science?"

"We're working on trying to help them recognize the value in further research."

The two men worked for some time, hand-drilling into the tree, aiming as closely as possible for the center. At length they rose, carefully removing the last sample in its long quarter-inch-diameter, clear-plastic tube that Dr. Cissna had had made especially for Adam's research. Adam set it into the large quiver that contained the half-dozen such samples already taken.

A brief silence fell.

"Do you know what they call this tree?" said Dr. Cissna at length as they stood back and again beheld the giant.

"Only its name."

"They call the baobab the tree where man was born," said the doctor. "According to the legends of the Nuer tribesmen, the actual tree where man was born still stood within memory of their ancestors, in the west region of southern

Sudan. And it is true that the baobab is the oldest of all known things living in Africa—perhaps on the planet. The legend has always intrigued me. To most, the phrase no doubt makes some reference to our chimpanzee ancestry—*so-called* ancestry, I should add by way of qualification. Yet I still like the phrase . . . for my own reasons. The mountain rising eastward from Olduvai near your camp—*Ol Doinyo Lengai*—the name means the mountain of God. We would have flown over it this morning. There are many legends and tales here, Mr. Livingstone, pointing not merely backward into the mists of antiquity but all the way back to origins. If you desire *spiritual* legends and tales hearkening to beginnings, Africa is full of them."

"What about the flood?" asked Adam. "Are there flood legends in Africa as everywhere else?"

"Of course. Such traditions abound, varying slightly from tribe to tribe, but always with the germ of the story intact—all other tribes destroyed, eight virtuous survivors, from which sprang a new race that peopled Africa and ultimately the globe."

"And the tree?"

"They say it survived the flood along with a small number of humans. Some traditions speak of the eight outlasting the floodwaters in the branches of the baobab rather than in a giant floating vessel. And look at the thing. If ever a trunk was stout enough *to* survive such a catastrophe, this would be it! Another tradition is told by the natives of Ujiji that says a great flood inundated the plains of the rift region, which were rich in livestock and cattle. The waters that were left formed Lake Tanganyika."

"How much truth do you see in these legends?"

"You found the ark, Mr. Livingstone!" laughed Dr. Cissna. "So I am inclined to doubt the tales of an African Noah and his family living for a year in the branches of a baobab. However, as I'm sure you know, there is evidence that seawaters once covered this region."

"Such evidence exists throughout the world."

"Which makes flood legends difficult to discount as mere local phenomenon."

"What about the survival of the baobab?" asked Adam as they now continued on their way.

"I conjecture it may have been more a matter of the root system surviving the flood waters, then sending up new shoots once the flood had receded," replied the botanist.

"A credible idea. Flood plains and volcanic eruptions all over the world every year prove such is possible."

"You know of the quaking aspens they found in Colorado—trees from a single root system covering more than one hundred acres. The banyan tree of India sends out aerial roots that descend deep underground and thicken and send up many separate trunks. The root system for a single tree can extend over several acres, as do the mangroves in Florida. Root systems may provide one of the great clues into botanical antiquity, though it is an area largely unexplored—another aspect to my theorizing."

"I'm intrigued, Doctor."

"Often there is more life under the ground, unseen by the eye, than above," Cissna went on. "By far the majority of earth's life *does* lie hidden from view, Mr. Livingstone. Just look around us. The very rift valley testifies to the life that is underneath trying to get out."

"I see your point," laughed Adam. "I confess I'd never thought of it quite like that before."

"We know so little because we rely on the mere sight of our eyes. The deepest truths, however—in any field—must be looked for differently than that."

"Now you *are* beginning to sound like a philosopher." Adam smiled.

"The greatest mysteries are hidden—it is one of the truths that makes life itself such an adventure! It is one of the exciting things about the study of botany as opposed to archaeology—if you do not mind my making such a statement—botany is about *life*. No offense intended, of course," he added with a smile.

"None taken," Adam assured him.

"My field is the study of *living* organisms," the doctor continued. "Your profession—if you do not mind a bit of a jab from one scientist to another—is about dead things."

Adam grinned. "But occasionally we stuffy archaeologists and paleoanthropologists spend most of our time with dead things, but what we find can tell us much about life. Surely you admit such discoveries are often as valuable as they are compelling?"

"I will concede that," rejoined the doctor. "But I still find that dry dust and old bones bore me. Give me a leaf or root or tuber or flower or peculiar grass or tree or shrub or bit of strange moss or algae that I have not seen before—give me such to examine and sniff and feel . . . and I am in heaven!"

"What accounts for the different appetites of explorers and scientists such as ourselves? Someone—a sociologist or psychologist, I suppose—would doubtless find *that* an interesting study."

"The *Homo sapiens* is, after all, the most intriguing study of all!"

(5)

Even as Adam and Dr. Cissna tromped through the wilds of Mount Kenya, Scott Jordan hurried toward the Olduvai airstrip in search of a telephone. A brief letter from his friend Marcos Stewart had been included with that day's delivery from Crystal.

*I've got to talk to you right away,* the senator had written. *I'm in trouble.*

*I've got no one else I can turn to. Call me on my private line as soon as you get this. Thanks, old buddy—I won't forget it. Marcos.*

Scott reached the airfield and made the call. He glanced at his watch as he waited for the connection to go through. It was one-thirty in the afternoon. Marcos should just be arriving at his office.

"Scott! Hey, man—thanks for calling," the senator answered.

"What's up, Marcos? Your letter sounded urgent."

"It is, I'm afraid," replied Stuart, and his voice took on a serious tone. "I got myself in over my head."

"How so?"

"Can't go into it now. Any chance we could get together?"

"I don't know, Marcos. I'm out in the middle of a research trip."

"I'll go anywhere. When will you be back in London?"

"Not for a month or two. What kind of trouble?" asked Scott, "financial . . . political?"

"No, not that. Let's just say I got involved in something I shouldn't have. Now the squeeze is on, and I don't see any way out. I've got to see you."

Scott thought a moment.

"Let me talk to Adam," he said. "I'll see what I can do."

"Appreciate it, old buddy."

"I'll be in touch."

(6)

Adam and Dr. Cissna had by now seen dozens of promising species of tree and vine. Adam was lugging nearly as much weight in samples as he had come with in supplies.

"For myself, the greatest intrigue has always come from the earth," the botanist was saying as they walked. "It is fairly bursting with life everywhere. Yet we see such a small portion of that life with our eyes."

He paused and glanced significantly toward Adam.

"We now find ourselves getting closer to one of those theories of mine I mentioned awhile back."

"I am eager to hear it," encouraged Adam.

"You must promise it will remain between ourselves. I plan to write about it one day, when I have, if not actual proof, at least reasonably verifiable data. Until then, I do not want to allow word to leak to the wrong sources."

"You have my word, Doctor," said Adam.

"All right—here it is then. It is no secret that life can remain hidden, dormant, for years. Organic life, I mean. You are well aware of the principle whereby old and long-neglected gardens suddenly pass into new hands. In their enthusiasm to refurbish the old, their new owners prune and trim and upturn the soil. Sunlight and air and water and oxygen are brought again to bear on places that perhaps have not felt such vital influences as these for years, decades, even centuries. And now a strange thing happens! Old forgotten seeds, bulbs, root systems spring to life. Even varieties of species altogether forgotten suddenly blossom anew. It is such a wonderful process to observe. You no doubt know of the herb garden at the Mount Grace Priory, the fourteenth-century monastery in England where species of herbs long considered extinct have burst to life after a new excavation of the priory's courtyard."

"I am familiar with it," replied Adam. "I had not theorized on the phenomenon. But now that you bring it to my attention, I see how it points in the direction of my own research."

"Indeed it does."

Dr. Cissna paused and smiled.

"If I can make the analogy, it is something like what would be the case if one of your colleagues found an ancient skeleton long buried in the sand of the rift valley. Yet the moment you unearthed it—voila!—suddenly it became alive again."

"It would be incredible," laughed Adam. "A human version of Jurrasic Park!"

"That is what makes the study of the earth's living botany so fascinating!" rejoined Cissna. "That very thing *does* happen in my field. If we uncover the botanical equivalent of an old fossil, it may yet have the power of life within it. Obviously organic matter dies too. We see examples of decay around us as well. Yet more life remains hidden than I think we have any idea."

"How long, in your opinion, can such dormant, hidden life remain vital?" asked Adam.

"I doubt there is a limit," answered the doctor. "Wheat found buried in the Pyramids is still capable of growth. I have little doubt that life can burst forth after being hidden not for mere centuries, but for millennia . . . or longer. Lotus seeds found in a Manchurian peat deposit dated to 2000 years germinated when exposed to water. And seeds of the arctic tundra lupine found in a frozen lemming burrow in the Yukon, carbon-dated at over 10,000 years old, germinated within a day of being exposed to warmth. I do not believe there is a limit to how long the capacity for life can remain hidden, waiting in readiness, until suddenly the appointed day of its reappearing is at hand."

"The appointed day? You make it sound planned."

"I will comment no further in that direction." Dr. Cissna smiled.

"Is that the gist of your theory, Doctor?"

"Only the foundation for it. The theory itself takes the speculation even further."

"Then by all means, go on!"

Cissna smiled, then nodded. "In the matter of living fauna—animals—once a creature is physically dead, its life is gone, passed—forever. Notwithstanding what may happen to its soul, bodies of creatures do not go dormant, so to speak, and then come back to life later, cryogenic experiments aside. When a species goes extinct, it is gone. What do the people say who study such things? That 50 million separate creature-species have become extinct since life has existed on our planet."

"It is some such fantastic number."

"There is an old Dinka song that speaks of the difference between creature-deaths and other deaths."

"I would like to hear it."

"I will just give you the germ of it. In the time when Dendid created all things, he created the sun. And the sun is born, and dies, and comes again. He created the moon. And the moon is born, and dies, and comes again. He created the stars. And the stars are born, and die, and come again. He created man. And man is born, and dies, and does not come again."

They walked on for a time in silence.

"To return to my theory," said the doctor, "I doubt it can ever be proven, but here it is in brief: I conjecture that all the living flora that has existed on the earth is still alive . . . somewhere. Or perhaps I should say, the potential for its life still exists."

"That is an astonishing theory, Doctor! What an incredible thought."

"With implications in the direction of your present research, if you follow my train of thought."

Suddenly Adam stopped in his tracks. His hand went to his head in gesture of sudden revelation and wonder.

"Eden!" he exclaimed.

"Precisely," rejoined Dr. Cissna. "What if all Eden's plants, all the trees and grasses and shrubbery the Creator provided as the perfect environment for man—what if they all still exist, dormant, waiting in readiness . . . for some fantastic moment of discovery?"

"Why would they suddenly reappear? What might cause such a thing . . . how could it happen after all these years?"

"I cannot answer that," replied Cissna. "Perhaps an answer lies outside man's domain. Reemerging life is all in the timing. If such a remarkable thing ever happens, it will be because the appointed season for it has come. A period of waiting often precedes such new life. In many parts of the world, dormancy is necessary. Winter must precede spring. Without the winter frosts, certain seeds and bulbs and grasses and roots are not revitalized to flow with life when the spring arrives. When the time for flowering comes, for the revelation of long-hidden mysteries, for the reemergence of life long hidden, for the discovery of ancient truths—it will be because the dormancy has done its work, and the proper time has at last arrived. Here in the equatorial belt we do not see much frost, but I believe something of the same principle yet can be seen."

"But why, Doctor?"

"Why is not always for us to know. As a botanist I heed the times and seasons of growing things. Then I remain watchful for the signs . . . so that I will be ready when the moment for germination arrives."

(7)

Candace Montreux had never been to this part of the world.

She didn't like the idea of flying alone into a land that had so recently been behind the Iron Curtain. Halder Zorin, however, was not a man you easily refused. It had not taken long for his assurances and charm to put her anxiety to rest.

"You shall be my personal guest," he said on the telephone. "You must see my new city. Believe me, it has every luxury and convenience and is more modern even than London."

"Your city, Mr. Zorin?"

"Speaking figuratively, of course," Zorin replied. It would not be long before he would be able to make such a claim openly as fact as well.

Candace fussed with her jacket as the plane began its descent. She'd tried on a dozen outfits before packing her suitcases. She chose for the plane trip a stylish black suit with a lilac-colored silk blouse.

The commercial jetliner had scarcely touched down on the tarmac at Baku when Candace saw a sleek black limousine approaching, flying on its hood the official flags of Azerbaydzhan. She stepped out a few minutes later to see that the interior minister of works had come for her personally.

"It is wonderful to see you again, Miss Montreux," said Zorin's powerful voice as she walked forward from the plane. "You are looking especially beautiful."

"Thank you, Mr. Zorin." Candace smiled, with flashing eyes.

He motioned her toward the waiting limousine, whose open rear door awaited them, held by a uniformed guard. "You shall stay at my estate, before we proceed together to Africa."

"What about customs? Don't I have to report somewhere?"

Zorin smiled. As crafty as Lady Montreux thought she was, she still hadn't a notion what a high-ranking man he was. "Everything has been arranged," he replied.

That evening they sat together in the intimate glass-enclosed dining room overlooking the bay on the top floor of Zorin's villa. They had just been served the first course in what would be a lavish dinner that Zorin's servants had prepared for the occasion. Zorin poured them each a glass of an expensive French Cabernet, then lifted his glass to his guest.

"To the charming and beautiful Lady Candace Montreux," he said. "May this be the first of many visits to Baku, the future center of European life."

Candace nodded appreciatively as she clinked her glass to his. Both took delicate sips of the deep red vintage. Zorin knew already that she was falling in love with him. He found the fact as amusing as it was gratifying. It would make his triumph over Livingstone all the more satisfying knowing that he had used the fool's own woman to destroy him. Livingstone and his inane expeditions had already caused him far too much agitation.

"Tomorrow you shall see the rest of the city," said Zorin. "And meet our president."

"From what I observed today," Candace remarked with a smile not nearly so bewitching on this man as she flattered herself it was, "I thought you must secretly be the president."

"All in good time, my dear . . . all in good time," rejoined Zorin, playing along. He could afford to let her imagine what she would. "But tell me, what would you think of being first lady of a small eastern European nation?"

"A small nation?" she repeated, with feigned innocence.

"Yes . . . say something, perhaps—well, like my own nation of Azerbaydzhan, for instance."

The two were both experienced and indeed well matched in this coy little game of cat and mouse, in which each considered the other the mouse.

"It might be something to which I could accustom myself," replied Candace at length. "But surely you are aware that I am nearly engaged to Adam Livingstone. I only agreed to help you in hopes of forcing him to make up his mind."

"Ah . . . I see everything clearly now!" said Zorin. "But give me time."

"Time . . . whatever do you mean?"

"I think we understand one another, Lady Montreux." Zorin smiled. "I can see it in your eyes. And to show you just what I mean, we will enjoy a couple of days here together. If the weather allows it, I shall take you out on my yacht on the Caspian. What would you say to candlelight dinner at midnight, followed by a night at sea?"

"It sounds enchanting. I accept your wicked proposal. It was intended to be wicked, was it not?" she added, lifting an eyebrow cunningly.

"Absolutely."

"I was certain of it."

"Then we shall return to the city and make preparations for the safari phase of our little adventure."

"What preparations?"

"For one thing, we will have to find you some suitable clothing. You, of course, will be beautiful in anything. But we need you to look more . . . like an archaeologist."

"You don't mean with boots and that horrid stiff brown cloth!"

"We must all make sacrifices for the cause, my dear Miss Montreux."

(8)

Two days later, Adam and Dr. Cissna were roaming through the underbrush in Murchison Falls Park.

On this day Adam had drilled a half-dozen or eight core samples, from not only baobab but also giant groundsel, several great heather trees, acacia, and thorn trees, as well as collected two packs full of moss and bark samples. Not all these species of trees even had annual growth rings, but Adam hoped they would prove useful in other tests and alternate dating methods.

Sometime early in the afternoon, Dr. Cissna paused in his step, an odd look on his face. He glanced at Adam but raised his hand to his lips, saying nothing. An expression of question crossed Adam's forehead. In a moment they resumed.

"The curious feeling has been growing on me that we are being followed," whispered Dr. Cissna at Adam's side. "It is probably ridiculous. I am certainly no sleuth, but sometimes these jungles can't help but give even experienced veterans like me, what you Americans would say, the spooks."

They continued on, though neither man spoke.

It was Adam who next heard sounds behind them. Now he paused and cocked an ear.

Dr. Cissna had been right. They were not alone. In a place like this, that might mean any one of a hundred things—and none of them good!

The two men's eyes met momentarily. Silently both asked the other whether they should stay put or run for their lives from whatever unseen cheetah or jungle gorilla was stalking them.

Suddenly a great tramping and crashing sounded behind them.

Adam's heart leapt into his throat.

He made a dash for the nearest tree. Already Dr. Cissna was several paces away in the opposite direction and moving rapidly. A shout sounded.

Adam spun around. No lion at all—there was a familiar dark face . . . a white grin under sweaty pith helmet . . . and a Denver Broncos T-shirt.

It was Scott! And just behind him—

"Rocky!" exclaimed Adam in delighted surprise and relief. He could say no more for a few seconds. Heart still pounding furiously, he continued to breathe in and out deeply.

"We thought we were about to be trampled by an elephant!" he exclaimed with a smile.

"Sorry to disappoint you," laughed the big American.

"Hardly a disappointment—but—what a surprise! How in the world did you find us?"

"It wasn't easy," laughed Scott. "I called the airfield in Nanyuki. They said you'd left for Uganda. I knew Murchison was next on your agenda after Mount Kenya."

"But we're in the middle of a forest!"

"We've been on the hunt about two hours. I had an idea you'd head upriver from Kabalega Falls. We got onto your track about twenty minutes ago. Rocky suggested we try to see how close we could get before you heard us."

"Always the detective! Actually we've known you were there for thirty minutes—haven't we, Dr. Cissna?" said Adam, throwing the botanist a wink.

"Whatever you say. You're the boss!"

"But . . . Rocky!" laughed Adam, now embracing the detective warmly. "How are you?"

"Tired feet . . . actually tired body, tired brain! It was a cramped flight down from London."

"What are you doing here!"

"You told me to meet you in Africa. Well . . . here I am!"

Still Adam's expression was astonishment.

"You heard about the break-in at your estate?"

"Right. I talked to Thurlow two days ago. And by the way—thanks for saving my household and all that. But that doesn't answer—"

"Someone tried to kill you. Now someone's broken into your house and nearly put a slug between my eyes. I figured it was time we got to the bottom of this before one of us does get killed."

"I couldn't agree with you more."

"Rocky, meet Dr. Petiri Cissna from Cairo. Dr. Cissna, Rocky McCondy, American private investigator." Rocky and Dr. Cissna shook hands.

"I suspect the two of you have more in common in the way of outlook," said Adam, "than you have let on, Dr. Cissna."

"What gives you that idea?"

"Let's just say I read between the lines. I detect a similarity of spiritual undercurrent whenever our conversations drift into certain channels."

The detective and the botanist laughed and glanced at one another, eyes bright with fun. Both understood Adam's meaning.

"Did you get the journal back?" Adam asked.

Rocky tapped his vest pocket. "Got it right here. From now on it doesn't leave me. I sleep with it. Though I did make one copy before I left."

"And put it someplace safe, I hope."

"I gave it to Pastor Mark—you remember, I told you about him. He may just have shed some light on this whole thing too."

"I want to hear everything. Let's get back to camp. I think I've got enough core samples here for one day's work. I can't wait to send them back to the lab to see what Emily can learn from them."

"What did you find?" asked Scott.

"We have some intriguing samples from several trees and a particularly interesting little shell fossil embedded in a chunk of groundsel bark."

"Are you thinking of flood evidence?" asked Scott as they began walking back the way they had come.

"It has crossed my mind. But right now I'm most anxious to examine that journal. I'm convinced it may hold the key to all this."

"What's it all about?" asked Scott.

"You remember my interest in the old archaeologist when we were at Cambridge? You mentioned it just the other day."

"Right—Rocky's great-grandfather."

"Rocky's got the man's journal in his pocket."

"Do I smell a new research paper coming on?"

"I have the feeling it's bigger than that."

"But, Scott," Adam said, a new thought suddenly occurring to him, "you didn't leave Jen alone back at camp at the mercy of Sir Gilbert?"

"I'm afraid so."

"Then we'd definitely better get back posthaste!"

"And speaking of leaving people alone," said Rocky as they went, "I took a liberty before I left Sevenoaks. I couldn't get hold of you, so I made a decision. Hope you don't mind."

"I'm listening," said Adam.

"I didn't want to leave Juliet, Mrs. Graves, and your girls upstairs. Scotland Yard had a guard around the place. But I still didn't like the thought of leaving. So I hired a private investigator that Thurlow recommended—a woman—someone we know we can trust. I moved her into one of your guest rooms."

"I approve completely. Excellent thinking, Rocky."

"Anyway, she's at your place now. She'll be in twenty-four-hour-a-day residency till I get back or give her further instructions."

"I can't tell you how grateful I am, Rocky," said Adam.

# twenty-one

# Surprise Callers

### (1)

Rocky had warned Captain Thurlow that the man they had arrested was involved in a scheme much larger than petty burglary. Unfortunately the captain's precautions to the governor at the Brixton Prison on Jebb Avenue, where the Livingstone burglar was being held, had not been so thorough.

They had still not managed to make the man talk. Now it was too late.

Three mornings after the arrest, the intruder was found dead in his cell, apparently of a poison administered sometime between the previous night's supper and dawn.

The man had had no visitors. Among those leaving the prison on the previous evening, however, one of the wardens had noticed a dark-complexioned individual with a distinctive gait whom no prison business could account for.

The only other factor he could recall was that the stranger wore an olive green beret.

Inquiries were undertaken, but nothing was ever learned. Nor did the eventual identification of the burglar yield any connection that could be traced.

### (2)

While Adam, Scott, and Jen were away in Africa, it was secretary Crystal Johnson's job to keep the research office functioning smoothly back home. With Rocky now gone and a large-framed, sober-minded woman detective under their roof making everyone nervous, the mood was again subdued. Every member of the household could not help silently wondering what calamity would befall them next.

Captain Thurlow's twenty-four-hour guard remained posted around the estate. But that could not stop the wind from occasionally howling eerily at night.

Beeves did his gallant best to supply sufficient bravery for the house. But the American's were large shoes to fill. The poor balding butler, as much as everyone loved him, was unable to sustain the women's spirits with anywhere near the same level of courage and optimism. If Mr. Livingstone was gone until spring, the months between now and then would be long indeed.

Juliet found no job and remained with her aunt. She wandered into the office more frequently, and she and Crystal gradually developed a blossoming friendship. If Mrs. Graves acted the part of older aunt to the Livingstone household, Crystal's role was that of wise and sober-minded older sister. At forty-two, and with a son already in university and a daughter just a year away, she was Adam's elder by eight years and had been with him almost since the inception of his career.

Of medium height and muscular, almost stocky, frame, with light brown hair cropped short in Beatles' fashion, the secretary was generally soft-spoken and of even temperament, though she was not afraid to speak her mind honestly when it was required of her. Adam had learned to trust both her instincts and her insights, though her formal education years before, oddly enough, had been in music and ballet. She was as devoted to Adam and his work as she was to her own family and found the fields of his endeavor thrilling and challenging. Even now, had a major role in the theater presented itself, she would have turned it down in an instant rather than sacrifice being part of Adam's research.

With the field team now gone, Crystal and Juliet spoke often about the work. Gradually Juliet found herself drawn more closely into it, learning more about the many projects Adam Livingstone had been pursuing for the past several years.

Materials arrived almost every morning from the field by overnight courier for testing in the lab. Notes from Jen kept them generally abreast of progress in eastern Africa.

Juliet walked into the office one morning about eleven. Crystal was obviously agitated.

"I'm making tea downstairs," said Juliet. "Want to join me?"

"I don't know," replied Crystal. "Right now I want Emily more than I do tea."

"Where is she?"

"I don't know. She hasn't come in yet today. I've been calling her flat, but there's no answer."

"She mentioned nothing when she left yesterday?"

Crystal shook her head. "There are some tests that need to be done," she went on. "Jen's going to be calling for results this afternoon at five."

"What kind of tests?" asked Juliet.

"Routine chemical analysis, one little fossil for dating. Actually, I don't understand half this stuff—here's Jen's note."

She handed it to Juliet, who perused the paper.

"I can do these things," said Juliet.

"You can!"

"Sure. That is if you don't mind . . . if you think it would be all right for me to be down in the lab."

"Sure," replied Crystal. "I don't want to disrupt Adam's schedule. Emily will probably arrive any moment. In the meantime, you can start on them. I hereby authorize it!"

Juliet was already nearly out the door, Jen's note and the packet in hand.

"Hey—what about my tea?" Crystal called after her.

"I'm no longer thirsty!" Juliet called back.

Crystal laughed as she watched her go. She picked up the phone and tried Emily's flat again. Still no answer.

(3)

Several days later a Land Rover approached the Livingstone camp.

At first sound of its engine, Adam and the others glanced at one another questioningly, as if to say, "Are we expecting anyone?"

Adam was in the process of rising, about to send Dr. Cissna darting for cover, when Scott put his mind at ease.

"It's just a single driver," he said. "No barage of reporters. I think we're safe."

None of the team, however, was prepared for the new guest about to be welcomed to their camp so far out in the wilds of Africa.

"Candace!" exclaimed Adam, running toward the vehicle as it pulled to a stop. "What in the world . . . I can't believe it!"

"It is really me, Adam!" said the newcomer, flashing a bright smile as she climbed out.

Adam embraced her affectionately, the miles between Olduvai and London accomplishing even more than the passage of time to remove the distasteful memory of their previous meeting. Somehow the setting at once eliminated differences that would have been obvious elsewhere. In addition to the environment, Candace's khaki garb, hiking boots, and floppy hat produced their desired effect. She seemed immediately one of them.

"You know Scott and Jen . . . ," said Adam ebulliently as they parted and he led Candace toward the others.

Scott stepped forward and shook her hand. Jen nodded, though without a smile, and remained where she was. She didn't like Candace Montreux any more than she did Gilbert Bowles.

"This is Rocky McCondy," Adam continued, "a friend of mine from the States . . . and Dr. Petiri Cissna from the University of Cairo. Rocky, Dr. Cissna . . . meet Lady Candace Montreux, my—"

Adam hesitated, then glanced toward Candace with a smile of playfulness.

"What are you exactly?" he said.

305

"I hope before *too* much longer, Adam, I shall be your fiancée," replied Candace, with a smile equally full of significance.

"There you have it, gentlemen!" said Adam, throwing out his hands to his side as if everything had instantly been perfectly explained. "That should make a murky situation as clear as it can be made at this time." They all laughed, except Jen.

"But, Candace," said Adam, "you still haven't answered my question—what in the world are you doing here? How did you find us?"

"Daddy has ways of finding out most anything he wants to know," replied Candace.

"You're the last person I expected to see. But . . . but *why?* I thought you hated all this," said Adam, laughing and gesturing about at the primitive surroundings. Gradually Adam led her, walking slowly, away from the others.

"Are you disappointed to see me, Adam?" said Candace softly with a flirtatious pout, slinking her hand through his arm.

"Of course not. I'm delighted—only surprised."

"You cannot have forgotten our previous talk," said Candace.

They continued to walk. Adam did not reply.

"I thought about what you said about a wife sharing your work," Candace went on in as sincere a tone as it was possible for her to muster. "It was unfair of me to expect anything else from you. I should have known you better. You have to be who you are—and you are a scientist and thinker. So I decided to come here to show you that I am interested in what you do."

"Candace—that is wonderful to hear."

"So, what are you doing? Is it going well?"

"Oh yes—it's so exciting. Dr. Cissna and I have been roaming about everywhere."

"And have you found the Garden of Eden?"

"Not exactly," laughed Adam. "But we've made some exciting discoveries."

"I'm eager to hear all about it, Adam."

The two continued to talk, returning in the direction of the camp about thirty minutes later.

"Will you be staying here with us, Candace?" Adam asked.

"I didn't want to presume, Adam. I'm in a hotel in Arusha."

"But you must, if you're going to join my team."

"I'm not sure I'm *quite* ready for that."

"I'll make it as comfortable for you as I can. I promise."

(4)

The phone rang in the downstairs lab of the Livingstone home. The voice that answered was one Adam did not immediately recognize.

"Uh . . . I'm calling for Emily." Adam's voice hesitated. "This *is* the lab?"

"Yes . . . she's not here."

"Who am I speaking to?"

"It's Juliet Halsay," answered Juliet, suddenly recognizing the voice on the other end of the line. Terror filled her at the reminder of her first encounter with Adam Livingstone. Now she had been found in the lab without his permission a *second* time!

"What are you doing there?" asked Adam. Had Juliet been able to see his face, she would have seen the humor in the question. As it was, however, she forgot all the pleasant exchanges they had had since that first day. Her optimistic resolve about life immediately crumbled.

"Oh, no!" Juliet could not help exclaiming.

Adam realized her awkwardness. "Don't worry, Miss Halsay," he laughed lightly, "I won't bite."

"I'm . . . I'm sorry—Emily has been out for a couple of days, and we knew she was in the middle of some work."

"We?"

"Crystal and I."

"Where is Crystal, by the way?"

"She had to go out for some things."

"I see. That explains why Mrs. Graves answered a moment ago."

"When the packet arrived from Jen the morning, Emily didn't come in. Crystal was anxious not to hold you up. I was with her at the time and told her I could do the tests Jen asked for . . . I'm . . . I'm sorry, Mr. Livingstone," she added.

In spite of Adam's genial tone, by now Juliet's voice was trembling. "I . . . I thought I could help so that Emily wouldn't get behind."

"Don't worry, I won't scold you," said Adam. "Besides," he added, laughing again, "I'm five thousand miles away. There's not much I could do to you from here even if I wanted to!"

"Thank you," replied Juliet, though her voice remained soft and shaky.

"But we've been getting reports back. Who has—do you mean . . . ?" The telephone fell silent.

"Have *you* been sending the reports, Miss Halsay?" asked Adam.

"Yes . . . yes, I have. I only wanted to help, Mr. Livingstone."

"And you have. This *is* a surprise—you are a young lady of versatile talents! I appreciate your diligence."

"You are very kind."

"Then let's get down to business, shall we," said Adam. "I'm sending some core drillings of a few trees, as well as some samples of vines, tubers, monocotyls, a shrub or two, and some unusual algae—any way we can ascertain dates, molecular structure, genus—*whatever* we can learn about them will be helpful. These are not my fields."

"What about Dr. Cissna? I thought he was the expert."

"You *are* up to speed on what we've been doing! Unfortunately Dr. Cissna's time with me is almost over, and of course we have no lab out here. He will soon be returning to Cairo. He could only give me a few days. But Scott and I will continue our foraging of the forests and plains and valleys. In any event, there are some interesting samples we want to know more about."

"I know someone I can call—a dating specialist in botany at my college."

"Dating is just the tip of the iceberg. Of course, that is the real bull's-eye in what we're doing here. If you do get help, that would be good—but make sure it's someone you can trust. And go to him with your questions. Nobody new gets in the lab. Come to think of it," he added in a thoughtful tone, "it might be best not to tell him who you're working for—keep my name out of it."

Adam paused again, thinking to himself.

"How much of Emily's work and the lab are you familiar with?" he asked.

"I don't know. I've tried not to snoop around too much."

"Don't worry. All that's now passed. The reason I asked is to see if you were aware of the long-core samples I sent in last week. There were about ten of them."

"Yes, I saw them."

"They've been stored away?"

"I think so."

"Do you know where?"

"I can find them."

"Good. We'll need some further tests on those too. What I want you to do is compare your findings on these new materials with Emily's results on the others."

Juliet put down the phone a minute or two later, more excited than she had been in years. She worked late into the evening, and all the following day on the assignment.

(5)

Candace Montreux walked toward Gilbert Bowles' camp from a direction opposite that of Adam's. She had parked, as per instructions, where the Rover would have little chance of being seen, then walked the last half mile.

The terrain was rocky and uneven. The new boots were already giving her blisters. She had had her fill of Africa in one day!

Candace hobbled toward the tent.

"Anybody in there?" she called out. Her voice sounded tired, hot, and irritable.

"Come in, my dear," said a deep voice. "We've been expecting you."

Candace lifted the flap and ducked inside. She glanced about, annoyed to

308

see the two men looking so cool and rested, with glasses that looked cold in their hands.

"Sir Gilbert, where can I lie down? I'm worn out!"

"Take my bunk over there," said Bowles, chuckling lightly.

"What is there to drink?" she said, plopping down and exhaling a long sigh.

"How about a beer—though I can't promise how cold it will be?"

"Anything! Oh, I've got to get these awful boots off . . . my feet are killing me!" She sat up and began untying and tugging at the laces.

Zorin observed the exchange with detached amusement. This lady was *not* cut out to be Adam Livingstone's wife.

"What did you find out, my dear?" Zorin asked.

"The man's name is Cissna," Candace replied. "Adam called him Doctor Cissna. He's from Cairo."

"Cairo? What does he do . . . why is he here?"

"The University of Cairo. That's all Adam said. I don't know what he does. Adam just said they had been roaming about together."

"Ring any bells, Bowles?" said Zorin, glancing toward the archaeologist.

Bowles shook his head. "I'll ask Cutter when I pass on the information to him. He should be able to—"

"Negative, Bowles," interrupted Zorin. "You'll say nothing to anyone. From now on, you work for me . . . exclusively." The command in the man's voice was unmistakable. It was obvious who was calling the shots for this secretive little trio.

"How long will he be here?" Zorin now asked Candace.

"I don't know," she grunted, yanking the second boot free from her swollen foot.

Zorin thought a moment.

"All right," he said, "we've done what we can do here. Nobody's going to follow them as long as they have that plane. There's not much use our sitting around any longer. We can get more done elsewhere."

He paused again, bringing his hand unconsciously to his chin, still thinking.

"Bowles," he went on, "you get up to Cairo. Find out who this Cissna is. That should tell us something. I want to know everything about him. Inform me the second you have anything."

"Where will you be?"

"I've got to get back to Baku for a few days. But my jet is always ready at a moment's notice. I want Livingstone stopped, and I intend to finish the job personally."

Bowles nodded. He hated taking orders like this. But the glint in the man's eye was evil, and he knew he'd better not cross him for the time being.

"Candace, it's time you and I returned to Arusha," Zorin said, now rising and draining off the last of the warm ale in his glass.

"I'm too exhausted to move!"

"Come up . . . on your feet." He reached down and took her hand. Candace groaned, doing little to help.

"When will you see Livingstone again?"

"Adam said he'd meet me in Arusha in two days. He has two more trips with Dr. Cissna planned, he said. Then he'll come for me. In the meantime he's going to set up a place for me to stay at his camp. He wants me to join his team," she added with another groan.

Bowles could not keep from chuckling at the thought.

"I don't know if I can stand to sleep outside . . . in a tent no less!" moaned Candace.

"You won't have to, my dear," said Zorin.

(6)

When Adam next called home and asked Crystal for the lab, he knew whom to expect on the other end.

"We've been getting the reports from you every day, Miss Halsay," he said. "Well done. First rate, in fact. Very thorough and professional."

"Thank you."

"How do you know how to carry out such complex analyses?" he asked. "Carbon dating is no easy matter. Did you get in touch with the professor you mentioned?"

"I called him and asked a few questions. It wasn't so complicated, really."

"You hadn't gone over those things with Emily?"

"No. I'd studied it at college."

"By the way—where *is* Emily? I forgot to ask Crystal a moment ago. I just asked for you."

"Crystal finally got through to her. She was sick, that's all."

"And didn't call in? I don't like her not letting Crystal know. I'm beginning to have my doubts. Hmm . . . so tell me," he went on, "what did you study?"

"Geography and geology. That's why I was in the lab before. You remember . . . that first day when you got angry with me."

"I wasn't angry," laughed Adam. "Just surprised."

"If you could have seen the look on your face, I think even you would call it angry," rejoined Juliet.

Adam laughed again.

"I was just so interested," Juliet went on. "I didn't touch a thing, I promise!" she added, a hint of fun in her tone.

"Geology," repeated Adam, "That's right—I'd forgotten. You and Scott both."

"I wanted to study earthquakes," added Juliet.

"Earthquakes *are* fascinating," replied Adam. "Can you *imagine* what we could learn about the earth if we could unlock secrets of the earth's interior movement."

"Oh, I know. I've always thought they were one of earth's greatest mysteries. I've wondered if it is because they are so silent and invisible."

"Have you heard of Cloe Komorowski?"

"Oh yes, I have her book," replied Juliet. "I once heard Dr. Komorowski lecture on her theory of catastrophism as a geologic foundation rather than uniformitarianism. I've never forgotten it."

"I'm familiar with the theory only in its general terms."

"Do you know her?"

"We met once . . . only briefly," replied Adam.

"That's so exciting."

"Not such a big thing. We hardly spoke more than a minute or two."

"After hearing her," Juliet went on eagerly, "I wrote to Dr. Komorowski, wondering if perhaps the volatility around the Pacific Rim was connected deep underground to the great rift of Africa, the one causing volcanos and earthquakes, the other causing a stretching of the earth's crust."

"That's good reasoning. I hadn't thought of it before," replied Adam. "What did Dr. Komorowski say."

"I never received a reply back from her."

"I'm sorry to hear that."

"I was saving my money to go on a two-week trip to California sponsored by King's College and the University of Prague, led by Dr. Komorowski next summer, but . . ."

The voice on the line paused. "But then . . . of course that won't be possible now," Juliet said softly.

"Why not?" said Adam. "It sounds like a great opportunity."

"When my father died, my mother and I were left with debts. There was no money, you see. That's why I've been looking for a job. I'm sorry," she added, sniffing, "I didn't mean to get all teary-eyed."

"Don't worry—I don't mind."

"I thought I was done with the tears," said Juliet. "Actually, I've had a wonderful last week or so. God has really turned my life around. I've been filled with a great new joy, in spite of a few occational lingering tears."

"*God* has turned it around?"

"Yes—he's even more personal than I realized when I told you about the sunbeams of peace before."

"How did he turn it around, exactly?"

"From a talk I had with a dear lady—Erin's mother, Mrs. Wagner—and from a prayer I prayed," replied Juliet.

"You visited Erin's mother?"

"Yes."

"Well, perhaps one day you shall tell me about it. In any event, I still say you're entitled to a few tears now and then," said Adam. "It's tough losing a father. I remember it. And my sister's still trying to come to terms with it all these years later. She's spent her whole life embittered about the past."

"Bitterness and unforgiveness are a terrible waste of energy, it seems to me."

"And so silly."

"Why do you say that?"

"Because it's so easily avoidable. But my sister won't hear such reasoning from me or from my mum either. I think she's determined to take her anger to her own grave. Yet it's hurting no one so much as her. I love her, but it's so stupid, if you'll pardon my saying so."

Adam laughed as he said the words, though not with humor.

"Now it's my turn to apologize," he added after a brief pause. "I didn't mean to get off on that! But back to *your* problem," he added, thinking as he spoke. "You forget looking for a job for the present."

"Why do you say that?"

"You're working for *me* now," said Adam enthusiastically. "That is, if you'll accept the position."

"What about Emily?"

"You leave that to me"

"But . . . I couldn't do it!" said Juliet, hardly able to believe her ears. "I don't know enough." Even as the words came out of her mouth, her heart was beating in disbelieving excitement.

"Sure you do," rejoined Adam. "Just keep doing what you've been doing. When I get back I'll show you around every inch of the whole lab myself. But I'd nearly forgotten why I called," he said. "I really need the results on that sample I sent in two days ago. I didn't want to wait—did you receive it?"

"It came yesterday."

"Do you know how to C-14 date the two different parts of the fossil—the little shell fragment embedded in the bit of wood? It seems to have grown right around it, making the shell part of the tree itself. I want to compare it with another shell that Emily—I assume it was Emily's work, though maybe it was yours—analyzed and dated last week. This new piece is really rather remarkable. If the shell was from some kind of water creature and was taken into the tree, so to speak, we might be able to discover how old the tree was at the time."

"That would have bearing on the flood!"

"Precisely what I was thinking. Do you think you can do it, Miss Halsay?"

"I think so. I've never actually dated something so complex. But I watched it done once. After what you gave me earlier, I think I can do it."

"It will be no problem. I'll walk you through it."

"All right—if you think I can," said Juliet, more nervous than she had been earlier in the week, now that Adam had suddenly placed such confidence in her.

"Sure," said Adam. "Put the phone on speaker, then go to the—wait, I just remembered that I wanted you to look at something on that ice core from Ararat too. Let's take care of that first. Is the phone on speaker?"

"Yes."

"Good. Then go to the freezer—you know where it is?"

"Yes."

"All right, the core is in the plastic cylindrical tube on the shelf to the left with the other Ararat samples. I'm looking for that little band of discoloration, with some speckles of dirt and other particles in it, like a dust storm perhaps blew over the snow cover. When you locate that, I need an exact measurement of how many centimeters it is from the top of the cylinder. What we're going to do is compare the core sample of the baobab from last week to what I took from inside the glacier surrounding the ark."

"I understand. What am I looking for?"

"I'm not sure exactly," replied Adam with a curious expression. "What possible connection could a core of ice have with a tree core from the jungles of Africa? I suppose it's an absurd notion. Still, I'd like you to see what you can come up with. If we can find a connection . . . well, let's do the research and analysis first and form our conclusions *after* we have the data!"

The two continued to talk for another thirty minutes, Juliet carrying out Adam's long-distance instructions and relaying the information back to him.

An hour later when Juliet left the lab, she skipped upstairs to her room, feeling more lighthearted than she had in months.

# twenty-two

# Grandpa Harry's Journal

(1)

The world's great waterfalls were not new to Adam Livingstone. He had stood in awe before the mighty and majestic cataracts of Victoria and Niagara. But never had those wonders exercised such a profound impact within his spirit as the remarkable sight before him at this moment.

He had ventured alone to visit the lesser known Kabalega, or Murchison Falls, on the Victoria Nile some twenty miles upriver from Lake Albert.

He had been standing nearly immovable for twenty or thirty minutes. Around him the noise was deafening, yet all was quiet within his spirit.

The waters from the upper Nile thundered with terrifying power as they tumbled into the narrow gorge before him, sending skyward a perpetual spray that moistened every growing thing within two hundred yards, twenty-four hours a day, three hundred and sixty-five days a year.

Adam's soul was still, subdued, thoughtful.

If ever, thought Adam, a single spot on the globe could put forward the remarkable claim to having preserved some hint of ancient Eden . . . surely it would be such a place as this.

Just over one hundred miles north of the equator, sunlight exactly twelve hours a day, no winter, and a pure and pleasing mist continually watering the verdant plant life—were such the conditions in which the *former* Adam lived? Was the original canopy something like this—a warm, gentle, sunny fog covering all the earth?

The *latter* Adam contemplating the enormous question could hardly imagine what it must have been like. Yet how could it be other than this—green and blue everywhere . . . plant life and abundant water to sustain it . . . the earth, the sky . . . a garden of perfection.

And water everywhere—Lakes Victoria, Tanganyika, Kivu, Edward, George, Albert, and Kioga.

*Water*—the great necessity of life! And rivers and streams! Surely these headwaters of the great Nile, the longest river in the world . . . was it possible he was looking at some remnant of the ancient Gihon of Genesis 2?

*A river watering the garden flowed from Eden; from there it was separated into four headwaters.*

However continental drift and earthquakes and crust movement and the stretching of the earth's rift had changed the globe since, a sensation of certainty grew within him as he stood watching the great river tumbling its way from Lake Victoria northward, beginning its four-thousand-mile journey to the Mediterranean. Nor could he discount the possibility that the Nile, like the Amazon, had reversed its direction at some time in the ancient past, which would have made its original headwaters somewhere near its present mouth.

Another ten minutes Adam stood in silent marvel and contemplation. Slowly he eased himself onto a nearby rock. He felt at this moment more than beauty, more than science, more than the thrill of discovery.

Something else, something deeper, was at hand.

He felt a sense—he didn't know what else to call it—a sense of *presence.*

Was this akin to the first stirrings within the original Adam? What had that most remarkable "waking" been like? The mere thought of it sent tingles into Adam Livingstone's brain.

How had the other Adam first recognized that he was not alone, that he was an individual unique and distinct from the other creatures, a being who could think in a higher way? How had self-awareness dawned? How had he first recognized that he was not *merely* a being, but one accountable to someone higher . . . to One who had made him?

What a remarkable notion!

Archaeologists weren't supposed to ask questions like this. God was not included within the matrix of their research.

Had the first Adam looked around, begun walking about in that garden full of trees and rivers and animals and food and pleasing things . . . and *also* felt the Presence?

A sensation Adam Livingstone had never known rose up from a deep inner well within him, urging from him a response to this revelation of what humanhood must *mean.* The incredible moment would remain with him as an eternal memory for the rest of his life.

Suddenly Adam knew that he was no mere *Homo sapiens,* no mere living future fossil that chance evolution had thrust up onto the topmost branch of its complex but random history.

He recognized himself as a *man,* an *Adam,* and understood that a *Creator* whom the Bible called *the Lord God* had made him, fashioned him, *purposed* him . . . in his own image.

He never knew whether he spoke in audible tones, or whether he spoke in some inaudible corner of his heart or brain. That he *spoke* there was no doubt. For the Presence became suddenly close, active, alive, personal . . . and seemed almost to command a reply from Adam's awareness of his own existence as a man and human creature.

"*God,*" said Adam softly, "*you're here—at last I know it. You are here. I'm not accustomed to thinking of you in this way . . . as real and personal . . . as a force in the world. But I know you are here. I feel you all about me. Your presence is unmistakable. Is this what the first Adam felt so long ago, newly awake and newly bewildered by the wonder of where he found himself? Did he feel the same wonder I feel here? I don't know what to do now—*"

Adam paused.

He glanced about at the greenery and spray and trees and tumultuous river and drew in a deep breath of satisfaction. His entire life seemed to focus on this single instant of time. Before this moment he had been one person. Ever after he would be awake in a new way. When he stood and walked away from this place, henceforth he would be a new man.

He reached down to the ground and probed the moist soil beneath the lush tropical grasses. He brought his hand up with a fistful of rich, black earth, beheld it a moment, and smiled to himself as again he remembered the profound words of Genesis 2:7.

Adam Livingstone's moment of waking had come, a moment of creating . . . a moment of wonder, perhaps no less for this *new* Adam on this day than for the *first* Adam on that day so long ago.

"*I want to understand,*" he said further. "*If you will show me what you want me to do, God, as you did your first Adam, I will try to do as you say and be faithful to you.*"

(2)

"No, he will not be a problem . . . he will not talk. He has been taken care of."

"Did he find it?"

"That I have not been able to determine. It is doubtful, though I have someone checking on the effects that were on him at the time of the arrest."

"What about Bowles? What does he report?"

"I have been unable to reach him."

"Is he not to contact you?"

"That was our arrangement. He is behind schedule."

The voice on the other end of the line was silent. She was one who trusted intuition, and hers at the moment smelled a traitor in the camp.

"Keep trying," she said at length. "In the meantime, you and your associate may be flying to Africa soon. Be ready at a moment's notice."

The woman put down the phone, thought for a moment, then picked it up again.

"What have you been able to learn from your daughter?" she said when the call was answered.

"Nothing yet. She is not here at the moment."

"Where is she?"

"Out of the country."

"Where, then?'

"She flew to Baku."

"Baku!"

"Then I think she was planning to go on to Africa."

So it was exactly as she suspected! The traitor was one of their own, who had decided to take matters into his own hands.

(3)

The sun had set hours ago.

A half-moon gave the African plain outside the canvas what light it was capable of. Adam sat in his tent poring over the journal of old Harry McCondy. On a cot several feet away Rocky snored away the night, not bothered by the light of Adam's lantern. The detective was exhausted from the day.

It was probably 2:00 A.M., though Adam had completely lost track of time.

This was no ordinary journal. It was as much a spiritual diary, full of as many thoughts and prayers and handwritten passages of Scripture as it was of archaeological travels and digs and theories, of which old Grandpa Harry McCondy had had many.

"As I sat listening to John Walter Gregory . . . ," Adam read in McCondy's tiny but precise handwriting under the date 1893,

> . . . though the hall was full of orthodox geologists interested only in his conclusions regarding the rock strata he had explored along the wall of Laikipia Escarpment, my heart was fairly beating within me. Other reasons existed for my excitement. For when I heard him use the word rift for the first time, as he said, "For this type of valley I suggest the name of Rift Valley . . . and that of East Africa may justly be called the Great Rift Valley," my thoughts immediately leapt to the passage concerning the temple veil following the Crucifixion.

Here followed the words of the verse, with Matthew 27:51 beneath it, boxed in to highlight its significance: And, behold, the veil of the temple was rent in twain from the top to the bottom; and the earth did quake, and the rocks rent.

Then Rocky's great-grandfather continued on with his notes:

> Was the Rift Valley of Africa, I thought to myself excitedly, as indeed was the rending of the veil, but one further earthly replication of that greatest of all rifts that scars the universe, that rending across the heart of man, that split which occurred when man was cast from Eden—the rift between man and his Creator, which only the cross

*would later be capable of bridging? Of course, I thought to myself.
All spiritual truths possess earthly types and foreshadowings.*

Adam but barely understood the spiritual import of what he was reading,
yet he continued on eagerly.

*The cross of Calvary . . . the Great Rift Valley of Africa and the
Middle East. The one a myth in the eyes of modern nineteenth-
century man so blinded by the lure of the evolutionary lie.*

*Evolution, however, is not the root of the deception and falsehood
being foisted upon the world. It is chance! This is the great evil—
removing God from creation. Might God have used something like
evolution to effect his will? Who am I to say he could not have done
so? He is sovereign over his creation, after all. Much in Darwin's
*Origins* is compelling and accurate science. But the enemy's people
have twisted his work so far and extended his conclusions as to
deepen the deception and widen the rift between man and his
Creator—purveying the humanistic perspective that chance, not the
Lord God Almighty, brought about life.*

*Could not Genesis 1:20, 24, and 2:19—Let the waters bring forth
abundantly the moving creature that hath life. . . . Let the earth bring
forth the living creature after his kind. . . . And out of the ground the
Lord God formed every beast of the field, and every fowl of the air—be
scriptural indications of some form of divine process not unlike evolution? Again, who am I to say what Almighty God can and cannot do?
But God must be seen as the sovereign creative force behind every
minutest aspect of the creative process, however it occurred!*

*What connection do the two rifts have with one another? The very
significance of the universe! The rift . . . the healing!*

*Where did the rift begin? Where else but in Eden itself. Gregory is
wrong only in this—it is not the Great African Rift . . . it is the Great
Edenic Rift. The rift began in Genesis 3 when man said to himself,
"I will separate myself from my Creator . . . I will eat the fruit . . .
I will not obey the Lord God," and when God banished him from the
Garden.*

*It should be called the Genesis 3 Rift!*

*But all rifts shall be healed. . . .*

McCondy's hurried script went on.

*The cross shall be victor. Separation shall cease. The rift in the heart
of man will be healed. He shall then return to the life of Genesis 2
for which he was created, a life of harmony and love and obedience,
walking with his God and Savior and Creator in the cool of the day in
the Garden mists. Then shall Eden be restored. The rift of Genesis 3*

*shall be healed. The Garden shall be rediscovered. Man and his
Creator shall again commune in Genesis 2 life.*

As he read, Adam's heart raced with the words *the Garden shall be rediscovered.*

He continued on until, at length, he fell asleep where he sat. Rocky found him several hours later, the half-open journal lying upside down where it had fallen against his chest.

(4)

"Scott, I want to know about this fellow Gregory," said Adam, as they sat sipping coffee, while Rocky and Jen busily finished up eggs and fry bread for breakfast at the portable stove.

"Who?"

"The geologist last century who first explored the rift."

"Oh yeah—John Walter. Don't know that much about him, really. Scotsman. First came to Africa in 1892, I think. Set out on his own expedition the next year. He was only twenty-nine. That's when he came upon the rift."

"Was he the first—the first European, I mean?"

"No. Gregory didn't exactly discover it. But he first made the Rift Valley widely recognized among American and European geologists for what it is and coined the name."

"Where'd he go?"

"Lake Naivasha, the Masai country, then north to Lake Baringo. That's where he collected most of his samples."

"And then?"

"He'd planned to do a wall-to-wall survey of the valley between Kamasia and Elgeyo. But he ran out of supplies and had to return home. He'd seen enough basically to figure out what the rift was doing, which he lectured about in England later that same year."

Adam nodded, taking in the information with interest.

"Why the sudden interest in John Walter Gregory?"

"It's not him so much," replied Adam. "It seems Rocky's great-grandfather was in the audience listening to Gregory's report." He tapped the closed journal on the table beside him. "It apparently had quite an impact on him."

"My own interest in Gregory was always the original supercontinents," said Scott. "Gondwanaland, Laurasia, and Pangaea. Gregory was a passionate believer in them. Naturally, if continental drift is your specialty, as it was mine, Pangaea is intrinsic to the natural history of the process. Of course, back in the 1890s drift theory was just in its infancy."

"I know the basics. It's part of my computer program on the oval theory. But review it for me. Pretend I'm a novice, and you're explaining it to me for the first time."

"Why?" laughed Scott.

"Maybe something new will leap out at me."

"Okay, I'll try to give you the picture in brief," said Scott. "The heat and forces deep in the center of the earth produce currents that can actually make the solid rock of the earth's crust move like heavy liquid. A glacier is a good example of how it works. The ice is solid, yet we talk of glacial ice flowing. It's so slow it can't be seen, but over time, there is indeed a liquidlike movement."

"Right—keep going."

Scott glanced up before he could continue, to see a couple vehicles approaching.

"Oh, no—the media has returned!"

"At least Dr. Cissna got away without his identity leaking out," said Adam. "I think we can handle our friends of the press from here on out."

"Mr. Livingstone," said a man jumping out of the passenger side of a jeep and approaching, "I am Jeremy Tout, just got in from Mombasa. Wondered if I might ask you a few questions about your current research?"

"Sure. Though I don't promise I'll answer them, Mr. Tout," replied Adam with a grin.

"I'll take my chances. By the way—where's Bowles off to? I was going to interview him also."

"His camp's right over there. I haven't seen him in a day or two."

"I'm Kathryn Anderson, Mr. Livingstone," said an attractive young woman approaching behind Tout. "We just came from there. We thought maybe he'd joined you."

"Why—what are you talking about?"

"His camp's deserted without a trace," said Anderson. "Not a sign of life."

"What about his team of researchers?"

"We were just at his camp, Mr. Livingstone—there's no one there."

(5)

When Tout, Anderson, and the few other reporters with them were gone thirty minutes later, puzzled expressions went around the Livingstone campsite.

"I don't suppose we need worry about Sir Gilbert," said Adam.

"I for one am relieved," said Jen.

"It is a little strange, though, don't you think? To come all this way for such a short and unproductive time? In any event, Scott . . . proceed with my Geology 101 lecture on continental drift."

"What were we talking about?"

"The flow of glaciers—slow movement in the earth's crust."

"Oh yeah, right. Okay, then picture this same sort of flow happening with continents. Way back probably during the Permian period when Pangaea was still in existence—"

"What's that?" asked Rocky, who had not been listening before the interruption and now sat down to join them.

"A giant supercontinent, back when all the continents were joined."

"Never heard of it."

"It didn't last," said Scott. "Eventually the subterranean currents rising toward the surface of the earth split the northern and southern hemispheric continents apart. So during the Triassic period there were two giant supercontinents—Laurasia in the north and Gondwanaland in the south. The movement and geologic forces continued, separating the chunks of land still further. Essentially this action was volcanic. More cracks developed in the earth. Molten rock spewed up. Drifting of the landmasses occurred, seawater came in to fill the gaps, and the flow gradually carried away the various pieces, especially of Gondwanaland, to their present locations. Madagascar, for example, is nothing more than a piece of Africa that was torn off and carried away. India, too, was originally connected to Africa. The whole Indian Ocean is one of these new seas, or so the theory goes."

"The theory?"

"Oh yeah—this is all relatively new stuff," replied Scott. "A German back early in this century, Alfred Wegener, developed the modern thesis of continental drift. But his ideas were ridiculed by most of the scientific community. The whole drift theory was discredited by the '40s."

"But it's come back?"

"It began to be revived in the '50s through paleomagnetism, which really was a brand-new science at the time. Once magnetism in the earth was understood, drift began to make more sense. Then Harry Hess brought Wagenerian theories, with a few revisions, back full circle in the '60s. And ever since, continental drift as I've explained it has been more or less accepted."

"And what about continental expansion?" Adam asked.

"There's some of that. Obviously the rift here in Africa is now thirty miles wide in places and two hundred miles wide farther north. Clearly a widening is occurring. Globally how much this has impacted drift and contributed to the present shape and location of landforms, we don't really know for sure."

"Have mountains risen up as part of this process that are not volcanic?" asked Rocky.

"Oh, sure," replied Scott. "Not only do continents drift apart, they squeeze together."

"India's slow drift into the Asian landmass," added Adam. "You know about that, don't you, Rocky—how the Himalayas are still being lifted up?"

"I suppose I've heard something about it. What about freestanding mountains, out in the middle of nowhere, so to speak?"

"Mountains are thrown up for any number of reasons, not only volcanic action."

Adam and Rocky listened with interest, the one hearing some of this for the first time, the other hearing it with newly attuned senses, looking for new clues to the Eden puzzle.

"That's about it, really," said Scott. "The Rift Valley could have been torn apart earlier and more violently and become an extended part of the Red Sea, with this whole eastern section of Africa then drifting off like Masdagascar."

"Why didn't that happen?" asked Rocky.

"I don't know. Maybe it just wasn't supposed to."

Adam took in Scott's answer with curious expression.

"All right, that's enough of a geography lesson for one day," Adam said. "I've got to hit the road if I'm going to get to Arusha and get Candace back here at a decent hour. You've got the tent ready, Jen?"

Jen nodded, still none too happy at the thought of being Candace Montreux's bunkmate. But she would make the best of it—nothing could last forever.

(6)

Adam walked into the hotel in Arusha about two hours later.

"Hello, Mr. Livingstone," the clerk greeted him. "We haven't seen you for some time."

"Candace Montreux checked in since I was here," he said to the man. "Would you please ring her room and tell her Adam is here."

The man looked at him a moment with blank expression.

"I'm sorry, Mr. Livingstone. You're right that she came since you were here. But Miss Montreux has already checked out."

"What . . . when?"

"Yesterday, sir."

"I don't understand. Are you certain?"

"I carried her and the gentleman's bags out for them."

"What gentleman?"

"The black-haired gentleman with the deep voice."

"What was his name?"

"Zorin."

The name meant nothing to Adam.

"Were they together?" he asked.

"Yes, sir. They arrived and checked in at the same time too—two days before."

"Well . . . give me the key to my room, then. Do I have any messages?"

The clerk turned to check, then handed Adam several slips of paper.

Still perplexed, Adam went upstairs to his room. He would return the calls and perhaps have a bath before heading back to Olduvai.

(7)

When Adam rang his home in Sevenoaks half an hour later, he was not merely expecting Juliet's voice when Crystal transferred him to the lab following some two or three minutes of business, he was looking forward to it.

"Mr. Livingstone, you're not going to believe what I found," Juliet exclaimed after answering.

"On the ice core?"

"No. You're going to have to figure out what that data means."

"You conducted the inspection?"

"Yes, but I'm sorry, I'm not really knowledgeable enough to know how to interpret it. I'll send you the results."

"Then what did you find that's got you excited?"

"It's about the age of those core samples you sent me."

"From the trees?"

"Yes. Actually, not just the age but the DNA."

"Were you able to make connection with ancient species or genus?"

"There's a problem with that."

"What kind of problem?"

"Not a problem exactly."

"What, then?"

"I hope you don't mind. I looked back at some of Erin's reports from your earlier research. I was trying to find something that might account for what this new data seemed to indicate."

"Of course not. Did it help you solve the riddle?"

"No, not really. I talked to my professor friend, but he didn't know what to make of it either. I called around to several of the London universities. I'm not sure I can explain it very well on the telephone. It's about the molecular structure of one of the samples. None of the people I spoke with could account for it. I think you'll need to see the results on paper."

"Give me a complete rundown and send all the reports along."

"And then those fossils we were talking about last time—"

"Right."

"I'm positive they're oceanic in origin."

"That's fantastic. It could be the link to the flood we've been looking for. Now if we can link the Rift Valley with Ararat and the Mesopotamian region, we'll be getting close to unifying this whole region as potentially of the same geologic origin. Good work!"

"Shall I fax what I have to the hotel?"

"Wait—come to think of it . . . no, don't say anything more," said Adam.

Suddenly he recalled everything that had happened. They still hadn't satisfactorily explained what was going on. They'd deactivated one bug in the office at home. What if there were more? And what if . . . ?

How could that be? Yet there was this strange new twist with Candace's disappearance. What if this hotel wasn't secure either?

The call to Juliet also reminded him of some information he wanted to make use of in deciphering Grandpa Harry's journal. He had a new laptop with him but had neglected to bring some vital pieces of material that had escaped destruction thus far.

"No, a fax might not be safe," said Adam after several moments' thought. "We can't afford to take any chances."

Again the phone went quiet.

"Miss Halsay," said Adam after a moment, "I want you to go up to the second floor, into the library. Do you know where I mean?"

"Yes."

"I need a particular quotation. I have a numbered set of the Waverley novels of Sir Walter Scott. What I want is on page 175 of volume 14. It is called *The Fortunes of Nigel*. Do you follow me so far?"

"Yes, sir. But how will I know the quotation you mean?"

"You will know, Miss Halsay. Listen to me carefully. I want you to make a copy and then send—"

Once more Adam paused.

"No," he said. "I think I would prefer the whole book. Miss Halsay, you've been on my staff now for a few days. Whatever is going on with Emily, it looks like I am going to need you for a while regardless."

"However I can be helpful," said Juliet.

Even as he was speaking, Adam was hastily revolving a new plan in his brain. Something was still going on here—something strange. They might not even be able to trust the mail and delivery service.

"This is what I want you to do," Adam went on after a moment. "Gather up all the information you have collected. Find the book I mentioned. Don't let it out of your sight. Bring all its contents. Then tell Crystal to copy the drift program and analysis she's been working up for—on second thought, transfer me up to her as soon as we're done. I'll talk to her myself. I want you to bring everything to me personally, Miss Halsay. I'm going to tell Crystal to book you on the next flight to Nairobi."

Adam paused.

Juliet caught her breath. Her heart was beating with an excitement not even the next sobering words could diminish.

"And, Miss Halsay," Adam added seriously, "we still don't know who is behind these things that have been going on. I want you to be extremely careful. Do you understand?"

"Yes, Mr. Livingstone."

"I will have Crystal give you some cash as well as one of my credit cards. Put anything you might need on it. I'm hoping Crystal can get you on a flight tomorrow."

"Yes, Mr. Livingstone," replied Juliet, trying to sound calm, though her heart was pounding furiously.

"Then I shall see you in Kenya."

# PART FOUR

# CAIRO

✦ ✦ ✦

*The day of the Lord as a rift extends,*

*Dividing mankind as the veil was rent.*

*Hoping that trump new salvation portends,*

*They are unprepared for his second descent.*

✦ ✦ ✦

# twenty-three

# Evil Machinations

(1)

Gilbert Bowles sat back in the chaise lounge at poolside and closed his eyes. He enjoyed being out in the field. But it was nice to relax like this once in a while, especially when someone else was picking up the tab.

He sipped at the scotch in his glass and gazed about.

His was not the sort of physique that displayed itself especially well bare-chested. Thus he wore a shirt in spite of the eighty-five-degree temperature. But his ponderous frame did not prevent him from looking. And a few scant-ily clad young women strutted about that might be worth inviting for a drink later in the hotel bar.

A call to the university had been sufficient to discover Dr. Cissna's field. He was a department head and apparently a man of some repute, sought after worldwide for species identification. What was his connection with Living-stone, Bowles still had to learn. But until the good professor returned his call, he could do nothing but wait. Therefore, he would pass the time as pleasantly as possible.

Two hours later, after dozing off in the afternoon warmth, a steward brought him a portable phone.

"Mr. Bowles, you have a call."

"Ah . . . thank you," said Sir Gilbert, rousing himself a bit clumsily in the deck chair as he took the phone. He grabbed the glass from the table beside him, gulped down a quick wake-up shot of scotch, then drew in a deep breath.

"Sir Gilbert Bowles speaking," he said.

"Mr. Bowles, it is Petiri Cissna, from the university, returning your call."

"Yes, Dr. Cissna, thank you for calling back so promptly." Bowles paused and cleared his throat.

"I am an archaeologist," he resumed.

"Yes, Mr. Bowles, I am familiar with your work and have read your book."

"I am flattered," returned Sir Gilbert. In truth, he had nothing to be flattered about. Dr. Cissna considered *The Link Is Found* little more than empty self-promotion. Nor did he respect Bowles' unvarnished bias against biblical explanations of archaeological evidence. But the botanist kept silent. "I understand you have been with my colleague Adam Livingstone recently," Bowles went on.

"That is, uh . . . that's correct," replied Dr. Cissna cautiously.

"Adam and I have been working on this Eden project together," Bowles continued effusively. "He said I should call you and let you fill me in on what the two of you have found. You were, I take it, looking for flora traceable back to antiquity?"

This was pure bluff on Bowles' part. But not so very far off the target. It was the only thing he had been able to think of to account for the botanist's involvement. Immediately, however, Dr. Cissna knew the man was lying. He had been around the Livingstone camp long enough to know the suspicion Adam and his colleagues harbored regarding Bowles. Throughout the past week Adam had been doing his best to *prevent* their steps being known—especially to Bowles.

"I am sorry, Mr. Bowles," he replied, "any information you will have to obtain from Mr. Livingstone. I promised strict confidentiality, as I do for all research projects in which I am involved."

"I understand perfectly, Doctor. It's simply that Adam specifically requested that I get the information from you."

"I am sorry."

"Tell me, then, what types of species were you searching for?"

"I simply am unable to comment, Mr. Bowles."

"When will you and Adam be meeting again?"

"There are no plans."

"What will be Adam's next—"

"I am truly sorry, Mr. Bowles, but I know nothing of Mr. Livingstone's plans. And I really must break off this interview. Good day."

Bowles set down the phone, cursing inwardly.

He didn't look forward to the *next* call that would be necessary. It couldn't be avoided, but he was under no obligation to put it through immediately.

With some effort he climbed to his feet, made a quick perusal of the pool, then walked toward the bar.

(2)

Juliet stepped off the British Airways 747 at the Nairobi airport all but certain she had been swept up in a make-believe world from a travel book. Could this really be happening? She had never been anywhere in her life—not even Scotland or Wales.

Suddenly she was in Kenya. And there was Mr. Livingstone by the gate!

Juliet walked forward enthusiastically, a big smile on her face.

As she approached, Adam cocked his head slightly as he beheld her, a half-smile on his lips and a quizzical expression in his eye. She was different, somehow, than he had remembered her. She saw the look and hesitated slightly.

"Miss Halsay, you look full of vigor," Adam said, recovering himself. "Apparently the flight did not take too much out of you."

After their gradually developing telephone relationship and growing ease talking with one another, actually seeing Adam in person with that inexplicable smile on his face made Juliet suddenly self-conscious, and she didn't know what to say.

"It was a marvelous flight," she began. "I had a seat by the window, and there was so much to see! It was clear and the Mediterranean was bluer than I had ever imagined. I could see the boot of Italy just like—"

She stopped herself, embarrassed. "But listen to me—I'm babbling away like a goose!"

"No, don't stop," laughed Adam. "It's wonderful to hear you talk so. I often feel exactly the same thing when I travel."

"I just don't believe I'm really in Africa," replied Juliet, now laughing at herself and shaking the hand he offered her.

"Take it from me, you are. And here is your friend, Mr. McCondy."

Now Juliet saw the private investigator standing behind Adam. Rocky was smiling broadly.

"Rocky!" she exclaimed, running to him and throwing her arms around him.

"How are you, Juliet?" Rocky smiled.

"I'm well, thank you. This *is* a surprise!"

"And how's that aunt of yours?"

"Still nervous—and never stops talking about you."

Rocky laughed. "From enemy to friend in less than a month!"

"More than just a friend, Rocky. She is convinced you not only saved all our lives, but single-handedly rescued the entire British Empire from collapse!"

Both Adam and Rocky roared with delight to hear of Mrs. Graves' complete turnaround on her opinion of the man she had so recently referred to as *"that American."*

"She will never admit it to my face!" said Rocky.

"Rocky has brought information from America almost as relevant to the case as what I hope you have," said Adam.

"Your book!" exclaimed Juliet, setting down her single carry-on bag and digging through it for the volume. "I did just as you said and never let it out of my sight after you called."

Juliet pulled it out and handed it to him. "Now I understand why you were being so cryptic about the quote."

Adam opened the Waverley volume to page 175, where a small cavity had been sliced from Sir Nigel's heart to house hidden treasures. He pulled out several four-and-a-half-inch CDs. Juliet also handed him a thick manila envelope with the reports of her recent lab work.

"No problems?" he said.

"None."

"No one followed you? Nothing that looked suspicious?"

"Not that I was aware of. But I might not have noticed if there had been. I'm not very used to this sort of thing."

"Neither am I, Miss Halsay," said Adam. "But I am gradually learning to look over my shoulder. Well, let's collect your bags and get going to the hotel. I've reserved us several rooms in the city. We'll rest up for the rest of the day, and I'll fill you in on what's going on. Tomorrow we'll drive down to the camp."

(3)

"Zorin . . . Bowles," said a thick-tongued Sir Gilbert into the telephone, "I have information."

"You sound funny—I can hardly understand you. Speak clearly."

"Yes, sir, Your Majesty."

"You're drunk!"

"Guilty as charged, Your Honor!" laughed Bowles.

"You fool! Get on with it. Drunk or not—what do you have for me?"

Bowles drew in a deep breath, as if the action might sober him. All it succeeded in doing was lightening his head still more. "Cissna is a botanist," he slurred. "He was hired to help Livingstone find old flora species."

"For what purpose?"

"I assume to lead them to Eden. Ha, ha, ha!" Sir Gilbert could hardly say the word without smiling when he had his wits about him. In his present state the very sound of it set off a fit of laughter.

"What were they doing in Olduvai?" asked Zorin, growing angrier by the second.

"What else but a ruse to throw us off the scent? Livingstone's a clever fellow, you know."

"What did they find?" demanded Zorin.

"Don't know, Your Majesty. The professor clammed up. But I can assure you on my word of honor as a gentleman and a scholar that they found nothing of substance relating to Eden. Ha, ha, ha! No one ever will! Ha, ha! It's a fairy tale. Ha, ha, ha!"

"You learned nothing of their movements?"

"His lips were sealed tighter than a drum, I tell you."

"You are a fool, Bowles—a drunken fool! I see I shall have to take the matter in hand myself."

332

"As you wish, Your Lordship."

"Say nothing of this to anyone."

When Sir Gilbert Bowles threw down the hotel phone this time, he swore loudly, though he could not help continuing to chuckle at the idiocy of the whole thing.

(4)

The message on Mitch Cutter's Internet screen could not be more unmistakable. He was on a plane for Zurich within two hours.

"My sources have traced our friend Bowles to our hotel in Cairo," said the Swiss woman when they met.

"That may explain why I haven't heard from him," said Cutter. "But why would he break off contact with me?"

"That we don't know."

"I gave him orders to call me daily."

"It would seem perhaps Mr. Bowles has developed other loyalties."

"Livingstone?"

"That I doubt. He is still in Africa."

"What can be Bowles' game, then?"

"I want you to fly to Cairo and find out."

"How were his movements traced?" asked Cutter.

"We have many resources at our disposal. Thus far, however, he has made no financial transactions."

"Do you have someone else watching him?"

She shook her head.

"He cannot elude us and our power indefinitely," she said. "Our network can trace anyone almost instantly, from a single banking transaction, use of a credit card, a passport, from almost anything involving money or electronics. We can follow checks and telephone calls more thoroughly and rapidly than anyone has any idea. I knew Bowles was in Egypt an hour after he had crossed the border."

"What do you need me for?" asked Cutter, betraying the merest hint of frustration at being kept out of the informational loop. Never before had he voiced such a sentiment, and it was noted.

"The Council requires individual men and women no less than computers," D'Abernon answered. "I need someone there watching what is going on." As she spoke, her eyes thinned imperceptibly. She probed the man's face for indication of weakness, suddenly wondering if his dependability was slipping. "We have been instructed to turn the human race to our cause," she continued, "not merely control its members like laboratory rats. The *mind* is our objective, Mr. Cutter—the universal human consciousness. To achieve our ends requires the dedicated efforts of loyal individuals . . . thousands, millions of them around the globe. To that end, we utilize every electronic and technological advantage we possess to track the affairs of ordinary men and women in every nation and city and town. Then we set about to influence how they think. How people *think,* Mr. Cutter—it is the key to the future . . . to *our* future."

"I understand, Miss D'Abernon."

"Do you, Mr. Cutter? Do you truly understand what the Council has been building toward all these many centuries?"

Cutter did not answer. Somehow the look of command in the woman's eyes told him no answer was wanted, that the question had been asked only for him to consider . . . and consider well if he valued his standing in the secret society about which, in truth, he knew very little. He had sworn a blood oath and held a prestigiously ranking degree in the Scottish Rite, yet it offered him as little light into the higher machinations of the Dimension as did his attempt at this moment to discern what was going through Anni D'Abernon's mind.

There was a moment of silence. Her eyes held his in a tight stare. Cutter felt a strange discomfort in his throat and momentarily found breathing difficult. The spell passed in two or three seconds.

"I will be in Cairo by tomorrow morning," he said.

"Call my private number the moment you know something."

Cutter nodded, then turned and left her.

D'Abernon watched him go.

*What is happening?* she wondered to herself. First Zorin, now Cutter. Loyalty was fraying. As much as she disdained Zorin's fondness for getting his own hands dirty in work best left to others, she might herself be forced to get more involved in this affair. Mitch Cutter had been one of their most skilled operatives for years. What could account for the change?

Within an hour Anni D'Abernon was on a jet for Amsterdam.

# twenty-four

# Revelation Approaches

(1)

Adam had asked the others for some time alone.

His brain was full. He needed an hour or two of quiet solitude to think, to piece together the information before him.

Scott and Jen had taken Juliet and Rocky over to the Olduvai Visitor's Center where three sections of gorge met. Afterward they planned to drive most of the length of the gorge, where Scott would show them some of the more famous sites of archaeological discovery, from Leakey to Bowles.

"It's too bad Sir Gilbert has deserted us," said Scott as they drove away. "He could give us the tour himself!"

Adam could not hear Jen's reply but could guess its tone well enough.

Forty minutes had now passed.

On the table in front of Adam were scattered the reports and analyses Juliet had brought. Adam had been poring over them most of the day, thinking of possibilities, speculating on the dating information, conjecturing in a hundred directions what some of the molecular structure data from the baobab core samples might mean.

He knew it was all guesswork. He was out of his field. He could tell there were indications of great age, though no ring count yielded anything older than 3,000. But Adam had not given up discovering some botanical connection to the wood of the ark . . . or even to his Eden theory. With the date now established for the ark wood, he hoped to find some correlation between the two.

He'd give anything for just an hour of Dr. Cissna's time now. But that would have to wait for the moment. He would stop over in Cairo on their way back to London, after he carried out all the rest of the research he had planned throughout southeastern Africa.

Adam sighed, sat back, and rubbed his eyes. On the table also sat the disks from home and from Crystal's research. He had still not copied them into the laptop. He would get to them soon.

Crystal had worked hard to get this information. She'd been in touch with two dozen research organizations and universities and meteorological experts, gleaning every scrap of data she could lay her hands on. She'd had programs and disks coming in from all over the world. She'd now been collating their contents for two months into a uniform picture that he could make use of.

Beside the disks sat Harry McCondy's hundred-year-old journal.

Adam reached out, picked it up, sniffed gently at its leather cover, then opened it almost reverently. Unconsciously he turned again to the cryptic poem of seven stanzas. It represented the last entry prior to the fateful departure for Cairo, which would prove to be the final expedition of Rocky's great-grandfather's life. If ever a man's last words held significance, surely these did. He had read the poem over and over since discovering it at the end of the journal. Yet still the mystery eluded him.

Adam was certain McCondy had left a clue for him somewhere in these verses.

*To him who has ears to hear,* Adam read, *in the sign given for that time, and in the number of days, will the mystery of Christ's coming be revealed.* Then came the free-flowing verse in McCondy's hand.

*One—Creation*
In the beginning, first day dawned bright;
Creation exploded through infinite sky.
Not by chance nor random atom flight,
But by the breath of El Shaddai.

*Two—Man*
Sin hid Paradise from God's highest creation;
A long season of separation began.
Though none knowns the day nor duration,
There will flower sign of his return to man.

*Three—Sin*
That in a new age men truth would require,
From sin through flood were delivered the obedient.
On holy ground I am appeared in smoke and fire,
Their seed expects pending parousial event.

*Four—Covenant*
Not harbingers nor signs as seers give pronouncement,
But by a wonder long concealed,
Of covenant deep buried will be made the announcement.
At its discovery, antiquity shall be revealed.

*Five—Salvation*
The day of the Lord as a rift extends,
Dividing mankind as the veil was rent.

Hoping that trump new salvation portends,
They are unprepared for his second descent.

*Six—Deception*
Eyes will be clouded in deception's day,
Of those seeking rapturous transfiguration.
Thus will the coming yet a season delay.
Until humbly fulfilled are John's simple conditions.

*Seven—Rest*
Rejoice! millennial saints—the sign is given.
Life sprouts at the center . . . the Tree is revealed!
Crowning eons of turmoil, a day of rest is risen.
Reconciliation is complete! The rift is healed!

*What does it all mean?* thought Adam. *What is the "wonder" by which antiquity would be revealed?*

He was still seated a couple hours later trying to piece together the clues when he heard the Land Rover approaching. Adam rose and sauntered to the back of his tent and looked out the mesh window. Jen and Juliet were walking toward camp talking gaily about the outing. Jen's braids bounced back and forth, her toes dusty in her open sandles, arms and legs tan from the sun. Wearing loose-fitting pants and a long-sleeved blouse, Juliet looked more like she was walking along a sidewalk in London than trampling into an African research camp. Yet she was smiling and chatting freely, to all appearances comfortable and settling into the new surroundings.

Adam's eyes found themselves pondering Juliet's face in a new way. Realizing they could not see him where he stood, he allowed himself to enjoy the sight a moment. Juliet really was quite lovely, now that he thought about it. Her smile, tentative during her first days at Sevenoaks, was now full and bright and infectious. There was no doubt she had added a buoyancy to the expedition. In *his* own mind, at least. He had felt a new enthusiasm and vigor the instant she had stepped off the plane. He had been genuinely happy to see her. She seemed to have changed even since he had left England. She seemed older, more mature, more confident and assured. What could account for the difference? he wondered.

She had been merely Mrs. Graves' niece back in England. Now Adam realized for the first time, that since her arrival in Nairobi . . . he had been hardly able to keep his eyes off her.

(2)

Mitch Cutter thought it best he not be seen until he knew more where Gilbert Bowles' loyalties lay.

Cutter, therefore, did not walk through the hotel doors until just after

2:15 A.M. local time. There would be little chance of running into the archaeologist at this hour. The two men had met face-to-face only once. Cutter doubted Bowles would make the connection with the Irishman he had met at the Lucky Doubloon, especially in that for all their telephone conversations since he had used his American accent rather than the brogue. But the fellow was a shrewd one. So he would find out what he could without Bowles knowing he was in Cairo.

Cutter checked in.

"You've got an archaeologist here, an Englishman named Bowles," he said as the night clerk handed him his key. "He's a friend of mine—what room's he in?"

"I'm sorry, sir," replied the Egyptian with a thick accent. "I cannot give out that information." A quick revelation of his employer would open the entire hotel staff and its records to him in an instant. But Cutter thought anonymity the best course for the present.

"Ah yes . . . of course," he replied, as if he had forgotten. "Well, I'll see him tomorrow." He turned and walked toward the elevator and his room.

He doubted Bowles would be up at the crack of dawn. But to be sure, Cutter placed himself in the lobby behind a newspaper where he had a clear vantage point to the elevator by 6:15. He would catch up on his sleep after he learned what he needed to know.

At 7:20 the hulking khaki-clad Englishman emerged and strode to the hotel restaurant for breakfast. Cutter rose, left the hotel, glanced about, squinting in the morning sun, then headed along the sidewalk.

He returned twenty minutes later with cup of coffee in hand and sat down to resume his watch.

At 8:10 Bowles reappeared and made for the elevator. Cutter rose. Fortunately several others gathered to wait. The doors opened. Cutter followed them inside. Bowles paid him no more heed than he did anyone else. The man's eyes looked hungover, a fact that worked all the more to Cutter's advantage.

The archaeologist got out on the fifth floor. Cutter followed him into the corridor, turning in the opposite direction. He walked a few steps, then paused and glanced behind him. Bowles lumbered heavily away from him without glancing back, then stopped. Cutter noted his location, then turned quickly around and continued on in the opposite direction.

Two or three seconds later he heard the door close behind him. Quickly he spun around and walked hurriedly back, past the elevator, and to Bowles' room—523.

That was all he needed to know. Cutter returned downstairs. He ordered a thermos of coffee from the restaurant. That should help keep him awake for a while. Now the waiting began again.

Bowles did not appear again until 10:35. Cutter was beginning to nod off where he sat in the lobby, but sight of the big man brought him quickly alert. Bowles left the hotel. Cutter rose and took the elevator to the fifth floor. Getting into the room would be easier here where they still used keys instead of magnetized cards.

Entry required less than a minute with his set of passkeys. Cutter stepped inside and locked the door behind him. A quick search of the room revealed nothing. He flipped on the television set and sat down at the desk. With the remote he selected "English," then "Customer Accounts" from the menu options. A display of Bowles' account showed that he had been here for two nights. This was his third day since check-in. The state of the room showed no hint that he was checking out soon. Cutter selected "Itemization of Charges," then "Telephone."

Voila—just what he had been looking for! That ought to tell them what they needed to know. He jotted down the information, turned off the set, and left the room.

He would make his own call from the lobby. Nothing must be traceable to *his* room. Bowles really had been careless.

"Cutter here," he said when the call went through. "He checked in on the seventeenth, two days ago. The only thing of note is that he has made two long-distance calls to the same number."

"The location?"

"Baku . . . Azerbaydzhan."

"So *that* is the connection! I half suspected as much."

The phone was silent a moment.

"Get on a plane for Baku," said D'Abernon.

"What about Bowles?"

"Leave him. He's a small fish. We'll decide what to do with him later."

"I understand."

"Your next assignment will be more difficult . . . and possibly dangerous. Mr. Zorin has become a liability that can no longer be tolerated. Take him out."

(3)

The Swiss executive put down the phone.

She had just sent Mitch Cutter on the most perilous assignment of his career. His success or failure would go a long way in determining his future. In the meantime, she could not sit idly by.

She took a key from her desk, rose, walked to the large safe on the opposite wall of her office, opened it, then inserted the key in the single locked drawer. From it she withdrew a single aging volume of handwritten notes and memoirs.

She returned to her desk, sat down, and began perusing its pages. She had done it so many times upon numerous occasions. The book never failed to evoke peculiar and unpleasant sensations within her. Somewhere between these fading and chipping leather-backed covers were important clues she needed to understand. Thus far, however, she had been unsuccessful. A transparent veil lay between her mind and the intent of the author that no amount of willpower had been able to penetrate. Nor had any of her Guides been successful at gaining insight from their dark world. Regarding this journal, the Dimension had remained curiously silent, though agitated.

She opened it and again read the final entries.

> ". . . *revealed to me the key to everything. Must go there . . . God will show me . . . origins of life. But they've got it all wrong . . . always been wrong . . ."*

Then came the meaningless jumble of phrases cast in verse. She had read the thing a dozen times, but it conveyed nothing to her.

> "*Not harbingers nor signs as seers give pronouncement . . . ,*"

she read aloud, as if the sound of her own voice might somehow beguile meaning from the page,

> "*But by a wonder long concealed, / Of covenant deep buried will be made the announcement. / At its discovery, antiquity shall be revealed.*"

And then on the following few pages, the personal notes resumed, ending with his final night in Cairo in the Nile Gardens Hotel:

> "*Last night here . . . leave journal at Nile Gardens for safekeeping . . . danger is close. Must escape as Israelites escaped . . . at night . . . across desert to the mount of Presence . . .*"

The only thing she recognized was the reference to the Nile Gardens, whose owners to this day belonged to the Order, which accounted for her possession of the book she was now attempting to decipher.

*The mount of Presence*—what kind of nonsense was this! Surely the man must have been raving even before he struck out across the desert.

Revealed . . . *what* would be revealed?

She slammed the book down on her desk. She hated that the book had power over her. Hated it all the more for being able to make her angry. She was irritated by the thing's capacity to engulf her brain in this spell of fog even more than she was nervous that somehow that very "revelation" spoken of a hundred years earlier truly was now *at hand* as the new millennium approached.

She picked up her private phone again. The call this time was to Milan. The words that followed were brief.

"What is the status of your new American friend—do we have information?"

The reply was brief.

"Continue pressure. In the meantime, meet me in Cairo. Check into the Nile Gardens. I need you."

(4)

It was the day after their tour of the gorge. Adam had been busy half the night and half the day and was at last ready to reveal to the others the results of his work.

"Come in . . . come in, Miss Halsay," said Adam, glancing up with a smile. He had been hoping she would return from her walk. "I was just about to show Jen what I've got on the screen here."

Juliet entered the large tent.

"Where's Scott?" asked Adam. "Anyone seen him?"

"He and Rocky are off in the gorge someplace," answered Jen. "Rocky's positive he's discovered a skull fragment two or more million years old."

"The blood of old Harry McCondy still flows hot!" laughed Adam. "Well, we'll have to fill them in later. Come—gather round."

The two girls did so. At first glance they could not see much on the tiny laptop screen.

"You know what I've been trying to put together—the Eden oval theory, and all that. Scientists, Miss Halsay," he added, glancing up and smiling toward Juliet, "have to always be continually refining their theories!"

"I understand completely." She smiled back.

"Being here in the rift," Adam went on, "and realizing anew how much the earth's landmass is widening have reconfirmed to me the importance of investigating the shape of things *before* the widening."

"Things such as the shape of Eden?"

"Exactly." Adam paused and set his fingers to the keyboard.

"All right," he said, "now I'll bring up a map of Africa and the Middle East. . . ."

A few clicks on the keys followed.

". . . and with the information from the disk Juliet brought from Crystal with continental drift set to run backward according to existing shelf and plate theory . . ."

Several more entries were made.

". . . and then we bring in the data I've entered concerning rift expansion between here and the Dead Sea, and likewise running that information backward through time . . ."

The two young women watched, fascinated—Jen, who had come to expect the unexpected from Adam from six years as part of his team, and Juliet, who was still sure she would any day wake from this wonderful adventure and find herself having dreamed the whole thing.

"The exciting part," Adam went on, "is to actually test my oval hypothesis by trying to discover what the earth might once have been like. The reverse drift and weather patterns are the key. Could the region stretching from Mesopotamia to southern Africa truly once have all been a garden?

"To answer that critical question, I asked myself what impact continental drift and the rift expansion and the changes in global weather might have had on that original garden site in the years since that time. The only way I could think to figure out what it might have been like then was to start with what we know now and see what happens when we go backward through time. I'd just started to think along these lines when Erin was killed and most of our files were destroyed. But I realized I had enough of the research on disk backup to gradually reconstruct most of it. It's been some work, but I think I'm about back to where I was."

(5)

A man and a woman in a small town in New Hampshire prayed. The church in which they knelt appeared unassuming. None passing it would know of the events of import in the heavenly realm being conducted at that moment in the pastor's office. Nor would even but few of its members recognize the high anointing resting upon the humble and soft-spoken man they all knew simply as Pastor Mark.

In truth, however, events of eternal consequence often remain unseen by human eye, and many of those mightiest of warriors chosen to ride at the forefront of the Lord's army are those who walk about among their fellows day by day unrecognized for their courage and valor in the fight upon which the fate of men's and women's souls hinges.

The battle is one of prayer, of faith, and of obedience. These two were of high rank in all three, for they walked in the daily spirit of their Lord's words: *"Whoever wants to become great among you must be your servant."* Their prayers, therefore, carried the authority of him who commanded them to go to the Father in his name. Thus did legions of devils flee when their knees bent to the floor and their hearts lifted themselves unto the heavenly throne.

*"Lord God,"* Mark prayed softly, *"such a burden has come upon us today for our brother Rocky McCondy and he whom our hearts tell us you have called and chosen as one of your own, Adam Livingstone. Though we do not know him, we earnestly pray for him now in the name of the Lord Jesus. Draw Adam Livingstone's heart to you, Father. Make him your son."*

*"Oh, yes, Lord,"* added Laurene. *"In faith we believe that he is yours already. Protect him, we pray."*

*"Block all attempts of the enemy to do him harm, Lord. Obscure the vision of Satan's servants so that Adam Livingstone may be free to do the work to which you have called him. Whatever mighty purpose is in your mind to do, Lord, we pray that your purpose would be accomplished and your will fulfilled."*

*"Amen . . . amen and amen, our God and Father!"*

*"Do your will, Lord. We thank you and praise you."*

*"Thank you, Jesus, our Savior. Praise you, our Father!"*

(6)

Half a world away, the object of their prayers was completely unaware of the entreaties being sent heavenward on his behalf. Nonetheless, was the covering canopy of the Spirit's protection over him as he continued to piece together the elements of that great truth toward which God was leading him.

"Enough explanations, Adam," said Livingstone's Swedish assistant in frustration. "Get on with it. We want to see something happen!"

"All right, all right, Jen," laughed Adam. "First we need to look at the situation as it presently exists." Adam hit several keys to erase the previous map and bring up a present-day map of the earth.

"You see the Sahara and Arabian deserts separating by thousands of miles two small fertile bands, the Fertile Crescent of the Tigris and Euphrates in the north and the African equatorial belt in the south."

They nodded.

"Watch what happens when I run the programs we developed backward."

He punched several more keys. "Keep in mind you're watching a reverse progression of changes that have occurred both continentally and climatically. First let's look at the changes in landmass."

In slow motion the map on the screen now began to transform, moving back, as it were, through not mere centuries but vast eons of earth's geologic development. The three watched in silent amazement to see India slowly separate from the Asian continent and move southwest through the Indian Ocean, which itself gradually shrank, toward the east coast of Africa.

"This is remarkable!" exclaimed Jen.

"Keep watching," said Adam. "There's more."

He now paused the progression.

"I just wanted to show you how it worked. I'll take it back to where we started."

He did so. Again the screen displayed the present configuration of the globe.

"Now we'll factor in weather changes. This is where it gets really exciting!"

Adam's fingers whacked at the keyboard, his thumb working the pad with experienced dexterity.

"We've also got Crystal to thank for most of the research on this weather part of it," Adam said. "She's really a pip with computers. All right . . . now you can see the oceans and landmasses and rivers and so on. I've highlighted deserts in tan—you see the Sahara, the Arabian Peninsula, the Sinai, and so on. Rain forests and areas of thick woodland and grassland—they're in dark green. And finally, river valleys and other highly fertile regions where man and animals would be able to survive easily and grow things—those are in light green. Everybody understand what we're looking at?"

The two young women nodded.

"As you can see, at present there are hardly any dark green sections—only a bit of the Congo rain forest and the Zambezi River basin. Then you have light green, more fertile regions in the Tigris/Euphrates crescent, along the Nile, and here generally around the lakes and rift highlands of eastern Africa."

As he spoke, Adam pointed with his finger about the map on his screen.

"All right . . . are you ready for the climax?"

"Yes, yes!" exclaimed Jen. "Come on, Adam—the suspense is killing us!"

"All right, I'll run the same progression as before, adding in the climatic changes along with the continental. Again we'll see India separate from Asia, but now as we go back through time, watch how the desert lessens and the areas of green gradually enlarge."

The changes continued on the screen as they watched. The Mozambique Channel disappeared as Madagascar floated westward, Cape St. Andre and Tambohorano coming together into the continent at Beira like the pieces of a jigsaw puzzle. At the same time gradually both northern and southern fertile regions grew, as Adam had said they would, and the Sahara and Arabian deserts simultaneously shrank.

(7)

Anni D'Abernon had the feeling things were getting away from her. It was a new and uncharacteristic sensation.

She was one of the most powerful members of the Council of Twelve. They dictated the way much of the world functioned. They and their ancestors and their ancestors before them set the agenda for mankind's perceptions and finances and institutions and governments.

Yet now suddenly a handful of individuals they couldn't seem to control threatened the very foundations of their power. She could not explain why the conviction was so strong that this was so. Nor could her mediums or Spirit Guides enlighten her.

The old archaeologist had been close. Now Adam Livingstone was getting close again. The secret that had been hidden could not be revealed. Livingstone continued to be one step ahead of her. She had to find it before he did . . . and put a stop to him and destroy that cursed place once and for all. Only so would their plan be secure.

Yet nothing in the Dimension seemed capable of penetrating the veil of obscurity surrounding it. What caused this feeling of vulnerability, this sense that her power had been clipped? Why was the Dimension quiet? Could this be one of those times when the enemy prevented their power functioning to the full? She had heard of such instances, though had never been aware of it. What could it mean?

It was time to make a conference call to her two most trusted colleagues. Within the hour she had them on the line.

"Yes, I am in Cairo. This is where all the trouble began. I thought being here would clarify voices from the Dimension. But all is shrouded in haze."

"You have the man's journal?" asked Vaughan-Maier.

"Yes, but all remains obscure. All, that is, except our friend Zorin. It is exactly as we feared."

"Steps are under way to take care of the problem?"

"As we discussed."

"The rest of the Twelve will have to be informed," said Lord Montreux.

"The eleven will be told of the traitor in due course."

"And a successor chosen."

"There are many worthy candidates. We will have to be more careful. We should have seen the look in Zorin's eye from the beginning."

"We thought it might be the Eye of Maitreya, the one who will rise to rule."

"Perhaps it could have been, had he been one with the Dimension."

"He will trouble us no further."

"What of Livingstone's movements?" asked Vaughan-Maier. "If he is truly about to discover the ancient door, he must be stopped."

"He remains in Africa," replied D'Abernon. "He will be watched. I have summoned a trusted assistant to my aid."

"And your daughter, Lord Montreux?"

He hesitated a moment. "She remains out of the country. She was to have reported back to me with information on Livingstone before now. Unfortunately, I must leave for Edinburgh in the morning. I must preside at the thirty-second-degree initiation into the Rite of a high-ranking member of Parliament—Robert Bons."

"Is he one of us?"

"He is."

"Where will it be held?"

"On the private grounds at Dunbar."

"You will keep us informed when you hear from your daughter?"

"I will."

"And I will be in touch with you both concerning Livingstone."

D'Abernon hung up the phone. Speaking with Lord Montreux and Vaughan-Maier did nothing to relieve her uneasiness.

She paced about the room a few moments, then drew down all the blinds, pulled the curtains, and turned out all the lights. She set a candle in the middle of the table, lit it, and sat down in front of it. From her purse she took a purplish crystal, set it beside the candle, then stared intently into it, softly chanting strange words no observer could have hoped to understand.

(8)

Again Adam's fingers set the computerized model in motion as Jen and Juliet watched with wide and eager eyes.

"I call this part of the program the time-reverse-climatic-impact," he said.

None of the three spoke further as they now observed three separate sequences of changes intermingle as the backward weather changes unfolded on the color screen before their eyes.

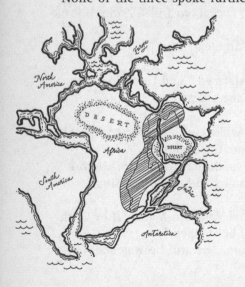

Areas of light green grew and widened, as did the dark green. As green took over more and more of the screen, the tan of arid desert regions shrank. Gradually now the northern and southern fertile regions joined near southern Egypt.

At the same time, so too did the backward crustal changes transform the shape of the globe's landforms as they had seen before. The continents shifted back toward their origins. The rift gradually closed.

Slowly the Red Sea shrank and became a river again. The Persian Gulf likewise closed, extending the Tigris and Euphrates all the way to the Arabian Sea. At length Mesopotamia, Arabia, and Africa had all united into a single landmass. The northern supercontinent of Laurasia and the southern supercontinent of Gondwanaland were now visible from the merging of the landmasses.

"You see, the desert has nearly disappeared, the green has grown at least to approximate something like the dimensions of my theory, and the rivers are coming into greater prominence. But we're not quite all the way back to the beginning. Keep watching."

A few moments more the computer model continued its movements. The mouth of the Nile now closed as the great river reversed its flow. At last it came to a stop.

"Look—do you see it?" Adam said excitedly.

"What . . . what are we looking at, Adam?" asked Jen.

"In theory at least—and I realize this is a gigantic stretch . . . you are looking at the original Garden of Eden."

(9)

Mitch Cutter's plane touched down in Baku, within an hour of Zorin's arrival in Cairo.

Cutter's inquiries established little. How long the interior minister would be out of the country was unknown. Knowing nothing of his movements, therefore, Cutter decided not to try to follow him. He would wait. Meanwhile, he would put the time to good use discovering how to penetrate the security of the Zorin villa.

✦ ✦ ✦

In Cairo Zorin took a limousine immediately to Bowles' hotel. If the man was drunk again, he just might kill him on the spot!

Zorin hastened to the fifth floor and knocked on the door of room 523. It opened. The two men eyed one another warily. It was an alliance grown cold. Yet it had not altogether outlived its usefulness. Bowles motioned him inside.

"What more have you learned?" Zorin demanded rather than asked.

Bowles shook his head. "Nothing."

"Did you make further attempt to talk to the man?" said Zorin, standing in the middle of the room.

"I tried," replied Bowles, sober and irritable with Zorin's importune manner. "He wouldn't take my call."

"Have you learned where he lives?"

"I have."

Zorin stood waiting.

Bowles walked to the desk, picked up a slip of paper, and handed it to his visitor.

Zorin took it, then turned to go.

"Are you through with me now?" Bowles asked behind him.

Zorin paused and glanced back, a look of disdain filling his eyes. "If you are asking if you can go back to working for Mitch Cutter," he said, "the answer is no. You stay put until you hear from me. I may have further need of you."

Zorin left the hotel and returned to the waiting limousine.

"Well, my dear," he said, closing the door behind him, "it looks like we now have some work to do to find out what your friend has been up to."

(10)

"Wow!" came astonished sighs of wonder from both Jen and Juliet at once.

"You see," said Adam excitedly. "The continents are all joined into the original massive supercontinent of Pangaea. It extends from Mesopotamia right down to this very region of Africa. We are sitting within its boundaries at this very moment!"

They all stared in awe, transfixed at what sat on the tiny screen.

"Now I'll highlight the major rivers," said Adam.

He did so, then pushed his chair back so Jen and Juliet could see the screen more clearly. There on the display before them was the Eden oval, green having now grown to encompass the whole, with four rivers running prominently through it—the Nile north-south in the west, what Adam called the Red bisecting the middle of the Garden, and the Tigris and Euphrates in the north—each of the four showing many tributaries and with lakes dotting especially the southernmost portion of the oval.

"I judge it now to be some two thousand miles from top to bottom," said Adam. "Still enormous, yet perhaps manageable. And of sufficient size to sustain all the creatures the Creator placed within it."

"And it's all green," said Juliet. "Lush . . . dark green. It truly looks . . . like a garden!"

"I truly believe, Miss Halsay, that this portion of the earth once looked something like this—yes, lush and green. This all comes about by understanding what global weather changes have done. The computer has reconstructed it for us."

"If what this indicates is true," said Jen, "then it means a huge part of the Garden is now comprised of the Arabian and Nubian and Ethiopian deserts, with the Red Sea running right down the middle of it."

"That's it exactly," rejoined Adam. "The Red Sea is the rift—a rift right through the middle of Eden, splitting it apart. Once that splitting occurred, everything began to change. If I may be so bold as to throw out a new interpretation of the Great Rift, I think it began when God banished man from Eden. And now we have an actual split in the earth's crust running all the way from the Dead Sea to southern Africa—right down the middle of Eden . . . a split in the earth representing and symbolizing, perhaps, the rift between man and God."

"Are you saying that the Great Rift has spiritual origins?"

"I hadn't thought of it in exactly those terms. But I suppose that is what I am saying—that the earth itself provides us a physical picture of something that actually began in the spiritual realm."

# twenty-five

# Search for the Center

(1)

Another day had passed.

From the moment Adam had awakened that morning, a peculiar feeling had gradually stolen over him. It was like the morning of the bombing when he had been unable to sleep. Suddenly many of those same thoughts now returned to him, things he thought he'd forgotten, things for a while he'd *tried* to forget . . . until now.

Something big was at hand. He could sense it.

All day long the feeling grew. God was trying to speak to him. He realized that now. But he was so inexperienced in such things that he hardly knew how to interpret the divine voice.

The seventh stanza of Harry McCondy's enigmatic poem had continued to go through his mind for the past forty-eight hours with such repetitive force that by now he had the words memorized.

> *Rejoice! millennial saints—the sign is given.*
> *Life sprouts at the center . . . the Tree is revealed!*
> *Crowning eons of turmoil, a day of rest is risen.*
> *Reconciliation is complete! The rift is healed!*

Center . . . *what* center was he talking about?

Who were the millennial saints? McCondy had been killed more than a hundred years prior to the dawn of the new millennium. He may have been a "saint," one of God's people, but surely he was no *millennial* saint.

Suddenly Adam realized, with new explosive force, that *this was the year* . . . the final year of the millennium. *He* would live through the millennial change.

Might believers living *now* be what McCondy had called "millennial saints"? Were Harry McCondy's words a prophetic pointing, not toward his own lifetime, but toward some *future* era? Was McCondy writing about God's people who would be alive at this very moment?

Adam could wait no longer. He must talk to Dr. Cissna again, even if only to bounce ideas off him. The conviction had grown upon him that the Egyptian botanist was a kindred spirit in more ways than their scientific backgrounds would account for. Adam stood and stretched. He would go to the airstrip and see if he could get through right now.

"Dr. Cissna," he said when he had his new friend on the phone half an hour later, "I want to talk to you about the beginnings of life."

As he spoke with Adam Livingstone, Dr. Cissna's hand picked up a pen and unconsciously began taking random notes on a pad next to him, brainstorming with himself as they talked.

(2)

Two hours later, a knock sounded on Dr. Cissna's door.

He rose, mind still full of the subject of the recent call.

In front of him stood a man of imposing presence, powerful of frame, perhaps six feet two in height, with jet black hair. The visitor's dark gray eyes bored straight into his own with probing interrogation. Dr. Cissna knew immediately he was in the presence of evil.

Behind him stood a woman—beautiful, stately, of obvious breeding, yet with the look of a fly caught in the web of a spider who did not know how to get out.

"Are you Dr. Cissna?" asked the Voice, yet more commanding than the gray eyes.

Without awaiting a reply, the man stepped forward into the room. "I see that you are," he said. "Lock the door, Candace," he said to the woman, without turning his head.

"I know that you have been with Adam Livingstone," said the man. "I want to know where."

"Won't you please sit down," said Dr. Cissna kindly.

"I have no interest in sitting down. Answer my question and answer it quickly."

"We travelled many places," said Cissna, realizing silence would be worse than useless. "We spent time on Mount Kenya, in the region of Lake Manyara—throughout a wide area."

"In search of what?"

"Ancient trees."

Zorin stood a second or two as one transfixed by the words. They cast a momentary spell over him. The words seemed to originate as in some ancient place of occult recognition within his depths that he could not account for. The simple answer to his question both silenced and enraged him.

"Why *old* trees?" he asked at length.

"He hoped to find trees still living—trees of great antiquity."

The single word *why?* nearly escaped his lips when Zorin thought better of it. He did not want to hear *that* place mentioned.

"Did he find it?" he asked instead, not realizing what the question betrayed.

"What?" asked a puzzled Cissna.

"The tree, you fool!"

"What tree?"

"*The* tree!"

"I don't understand—"

A violent slap of the back of Zorin's hand across his face sent the botanist sprawling onto the floor. Behind him, Candace sucked in a sharp breath of air as her hand went to her mouth in shock.

Already Zorin's hand had grabbed the back of the poor man's neck. He yanked him off the floor in a single motion, then threw him viciously into a nearby chair.

"Don't toy with me, Doctor!" he spat. "I will learn of Livingstone's movements, with or without your help! It will go the worse for you if you continue to resist me."

"I am sorry. I intend no resistance. Mr. Livingstone took samples of a great many plants," said Dr. Cissna softly. "We found nothing of particular note. He planned to run tests and analyses, but—"

Another slap silenced him, this time from the palm of Zorin's hand. Blood began dripping from his nose and one eye.

"You are lying, Doctor!" Zorin shouted. "Something is afoot here. I demand to know what it is!"

As he spoke, Zorin drew from inside his coat a small but powerful handgun. Its silencer was already in place.

"No, please, Halder!" cried Candace, stepping forward and lightly touching Zorin's arm as if to restrain him.

"Silence!" he cried, shoving her back. She gave a little cry but dared not speak again.

"I will give you one more chance to talk, Cissna!"

But already the man had bowed his head and begun to pray.

"Close your eyes if you're squeamish, my dear," said Zorin over his shoulder. He laughed an evil laugh. "But whether you watch or not, you're in this now!"

"*Lord God of Abraham, accomplish your purpose,*" prayed the Egyptian softly, "*and forgive this man for—*"

No more sounds left his lips.

The pistol recoiled slightly in the assassin's hand. There was a sound of muted, fleshy thuds. Blood splattered from the center of the man's chest.

Candace screamed in horror as she watched the botanist slump over in a pool of blood. Bright red oozed down the front of his body and into the yellow fabric of the chair upon which he sat.

Gun clutched tightly in his fist, Zorin stared into the redness without remorse. The color seemed to *enter* his eye rather than *reflect* off it.

The eye of steel had become the eye of the ruby. The would-be Man of Peace had become, instead, Death's slave.

(3)

Sagging into a chair on the opposite side of the room and trembling uncontrollably, Candace Montreux desperately clung to one of its arms to keep from both fainting and vomiting at once. Her face turned several shades paler than usual, though she was still thinking clearly enough to realize her own life was in danger too.

Meanwhile, Zorin walked about the room looking for the clue he had been unable to extract from the fool who was now dead behind him. Dispassionate after his evil deed, he approached a low table upon which rested the telephone. Beside it sat a notepad. Zorin glanced down at it more closely, then tore off the top sheet.

This might be what he was looking for!

*Livingstone* was written across the top, with today's date. The man must have called recently.

Zorin perused the sheet, but nothing made sense to him. There were scattered words and phrases, but in random order.

"Come over here," he said to Candace.

With effort she rose and approached.

"Any of this mean anything to you?"

She took the sheet and read through most of it.

*. . . significance of rift . . . Sinai . . . spiritual rift . . . Garden hidden . . . growth . . . trees . . .*

Then came a line drawn across the sheet, under which had been written the word *ideas,* followed by what appeared random scrawlings—*alternate site . . . sandbar . . . Monastery of St. Catherine? . . . Lawz theory? . . .*

"No," Candace replied in quivering voice, "only Adam's name."

"Bah! It's all useless!" Zorin exclaimed, stuffing the paper in his pocket. "Let's get out of here. I'll find out from Livingstone himself what it means!"

Even as they left the scene of the murder, Zorin was considering his next moves. It may be that he would have to kill Bowles too. The fat archaeologist might put two and two together. But first he had to deal with Livingstone.

There was nothing to do now but confront the man face-to-face. If he couldn't find out what he needed to know that way and put a stop to the man's activities, he would kill him too.

Zorin stopped at the first available telephone. The call was to Baghdad. When the private line into the underground compound of Il-Khadim was answered, a deep Voice asked for Sidqi.

"I need three men," it said. "I need something taken care of."

"Your wish is ours to obey, Powerful One."

"Meet me in Nairobi tonight. The matter is urgent and cannot wait. I will be at the Ngong Towers."

(4)

That evening Adam Livingstone sat at his laptop computer.

He was still running over and over the same progression he had shown Jen and Juliet the day before. All the while his thoughts ruminated upon the strange sensations he had had during those early-morning hours several months ago—the two trees, the Garden . . . the insights and revelations . . . the questions, the spiritual implications. What did it all have to do with *this* . . . the computer model of the Garden?

Somewhere a connection existed . . . something deeper and more significant than he had yet been able to discover.

He sat staring at the screen. Everything was exactly as it had been before.

For a long time he sat pondering the map he had created. Something was missing . . . something he wasn't apprehending . . . something he *needed* to see. He had come to an impasse, a mental brick wall beyond which he could not see . . . a veil his brain could not penetrate.

For ten long minutes he sat staring at the screen in front of him, eyes focused on the shaded embryo-shaped proposed Eden. He should be rejoicing. In front of him was a computer model verifying his large-oval theory. Had he not said to Jen and Juliet, "You are looking at the original Garden of Eden"?

Why then did he not feel the same triumph he felt earlier? Why did the model seem now suddenly incomplete? What was the missing ingredient?

At length, Adam turned off the computer, rose, and went to bed. Through the night his sleep was disturbed by fitful phantasms of a faceless archaeologist fleeing from danger, glancing repeatedly over his shoulder . . . running . . . searching . . . stumbling . . . seeking a place to hide . . . yet he did not know the name of the place he was bound.

# twenty-six

# Life Is Found

(1)

Adam awoke in the dim light of early dawn.

He hadn't slept well and felt a headache coming on. Rocky's snore came from across the tent, but that had not been the cause of his unsettled condition.

More sleep was out of the question. Adam climbed from his cot, rose, and dressed. Was that a fire he smelled? But who else could possibly be up?

He lifted the flap of his tent, ducked out into the damp morning air, and gave a great stretch of arms into the air.

"Good morning," came a soft voice.

Startled, Adam dropped his hands and glanced around. Juliet sat some yards away from the tents with a cup in her lap.

"Miss Halsay!" he whispered in soft exclamation, half laughing to have been caught in such a candid moment. "I didn't expect anyone else about at this hour." He grabbed a camp chair and walked toward her.

"I couldn't sleep." Juliet smiled as he approached. "I'm still so excited to be here. And there's something so quiet and special about the early morning—I wanted to be out drinking it in."

"I've always thought it the best part of the day," said Adam, sitting down beside her.

"The words of that hymn we sing in church have been going over and over in my mind—'This is my Father's world.'" Juliet paused momentarily, then added, "Early morning is also a good time to pray."

"Unfortunately, neither excitement nor prayer drove me out of bed." Adam grimaced, his head beginning to throb in earnest.

"Would you like some tea?" asked Juliet. "I've water boiling."

"You can't imagine how wonderful that sounds!"

Juliet was already on her feet walking back to the stove on one of their two large camp tables. A minute later she was again seated, and Adam held a large steaming mug in his hands, blowing into it lightly and jiggling the contents, as if to coax flavor from the tea bag more rapidly.

"Why didn't you sleep well?" asked Juliet.

"I don't know," sighed Adam. "I was going over the computer model again. I had the distinct feeling I was missing something."

"You were so enthusiastic when you showed it to us day before yesterday."

"Since then I've felt a growing sense of ambivalence."

"I thought the backward computer model proved your theory."

"I don't know about *proved,*" rejoined Adam, now taking a tentative sip of the tea, then removing the bag. "It seemed to show that it was possible, at least," he said. "I was excited at first. Now I have the sense there's yet more to discover. I just don't know what it is."

Adam rose in search of milk for his tea. When he returned a minute later, Juliet was deep in thought. Adam's last words had stimulated her own brain in new directions. However, she said nothing for the moment.

"In any event, that's why I didn't sleep," sighed Adam, resuming his seat and now sipping his tea in earnest, "*and* why my head is splitting. We're on the threshold of something major—I can feel it. I only wish I knew what it was."

Neither spoke for a few moments.

"Have you thought about praying for an answer?" asked Juliet at length.

As much as Adam's thoughts had lately been turning toward the reality of God's presence, the question nevertheless caught him off guard.

"No . . . no, I haven't," he answered.

"If the Garden of Eden was hidden from man by God," Juliet went on, "it would seem to me that no intellectual search, not even with the help of a computer, is going to disclose that mystery."

"Why?"

"Because it's a revelation only God holds the key to. If he wants us to know more, he will have to show us *himself.* It's not something we're going to be able to figure out on our own."

"I see . . . yes, of course. That makes perfect sense. If he closed the Garden, only *he* can open it."

Adam paused. He stared at Juliet, that same odd look coming over his face as when he had first seen her at the airport. She saw the expression again and now laughed lightly.

"What is it?" she said. "Why are you looking at me like that?"

"I knew there was something different about you the moment I saw you in Nairobi," replied Adam. "Now I think I know what it is. Something's changed between you and God, hasn't it?"

"Yes—yes, it has." Juliet smiled in return.

"I want to know about it."

"I prayed and invited Jesus into my heart," said Juliet simply. "I know it may sound like an odd statement in this day and age and perhaps a peculiar thing to do."

"Perhaps not as odd as you might think," replied Adam. "New thoughts and insights about God seem to be everywhere these days."

"It was Erin's mother who explained it to me and helped me see the difference it could make. After talking to her it seemed like the most natural thing in the world, the thing we were created to do—live in intimacy with God the Father and his Son. Mrs. Wagner said the cross bridged the separation between God and man."

"But I had understood you to say you believed before?" said Adam.

"I did. I'd believed in God before and had prayed and felt his peace, as I told you. But it's different now. There has been a change. Now I am aware of God's Spirit actually living within me. I can feel that that rift has been closed. For the first time, I truly feel that I am God's daughter and that he is with me every moment. It's almost, if I can say it, as if I am living with him back in the Garden again, like it was supposed to be."

"I am fascinated," said Adam. "Tell me what you actually did."

Juliet told him more of her conversation with Mrs. Wagner and of the prayer she had prayed after pulling off the motorway.

Adam listened with great interest. "And you believe that God might really show us what we are looking for?" he asked at length.

"He obviously has the answers to all the questions in the world. What is the harm in asking him?"

"None that I can see," rejoined Adam.

"Why don't we pray right now," said Juliet, "and ask him for insight?"

"Fine by me. But I've never prayed with anyone before."

"I don't mind. I'll pray if you like."

Juliet closed her eyes. *"Lord,"* she prayed simply, *"please show us whatever you want us to know about the Garden where you first gave man life. If there is something Mr. Livingstone is missing, reveal to him what it is. Amen."*

*"Amen,"* repeated Adam.

They both looked up and smiled at one another. "That was easy enough," said Adam.

They sat for several minutes in silence, pondering what they had just done. It was a first for both. Each realized that something in their relationship had changed as a result. No longer did a barrier of age or station or background seem to separate them. A new invisible bond had been established. Intuitively both Juliet Halsay and Adam Livingstone knew their lives would never be the same again.

"Oh, I want to show you something," said Adam at length, rising and walking hurriedly back to his tent. He returned a moment later, carrying Harry

McCondy's journal. He turned to the seven-stanza poem, then handed Juliet the book.

She read it carefully.

"The last lines have me stumped," said Adam. "I think they may contain the key."

They continued to talk softly. Gradually the sun rose over the eastern horizon. By and by stirrings of wakeful activity began to sound from the two tents.

(2)

It was midafternoon of the same day when Adam returned to camp with Rocky and Scott. Neither of the young women were to be seen.

"I'm ready for a nap!" sighed Adam as he walked toward the tent. "Last night has finally caught up with me."

He ducked under the flap. There sat Juliet at his small table, staring intently at the computer screen in front of her. She heard Adam enter and spun around. On her face this time, however, was not a look of embarrassment at having been caught where she didn't belong but a wide-eyed expression of wonder and revelation.

"I don't know what you're onto, Miss Halsay," said Adam, "but from that expression, it looks important."

"I'm sorry for coming in like this," exclaimed Juliet, "but I just couldn't wait until you got back. Suddenly it hit me . . . everything made sense. I think I know what you were looking for. I think I know what the last stanza of the poem means!"

Any thought of sleep was gone from Adam's brain in an instant. He approached, now seeing the McCondy journal lying open on the table beside the computer. Beside it sat a magazine he did not recognize.

"What's that?" asked Adam, pointing to it as he pulled a chair over and sat down at Juliet's side.

"I'd forgotten," Juliet answered. "You received this just before I left Sevenoaks. Crystal said you'd subscribed recently and this first issue came before I left. She thought you should have it."

Adam picked it up and flipped casually through its pages, then set it down again.

He now glanced at the screen. On it was the same embryo-oval he had himself been puzzling over the previous night, but whose secrets he had been unable to unlock. Rocky, Scott, and Jen entered the tent and approached behind them.

"I thought I might be able to take the computer model further than you had," Juliet was saying, "but it stopped at this same place."

"That's the endpoint of the model," said Adam. "That's as far back as continental drift theory goes, back to the Permian period."

"But what if you took it *further!*" said Juliet excitedly.

"I don't know what you mean, exactly. That's as far back as drift is thought to extend, to the Pangaean supercontinent."

"But what if you postulated it *further* back—not the whole earth, not all the landmasses . . . just the Garden portion . . . all the way back?"

"All the way back to what?"

"To the beginning, Mr. Livingstone! *That's* what you've been looking for . . . *that's* the missing thing you were telling me about this morning—the *beginning* . . . the *center* of the Garden. Not the whole thing that stretches from Africa to Turkey, but the *center.* Look—"

Juliet grabbed up the McCondy journal and read from the last stanza again.

"It's right here," she said. "It's been right here in front of us—*Life sprouts at the center.* The *center* is what you need to find, Mr. Livingstone!"

"What are you suggesting—that there is a way to *find* that center point, Miss Halsay?"

"Yes—by running your program *further* back in time—even if there is no continental drift data to account for it—continuing the changes *as if* the origin of the earth was a single point, like astronomers do to back up the expansion of the universe trying to collapse it in on itself to re-create the moment of the big bang."

"I see what you're saying!" exclaimed Adam at last. "Continue the backward model *beyond* the large oval, even though that's where the actual data stops—"

"Yes—to a beginning point!"

"Not just back to the oval . . . but *much* further back in time!"

"Can you make the computer do it?" said Juliet, rising.

"I don't know," said Adam, slipping over to the chair. Already his fingers were busy with new instructions for the sophisticated program, while all the others watched silently, anticipation rising.

Adam was in a world of his own, eyes alight and face aglow, Juliet's suggestion possessing him with sudden new possibilities. It was a wild thought. What might happen if he *did* continue the backward model further?

All the way back!

Why could he not collapse the Eden oval into itself . . . literally to a region of beginnings . . . a vibrant life-core . . . a center out of which perhaps had initially radiated the life of Eden itself . . . an Edenic big bang of sorts, just as Juliet had suggested?

After making what he felt to be the necessary entries, Adam reached out and pushed the button marked return.

Now the computer produced the result. At last the model began to move on the screen before their eyes—the oval shrinking . . . shrinking . . . to the center.

Adam Livingstone sat as one dumbfounded. The others standing around him beheld the same result.

As the Edenic oval now shrunk . . . smaller . . . smaller, the four rivers came closer together. All ten eyes remained riveted to the changes displayed of the boundaries of Adam's proposed Eden as it steadily reduced to a fraction of the expanded oval.

"But . . . but look!" exclaimed Jen. "Look how it's—"

"Mr. Livingstone . . . the center!" exclaimed Juliet.

"I know, Miss Halsay," said Adam. "It could be the middle of the Garden . . . prior to the split, before the rift. It looks as though you indeed hit on the secret to unlock the mystery."

"But that's just the Sinai and Arabian deserts," said Rocky. "There's no garden there."

"Maybe not now. But we're looking at what the region might *originally* have looked like."

"Three cheers for Juliet!" cried Scott.

Suddenly Juliet found herself spun around and grabbed about the waist. The next moment Scott was twirling her around the tent in an impromptu jig of celebration. Jen and Rocky joined in, stomping and clapping in rhythm, then grasped hands themselves and danced about in place with them. Not to be left out of the fun, Adam now sprang from his chair, clapping, and chanting a Scottish dance tune.

"My turn!" he cried after a moment, shoving Rocky aside and taking Jen's left hand in his right, leaping about gaily. "Rocky, you keep the music going!"

"I can't sing! Besides, I want to dance with the guest of honor."

Now Rocky took Juliet's hand as she giggled with delight, and the two danced about amid dust flying up from the tent floor, while Scott kept the melody going. Watching Rocky's large frame bouncing about on his toes, however, was almost more than Scott's funny bone could take. The music was soon lost in a fit of laughter.

"You got no rhythm, my man!" Scott exclaimed.

Suddenly Juliet felt Adam's hands taking her away from Rocky and lightly into his arms as he led her about the small space in a quick polka step. A sudden rush of heat filled her head that it took more than the exertion to account for. She was glad they were all moving about and that the light inside the tent was dim. Her face and neck must be bright red!

The wonderful moment of closeness lasted but a few seconds. Adam spun her once, then twice, then sent her off in Scott's direction. After Adam and

Rocky circled around one another in a boisterous jig, all five collapsed on cots and chairs, trying to catch their breath while laughing hilariously.

### (3)

*"Again I come to you, Lord,"* prayed Laurene Stafford in the living room of her home, *"lifting up Rocky and Adam Livingstone to you. You have put them constantly and forcefully on my mind. I know the battle at this moment is waging around them. Be in the battle with them, Lord, and send the enemy fleeing by the power of your might. I sense some revelation at hand. Oh, Lord, I pray that you will give Adam Livingstone the mind of Christ. In the name of Jesus I ask for wisdom on his behalf that he will rightly divide the truth you are showing him, and that he will know what he is to do. . . ."*

At the same time his wife prayed, Mark Stafford had been strongly reminded to also pray for the two men. He had pulled off the road immediately. He now sat, while cars whizzed by on the highway, praying after a similar fashion as his wife.

*"I am filled with a sense, heavenly Father,"* he prayed, *"that even now you are raising Adam Livingstone up into the knowledge and understanding of your ways. He has not known you long, Lord, but I believe your hand has chosen him and that you are filling him even now with a special anointing for your purpose. Protect him and guide him, Lord. Lead him into truth. Make of him a saint for the new times that are coming, Lord. May he be one of your bold sons in a rising new generation of spiritual men and women who will carry your Word forward into the new millennium, with eyes clear and unclouded by the deception that approaches. . . ."*

### (4)

As Adam Livingstone wandered into the warm moonlit night, more was going through his mind at a deeper level than on any recent period of reflection.

Throughout his life, until recently, he had not considered himself an introspective man. Thoughtful, perhaps, but not given to much personal analysis. Rarely did he ruminate pensively about matters of the soul. He prided himself on being a practical intellectual.

Now everything was changed for Adam Livingstone. He had nearly succeeded in making the discovery for which he had longed all his life. He was on the threshold of arriving at the theoretical synthesis to which he had dedicated his efforts.

Yet suddenly his brain was filled with the personal, private, and deeply spiritual implications of his search. The entire focus of the quest had shifted. Nothing mattered now half so much as what was stirring and rousing to wakefulness in his own heart.

The arrivals of Rocky and Juliet in his life could not have been accidental.

Both had contributed toward the gradual discovery, over the past several months, of his spiritual self. Now he found himself in a brand-new quandary. The stark and visible reality of the biblical Genesis account now stared him in the face with a thousand very pointed implications.

He had long used the Bible as a historical document, as one of many such documents, no more than half believing it. The Hebrew account gave intriguing glimpses into Middle Eastern antiquity. But he had scarcely stopped to ask himself what he thought of its spiritual content.

Until that day he set foot in the ark.

It all began to change from that moment—when he suddenly began to realize that the Genesis account of creation could be historically true. Even though he had spoken of that very thing since, somehow the overwhelming reality of it had not struck rock bottom in his own heart . . . until now.

He was on the threshold of discovering proof, to his satisfaction, that the early Genesis account of the Garden was factually true as well, earlier than the ark . . . all the way back to the beginning.

What an astounding claim!

Would anyone believe him if he put forward such an astonishing thesis? Suddenly it no longer mattered. It only mattered for one person—it only mattered whether he himself believed that Genesis was true. At last he realized he *did* believe it! He knew it was true.

And if the foundation was solid, did that not speak volumes about the veracity of the rest? If Genesis was true, did not that fact indicate the truth of the entire Bible?

Then followed the most significant and vital question of all: what did such a conclusion imply . . . for him? What were the personal implications?

At last Adam realized that to the honest heart, to the true truth seeker, truth and revelation demanded a response. There were consequences to looking for truth. It could not be ignored. Something was required of you if you discovered it.

If God really was God, suddenly Adam realized, the knowledge of that astounding and universe-shaking truth placed an incumbency—not upon some vast impersonal cosmos but upon him as a created being of that God. It was an incumbency to acknowledge, not merely to that Being's existence, but to his primacy, his authority, his complete sovereignty over all of life . . . most of all, over him—Adam Livingstone himself.

Adam had trained himself for years in cause-and-effect thinking. Now he found himself up against the most thunderous cause-and-effect question of all: If God is the causing originator of life, then what is the requisite effect upon the man or woman who recognizes that causitive Truth?

If the discovery lying before them was the fantastic revelation he was certain it was going to be, then that "causing origination," that divine beginning of the universe, was not one any honest man could ignore.

At this moment Adam Livingstone had never felt more alone, more vulnerable, more naked to the vast yet personal creation he had given his life to study. His past, his future, his relationships, his discovery, what to do with it all—everything had risen to a culmination at this moment of time as he walked in the quiet African moonlight.

His very personhood was at stake—the most vital question every man or woman must ultimately face: Who am I? Am I my own . . . or do I belong to another?

Slowly Adam looked up. He knew God was not really up there, in the sky, among the stars, in the literal heavens. He was everywhere—beside him, around him . . . within him. The upward glance was a sign of respect, a human response to the awareness that there was a divine Creator-Father above, seeking intimate relationship . . . with him.

There comes a moment in the lives of all humans when distinction between themselves and the lower creatures is more evident than at any other. Not creativity nor thought nor artistry nor genius nor spiritual yearning makes men or women most fully themselves. The pinacle of personhood is reached not by climbing high but by stooping low. Humans are the only creatures endowed with the capacity to yield themselves by willing abandonment into the higher life of their Creator.

When people relinquish claim as master of their own lives, at that moment they step into the highest calling to which their humanness can lead them. Then are they ready and capable of walking with their Creator, their Lord, their Father, in the cool of the Garden. In abandonment of self, life is born.

Adam Livingstone was prepared to relinquish his claim of sovereignty over himself. He had pondered the meaning of his first name in recent months, feeling a gradually deepening kinship with that Adam of old. But now the implications of his family name began to penetrate more deeply as well. Thus was he at last ready to step into the full meaning of that name and become a living stone.

Adam gazed upward again, then drew in a deep breath.

And there, in the quiet night on the African plain where archaeologists came from the world over to seek and to study that which was dead and gone, he knelt down and offered himself in humble acknowledgment to the Creator of men and women, past and present, to the Lord of eons gone by and eons yet to come . . . to one who was living and present with him at that moment.

*"God,"* Adam prayed in a barely audible whisper, *"I am ready at last to make you my own personal God. I hardly yet know what that means. But I realize I can do nothing else. Such a decision is one I must make, one I want to make. I now know that you are God. You are the God of Genesis 1—no life force, no impersonal cosmos, but a personal Creator who reached down into the dust of the very earth of your making and fashioned a man, an Adam, in*

*your own image. You breathed life into him. And now, God, I ask you to breathe life into me.*

"No longer do I want to be an incomplete man, living but not apprehending what it truly means to be a man. No longer do I want to exist outside the garden of your presence. Bring me back, God. What Juliet told me about your Son's making that possible now makes sense, about the cross being the bridge across the gulf between you and your creation.

"Close the rift in my heart, God. I cannot be answerable for the rift on the globe's crust. I cannot undo the rift that the first Adam caused between yourself and him when he did not obey you and you had to send him from the Garden. But I can ask you to heal the separation within me, within this one man, this one Adam. Make me one with you, God, my own personal Creator, so that I may walk with you in the cool of the day in my own personal Eden.

"Even if I never set foot in a place on this earth where Adam and Eve actually trod, I see now that you have led me on this quest, not to find that literal Eden, wherever it might be, but to find you, Lord God, at the center of it . . . at the center of all things . . . at the center of my own being. It wasn't the Garden or the trees you gave to that first Adam—it was you, yourself. And you are offering that to me now as well."

Adam rose. His spirit was quiet and at peace. He was Adam Livingstone, a man now fully alive.

(5)

Marcos Stuart stood in front of his mirror in his Washington, D.C., apartment staring at his reflection staring back at him.

Even a simple act like shaving, never the highlight of the day, had become not merely tedious but a serious emotional drain . . . for the simple reason that he couldn't avoid looking himself in the eye.

That was the one thing these days more unpleasant than anything. But there he stood, chest bare, face lathered up, trying to make himself presentable for this evening's reception at which he would smile and laugh and be charming . . . playing the political game.

Who was he trying to kid? It was all a sham. He'd sold out. He'd become the very thing he always despised about politics.

He brought his razor scraping roughly down across his right cheek. He leaned closer to the mirror and eyed the swath through the white, looking for signs of red. The blade was dull. It was a relief he hadn't cut himself.

He washed the razor under the faucet, dumped the blade in the trash, and took a new one from the cupboard. He stood for a moment, eying the blade clutched between his thumb and forefinger.

A morbid grin spread over the senator's lips.

This was how a lot of people got themselves out of a jam. A few deft strokes and the deed was done. A pool of blood left behind on the bathroom floor someone would have to clean up when they found him. But his troubles would be over.

Actually, it would be the honorable thing to do—put an end to it before he hurt anyone else . . . before he hurt the man who had once been his best friend.

What had happened to him? How could he have gotten himself into this? This was not how he'd planned to climb the political ladder. Here he was, considered one of the fastest and brightest rising stars in Washington. But it didn't feel like he'd imagined it would. He felt like a traitor, like a Judas, like a weakling and coward.

It was all about choices. Everything came down to a hundred tiny moments of decision. You made the choices that determined which direction your life took a thousand times a week without even realizing it.

Then some pensive moment of reflection caused you to wake up and glance back . . . and there you could see the bread crumbs of your choices and decisions spread out behind you as far as the eye could see. If only you could see where your choices were leading when you gazed forward. That was the tricky part. Good old 20/20 hindsight!

Stuart's eyes again focused on the blade in his fingers that had sent him off into his momentary trance. No, slitting his wrists wasn't the manly way out. Instead of attending the reception tonight, he'd go for a long drive, maybe down the coast. He'd take his gun along, just in case he couldn't summon the courage to drive over a cliff. A single shot to the head. That was the manly way. It was quick, easy—he'd never feel—

Suddenly he stopped himself. What was he thinking? This was ridiculous!

Had he gone insane? Marcos Stuart wasn't going to commit suicide! He was a United States senator. He would weather this thing!

Quickly he popped the new blade in the razor and continued with his shave. Two or three minutes later he rinsed his face, dried it off with a towel, and continued to stare into his own eyes. Already he had weathered the storm of conscience and had begun to rationalize with himself.

*Hey, man! Look at you. You're a good-looking guy. You're sharp, intelligent, compassionate—exactly what Congress needs. Put all those ridiculous thoughts out of your head! Okay, so you blew it . . . okay, so you blew it big! Nobody knows. Nobody has to know. All they want is a little information. What's the big deal? You can do this country a lot of good. And you will too. You'll do the people of the United States good. And you'll make it up to Scott, too. There's plenty you'll be able to do for him when you're president, maybe even bring him along on your staff. The situation isn't so bad!*

Stuart exhaled a long breath, then turned and left the bathroom. He felt better already. He'd do what he had to do.

Then he'd make it up to Scott later.

# twenty-seven

# Jebel al Lawz

(1)

When Adam returned to camp two hours after having wandered off, the others had already bedded down for the night.

As he'd turned and headed back, his thoughts had shifted to someone nearer at hand than the heavens. Her face had continued to intrude more and more regularly into his mind. And strangely, now at this moment, the only person he wanted to see was Juliet Halsay.

He walked slowly to the tent where the two young women slept. He wasn't sure if this was the right thing to do or how she might respond. But he had to talk to somebody.

*No,* Adam corrected himself. It wasn't just *anybody* he wanted to see—he wanted to talk to *her.*

"Miss Halsay," he whispered just loud enough to rouse her. "Miss Halsay . . . Juliet."

A moment later he heard a stirring inside.

"Yes . . . yes, what is it?" said her voice.

"It's Adam. Would you mind coming out? I'd . . . I'd like to talk to you."

"I'll be right there."

Adam backed away from the tent and walked a short distance away. A minute or two later he heard the tent flap open behind him. Footsteps approached. He turned.

"I'm sorry," he said, smiling. "Were you asleep?"

"Not quite," Juliet replied with a smile. "I don't mind. But what is it?" she asked, the smile disappearing.

"Nothing serious," said Adam, seeing the anxious look on her face. "I wanted someone to talk to. I found myself wanting to talk to you."

They began walking slowly away from the camp. Pale moonlight shown over the landscape, casting an eerie gray glow over the brown rocky terrain. They continued on for two or three minutes in silence. Now that he had her at his side, Adam found himself at a loss.

"Do you remember that day," he began at length, "when you told me about God's being personal? You said he *had* to be personal."

"I remember," replied Juliet softly.

"I finally understand what you were saying. I've been a bit thickheaded. But now I see that you were exactly right in what you said way back at Sevenoaks: God is no impersonal creative force—he is a very personal Creator. Isn't that what our whole research is about, in a way? Isn't *that* the meaning of the Garden of Eden?"

"I hadn't really thought of that exactly. But I suppose you are right."

"If Eden existed, as a real place, I mean, with *real* people, a real man and woman . . . if it's more than mere myth, then the one thing it was above all else was personal—God and man living and walking and talking together. You said it earlier this morning when you told me about asking God to live in your heart—that it had begun a new intimacy between you and him. Isn't that what it must have been like in the Garden—that same kind of intimacy between Adam and Eve as God's newly created son and daughter? Genesis is a pretty remarkable account when you stop and think about it."

Juliet nodded but found herself unable to speak. Her heart had begun to climb into her throat.

"Yes, well, at any rate," Adam went on, "I believe I have *you* to thank for setting my feet down the road of thinking about God as personal. And that's what I wanted to say. So, Juliet Halsay . . . thank you. I appreciate your telling me how you prayed. Your openness meant a great deal to me. It helped me realize that I wanted to be God's son, too, and that I desired to experience that same garden intimacy."

Adam paused, turned, and looked down into her face. Their eyes met.

Only for a moment did they hold the gaze. Juliet glanced away. She brought her hand to her heart as if its beating was strange and unexpected.

"I'm sorry if I embarrassed you," said Adam, now also suspecting something rising within his own heart. He felt like a schoolboy.

"No . . . that's all right," floundered Juliet. "I . . . I mean—"

She didn't know what she meant and could say nothing more. Too many thoughts and feelings were rushing through her. She couldn't think straight! Did she care more about this man than she had allowed herself to admit?

"Will you . . . walk with me awhile longer, Juliet?" It was the first time he had spoken her name aloud to her face.

Adam led the way. She followed at his side. For a few moments neither said more. Their hearts were too full.

Gradually as they walked both found their tongues again. They continued to speak of many things, all the former invisible barriers between them gone as if they had never existed. They felt they had known one another all their lives.

(2)

The interior minister for the sovereign nation of Azerbaydzhan had still heard nothing from his hired Iraqi muscle.

He glanced at his watch again. It was nearly ten o'clock at night. Where were the imbeciles!

At ten thirty-five, a turbaned Arab entered the Ngong Towers Hotel in Nairobi.

Zorin turned immediately. He did not acknowledge the man but, instead, strode toward the elevator and pushed the *up* button. The Arab approached behind him. Neither glanced at the other.

The elevator doors opened. Both entered. The moment they were alone, Zorin spoke. "What took you so long?"

"Baghdad air travel is never the most dependable, Powerful One."

"You have others with you?"

The man known as Sidqi nodded.

"Here is your room," said Zorin, handing him a key. "Sleep well. Since you bungled the last job, I will oversee this one personally. Besides, I want to look into Livingstone's eyes myself. We must leave before dawn."

"You have . . . what we need?"

"All the arrangements have been made. Be in the lobby at four-thirty. We will fly to Arusha, pick up two vehicles, and hit the camp by seven o'clock. When it is over, you and your associates will make your own way back to Baghdad."

The terrorist nodded.

"Payment will follow in the usual manner."

(3)

An hour after he and Juliet had set out for their walk, Adam returned to his tent, overflowing with deeper contentment than he ever remembered in his life.

He knew he would not be able to sleep for hours. But how different was tonight's than last night's sleeplessness. Suddenly he had many new things on his mind . . . and unexpected sensations in his heart.

He walked inside his tent, flashlight in hand. There still sat Grandpa Harry's journal next to his cot. He lay down, flipping to the last several pages. He had read them before.

Suddenly the words of urgency and danger rang with present warning.

> *Leaving for Cairo in the morning. Even here in New Hampshire,*
> *they're after me. Hope they will not trace me there. Taking steamer*
> *from Boston to London, then to Rome en route. From Egypt I must*

*get there without them following me. But they know much . . . secret*
*societies joining together as never before . . . history converges . . .*
*millennium of confrontation between heavenly powers approaches,*
*though none knows the hour of its beginning . . . they cloak them-*
*selves in exteriors of calm, but they are desperate . . . they are terri-*
*fied of God's true saints because they know they have no power over*
*them . . . secrecy is their only weapon . . . God's light will expose*
*their deceit . . . they will stop at nothing to keep this news from*
*getting out . . . they are powerful . . . but I am confident the Garden*
*will be found . . . Eden will bloom again!*

Then followed, on the final two pages, the twenty-eight lines of verse, after
which the remaining pages were blank.

*Get where?* thought Adam. *Where* was Harry's great-grandfather bound
with such urgency that it had gotten him killed?

His body had never been found.

Now Adam remembered. He had written about it himself in his *own* paper
on the old archaeologist that he and Rocky had been looking for. How could
he have forgotten such graphic details? As from a dream out of the distant
past, the phrases returned to him as if he had written them yesterday:

> *. . . last reports from Nile Gardens Hotel in Cairo . . . brief note sent*
> *from archaeologist to colleagues in London . . . hasty message to*
> *the manager. Off to Mount Sinai . . . handed man a few things to*
> *safeguard until return . . . Harry McCondy never heard from again.*
> *Thorough search of Ras es-Safsaf on Sinai Peninsula . . . from*
> *Monastery of St. Catherine to summit . . . turned up nothing. No*
> *one in vicinity saw or heard from McCondy . . . neither were the*
> *papers left in hotel safe ever seen again . . . all traces mysteriously*
> *disappeared. Harry McCondy vanished from sight . . . world of*
> *nineteenth-century archaeology left with one of its most curious*
> *unsolved mysteries. . . .*

Those may not have been the exact words in his paper, thought Adam, but
they captured the gist of it. Now he remembered so clearly why the strange
fate of Harry McCondy had captured his youthful imagination.

If only he could lay his hands on his paper. But he hadn't seen it in years,
and now it was gone.

And how could those words of his have tied him into old McCondy's research to such an extent as to put his life in danger?

Adam now flipped through several pages in Rocky's great-grandfather's
journal, reading here and there. About ten pages before the end, he encountered a passage he remembered reading earlier but without making much
sense of it. He read through it again, now trying to link it to the poem that

ended the words of Harry McCondy. It came as he discussed preparations for his impending trip to Cairo.

> *I believe God has revealed to me that the holy mount of fire and smoke is the key to everything. Must go there . . . God will show me . . . origins of life. But they've got it all wrong . . . always been wrong. The crossing was through Aqaba, not Suez. The encampment of Exodus 14 sat on the beach at Nuweiba el Muzeina, or Neviot. They crossed Aqaba on the submerged shallow plain and reached the mount on the opposite shore in Arabia as Paul states in Galatians 4:25.*

The text in the old archaeologist's hand was accompanied by a hand-drawn map of the Sinai Peninsula region, showing both the Suez and Aqaba shoots of the Red Sea, with a dotted line indicating the route of the Exodus and the mount on the Arabian side called Jebel al Lawz. Beside the map, in big letters, was the word *H-O-R-E-B*.

What did the word *Horeb* mean? It must have some biblical connection.

Adam set down the journal and glanced about in the darkness of the tent for

his research Bible. A moment later he had it in his hands and was hurriedly flipping through the pages following the text for any information. He found no listing in the concordance. He tried the subject index. There it was—*Horeb,* followed by several Scriptures.

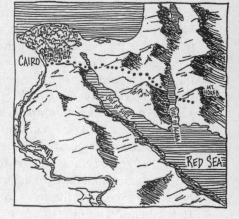

Hastily Adam flipped to the front of the book, to Exodus 3. It was the account of Moses and the burning bush. A footnote explained: "Horeb, which means *desert* or *desolation,* is an alternate name for Mount Sinai."

*Of course!* thought Adam, closing the book. How could he have been so blind?

*That's* what McCondy was onto—he had discovered an alternate site of Mount Sinai! That would explain why his enemies had gone after him—to prevent revelation of the true site.

He read back through the journal entry again, gazing with incredulity at the hand-drawn map. Now it all made sense.

Harry McCondy had uncovered an astonishing biblical secret.

*That's what this whole thing was about—not mere archaeology, not even Noah's ark . . . it was about biblical origins.*

His ark discovery had roused the same hornet's nest of evil that old Harry's attempt to find the original Mount Sinai had stirred up.

They had killed old Harry McCondy to silence him. Now someone was trying to do the same to him.

(4)

In the late quiet hours after midnight, Anni D'Abernon sat in her hotel room in Cairo, still puzzling over the cryptic words in the second copy of the journal, which fate had passed down through the years into her hands.

She pored over the pages at the same moment Adam Livingstone read with new insight from the original, which had been buried for a century in a forgotten attic trunk in Peterborough, New Hampshire. To Adam, the old handwriting was newly filled with life and revelations of truth. To her darkened eyes, the journal contained mysteries no séance with unseen Dimension would enable her to comprehend.

She went over the words again and again with mounting frustration.

*. . . leave journal at Nile Gardens . . . must escape . . . at night . . . to the mount of Presence . . .*

What else could it mean but Sinai? So they'd thought back then. So she concluded now.

But the man had never gone to Sinai. He'd never even set foot on the lower Sinai Peninsula. Their own people had followed him.

Then followed the cryptic words about the Garden being found: *Eden will bloom again.* A garden blooming anywhere in the region of Sinai was preposterous! The man must have been raving even before leaving Cairo!

*So what was Livingstone's game?* she thought, flipping back and forth, trying to make some sense of the poem. *Does the fool think he is going to find the Garden of Eden in the middle of the desert, atop a mountain, for heaven's sake! Were all Christian archaeologists lunatics? How are these two men— separated by a hundred years but now seemingly following in the same footsteps on the same quest—how are they connected?*

She had come across these words earlier in the journal on previous occasions, but the names and places and Scriptures were meaningless to her, and she had no reason to connect the entry with Sinai. When she had come across the word *Horeb,* it meant nothing to her, and a divine blindness halted further curiosity.

Revelation had come, but not to those of the Dimension. Rather to the inheritors of the Kingdom of the Most High God.

(5)

Adam set down the journal and shone his flashlight excitedly about the tent, looking for the magazine Juliet had brought him from London. It still sat on the table where he had dropped it earlier.

He'd seen the title of the lead article, but it hadn't registered in his brain. Adam now grabbed the copy of *Biblical Archaeology Review* and feverishly tore through the pages . . . yes, there it was.

He sped through the account. It repeated the information in the *Geographic* article but brought a report of the peculiar Saudi growth pattern up to date. Already the mystery tree was more than ten feet high. Then was added the conjecture that suddenly sent explosions off in Adam's brain. His eyes widened as he turned to the next page where a small cutout map of the region in question was shown.

Quickly he looked back at his own computer screen.

He could hardly believe the words he had just read! ". . . below the ancient mount Jebel al Lawz, a long-dead volcano, which some have theorized to be the Mount Sinai of Moses . . ."

Why would the desert spring to life there . . . now?

Adam's brain spun in a hundred directions—the vision of his own computer model of Eden collapsing to its center at that exact spot. Flipping to the last entry in the journal before the poem, there were McCondy's words: *Eden will bloom again!*

The thought was too fantastic! Eden . . . in the desert . . . with Sinai, or Horeb, the mount called Jebel al Lawz, at its very center!

This Sinai, McCondy's alternate site—not the traditional site at all. Adam flipped back several pages again to the hand-drawn map. *There it was!* He had finally deciphered the mystery of what burdened Harry McCondy's mind prior to his disappearance!

Now a wave of new thoughts filled him.

What if Harry's words and warnings were not merely an account of his own steps . . . but now had become a prophetic warning to those who might follow in his path?

Suddenly Adam realized there wasn't a moment to lose. He leapt up and ran back outside and to the girls' tent.

"Juliet . . . Juliet, are you there . . . are you still awake?"

The next moment Juliet appeared.

"Juliet, wake Jen," said Adam. His voice was filled with urgency.

"Why . . . what?"

"I just realized—I know where it is!"

"Where what is?"

"Sinai—the real Sinai . . . where McCondy was killed . . . the article . . . where the computer simulation collapsed . . . where the desert is blooming again—everything!"

"But what—"

"I'll explain it all. But first we've got to get out of here."

Two minutes later Adam was shaking Scott and Rocky into wakefulness.

"We're breaking camp," he said. "We've got to get out of here . . . tonight."

"What . . . where are we going?"

"Sinai," replied Adam.

"Sinai!" exclaimed several voices at once.

"But, Scott," said Adam, turning to his assistant, "I need to give you the most thankless, and what might be the most dangerous, job of all."

"Anything you say."

"I want you to stay behind—and get everything sent home."

"What's the dangerous part?"

"If I'm right," said Adam, "we may be in just as much danger as Rocky's great-grandfather was. So if anyone does have us under surveillance, I'm hoping that by keeping the campsite active for a day or two longer and our making a getaway in the middle of the night, they'll lose us. Get this stuff on its way. Then get back to the estate and make sure everything's safe there. I'll feel better with you on hand at the house."

"How will I reach you?" asked Scott.

"You can't. After a brief stop in Cairo for supplies, we're heading into the desert."

"Why the desert?"

"It would appear that our next stop, possibly the final one in our quest is somewhere in Arabia . . . across from the Aqaba Gulf of the Red Sea."

# twenty-eight

# Gone!

(1)

A flurry of dust and cursing voices rose into the air together as a dusty, rust-colored Land Rover careened around a curve in the dirt road.

It continued to bounce and tumble over the rocky terrain, jarring both nerves and bones of the man in the passenger seat far beyond the comfort level. He was used to limousines and Mercedes. But he had himself ordered the vehicle, and for good reason. It was already 7:20 in the morning, and he feared his quarry would already have left for his day's work if they did not reach Olduvai soon. Bumps or no bumps, they had to make haste, and no limousine would survive five minutes in this terrain.

"Watch where you're going, you fool!" he cried as the Arab at the wheel swerved to miss a large pothole. Recovering himself, he glanced down, doing his best to look at the map in his hand.

"How much further?" the driver asked

"I don't know—not far . . . twenty, maybe twenty-five, minutes," Zorin replied.

Half an hour later the Land Rover slammed to a stop. A second vehicle pulled up behind them. As the engine idled, Zorin grabbed a pair of binoculars from the seat beside him and gazed toward the area southeast of the Olduvai Gorge where a number of sites and digs were in progress. It was not yet eight in the morning. But campfires and the faint aroma of coffee signalled that many of the archaeologists were up and about and well started on the day.

"There it is," he said, pointing to the Livingstone site, "the large blue tent, two small orange ones, sitting twenty yards from that scraggly thorn tree." It was unchanged since he was here just a few days earlier, and Bowles had pointed it out to him from across the way. No sign of life shone about the place, though smoke rose from a fire. A jeep and a small trailor sat parked beside one of the tents.

"What do you want us to do?" asked the Arab.

Zorin thought a moment. "We will drive straight in," he said, pointing.

"They seem to still be in their tents. We will be upon them before they see us coming."

He said no more. Both men knew well enough the errand they were on.

Zorin set the binoculars down. "Let's go, Sidqi," he said.

As the Iraqi turned the vehicle back onto the road and sped in the direction Zorin had shown him, Zorin pulled his gun from his pocket.

Three minutes later the two cars roared into the Livingstone camp at dangerous speed, skidding to a stop as dust flew all about them and a spray of small stones scattered. Zorin leapt out even before the car had come to a complete stop, brandishing his weapon in one hand. The fire glowing in his eyes indicated well enough his eagerness to use it.

He ran straight into the largest of the tents. Behind him, four Arabs carrying automatic rifles followed him into the camp. Even as Zorin emerged a moment later with a look of astonished fury on his face, Sadqi ran out of one of the smaller tents.

"They're gone," said the Arab.

"It can't be!" cried Zorin. "They couldn't possibly have known I was coming!"

He glanced frantically around in disbelief that Adam Livingstone had outwitted him again.

"Search the tents!" he cried. "Turn over every inch!"

Ten minutes ransacking the place, however, turned up nothing but what remained of the food, cots, and some miscellaneous equipment. No books, computers, files, notebooks, itineraries, or anything connected with their research or plans was to be found.

"How could they have slipped past us?" said Zorin, adding a volley of curses.

He walked toward the fire, staring into it intently. Somebody was still around. That fire hadn't lit itself. And the jeep and tents were still here. But Livingstone was gone. He knew it. He could tell.

Fury rose within him. He kicked violently at the fire, sending ashes and coals spewing about, then suddenly turned and sent a volley of shots around the camp, spraying through Livingstone's tent. Behind him, needing little excuse, the four Arabs now opened fire as well. Sharp screaming gunfire echoed up and down the little canyon.

The three tents and their contents were quickly reduced to rubble.

(2)

From a concealed vantage point a hundred and fifty yards away, Scott Jordan watched the ransacking of their camp. Adam had been right. If he hadn't heard them coming and dashed out of camp just seconds before their appearance, he would be dead by now.

He'd pack up camp—though they had nearly destroyed it—as soon as they were gone. He was getting out of here!

✦ ✦ ✦

The echoes of gunfire died away. The dust from the frenzy of destruction gradually settled. His wrath momentarily satisfied, Zorin walked into the largest tent and sat down on what had recently been Adam's cot. He sat for several long minutes, as if willing by sheer force of his own consciousness the spirit of his adversary to reveal where he had gone.

He reached into an inside pocket of his jacket and pulled out the paper he had taken from the murder site in Cairo. Again he read the words in Cissna's hand.

Suddenly the words jumped out at him—*Sinai . . . Monastery of St. Catherine.*

He jumped to his feet and stuffed the paper back in his pocket, eyes wide with sudden revelation.

"He's on his way to Mount Sinai!" he said. "Why didn't I see it before! That's where he's bound—St. Catherine's Monastery at the foot of Sinai. That's what the two of them were talking about. Come!" he cried to his hired thugs, "there's not a minute to lose. Get me to the airstrip. I'll hire a plane. I'll buy one if I have to! I've got to intercept him. You can drive back to Arusha and then get yourselves back to Iraq. Our mission here is over!"

✦ ✦ ✦

Scott remained hidden where he was for another hour, making sure they were gone, then returned to salvage what he could and begin packing up.

By late afternoon he had packed and had seen no more sign of danger. He was in Arusha without further incident by early evening. He would ship everything from there, then be off for Nairobi and then England.

Scott made two telephone calls from the hotel. The first was to Mrs. Graves. Everything was fine at the estate, she assured him, though she was delighted to hear he would be returning. She couldn't help still being nervous. She would be glad to have him back.

Next Scott placed a call to Washington, D.C.

"Hey, Marcos, old buddy," he said, once the call went through, "it's Scott. My plans have changed, if you're still desperate to get together."

"Yes, I still do want to see you," replied Stuart. "What's going on?"

"Like I said, a change of plans. Adam's on his way to Mount Sinai, and I'm on my way back to London, where I'll be for a while. So if you still want to fly over . . ."

"Let me look at my schedule," Stuart replied, keeping his voice calm in spite of this new development. *Sinai,* he thought to himself, *what could Livingstone be up to there?* "I'll be able to reach you at the Livingstone office?" he added into the phone.

"Yep," replied Scott. "I'll be back home in a couple of days."

# twenty-nine

# The Nile Gardens Hotel

(1)

"What are our plans in Cairo?" asked Rocky, as they awaited their flight out of Nairobi.

"In and out as quickly as possible," replied Adam. "If someone is tracking us, we've got to move fast. We'll pick up a little camping equipment and supplies, another vehicle. Saudi and Israeli visas for you and Juliet, maybe a quick visit to Dr. Cissna to see if he can join us. Not more than a day or two."

"Why don't we stay at the Nile Gardens?" suggested Rocky. "If Grandpa Harry spent his final Cairo hours there, not to mention having his papers disappear there, who can tell—there *might* still be a few clues hanging around."

"Always the detective!" laughed Adam. "But there may be people around too, besides clues. Though what you say makes sense. If we've followed your great-grandfather this far, why not stay where he spent his last night in the city?"

The ancient Nile Gardens Hotel in Cairo stood on the Corneish el Nil, the scenic riverside boulevard stretching along the east bank of the fabled river near the heart of the Egyptian capital. It had been well known to Western travellers for a century and was a mere block from the British Embassy. On the river island directly across from it could be seen the Tahir Gardens, and slightly north on Gezira, the Cairo Tower and the grounds of Gezira Sporting Club. Eastward, the center of the city lay within a radius of a mile and a half.

As they approached, Juliet gazed around with awe. The blaring horns and traffic and shouts and high modern buildings made it seem like many cities in the industrial world. But it wasn't just any city—this was Cairo!

Juliet's brain filled with images from a hundred legends. She had managed, with Adam's help, to see the great Pyramids from the air as they made their approach. The wonder and history still had not left her.

Egypt . . . ancient Egypt. Pharaohs and slaves . . . Moses and the Exodus. Truly this was a land of antiquity. This was different from any other place in the world, and as Juliet gazed about, its mood quickly engulfed her.

White robes and dark faces, strange tongues and unfamiliar music, rounded

mosque domes and white-plaster walls glaring in the bright sun . . . all the sights cast upon the sheltered girl from Brighton a spell even deeper than she had felt in the middle of Tanzania. Her mouth hung open as she tried to keep pace with the others, unable to prevent her head from constant motion in every direction.

As they entered the hotel doors, Adam glanced up. A strange set of symbols was carved into the sandstone above the entryway. He had time to puzzle over it only momentarily, but the sight struck a chord of strange recognition. Where had he seen that emblem before?

They continued into the lobby. As the doors of the Nile Gardens closed behind them, Adam, Rocky, Juliet, and Jen all felt the immediate sensation that they had entered a mysterious enclave even more foreign than Cairo itself. Unconsciously they glanced about, the odd feeling that they were being watched engulfing them.

"Do I feel the ghost of Grandpa Harry already!" said Rocky, in scarcely more than a whisper.

"I sense it too," remarked Adam, "although I'm not sure it's Harry we feel."

Nothing in the surface appearance indicated anything out of the ordinary. The atmosphere was pleasant enough—Persian rugs accented a handsomely furnished sitting area of couches, chairs, and oriental lamps. The decor conveyed welcome and warmth. Gleaming brass-and-glass chandeliers hung down from a high ceiling. Wood blades of several fans spun slowly. Men and women mingled about in business suits and expensive dresses. The clerk, a young Egyptian with wavy black hair and thin moustache, greeted them warmly.

Yet all four felt unpleasant vibrations in the strings of their collective spiritual consciousness. Their spirits grew subdued.

A presense was near. And not one friendly to their cause.

(2)

Candace Montreux walked into the hotel restaurant and glanced about.

She had only just arrived in Cairo, had tossed her few belongings into her room, and come back downstairs. She hadn't even fixed herself or changed for dinner. What was the use?

Boredom was written over every inch of Candace's face. She wasn't the least bit hungry, but she had to do *something*. She had hardly eaten in thirty-six hours. She was getting a little light-headed. If for no other reason than that, she ought to try to eat some dinner.

Actually, she was more frightened than hungry. Why didn't she get on a plane and fly back to England?

Because Zorin would find her. She knew that well enough. And kill her, she didn't doubt—after the horrible murder she had witnessed.

She had seen the man's raw self, and she was terrified of him. How could she have been such a fool? All because she'd gotten impatient with Adam. Now he looked like a man who could be her savior.

Unfortunately, Adam was nowhere around.

Why would he help her now, anyway? She'd burned her bridges. How stupid she had been! She'd actually imagined that playing hard to get might wake Adam up. Didn't she know him better? Adam was his own man. She wasn't going to manipulate *him!*

She'd been so foolish. All it had succeeded in doing was trapping her hopelessly in Zorin's clutches!

"You get back to Cairo," Zorin had ordered her, the instant he'd figured out Adam's next move. "You watch and see who comes and goes. You'll tell me everything. Believe me, Candace," he had threatened, "you will regret it if you cross me. I will call you every evening. You will be in your room when I call."

Now might be her only chance to get away. She should hurry back to England, throw herself on her father's mercy.

And Adam's. Tell them everything. But what about the awful murder of Dr. Cissna? If she told them *that,* she could go to jail for complicity in the affair.

Maybe she'd go out and go shopping tomorrow. That would help. She had not considered stopping in Cairo and had hardly anything suitable to wear.

Suddenly not far in front of her she spotted the unmistakable mammoth bulk of a fellow Englishman at a table off toward the terrace. She debated momentarily the pros and cons of being seen with him. Among Zorin, her father, Adam, and whoever else, she couldn't tell who was on whose side anymore.

It was too late. He had spotted her and now beckoned her forward.

"Please, join me for dinner, Miss Montreux," he said. "I am about to go crazy for lack of an English tongue in my ear."

"I, uh . . . all right," she replied, forcing a smile. "Thank you, Mr. Bowles." She sat down, brushing away a fly and dabbing at the perspiration on her upper lip.

"When did you arrive?" he asked as she took the seat opposite him. He seemed not the least surprised to see her.

"Only a short time ago," Candace replied.

"You are . . ." Bowles allowed silence and the raising of a single eyebrow to complete his question.

"I am alone, Mr. Bowles. Mr. Zorin is elsewhere. I am to wait for him here."

Bowles laughed lightly, more in the fashion of a grunt. "It would seem the man has managed to get both of us in his grip," he said.

Candace did not reply. The truth could be bitterly painful. What Bowles said was true. Right now, they were both at his mercy.

"Perhaps," Bowles went on, "it is time we joined forces to see what we might be able to do about the situation."

"What do you mean?"

"All I know," he replied, "is that I am beginning to tire of Zorin and his demands."

(3)

Anni D'Abernon immediately recognized Candace Montreux sitting in the hotel restaurant. Some inexplicable blindness caused her to not recognize the human rhinoceros at her table with his back momentarily turned as he spoke to the waiter. Her gaze was fixed on a woman who could be her equal, or a mere token, depending on which way power was played.

The Swiss woman paused, then retreated. She would eat elsewhere. There was no way Lord Montreux's daughter could know her by sight. Still it would be best to remain unseen. In the things they had been given to do, exposure was never to be sought.

Before doing anything, however, she would call England.

Ten minutes later, Lord Montreux, just returned from Scotland, took in the news relayed by her call with grave concern.

"What is she doing there?" he asked.

"I hoped you might enlighten me," replied D'Abernon.

"I begin to wonder if somehow our friend Zorin is involved in this. You have not seen him?"

"Oh, he is involved all right," replied D'Abernon cynically. "But he is not in Cairo. He shall not trouble us further. Mr. Cutter is even now dealing with that difficulty for good."

"I think I should fly down," said Montreux. "Whatever Candace knows—about Livingstone, about Zorin, about any of it—we must find out."

"Bring Rupert with you. I sense we are close. I have felt disturbances this afternoon and evening, as if forces were trying to prevent our people from getting through to us. We need the strength of the Dimension working as one."

"You are at the Nile?"

"Of course."

"We will fly overnight and see you for breakfast."

(4)

After a midday check-in at the Nile Gardens, Adam Livingstone's small entourage spent the remainder of the day securely behind the closed doors of their two rooms. Adam did not want to risk being seen. The sense lay heavy upon all four that unfriendly eyes were everywhere.

Quietly they ate dinner in the larger of the two rooms.

About eight o'clock Rocky had finally had enough. "I can't stand this," he exclaimed. "I've got to get out. I'm going to prowl around."

"What do you expect to find?" laughed Adam.

"Who knows—maybe some bad guys are lurking about."

Rocky left the room and wandered downstairs, through the lobby, into the restaurant, then toward the bar. He felt as if he'd stepped into a scene from *Casablanca* or an Indiana Jones movie. He ordered a Coke, while continuing to glance about. Before long, he saw sinister intent behind every glass and under every white straw hat. His mind was full of his great-grandfather, wondering what his last night here had been like.

Leaving the bar a short time later, Rocky made a discovery that took him by complete surprise. There was the same olive green beret that had spied on him in Peterborough!

He didn't have long to think. Rocky ducked into hiding. The figure rose and came his way.

He couldn't believe his eyes. It was a *woman* . . . with Mediterranean complexion and black eyes.

He pulled his hat down over his eyes and turned away. She passed. Rocky glanced after her. It was the same walk! There was no doubt about it. How could he have been so completely fooled? A woman! He couldn't believe it. She was a beautiful woman too, with no masculine characteristics. What could have so blinded his eyes?

Rocky returned upstairs to the room after some more sleuthing. Adam and the others were watching what news they could find on TV. The girls were starting to doze off.

"What did you find, Rocky?" asked Adam.

"You'll be interested to know that your old friend Bowles is here."

"Bowles!" exclaimed Jen and Adam at once.

". . . *and* your friend Candace Montreux."

"Candace—what is this!" exclaimed Adam. "Has everyone converged on the Nile Gardens!"

"And they're not all," Rocky continued. "There's also one of those people here who followed me to New Hampshire and was in cahoots with whoever trashed my place."

"The ones that stole the journal?"

"Right—which I stole back!"

"Who?"

"Don't know. But I'm going out again. I managed to locate her room. Now I have to find out what she's up to. Whatever's going on, this hotel is part of it. Now that I'm here, I remember some correspondence with the Nile hotel I ran across in Grandpa Harry's trunk. I thought nothing about it at the time."

"You're right," said Adam seriously. "Something about this hotel feels very strange."

"What I can't figure out is how they always manage to keep dogging our heels. They anticipate our every move. Olive Beret's people were in New Hampshire before I got home. Now she turns up here . . . ahead of us again. It's as if they have a copy of Grandpa Harry's journal too, one that's telling them more than ours is telling us."

(5)

More things were afoot even than Anni D'Abernon realized.

She returned from dinner in the city as nightfall descended over Cairo. Two messages awaited her. Both changed her plans dramatically.

A signal from the desk clerk as she walked across the lobby brought her toward him.

"The manager has been waiting to see you," he said. "He said I must not miss you when you returned. There is important news."

D'Abernon—who sat on the board of directors for the conglomerate that owned the Nile Gardens—nodded and walked straight in the direction of the manager's room. She knocked once, then entered without awaiting reply.

"I am told you have information," she said.

"Adam Livingstone checked in this afternoon," the man replied.

"Adam Livingstone!" repeated D'Abernon in astonishment. "I can't believe it. What can he possibly be doing here?" Of course, what difference did it make *why* he was here. This was a fortuitous development indeed. They had been tracking him over half the globe. Suddenly he now turned up under their noses!

"Is he alone?" she asked.

"There are three with him—a gentleman, an American as I understand it, and two young women."

"Their rooms?"

"Eight-seventeen and 819—adjoining."

"You have done well. Have they been seen, gone out . . . telephone calls?"

"Four dinners from room service. No other activity."

"Length of stay?"

"They reserved both rooms for three days."

"You will inform me of any movement."

It was not a question. The man nodded.

"If by chance they attempt to check out earlier, delay them until I am notified. I do not care how—a failed computer, an error in the bill . . . if they try to pay with card or check, that should not be a problem. In the meantime, I shall take steps to freeze Livingstone's accounts. Within twenty-four hours he won't be able to make a move."

"All shall be done as you wish."

D'Abernon left the room in good spirits. Things were looking up. Maybe they would be successful in squashing this thing after all.

(6)

As Jen, Juliet, and Rocky listened, Adam read the ancient account from the Bible:

> *"During the night Pharaoh summoned Moses and Aaron and said,*
> *'Up! Leave my people, you and the Israelites! Go, worship the Lord*
> *as you have requested. Take your flocks and herds, as you have said,*
> *and go. And also bless me.' The Egyptians urged the people to hurry*
> *and leave the country. . . .*
>
> *"The Israelites journeyed from Rameses to Succoth. . . . With the*
> *dough they had brought from Egypt, they baked cakes of unleavened*
> *bread. The dough was without yeast because they had been driven*
> *out of Egypt and did not have time to prepare food for themselves.*
>
> *"Because the Lord kept vigil that night to bring them out of Egypt,*
> *on this night all the Israelites are to keep vigil to honor the Lord for*
> *the generations to come."*

Adam paused and glanced around.

"It's the same with us," said Juliet. "We have to make a night escape from Egypt also."

"It's eerie to think that my great-grandfather was here too," said Rocky, "on a similar quest and also in danger."

"Although he never made it to the promised land," remarked Jen.

"Maybe he did." Adam smiled.

"But what was his last night here like?"

"At least we know where he was bound. If we follow his footsteps, perhaps the Lord will lead us just as he did the Israelites. And since we have no more words of Harry to follow, this here may be our guidebook." Adam patted his Bible gently. Then he continued to read:

> *"When Pharaoh let the people go, God did not lead them on the road*
> *through the Philistine country, though that was shorter. . . . God led*
> *the people around by the desert road toward the Red Sea. . . . After*
> *leaving Succoth they camped at Etham on the edge of the desert. By*
> *day the Lord went ahead of them in a pillar of cloud to guide them*
> *on their way and by night in a pillar of fire to give them light, so*
> *that they could travel by day or night. Neither the pillar of cloud*
> *by day nor the pillar of fire by night left its place in front of the*
> *people."*

As Adam read, Rocky continued to puzzle about what had long confused him—that he had not himself been in danger until becoming associated with Adam. Now he remembered the words he'd read in Harry's hand about a *travelling* journal. He'd always taken that to mean simply the notes he took while travelling.

But what if there was a *duplicate* journal that Harry travelled with and had left here in the Nile Gardens Hotel safe with his other papers?

They could have had it all this time, whoever they were. It would explain why they hadn't come after him. They would have assumed, as he did, that there was but one journal and that no one else knew anything about Harry McCondy, except Adam Livingstone because of his paper.

If the hotel had been involved, it was probably still involved.

What if the duplicate journal was here . . . now? Might he be able to lay his hands on it? Not without finding out who had it first. Olive Beret? No, she had stolen his from his safety deposit box. Bowles? Unlikely. He'd only turned up recently, and Rocky couldn't be certain how involved he was. Who then? He'd go out again after the others went to bed.

Rocky was hardly paying attention as Adam continued to read the ancient account of the escape route.

A plan for their own modern-day exodus was already coming into focus in Adam's brain. They would follow the path of the Israelites!

He was now convinced such was exactly what Harry McCondy had done. They, too, would follow the ancient route to the place where God dwelt.

(7)

D'Abernon's second message did not reach her until later that evening.

A light knock sounded on her door. She opened it, then pulled a thin woman with a mysterious expression quickly inside.

Watching from behind a large potted palm at the end of the corridor, Rocky McCondy puzzled over what he had seen. What was Olive Beret up to? He'd followed her to her own room, still getting used to the fact that she was a woman. How had she been able to fake a man's appearance and build so thoroughly!

Now, after midnight, she was two floors above her own. Who was the occupant of that room? Rocky crouched lower, hoping to get sight of him or her when Beret left.

When they were alone inside D'Abernon's room, the visitor spoke. "I have received a message from Washington," she said.

"Has he finally cracked?"

"It would appear our efforts have been successful."

"What have you learned?"

"Livingstone is on his way to Mount Sinai."

*Sinai!* breathed the Swiss woman. "You are certain of the information?"

"It comes from the highest level within the Livingstone camp."

"You have done extremely well, Ciano. I will not forget it."

"I am yours to serve, Miss D'Abernon."

"Remain alert. We may be on the move again. I have also learned that Livingstone himself is in the hotel. If Sinai is his objective, we must move the instant he does."

D'Abernon let the Italian woman out of her room.

For the rest of the night she continued to pore over the McCondy journal, Adam Livingstone's university paper, and the other documents in her posssession concerning the two archaeologists whose work had become her passion and whose success could be her undoing.

(8)

When the desk clerk informed her shortly after dawn that two gentlemen checking in had asked for her, D'Abernon ordered that they be sent to her room immediately.

She brought them inside. None of the three took chairs. The newcomers knew from her expression that their comrade had news.

D'Abernon eyed Lord Montreux and Rupert Vaughan-Maier with eyes aglow.

"It's Sinai!" she said with triumph in her voice.

"What's Sinai?" asked Vaughan-Maier.

"Livingstone's destination! We've finally gotten to the bottom of it. It ties into McCondy's research. I think we've finally managed to get a step ahead of him!"

"What does Sinai have to do with it?" asked Lord Montreux.

"That's where his research is leading," she replied. "His objective at last is clear."

"He thinks the Garden of Eden is at Sinai!" exclaimed the Dutchman.

"The idea's nonsense," added Lord Montreux. "It's worthless desert, rock, and mountains! I shall find out if Candace can shed additional light on the matter. I shall go directly to her room and question her thoroughly." He turned to go.

"I tell you, that's where he is bound!" insisted D'Abernon. "For a hundred years we've been waiting for this final piece to the puzzle. Now we have it!"

"What do you propose?" said Vaughan-Maier.

"We must get a helicopter here with missiles capable of reducing Livingstone and his team to dust and rubble. No one will know what he was looking for. No more approach will be made to that ancient place. The Plan will be safe. The entire affair will be reported as a stray Libyan missile whose guidance system went berserk."

"All that can be arranged," mused Vaughan-Maier. "Carrying out what you say will be the easy part. There is, however, the matter of the monastery. It is of great antiquity, I understand."

389

"It may be that the Libyans will have to suffer repercussions for destroying a historic site."

"Is it possibile something other than the Garden is his objective?"

"Such as?"

"Some other kind of treasure, an archaeological find of great importance, another Tutankhamen. Our response mustn't be rash."

"We know he seeks the Garden. Have not our Wise Ones warned us of the danger and ordered us to stop him?"

"This predilection these old archaeologists have with Sinai—it's beyond comprehension!"

"Perhaps he thinks he has found the tablets of the commandments. If so, our work will be done—the world will call him mad."

The other two laughed, though without humor. There were some things that were *not* to be spoken of, and the tablets of stone were preeminent among them.

(9)

Adam Livingstone was gone most of the day.

The arrangements he had to make for transportation and further experimentation were best made alone. His credit card, however, halfway through the day, had suddenly been rejected.

A computer glitch?

Adam doubted it. He had a premonition that the forces trying to stop him weren't far behind. They seemed to be closing in. More and more of what Rocky had said about the conspiracy was confirmed. A few suppliers of equipment granted credit on his name. But this change of circumstance would make matters difficult and more complicated.

Adam called his staff assistant who had been overseeing operations in Turkey.

"Figg," he said, once he had him on the phone, "I need you in Cairo—immediately. Things are heating up. I don't have time to explain. Get some paper and write all this down carefully. I may not be able to contact you again."

"I'm ready," replied Figg.

"First, bring me as much cash as you can—preferably in dollars or pounds. But at this point I'm desperate. Anything will do. Then I've got a list of other things—you ready?"

"Shoot."

Adam enumerated his needs.

"I'm going to tell you when and where to meet me. You've got to be there, Figg. Lives are at stake."

"I'll be there."

(10)

Adam returned to the hotel in midafternoon.

As he entered the lobby his eyes immediately were drawn as by the lure of occultish power to a tall stately woman talking in hushed tones to a distinguished white-haired gentleman. He recognized neither, yet had the distinct impression they knew him . . . and were watching him.

The hair on the back of his neck rose slightly.

A dozen inexplicable inner sensations told him he had come face-to-face with the Power of the new-age forces that were trying to destroy him.

This was a place of antiquity where good and evil had waged one of the classic wars of all time some thirty-five hundred years ago. Had he been destined to live out that same battle in this new time?

The question brought a thousand *why*s in its train. Adam had no time to pause and ponder them. Escape must be made. The safety of his friends fell to his shoulders.

He strode through the lobby and past them, feeling an imperceptible chill as he did. How had they followed him here?

He waited nervously at the elevator. Behind him he felt four eyes boring holes of demonic sorcery into his back. The moment the elevator doors opened, he fairly leapt inside. As he turned to watch the doors close, both strangers were staring directly into his eyes. An involuntarily trembling sensation pulsed through him.

Adam entered his room and saw Jen, Rocky, and Juliet seated silently with somber expressions on their faces. Something was seriously wrong.

His questioning glance was answered by Rocky, who tossed him the afternoon's English edition of the Cairo paper.

Adam grabbed it and read the caption of the front-page story: LEADING UNIVERSITY BOTANIST FOUND MURDERED IN HOME.

A photo of Dr. Cissna and brief story followed. A gunshot wound straight to the heart. A specially manufactured caliber of weapon, virtually untraceable. Only one smudged fingerprint that could not be accounted for. It was being checked. Otherwise no clues.

Adam slumped into a chair. Was this the *second* death he was responsible for?

A heavy silence pervaded the room.

"It would seem the plague of the firstborn has begun," sighed Adam at length. "We must not delay our own exodus a moment longer."

No one replied.

"All right, everyone," said Adam. "This news is a blow. But if we're going to get out of here, I'm going to need you all with me. There are things we've got to do. Almost everything is ready. I have the visas for Saudi Arabia and Israel. I have obtained clearance for our exploration. The equipment we will need is being seen to. But I need your help now too."

The three looked up toward him and nodded.

"Okay, first, I want each of you to leave the hotel separately. Go to whatever bank or automatic teller you can find. We need as much cash as we can get. If you all can get a thousand pounds, that should be more than enough to get us home in an emergency. My card is showing up over its limit. I hope they haven't gotten to yours yet. If they have, we'll have to regroup."

The three rose.

"All right, get going," said Adam. "As soon as you're back, we're going to dress up and go downstairs for a big dinner. We're going to do our best to put the tragedy behind us and have a good time."

"But why, Adam?" said Jen. "I don't feel like celebrating."

"We will celebrate our own Passover feast—though not with bitter herbs. We must truly pretend we haven't a care in the world if we are going to pull this thing off. Cunning is called for if we're going to get out of this alive."

(11)

At seven o'clock that evening, the Livingstone entourage strode through the lobby of the Nile Gardens in seemingly boisterous spirits, talking and laughing gaily.

Adam led Juliet on his arm. They were followed by Rocky and Jen. Reservations had been made, and one of the most central tables in the restaurant awaited them. Word had spread, not merely through the hotel but into the city, that Adam Livingstone would make an appearance this evening.

"Ah, Mr. Livingstone!" the maitre d' greeted them warmly. "We have been expecting you. Your table is ready—and let me say it will be a great honor to serve you."

"Thank you," replied Adam with enthusiasm.

He led the way to their table. Adam seated Juliet, who could not prevent a smile from breaking out. Rocky helped Jen into her chair with all the grace and aplomb of an English gentleman.

Already, however, the maitre d' was on the telephone to the room of the Swiss woman.

"He is here," said the man.

Wine and hors d'oeuvres were served. Conversation flowed freely. A number of other guests wandered by nodding and smiling, wanting to see the discoverer of Noah's ark up close.

"I don't believe my eyes!" exclaimed Adam. "If it isn't Sir Gilbert Bowles! Sir Gilbert . . . over here!"

Adam stood, hailing his colleague.

Now Gilbert Bowles, along with everyone else, had heard the rumors circulating all afternoon. If there were festivities afoot, he wasn't about to be left out of them. Zorin had made no further trouble. Why should he not resume his former role of archaeological and spiritual foil to the supposedly *great* Adam Livingstone!

He had dressed in his cleanest khaki, washed his hair and brushed his ponytail, and sauntered into the restaurant at the appropriate moment to see what might develop.

"Ah, Livingstone!" he said, extending his hand in uncharacteristic generosity. "We meet again, in more cultured surroundings than the African bush."

"Right you are, Sir Gilbert—join us, won't you?"

"Well, I don't want to—"

"Nonsense, we are having a celebration before we embark on our Egyptian adventure. Please, I insist!"

Already Adam was signalling for a waiter to set another place, an undertaking that required some effort. Bowles' objections were voiced no further.

"What brings you to Cairo, Sir Gilbert?" asked Jen, with a devilish look in her eyes. "I thought you were going to be busy for months cataloguing Olduvai."

"The project suddenly fell through," replied Bowles. "The people I had lined up all deserted me. What about you, Livingstone? Still in search of your mythical garden?"

Adam had no chance to answer. For at that moment Candace Montreux appeared, her face still red from a heated blowup with her father. They had argued over Adam Livingstone, about whose plans each knew nothing. Both, however, suspected the other of withholding information. The interchange had been anything but pleasant. Now suddenly here was the object of their dispute striding toward her with a smile and an outstretched hand.

"Candace Montreux, what a surprise to see you here—and looking lovely as always! My party and I have just begun. We would be honored to have you join us."

Adam led Candace to the table. They squeezed in one more as Sir Gilbert's double place setting was somehow shrunk to one and a half. Jen and Juliet stared at Adam with wide eyes full of question. Adam returned their incredulity with a smile that said *I know what I'm doing—the more the merrier!*

Introductions were made all around. Candace finagled the seat to the opposite side of Adam from Juliet, whose presence and familiarity with her almost-fiancée did not please her. The gathering was altogether an incongruous one.

Everyone but Candace Montreux warmed to the ambiance of the festive Cairo evening. Music, exotic foods, and a fascinating mix of international tongues and dress caused most of the party to temporarily forget their troubles. Candace, however was clearly agitated and distracted.

"You still haven't answered my question, Livingstone," persisted Bowles. "What are you in Cairo to search for?"

"I musn't divulge my secrets, Sir Gilbert, you know that," replied Adam gaily. "But I don't suppose any harm would come of telling you what we plan for the next few days. First we're going to do some sightseeing. Tomorrow I have a full day, interviews, the press. After that I plan to show the girls and my American friend the great Pyramids. Beyond that, our plans are loose—we may be flying back to London."

"And the Garden?"

"Unfortunately we found nothing in eastern Africa."

"And your research here in Egypt?"

"Purely a pleasure junket, I assure you, Sir Gilbert. Anything unearthed between here and the Pyramids, I shall give to you!"

Certain ears had perked up throughout the conversation. Seated in a shadowy corner of the restaurant, they picked up everything via a transmitter located underneath the table. A slight nod from D'Abernon to her colleague indicated that information was coming clearly through her hidden earphone.

The only person not present in the restaurant among the principle players of the drama besides Candace's father, who had remained upstairs, was Ciano Bonar.

The wearer of the olive beret was at that moment upstairs doing her best, with the hotel manager's help, to secure entrance into the two Livingstone rooms. Rocky, however, had seen to it that such was impossible with a device guaranteed to keep the two rooms locked even with a key. Without the electronic mechanism in his own pocket, no one would get into their rooms without literally breaking them down. The manager of the Nile was not prepared to go quite that far.

He of the ominous voice, meanwhile, was some eight hundred miles southeast, outfitting himself with the clerical robe of a desert monk. The contrast between outer adornment and inner character could not have been greater. But such things were not on Halder Zorin's mind at the moment, but rather gaining entry to the highly secure compound at the foot of the mount known as Jebel Musa to the south of the Sinai Peninsula.

At the Nile Gardens, music now flowed in earnest. Casting etiquette to the wind, Candace begged Adam for a dance. The two rose and drifted away from the table toward the dance floor. The instant she felt Adam's arms around her, Candace clung close, pressing her face to the side of his head.

"Oh, Adam," she said, "I was such a fool before. I am so sorry. . . ."

Adam gently led as the strains of the waltz surrounded them.

"I should never have said all the things I did," she went on. "Forgive me."

"Of course, Candace—think nothing of it."

"Oh, but Adam, you must get away from here. There are bad people trying to harm you."

"Where, Candace?"

"Here, Adam—here . . . everywhere. Please, take me with you!"

"I don't know what to say, Candace," replied Adam, taken aback by the sudden change in her. He could tell by the tone of her voice that she was afraid. Candace Montreux was as skilled a manipulator as he had ever met. But fear? He had never heard such in her voice before now. "I thought you said as much down at Olduvai," Adam went on. "You were going to join me there. Then you disappeared. I thought you'd joined forces with Sir Gilbert."

"Adam, please—it was all a terrible mistake," Candace pleaded. "Can't we just forget all that?"

"Here you are again with Sir Gilbert—and now suddenly you want to go with me. What am I to think, Candace?"

"Adam, please . . . just believe me when I tell you it's all been a horrible nightmare. It's over now that you are here. I feel I can be safe again. Please . . . just take me with you!"

The music ended and they walked back toward the table.

"You must give me some time to think, Candace," said Adam. "I'm going to be tied up tomorrow. We'll talk further after that."

"Thank you, Adam," replied Candace. She was obviously relieved, though he still detected fear in her eyes.

Adam fought back a stab of guilt and regret. But too much was at stake to bring Candace in now. After recent developments, he didn't know if he could trust her. Somehow she was going to have to get through this on her own.

As the evening progressed, newsmen and journalists arrived on the scene. Questions became more persistent, until eventually Adam Livingstone had divulged a complete itinerary of interviews and sightseeing for the next three days.

Talk of the Garden of Eden did not surface.

# thirty

# Exodus

(1)

The hour was early. It was sometime after three o'clock in the morning. No moon brightened the dark, silent streets of Cairo. All was still.

A figure clad from head to foot in black made his way with extreme care down a rickety fire escape. One false move and he would send clanging warning to the occupants of the building that something untoward was afoot.

He took each step painstakingly, as if it might be his last. After a tedious descent, he reached the bottom landing. He would jump the final ten feet.

Climbing carefully over the edge of the steel frame, he eased himself into the void, grasping the lowest iron rail tightly with his fists, legs dangling in space, then released his grip.

With a momentary dull thud, his feet hit the concrete of the alley below. A dog barked somewhere. The figure crouched to the ground.

Three long minutes he waited. All seemed safe. Uncoiling himself, he walked along the wall to the entrance of the alley and peeked around the corner.

No sign of life was visible. He emerged and, clinging to the shadows, walked away from the hotel and into the night.

Inside the room of the same hotel a young woman lay awake in the dark. She knew the plan and was afraid. Gradually she dozed off, but dawn was a long time coming.

Several hours later, a voice whispered into the sleeper's ear.

"Juliet, dear—it's time," she said softly.

"Oh, thank you, Jen," replied Juliet, awake instantly.

"We must get you ready," Jen whispered.

After both girls were thoroughly up and awake, they began to converse in uncharacteristically robust fashion.

"Today's the big day," said Jen loudly. "We're off to see the Pyramids!"

"Will we have time for a short walk before breakfast?" asked Juliet, speaking yet again more loudly than was her custom.

"Sure," replied Jen.

In the adjoining room they could hear sounds of shaving and bustle, though it was just six o'clock.

"Hey," she called out, knocking on the door between the two rooms, "you guys going out or eating in?"

"Adam's still in bed. Adam, what are you doing for breakfast?"

A pause followed.

"He says he'll order room service," Rocky called back. "I think I may go out."

"I think we'll do room service too," Jen called back. "But we're going out for a short walk first."

(2)

In the lobby of the Nile Gardens Hotel, Ciano Bonar had seen or heard nothing all night. No one had come or gone after midnight.

The first sign of the four under surveillance came at about six twenty-five when the two young women emerged from the elevator wearing loose-fitting sweats and left the hotel. Immediately Bonar was on the phone with a report.

"Shall I follow them?"

"No, Livingstone's still in the room. The American's going out for breakfast too. Lay low so he doesn't spot you."

"Let him go?"

"Livingstone's all I care about. If he should appear, glue yourself to him. I'm listening to every sound in those rooms. If he goes anywhere, I'll call down on your pager."

The Italian returned to her watch.

Ten minutes later one of the girls returned just as the American entered the lobby from the elevator. Bonar crouched out of sight, though Rocky had already spotted her out of the corner of his eye.

"Hey, Jen," he said, making no attempt at subtlety, "Where's Juliet?"

"She's back a few doors looking at some clothes in a shopwindow. She'll be along in a minute. Adam still upstairs?"

"He's in the shower," replied Rocky. "I'm going out to get something to eat. See the rest of you when I get back."

"See you in a while, Rocky."

Jen turned and went to the elevator, where she rode back to the eighth floor.

Bonar made another brief report.

"You may come up, Ciano," said D'Abernon. "Everyone seems accounted for. Try to get some sleep."

(3)

Five blocks from the Nile Gardens Hotel, in a dirty alleyway beside a gray, plaster-coated warehouse, a young woman was snatched from the sidewalk and pulled into the shadows.

"I've been so worried!" she exclaimed, clinging to the black-clad figure for dear life. "I hardly slept after—"

"Don't worry—everything's fine. Just keep your voice down for yet a while longer."

The girl obeyed, but with obvious difficulty. Relief and anxiety were written in every line of her face.

"Come," the man said, "we've got some distance to go, and I don't trust anyone in this city."

Keeping to shadows and alleyways, they made their way farther from the hotel, glancing this way and that as they went, making sure they weren't followed.

The girl hardly noticed that a large man had fallen in about half a block behind them. Her escort glanced back, took no particular heed, and continued on, now crossing the wide boulevard Al Qasr al Eini, beginning to fill with the morning's traffic. They turned left to the south, hurried on another block, then darted into a narrow alley between two buildings. Both were breathing heavily from the quick-paced walk. Two minutes later the big man lumbered into the alley behind them.

An automobile was waiting. All three got in quickly, then crouched low. No eyes could have followed, yet still they took every precaution.

The car emerged from the alley, to all appearances carrying but a single driver. He turned eastward and in three minutes pulled into Port Said Street. This course would intersect with Ramses Street toward the northeast and eventually take them out of the city . . . on the highway toward Suez.

Thirty minutes later at the outskirts of Cairo, the automobile pulled up beside another car and stopped. A transfer of passengers was made. The man in black also made a telephone call.

(4)

"Adam . . . are you through with your breakfast?" Jen Swaner's voice called out to the adjoining room. Still she spoke with more volume than seemed necessary.

A pause followed.

"All right then, Juliet and I will read for a while."

Indistinct sounds and movements in both rooms could be heard. Ten minutes later the door to room 817 opened, and a room-service cart containing the remains of the breakfast ordered earlier by the gentleman, apparently well enjoyed, was wheeled out into the hall. A similar proceeding occurred a few minutes later outside the door of 819, where the two women's breakfast trays were dispensed with.

Half an hour later, the telephone rang inside 819. A Swedish voice answered.

"Yes, this is Adam Livingstone's assistant."

The caller spoke further.

"His schedule is rather tight today. He has a number of appointments. No, they will all be here in the room. Actually, Mr. Livingstone is not feeling well and plans to remain in all day."

Another pause.

"Let me see—I will ask him."

The caller waited.

"He would be willing to see you," she said. "Could you be here at ten-thirty We have an opening then."

The sound of the telephone hanging up sounded over the earpiece. Anni D'Abernon's forehead twisted into puzzled expression. Something sounded peculiar about the conversation.

Something seemed odd about this whole day!

(5)

The hot sun of the upper Sinai Peninsula an hour east of Suez bore down upon three pilgrims.

This same trek had been made twice before—by a million people thirty-five centuries earlier and by an American archaelogist in the previous century.

A trailer hauling a twenty-two-foot motorized boat followed the Land Rover in which they bounced along the lonely desert road. What purpose the

boat could serve in this arid wasteland would have been anyone's guess.

"Feeling better yet, Juliet?" asked Adam.

"I suppose," she answered, snuggling closer to his side. "I was so frightened earlier. Ever since we heard about poor Dr. Cissna, I've been afraid we would all be killed."

"Don't worry," rejoined Adam, reaching his arm around her. "We're in the clear now."

"They'll be looking for us in Cairo for days!" added Rocky from the backseat.

"I hope so!" answered Adam.

(6)

At 10:25 that same morning, a man of approximately thirty strode into the lobby of the Nile Gardens Hotel in Cairo.

"I'm here to see Adam Livingstone," he said to the desk clerk.

The clerk called up. Jen answered the phone.

"There's a gentleman here for Mr. Livingstone," he said.

"That would be Mr. Livingstone's ten-thirty appointment. Please send him up. Mr. Livingstone is expecting him."

A few minutes later a knock came to room 819. Jen answered it.

"Figg!" she exclaimed, then caught herself. She pulled him inside, then embraced him warmly. "It's so good to see you again," she whispered. "Just a minute. How good of you to come so promptly, Mr. White," she said loudly. "Mr. Livingstone . . . Kevin White is here."

She grinned to the man she had called Figg as she spoke, pointing to her ear as she did to indicate she was talking for the bug.

She led him into one of the bathrooms and turned on the faucet.

"Did they get off all right?" she whispered.

"Without a hitch," replied Figg in a low voice. "They should be in the middle of northern Sinai by now."

In her own room Anni D'Abernon's reservations had grown serious. This whole thing didn't sound right.

Suddenly words from early this morning came forcefully back into her brain. *Today's the big day. We're going to see the Pyramids.*

They weren't going to see the Pyramids today! There had *never* been any intention of sightseeing. All this talk and room service and the comings and goings . . . she'd still only heard *one* voice over the speaker all day.

Already she was on the phone to the hotel manager.

"I want a maid into 817 and 819 immediately," she said. "I don't care what excuse the girl of Livingstone's makes, I want those rooms searched!"

The manager called upon his Swiss guest personally ten minutes later.

"One room empty, the other with a young woman and the fellow called White who had just arrived. No sign of Livingstone, the American, or the other girl."

D'Abernon swore lightly. It was all a setup. Livingstone had skipped Cairo right under her nose!

In a heartbeat, she was out of her room and on the way to see Vaughan-Maier and Montreux.

"Livingstone's gone!" she said. "I'm ordering that helicopter within the hour. I'll handle this personally from here on. I'll be at Sinai ahead of them and be ready the instant they arrive!"

Jen knew the moment the maid left the room that the charade was over. She could tell from the way the woman looked around and was watching them that something other than cleaning the room was on her mind.

Mindful of the bug in the room, she scribbled a hurried note to Figg: *They've made us. Get out of here. I'm on my way back to London.*

Already Jen was throwing her few belongings into her suitcase. If she could just get out of the hotel safely, she'd call a quick news conference at the airport. She'd announce that Adam Livingstone had left Cairo secretly early this morning in order to avoid the press . . . and was on his way back to England.

# PART FIVE

# SINAI

◆ ◆ ◆

*Eyes will be clouded in deception's day,*

*Of those seeking rapturous transfiguration.*

*Thus will the coming yet a season delay.*

*Until humbly fulfilled are John's simple conditions.*

◆ ◆ ◆

# thirty-one

# In the Steps of Harry McCondy

(1)

The sacred Monastery of St. Catherine at the foot of Jebel Musa had never witnessed such a cruel deception against the simple faith of its members in all its one hundred and fifty years.

Churches and communities of contemplatives had been located at the sacred site below the traditional mount called Sinai since the fourth century. There had even been attacks on it through the centuries. But for such to happen in this modern day was beyond belief.

The man had appeared, dressed in the garb of a friar, without appointment or forewarning, explaining that he was on an urgent pilgrimage. Hesitant, the monks of St. Catherine's nevertheless allowed entry. Once inside, the man began plying them with questions. He said another was coming whom he must stop, one with motives to destroy Sinai by turning it into an archaeological dig. He

had come to prevent the desecration, he said, and to preserve the tradition of St. Catherine's. His voice, however, betrayed more sinister motive. The spirits of the holy men recoiled. Immediately they knew a serious error had been made. The newcomer's importune manner became angry and demanding.

Suddenly a gun appeared. An elderly monk dared voice an objection and was slapped viciously to the ground. Before many more minutes had passed, one priest was dead, all the others terrified. The entire monastery was now under the visitor's command. The peaceful men of contemplation could not imagine what an evil man like this would want with them or could find to interest him at the holy site.

They could continue their prayers, he said. They must only stay out of his way and no one else would get hurt. Otherwise more would end up like the one for whose burial they were already preparing.

(2)

It was midafternoon on the upper Sinai Peninsula.

Rocky now drove. Juliet sat in the front passenger seat.

Adam had stretched his long legs across the backseat and opened his Bible. As they went, he now read from the opening chapters of Genesis. He had pored over these words intently during the last six months. But now he continued further on into the story of early man's development and how he related himself to his Creator. As the hours passed, he read of Noah, Abraham, and Moses, fascinated at the intimacy with which these giants of primitive faith walked with God in mingled friendship and childlikeness. Adam was eager now himself to walk in that same humble friendship with his Creator.

He was a *personal* God. No reason remained in the consciousnss of Adam Livingstone to doubt a word of the biblical account. He found himself absorbing the stories with the same mind as if reading a factual account of today's events. The Bible had become for him a document, no longer of mere curiosity, but of fact . . . *verifiable* fact. Its antiquity changed nothing of its authenticity, only made verifying that authenticity a greater challenge.

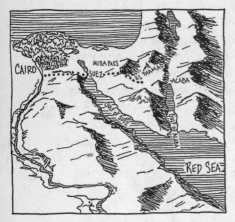

It was a challenge to which he was now determined to dedicate what remained of his life.

The route they pursued was following, according to Harry's journal, what had long been known as the traditional trading route between Egypt and Arabia across the wilderness of Paran—from Suez through Mitla Pass to Heitan and Nakhl.

Adam turned back from his interest in Abraham to a more detailed reading of the Exodus account. He wished he had taken the time to investigate these Scriptures first and gotten to know the story better before embarking on this trek through the desert. But events forced haste.

Attempting to follow Harry's steps as precisely as possible, and thus those of Moses, they turned southward at El Thamad. Their way now led through a rocky region, mountainous, passable enough but desolate. They encountered not another human soul. It was indeed wilderness. At length they came to a narrow gorge. Continuing on, they saw rising high mountains on each side.

They felt that same eerie sense of being hemmed in that caused the children of Israel to doubt Moses' directions and leadership.

Eventually this track would lead them to the sea, to a wide beach at Neviot on the shore of the Gulf of Aqaba.

> Then the Lord said to Moses, "Tell the Israelites to turn back and encamp near Pi Hahiroth, between Migdol and the sea. They are to encamp by the sea, directly opposite Baal Zephon. . . .
>
> The Egyptians—all Pharaoh's horses and chariots, horsemen and troops—pursued the Israelites and overtook them as they camped by the sea near Pi Hahiroth, opposite Baal Zephon. As Pharaoh approached, the Israelites looked up, and there were the Egyptians, marching after them. . . .
>
> Moses answered the people, "Do not be afraid. Stand firm and you will see the deliverance the Lord will bring you today. The Egyptians you see today you will never see again. The Lord will fight for you; you need only to be still."

As Adam read the words, he reflected on the amazing pilgrimage he and his two friends were making. A reverent and thoughtful silence had gradually stolen over all three. What an unlikely trio this was. None of them had known each other six months earlier, but now their lives intertwined on so many profound levels.

Theirs was a historic journey. Adam had felt it to such an extent that he had rented the craft now bouncing behind the Land Rover that would enable them to actually cross the Red Sea at the site he believed the Israelites of old walked across on the seabed. If the Garden and Sinai *were* indeed linked, he wanted to experience the original accounts as fully as possible.

Adam glanced up briefly at Juliet and Rocky in front of him. Rocky was perspiring in the heat but remained in good spirits. Juliet's brown hair tumbled and fell about her face, which bore a smudge or two of dust, in a way that made her beautiful in Adam's eye—more beautiful than Candace could ever be. He could hardly believe she had been part of his team less than two weeks.

How he loved these two new friends!

How thankful he was that they were now sharing this quest. They were all bound up in events and times so much bigger than themselves. If they were indeed on the verge of making a discovery that would change how mankind interpreted the Genesis account, how quietly grateful he felt to be one of those chosen to occupy such a pivotal role.

(3)

Back at the Nile Gardens, Candace Montreux picked up the ringing phone to hear Halder Zorin's commanding baritone.

"Where is Livingstone?" he demanded.

"I don't know—he's gone."

"Gone! Where?"

"I don't know. They said they were going sightseeing at the Pryamids."

"Bah, the Pryamids! He's no more going to the Pryamids than the moon!"

"That's what they said. Then suddenly they disappeared."

"There was no mention of Sinai?"

"None."

A few more tense exchanges followed, each with an increasingly threatening tone.

Candace hung up the phone a moment later, face red and angry. She was being used. And she'd had enough.

She left her room and wandered down to the lobby. The place had grown desolate. She didn't know where her father was. Adam and all his people were gone. Why was she staying around this miserable place, anyway?

Maybe she would have some lunch.

She wandered into the restaurant and sat down. Ceiling fans blew the stale air about, but they could do nothing to combat the flies. She hated them, buzzing, buzzing everywhere. This was supposed to be a first-class hotel—why didn't they do something about them! It was hot. She was perspiring. All the people here smelled. Didn't they have deodorant in Africa? In the background some melancholy Egyptian music played. How could it have seemed so gay and festive just last night.

Behind her, heavy footsteps approached. Candace paid them no heed. She wasn't interested.

"Mind if I sit down?"

She glanced up. There again was the large form of Gilbert Bowles, chest and armpits showing the stain of sweat on his khaki shirt. "Please do . . . I hate to eat alone," she said, greeting him with testy irritability.

Bowles crunched into the chair opposite her, which miraculously did not collapse.

"How do you stand it?" she asked and exclaimed all at once.

"Stand what?"

"Places like this, Africa . . . strange foreign countries—the dirt and heat and flies and smells!"

Bowles' frame shook with a light chuckle as the chair groaned under his weight.

"I deal with it by always wearing the same clothes."

Candace looked the man over from head to foot, then began laughing herself.

"What's funny?" he said.

"I don't know—maybe what you say makes sense. Your khaki does look like it came out of the ground—fitting for an archaeologist. Maybe it *would* help if one didn't have to think about a wardrobe."

Bowles got the waiter's attention and ordered a bottle of wine. He poured two glasses.

"How long are you here?" he asked.

"I was supposed to be helping Zorin. But I've had it. He can kill me if he wants like he did—"

Suddenly she caught herself. Bowles saw it, glanced at her with dark inquiry, but then thought better of pursuing it. If he had just turned over a rock with vital information that might reward him later, its usefulness would be greatly enhanced if no one knew he possessed it.

"Zorin, ha!" he chortled with disdain. "He's a bloke I'd just as soon never see again. Myself, I'm booked on a flight this evening straight back to Heathrow."

"I'd do anything to get out of here!"

"Would you like me to see what I could do for you?"

"I would be forever grateful, Mr. Bowles."

They proceeded, if not particularly, to enjoy the lunch that followed, at least to consume it with more vigor than either had anticipated when they walked into the place alone.

That evening Sir Gilbert Bowles and Lady Candace Montreux, the two expendable pawns in the drama now escalating elsewhere in northeastern Africa, were seen together boarding the London-bound British Airways flight out of Cairo.

(4)

On the three pilgrims drove. The sun beat down upon the desert.

What were they on their way to discover? Adam wondered again. Were they merely following the footsteps of Moses of old, as recounted by Harry McCondy in contradicting the traditional theorists who had the route of the Exodus to the west of here? Or would they truly find physical evidence, as he dared dream his computer model suggested, that verified this very region as the heart and center of Genesis beginnings, covered over later by desert yet kept hidden and alive . . . awaiting this *new* moment of discovery?

They reached Neviot . . . and the sea.

> Then the Lord said to Moses, "Why are you crying out to me? Tell the Israelites to move on. Raise your staff and stretch out your hand over the sea to divide the water so that the Israelites can go through the sea on dry ground. . . ."
>
> Then Moses stretched out his hand over the sea, and all that night the Lord drove the sea back with a strong east wind and turned it into dry land. The waters were divided, and the Israelites went through the sea on dry ground, with a wall of water on their right and on their left.

409

> *. . . That day the Lord saved Israel from the hands of the Egyptians. . . . Then Moses and the Israelites sang . . . to the Lord.*

How could so many historians and biblical scholars—who believed Sinai located at Jebel Musa forty or fifty miles southwest of here—*how could they all be wrong?* thought Adam.

They had built shrines and churches and chapels on the site for centuries. Now the Monastery of St. Catherine sat in the valley overlooked by the 8,600-foot peak.

According to Grandpa Harry, however, St. Catherine's sat at the *wrong* site. There were those amazing words in his journal, which now at last Adam understood:

> *They will look and look, but not see. They have built their shrine on the wrong mount. Look for the mountain of fire—twice did the fire of God burn there. It is the mountain of fire.*

The mountain of fire . . . what would they see when they crossed this thin stretch of sea and cast their gaze tomorrow upon Jebel al Lawz, the ancient Arabian volcano?

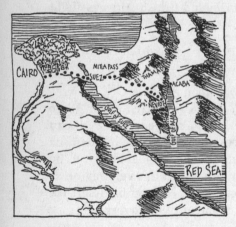

By now it almost ceased to matter whether they found links to the original Garden. He was *Adam* in the midst of his own personal garden.

And was not Genesis, at root, the story of every man's, every woman's, personal and individual creation, from conception in the womb to the moment when God's Spirit was breathed into them?

Did not each man, each woman, have to decide for himself or herself whether to eat the fruit of independence . . . or choose instead to *obey* their Creator and thus partake of Garden life?

Such was the choice before every man and woman. *Was not this the meaning of Eden?*

The Tree of Life had blossomed within Adam's heart. Whatever else he might find was secondary to that single, astounding, eternal fact.

Adam Livingstone remained, however, in great danger. Like Harry McCondy before him, he had unearthed truths in the heavenly realms that the powers of darkness were fighting to keep from being made known. He and his two friends were on their way into the eye of a great storm. An eternal hurricane was blowing in the heavenlies. At the center of it, they alone now carried the legacy of Harry McCondy forward to its destined conclusion.

(5)

The urgent phone call to Baku came from Cairo.

"President Voroshilov?"

"Yes, of course," answered the president of Azerbaydzhan on the secure line meant only for his top three military advisors. It was to be used only in cases of crisis and emergency. "Who is this?" he asked. He knew it was not one of the three.

"It is Anni D'Abernon speaking."

A brief silence.

"You are familiar with the name?"

"Yes . . . yes, I know who you are. How did you get this number? It is only—"

"I have access to all such numbers, Mr. President. I thought that was understood."

"Yes, but—"

"I must speak with Halder Zorin," she interrupted. "It is extremely urgent. I have been unable to locate him. I hoped you could help."

"I have not seen him in a number of days."

"Then I need you to send me General Pervukhin with one of your nation's swiftest military helicopters, fully armed. The weapons must be disguised as either Libyan or Iraqi."

Again, silence.

"You know whom I represent, President Voroshilov?"

"Uh . . . yes."

"I trust, then, there will be no delay."

"All will be done as you specify."

"I need the general here immediately. The distance is seven hundred miles. I will expect him in four hours. I will be at the airport in Cairo at eight o'clock this evening."

D'Abernon hung up the telephone, then turned once more to the hundred-year-old journal that had become her constant companion of late. She had come to despise the thing, yet could not help thinking it still possessed a clue for her that would tell her the exact location of the place she must destroy.

She had an eerie sensation of playing out a role in the century-old chase after Harry McCondy, which had ended in futility. He had come here too, right to the Nile, before he began wandering off northward and into Arabia. That's where they had finally killed him in the middle of nowhere. He had devoted his whole life to the study of the Bible, and the fool didn't even know where Sinai was.

Now she was after *another* archaeologist, who was also said to be bound for Sinai. The similarity was all too uncanny.

Her Guides had been active for several days, warning her repeatedly: *The evil place must be destroyed . . . the Master's power must be preserved . . . the shroud must remain . . . you must find it and destroy it.*

But she didn't know where it was.

And now she had lost track of Livingstone. He was bound for Sinai, that much she was sure of. But she couldn't blow up the whole mountain!

Frantically she began flipping through the journal again. But she might as well have been reading Greek. Too many prayers of too many saints surrounded the words on the pages, and her eyes could not probe their depths.

(6)

The evening was early. The sun had not yet set. The afternoon's warmth still clung to the earth, though shadows were lengthening from the high cliffs behind them.

The three modern-day pilgrims had arrived about an hour before and set up their night's camp some distance back from the edge of the water of the Red Sea's eastern finger, the Gulf of Aqaba. Adam felt that in this very place referred to in Exodus 14:2 as Pi Hahiroth, on the great flat sandbar stretching two or three miles in each direction of the village of Neviot, the Israelites had encamped prior to their miraculous crossing.

No wonder they had lost heart—behind them rose the cliffs and narrow gorge through which they had come, and before them stretched miles of open sea.

What would they find tomorrow when they crossed into Arabia and made their way on that last leg of their quest to the mount called Horeb, the mount where God dwelt, the mount where he had spoken to Moses, perhaps the place where he had dwelt . . . since the beginning?

A low fire burned between the three as they sat with coffee cups in hand, a quiet sense of history and antiquity—and destiny—descending upon them.

It was a night heavy with portent. As the night closed in, the embers in the small fire glowed bright in the darkness. Another glow was present within the hearts of this unlikely trio of pilgrims—a sophisticated British archaeologist, a crusty aging American detective, and a young woman a year out of college without even a place to call home.

Juliet was the first to break a long silence.

"I sense God's presence so strongly," she said. "It is so hard to imagine that such a short time ago I hardly gave him a second thought."

"I know what you mean," added Adam.

"I am still in such awe to be here at all," Juliet continued. "I don't know what I have to offer this search. It seems that so many others ought to be by your side right now, Adam . . . and yet here Rocky and I are sharing it with you."

"That's just how I feel," said Rocky. "I had the journal in my attic all these years, yet didn't possess the spiritual knowledge to interpret what it had to say. God has been providing that aspect of it in my life only very recently."

"How do you mean?" asked Adam.

"Through my friends Mark and Laurene."

"You've told us some of what the three of you talked about," said Adam. "Could you tell us more?"

As they stared into the fire, Rocky began to recount his conversations with Mark and Laurene Stafford in greater detail than he had had opportunity before.

(7)

Anni D'Abernon and Ciano Bonar climbed aboard the deadly, tan-and-green military helicopter only moments after it touched down. General Pervukhin had no time to even stretch his legs.

"Take it up, General," Anni commanded.

"What is our destination?"

"Bear southwest toward the southern Sinai Peninsula. I'll tell you more when we're aloft."

Already the rotor blades were screaming with increased speed as the skids lifted off the tarmac. Quickly the high-tech battle-machine rose into the Egyptian dusk, then bent at a steep angle in the direction D'Abernon had indicated.

"Are we armed with missles, General?"

Pervukhin nodded. "What is our target?"

"You will be told when the time comes. I do not yet know the precise location. That is what we must learn at Sinai."

The Swiss woman sat back to relax, as much as one of her temperament was capable of doing. Beside her, Bonar now spoke.

"A message arrived a short time ago from one of our people in Baku. I hoped to learn more before our departure so did not trouble you with it. Unfortunately, nothing more came."

The Italian woman handed D'Abernon a slip of paper folded in half. She opened it and read the brief message.

*Body of Mitch Cutter dragged from Caspian north of Baku Harbor this morning. Single bullet to head. No details known. Will advise.*

D'Abernon shook her head with a smile of irony. She should have known Cutter was out of his league. It was her fault for sending him on such an errand. But he was expendable.

The worst of it was the realization of what this development meant. Zorin was still alive.

(8)

"The year 1999 may be highly significant," Rocky was telling Adam and Juliet around their small campfire. "Actually it's the year 2000, or, some say, it won't be until 2001 that the new millennium begins. Although, there have been enough miscalculations and changes to the calendar over the centuries that only God knows *exactly* when the significant year will truly be upon us."

"What is all this leading to?" sighed Adam in wonder as he listened.

"I asked Mark the very same thing," replied Rocky. "The timing kept confusing me. I asked him why all these things were taking place now.

"'Because now is the appointed time,' he answered. 'This is the moment for the next break in the history of the universe—the next epoch, a new era. The New Age people are talking about the new dawn of time—but they mean something completely different.'

"'So you truly think,' I asked him, 'that there is more going on here than merely that one archaeologist named Adam Livingstone has made a few discoveries that are uncomfortable to certain people?'

"'Absolutely,' he replied. 'There are times and seasons in the spiritual realm. There are things that happen. There are things that must happen before others can take place. Some events proceed slowly. Others come quickly. And always they follow a preordained sequence. God holds the timetables for all the eras and the keys to unlock the doors to them.'"

"What do you mean by keys?" asked Juliet.

"Divine signs of indication," replied Rocky. "Mark explained it as the events people look to, for example, as signs pointing to the end times—the rebuilding of the temple in Jerusalem, wars, rumors of wars, earthquakes, all the signs mentioned in the Bible."

"He thinks such signs are coming now?"

"He said we're at a significant historical crossroads. It has been two thousand years since Jesus came, as his birth was approximately two thousand years following God's covenant with Abraham. Though Mark did say," Rocky continued, "that he thinks the signs of the next era will not be so readily visible as what many are looking for. Laurene said the signs that foretell and pave the way are usually misunderstood by the religious people of a particular day. Especially will this be true, she said, for the next season we are approaching."

"What did she mean?" asked Juliet.

"What I told you about earlier," said Rocky, "remember, the progression of eras through history. The next, according to my friends, will be that of deception."

(9)

The evening was well advanced into darkness when the harsh sounds and bright lights of the whirring machine of destruction set down fifty yards from the entrance to the quiet place of sacred contemplation and prayer.

Inside, everyone heard its approach. Recent events had greatly increased the threshold for terror of St. Catherine's monks, and these were not sounds whose omens boded well.

Two of the monks who were not yet in their private cells rushed to the outside entrance, through the courtyard, and into the night.

There sat the strange, horrid spider of warfare, its blades gradually slowing yet continuing to blow a great cloud of sand in every direction. Already a woman was approaching them.

"My friends and I will be spending the night," she said. It was clear she was giving orders, not asking permission.

"We have no—"

"I am afraid I must insist."

"But women are not—"

"Do you want me to order a missile to blow apart your whole monastery?" she shot back. "We are on a mission of worldwide significance. We will be here until it has been accomplished. Now show us to whatever rooms we may occupy, or warn your fellow monks that we will open fire."

Faces white, the two humble men turned, gesturing for them to follow, and led toward the open gate into the walled courtyard.

As D'Abernon approached the ancient building, a familiar figure strode forward.

"I should have expected to see you, Zorin," she said with scorn.

He nodded and smiled with an expression of odd amusement. He knew well enough who had sent the fool Cutter on his ill-fated mission.

"I don't know how you found out about the monastery," said D'Abernon. "I assume you are here on the same errand as I."

"I could just as well ask how you learned of it," rejoined Zorin. "I must say, this doesn't seem your style. I didn't think you went in for frontal tactics."

"I had to get here fast. I'm afraid the time for subtleties is past."

"I see you commandeered my own general for your dirty work," said Zorin with an unpleasant sneer, no longer making an effort to hide his disdain for his rival on the Council of Twelve. "Trying to implicate me, are you?" he added, nodding in the direction of the helicopter.

"I tried to reach you first," countered D'Abernon. "Then I did what I had to do."

"From your hasty and high-profile arrival, I presume you expect Livingstone any moment."

"He has not arrived . . . you have seen nothing of him?"

"Nothing."

"It would seem then, Zorin," she said, "that there is no choice left us but to join forces. We are both seeking the same resolution to this affair. We will no doubt be more likely to succeed if we work together."

In her heart, even as she spoke, she was already contemplating how to get rid of him the moment it was over.

(10)

"'I believe such a sign for the times was revealed to Laurene and me as we were praying,' Pastor Mark told me," said Rocky. "Then he mentioned you again, Adam," Rocky added.

"What did he say?" asked Adam.

"He said, 'I have a feeling God's hand is on your friend Adam Livingstone to an even greater degree than he realizes.'"

Adam took in the words with sober expression full of deep thoughtfulness.

"That stanza of Grandpa Harry's poem comes to my mind," said Adam. "Where's the journal?"

Rocky pulled it out and handed it to him. Adam located the passage, then read the words aloud:

> *"Eyes will be clouded in deception's day,*
> *of those seeking rapturous transfiguration.*
> *Thus will the coming yet a season delay,*
> *until humbly fulfilled are John's simple conditions."*

"But if deception is coming, why would these greater revelations of truth come at the same time?" asked Juliet.

"As I understand it," Rocky replied, "Perhaps it is to be expected. Even as the era of salvation dawned, the eyes of the Jewish nation were blinded to their own Messiah. Deception and revelation always accompany one another, is what Laurene said. Whenever God appoints one to herald truth, Satan increases his attempt to destroy and discredit that truth. Revelation and deception usually arrive hand in hand."

"So you believe this new era is near?" asked Adam.

"I think I do," replied Rocky. "If Mark and Laurene are right, I would say yes, the new era is coming, with spiritual deception at the heart of it. The enemy will increase his efforts to discredit God's most significant voices, especially by the hand of their own brothers."

It fell silent. The fire now burned low.

"Mark's last words to me before I left New Hampshire haven't left my mind," said Rocky. He said, 'I try always to keep the Lord's words at the forefront of my thoughts: Be alert, be watchful, be vigilant. Deception may be lurking where you least expect it.'"

Adam and Juliet took the words with somber nods.

Gradually a smile spread over Juliet's face.

"What is it?" asked Adam.

"It sounds to me like Aslan's on the move."

"What?"

"That spring is about to burst forth."

"Who's Aslan?"

"A story I'll share with you when we get back to London."

"But they will do all they can to stop Spring from coming," added Rocky with a smile. It was one of the first books Mark had given him to read after his wife's death, and he understood Juliet's analogy clearly enough. "We are squarely in the middle of the battle. Like Mark said, we must take care."

"Whatever the enemy's strategy," said Juliet, "there is a deeper magic, to use Aslan's term, from before the dawn of time, about which he is unaware. Over those deep truths he is powerless."

"God will be the victor," said Adam, rising into the confidence of his new-found faith. "I believe that his purpose will be accomplished."

(11)

Adam and Juliet would cross by boat tomorrow from Neviot, bearing northward from the actual site opposite to Al Humaydah in Saudi Arabia. Rocky would drive around the northern expanse of the gulf, pass briefly into Israel, then into Saudi Arabia at the town of Aqaba, presumably exactly as his great-grandfather had done, then drive south to meet them.

From there, they would begin the final leg of their trip, following in the footsteps of the Israelites to the final encampment at Rephidim, and ultimately to the slopes of Horeb itself—the mount of the burning bush, the mount of the Presence, the mount of fire and smoke.

*The whole Israelite community set out from the Desert of Sin, traveling from place to place as the Lord commanded. They camped at Rephidim, but there was no water for the people to drink. So they quarreled with Moses. . . .*

*Moses cried out to the Lord, "What am I to do with these people?". . .*

*The Lord answered Moses, "Walk on ahead of the people. Take with you some of the elders of Israel and take in your hand the staff with which you struck the Nile, and go. I will stand there before you by the rock at Horeb. Strike the rock, and water will come out of it for the people to drink." So Moses did this in the sight of the elders of Israel. And he called the place Massah and Meribah. . . .*

*In the third month after the Israelites left Egypt—on the very day— they came to the Desert of Sinai. After they set out from Rephidim, they entered the Desert of Sinai, and Israel camped there in the desert in front of the mountain.*

*Then Moses went up to God, and the Lord called to him from the mountain. . . .*

*Moses led the people out of the camp to meet with God, and they stood at the foot of the mountain. Mount Sinai was covered with smoke, because the Lord descended on it in fire. The smoke billowed up from it like smoke from a furnace, the whole mountain trembled violently, and the sound of the trumpet grew louder and louder. Then Moses spoke and the voice of God answered him.*

*The Lord descended to the top of Mount Sinai and called Moses to the top of the mountain. So Moses went up.*

Adam set down the Bible in which he had been reading the ancient account by the fading light of the flickering fire, rolled over, and was soon asleep.

•

# thirty-two

# The Slopes of Horeb

(1)

A pale half-moon lit the early night.

Adam and his two novice archaeologists approached an area that had been barricaded near the foot of the 8,500-foot mount known as Jebel al Lawz. The peak was the highest of many surrounding it. It was a rugged and forbidding region whose volcanic past seemed to preclude any hope of life. Yet beyond the fence they beheld the exuberant area of new widening shrubbery and new green growth below the mountain, somewhere near where the nation of Israel had camped long ago. It was exactly as described in the two accounts of the phenomenon Adam had read and as explained by their dead friend Dr. Petiri Cissna.

Adam walked to the fence and probed it. It was standard chain link, barbed wire running the length on top, not electrified.

He put his face to it and gazed through. Even in the dusky light he could make out a single tree in the distance, growing straight and tall out from the midst of the other miraculous new plant life.

A tingling thrill of awe surged through him just as it had upon first seeing the photo. Here indeed was a lush oasis—perhaps even a brand-new forest—in the making!

No one else was about. They would try to take their samples and be gone quickly.

He had a clearance to be in the country for research. But the Saudis were fickle. This area had already been fenced. He wanted to arouse no suspicion. He might produce the documents obtained at the Saudi embassy in Cairo and *still* find all three of them in jail. Such things happened in this part of the world.

He was not about to cut through the fence. The perimeter of chain link comprised only three of the four sides of a rectangle. The fourth was occupied by the slope of the mountain itself. They ought to be able to simply climb up and around, ascending the slope far enough to get around the fence end, then descending down into the middle of the oasis. There, hopefully without being seen, they would conduct their experiments, take as many vegetation samples as possible, and drill core samples from the trunk of the mystery tree.

First they would hike around to the opposite side of the peak. Within the protected crater of the dead volcano they would camp for the night, hoping the Land Rover would be safe and out of anyone's sight where they had parked it between two large boulders about a mile away.

(2)

At the Monastery of St. Catherine the watch continued. Twenty-four hours had passed. All remained quiet. No one had been seen.

The monks tiptoed around in fear for their lives. Zorin and D'Abernon prowled about, avoiding one another as much as possible, conducting what business was necessary between them with terseness. Bonar kept to herself. General Pervukhin took the helicopter up every two or three hours with one of the three for a quick scan about the region of the two peaks for any sign of expedition or activity.

If Livingstone was bound for Sinai, he was taking his time getting here.

Meanwhile, Lord Montreux and Rupert Vaughan-Maier flew back to Europe without their Swiss colleague.

Vaughan-Maier was worried. D'Abernon, like Zorin, seemed to have forgotten one of the central precepts of their master's design, that The Plan could not be rushed nor implemented by force or coersion. He did not know where she was at this moment. She had been supposed to fly back with them but had disappeared. Neither had either of the men seen Lord Montreux's daughter during the same period.

Something was amiss, and Vaughan-Maier feared no good would come of it.

(3)

The thin gray light of predawn spread over the far west corner of Saudi Arabia.

Three tired sleepers gradually came to themselves. Even in their well-padded bedrolls, they felt the hard ground. A few groans from Rocky accompanied wakefulness.

This day represented the climax of a long quest. Soon all three were bright eyed, despite lingering weariness. They were ready to discover Horeb's ancient mysteries.

With daylight to assist them, they saw that they were indeed within the rim of an ancient volcano, surrounded by peaks of varying height, in the midst of a flat plateau of several hundred acres in extent. A quick glance about confirmed to all three that this certainly could be the Sinai of the biblical account. The highest peak of the mountain was still blackened, as if by fire. Between two massive boulders upon the peak grew a solitary tree some four or five feet high.

Adam gazed up at it with wonder, thinking of many things—especially the burning bush of the Moses account. Why would *this* be the place to which God would bring his people to reestablish his covenant? Were the Exodus and the Garden intrinsically and symbolically linked? Why would God speak *here?* Why else unless this was the place where he had *first* spoken to man!

Questions surged through his brain. But he quickly caught himself. He was a scientist. He would finish gathering the samples before he let himself get too carried away in speculation.

Gazing about further, he noted several caves spotting the cliffs and slopes. He had just run across a passage in his reading yesterday about a man by the name of Elijah taking refuge in a cave on the mountain called Horeb.

Truly they could be standing on historic ground.

Already Rocky was building a fire with supplies they had carried in. Juliet was gathering together what provisions they had for coffee and a scant breakfast.

While Rocky and Juliet were busy with their chores, Adam took his notebook from his pack. Without his computer before him, he began doodling and drawing, imagining what might have been going through Harry McCondy's mind during his similar trek. A map began to form on the paper, as Adam reflected back on how this adventure had begun at Ararat.

He sketched in the Turkish mountain on his drawing.

Then had come his revelations on the computer, then the bombing . . . then Rocky . . . then the trip to Africa . . . now Juliet was part of everything. So much had happened in such a short time.

He remembered the day he stood at Murchison Falls and had prayed for the first time in his life.

Adam now sketched in the region around Lake Victoria and the headwaters of the Nile.

He glanced down at his hand-drawn map and smiled. He could still hardly believe it. Jebel al Lawz sat on a straight line between the two extremities of his research.

The quest had brought them to this exact spot.

The very center!

(4)

It was still early as the sun inched over the edges of the lower summits.

Adam and his two assistants gradually crept their way down the side of the holy mount toward the fenced area of new green growth below. The place was not guarded, though they continued to move warily.

They reached the outcroppings of lush vegetation. It was exactly as described in the *National Geographic* and *Archaeology Review* articles—completely without explanation, astonishing, beautiful, verdant. As they walked into its midst, they suddenly felt they had entered a tropical paradise.

Adam led the way in silent wonder as they brushed through grasses and shrubbery—not mere scraggly desert varieties but moist and lush and infinitely hued deep greens.

"I don't believe what we're seeing!" said Adam.

"I *wouldn't* have believed it," rejoined Rocky, "without seeing it with my own two eyes."

"I can hardly keep myself from thinking what we *might* be seeing!" added Adam.

Juliet walked behind them, unable to voice the wonder rising in her heart.

Trees were springing up amongst the low growth, in all throughout the several acres probably fifty or more, from seedlings a foot high to four- and five-foot varieties that gave every indication of preparing themselves to get much larger.

They approached the stout, twelve-foot mystery tree.

They paused and gazed upon it with wonder, filled with awe. They could not take their eyes from it. The sight was full of nothing less . . . than *Life*.

This was certainly no baobab. It was unlike any tree they had ever laid eyes on. In some mysterious way it seemed to resemble *every* tree they had ever seen. It was as if all the species of all the trees of the world had somehow gone out into all the earth from this single point of arboral beginnings.

For several long minutes they stood, reverently gazing upon it.

"I suppose we should do what we came to do," sighed Adam at length. "It seems almost a sacrilege at this point. But the scientist in me has to learn what I can."

He set down his bag of equipment, then knelt and removed the large pack from his back.

"If you two will help me, let's take some samples."

Adam readied the drill, then approached, almost trembling. At the ground level, gnarled and twisted roots of great thickness seemed fairly bursting out of the earth, out of which the twelve-inch-thick trunk shot upward. Never had Adam seen a root system quite like it. Though growth was noticed here for the first time only three years ago, both root and trunk appeared unbelievably old.

Adam drilled two separate samples through the trunk as he had learned to do with Dr. Cissna and extracted them in one of the specially designed plastic tubes. By logic he should have seen three to five rings indicating the tree's apparent age.

He stared at the sample a moment. The lines of his face twisted in incredulity.

"This . . . this can't be!" he said softly, almost to himself.

Lines of ring growth were so compact and dense they were impossible to count. Within the short piece he had drilled, his eyes fell on what appeared to be hundreds, perhaps even a *thousand,* lines!

"This is impossible," he repeated, squinting and attempting to begin a count.

He gave up after counting roughly twenty or thirty lines within an eighth-inch space, shaking his head. "It just can't be."

All the while Rocky and Juliet stood watching in silence.

Adam leaned back on his knees and held up the sample for them to take a look. They saw well enough.

"But . . . the tree *can't* be that old," said Rocky.

"I've got an idea," said Adam. "I'll drill into the root. It may be that the root system has protruded up into the trunk, which is what I'm getting a reading of."

He drilled again at ground level, at an angle down into one of the gnarled twistings of root. The bit disappeared and soon reached its full length. Adam withdrew the bit and examined it. The tip had not yet penetrated through to the opposite side of root into the earth.

He removed the sample of wood, screwed an extension onto the increment borer, and repeated the procedure, again with the same result. A strange look came over his face.

"This can't be," he said. "I'm still not penetrating through to earth. *No* root can be so thick!"

Adam now attached every extension he had left and sent the borer yet a third time into the tree's root, turning the auger carefully. The operation took some thirty minutes. By now he was perspiring from the work, and the muscles of his arms were turning to lead. Still no end was to be found. Slowly he withdrew what was now a four-foot core drilling.

"The root system is far more massive than we can investigate with the equipment we possess," said Adam. "For all I can tell, the root might extend down many feet—maybe hundreds of feet—into the depths beneath us."

He paused, shaking his head in continued disbelief.

"I don't know what to say," he added softly. "We may be dealing with something here that makes the baobab and bristlecone pine look like seedlings. I've got to take another sample or two, going in from different angles."

"Aren't you afraid of harming the tree?" asked Juliet

"I have the feeling," said Adam, "that nothing any man could do will destroy *this* tree! In the meantime," he added, "while I'm doing this, why don't the two of you walk about and collect leaves and grass and small branches and twig samples from as many of the plants as you can. We may not get back here. When we start analyzing all this back at the lab, we want to have plenty of samples."

(5)

The monks of St. Catherine's were up for prayers and mass on the second day of their monastic captivity hours before their four troublesome guests. By midmorning, however, all were awake and both Zorin and D'Abernon were growing restless.

An unaccountable feeling told the Swiss woman that something was wrong. What if Livingstone wasn't coming here at all? What if—horrible thought . . . it only now just dawned on her!—what if McCondy of old *hadn't* been struck with sunstroke, but had never intended Sinai as his destination at all?

She immediately sought Zorin.

"There may be a problem," she said.

"There *is* a problem!" he rejoined irritably. "Livingstone's nowhere to be seen."

"We may be waiting for him at the wrong place. I thought you possessed confirmed evidence the destination was Sinai."

"I did. You must have also."

"What if some other place was meant?"

"Meaning what—some *other* Sinai?"

"I only suggest the possibility."

Zorin's face took on a thoughtful expression. Suddenly he spun around and went quickly in search of the abbot.

"Who's your historian!" he demanded.

"Friar Skeggs is in charge of antiquities and research," answered the man timidly.

"Does he know biblical history?"

"As well as any."

"Where will I find him?"

"In the library. Please, don't—"

Already Zorin was gone. D'Abernon quickly followed.

He entered the library already in a rage that so much time had been wasted. Within seconds he had the front of the historian's robe clutched in his fist. Friar Skeggs, however, though momentarily terrified, was not cowed. Notwithstanding his balding head and unimpressive stature, he was a true man, because he was God's man, one who had been growing strong in that humble manhood for many years. He knew something about the invisible warfare that had been waged upon the earth since antiquity. And now he did his best to regain his courage and return the evil man's gaze with stout heart, for the moment of his testing had come.

"I want information!" Zorin said. "I want to know if there are other possible sites of Mount Sinai."

"This has always been considered by scholars the traditional—," began Skeggs.

"I realize that, you fool! But what other sites have been suggested?"

"There are three . . . proposed routes of the Exodus," he answered, struggling for words. "Some have said the mount called Horeb was . . . Jebel Halal to the north of the Sinai."

"I'm not interested in a history lesson!" cried Zorin.

"No, that cannot be it," said D'Abernon. She knew McCondy's movements had not gone in that direction.

"There is one place some have . . . some have conjectured," said the monk, "in Saudi Arabia. But it could not possibly—"

D'Abernon's eyes widened.

*"Saudi Arabia,"* she repeated. "Where in Saudi Arabia?"

"Across the Gulf of Aqaba, but it could not—"

"It's exactly where McCondy was followed!" she exclaimed. "Somehow they've picked up the old fellow's trail."

"Where is this place?" demanded Zorin.

"Due east—perhaps eighty-five or ninety miles," replied the monk. "Archaeologists have been coming and going in recent years, exploring and asking questions—"

Already Zorin had spun on his heels. D'Abernon made haste to follow him.

"Wait," sounded a voice behind them. It was Friar Skeggs. He had found his voice, his valor, and his sonship all at once, and now spoke heroically on behalf of his Father.

Zorin and D'Abernon paused in their step, then turned back to face him. The tone had been one of command, and without forethought they had obeyed. The little monk's eyes stared straight into theirs.

"In the name of God the Father and his son Jesus," said Skeggs in the same strong voice, "I declare that you will harm no hair on the head of whom it is you seek."

Zorin stood for a moment immovable, as one stunned that so slight a man would dare confront him. Chills swept through D'Abernon's body, and she felt a psychic strength drain out of her.

Only a moment did the spell last. Zorin found the movement of his limbs again and now walked forward, hatred gleaming from his eyes. Skeggs returned the stare, praying silently that he would not quail before the enemy.

Zorin reached into his vest pocket and withdrew his .38 automatic. Slowly he lifted it and pointed it directly toward the librarian's forehead. The barrel stopped less than twelve inches away, while Zorin's finger fidgeted with the trigger. For several long seconds the two men stood locked in silent combat.

Suddenly Zorin spun about again and strode hurriedly from the room, replacing the unfired handgun as he went. D'Abernon followed, though as one deflated.

"No wonder we haven't been able to get him . . . to penetrate the haze," she reflected, as if thinking aloud.

"What are you talking about?" said Zorin angrily as they made their way along the corridor.

"He has been protected," replied D'Abernon. "Our hands are tied . . . our hands have been tied all along."

"Bah, that's absurd nonsense! I will find him, and I *will* kill him."

"It's no use," rejoined D'Abernon. "The hedge is up. The enemy's people have summoned forces even we cannot overcome."

"No one can withstand us!"

"Zorin, you are a fool. You have no idea what power exists . . . on *both* sides."

(6)

Inside the lush oasis, the three pilgrims sensed a peace so deep it seemed they were dreaming. Feeling as if they could have remained in the wondrous desert garden indefinitely, at length Adam, Juliet, and Rocky loaded up packs and equipment and headed out of the greenery back up the slope by a slightly different route than that by which they had come.

"We have to climb to the summit," said Adam. "I've got to stand up there. I've got to see the tree growing on top. All I can think of is whether it's similar to any of those down at the base."

"And take a core sample," suggested Juliet.

"Of course."

"Hey, look," said Rocky, pointing off to one side. He trudged ahead. "It's a path up the side of the mountain."

"I see it, though it's faint," said Adam. "Let's take it."

"It looks like it's headed toward the peak," said Juliet.

They fell into single file, Rocky now leading the way up the circuitous track.

For thirty minutes they walked in relative silence. The sun had now begun to warm the earth. All three were tiring and perspiring, and Rocky had dropped to the rear. They had climbed perhaps halfway from the valley floor of the oasis toward the summit, working their way around the opposite side of the mount around many twists and turns, up and downs, beside huge boulders, and up some very rugged terrain.

"Why are so many big roots growing across the path?" said Juliet as she stumbled over one. "I've nearly fallen several times."

(7)

Within minutes of racing out of St. Catherine's library, Zorin had General Pervukhin in tow, and the two headed outside.

D'Abernon located Ciano Bonar. By the time they emerged from the gate, already the General was at the controls of the helicopter revving the engine, with Zorin strapping himself into the seat beside him.

"Are you coming?" Zorin shouted down to the two women.

"I'm not going to let you go alone," D'Abernon replied, "though I assure you we will not find him."

They boarded. Immediately the giant blades began to rotate and quickly increased in speed. In another few seconds their revolutions were invisible. It took but a minute or two more and they were lifting into the air. Instantly they began a steep climb to clear the surrounding mountains of the would-be Sinai.

Once at elevation, they flew screaming over the rocky wasteland toward the coast, then sped over the Gulf of Aqaba at more than a hundred and fifty miles an hour. Within a very few minutes the slopes of Jebel al Lawz loomed off to the left in front of them.

"It's the tallest mountain for miles," said Zorin, pointing to a blackened volcanic-shaped peak some three miles distant. "Head straight for it, General! They're there. I'm sure of it!

(8)

Rocky paused after briefly examining the root Juliet had stumbled upon and turned back toward her and Adam.

"I just had an incredible thought," he said. "If we are right, and Grandpa Harry *was* headed here . . . and if by chance he made it to the mountain . . . then the one thing he would have done was scale the summit."

"Are you saying what I think you're saying?" said Adam.

"That depends on what you think I'm saying." Rocky grinned.

Adam and Juliet glanced at one another.

"That he may have gone along this very path," they said at once.

"We may finally have gotten onto Grandpa Harry's track!" cried Rocky.

"Let's go!" said Juliet with renewed enthusiasm. She struck out up the rocky incline ahead of the two men.

They fell into step behind her in quick march stride.

This time it was Adam who suddenly stopped.

"Hold on!" he exclaimed. "If what you say is true, Rocky, and your great-grandfather did walk this way, then he must have been followed right here . . . and may have been killed on the very slopes of Mount Sinai."

The other two were silent a moment. Each sensed that they had indeed stumbled onto the old archaeologist's trail. As yet, however, they had nothing to substantiate such a claim.

"His body was never found, was it?" said Adam.

"At least not to be made public," replied Rocky.

"Do you think he knew he was being pursued?"

"If so, he was probably trying to get away."

"Maybe running from them up this very path!" suggested Juliet.

"A last pilgrimage toward his final destination."

"And never heard from again."

A thoughtful silence came over them. All at once the same thought occurred to all three.

"The caves!" they exclaimed. "He might have tried to hide in one of these caves!"

Again they broke into a run up the hill. Rocky was as eager now to solve a hundred-year-old murder as Adam was to examine the tree at the summit of the mountain!

Before they had gone far, in the distance a menacing sound intruded into their ears.

Adam turned and glanced toward it.

"Give me those binoculars," he said. Quickly Rocky handed them over. Adam pointed them toward the sound.

"It's a military helicopter," he shouted, "and it's rapidly coming this way."

# thirty-three

# A Rift in Time

(1)

Inside the helicopter the mood after the incident in the monastery library was subdued. Anni D'Abernon said not a word throughout the flight. She had come up against something so powerful—something she had never confronted before that moment when the monk's eyes bored into hers. She had still not altogether recovered.

As powerful as were these servants of the powers of darkness, when commanded they yet had to yield to him who was sovereign over all things in both the heavenly and the earthly realms. As their Master in days of old had been given leave to harass God's servant Job for a season but was not permitted to harm him or take his life, they had likewise now been prevented from interferring in God's plan for his servant Adam Livingstone.

She had accompanied Zorin on this final stage of their mission, but in her heart she knew they would not find him who had become their nemesis, nor would they be able to harm him if they did. Beyond that, the future had now become very obscure to her once keenly occultic vision.

At last she understood why the Dimension had become so quiet.

(2)

Breathing heavily and hoping they had gotten out of sight without being seen, Rocky, Adam, and Juliet sat in total blackness.

They had spotted the cave only moments before the huge helicopter had emerged from behind a slope of the mountain. The screeching of its approach roared in their ears as the chopper whizzed past, its shadow briefly darkening the cave entrance.

"I don't think they saw us." said Rocky. "They're not hovering about."

"Who is it?" asked Juliet.

"Saudis, do you suppose?" asked Rocky.

"I have a feeling it's the same people who have been after us all along," said

Adam. "If they've got a copy of the journal, like you said the other day, they'd know old Harry's movements too."

"They probably came straight here after they discovered we hightailed it out of Cairo," said Rocky.

They listened anxiously to the sound of the helicopter flying back and forth over the mountain, receding then circling again two or three times.

"We may be here awhile," said Adam. "These people have demonstrated remarkable persistence."

"I hope they don't spot the Land Rover under the camouflage net," said Rocky.

"I'm getting cramped," said Juliet. "If we're going to spend the day here, I'm going to stretch out." She inched toward the back of the cave.

"Wait a minute, young lady!" said Adam. "You're not going anywhere until we see what kind of place this is. I don't want you scooting into a nest of snakes."

Adam dug a flashlight from his pack. He now sent a beam of light probing into the blackness behind them.

Suddenly Juliet caught her breath. "Did you see that!" she exclaimed.

"No, what?"

"Give me the light."

Juliet took it and pointed toward a hidden recess among the rocks. "No snakes," she said. Crouching low, she crept toward it. "I'd say it's something that looks far more interesting."

Neither of the two men spoke. Juliet's body momentarily hid the cache from their view. A moment or two later she inched back toward them, dragging something behind her.

She sat back with an expression of triumph all over her face. She shone the light on what she had recovered from the cave's depths—an old, dusty, half-dilapidated rucksack.

"Good job, Juliet!" exclaimed Adam.

Very gently, he felt at it, then turned it carefully over as Juliet kept the light shining upon the newly discovered treasure.

The faint words *Harry McCondy, Peterborough, N.H.* could be read on the inside of one of the flaps.

"I don't believe it!" gasped Rocky.

"You may have just made the first archaeological discovery of your career, Juliet," said Adam.

"Unbelievable," said Rocky, stooping forward and probing tentatively with his fingers as if the slightest touch would turn it all to dust. "One hundred and one years!"

"Well, Rocky," said Adam, "by right of inheritance, I suppose this belongs to you. What do you want to do?"

"Open it, of course. But I'm just a clumsy old detective," he added, now pulling back. "You're the archaeologist—you do the honors."

(3)

Gently Adam proceded to open the rucksack.

He pulled out a canteen and shook it—empty and one hundred years dry. Several antiquated instruments and measuring devices were next, a notecase with a few bills of money and some cards, various small papers, a pair of binoculars, one eyepiece broken out, a Bible with decaying cover, a half-rotted extra shirt, two handkerchiefs, and various other items.

Adam now pulled out a small notebook. At last they had came to the prize they had long sought.

Only the first several pages contained notes. The most lengthy entry had apparently been penned the night before McCondy's disappearance.

Juliet crept close to Adam. Rocky moved closer on the other side. Oblivious now to the sounds of the helicopter outside still seeking their presence, the three pilgrims sat together in wonderment. As Juliet shone the flashlight upon the yellowed paper, Adam read in a quiet, reverent voice:

> *"I am two days out of Cairo. It is late. My campfire has nearly turned to embers. Tomorrow I shall cross into the ancient land of Arabia. If God is with me, at last I shall witness that for which my heart has longed and finally set foot on the slopes of his mountain, ancient Sinai itself.*
>
> *"Though not a soul on the earth of his creation would believe such a claim, for no physical evidence exists to support it, there, I am convinced, God's presence was first revealed to man, to Adam himself.*
>
> *"There—not on the mountain itself, but on the site in the middle of Eden where the mountain later was raised up to hide that Garden of beginnings until the day of its eventual revealing—did the Almighty plant his Tree of Life. Truly was that tree symbolic of the life he breathed into man. It was a tree he miraculously hid both by the uplift of Jebel al Lawz, as it is known today, and by turning the Garden into a desert. But it will blossom again, I am convinced! For there will the sign of preparation for his coming begin!"*

"How could he have known?" said Juliet. "He wrote this a hundred years ago!"

Adam continued reading:

> *"In days of old the place was known both as Horeb and Sinai. To that sacred place, because it represented the center of all things, the center of life, the center of the Garden, God brought his holy men Elijah and Moses, men after his own heart. Though the location has long been obscured to the men who have attempted to find it, he will*

lead others to it, as he has me. For God yet has a purpose for his Garden, his holy mountain, and his sacred life-giving tree, a purpose he will accomplish before the end comes.

"Thus has he kept alive that tree, under the desert, covered over and protected by the mountain, nourished by subterranean waters of Eden, the remnants of the original headwaters spoken of in Genesis. Those underground springs and streams flowed from the rock, the very rock of Rephidim that yet sits between the gulf and the mount for all to see, split from Moses' smiting, hid from all but those with eyes to see.

"The wonder of these sights and the knowledge of their existence have been hidden but kept alive. In the fullness of time the Creator will again reveal his glory to man. The Life of Creation has been kept alive though the Garden was rent asunder by man's sin and by the great rift that God caused to split the earth, hiding the rivers and headwaters, changing the direction of the Nile, turning the Pishon into a sea, and obliterating all evidence of Garden life.

"Yet from that dynamic center of beginnings flowed the Jordan northward, connecting to the Tigris and Euphrates, and flowed the Red Sea and Nile south before the drift of continents so obscured their origins as to make recognition impossible."

In her excitement, Juliet could not keep from interrupting. "It's just like in your computer model!"

Adam continued to read:

"Thenceforward did Adam's descendents wander—northward into Mesopotamia and southward into Africa, as the earth's crust shifted and changed.

"I believe that out of a fragment of that same tree that he caused to blossom forth on the mountain, he spoke in fire to Moses. For the tree yet lived and still gave life. Indeed was it holy ground, for his Presence still occupied the holy place of beginnings:

And the angel of the Lord appeared unto him in a flame of fire out of the midst of a bush: and he looked, and, behold, the bush burned with fire, and the bush was not consumed. And Moses said, I will now turn aside, and see this great sight, why the bush is not burnt. And when the Lord saw that he turned aside to see, God called unto him out of the midst of the bush, and said, Moses, Moses. And he said, Here am I. And he said, Draw not nigh hither: put off thy shoes from off thy feet, for the place whereon thou standest is holy ground.

"We are told that he spoke to the Israelites from the mountain in fire and smoke. In fire did he reveal himself to Moses in the tree. But

*I think Moses' bush was the Tree of Life. That is why the fire did not consume it.*

*"I believe evidence of that same Presence will be revealed to the eyes of man. I believe that tree is still alive, as life still trembles invisibly beneath the holy mountain. One day it shall be revealed. I think the Garden will be found again, and it will be the sign of his coming.*

*"Scriptures perhaps confirm that the Garden is not lost but has only been hidden for a season:.*

> *All the trees of Eden, that were in the garden of God, envied him. Therefore thus saith the Lord God . . . I have therefore delivered him into the hand of the mighty one of the heathen. . . . None of all the trees by the waters exalt themselves for their height, neither shoot up their top among the thick boughs, neither their trees stand up in their height, all that drink water: . . . In the day when he went down to the grave I caused a mourning: I covered the deep for him, and I restrained the floods thereof, and the great waters were stayed: and I caused Lebanon to mourn for him, and all the trees of the field fainted for him. . . . And all the trees of Eden, the choice and best of Lebanon, all that drink water, shall be comforted in the nether parts of the earth. To whom art thou thus like in glory and in greatness among the trees of Eden? Yet shalt thou be brought down with the trees of Eden unto the nether parts of the earth. (Ezekiel 31: 9-18)*
>
> *I the Lord have brought down the high tree, have exalted the low tree, have dried up the green tree, and have made the dry tree to flourish: I the Lord have spoken and have done it. (Ezekiel 17:24)*
>
> *Then shall the trees of the wood sing out at the presence of the Lord, because he cometh to judge the earth. (1 Chronicles 16:33)*
>
> *Thou didst divide the sea by thy strength: . . . Thou didst cleave the fountain and the flood: thou driedst up mighty rivers. (Psalm 74:13, 15)*
>
> *In the midst of the street of it, and on either side of the river, was there the tree of life, which bare twelve manner of fruits, and yielded her fruit every month: and the leaves of the tree were for the healing of the nations. (Revelation 22:2)*

*"Such revelation will come before the new millennium. I pray perhaps my own eyes may be privileged to witness a foreshadowing*

*of that great revelation. Tomorrow my steps shall take me there, and I shall see these sacred and wondrous things of which I write.*

*"But men of evil intent would destroy what God has revealed."*

Adam paused. He glanced up toward Juliet, then toward Rocky.

"Can all this be possible?" said Rocky. "I can hardly believe what I'm hearing!"

"I am learning not to be skeptical of anything!" said Adam. "When I began this quest, I don't know if I *really* even believed that the Garden of Eden ever existed at all. Yet here we are sitting in a cave in the middle of the Arabian Desert nearly at the top of a volcano, asking ourselves if surrounding this place and stretching for hundreds, perhaps thousands, of miles once existed the most lush garden in the world, the very birthplace of man."

(4)

Above them, Halder Zorin's eyes scanned the mountain and every inch of the countryside surrounding it with powerful binoculars.

But he beheld no forms of life. All he could make out was desert. He had no eyes to see, as D'Abernon who sat beside him, knew he would not. For Life did not exist within them.

They stood on grass. The deep blue sky was overhead, and the air that blew gently on their faces was that of a day in early summer. Not far away from them rose a grove of trees, thickly leaved, but under every leaf there peeped out the gold or faint yellow or purple or glowing red of fruits such as no one has seen in our world. But the Dwarfs were sitting very close together in a little circle facing one another. They never looked or took notice. They couldn't see anyone, for they were blind in the dark.

"But it isn't dark, you stupid Dwarfs. Can't you see? Look up! Look round! Can't you see the sky and the trees and the flowers?"

"You see," said Aslan. "They will not let us help them. They have chosen cunning instead of belief. Their prison is only in their minds, yet they are in that prison; and so afraid of being taken in that they cannot be taken out. But come, children. I have other work to do."

He went to the Door and they all followed him. He raised his head and roared, "Now it is time!" then louder, "Time!"; then so loud that it could have shaken the stars, "TIME." The Door flew open.

(5)

Rocky now pulled out his copy of his great-grandfather's journal and read aloud again the poem that comprised the final entry.

*"Rejoice! millennial saints—the sign is given.*
  *Life sprouts at the center . . . the Tree is revealed!*
*Crowning eons of turmoil, a day of rest is risen.*
  *Reconciliation is complete! The rift is healed!"*

*"There will flower the sign,"* repeated Adam softly.

*"A wonder long concealed,"* mused Juliet.

Even as they sat in the darkness of the ancient cave, a heavenly veil was being pulled back. In the appointed time, the original rift in Eden, made provision for by the Cross, would indeed be healed, and, as McCondy had written, reconciliation would be complete.

A lengthy silence followed.

"Listen—I think the helicopter is gone," said Juliet.

(6)

"We've got to get the rest of the way up the mountain and take samples from the tree up there," said Adam rising. "And its roots," he added, almost as an afterthought.

Again the three found themselves looking at one another in sudden wide-eyed awareness.

*"Roots!"* they exclaimed.

"We were stumbling over roots all the way up the mountain."

"The whole mountain is covered with roots . . . *big* roots!"

"But except for down at the bottom, there are no plants anywhere, except for wiry little shrubs."

"That's just it—don't you see? They're all part of the same root system!"

"The entire mountain."

"Oh, my goodness—what if it's all from one original tree?"

"We've got to drill core samples of the roots up and down the mountain and from the tree at the top. If they're all interconnected . . . I don't even dare imagine it!"

✦  ✦  ✦

Three hours later, exhausted but exhilarated, the three pilgrims tramped toward their Land Rover. There had been no more sign of the helicopter since its disappearance.

They gazed back toward the mountain, half shaking their heads in continued wonder.

"We've got to get back to Cairo with these samples," said Adam. "We'll hurry on to London. What we're carrying may be a more important archaeological and spiritual discovery than Noah's ark and the tomb of Tutankhamen and

Lucy and all the rest put together! This will be the most exciting lab work of my life."

"I don't want to put a damper on your eagerness, but we'll have to drive at night," said Rocky, injecting the euphoria of the discovery with practicality. "They're still out there somewhere. And we'll also have to ditch the boat."

# thirty-four

# Sudden Change in Plans

(1)

Two days later, Adam Livingstone, Rocky McCondy, and Juliet Halsay checked into the Ramses Hilton Hotel—across the city from the Nile Gardens—anxious for a bath, a warm meal, and a soft bed—in that order. Adam was eager to get back to London, and paid for the rooms for only one night.

Exhilarated in spirit, all three were nevertheless spent—physically and emotionally. For the moment, fear of being pursued was not on their minds.

"Okay," said Adam, handing them their room keys. "Separate rooms all the way around—even for you and me, Rocky. Let's all take a hot bath, change into fresh clothes, and meet back for dinner—" Adam glanced at his watch—"it's three forty-five now," he said. "What shall we say . . . around six?"

"Tell you what," said Rocky, beginning to realize well enough how things stood between Adam and Juliet, "I'm beat. I'm going to my room, take a bath, take a nap, then order room service. I think I'll see if I can find an old detective flick on TV."

"A busman's holiday, eh?"

"Yep. You two kids enjoy your dinner. I'll see you in the morning."

Adam looked at Juliet with a smile. "Shall we make it seven-thirty then? Somehow that seems more romantic than six!"

(2)

Juliet and Adam walked into the hotel restaurant. For Juliet Halsay, the place was full of romance and happiness. This had to be the most wonderful and picturesque place in the whole world.

The two were not dressed as prince and princess. They had no clothes with them that would have sufficed for such a lofty purpose. But Adam could dress in khaki from head to foot like Gilbert Bowles and be none the less a prince in Juliet's eyes. She had fallen through her own little Alice-like rabbit hole—out of reality and into an enchanted world all her own.

The ceiling fan made a light whirring hum, which fit exactly with the strains playing through the restaurant's speakers.

At Adam's request they had been placed at a table near the open-air veranda. Warm, fragrant breezes drifted toward them. Juliet could see the wide expanse of the Nile shimmering in the glow of the rising moon, reflecting the lights of the city on the opposite bank. Like the Thames, it was so much prettier at night.

Adam pulled out a chair for her. She had always thought of it as an awkward gesture, not knowing exactly when to put her weight down, all the time imagining being shoved headlong into the center of the table. But Adam handled it with such a graceful motion that suddenly she was seated comfortably without quite realizing what had happened.

Juliet glanced around. Being here alone with Adam, everything had taken on a wonderful glow of bliss that only being in love could produce.

Yes, she was in love. In the back of her mind practicality suggested all the impossibilities. But for this evening, she would let the dream continue!

She brought her gaze back to their own table. A single candle stood in the center, flickering occasionally from the outdoor breeze but managing to remain alight.

"What are you thinking about?" said Adam, smiling with the smile that had melted many a woman's heart in its day. This was the first occasion, however, that his own heart was simultaneously in danger of becoming entangled. "You look far away."

"It is all . . . so wonderful!" exclaimed Juliet with a sigh. "I can't believe I'm here."

"Shall I pinch you?"

"Don't you dare!"

"So what were you thinking about?"

"My mind is full . . . of so many things—the discovery out there, Africa, all I've seen, crossing Aqaba in that little boat—"

"Were you scared?" Adam smiled.

"Only at first. But how could I possibly be frightened with you there with me?"

"What else?"

"Rocky, and the journal, everything we read in Grandpa Harry's notebook in the cave, the tree . . . oh, Adam, why are you pressing me?" she laughed. "I'm thinking about *everything* that's happened, all I've seen, all the places I've been in such a short time, all the people I've met."

"Nobody else?" Adam's questioning smile now turned mischievous.

"Well, let me see . . . I suppose I should be thinking about Aunt Andrea, and my mum—"

"Juliet!"

She laughed and Adam joined in. They found it easy to laugh together.

"Oh, Adam, of course—*you!* You're in *all* my thoughts, don't you know?"

Adam gazed across the table. His eyes held hers for a moment. Slowly he reached across the table and took her hand.

"Juliet," he began, "I know there's never a good time to say the kind of thing I want to tell you."

Juliet's neck was suddenly hot. She knew she was getting red! She hoped it didn't show in the candlelight.

"For a long time," Adam went on, "I suppose I took you for granted. I don't mean in a bad way. I just mean you were *there,* in the background—do you know what I mean?"

Juliet nodded, but with effort. What was Adam going to say?

"And I was busy with my work, and all that was happening . . . and, of course, there was Candace," he added.

*Oh, this is really too awful!* thought Juliet. *Too wonderfully, deliciously, agonizingly awful!*

"It was all so different when you got to Africa. I realized once you arrived that I wouldn't have wanted to go any further without you. I knew that you were a friend, a part of the team. And then came that night—you remember—outside the camp down at Olduvai, the night after your brainstorm that put the whole Eden research into perspective . . . but I don't suppose even then I . . ."

Adam stopped and let out a long sigh.

"This is harder than I thought it would be!" he said, laughing a little. Juliet tried to laugh with him, but her throat was too dry.

And he still held her hand. Her *perspiring* hand!

"What I'm trying to get around to saying," he went on, "is that—"

All at once the waiter appeared. In the center of the table he set down a huge steaming plate of rice piled high with vegetables. In the nick of time they quickly withdrew their hands. Embarrassed, Juliet turned away.

The waiter continued to pile the table with food, talking boisterously with Adam throughout the process.

When at last he was gone, their talk turned to the food. They began serving themselves. Gradually the conversation drifted into other channels, Adam telling himself he would get back to more serious and personal matters when they were through.

By nine-fifteen dinner was over. They rose. Adam led the way onto the open veranda. It led down a few steps into a lit garden. They strolled about casually, saying little. Much was on their minds. But Adam could not surmount the difficulty of re-creating the prior mood. When they arrived back up on the veranda, the waiter appeared. He had been looking for them.

"Mr. Livingstone," he said, "you have a long-distance telephone call."

"Where can I take it?"

The waiter led him to a phone.

The voice on the other end of the line could not have been more unexpected. "Livingstone . . . Gilbert Bowles here."

"Just a moment . . . please," said Adam.

Adam handed the waiter the telephone. "Can you please have this transferred up to my room?"

Adam turned to Juliet and led her toward the lobby. "I don't know what this is about," he said, "but it could take some time. I'm afraid I'm going to have to say good-night. Let's walk upstairs."

The elevator ride was awkwardly silent. There was so much both wanted to say. They exited on the floor where their rooms were located, then parted—Adam to his mysterious call, Juliet to finish the enchanted evening in her dreams.

(3)

"Sir Gilbert—this is a surprise," said Adam, once the call had been put through to his room.

"As much to me, Livingstone—believe me—as it is to you."

"I apologize for the delay. What can I do for you, Sir Gilbert?"

"It's what I may be able to do for you."

"I'm listening. By the way, how did you track me here?"

"I've got spies everywhere, Livingstone," laughed Bowles, trying to brush off the question. "More than that, I know where you've been, Adam—at that mountain off in Saudi Arabia." This much was an educated bluff on the part of the two who at that moment stood on either side of the ponderous archaeologist whom they had coerced into making the call. Livingstone's response would reveal whether their hunch was correct.

"Indeed you must have eyes everywhere, Sir Gilbert," said Adam, growing more cautious.

"You know the mountain I'm speaking of, the one they call Jebel al Lawz?"

"I am familiar with it."

"I've been out there today myself, Livingstone," said Bowles. "Didn't know I was following you, did you?"

"No . . . no, I didn't," said Adam. His voice took on a more serious tone. Being traced to the hotel was bad enough. He didn't like the implications.

"Well, I was. I found something you missed—something that could be huge. Here's the part you're not going to believe. I want you to be the one to make the discovery, to break the news."

"That's not like you, Sir Gilbert."

"I know you've gotten a little religious lately. This thing I found has religion written all over it—ancient religion. If it turns out to be what I think it may be—who knows, maybe even I shall change *my* mind."

"That really doesn't sound like you, Sir Gilbert!"

"Yeah, well, sometimes a man's got to do what he's got to do. Anyway, I want you to have it."

"What is the discovery?" asked Adam.

"Can't tell you that. I'll have to show you. I will say this much—it may prove there was an encampment of people at the foot of the mountain and that they had some kind of idol or god in the shape of a golden calf. Sound interesting?"

"Of course it does."

"Then you be here tomorrow morning, because there's something else you missed, too, that might have bearing on your Eden project. I can't say more. Eleven o'clock ought to give you time to charter a plane down to Al Humaydah. That's where I am tonight. Then get yourself a jeep and drive down to the mountain. The fellow at the hotel will rent you one. It's only fifty, sixty miles. I'll be there between eleven and noon. I'll meet you in front of the wire fence—you remember, the enclosed area at the foot of the slope where all that stuff is growing."

"I know the place."

"What do you think that is, anyway—some kind of botanical experiment the Saudis are conducting?"

"Surely you've read the articles."

"I don't believe what I've read. The Saudis are behind it somehow."

"Well, I don't know, Sir Gilbert."

"Can't figure why it'd be fenced off. Anyway, you be there, Livingstone." The line went dead.

In his room Adam was left puzzling over this very unlikely turn of events.

Meanwhile, Sir Gilbert Bowles let out a long sigh. "You can put away the gun now," he said. "I did exactly as you said."

(4)

Adam rang both other rooms at six o'clock the next morning. He told Rocky and Juliet to come to his room as soon as they could.

When they were gathered, he explained the situation.

"What can I do but go?" he said. "He made it sound important *and* urgent."

"I don't like it," said Rocky.

"I'm suspicious too, but I've got to go. We have to know what he's found, *whatever* he's up to."

Adam turned to Juliet.

"Juliet," he said, "you've got to take our samples back to the lab. Rocky, I think maybe you ought to stay here in Cairo, just in case I get into some kind of jam."

"I can't leave you," protested Juliet. "You don't expect me to go alone?"

"You're going back to England where you'll be safe. The sooner you're away from here, the better I'll feel."

"Why can't I just wait for you?"

"Time is important here. We can't risk their destroying the evidence. We've got to be certain of what is going on . . . we've got to know what we've discovered . . . as soon as we can. Besides, I'll be less than a day behind you."

"When are you leaving?"

"Immediately," replied Adam. "I made a call just a few minutes ago. I managed to arrange to charter a small plane down to Al Humaydah for the day. I'll find out what Bowles has, then get back to London. I'll be down there in two hours, drive out to the mountain, drive back, return to Cairo, rejoin you, Rocky, and we'll fly home. We'll all three be enjoying one of Mrs. Graves' English breakfasts at Sevenoaks twenty-four hours from now."

"I'll do whatever you think best," said Juliet."

"You and Rocky pack and crate up everything carefully, especially the samples."

Adam paused.

"Come to think of it, since we have so many samples, package them in duplicate—in two sets—just to be on the safe side. I don't trust the airline baggage system. We don't want any of these things lost. Juliet, you take half the samples with you. Rocky, you ship the others by two-day courier. Make sure the rucksack and the core samples are well packed."

Rocky nodded.

"Rocky will take you to the airport and put you on a plane," said Adam to Juliet. "Rocky, you call Scott and alert him when to be at Heathrow to pick up Juliet. Then you wait here. I'll be in touch if I learn anything. Then I'll see you when I get back from this Bowles' affair later this afternoon. We'll head for London this evening."

Adam approached Juliet and took her in his arms.

"Everything's going to be fine," he said softly. "Scott will take you back to the house. Why—you should be there by early afternoon. You and your aunt can catch up on everything. Who knows, you might even have time to start running the analyses on these cores. We should be there later tonight. If not, I'll ring—I promise."

Juliet melted into his embrace. She hated to be away from him . . . but it would only be for twenty-four hours at the most.

# thirty-five

# Disappearance!

(1)

Adam had never done so much smooth talking as he'd done recently.

His finances were a mess. He couldn't get cash. He couldn't write checks. If he didn't have a reputation that was recognized even in remote parts of the world and a stash of hundred-pound traveler's checks sewn into the lining of his briefcase for an emergency, he'd have been in trouble.

There was going to be a lot of sorting out to do when he reached home. *If* he reached home. In the meantime, he had to get to the bottom of whatever was going on.

He glanced out the window of the two-seater Cessna at the sparse ground of the Sinai Peninsula. They had driven over it such a short time ago on their way to the discovery of Adam Livingstone's lifetime. Now he was flying back for a return engagement—this time to meet Sir Gilbert Bowles, of all people.

Adam's thoughts drifted toward his friends. He prayed everything would go smoothly on their ends. Praying was a new activity, but his concern, especially for Juliet, made it as natural as thinking about her.

In another two or three hours he would know what Bowles had found. In the meantime, he might as well enjoy the view.

(2)

At the British Airways ticket counter, Rocky McCondy and Juliet Halsay stood speaking with the agent in mounting frustration.

"I am sorry, Mr. McCondy," the woman was saying, looking up from her computer terminal, "at this late notice, all direct flights to England today are full."

"What *can* you do to get Miss Halsay to London?" said Rocky.

"I do have an opening on a flight . . . tomorrow afternoon," said the lady as she examined the computer.

"How can she arrive there *today?*"

"Hmm . . . let's see, there are several routing possibilities." A few clicks on her keyboard followed. "I see a flight through Paris, four-hour layover . . . arriving Heathrow this evening at ten."

"Too late—what else?"

"We could go through Rome—no, that would mean a night layover. Still checking . . . this looks like a good possibility. We have a flight that leaves Cairo in an hour for Amsterdam. It would require connecting to a Virgin Atlantic flight from Amsterdam to Heathrow two hours later. Still it would get Miss Halsay into Heathrow at 2:55 this afternoon."

"What do you think, Juliet?" asked Rocky. "Are you up to a plane change?"

"I can manage it. Anything to be back at Sevenoaks!"

"All right, then, book the flight," said Rocky to the ticket attendant. "Can we check her bags straight through?"

"I'm sorry, Miss Halsay, you will have to claim everything in Amsterdam, since you will be changing airlines, and recheck them."

"I can manage it," said Juliet.

(3)

Even as he sat in the taxi riding back into Cairo from the airport, a feeling of disquiet gnawed at Rocky McCondy's gut.

He'd been playing the role of archaeologist's flunky so long he'd almost forgotten he was a private eye. Now that he was alone, his detective's personna again began to assert itself.

He had a growing sense that some foul stench was nearby—a gut feeling that said something was wrong.

Any private cop worth his salt learned to trust his hunches. Rocky trusted his. This particular one said that someone was playing them for suckers!

As soon as he got back to the hotel, he'd call Scott and give him the details of Juliet's Virgin flight. Otherwise, there wasn't much he could do. Adam was on a plane heading east. Juliet was on one heading west. And here he was stuck between them in Cairo.

Twenty minutes later Rocky ran into the Ramses, checked for messages—there were none—and hurried up to his room. He placed the call to Sevenoaks. But speaking with Scott didn't alleviate the qualms in his belly.

"Scott, you and Jen get there okay?" he asked.

"No problems. After I left Olduvai, that is." Scott told him about the visit from the terrorists. "Most of our supplies are ruined."

Rocky's brow wrinkled in concern. "And Jen?" he said.

"She and Figg have safely arrived. What's up on your end?"

Rocky explained. He gave Scott Juliet's flight information.

"I don't know—I don't like it," said Scott. "My senator friend has been acting peculiar lately too. I've had a couple very curious telephone calls. Though I'm not sure it ties in."

"There are strange things afoot, that's for sure," said Rocky.

He replaced the phone and sat down to think.

Last night's call to Adam from Bowles. That's what started it. From what he knew of Bowles, the call didn't fit. Handing over an important discovery wasn't the guy's style.

He'd see if he could find out exactly where the call had come from. He picked up the phone again and called downstairs.

"Hello, this is Adam Livingstone," said Rocky, doing his best to disguise his voice. It ought to be good enough to fool the Egyptian desk clerk. "I'm in my friend McCondy's room. I had a telephone call last evening about ten-thirty. Could you please tell me the country of origin of that call?"

Rocky waited.

When the man spoke again, Rocky's eyes lit with confirmation.

"England!" he exclaimed. A few seconds later he set the phone down.

"I thought as much!" he exclaimed, already scurring about the room gathering his things, including the botanical samples. *Sorry, Adam,* he said to himself. *I don't have time for the courier! We're going to have to trust the airline on this one!*

Two minutes later he was flying down the stairs without bothering to wait for the elevator.

He would find a way to Heathrow if he had to stand in every standby line of every flight for the rest of the morning! He had to get to London before Juliet did.

There wasn't a second to lose!

(4)

There was only one hotel in Al Humaydah on the Saudi coast of the Gulf of Aqaba. Rocky would call it a flea trap.

As Adam approached, he thought he'd been drawn back into a 1940s B movie staring Humphrey Bogart. Although it did seem a fitting place, he thought with a wry smile, for Gilbert Bowles to have spent the night. His colleague would add just the right flair to the surroundings.

The misgivings in Adam's stomach were growing stronger by the minute.

He approached the run-down building, which looked as if it had been constructed a hundred years ago out of the very sand of the Sahara itself and then had allowed the wind and elements to gradually eat away at it ever since.

An undefined sense of isolation swept through him. How far away from everyone he felt!

He was in the middle of nowhere, his money nearly depleted, no friends nearby, only a rented airplane.

Suddenly it seemed a very precarious arrangement. Coming here was perhaps not the brightest of things to do. He wasn't sure he liked what he was feeling.

Adam strode into the hotel.

"Has my friend Gilbert Bowles left for the day?" he asked a sloppily dressed bearded man who stood disinterestedly behind what passed for a counter.

"Bowles?" repeated the man.

"Yes, he spent the night here."

"We have no Bowles," said the man in scarcely decipherable broken English.

"Gilbert Bowles," repeated Adam. "Last night—here in this hotel? He said you could rent me a jeep or truck for the day."

"Bowles . . . no Bowles!"

"Perhaps he used another name," suggested Adam. "A large man—a very large man." He gestured widely with his hands.

"No Bowles . . . no fat man. *No* guest last night. You first in three day."

Adam's misgivings now gave way to outright panic!

"I need a phone!" he said to the man.

The clerk pointed to his desk.

"Will you place a call for me? It is urgent."

The man stood staring blankly.

Adam hastily pulled out several bills from the few he had left. He slapped two down on the counter. The man's greedy eyes lit.

"I see you understand my English well enough now!" said Adam. "This is twice what the call will cost. Now get me the Ramses Hilton Hotel in Cairo and be quick about it!"

The man placed the call, not once removing his eyes from the waiting cash. When the connection was made, Adam grabbed the phone. The clerk simultaneously trousered the bills.

"This is Adam Livingstone," said Adam. "I received a call last night, there at the Ramses. I must know where that call came from."

"I do not understand, Mr. Livingstone. Have you forgotten the information so soon?"

"I don't know what you're talking about. Just tell me where the call was made?"

"As I told you only a short while ago, Mr. Livingstone, the call came in from London."

Already Adam was out the door in a dead sprint back toward the small airstrip where his chartered Cessna had landed only fifteen minutes earlier.

How could he have been so stupid to leave Juliet by herself? He loved her.

Suddenly that fact dawned on him with powerful force. She wasn't just a part of his household or even his research team . . . he *loved* Juliet Halsay!

And he had flown off into the middle of nowhere on a wild-goose chase . . . leaving her alone!

(5)

At the Virgin Atlantic check-in counter in Amsterdam, Juliet Halsay stood nervously waiting. A perplexed agent stared at the ticket she had just been handed.

"Is there . . . some problem?" asked Juliet.

"There does seem . . . hmm, let me double-check here."

The lady punched a rapid barrage of keys, then stared at her computer monitor.

"Yes, I'm still getting the same thing . . . it seems your ticket has been cancelled."

"Cancelled!" exclaimed Juliet, her heart jumping up into her throat. "Can . . . can you issue me a new one?"

"Let me see . . ."

The agent again busied herself at the keyboard.

"It seems we do have several seats still available."

Juliet sighed with relief.

"Shall I reticket you?"

"Yes, please!"

The lady proceded to do so.

"How will you be paying, Miss Halsay?"

"What about the other ticket? It *was* paid for, wasn't it? Can't you just . . . I didn't think I would have to pay *again.*"

"The other ticket was cancelled. It shows as *Cancelled—no refund.*"

"All right," replied Juliet. Adam could sort it out later. She set her purse on the counter and dug into it for the credit card Crystal had given her. She handed it to the lady.

Quickly the woman ran the metalic strip through the card processor. Her eyebrows wrinkled slightly as she stared at the small machine on her desk. She tried the card again, now staring intently to see if the same message reappeared a second time.

"I am sorry, Miss . . . wait just one moment please." The lady turned and walked to a wall phone a few yards away. She turned her back. Juliet could not hear what transpired.

"Security," said the agent softly, "this is Virgin Atlantic ticket counter. I've got someone trying to use a card that comes up on my computer as stolen. There's a note saying dangerous, apprehend with caution, with a number to call."

The woman returned to Juliet.

"Have patience a moment, Miss Halsay," she said with a warm smile, "it's being looked into. I'll just keep watching my computer."

"What's . . . being looked into?" said Juliet, the lump in her throat tightening.

"Your card doesn't seem to want to go through, that's all."

Less than two minutes later, suddenly Juliet felt a grip on both her elbows. Turning frantically, she realized she was in the clutches of two uniformed guards.

"You'll have to come with us, Miss."

"But why . . . what . . . where are you taking me?"

Already she was being led forcefully away. Two additional guards followed, carrying her luggage and boxes.

Juliet was led to a room, taken inside with her things, then left alone. A deadbolt sounded in the door behind her.

Thirty minutes later, the lock clanked again. Juliet spun around in panic. The door opened. A tall, white-haired man walked in, dressed in an expensive suit and bearing an air of impersonal authority.

"Miss Halsay," he said, "my name is Rupert Vaughan-Maier. You will please come with me."

Juliet glanced toward her things, her face white.

"Leave them," said Vaughan-Maier. "They will be taken care of."

(6)

It was already late in the day when Adam reached the Ramses Hilton.

He hurried up to Rocky's room. No reply came to his knock. He rushed back downstairs.

"Have you seen Mr. McCondy," he asked the desk clerk, "the American?"

"He left several hours ago."

"Where did he go?"

"To the airport, I believe, Mr. Livingstone."

Adam glanced hurriedly around, then ran to the pay telephone. It took several minutes to get through to England.

"Mrs. Graves, it's Adam Livingstone," he said when the call was completed. "I need to talk to either Scott or Crystal . . . or Jen if she's there. It's extremely urgent."

He waited, moving about on his feet in obvious agitation.

"Crystal!" exclaimed Adam into the phone when Crystal answered, "what's up—is Scott there?"

"He's on his way to the airport . . . again."

"What do you mean . . . again?"

"He drove out earlier to meet Juliet's flight. But she wasn't on it."

"Oh, no! I had a feeling. . . ."

"Then Mr. McCondy called to tell us *he* would be arriving at three-fifteen."

"And?"

"Scott just called me a little bit ago. Mr. McCondy arrived okay. They are on their way back."

"Any word from Juliet?"

"Not a trace, Adam . . . I'm sorry."

A knot was already forming in the pit of his stomach.

"Stay by the phone, Crystal. I may need you to wire me some money from the emergency cash fund. Something's gone haywire with our credit card."

"What are you going to do?"

"Get there as soon as I can find a flight!"

# thirty-six

# The House of the Rose and Cross

(1)

Adam arrived back in Sevenoaks at 9:35 the following morning, frantic over Juliet's disappearance.

He had hardly slept all night, bouncing from city to city on standby flights as he maneuvered his way gradually toward London. Scott and Rocky met him at Gatwick. Rocky explained his own premature departure from Cairo, which had accomplished nothing but getting him back to London eighteen hours ahead of Adam.

"Still no word?" said Adam, his voice raspy and full of fatigue. His face was haggard and worn. Bags drooped under his eyes.

"There's been a call," said Scott. "It's not much. The guy's supposed to call back. Mrs. Graves took the call and will fill you in."

He recounted the brief exchange.

The moment they arrived at the estate, everyone in the house, including the normally taciturn Beeves, surrounded and smothered Adam in hugs and well wishes as though he were a returning conquering hero. A great deal had been happening in the past few months, and they all felt better having the master at home. An undercurrent of anxiety, however, showed clearly upon everyone's face.

Gradually they stepped back.

"All right, Mrs. Graves," said Adam, "I want to hear about the call straight from you. Every word."

"Well, sir," replied the housekeeper, more fretful than anyone over the apparent abduction of her niece, "I answered, and the man said he wanted to talk to you."

"Exactly, Mrs. Graves," interrupted Adam. "Tell me his words *exactly.*"

"'Get me Livingstone,' sir—that's what he said . . . 'Get me Livingstone.'"

Adam nodded. "Go on, Mrs. Graves."

"I said, 'He's not at home, sir.' And he said, 'Well, you tell him I got what he's looking for.' Then he hung up."

"That's all?"

She nodded.

"Nothing more?"

"Nothing, sir?"

"Anything to distinguish the caller, Mrs. Graves?"

"Not that I noticed, sir."

"He was English . . . American . . . ?"

"It was a Scottish accent, sir, now that I recall."

Adam nodded. The fact might mean nothing, but it was something.

Adam glanced at Rocky and Scott, then around to Crystal and Jen and the others, and shrugged. "Well," he said, "I think I'll go upstairs and take a shower, while you, Mrs. Graves, make some tea. After that, either the man will call again . . . or I'll take a nap."

Adam was scarcely dry and but half dressed when suddenly his consciousness exploded into revelation.

He tore out of the bathroom with bare feet and bare chest, shirt in hand. He ran into the kitchen where all the others were seated. Mrs. Graves' eyes opened like saucers to see her master in such condition.

"Rocky, Scott . . . how could I have overlooked it!" he cried, throwing on his shirt and fumbling with the buttons. "*Bowles* is the one who called me and sent me on that wild-goose chase. Whatever his role in this, he knows something. Let's go!"

Already Scott and Rocky were headed for the door as Adam flew back upstairs for his shoes.

"What about the tea?" said Mrs. Graves. "And, Mr. McCondy . . . your coffee."

"It'll have to wait, Mrs. Graves," replied Rocky over his shoulder as he disappeared from the room. "We'll be back!"

(2)

Sir Gilbert Bowles rarely felt intimidated—by man, beast, or conscience.

But he was getting close to that point now on account of two out of the three. The moment they were inside Bowles' home, Adam had questioned his colleague as calmly as he was capable of. Within seconds, however, his American friend unceremoniously shoved him aside to take over the interrogation.

"Look, Bowles," Rocky said angrily, climbing into the archaeologist's huge face, "I don't believe you're telling us all you know! I can play rough if I have to . . . and believe me, if you don't come clean, that's exactly what I'll do!"

"I know nothing," repeated Bowles. "I had a gun pointed to my head! Look, Livingstone," he added, turning toward Adam with an imploring expression, "I know you and I've had our differences. But I'd never do anything like this— you've got to believe me. I'm no criminal, whatever you think of me."

"These people are murderers, Sir Gilbert," rejoined Adam. "Whatever your intent, the matter is serious."

"They had a gun pointed at my head, I tell you. They told me exactly what to say. I've never even been to those places they were talking about."

It was silent a moment. Bowles' face suddenly looked old and fat, with its bulging eyes and hanging jowls. The look of anxiety in his eyes was real enough. Adam believed the pathetic man was telling the truth. For a fleeting second, he almost felt sorry for him.

But the next instant he remembered why they were here. He would have to let his compassion express itself at a future date. First he had to find Juliet.

"Who were they, Sir Gilbert?"

"I've told you already—two men and a woman. I've never seen them before. Business types. Executives. Gray-haired man, slight accent. Tall muscular lady. A third man, slightly balding, shorter than average, purebred Englishman—hey, wait a minute!" he exclaimed. "I just remembered where I've seen the fellow before!"

"Which one?"

"The Englishman."

"Where?" cried Adam.

"At that garden affair at Buckingham in your honor, Livingstone. I saw him arrive with your friend, Lady Candace. She was on his arm."

Short . . . balding!

*"Lord Montreux!"* Adam exclaimed.

Adam, Rocky, and Scott ran from the house, leaving Sir Gilbert Bowles staring after them in mingled relief and bewilderment.

(3)

Rocky and Adam walked toward the door of the Montreux estate of Swanspond.

Scott waited in the car, already on the phone to Captain Thurlow of Scotland Yard.

Adam sent the large iron knocker rapping loudly on the door. As he did, Rocky glanced about, noting the symbolic engraving above the door. His expression darkened. He nudged Adam and pointed to it. He was about to speak, when the door opened.

"Phelps, I have to see Lord Montreux immediately!" said Adam, walking inside without benefit of invitation. Rocky followed.

"I'm sorry, Mr. Livingstone, my lord is away at present."

"Where is he?"

"My lord did not confide that to me, sir."

"Then I shall speak to Miss Montreux."

"Lady Montreux is not feeling well, sir, and I am afraid she is not up to—"

"Look, Phelps," Adam finally exploded, "get your sleepy legs into gear and tell her to get up here immediately! On second thought," he added "I'll go myself!" Adam did not await further answer or action but sprinted up the stairs and off down the long corridor toward Candace's room, Rocky chugging after him.

He banged two or three times on the door with his fist.

"Go away," came a voice from inside.

"Candace . . . it's Adam—are you decent?"

"Yes, but—"

She had no opportunity to say more. The door crashed open. Adam and the strange American burst in, faces red.

"Candace, where is your father?" said Adam.

"I don't—"

"Candace!" he interrupted, "I'm in no mood for beating around the bush. I want to know where your father is!"

"I don't know—at one of his Lodge things, I think."

"What Lodge . . . where?"

"Oh, Adam, please . . . I don't know. I didn't know they were going to take her. I'm sorry, Adam . . . I didn't realize—"

*"What do you know?* Taken who—they have Juliet, don't they?"

"Yes, but Daddy wouldn't tell me anything. I never saw her . . . I just heard him talking on the phone and he said your name, so I picked up another phone and heard a man with a thick accent . . . and then I heard him say *Halsay* . . . and then that was all . . . oh, Adam, please—I would tell you if I knew. I didn't know any of this was going to happen!"

She broke into tears and sobbed. Adam saw further questioning was useless.

"Let's go, Adam," said Rocky, turning and heading for the door.

"Adam . . . Adam, please!" called Candace, looking up after him. "Adam . . . I did it all for you . . . for us!"

Adam paused and turned. He stared at the piteous form on the bed.

"For *me!*" he said incredulously.

"For *us,* Adam . . . for you . . . so you could be part of Daddy's world. It was what he wanted for you."

Adam continued to stare in mingled horror and pity. A tense silence followed.

"It's not a world any of us should *want* to be part of, Candace," he replied.

Rocky yanked on his arm and pulled him away. The next instant they were sprinting along the corridor back toward the front door.

Once outside, Rocky stopped, turned, and pointed up to the emblem.

"See that, Adam—it's the rose and the cross. Know what it means?"

Adam shook his head.

"It's the ancient mystery symbol of Rosicrucianism, one of the secret societies connected to the Illuminati. The same symbol was above the entry to the Nile Gardens."

"I remember it now!" exclaimed Adam.

"You've heard of the Scottish Rite—it's connected too. Whoever these people are who have been after you and who have Juliet, they are high up the chain of command."

The two men stood gazing at the symbol a moment.

"Scottish Rite . . . ," mused Adam thoughtfully.

Only a second or two longer it remained silent. Suddenly they looked at one another, eyes shooting open wide.

"It was a Scottish accent, sir!" exclaimed Rocky, imitating Mrs. Graves' voice. "A *Scottish* accent!"

(4)

The room where she sat was pitch black . . . and cold.

Juliet hadn't an idea in the world where she was. Since Amsterdam she had hardly slept.

They had taken her through several long airport corridors, down a flight of stairs, outside, and to a waiting private jet. Once inside, she had been blindfolded and had remained so for the entire flight.

She was so terrified she had hardly been able to think straight.

All she could think of was Erin and what had happened to *her*. The only consolation the grim memory brought was a reminder of Mrs. Wagner's words during their morning together: "If ever you get afraid, dear . . . afraid of anything—call on the name of the Lord. Ask Jesus to help you. No matter what the circumstances, he will."

Never had Juliet prayed so much in her life. And never had she been so sure she was about to die!

Her thoughts were in such turmoil that she couldn't accurately judge time, but it seemed they had probably flown for about an hour. Then she felt the plane's engines begin to slow. Suddenly came a soft bump, and she realized they had landed.

Still blindfolded, she was taken outside and transferred her to what she thought was a helicopter, though she had never been on one before. They took off again, flew for perhaps half an hour this time and again landed. Then they brought her, walking, to wherever she was now, tied her to a chair in the middle of a dark room, and removed the blindfold. She had been here ever since.

She was given water occasionally and untied enough to nibble at a few bites of something during the night and go to the bathroom. But everything remained black, even when people came and went. She had not been allowed to sleep. Every thirty or forty minutes someone came to jar her senses awake.

It had gone on that way the rest of the day, all night, and this day . . . if it *was* day. She could no longer keep track. Had one day passed, or three? Her brain lost the capacity to make sense of anything.

Again Juliet heard a door open, as she had twenty or thirty times already. Footsteps echoed across a hard cement floor—it sounded like two people, maybe three. They stopped in front of her.

All was silent. Juliet felt a presence nearby.

"Miss Halsay," said a voice at length.

Juliet jumped at the sound.

It was so close. She could feel it in front of her, but it sounded far away. It was a woman's cold voice. Its timbre sent a chill down Juliet's spine.

"Are you tired?" it asked.

"Oh, yes," Juliet groaned.

"Would you like to sleep?"

"Oh . . . yes, please!" she whimpered, starting to cry.

"Then tell me where Adam Livingstone was. I need to know. And what he discovered."

"I . . . I can't."

"You cannot refuse . . . you *must* not refuse me."

"But . . . I can't tell you."

"No harm will come to him, Miss Halsay," said the woman in an attempted soothing tone. "No harm will come to *you*—only sleep . . . sleep. All you have to do is tell me. You were in the desert, weren't you—on a mountain?"

The words were soft, measured, cold, and hypnotic.

"Yes," said Juliet dreamily, "no . . . I mean . . . I don't know . . . I don't know where we were . . . I can't remember."

"What did you find?"

"Nothing . . . I don't know . . . please, won't you let me sleep?"

"Nothing? But what are those things in your luggage—instruments, leaves?"

"I don't know . . . samples."

"Samples of what?"

"Trees, bushes."

Again it was silent. Five minutes went by. Juliet thought maybe she was alone again.

Suddenly a bright light exploded into her face. Two eyes stared into hers from less than a foot away!

Juliet screamed in terror. She shut her eyes, as much from the pale leering face as from the sudden brightness.

"Open your eyes," demanded the voice. Its soothing quality was gone. There was only command.

Squinting, Juliet obeyed.

The face had not moved. Its two eyes probed straight into hers. Juliet shuddered. She knew she was in the presence of something evil, something frightening, a force that was her enemy . . . and Adam's enemy.

Without removing the gaze of its eyes, now the two lips of the face began to softly chant in an eerie otherworldly cadence and melody words that were nothing Juliet recognized as from earthly language. Again she shivered. The cold went through her like sharp icicles. She knew an evil spell was being woven upon her.

Again she closed her eyes and tried to turn her head.

"Open your eyes," commanded the lips. "Look at me! Do not turn away." Then came again the strange, horrible, terrifying crooning . . . chanting . . . in dreadful words of sorcery!

Juliet could not resist its demands. Her eyes opened wide as a frog's when it's about to be swallowed by a snake.

"Where did he go?" suddenly asked another voice—a deep, terrifying man's voice.

Juliet let out another scream, struggling to turn toward the sound. It came from close behind her, next to her ear. She felt its breath as it spoke! But it was no warm human breath—only the cold-blooded breath of a serpent.

"Do not turn away from my gaze!" hissed the woman as she stared into Juliet's eyes. "You *must* answer the question."

"What did he find?" intoned the Voice at her ear. The serpents had surrounded her!

"Stop . . . please . . . please, stop!" cried Juliet. "I don't know . . . why are you doing this . . . please . . ."

"You *must* answer," said the woman and again began the diabolical chanting.

"Miss Halsay," whispered the cold breath in her ear. "Harm may come to you if you continue to disobey our commands. Do you hear . . . *harm* . . . you are in grave danger."

"Stop . . . stop!" cried Juliet.

All at once she thought of Erin's mother. Then Adam's face came into her mind. Remembering them both gave her courage.

*"Stop . . . help. Jesus, help me . . . please, Jesus!"* she cried. "Leave me, you evil people—*Jesus, send them away . . . Jesus . . . Lord Jesus, help me! Make them go away!"*

The chanting ceased. The cold breath pulled back. The light went out. Two sets of footsteps retreated across the floor. The door opened and shut.

Then silence.

A great calm came over her and Juliet dozed.

Sometime later, two hours, perhaps three. Suddenly a harsh blaring sound in the room awakened her. Moments later the door opened yet again.

Everything had changed. Light came through it now. A man ran toward her, quickly cut the ropes binding her hands and feet, yanked her up, and pulled her to a standing position.

Half dragging her, he pulled her out of the room and into the open air. People were running and shouting. Commotion was everywhere.

# thirty-seven

# Winged Rescue

(1)

In the middle of that afternoon in which Adam had arrived back in England, two small planes touched down in Edinburgh within thirty minutes of one another.

The first carried Adam Livingstone, Rocky McCondy, and Scott Jordan; the second, Captain Thurlow and various agents of his Scotland Yard crack hostage-rescue team. A contingent of Edinburgh's police force awaited them.

It had taken Adam and Captain Thurlow less than an hour after Adam's departure from Swanspond to isolate the stronghold in Dunbar as the probable location where Juliet was being held.

Files indicated several unsubstantiated rumors about the place. It was a hunch, though one aided considerably by Inspector Saul's report after listening in on a second telephone call to the Livingstone estate. A shrewdly coached Crystal Johnson took the call and was able to extract more information than the caller realized he was providing.

Captain Thurlow stepped out of his plane and ran toward those waiting at the other.

"Your end of this thing ready, Livingstone?"

"We're about set," replied Adam, checking the last of his equipment. "How long will it take you to get there? We've got to have it timed perfectly."

"Around Edinburgh on the loop, probably thirty minutes, then another thirty or forty to Dunbar."

Adam looked at his watch. It was three-twenty. "What do you think . . . an hour and a quarter?"

"An hour and a half—let's say five o'clock to be sure. We'll hang back four hundred yards or so till we see you—then we'll move."

"I'll go at five," said Adam.

"You have your microphone—you and McCondy check everything?"

"We're ready."

"Legally I've got to take my men in the front door and announce ourselves," said Thurlow. "It's a huge enclosed compound. If they try to move her or get her out, you're going to have to give us directions fast."

"I thought up this crazy plan, remember," replied Adam. "That's what I'll be doing. I'll relay whatever I see."

"Do you have a firearm?"

Adam nodded. "But I don't want to have to use it."

"Nobody ever does in these situations, but we've got to be ready for anything."

Thurlow glanced around. "All right, that it then?"

Adam and the others nodded.

"Then we'll head out."

He turned and ran toward one of the waiting police van units.

"Good luck, Adam," said Rocky, shaking Adam's hand.

"Same to you!"

(2)

At five minutes before five in the afternoon, the faint sound of a small airplane engine could be heard some five thousand feet above the Scottish coastal town of Dunbar, twenty-nine miles east of central Edinburgh.

Several miles away, on a grassy bluff bordered by rocky cliffs of the picturesque coastline, sat the secluded fifty-acre walled compound. Many of the most powerful individuals in Europe, including not a few heads of state, had taken their oaths of initiation at this very place.

The plane now began a circling descent to three thousand feet. At five o'clock sharp, it had reached two thousand feet.

A figure suddenly appeared at the plane's open side door, then leapt from the plane. Seconds later a white paraglider canopy opened silently as the plane climbed and sped away toward the coastline.

"There he is!" cried Captain Thurlow from his vantage point. "Let's go!"

Less than a minute later, two police vans stormed to the front gate of the compound, skidding to a screeching stop on the pavement. Immediately they emptied of twenty uniformed policemen carrying rifles. Thurlow sprinted toward the guardhouse.

The man on duty stood the moment he saw them and stepped outside the small building. He had taken the time, however, to punch the red warning button that signalled emergency buzzers in every building of the highly se-cretive grounds.

The guard now stood and awaited them, while behind the tall stone walls the compound sprang into protective action.

"I'm Captain Thurlow of Scotland Yard! I have a warrant here authorizing a full search of the premises," said the captain. "I order you to open the gate im-mediately!"

Unconsciously, Thurlow glanced upward.

(3)

The moment Adam's ropes tugged comfortably in all the right places about shoulders and arms and he had control of the canopy above him, he looked down at the compound to get his bearings. Above him in the plane, Scott banked up over the North Sea and was already nearly out of earshot.

The walled precincts of the main Temple and half-dozen or more smaller buildings spread out below. He saw the police vans skid up to the guardhouse.

"Rocky . . . Thurlow—you there?" Adam called into the miniature micro-phone attached to his shoulder.

"We're heading in," returned Rocky's voice into his ear.

"They're scattering everywhere, Rocky. They've been alerted. I see a dozen people flying out of the main building and across the lawns . . . wait . . . there's a huge flat-topped building across a field of grass—looks like about a quarter mile east—they're heading that way. I see you all running from the gate toward the Temple! Can you get around behind it without going through?"

"Don't know," came Rocky's voice, puffing from below as he ran.

"Thurlow!" yelled Adam, swooping in a wide arc above the scene. "I don't think she's in the main Lodge. They're scattering like bees from a nest. Can you get around back?"

"I'll send one squad of men to search the main Lodge—"

"Just get out back into the central part of the compound however you can!" shouted Adam. "Things are happening fast."

"Any sign of the girl?" cried Thurlow as he led the way through the front door of the Temple and pointed out directions to several men.

"Not yet."

Rocky was already halfway around the huge brick mansion with another contingent of officers.

"I've got you in sight, Rocky," said Adam. "Keep going the way you are, then straight on—wait!" he cried. "Rocky . . . Thurlow! The roof of that flat building across the way . . . it's separating . . . rolling back . . . great Scott! It's a hangar! There's a helicopter inside!"

Even as Adam cried out the warning, he could see the rotor blades starting to move. These people wasted no time! The wide front doors of the building now opened.

"Livingstone!" cried Thurlow. "Can you see weapons? Should we expect gunfire?"

"Don't see any from here, Captain. But I'm still five hundred feet up. I'm heading for the hangar!"

"Stay out of the way of that chopper!" called Rocky, puffing now more noticeably.

Adam arced his descending glide in the direction of the large building that had suddenly become the focus of action.

"There's Juliet!" Adam cried suddenly. "They're dragging her from a small house about a hundred yards behind the hangar!"

✦  ✦  ✦

Fresh air, sunlight, and sudden activity roused Juliet into instant wakefulness.

Oblivious to the helicopter's blades screaming nearby, readying for takeoff, all Juliet knew was that her hands and feet were finally free. It took but a moment or two for her head to clear.

With a sudden thrust of unexpected power, she jabbed her elbow into the ribs of her guard with all the strength she could muster. The blow staggered the man momentarily as his grip on her arm loosened. Juliet yanked it from him, then sprinted away.

"Why you little—," he cried. "Come back here!"

He took off in pursuit.

✦  ✦  ✦

Rocky and his men coming from the side of the Lodge and Thurlow with a half-dozen more now bursting out the back door of the Lodge, all sprinted in the direction of the sound.

It was a race against seconds. If the chopper lifted but a few feet off the ground, they would be unable to stop it without killing everyone on board.

✦  ✦  ✦

From above, Adam saw well that, not knowing her danger, Juliet was running *toward* the hangar. None of the policemen would reach it before Juliet's captor caught her again and dragged her inside.

With all his might he bent the canopy above him into a dangerously steep downward angle. He had to cut them off before they reached the building. Once they got her inside there would be little he could do. They would be airborne within seconds.

Adam plunged toward the ground at a dangerous speed. A tiny miscalculation would send his body crashing to earth, slam him against the building or straight into the screaming helicopter blades.

The man was gaining on Juliet. But he neither heard nor saw Adam's silent approach. He had expected no rescue from the sky and was unarmed.

Suddenly a great shadow darkened the grass. The form of a menacing angel swooped upon him with a single huge white wing of flight.

"Juliet . . . grab on!" cried Adam.

It was over before the man knew what hit him. Adam steered his canopy skillfully to bottom out its descending arc. With a great kick from his feet, he sent the man sprawling onto his back.

As he flew by, Juliet threw her arms tightly around his passing torso. Snatched suddenly from the ground, a breathless scream escaped her lips. She felt herself lifted ten feet into the air and clung to Adam for dear life.

The speed of Adam's descent gave him sufficient momentum to continue the flight some distance, even with a passenger aboard. But the added weight and precarious equilibrium made it a risky operation. Twisting at his ropes and pulleys, he brought them downward again, yelling out landing directions to Juliet.

The canopy now dipped toward the ground, if not gracefully, at least with not so steep an angle as before. In five more seconds Adam and Juliet were rolling about in a tumbling mass of legs and arms, ropes and nylon, fifty feet from the hangar door.

"Are you in one piece?" Adam cried.

"Yes . . . yes . . . oh, Adam—how did you . . . I was so scared—how did you find me?" Already she was smothering him with hugs and tears.

"I'll tell you everything—just help me get out of all this first!"

Adam struggled to his feet, extricating himself with some difficulty, then pulled his gun.

By now the enraged Scotsman had risen from the ground to again give chase. But seeing Adam's gun, he suddenly thought better of it, stopped, and began backing away. Shouts of the two contingents of policemen running toward them now sounded.

Suddenly the whirring of the helicopter roared above them. Its blades rose above the hangar's flat roofline. Realizing their prey had been snatched from under their very noses, the principle players in the kidnapping judged it prudent not to hang around for questions.

As the machine climbed out of the building, through its glass windows Adam saw the faces of a gray-haired man in a business suit and a man of dark countenance and darker hair staring down at him with piercing eyes of hated. Beside him the face of a woman—whose eyes had so unnerved him in the lobby of the Nile Gardens—stared at him with an expression that conveyed clearly enough, "The fight is not yet over!" Behind them, a short, balding man bent down trying not to be seen.

The silent exchanges between light and darkness lasted but a second. The instant the skids were clear, General Pervukhin pulled his proud machine skyward in retreat, arcing immediately away from potential danger of gunfire. It headed east over the North Sea, gaining speed rapidly, and within seconds disappeared from sight.

Adam looked at Juliet's terrified, relieved, and exhausted face where she now stood at his side. He smiled and stretched his arm around her and pulled her close.

Rocky and Captain Thurlow ran up. Already Thurlow's men were beginning arrests and questioning the captives.

"Recognize the chopper, Captain?" asked Adam, still gazing after the speck in the sky.

"Military—that's all I could tell. One of those small eastern European republics, most likely. We'll probably never know. I doubt these people here even know. But we'll interrogate everyone and see what we can find out."

"Are you through with us?" said Adam. "If so, we'd like to go home."

"I'll have to ask you some questions, Miss Halsay," said Thurlow. "But I think they can wait until tomorrow."

"Thank you, Captain," sighed Juliet. "I am so tired!"

"Let's go, then, Juliet . . . Rocky, Scott will be waiting for us back at the airport. Let's see, what time is it? . . ." He glanced at his watch. "It's only five-fifteen. We ought to be back at Sevenoaks by . . . hmm—I would say eight or eight-thirty. Before we left, I told Mrs. Graves to plan roast beef and Yorkshire pudding for nine!"

# thirty-eight

# Proposal in Eden

(1)

In her wildest romantic fantasies, Juliet Halsay had never envisioned a setting like this.

How Adam had arranged it she hadn't a clue. But she had given up trying. The man was able to pull off the most amazing things! Like discovering arks and Edens and making daring rescues . . . and captivating a young woman's heart.

The last wasn't really so amazing when she thought about it. What woman *wouldn't* fall in love with a man like Adam Livingstone.

The amazing part was that he seemed to feel the same way about *her.* At least, so she dared hope. But she had to keep pinching herself all the time, thinking she was going to wake up from this adventure and find herself—

But it *wasn't* a dream!

A fairy tale . . . perhaps. But all of it had happened. It had really and truly happened!

Adam Livingstone and Juliet Halsay walked together hand in hand through thick green grass, surrounded on every side by luxuriant shrubbery and trees of all sizes and shapes. Above them and to their left towered the rocky slope of a barren Arabian mountain. Everything around their feet grew wildly. They followed no path, for none had yet been worn through *this* garden. Theirs were among the first steps to tread this ground since its miraculous reawakening.

Though they were out in the open, the very air seemed full of a strange hush. They could not help but make their way slowly, and their words were soft. Awe filled their spirits. Everywhere they looked produced a sense of wonder at what they had been privileged to experience.

As they filled their lungs with the Garden air, even the oxygen felt cleaner, purer, more vibrant with life. Never could they have dreamt themselves in the middle of the desert. The greenery beneath their feet and that now growing up to waist and even head height was so lush that it seemed to produce moisture, both above and below, of itself. They would not have been surprised to encounter a stream flowing somewhere in the midst of it.

"How did you ever arrange for us to come here again?" asked Juliet at length, her voice quiet and peaceful.

"Since our last visit, let me simply say I pulled a few strings."

"You are truly a remarkable man, Adam Livingstone."

"I promised that we would be in and out within two hours, that no harm would come to anything, that I would bring no equipment, not even a camera. Besides, the Saudi government owes me a favor or two."

"I don't even want to ask what for," giggled Juliet.

"Good—don't."

"Oh, Adam," Juliet sighed, "will I ever know everything there is to know about you?"

"I hope not. But we shall have years to find out."

Juliet's heart skipped a beat at the words.

"But you still haven't told me what we're doing here."

"Didn't you want to see it again?" said Adam. "We were so rushed last time. It was hardly light when we were down here on the flat. Just look how it's grown since. I can hardly believe it. The trees are taller, the grass thicker . . . it's spreading out beyond the fence line. If they intend to keep this area bordered, they're going to have to widen the boundary every week."

"Little chance of that. If it is a sign of preparation for the Lord's return, I don't think a fence is going to stop it."

"It is truly amazing. It cannot be anything *but* a sign from God."

"Just like old Harry's poem says."

Again they walked for a while in contented silence.

"Admit it, Juliet," said Adam at length, fun in his tone, "you know why we're here."

Juliet reddened slightly. She smiled shyly but did not reply.

"I'm glad," Adam went on, "that I was interrupted by the waiter that night at the Ramses. Who knows what I might have blurted out. Ever since then, once I realized that God had given me a helpmeet, my very own Eve, I knew there was only one place on the whole face of God's earth that would be fitting to propose to her."

"Adam . . . are you . . . what—"

"I'm answering your question about why we are here. I brought you here to propose to you!"

"Oh, Adam," sighed Juliet. "Yes . . . yes!"

"*Yes?*" he repeated. "What do you mean . . . yes?"

"Adam . . . that I accept."

"Wait!" he cried, clamping a playful hand over her mouth. "Not yet. I haven't proposed. I just said that's what we came here for. Be patient, Juliet."

Slowly now he released his hand. His eyes twinkled with fun. Juliet gazed up into them. Her eyes filled with moisture.

All she could do was return his smile.

(2)

They reached the tree in the center of the Garden.

Already it seemed to have added a foot since they saw it last.

Something sat at the base of the tree. "What . . . what's that?" said Juliet, breaking into a run toward it.

"Why—it's amazing!" exclaimed Adam, following her. "It looks like a picnic basket."

"Adam Livingstone, you planned this whole thing behind my back."

Juliet was laughing as she reached the basket and now dropped to her knees and started to lift the wicker lid.

"There you go again, getting too hasty," cried Adam, catching up and preventing her from opening it.

"How did you get it here? I've been with you the whole time."

Adam glanced at the mountain. Juliet followed his gaze.

"Rocky!" she exclaimed. "He's been in on this whole thing. I should have known."

"I needed an accomplice."

Rocky waved down, then turned and disappeared.

"All right, now you can open it," said Adam.

Juliet did so.

On top of a white folded linen cloth was laid out the most perfectly shaped deep red rose. Juliet's eyes now filled with tears in earnest.

"The rose is for you," said Adam, kneeling beside her. He reached in, took it, and handed it to her. "Its message is simple enough—I love you, Juliet."

She took it, lifted it gently to her nose, and breathed in deeply. A moment later they were in one another's arms, still kneeling. For several long seconds they remained silent, unmoving, and more content than either thought possible.

"Aren't you going to see what else Rocky has provided us with?" asked Adam at length.

They parted. Juliet turned, sniffed a few times, took out a handkerchief to dab at her eyes, then probed the basket's contents—a cold luncheon so complete no gourmet could have done better.

"No apples, I hope?" she said.

"No, Eve . . . no apples," laughed Adam.

Juliet spread out the cloth on the green grass, then proceeded to remove the contents, placing them one at a time on the white linen. At the bottom of the basket lay an ornately framed certificate of some kind.

"What's this?" she asked, picking it up.

"Read it," said Adam. "It's to hang on the wall of the lab."

"'To Juliet Livingstone,'" Juliet read aloud, "'archaeologist apprentice and lab technician extraordinaire. This is to certify that the aforenamed individual is hereby promoted to the aforenamed status on a permanent basis with Livingstone Explorations, Investigations, and Discoveries, Ltd., and shall never have to wash test tubes or sell fish-and-chips to earn her daily bread.' Oh, Adam," laughed Juliet, turning to him, "you are so funny!"

Suddenly a look of delight and astonishment crossed her face. Her eyes both lit and filled with tears at the same instant.

"It says Juliet . . . *Livingstone.*"

"I am hoping that is the name by which you will want to undertake your future employment," replied Adam. *"Will* you be my wife, Juliet?"

Again Juliet's eyes filled with tears.

"Oh, Adam, I can't think of anything in the world I would rather be!"

(3)

Two hours later, Adam and Juliet walked together toward the slope of the ancient mount. Ahead they saw Rocky sauntering down the memorable, fateful path toward them.

"I take it from your two faces," he said, "that congratulations are in order?"

"They are indeed," replied Adam.

"Then may I be the first to offer them."

"Thank you, my good man."

"Thank you, Rocky!" said Juliet softly. Her voice was dreamy, as indeed, at this moment, was her entire life.

"It might be worth your while to walk up to the summit," said Rocky, "although I know the time you arranged for us is about up."

"Why?" said Adam.

"You know the tree up there?"

Adam nodded.

"It's bursting into leaf all over."

"Seriously . . . that's remarkable."

"It shows all the signs of turning into an exact replica of the one down at the base."

(4)

Adam and Juliet did as Rocky suggested, while he walked the rest of the way down and then began his drive back to Al Humaydah, where they would rendezvous before returning to England.

Because they were in love, the passage of time ceased to have meaning as long as they were together. As they ascended the mount, Adam and Juliet spoke quietly of many things, not the least of which was what to do concerning the discovery they had made.

The whole of Jebel al Lawz confirmed the resounding truth that Harry McCondy had indeed spoken prophetically in his journal concerning the last days: *Then shall Eden be restored.*

Sprouts and tiny blossoms were bursting from the surface and subsurface root system wherever they looked. The mountain *felt* alive, as if underneath, it was trembling to explode again, though now not with the smoke and fire of volcanic force but with the burgeoning growth of life. They sensed that they were walking atop a massive living organism.

"After the tests," Juliet was saying, "connecting the DNA composition of the tree at the bottom with the one up there on top, with all the root samples we took, is it really possible the whole mountain is a *single* tree?"

"I can't think of what else to believe," replied Adam. "According to the DNA, that is precisely what it is. Why should we be surprised if it is indeed miraculous . . . if it is the center of Eden's life? It would have to be such a life as has never before been known—life so vibrant and energetic as to spread throughout the planet."

They walked on.

"What are you going to do?" asked Juliet at length.

"I don't know," sighed Adam. "I am feeling strong reservations whether to make public what we think is occurring here. There would be those who would seek to exploit a finding like this in ways that would be anything but spiritual of motive. As we know all too well, there would also be those who would seek to destroy it. I know the place could *not* be destroyed. That much I'm certain of. If millennia of changes on the earth has not destroyed this original site of life, man will not destroy it. However, God's perfect purposes might be thwarted if this is not handled according to his will. If he gave the revelation to us, for whatever reason, then we must find what *his* will is in the matter. I have to change my thinking entirely from what would be the case with a traditional scientific discovery."

"It isn't a scientific discovery at all, really—is it?" said Juliet.

"No, we've been swept up into something more than mere archaeology."

"It truly is a *spiritual* discovery—a revelation of *God's* world, *God's* truth, not a discovery, in a way, that has anything to do with the science of *man.*"

"Which is why we must seek God's guidance about what to do with it."

"But would he have shown you all this if he *didn't* want you to make it known?" said Juliet. "Just imagine what an impact this might have on the world's response to the truthfulness and authenticity of the Bible."

"Don't forget, I am still pretty new to knowing how God does things," rejoined Adam. "What I am thinking is that maybe God sometimes makes revelations that are meant to be private. It just may be that he wanted me—maybe I should say us—to recognize the truth of his Word more than he wanted us to proclaim that truth to the rest of the world."

"But something like this? Of such magnitude?"

"I don't know, Juliet. If there is anything we have learned through this, it is that eternal timetables are God's, not man's. Remember what Rocky's pastor said. I would be extremely reluctant to interfere in what God had in mind. If I err at all, I would rather err by going too slowly, following a step behind God, than going too fast and running the risk of getting a step ahead of him. It really isn't a question of whether or not the world will recognize the truth of the Bible—that revelation will most certainly come one day. I have a feeling one day very soon. But it is important that God make the revelation, not Adam and Juliet Livingstone. We want him leading the way."

(5)

In a secret windowless enclave high in Amsterdam, a lone candle burned on a table around which the twelve members of the World Council of Twelve sat silent.

It was time to draw back into their web of secrecy for a time.

Their efforts of late had been less than successful, and many had been the disruptions in the Dimension. But their Master's Plan remained unchanged. The new age would dawn, though confusion had spread through their number concerning when their own Great One would be revealed. The rivalries between them were not voiced upon this occasion. Even Halder Zorin was still numbered one of the Council notwithstanding the reservations of some. About many things the Dimension was curiously quiet. It was a season for waiting, to see what would come next.

It was time to devote their efforts to less prominent displays and more subtle persuasions of the enemy's people to ally themselves with their cause without knowing it.

Their Spirit Guides and Wise Ones of darkness assured them, despite recent setbacks, that The Plan would prevail.

(6)

Passing the fateful cave where they had discovered Harry McCondy's rucksack, at length Adam and Juliet reached the summit.

In the distance they saw the tree between the two boulders, growing as if newly flourishing with life, just as Rocky had said. The drilling and samples they had taken from its trunk the last time they were here seemed almost to have invigorated the tree, which now appeared an exact replica of its twin at the foot of the mountain.

They paused some distance before it.

Anew the sense stole over them that they had been given a sacred revelation. They stood together, realizing that they were in the presence of God.

Silently the words entered into their minds: *"The place where you are standing is holy ground."*

As of one accord, both knelt and removed their shoes, then bowed and began to pray. The words of Adam Livingstone, archaeologist of worldwide fame but now humble child of God, were simple and sincere. *"God,"* he prayed, *"show us what you want us to do."*

They were nine simple words, yet they comprised the highest of all human entreaties to him who had created them and from whose divine breath all life had gone forth from this place.

They rose ten minutes later, put on their shoes, and stood awhile longer gazing upon the tree.

At length, Adam took Juliet's hand, turned, and led her slowly back down the way they had come.

"I think the Lord has answered my prayer already," he said.

Juliet waited, knowing he would tell her in his time.

"It may be," he said after they had walked some ways down the path, "that the knowledge of Eden is not yet meant for the world. Men will see this growth and not apprehend its significance. Yet such has truth always been—right before our eyes. Some see it, some remain blind to it. So was I for many years. The revelation will, I believe, come singly—as each man and woman allows its Life to be breathed into his or her own heart."

Juliet smiled.

"On the other hand, I believe that huge things are at hand in the eternal realm."

"The end of one era and the dawn of another," suggested Juliet.

Adam nodded. "But we mustn't interfere with God's timetable," he said. "If what Rocky and his friends have said about the eras is true, we cannot be the ones to make that determination. We must not let the fact that the new millennium will soon dawn make us rush ahead of the Lord's leading by charging out of the hills like the old gold prospectors in Rocky's country used to do, shouting, 'Eden has been found . . . Eden has been found!'"

Adam paused.

"Am I making sense, Juliet, dear?" asked Adam.

"I think I understand exactly."

"I am feeling strongly that we are to await further guidance. This revelation, obviously begun by God, is his to make known to the world in his own way . . . and in his time."

They walked again in silence.

"It is exactly what I felt as we were praying back there," said Juliet.

"God was the one who closed the Garden from man originally," said Adam. "We must make sure he is the one to open it."

They continued down the mountain known to the ancients as Horeb and today as Jebel al Lawz. As they rounded a bend in the path, they glanced back. Two projecting ledges of rock face slowly appeared to come together, gradually shutting off the tree at the summit from view behind them.

Adam and Juliet looked at one another and smiled. For the present, the center of the Garden was closed again.

But nothing is hid that shall not be revealed. A new millennium approached . . . and the heavenly realms were busy preparing for eternal change.

(7)

As Adam Livingstone and Juliet Halsay drove the final yards toward the Livingstone estate at Sevenoaks, they saw a cluster of journalists about the gate.

Rocky had preceded them from Saudi Arabia by a day. Adam and Juliet had flown into Heathrow early that afternoon and driven down to Sevenoaks together.

"Here we go again," laughed Adam.

Juliet had no chance to reply before the reporters were on them, Alex Glendenning of the BBC leading the way, microphone in hand, cameraman close on his heels.

"Mr. Livingstone," he called, approaching the open window as Adam slowed the automobile to a stop, "rumor has it you made a great discovery in Africa."

"Right you are, Glendenning." Adam smiled. "And she's sitting right beside me."

"Ah yes—well . . . ," said the reporter, caught off guard and now leaning down and peering further inside the car. "This is, I take it, the new assistant I've been hearing about?"

"No, Alex—this is my new partner. Meet Juliet Halsay—soon to be Juliet Livingstone. Juliet . . . Alex Glendenning."

Juliet reached across Adam and shook the man's hand.

"This is big news!" said Glendenning. "Do you have any comment for the record, Miss Halsay?"

"Adam has already warned me about you, Mr. Glendenning," replied Juliet. "He said I should say only what I want to hear repeated on the telly! So I think I shall say nothing."

"But did you find the Garden? That's what everyone wants to know."

"We found the garden of happiness," replied Juliet with a demure smile. "After a discovery like that, what else can there be to search for?"

Adam laughed to hear Juliet banter so deftly with the skilled Glendenning.

"There you have it, Alex," he said good-naturedly. "The lady has spoken— end of interview. You won't mind if we proceed?"

He began inching the car forward through the mass of television and newspaper people, all of whom were clamoring to be heard with their questions.

"What's next on the Livingstone agenda?" called out a tall blond man behind Glendenning.

"This lady and I have some personal business to attend to," replied Adam.

"I mean what's next for the research team?"

"Come on, Al," said Adam, "you know we can't divulge that. We're not even home from this adventure. Besides," he added with a wink, "you might leak my plans to Sir Gilbert!"

Adam now accelerated slightly. The crowd parted as Adam and Juliet made their way through the gate that Scott had opened and now closed behind them the moment the car was clear.

Adam pulled forward and stopped.

As he climbed out from the driver's side, Scott and Figg were both there already, shaking his hand and welcoming him home as if he had been gone for months rather than just a week. Adam walked to the other side and opened the passenger door. As Juliet stepped out into the spring sunshine, Crystal and Jen ran to her as if she had been part of the family for years. Rocky had spilled the news of what had taken place at Jebel al Lawz, and the three women now embraced one another happily.

Twenty yards away, in front of the door, Rocky and Mrs. Graves stood quietly observing the proceedings. They would extend their greetings after the hubbub died down.

"But, Adam, look who's here to welcome you back," said Crystal.

Adam glanced toward the house.

"Mum!" he exclaimed. For there, indeed, was his mother walking toward them. "I thought you were still in India!"

"Well, I am back. And the moment I heard there was soon to be another lady added to the Livingstone clan, I knew this was something I had to see for myself."

"This is great! Juliet," he called to her, "come meet my mother!"

But already the two women had approached one another.

"Hello, Mrs. Livingstone, I am Juliet Halsay," said Juliet.

"And I am Frances Livingstone. I am delighted to meet you, my dear."

They embraced lightly.

"You must really be some young lady, Juliet," said Adam's mother. "To be honest with you, I never thought any woman would succeed in tearing this boy of mine away from his work. I offer you, not only my welcome to the family, but also my esteem and sincere congratulations!"

Adam laughed with delight. The rest of the entourage joined in.

He extended his arm toward Juliet. She approached and snuggled close as he pulled her to his side. They turned toward the house and walked slowly toward it, the others following several paces behind.

"Welcome home, Juliet," said Adam softly.

"Thank you, Adam," Juliet replied in scarcely more than a whisper. "You can't know how good it is to have a home again. But anywhere would be home with you."

They paused in front of the house, then separated.

While Juliet and her aunt embraced, Adam and Rocky shook hands as only dear friends of the Spirit can do, holding one another's gaze for a second or two. Neither spoke. What they had to say to one another was conveyed well enough with their eyes. Then Adam turned toward his housekeeper, whose own eyes were full of tears.

"Well, Mrs. Graves," he said, "what's for tea!"

> *As the rain and the snow come down from heaven, and do not return to it without watering the earth and making it bud and flourish . . . so is my word that goes out from my mouth: . . . the mountains and hills will burst into song before you, and all the trees of the field will clap their hands. Instead of the thornbush will grow the pine tree, and instead of briers the myrtle will grow. This will be for the Lord's renown, for an everlasting sign, which will not be destroyed. (Isaiah 55:10-13)*

> *Rejoice! millennial saints—the sign is given.*
> *Life sprouts at the center . . . the Tree is revealed!*
> *Crowning eons of turmoil, a day of rest is risen.*
> *Reconciliation is complete! The rift is healed!*

# Research Notes for Rift in Time

## Noah's Ark

At present there are two general theories among those who believe that Noah's ark, or remnants of it, still exists on the earth. Both have devoted and passionate advocates, able to cite a considerable body of evidence to back up their claims. Since there is only one ark, many of these legends, apparent sightings, photographs, and other scientific data to validate them—even stories of those who tell of actually climbing inside the ark—are obviously not what they purport to be. It will clearly take further research and future archaeological breakthroughs to decide the matter.

It has long been assumed that the ark lay buried either in glacial ice or under a layer of volcanic ash, thus preserving it *somewhere* upon Mount Ararat. Numerous have been the "eyewitness" sightings through the years (as recounted in chapter 1), mostly in the region of the rocky canyon known as Ahora Gorge.

The biblical account, however, does not specifically indicate that the ark came to rest upon the peak known today as *Mount* Ararat, but rather says, in Genesis 8:4, that "the ark came to rest on the mountains of Ararat," a reference to the ancient country known as Urartu. Since the mountain known as Ararat is the highest peak of the region and would obviously have been the first to dry out after the floodwaters receded, it is logical, as many have assumed, that the ark *may* have come to rest upon it. Yet the Bible tells us only that it was in this *region* that Noah's family and the animals eventually disembarked. And others say it is equally logical to conjecture that the steep slopes of a mountain peak would *not* be a likely resting site, but that a rudderless vessel would naturally drift with receding floodwaters to a lower and flatter location before coming to rest.

A compelling alternate possibility that has received much attention in recent years suggests that the ark actually came to rest some fifteen miles from Mount Ararat at Al Judi. There among the low-lying barren Turkish hills at

6,000 feet elevation—10,000 feet lower than the peak of Ararat itself—an intriguing "boat-shaped object" can be seen emerging, as it were, out of the ground. Its measurements (both length and width) almost precisely coincide with the biblical dimensions of Noah's ark. No wood remains, only rock and soil, which have retained what must be considered a very remarkable shape indeed.

We are left with the fact that *conclusive* evidence substantiating either the Ahora Gorge site or the boat-shaped object as the final resting site of the ark remains yet to be found. Meanwhile, the debate goes on about which set of evidences, proofs, and sightings are in fact valid. Archaeological expeditions to Turkey will no doubt continue.

## Mount Horeb/Sinai

Much of the general plot for *Rift in Time* derives from a fairly recent theory concerning the Exodus of the nation of Israel out of Egypt and an alternate site for Mount Sinai than what has traditionally been assumed.

Three general routes for the Exodus have been proposed by Old Testament scholars. Numerous potential Horeb/Sinai sites have been suggested, including a number of mountains in the vicinity of Kadesh-barnea (between Egypt and Arabia, exactly north of the Gulf of Aqaba.) Sinai is also mentioned in connection with Edom, Paran, Seir, and Teman. The Genesis accounts themselves are of scant use in pinpointing specific locations since many biblical names and place sites (the en route points of the Exodus, for example) are now unknown.

As is the case with Ararat, no specific mountain exists by the name of *Mount Sinai.* The Sinai Peninsula represents the entire region between the Gulf of Suez and the Gulf of Aqaba. Conjectures of the biblical Sinai/Horeb have ranged from the traditionally accepted site of Jebel Mesa on the Sinai Peninsula, at the base of which sits St. Catherine's Monastery, to Jebel Serbal twenty miles northwest, all the way north to Jebel Helal only forty miles from the Mediterranean.

A singularly tantalizing theory in recent years, gaining support among some scholars and archaeologists, brings back the nineteenth-century view (represented by fictional Harry McCondy) that Saudi Arabia's Jebel al Lawz is, in fact, the biblical Horeb.

We are told that when Moses left Egypt he went to "the land of Midian" (Exodus 2:15). There he married and lived for forty years. Midian is in *Arabia*, not the Sinai Peninsula, a fact confirmed by Paul in Galatians 4:25. It was during his years in Midian that Moses was called "to Horeb, the mountain of God" (Exodus 3:1).

After returning to Egypt at God's instruction, Moses knew he had to bring God's people back to Horeb (Exodus 3:12). The most natural and direct means to accomplish this was along the route traced by Harry McCondy, on the traditional caravan connection between Egypt and Arabia. Along the way, however, God directed Moses southward through a narrow, rocky pass, where the Israelites eventually found themselves, as they saw it, trapped on the coast of the Gulf of Aqaba.

One of the most apparently convincing aspects to this newly re-proposed route of the Exodus concerns the site of crossing, through the Gulf of Aqaba rather than either the Gulf of Suez or the so-called Sea of Reeds further north through what is now the Suez Canal.

The Gulf of Aqaba, as well as the rest of the Red Sea, is very deep in most places—as well it might be since it is part of the Great Rift. Indeed, in its center, there is evidence that rifting is still in process. Chasms exist in the Red Sea of over 7,000 feet, whose depths still send up hot, mineral-laden deposits from below—including gold! In the middle of the Gulf of Aqaba at Neviot, however, some say a curious break in this "rift" exists. At that point a sandbar or spit appears to extend out from each shore (laid down, no doubt, by ancient rivers emptying into the gulf at exactly opposite points and directions). Though now submerged from the continual widening of the rift, 3,500 years ago this causeway would likely have been much shallower, offering the Israelites an ideal crossing point, aided by a miraculous, divine freezing wind, temporarily solidifying both the water as it blew back and the seabed itself. Upon this frozen sandbar the Israelites could well have made their crossing during the night and in early morning. When day came and the wind ceased and the earth warmed, the chariot wheels of the Egyptians would have bogged down in the thawing sandbar as they gave charge. If this seemingly plausible scenario is correct, the melting water of the sea would then have returned to complete the destruction of the Egyptian army (Exodus 14:21-30).

Jebel al Lawz, some thirty-five miles southeast of this conjectured crossing site, has a volcanic history. Might this blackened peak be a reminder that the mountain trembled before the Israelites, and that God appeared (Exodus 19:18) to them as from fire and smoke? No flourishing oasis, however—yet!—has sprouted at its base.

## The Garden of Eden/The Oval Theory

I am aware of no current research documenting evidence pinpointing Eden's location. Adam Livingstone's conjectures are my own, as is the conviction that most, if not all, floral life created by God still lives . . . *somewhere*, even if in the dormant stage.

When I began writing *Rift in Time*, the Oval-Eden theory had already taken shape from reading, research, and the challenge to harmonize the biblical account with archaeological findings. I did not at the time anticipate an attempt to locate Eden more precisely than roughly between Mesopotamia and the Rift Valley of southeastern Africa.

During the writing of the book, however, I underwent a process much like Adam Livingstone—refining, rethinking, asking myself many questions pointing in newly considered directions, all the while adding new data to my research. The result turned out to be a dual quest—Adam Livingstone's fictional pilgrimage within the pages of this book . . . and *mine* as I wrote it! I stood for hours in front of various of my many wall maps or bending over my globe, peering at various places on the earth's surface, trying, as it were, to gaze back through the mists of history, all the while saying to the Lord, "God, what did you do on the earth all those eons ago? What does it *mean?* What is in your heart to reveal to your people yet in the future?"

Many of Adam's "discoveries" I was breathlessly making on my own computer at the same time he was. At places in the manuscript I was literally only one or two words ahead of him. I found myself jumping up to consult maps and books yet again from some daring new idea that had just entered my brain, flipping through atlases, consulting now a globe, next a geology text on continental drift or a meteorological depiction of global weather changes, sketching possibilities in a feverish excitement for what I might find. My research file is full of sketches and possibilities, notes and dead ends . . . until finally the "theory" began to come together into a unified whole.

It was an exciting process, one that even included a heart-stopping computer crash in the middle of a tremendous rush of ideas. What you have read is not merely Adam Livingstone's story. It is an account of how the ideas in *Rift in Time* developed as well.

But it was not until the further spiritual implications of Eden began to dawn on me, and with them, the role Eden's truths might yet have to play in the history of the world, that I concluded there could be no other location of the Garden's center. When I suddenly realized, *It's Sinai . . . it has to be Sinai!* and then drew the diagonal down from Ararat to the present origins of the Nile and saw the line pass almost straight through Jebel al Lawz, I could scarcely believe my eyes. At that moment, I truly did feel like Adam Livingstone, that I had come upon what may be a stupendous revelation.

Everything God does has significance. If the tiniest details of the Hebrew alphabet and numerology are incorporated into every word of Scripture, if every living thing is a reflection of its Maker, is it likely that God would plant a Tree of Life upon the earth, only to allow it to wither and its species become extinct and forgotten?

Would God create a Tree of Life and then let it . . . die?

I cannot imagine it.

It is not the way our Father works. The Bible never said the Garden died but that it was hidden. Things of God do not just fade away into the desert. Everything has purpose. Everything God does lasts and has eternal import.

The most significant things return into God's plan a second time, elevated to their higher, spiritual, eternal level. There was a first Adam, there was a second Adam. Jesus will come again. Moses and Elijah will return before that coming.

This is a wonderful truth—but not one we have thought of in relation to Eden. God's designs are fulfilled. The circle of purpose always returns to close upon itself in fulfillment of what was in God's mind to accomplish.

Is this not the astounding truth of Isaiah 55: *"[My word] will not return to me empty, but will accomplish what I desire and achieve the purpose for which I sent it."*

God's purposes always come back around. The closing of the Garden's door in Genesis 3:24 only represents half the story of Eden. The other half is yet to be told—the reopening of that door!

And this second phase of the story will be told in God's way and in God's time.

I truly believe the Garden of Eden still lives upon or within the earth. We have not yet been permitted to behold it, for it remains sealed. But what God creates does not die. With the exception of Jesus, in whom God became man and walked among us on a daily basis, we are told of only two places where God actually set foot and dwelt for a brief period upon the earth—in Eden and upon Horeb.

It is my conviction that they are indeed one and the same place.

Much of what God said to Moses with regard to his presence upon Sinai hearkens back with reminders to an earlier time—God's presence was there, life was there, command was there, divine warnings were there, holy ground was there . . . at both Eden and Sinai. The parallels are staggering and wonderful.

At what other earthly place would God tell Moses he "dwelt" than where he "walked" in his Garden in the cool of the day? From what other tree would he speak to Moses than the Tree of Life? What other place would he call "holy ground" than where creation was brought to its resounding climax? From what other place would he deliver his complete law than where he delivered his first command? To what other place would he summon his people upon their symbolic deliverance from sin than that place where sin had first come upon him?

I can think of no other place than Eden where God would do these things.

How can Eden and Sinai not be the same place? How can the one not be the fulfilling completion of the circle of purpose of the other?

It may not yet be the time for that flowering revelation that will surely come—though I believe that time approaches. It may not yet be time for Horeb and Sinai to be revealed. But when Horeb and Sinai are revealed, whether that place is Jebel at Lawz, the traditional Sinai site, or some other mount yet to be shown us, surely the center of Eden will have been found. For the holy mount of God's presence can exist nowhere but within the Garden of beginnings.

*Rift in Time* is fiction. Yet it is by such types and wonders that God will demonstrate to his "seeing" people that the seventh day in his eternal plan draws closer.

I believe that prior to the return of the Son of God, we will witness many signs of flowering in unexpected ways—in hearts, in the earth, and in the unfolding of events. Many of these signs will not come as the "traditional" Second Coming precursors anticipated by prophets of literalness. God's ways are often unexpected. Thus they will be apprehended only by those with eyes to see.

We are on the very threshold of those days of revelation. A new era is coming . . . and soon. The call upon God's people is to vigilance and obedience . . . that we might be ready!